Blood Brothers

Jody Zimmerman

CONTENTS

CHAPTER 1

Billy is so much like Mother the smile; the green eyes; the long, thick, auburn-brown hair; the flawless, warm-olive skin; the chaotic, anxious, angry moods; but most of all, the gift with canvas.

I pick up his limp, warm, right hand to kiss it tenderly. My tears fall on his fingers, rolling off onto the harsh, crisp-white linens. I study his hand—the slender, long fingers; pink nails topped with white crescents, speckled with bits of dried red and yellow oil paint underneath them; the faintly green veins on the back of his hand; the downy covering of brown hair on the tops of his fingers and hand, becoming thicker and slightly curled on his wrist and forearm; and the thumb he sucked until he was four years old. There is no expression on his face. Stubble sticks out in sharp contrast to the etiolated complexion.

"Please God, please God, let this hand paint again," I beg.

"Oh please, let my brother wake, pick up his brushes and paint again," I plead.

"Mother, I'm so sorry, forgive me," I rub Billy's hand all over my wet face.

"I've tried my best to look after him. You know I have. Dammit, Goddammit, don't you Mother? I miss you so much. I miss you so, so much." Futile queries spark through my mind. How would she react if she were to see her baby boy lying here in a coma? How would age have affected her beautiful face? Would I have turned out the same? Would she and Dad have stayed together? Would Billy be lying here now?

"Please don't leave me, Billy," I whimper, hands trembling, nose dripping. I rub my nose on my right shoulder. Fear hammers through my soul with each beat of my heart. My connection with Billy began the day Dad brought Mother home from the hospital with a tiny, pink creature, eyes shut tight with a head full of dark brown hair, squirming, reeking of sweet, silky Johnson's Baby Powder, his tiny little fingers grabbing tightly around mine, leaving me breathless—the first vivid memory I recall, though I was only two years old.

I've been sitting for hours willing that my touch and voice might get through to him, that his fingers might once again grab mine. I visualize my love for him to be a life-giving force emerging from my body through my hands, permeating his body, repairing all the damaged cells, nerves, and tissue in his brain. I focus all my consciousness into him, communicating to him that I am here with him, that together we will make him well. I imagine that he opens his eyes—imploring God to make it happen. I remember my lucky rabbit's foot. I fish it out of my left pants pocket, put it in his hand and fold my hands over his.

"How could this be?" I ask myself over and over. "How could you have overdosed, Billy? You've gotten your life so together the past few years. What were you doing taking GHB? You never mentioned that drug to me before."

My brother is attached to life through an array of plastic tubes. Electrodes monitor all the electrochemical pulses emanating from his heart and brain. Machines surround him. The metronomic sound of a ventilator pumping oxygen through a white, plastic tube inserted into his trachea through his mouth sends stinging waves of adrenaline-laced fear through my body. This high tech cubicle in the neurological intensive

care unit at St. Vincent's Hospital is one of several fanned out in a circle around a central operations post manned by technicians and nurses overseeing dozens of panels, monitors, and computers. The area looks like mission control, and I think about how Billy loved to play space travel when we were kids.

Armed with a walkie-talkie and a laser firing cap gun, he would set out from my bedroom—mission control—to explore outer space—our back yard. I would direct him on his journey and he would report back his findings. We were careful to steer clear of Planet X—Mother's cottage studio, whenever she had shut herself in to paint.

"Mr. Hampton, Mr. Hampton," a soft, high pitched female voice interrupts my thoughts. I look up to see a short, obese, middle-aged woman in a large blue and green flowery smock looking down at me, her brown eyes full of compassion.

She bends over, gently takes Billy's hand from mine, gently placing his hand on the bed. She smiles when she sees the rabbit's foot as it rolls from Billy's hand onto the bed. Her bosom is huge, so I am unable to read her nametag that faces upward. She takes both my hands in her right hand and puts her left arm around my shoulders pulling me into her large body. I collapse into the warmth, sobbing like a lost, frightened child. The scent of fabric softener crawls through my swollen nasal passages, my eyes fix on her perfectly manicured red nails, dwarfed by the circumference of her fingers. Her breathing is labored. After a while, she slowly releases me.

"Mr. Hampton, they tell me you've been sitting here since noon yesterday," she informs me as she hands me a wad of tissue.

"You should go get some rest. We'll notify you the second there is any change in your brother's condition. I promise you," she says. I stare into her eyes that tenderly acknowledge the desperation in mine, yet reflect no solid hope for me to grab.

I try to speak; nothing comes out. I blow my nose into the tissue and try to clear my throat but it clenches shut emitting a raspy dry cough.

"Water?"

"No."

"We have a nice lounge where you could rest. We can also offer you something to eat if you are hungry," she says. "If you prefer, you can go home and get some rest there. Do you live here in town?"

I shake my head back and forth.

"I see," she says. "Well, we have a family coordinator who can help you make arrangements," she adds in muffed, gentle soprano tones. Her face is full and round, framed by cropped brown hair, with penciled in crescent eye brows, and red lips stretched into a slight smile over large jowls, resting under ample earlobes, hanging like beagle ears over her neck. She exudes compassion, and I wonder if she is a hand picked harbinger carefully groomed and trained in the skill of gently relaying devastating news.

"Where's the restroom?" I ask.

"This way." She pulls me up, and I look down to read her nametag—Janet Ostro, RN.

My knees lock, my lower back hurts, and my bladder aches. I bend over to gently kiss Billy's face.

"I love you," I whisper into his right ear.

She picks up the rabbit's foot and hands it to me. "It's beautiful. I've never seen one with a gold cap and chain. Are these your initials, Mr. Hampton?"

"Yes. My grandmother gave us each one for Christmas when we were kids," I struggle to get the words out as I stuff the rabbit's foot in my pocket, desperate for its magic to work.

Slowly, we walk out of the intensive care unit and down a corridor. She leads me by my right elbow. We come to a men's room, and I go in. It is dark. She reaches her right hand in and turns on the light. I go to the urinal and begin to pee. My concentrated urine splashes my hands, overpowering the pink urinal cake, its odor illuminating the memories of Billy and me engaging in pee contests in grade school to see who could back away farthest from the urinals without hitting the floor. I feel

tears running down my face again. If his brain is damaged beyond repair, how can I let him live that way? How could I ever let him not live? Dear God, how could I make such a decision? I finish peeing, move to the sink, turn on the cold water, soap my hands, rinse them, then bend over splashing water on my face several times. I stand up, water dripping down my face and neck onto my green Polo shirt, and look at myself in the mirror—swollen face thick with stubble and stinging red tear trails, dark semicircles under blue-grey eyes, my curly, dark blonde hair in disarray. I gaze at my face distinguishing Mother's features, Dad's features—the genetic commingling producing indisputably recognizable brothers. I grab my neck with my left hand, apply pressure on my carotid arteries until I feel the thump of my heart in my throat, startled by a feeling of déjà vu that sends rings of shivers over my skin like the iridescent rings of color accelerating from a drop of gasoline on a sunlit mud puddle.

"My God, I've got to get out of here," I mumble. I release the grip on my throat, grab some paper towels, wipe my face and hands and emerge to find Janet waiting.

"I'll, I'll stay at my brother's, at Billy's," I hear myself say.

"He lives in Tribeca. Could you find out where they put my duffle bag and please call me a cab? I have to get out of here now."

Puzzled, she says "Why certainly."

I follow her to a closet. She takes out a set of keys from a pocket in her smock, unlocks the door, reaches in and pulls out my black duffle. I grab it.

"Wait a second Mr. Hampton. I also need to give you your brother's personal items. They are locked up in an office. Please wait here, I'll be right back."

"Yes, thank you."

"Oh, I almost forgot. The man who accompanied your brother in the ambulance left this note for you," she says, almost in a whisper and pulls a small, white envelop from her smock pocket and hands it to me.

"Thank you, thank you very much," I say looking down into her eyes. She hesitates a moment and looks at the note. I look at the note and look back at her.

"Yes, well, I'll be back in a minute," she turns, breathing heavily. Stride induced echoes of rubbing fabric resound and slowly fade.

I tear open the sealed envelope to find extraordinary penmanship: consistent, uniform letters and numbers printed by a steady hand with a black felt tipped pen.

7 April 2006, 8:00 am

Philip:

I am the friend of Billy's who called you this morning. As you may know, we've been dating for the past couple of months. I am so sorry this happened. I really don't understand it and cannot explain how this happened. He went looking for some coke and that was the last time I saw him. I think someone must have slipped him something. I'm sorry I can't meet you here, but I have to fly to Bermuda in a couple of hours for an important shoot. I feel like a bastard for leaving him, but I know you're on the way. This is the biggest shoot of my career. Billy would want me to go, I believe. He is getting the best medical care in the city and they tell me there's nothing we can do now but wait. I'm afraid his situation is not good at all. My cell phone number is 212-555-1432. Please call me if there is any change at all in his condition. I'll be back in town on Wednesday.

Elliott Fields

"Christ, how could you leave him here and go off to some fucking shoot, you bastard?" I whisper through clenched jaws. I reach into my left pocket and pull out my cell phone and dial the number. I hear faint ring tones through crackling static, then nothing.

"Damn."

I look at the number and dial again. I stick the note in my back pocket, rest my back against the wall, bending my knees, sinking to the floor. I clutch my forehead with my left hand, press the phone against my right ear, close my eyes and rest my elbows on my inner thighs. I hear more crackling static, a couple of rings, then silence.

"Mr. Hampton, are you alright?"

"Huh? Oh shit!" I look up and recognize Nurse Ostro looming over me.

"I'm sorry, I didn't mean to startle you," she expresses concern in her eyes as she stands there holding a large white bag with handles and a clip board holding some kind of forms.

"Here are your brother's personal belongings." She sits the bag down beside me as I struggle to get up. My cell phone slips out of my hand, slams against the floor and slides down the terrazzo hallway, spinning like a top.

"Oh dear, I hope it's not broken" she says moving toward the phone.

"It's okay. I'll get it. I go through a lot of cell phones in my line of work, so I always insure them," I reply as I walk down the hall to pick up the phone. It appears to be all right, just a few more scratches added to the existing array.

"What do you do?" Her eyes brighten.

"I'm a free lance journalist—a rogue reporter of sorts."

"A rogue reporter?" She smiles arching her right eyebrow.

"Yes, it's my way or it's the highway."

"I see," she replies in a softer tone with her head tilted toward the floor.

"What I mean Miss Ostro," I add as my eyes dart to her left hand, but I see no ring. Perhaps ICU nurses aren't allowed to wear rings I surmise.

"I'm sorry, is it Mrs. Ostro?"

"I'm not married," she replies, shifts her weight from leg to leg, clasps her hands together and sighs.

"Yes, well, what I meant to say is that I have been fortunate enough to fashion my career so that I can pursue the challenges that appeal to me most—not really a rogue at all."

"You are indeed fortunate," she smiles.

I nod, looking into her big brown, intelligent eyes and realize they have guided me back to a brief emotional respite. I am thankful, yet I feel the tears working their way out as my mouth tightens and puckers.

"Mr. Hampton, if you feel this is not the time, just tell me and I'll stop. But, since you are your brother's medical surrogate, you probably know his desires about organ donation," she sighs, squints her eyes, and shakes her head.

"Yes, I know. He would gladly donate; we've discussed it before. Are those the papers?"

"Yes. Do you feel like signing them now?"

"Is he really going to die so soon, Miss Ostro? I better stay with him."

"No one knows for sure. But he has an extremely high chance of experiencing a life-terminating event at any time. I'm so sorry." She pulls a tissue from her smock and hands it to me.

"Yes, yes, the doctors all told me that. I'll sign them."

"Sign in these three places." She hands me a pen, holding the clipboard up for me along with the white shopping bag like sacrificial offerings. Her expression is calm, and I sense her warmth of soul. I dab my nose with the tissue, steady my hand, sign the forms, hand her the pen back and take the white bag in my hands.

"The man who accompanied Billy, Elliott Fields, says in this letter that he thinks someone may have slipped Billy something."

"Yes, his chart shows that. We have reported it to the police department. I expect they'll be contacting you and Mr. Fields," she replies as she witnesses my signatures, then tears apart the forms to give me a copy.

"Please try to get some rest. I'm on a ten-hour shift so I'm here until ten in the morning. I will call you if there is any change at all with your brother."

She picks up my duffle and says, "I'll walk you to the elevator."

We walk down the hallway and make a couple of turns in silence. As we approach a bank of stainless steel elevator doors, she hesitates a moment and says, "Mr. Hampton, I'd like to tell you that I know the art of your brother and mother. They both have inspired me—I love their work. I'm a bit of an amateur painter. I work night shifts so I can take art classes and paint during the day." She looks down at the floor as she finishes speaking.

My tears release themselves again. She presses the down button. I'm speechless. The elevator door opens. I get in and turn around.

"Go to the information desk in the lobby. They'll show you how to get to the cab stand," she says, and I notice a single tear trail from her left eye down into the folds of her neck.

"Thank you," I whisper as the door closes.

Outside the April air, engulfed with a fine mist falling through the night sky, is crisp and fresh on my face. I spot a cab at the stand, throw in the bags, climb in the back, and ask the driver to take me to Billy's condo on Warren Street in Tribeca. The lights and sounds of the city fill my head. I put my face in my hands, feeling the texture of my stubble. I look at my watch—4:30 am. It is Monday. The nightmare of the past twenty-four hours replays in my head—the shrill ringing phone at 5 am; the muted voice of a stranger—I realize it must have been Elliott Fields—calling from a hospital in New York informing me that my brother had been admitted in a coma from an apparent drug overdose; the mad dash through my house trying to get ready to go to the airport; the frantic, dawn cab ride from my house to Hartsfield; the call to my best friend Luscious, the scrambling at the airport to get on the first Delta flight; the sick anticipation in my stomach and heart as I flew to New York; the unending cab ride from LaGuardia to the hospital and the breathless anxiety, uncontrollable, enveloping me almost to the point of hyperventilation; the cell phone call to Dad in St. Louis only connecting with his voice mail; the matter-of-fact, heavily accented, rapid staccato in which the young neurosurgeon of Indian origin explained to me that my brother had ingested large amounts of alcohol, cocaine, GHB (a strong respiratory depressant), and possibly some other drugs rendering him unconscious, leading to aspiration of vomit and the onset of seizures and cerebral hypoxia, depriving his brain of oxygen for sufficient time to cause a state of stage three coma, and that, recovery from the persistent vegetative state would be unlikely, and, as the patient's designated legal health care surrogate would I consider donating Billy's organs should he die or should the decision to remove him from life support be made; and, finally, the walk through a maze of corridors, walk-ways, and rooms to Billy. The nausea I felt yesterday afternoon when Dr. Seng asked my permission to let him bring several residents to observe Billy stirs in me. Trying to get any reaction from Billy at all, Dr. Seng poked his chest and shouted his name, squirted cold water into his left ear, shined a bright light into his eyes, squeezed the quick of his finger nails and toe nails, and moved his head back and forth rapidly. He pointed out that brainwave activity was evident, but had decreased during the day, indicating that the most likely scenario in this case would be a steady decline into a persistent vegetative state. He thanked me profusely as he left. Three of the residents thanked me and the other one, also of Indian origin, gave me an embarrassed look as she walked out. I feel suffocated. I roll down my window to let fresh air into the stale cab. I remember the note in my back pocket, pull it out, and reread it in the mottled light of streetlights and signs we pass. I pull my cell phone out to dial Elliott's number again. The phone doesn't work at all.

I realize Elliott must be another one of Billy's sexual conquests. They rarely last more than a couple of months. Billy usually prefers men, and there have been a lot of them, but occasionally he encounters a woman who fascinates him either by great beauty, by great talent, or by great wealth or some combination of the three, and he enters into a hasty but passionate relationship, often ending when the woman finds Billy in bed with a man. Neither Billy nor I have ever been able to maintain long term relationships of a romantic nature, another legacy from our past, I believe. My relationships with women have been sporadic, tumultuous, and brief. Except for Luscious, I have only been able to connect with women on a sexual level—a definite prerequisite for rapid relationship deterioration. Nonetheless, this pattern seems to complement my work as a free-lance journalist—forever chasing the next story.

My brother not only inherited the artistic talent from my mother, he also inherited the best looks from both sides of the family. Billy is in his prime at thirty-one years old, standing six feet two inches, with long muscular limbs, long, thick auburn-brown hair, and unforgettable crystal-green eyes. The symmetry of his facial features is remarkable and bankable.

He started modeling when he first moved to Manhattan after graduating with a degree in fine arts from Syracuse University ten years ago and managed to make more money in five years than most people make in a life time. We equally inherited the estates of our Mother and our Grandmother, Fatgram, which made us both teenage millionaires, although Fatgram structured it so that we would not gain control of our entire inheritance until we each reached thirty years of age. I took over the financial duties for us both after Fatgram died and kept up the contact and meetings with our trust officer, Mr. Barksdale, from the Citizens and Southern Bank in Spartanburg, South Carolina, which by then had been purchased by Nations Bank and now is part of Bank of America. Billy's modeling success earned him five-fold the amount he inherited. Thank God he invested most of those earnings in his co-op and a healthy portfolio of stocks and bonds. It came as no surprise to me when the glamour life succumbed to Billy's deepest calling—one that relentlessly pursues his soul, his entire being, generating cycles of low and high, of creativity and sterility, and of volatile, discordant rhythms of emotions and feelings, forming the fishbowl world peculiar to each and every artist—a calling many people have said drove Mother to suicide, an act my brother has attempted twice before, once as a freshman in college and once during his transition from super model to artist. Few people know that both incidences were botched episodes of autoerotic asphyxiation. Billy is now on the brink of international success in the art world. Art critics and collectors have praised the contemporary, impressionistic paintings he has produced over the past five years—in my mind he has extrapolated from the raw sensitivity in Mother's best works. My whole body tingles with a blast of anxiety-laced adrenaline, and a sick, gnawing feeling spawns a spasm of nausea in my throat as I reconnect to the present. I attempt to calm my insides by taking deep, slow breaths.

The cab pulls up in front of Billy's building. It is not one of the renovated factory buildings, but a new twenty-story luxury building where each floor comprises one unit. Billy has the penthouse with incredible views of the Hudson River and the City. The cab driver is a small, coffee-colored man with dark, beady eyes, greasy dark hair slicked back, and a ratty goatee. He turns toward me and barks at me in a high voice, thick with a Middle Eastern accent, "Tweluv feefty." I swallow hard, pull my money clip from my front pants pocket, push a twenty through the Plexiglas panel and catch a whiff of body odor and wonder if it's from him or me. He glances back at me to see if he owes me any change.

"Keep it," I say, grabbing my bags. I get out and shut the door. He drives off without a word.

I walk up the stairs and push the doorbell. The electric lock immediately slides open; I pull open the heavy glass door and enter the foyer of the building.

"Nice to see you, Mr. Hampton. Late one tonight," stutters Tim, the boyish, blonde doorman, who greets me from behind a mahogany counter concealing security monitors for the building.

"Right," I reply as I walk past toward the elevator.

"Is Billy still out on the town?" Tim stammers with a big smile.

12

"What? No. He's in the hospital."

"Oh my God, is he alright?" Tim spits out a line of Gs before he hits God then stands up and leans toward me. He is wearing a grey jacket with brass buttons and gold epaulets. Anger flashes through my body like an anaphylactic shock as I recall Billy often buys drugs from Tim. Enraged, I turn toward Tim.

"No, he's not. He's in a coma. They found him unconscious lying in a bathroom stall at Splash," I scowl, tensing with anger which extinguishes the sick feeling in my gut.

In a reflex I sit the bags down and reach over the counter and grab Tim's jacket at the collar, pull him up to my face, gritting my teeth, "Goddamn you Tim. Did you sell him some bad shit?"

I shake him hard and his eyes pop open wide, his stuttering intensifies as he tries to answer me. I think if he is the perpetrator, I'll choke the life out of him.

"No Sir! No Sir! Only good stuff," he is barely able to get out recognizable words. I feel flecks of his spit on my face as his stammering intensifies. He begins to gasp for air and veins bulge on his forehead and throat. He tries to free himself by pushing my chest with his hands.

"Did you ever sell Billy GHB?" I scream, shaking him harder, increasing the pressure on his throat.

"Never," he gasps, turning redder in the face, then grabs my hands to try to remove them from his neck. "Just pot, coke, and E," he stutters almost in a whisper.

I stare into his blue eyes thinking about how fond Billy is of Tim, even calling him sweet little Timmy. "So what if the kid deals a little on the side to make ends meet?" I think, quickly releasing him. He folds over the counter, bursts into tears, gasping for air.

"My God, I almost choked him to death," I think.

Tim cries like a child, his chest heaves and convulses, his mouth opens spasmodically sucking in air with a gurgle. He tries to speak, but only drools. I feel guilty, and I remember one night a couple of years ago while I was visiting Billy for one of his openings, Billy invited Tim up to have drinks with us. After several martinis and a puff or two on a joint, I fell asleep on a sofa and woke up sometime before dawn. As I passed by Billy's bedroom, I noticed lighted candles on the dresser and bedside tables. Some were dripless and some had burned down into amorphous gobs of wax. I tiptoed in to blow them out and saw Billy sound asleep with his arms wrapped around Tim. They were both naked and looked so peaceful. Tim opened his eyes and smiled at me as I blew out the last candle.

"Goddammit Hampton, you stupid son of a bitch. This kid loves Billy, he'd never do anything to hurt him," runs through my mind. Then I wonder if Timmy could be jealous of Billy's constant string of lovers, but this makes no sense. I know Billy often includes Tim in three-ways, and Billy has told me that Timmy turns tricks and gets three-hundred dollars or more an hour from his clients, so why would he be out to get Billy?

"Tim, Timmy I'm sorry," I offer and walk behind the counter, turn him towards me and hug him. I draw him close to me and feel his small, but muscular body heaving with sobs. He lays his head on my chest, collapses into me, and I stroke his head.

"Hush, hush," I whisper. "It's alright. Hush, hush..."

I stand rocking Timmy gently. Slowly, his sobs subside and my mind wanders. I hear Mother singing to me in her sweet, soft soprano.

"Hush, hush. Hush, hush, little man. Hush, hush, sweet darling. Hush, hush, little baby, don't say a word. Mother's gonna buy you a mocking bird. If that mocking bird won't sing, Mother's gonna buy you a diamond ring. If that diamond ring don't shine..." I can smell the Chanel No. 5 and feel the softness of her dress. She is rocking me in her wooden rocker. I am eight years old and have just skinned my knees badly—the Bactine® stings. Little Billy has a hurt look on his face, and he gently holds on to my legs and kisses my knees every so often as Mother rocks and sings.

"I'm sorry. I didn't mean to hurt you. I'm just so scared, so scared. Why did this have to happen to Billy? Why did this have to happen to my little brother?" I am crying now. As Timmy and I hold each

other, swaying and sobbing, the same coldness I came to know so well after Mother's death enters my spine and begins to wrap around my soul, and I look into the monitor showing Timmy and me. I become weak in the knees and feel faint.

"I need to go upstairs, Timmy."

He pushes the elevator button, the door opens, and he guides me in with his hands on my back and shoulders. He pushes the hold button and gets my duffle and Billy's clothes. He sets the bags down, retrieves a plastic card from his jacket and then inserts it into a slot, the door shuts, and the elevator rises to the twentieth floor, stops, and opens directly into Billy's foyer. Low light emanates from antique Venetian sconces on the mirrored walls, reflecting the limestone floor and the lightly gilded barrel-vaulted ceiling. Clark, Billy's mongrel dog, sits on the floor smiling at us the way dogs smile, wagging his tail furiously.

"Hey Clark, poor little lonely guy," I drop to my knees and receive several licks on my face as I hug and stroke Clark's ruddy-brown coat. He licks my ears and slips a quick lick on my lips. I chuckle.

"Mr. Hampton, I'll take him out to the terrace," Tim offers.

"Thanks. Tim, just call me Philip, please."

"Yes sir, I mean okay, Philip."

"Where do you want to rest?"

"In Billy's room, please," I muster with what little energy I have left.

"Okay, I'll put your things in his room and then take care of Clark. Come on Clark. Come on boy; let's go." Timmy heads off. Clark turns around, gives me a quizzical look, his tail wagging, then trots after Tim.

I walk slowly through the large, exquisitely decorated living room, frequently stopping, remembering my past. Billy created this room as a tribute to Mother and Fatgram. He calls it the museum of our lives. I always feel grounded when I'm in here. Groupings of richly upholstered chairs and sofas sit atop large Oushaks woven from wool dyed with muted shades of yellows, oranges, and blues. Several of Fatgram's prized early American pieces, including a beautiful Philadelphia highboy chest in the Chippendale style, a lovely pair of Hepplewhite mahogany inlaid Pembroke tables, and a trick leg card table with a carved swag panel, all of which I remember so well from her antebellum mansion—where our father deposited us to live after Mother's death, just four blocks down Maple Street from our own home in Union, South Carolina—are situated in the room along with some of Fatgram's best silver pieces. A black Steinway grand piano sits in the northwest corner of the room framed by large Palladian windows, which reveal incredible views of the Hudson River and Manhattan. Antique Chinese blue and white porcelain Mother collected, cherished, and included in her still life works is scattered throughout the room, and major works of art adorn the walls. I glance up at Mother's painting of Billy and me playing on the beach at Pawley's Island. It hangs over the large, white wooden mantel with carved columns and black marble facing. It is one of her largest paintings, forty-eight inches wide by thirty-six inches tall, and my favorite. This painting took first place in a major international art competition in 1980, after which her works became highly sought in the art market and regularly brought tens of thousands of dollars each. The painting is framed in a hand-carved, gilded frame that Mother had custom made in Florence. Billy is seated in the sand, legs crossed Indian style, in short red trunks, long lashes pointed toward the drip castle he is building. I'm kneeling down beside him in blue trunks, digging a hole with a green sand shovel to supply fresh wet sand for him. Through an array of small, thickly applied crosshatched patterns using the spectrum of visible colors, Mother painstakingly replicated the light patterns created by the mid afternoon sun on the ocean that bounce from the painting with such intensity that you can feel the August heat radiating. The sound of the crashing waves, seagulls' cries, and the shrill laughter of playing children fill my mind, and I'm carried back to those long days on Pawley's where Billy and I spent our summers seining for shrimp in the marshes, fishing off of docks and piers, collecting sand dollars and shells, crabbing using chicken necks and backs for bait, wandering the beaches, and occasionally, when we had behaved especially well and Mother was in a bright mood, making the trip up to Myrtle Beach to the amusement parks. Ala Mary,

our maid, managed the household, kept us from disturbing Mother's drawing and painting sessions, and from interfering with the constant string of guests from the world of art, few of whom ever arrived with children who might offer us new excitement in the summer. Dad would come in off the road from his job as a furniture salesman for weekends once or twice a month and would spend most of his time with us playing on the beaches and fishing, crabbing and clamming in the marshes. Mother would host her little cocktail soirees two or three times a week, which would often prolong late into the night. Billy and I spent most nights out on the sleeping porch attached to our bedroom. We would talk, ponder the enormity of the starlit sky, search for shooting stars, and try to decipher bits of speech, often slurred, from the grown ups which intermittently rose up over laughter and between the rhythmic crashes of the waves, carefully listening for and desperately hoping not to hear the familiar screaming accusations from Mother that signaled a bad fight between my parents. Whenever this occurred, Ala Mary, sometimes still in her white dress she always wore as a uniform or sometimes in her night gown, depending on the lateness of the hour, her large brown eyes and ageless face offering love and compassion, would slip onto the sleeping porch to check on us and offer us reassurance and comfort.

"You chillren okay out here?"

"We're okay," I'd reply followed by Billy's "Yep, just fine Ala Mary."

"They're really going at it tonight, ain't they Ala Mary?" Billy would ask.

"Aren't they, not ain't they," I would correct Billy.

"Don't say ain't or your Mother will faint and your father will fall into a bucket of paint," Billy would sneer back at me.

The sound of breaking glass, Mother's screams, or Dad's bass voice pleading, "For God's sake give it a rest, Eva," would punctuate the night ocean sounds.

"Lawd, lawd-a-mercy, mmmm,mmmm,mmmm," almost in her singing voice with the final "mmmm" in crescendo to a high note, Ala Mary would reply, looking out at the foamy whiteness of the breaking waves, a vision only the thickest fog could hide from our view.

"You boys better promise me to never let that evil booze lay holt a you. It ain't never done yo Mamma no good. No sir. Make her say thangs she don't mean, don't even know she be saying. Sweet Jesus gonna help us, I know he is."

"Are they going to get divorced Ala Mary?" Billy would ask. "If they do can Philly and I come live with you and Newt?"

"Oh, sweet baby, my little man. Dey jes gettin the bad blood out. Yo Mamma and Daddy loves you both a lot. Dey ain't gonna let nuthin bad happen to you." Ala Mary always fabricated something to make us feel better.

"Now go on and go to sleep and have you some sweet dreams. Mornin' come and I'll make you buttermilk pancakes. Okay sugars?" She'd kiss us both and head back to her bedroom on the top floor. Ala Mary's room had a porch too, and sometimes I'd wake up in the night to see her looking down at us or staring out into the Atlantic.

I walk down the hallway into Billy's bedroom. I sit on his bed adorned with luxurious spreads, linens, goose down pillows, and bolsters in varying shades of green and blue. Mother's painting of Willie B, Ala Mary's oldest son, loading a bushel basket of peaches onto a flatbed truck hangs by the entrance to the bathroom. The recessed ceiling light shining down on the painting illuminates Willie B's muscular arms, the dark shades of his skin in stark contrast to the white tank top he wears. Sweat pours from his forehead and the front of his tank top is soaked with perspiration. The expression on his face is one of satisfaction, even enjoyment of this labor. Billy says this painting is even more sensual and sexual than most of Mother's nudes. I vaguely remember Willie B and his younger brother, Clevis. They both died in an industrial accident at a toilet factory where they both worked when I was in the first grade. What I remember most about Willie B was the almost alarming contrast between his great strength and gentle

demeanor as he meticulously went about tending to Mother's prized camellias, azaleas, gardenias, and rose bushes in the evenings and on weekends. Some of Mother's most acclaimed and sought after paintings depict the everyday life of African Americans in the South Carolina piedmont region. Timmy enters the room and removes most of the pillows to a large, ornately carved antique French armoire and stretches me out on top of the covers. He unlaces my Timberlakes and slides them off my feet. He goes into Billy's bathroom and fills a glass of water and opens the medicine cabinet. I hear the steady clinking rhythm of Clark's toenails on limestone echoing in the hallway. He comes into the room and with a graceful leap lands by my left side, curls himself up, rests his triangular shaped head on my chest, sighs, moans, and searches in my eyes with his.

"Here Philip, take one of these sleeping pills to help you rest." Timmy hands me the pill, raises my head, puts the glass to my mouth, and I wash it down. Clark raises his head to observe Timmy and then puts it back down on my chest. The last thing I remember is the fading of Timmy's syncopated stammering as I fight the dread of waking up.

CHAPTER 2

"Philip, Philip darling. Wake up, Philip. Wake up darling." I hear Mother—her sweet soft voice tinged with a slight, but sophisticated southern drawl beckons to me. Deeply asleep, I try to force myself to begin the climb back to lucidity.

"Philip, darling. Wake up. Mother needs to talk to you darling." Her voice is much louder now, with more energy—urging in reverberating tones. I bolt upright in bed, shivering. I notice I have on only a pair of red and grey striped, flannel Calvin Klein boxers. I look around to find a tee shirt, a sheet, anything to cut the chill, but the bed is gone, and I am sitting on a cold stone floor in a dark hallway.

"Please, I need to speak with you. Please come to Mother." Her speech is now slurred, drawn-out, out of phase, deep, now moving fast and high pitched, time warped like a record spinning from 33 to 78 rpms, up and down. I look up at a strip of light shining through a doorway at the end of a long hallway.

"Philip darling, please listen to Mother. Philip, come to Mother!" I jump up and sprint down the hall. My senses read old mausoleum, and I bristle. The sound of my flat, bare feet slapping the cold stones overlaps Mother's beckoning calls. The strip of light does not seem to be getting any closer, but I keep running hard. My heart pumps madly as I sprint towards Mother's voice. The mist thickens. I am startled—something feathery brushes my face. "What the hell was that?" I spit out. I keep running. I hear a primordial screech far down the hall. The sound is unfamiliar, threatening and demonic.

"Mother, Mother, are you down there?" I scream as I run. Something dark flies past my head, and I feel another brush of a feather followed by a sharp pinch on my left side. Another screech resounds, then another and another—a blood chilling cacophony.

"What the fuck?" I choke out, hyperventilating, still running. I look back to see nothing but the dark mist. I look forward again, and, to my horror, the light is gone as is Mother's voice. Whoosh, whoosh, whoosh—I sense things flying all around me now, brushing all over my body, pecking at me and drawing blood.

"Oh shit, oh God, Mother!" I scream out covering my head with my arms. I keep running, but I'm out of breath and the screeching, dark winged creatures have descended upon me, smacking directly into me from all sides, tearing my boxers off in pieces with their beaks and talons.

"Help me!" I scream and stumble over a dark winged creature. I cover my head again and crouch down, burying my face into my thighs. I feel them land on my back and all around me, pecking me, feasting on me, ripping the flesh off my back and arms.

"Why me God? Why me?" I whimper.

Suddenly, I feel an incredibly warm sensation all over my body—blood oozing over my torn flesh. I sense a strong light.

"Philip, darling, where have you been, sweet heart? I've been calling you for such a long time." I open my eyes and look up. The sun is bright and warm; the terrible birds are gone. I am unharmed.

Standing up, I look around in disbelief. I am home, back in Mother's garden beside her cottage studio. Mother stands in front of her easel deeply engaged in a landscape. She holds her round palette board in her left hand and dabs at it with a brush in her right hand. It is April because blooming azaleas and climbing roses are abundant; the sweet fragrance of honeysuckle hangs on the breeze. The sun sparkles throwing shadows over the thick spring grass. My ears rejoice with the calls of cardinals, robins, wrens and mockingbirds. Mother wears a white sleeveless blouse and a beautiful pink skirt. I know she is barefoot; I know her toenails glisten bright red. She turns toward me smiling, motioning with her brush for me to come to her.

I feel embarrassed because I do not want her to see my naked body. She has never seen me as a grown man, especially a naked one. I start to cover my genitals and look down to discover that I am not a grown man at all, but a boy dressed in khaki shorts with white Buster Browns, white knee socks, a white shirt with a clip on yellow tie with blue stripes and a blue blazer with gold buttons—my Easter Sunday outfit when I was seven years old. Everything is moving in a type of slow motion—video clips playing with frequent pauses. Diaphanous, gossamer-like, fabric panels, in an array of tinted pastels, stir and float in the breeze, gently brushing my face and legs. I run toward Mother. It takes an eternity to get closer to her. Mother looks out over her garden and continues painting. I look at the painting, but it is not a painting of the garden at all. It is a beautiful water scene, a river flowing through a wooded area. On the near bank of the river is a sort of small fishing pier. On the far side is a blue shack. The reflections of the shack, the trees, and the sky in the water are extraordinarily beautiful. Mother's water scenes are my favorite—this is one I do not recall ever seeing.

"Mother, I've missed you so much," I cry out and run with my arms outstretched toward her. She puts the palette and brush down on her red Adirondack chair and picks me up, hugging me, and twirls me around. I bury my face in her neck and my whole body absorbs her warmth, her essence, her force of life. I hear the screen door on the back porch slam shut and look up to see Ala Mary, Billy, and Bonnie Belle, Mother's fat beagle, walking toward us. Billy is five years old and in his Easter outfit also. Ala Mary is dressed in her usual white dress with white shoes and is carrying a plate of chocolate chip cookies and a glass pitcher of milk. The smell of freshly baked cookies envelops me. My mouth waters. Mother puts me down and runs toward Billy and Ala Mary. She picks up Billy, hugs and kisses him and twirls him around. I run over to them. I lean over to pet Bonnie Belle whose tail and back end wag as she licks my face.

"Miss Eva, I told you if I was to mix up a fresh batch of chocolate chip cookies, these little uns be coming out the woodwork for them," Ala Mary says grinning.

"What would I ever do without you Ala Mary?" Mother smiles at Ala Mary, picking Billy up as he reaches his arms up to her.

"You never have to worry bout that purty chile," replies Ala Mary in the same loving tone Mother must have known her entire life.

Mother, holding Billy with his sleepy face resting on her right shoulder as if he's just awakened from a nap, Ala Mary, and Bonnie Belle turn away from me and walk toward the house. I immediately start to follow, but the faster I walk, the farther away they are from me. They are getting closer to the house now, yet I am no closer to them.

"We love you Philip," Mother's voice echoes.

My feet start pounding the ground furiously.

"Mother, wait for me!" I scream as loud as I can. They do not turn around, but walk up the back porch steps.

"Wait! Mother! Ala Mary! Billy!"

"Don't leave me!" My throat clutches and aches. Tears stream down my face, and I keep running, getting no closer to the house. Suddenly, two of the sheer panels curl around my wrists tightly, pulling my arms back. I can no longer run. A panel curls around my neck and constricts like a boa. I scream to Mother as everything turns cold, fading to black, and I am running once more down the dark hall. I am running and running, and I hear an excruciatingly loud blast of a horn or a siren. My eyes fly open; I look over to my left. Billy's telephone is ringing. The digital alarm clock reads eleven am. I am shivering, my shirt soaked in a cold sweat. Adrenaline rushes into my bloodstream. I am fully dressed except for shoes. My erection pushes against my pants; my bladder is painfully full. I am shaken to my core by the dream. I reach over Clark who looks at me with sleepy eyes and pick up the phone but cannot speak.

"Mr. Hampton? Mr. Hampton are you there?" I recognize Nurse Ostro's soft voice, which hits me like a sharp punch in the gut and strangles my throat. I can't breathe.

"Yes," I whisper.

"I'm so very sorry. Your brother passed away about twenty minutes ago," she says. My mind recalls the smell of her fabric softener and creates the image of this large, peaceful woman, with tears in her eyes delivering this news to me, which somehow relieves my tight throat. I gasp for air.

"Oh God," I say into the phone and begin to cry out loud. Clark pushes his cold black nose to my face, licking my tears.

"I'm so, so sorry," she says softly and then remains silent until my crying subsides.

"He went into a convulsive state, that is, he started having severe seizures nearly an hour ago. We tried our best. I tried your cell phone several times, but just got your voice mail. I finally found your brother's number in our records."

"Were you? Were you with him when he died?"

"Yes, he was not alone. We had a team of doctors and nurses and technicians in with him. I, I held his hand as much as I could. He was not alone," she replies, and I hear her sniffing back tears.

"Thank you Miss Ostro."

I hang up the phone, Clark whimpers, wags his tail slowly, looking into my eyes. I pull his compact, muscular body next to mine, cuddle around him, letting his soft fur absorb my tears. A sigh rocks his entire body, then he relaxes into my pain—his pain.

CHAPTER 3

The night mist has dissipated leaving the city framed in a pale blue sky, tinged with shades of pink. A chilly breeze rustles the potted evergreens on Billy's expansive rooftop terrace. I remember teasing him that the only reason he wanted this unit was so that he could land a helicopter up here. City noises fill my head as I watch Clark sniffing the tender young blades of grass emerging on the lawn area Billy created for him. The coffee mug warms my hands, and I crave a cigarette. I haven't smoked in years—Billy does occasionally. I start back inside to search.

"What am I doing? The last thing I need to do is start smoking again," I tell myself. I feel numb all over, zombie-like. I inherently sense the nicotine will somehow assuage the pain in my body, in my soul. When I had a painful case of shingles around my neck several years ago, the only thing that gave me relief was smoking. I smoked until they went away, about three weeks, and then no longer craved nicotine. I head back inside. Clark hunches up on his haunches on the grass, splays out his back feet, sticks his tail straight up, makes a 360 degree turn so that he resembles a hovering helicopter and initiates his morning constitutional, as Fatgram would call it, so I leave the terrace door open for him.

I find a couple of unopened packs of Marlboro reds, a sleek, onyx butane lighter, and a stash of European chocolate bars in a drawer in the wet bar. I smile, Billy is such a chocolate whore, and I grab a pack of the Marlboros, instinctively pound it on my left wrist, peel it open, pull out a cigarette and light it. The lighter emits a steady rushing sound sending up a uniform, intense, compact blue flame—a mini welding torch. I inhale deeply. An instant nicotine rush cascades through my body. After a couple of puffs and sips of coffee, I begin to focus on the things I must do. Clicking toenails on limestone divert my attention. Clark arrives looking up at me, wagging his tail.

"Bet you want some breakfast, boy?"

He jumps up planting his front paws on my waist.

"Okay, let's go get you some food."

He jumps down. I snuff out the cigarette in an ashtray and bend over to scratch his back. He performs a little dance by curling his rump around toward his face, wagging his tail, repeatedly sticking out his tongue, and making intermittent grunts. I smile, thankful he is here with me.

"What am I gonna do with you now?"

Clark continues his dance and then pops a lick right on my mouth. I laugh out loud—a small joy. Some internal dam temporarily holds my tears back. I get up and walk to the kitchen trying to remember in which cabinet Billy keeps Clark's food. The kitchen is large by New York standards with stainless steel appliances, black granite counter tops with flecks of sparkling gold, and beautiful wooden cabinets stained a light golden color. It has the most contemporary feel of any room in the condominium. I look inside several cabinets before I find his food in a concealed pantry. He waits patiently beside his bowl while I pour in some of the dry food. When I'm finished he begins to eat, and I wonder how a mutt from the projects of Louisville got such good manners. I pick up a phone on the counter and dial Luscious's number.

"Hello, Philip?"

"Hi Lush, Billy's gone. He died around ten thirty this morning," I say as I squeeze the muscles in my face and push my left fist into my forehead.

"Darling, I'm so sorry. I just can't believe this has happened—it's so unfair," her voice cracks.

"I, I feel so lost. I keep hoping it's all a bad dream…. that I'll wake up any second, but, I know it's real."

"You know I'm here for you. I'll be up this afternoon. I'll take the three pm nonstop—US Air," her words are interlaced with sniffles and sobs.

"Thanks, I hate to impose, but it would mean a lot to me to have you here."

"It's done. I'll go pack right now."

"What about David? Won't he mind?"

"Fuck David. He's a big boy, he can fend for himself," she asserts followed by a big sniff and loud throat clearing.

"Sounds like you two are getting along well."

"I'll fill you in tonight."

"Okay."

"I've been dialing your mobile all morning and just got your voice mail. I guess you were with Billy."

"No, I came back to his place to get some rest around four this morning. I dropped my phone and busted it at the hospital. I got a call at eleven this morning that he had gone into seizures and then died."

"Oh, God."

"Lush, this is so weird. When I got that call I was dreaming that I was at home again watching Mother painting in the garden. Ala Mary came out with Billy and Bonnie Belle. Then they all went into the house. I tried to follow, but couldn't, and they wouldn't wait for me. It was awful."

"Oh my."

"Yeah, well, can you get a cab to Billy's?"

"Sure."

"Need the address?"

"No, I know it."

"Good. Well, I need to get in touch with Dad. I couldn't reach him yesterday."

"Okay. Philip, I'll stay as long as you need me."

"Thanks Lush."

"How's Clark?"

"He's sitting right here waiting for you."

"Good. See you tonight."

"Bye."

I hang up the phone and bend down to pet Clark again.

"Clark, your mommy's coming to see you tonight," I say as if talking to a baby. He wags his tail and pants.

"Aren't you the lucky one? She saved you from the streets. Yes she did." He seems completely happy as he jumps up putting his front legs on my thighs and positioning his face next to mine. I give him a bear hug, and then stand up to call Dad.

"Hello," Dad answers his cell phone after the first ring.

"Where are you?"

"We're just walking off the plane."

"Brenda's with you?"

"Yes. How's Billy?"

"Dad," I break into sobs. "He died this morning."

I discern the sound of Dad weeping through the recitation of boarding instructions by a woman of Hispanic origin.

"Dad are you there? Dad?" There is no answer, just more announcements and shuffling sounds.

"Philip, it's Brenda. I'm so sorry. It's almost incomprehensible."

"Yes it is. Is...how's Dad?"

"He can't talk right now."

"I guess y'all were going straight to the hospital?"

"That's right."

"Did you book a hotel yet?"

"No, it all happened so fast. Charles didn't get your message until late yesterday afternoon. We had just arrived at Disney World with the kids for Spring break. We got the first flight we could this morning."

"Are the kids with you?"

"No, we put them on a plane back to St. Louis. My sister-in-law will keep them."

"I see. Well, why don't y'all just come here to Billy's first?"

"Yes, I suppose that's the best thing to do now. We'll see you in a bit."

"Okay, bye."

"Bye."

"Shit," I say to Clark. I have not seen Dad since one of Billy's openings a couple of years ago. I dread this encounter, but I resolve as I light another cigarette that I will try not to let my bitterness towards Dad thwart my responsibilities to Billy. I walk back into Billy's bedroom and find my backpack. Holding the cigarette between my teeth, I unzip the pack and search for the will. A dark shadow crosses my mind.

"Did going into my office at the last minute early Sunday morning, getting the copy of Billy's will and stuffing it into my back pack constitute the karmic 'straw that broke the camel's back' resulting in his death today?"

I cannot pursue this pattern of thinking. Luscious says I've always exacerbated my feelings of filial responsibility to an unhealthy realm. If I tell her this newest fear, she would call it ludicrous and tell me how conceited I am thinking my taking the will would contribute to Billy's death. Now my brain is telling me that if I had not insisted that we both hire estate-planning attorneys while only in our mid twenties, this would not have happened. The ash of the cigarette has grown and falls to the floor. I go into the bathroom, turn on the faucet, stick the lit cigarette under it, and then toss it into the toilet and flush. My face is red and puffy again. I set the will on the counter and splash cold water onto my face.

"Dad and Brenda will be here within an hour. Pull yourself together, Hampton."

I dry my face with a towel, pick up the will, and go sit on a chaise lounge in the bedroom. Clark hops up beside me and sniffs the will. I think about how my teenage years were punctuated by death—thirteen years old, mom; sixteen years old, Ala Mary; and nineteen years old, Fatgram. Dad might as well have been dead as little as we saw of him during those years. These deaths drew me closer to Billy yet away from my core self. Billy grew more defiant and reckless with each death, seeking a realm of emotionless feeling that I believe drove him to so many peaks and valleys. But my gut feeling is that he did not intentionally commit suicide. I thumb through the will and find the letter attached to it where Billy tells me his desires. My own will has a similar letter for Billy. I read the letter, even though I already know what it says.

May 23, 2000

Dear Philip:

This letter sets forth my wishes in the event of my death.

It is my desire, upon my death, to have my body cremated and my ashes put into Mother's large Kangxi Blue and White Ginger Jar with the Three Friends of Winter scene, which is usually kept in my living room and is cataloged in our collection of Chinese porcelain as C-1044 (marked on the bottom of the piece). Within a week of my death, I desire that a wake in the form of a cocktail buffet be held at my residence in New York. At a minimum those people listed in my Mac's Address Book database as Friends, Family, or Business Associates should be invited. Should you survive me, I ask you to carry out these instructions as you see fit. Should you not survive me to implement these instructions, the designated Executor, who shall be my trust company, Bank of America, shall carry out my wishes.

I desire for this wake to be a memorable event with the same high level of entertaining utilized for which I am generally known. No expense should be spared for food, drink, and flowers.

Within six months after my death, I desire that my ashes be taken and scattered in thirds at the following places: 1) over our beloved swimming hole at Harmon's Fork Creek on

the farm formerly owned by our late grandmother, Ina Robertson Eades, in Union, South Carolina; 2) over the Marquesa Atoll off the coast of Key West, Florida, transported on a flats fishing boat by my trusted fishing guide, Stan Shultz, should Stan survive me; and 3) along the shore of Gouverneur Beach in St. Barts. My preferred wish is that my ashes be scattered in the order I have listed above and within a period of two weeks. My estate will provide the funds for all aspects of the trip with only first class travel and accommodations, including all meals and drinks, allowed.

My intent is that the wake be a joyous celebration of my life. Should you be the one dispersing my ashes, Philip, I hope you see it as a celebration of three places I dearly love.

Your loving brother,

Billy Hampton

Heaviness descends upon my chest, like a big iron hook waiting for some force to manipulate it into action—an action I sense will result in my evisceration and the leaking out of my soul. I hug Clark again and swallow hard.

A page showing Billy has previously contracted with Riverside Funeral Home for his cremation follows the letter. I force myself to get up, grab the telephone off the bedside table and dial the number.

"Riverside Funeral Home. How may I help you?" The voice of an elderly woman greets me.

"Yes, I'd like to make cremation arrangements for my brother." I feel hollow and emotionless as I say these words.

"Certainly. One moment while I transfer you to one of our counselors."

"Thank you."

"This is Mr. Henderson. May I help you?"

"Yes, my name is Philip Hampton. My brother, William Hampton, died this morning. He has made arrangements with your funeral home."

"Please allow me to express my deepest condolences, Mr. Hampton," he says in a rehearsed baritone.

"Thank you."

"One moment sir while I pull up his account."

"Yes, Mr. Hampton, your brother has arranged for a simple cremation."

"Yes, that's right. He is at St. Vincent's Hospital."

"Fine sir, we will take care of everything."

"Thank you. Would you be able to deliver his ashes to his residence by Thursday?" "Of course. We can do it on Wednesday if you prefer."

"That's fine. What time?"

"Whatever you choose, sir."

"Let's say 2 pm."

"Yes sir. Is his residence still on Warren Street?"

"Yes, it is."

"Will you need any permanent receptacle?"

"No thank you."

"May we assist you with any arrangements for a memorial service?"

"No thank you."

"Fine. We'll see you Wednesday at two pm. Again, may I express my deepest condolences."

"Thank you." I hang up quickly, thankful that call is out of the way.

"Okay Clark buddy, let's go check his address book on his Mac."

Clark hears the "let's go" part and must think I'm going to take him for a walk because he starts prancing around, whimpering with an urgent high pitch, then dashes out of the bedroom. I proceed out of the bedroom, down the hall, toward the living room. Clark runs towards me with his leash in his mouth.

"What a smart dog you are! Hey buddy, we aren't going out just yet. I'll take you after while."

His head drops a bit and the speed of his tail wagging slows.

"Come on, let's go into the kitchen. I'll get you a treat."

Clark follows me, still holding his leash in his mouth. I go to the pantry containing his food and retrieve a rawhide bone from its package and hand it to Clark. He smells the bone, drops his leash, takes the bone and disappears. Closing the pantry cabinet I see a package of plastic bags made for picking up dog feces, and I remember Clark's morning constitutional. I grab a bag, pick up the leash, put in on a counter and head out to the terrace, but I think about Elliott Fields. I reach into my back pocket. The letter is still there. I head back to the kitchen and grab the telephone and dial his number. I hear faint ringing and lots of crackling noise.

"Hello?" I hear the faint sound of a man's voice.

"Elliott? Elliott? Can you hear me?" I inquire in a loud voice.

"Yes, bad connection, But I can hear."

"It's Philip Hampton—"

"Is there any change with Billy?"

"He died this morning—"

"Christ no. I—" The connection sounds like bacon frying, and I can't make out what Elliott is saying.

"Elliott, I'm having trouble hearing you."

"Can you hear me now? Philip—"

"Yes, that's better—"

"Philip, I'm so sorry. I feel like a jerk. I, I should've stayed with him. But, but the doctors told me it was unlikely his condition would change—he seemed stable. They said he would probably be in a vegetative state for years. Unless, unless the family decided to…to take him off life support."

"Yes, I know—"

"This is the biggest shoot of my career—I'm the feature model for next year's Ralph Lauren Men's Resort Collection—I'm under contract—I…I just had to go—"

"Elliott, it's okay. Billy would've wanted you to go—"

"I kind of thought the same thing. What a guy. We've just been dating a couple of months and now this—" The sizzling sounds intensify. I wait a moment as they fade.

"Elliott, can you hear me?"

"Yes."

"Tell me what happened."

"Well, Billy had been working all day long, and I was getting ready for this shoot—to leave on Sunday. We went out to dinner Friday night—we'd already said our goodbyes. I mean I stayed at his place Friday night. We got up Saturday morning, took Clark for a walk, grabbed a bagel and coffee on the way, and then I went home."

"I see."

"Well you know how spontaneous Billy is."

"Oh yes—"

"Well, he calls me just before midnight on Saturday. He's ecstatic. He's just completed the final painting of his series on sexuality he's been working on for the past couple of years. He says he now understands the key to this series. I mean, I've never heard him sound so happy. He tells me to throw on

my clothes and dancing shoes and meet him at Splash in forty-five minutes. I say okay." As he talks, I walk into Billy's studio to observe the painting. I gasp audibly when I see it. Clark looks up from chewing his bone in his dog bed.

"My God, this painting—"

"Yes, it's incredible. I saw it Saturday when it was almost finished. He called the painting Blood Brothers. It's almost abstract, isn't it? He's so protective of his work; it's the only one in the series he let me see. I think there are about fifty others."

"Yes, he told me that too."

"I guess that's why he was in such high spirits. Anyway, I arrived at Splash about one-fifteen a.m. The place was packed. Billy was at the bar, talking to some people and drinking a martini. From his looks, I'd say he had already had a couple. Anyway, he hugs me, grabs my hand—I didn't even have time to order a drink. We go to the dance floor and start dancing. He is wild—such energy. After dancing for about half an hour, we're both covered in sweat. I tell him I need to rest and get some water. He says no water, champagne to celebrate his new painting and the end of the series. I tell him maybe one glass because I don't want to be hung over for my trip."

"It sounds like he was on a roll—" I cannot stop looking at the painting.

"Definitely, but a good one—"

"Was he doing any drugs, coke, E?"

"Well, well we go stand at a table and he orders a bottle of Cristal and two waters. The whole time he's telling me the significance of this painting—how it's unlocking his fucked up childhood. Sorry, but that's what he said. You know he's been in therapy the last couple of years. You probably know he hated it at first, but lately I think he was getting a lot out of it. Anyway, he said he wouldn't mind having a little snort or two to celebrate. The champagne came and we toasted the painting and my big shoot. Some friends came over to see what we were celebrating. Billy tells them and orders another bottle so they can join us. Then he whispers to me that he's got to pee and find a little coke. I tell him okay, but that I can't stay too much longer. He smiles, says okay, kisses me on the cheek and says he'll be back in five minutes. That, that was the last thing he ever said to me," I hear Elliott weeping as the crackling intensifies again.

"Elliott, it's okay. Are you there?"

"Yes. Well anyhow, he doesn't come back in five minutes. I drink my glass of champagne and keep talking to our friends. The place just keeps getting more packed. I look at my watch, it's three a.m., so I go searching for Billy. I look everywhere: in the bathrooms, on the dance floor, other sections of the club—nothing. I get a little pissed and think if he's ditched me, especially for drugs, I'm gonna leave and just not call him until he calls me."

"That sounds like my brother, especially when he's having a good time."

"Yeah, well all the sudden I see commotion around one of the men's rooms. I don't know, but I just had a bad feeling. So, I push through the crowd and into the rest room. There are several people by the handicapped stall. I look in and see Billy slouched back by the toilet. Two guys are trying to slap his face to revive him—there's vomit on his chin and on his shirt. Some guy who was a doctor takes over. We pull him out and the doctor starts CPR. He wasn't breathing—" Elliott begins to cry again. The tears flow from my eyes as I look at Blood Brothers.

"The doctor is working furiously, breathing into his mouth, pounding his chest, but he will not breathe. I don't know what to do. Suddenly the paramedics arrive. They stick a needle in his chest—it was so awful." Elliott's speech is interrupted by sniffs and gurgling sounds. My tears stream to the floor. Clark stands beside me looking up at me.

"They get a faint pulse and keep applying some kind of mask—oxygen I guess. They put him on a stretcher and take him out. They're asking me all kinds of questions. I answer as best as I can. We get in the ambulance and on the way they have to do a tracheotomy and put him on a mobile ventilator. They've

given me his wallet so I go talk to the admissions people in the emergency room while they take him away. By four twenty a.m., the doctor, Dr. Seng, is telling me that Billy is essentially brain dead from lack of oxygen—they expect from ingesting GHB. I call 411 and thank God you're listed in Atlanta, so that's when I called you."

"Yes."

"Well, they put him in the ICU, and I stayed with him until ten o'clock. I called my agent to explain—to see if she could get them to postpone the shoot. She was sympathetic, but she said the shoot couldn't be postponed and that they would simply use an alternate if I didn't show up. So I wrote you a note, and I left. I'm really sorry; I should've stayed." The sound of a man weeping pulses through the static on the line. He sniffs, and I imagine him wiping his nose on his sleeve. He must have extraordinary looks, and I try to picture what he looks like.

"Elliott, Elliott, it's okay. It's not your fault. Please, it's okay."

"You really think so?" His voice is childlike.

"Yes, I do. Listen, did you and Billy ever take GHB?"

"No, never. Just some coke and pot, not even ecstasy."

"That's what I thought. Where do you think he got the GHB?"

"Don't have a clue. I wonder if someone could've spiked his drink? It happens, you know."

"Yes, I know. Usually it's a case of a guy doing that to a girl so he can have sex with her—the so-called 'date rape drug'. Isn't that right?"

"Yeah, I believe. I just don't know how it happened, Philip. I should've gone looking for him earlier. I should've—"

"No, don't go there, it's not your fault."

"Well, I guess…."

"When are you coming back, Wednesday?"

"We're running behind—they say Thursday now, but I can—"

"No, finish your shoot. We're having a wake at Billy's at six o'clock on Friday. I hope you'll come."

"Of course. When's the funeral?"

"There won't be one. He wanted to be cremated."

"Oh, I see."

"Well, thanks for talking to me, Elliott. I know how hard that was."

"Oh, well, sure. I mean, it's just so sad—"

"Yes. Well, I'm looking forward to seeing you on Friday."

"Right. Me too."

"Listen, Elliott, take my cell number."

"Okay, I'll program it in my phone, go ahead."

"404-555-0123. Got it?"

"Yes."

"Good luck with the rest of your shoot. Goodbye." I start to hang up the phone.

"Hey Philip, Philip, you still there?"

"Yes."

"Well, uhm, well, that painting Blood Brothers?"

"Yes."

"Well, uhm, Billy told me it is about you and him having sex together as children." I'm stunned, almost speechless.

"Jesus. Well lots of brothers beat off together as kids. I guess that's what he was talking about."

"Yeah, but he went into it a little deeper than that. I just thought I ought to let you know what I know."

"Right. I mean sure. Uhm, let's talk more about this when you get back to New York," I offer in a weak tone.

"Oh sure. I'm not trying to pry or anything. I just wanted to let you know what Billy told me. One other thing, Philip. Billy gave me a small package. It looks like a necklace case, and it's wrapped in silver wrap with a white ribbon. He asked me to leave it with the concierge here, but not before ten in the morning on Tuesday. I am to leave it for someone to pick up. He said he was returning something to a friend he had borrowed. Do you know anything about that?"

"No, I don't. I don't have any idea, but I guess you better drop it by the desk in the morning like Billy asked."

"Right, I'll do it. Philip, I'd really like to sit down and talk with you when I get back. This is all so weird."

"Okay. We'll do that. I appreciate everything you've done, Elliott. See you on Friday. Good bye." I hang up the phone. I feel washed out, drained, weakened beyond repair. I sit on a stool staring at Blood Brothers. The large painting conveys motion and is awash in red shades of blood that appear to flow over and through the painting. Three figures are holding hands as if in a circle playing ring around the roses or something. The figures are abstract, but definitely two small boys and one tall man—they all have manifestations of penises and hearts, all interconnected by very faint blood vessels. The faces are less abstract, but each face is painted as a moving image and portrays a varying range of emotions from dejection to ecstasy. I recognize my face as a boy, Billy's face as a boy, and undeniably, Uncle Adrian's face as the man. Chills race up the back of my neck as I realize the figures are circling a camera on a tripod and are at the edge of a creek. I let myself go back there. The buzz of dragonflies, chirp of birds, and rush of water resound; the summer sun beats down; the dense smell of the wet, red, creek bank clay hangs in the air. This is the place where we became Blood Brothers.

"Boys, this heat feels as if we're on the Indian subcontinent; it's just as oppressive," Uncle Adrian exclaims as he turns knobs and adjusts the aluminum (Uncle Adrian pronounces this as aluminium which always makes Billy and me laugh) legs to level out his tripod on one of the large boulders surrounding our swimming hole. He looks up at us, squinting his pale blue eyes in response to stinging sweat and glaring midday sun, pulls a blue bandanna from his right pocket and mops his forehead and eyes.

"Yep and you're white as a lily, Uncle Adrian. You're gonna get a bad burn out here," I say.

"Right. I'll try to keep to the shade. Ala Mary was kind enough to send along some sunscreen lotion. Perhaps you can rub some on my back in a bit?"

"Okay."

"Why is India called a subcontinent, Uncle Adrian?" Billy asks in a loud voice without turning around to look at us as he squats in the shallows poking around for crawdads with a stick. I'm almost ten years old, going into the fifth grade, Billy's just going into the third grade, and I rush to say, "It's because it is the bottom part of the continent of Asia, the part below the tallest mountains in the world, the Himalayas."

"Oh, I know about the Himalayas," Billy looks up with a twisted expression on his face, annoyed that I spit out the answer. "That's where the world's tallest mountain, Mount Everest is, and I'm gonna climb to the top of it when I grow up."

"Both of you chaps are right. The Indian subcontinent is the vast peninsula surrounded by the Arabian Sea and the Bay of Bengal which lies south of the Himalayas, which, in turn, indeed make up the world's highest mountain range where that most magnificent and tallest of all the mountains, Mount Everest, sits."

Billy and I look at each other and break out in belly laughs.

"What's so funny you little scoundrels?"

"You said Himalias when it should be Himalayas," I say still laughing.

"Ah, how many times do I have to tell you that Brits pronounce things differently than you Yanks," he replies with a big smile that reveals his teeth, crooked and nicotine stained.

"Fancy a crisp, Billy, or perhaps a sweet?" I say, continuing to mock Uncle Adrian who is looking at Billy who holds up a large crawdad, its legs and claws combing thin air.

"Look how big this one is!" Billy stands up and brings the specimen to me for closer inspection.

Uncle Adrian walks over with a worried expression on his face, "Yes, quite big isn't it Billy? But, for Heaven's sake, put the poor bugger back in the creek. You're scaring the wits out of it."

Laughing, Billy thrusts the wriggling crawdad towards Uncle Adrian's face. Uncle Adrian gasps and jumps back, "You nasty devil, I said put that little langoustine back in the creek."

Billy wrinkles his forehead, shades his eyes with his left hand, looks up at Uncle Adrian, and says, "This ain't no langoustine; it's a craw daddy, a granddaddy craw daddy."

"Langouste is the French word for crawfish, and you better not let your grandmamma hear you using that bastardly contraction, 'ain't'," Uncle Adrian walks back to his tripod. "Now put him back in Billy. Be a good chap."

"Okay, okay, but he'll just end up being supper for some old fat daddy coon anyway." He shrugs, walks back over to the shallows, kneels down, and lets the crawdad go. It quickly scampers under some submerged decaying leaves. Billy starts turning over rocks in the creek, exploring for other creatures. I pick up some pebbles and start skipping them over the swimming hole. A Belted Kingfisher swoops over the swimming hole protesting our presence with its loud trill.

"Uncle Adrian, when can we get in? It's hot enough to fry an egg out here," I complain as I try to get a pebble to skip more than four times.

"Yeah, we shudda got an egg, Philly, and cracked it on one of these rocks. I betcha a dime it'll fry today," Billy says.

"No need to bet, it'll fry alright," I reply.

"You boys hang on a bit. Let me get the Hasselblad set up here, and then we'll get in. I want to document our historic ceremony today," Uncle Adrian smiles as he mounts the camera on the tripod. His shirt is unbuttoned and I see glistening trails of sweat running through the light red brown hair on his chest. This spring I began developing a fine layer of peach fuzz along my upper lip, and a few darker blonde hairs had appeared in my pubic region and under my arms. I wonder if I'll have a hairy chest like Uncle Adrian and Dad. I wonder when I will sprout a beard and get to shave.

It's a Sunday morning, a special Sunday, the fourth of July, and Uncle Adrian just arrived a couple of days ago. We are going to have a big party with fireworks tonight at Fatgram's. Billy and I are so excited but we are also excited because this summer Uncle Adrian says Billy and I are old enough to join a top-secret club just for guys. It is called The Blood Brothers Club. Today is the special day we will conduct our initiation ceremony at Fatgram's swimming hole. Billy and I have been full of excitement and anticipation all day, lying awake last night, speculating about all aspects of the club.

"Are we gonna go skinny dipping today?" Billy asks as he pees into the creek, aiming to hit some exposed rocks in the middle. I hear the camera shutter clicking.

"Oh yes, that's part of the secret ceremony. Let me just get some test shots here, then we'll get started. I think the light will be perfect on the other side of the swimming hole." Uncle Adrian makes some final adjustments to the camera, attaches a long black wire to it with a button on the end, and begins to unroll the wire.

"What's that cord?" I ask as I observe him placing it on the bank, heading to the other side of the swimming hole.

"It's a shutter release. I can take pictures of the ceremony over here while the camera remains on the other side of the pool."

Uncle Adrian takes black and white photographs with this old camera and develops them himself. He has a dark room in his apartment in New York City. Sometimes, he lets Billy and me help in the dark room, which is great fun so long as we don't touch anything. Mother says Uncle Adrian is known for his fine art photography.

"You boys go grab the lunch basket, the blankets, and my leather attaché. Put them on this big rock in the shade here. Then we'll get started."

"Yippee!" Billy yells and we both run up to Mother's red Alpha Romeo Spider parked up on the dirt road. I grab the large basket which Ala Mary has filled with cold, fried chicken, potato salad, slices of cantaloupe, biscuits and honey, pecan pie and a thermos filled with sweet iced tea. Billy takes the blankets and the briefcase and we scamper down the side of the creek bank as fast as we can.

"Hand me the satchel, love," Uncle Adrian says to Billy. "Spread the blanket there on the sand in the shade. Philly, you put the basket over on that rock."

"Okay," I say. "Uncle Adrian, I've gotten really good at archery this summer," I boast.

"Oh have you?" he replies as he opens the briefcase, peers in, sticks his right hand into it, moving it around as if he's searching for something.

"Yes, I have, haven't I, Billy?"

Billy, on his knees in the sand spreading out the blanket with his hands, turns his head toward us, sighs and says, "Yeah, he's pretty good." I am thrilled at his response because, even though Billy is younger than I, he's blessed with physical coordination and is much more of a natural athlete than I, especially in sports involving balls. Everyone was amazed last autumn, when Dad first exposed us to archery, that I could consistently hit the target more than Billy could, and I enjoyed a great deal of satisfaction in that revelation, so I've practiced whenever I can, which hasn't been that often because Dad won't allows us to use the bows and arrows without adult supervision.

"Really, you're quite the little toxophilite," Uncle Adrian replies as he continues to fish around inside the case.

"Little what?" I ask.

"Toxophilite," he replies.

"What's that?" I ask.

"Oh, just a word describing a lover of archery," he replies with a slight grin on his face.

"Wow that's a strange word," I observe.

"Not really," he replies, "It's from Greek, you see. *Toxon* means bow and *philos* means love. That gives you bow lover, and that's what you are, no?"

"Well, I guess," I reply. "Gee, you are the smartest person I know, Uncle Adrian."

"Yeah, pretty smart," Billy says as he joins us.

"Anyone can learn who has the desire. Anything is possible with knowledge. Now, moving on boys, are you quite certain you want to go through with this secret ceremony?"

"Yes, yes," we eagerly reply.

"Now this is the type of secret ceremony that customarily is engaged in by fathers and their sons. But, since your father is so often away, I've agreed to do this on his behalf." His eyes move from mine to Billy's and back. We both can hardly breathe.

"You must swear on this Bible," he pulls a small black Bible from the case, "that you will never breathe word about this ceremony to anyone, outside of yourselves, for as long as you live. If you do, our secret pack will immediately become null and void, but especially, if your Mother finds out, it would upset her terribly because she thinks that it is your father's responsibility to do this, which it rightfully is. As I said, I've made a secret pact with him to do this on his behalf, since he has to be away so much of the time."

Billy and I look at each other. I am thrilled to the bone that Uncle Adrian is entrusting us with such a wonderful secret.

"I promise, Uncle Adrian. We won't tell anyone, ever, not even Ala Mary or Fatgram," Billy exclaims putting his right hand on his heart.

"Good, you certainly don't wish to upset your dear old grandmother. Yes, you see, if this gets out, I think it might cause your parents to divorce," he states with great authority, giving us a stern look.

"Divorce?" I say and look anxiously at Billy.

"Yes, divorce," Uncle Adrian replies.

"Philip, put your left hand on this Bible, hold your right hand up, and repeat after me." I do as he says and look up at him. A slight breeze rustles through the poplars and sycamores overhanging the banks of the creek, and several crows sound off in the highest branches of a dead sycamore. Their loud, shrill warning caws bounce off the stark whiteness of the limbs and blend with the gurgle of the water as I repeat after Uncle Adrian.

"I, Philip Robertson Hampton, do solemnly swear on the Holy Bible of our Lord and God that I will never reveal the secret purpose of the Blood Brothers Pact nor shall I reveal the members of the pact or any of the reasons why the pact exists. This I promise until my death, so help me God."

I feel as if I'm being inducted into the knights of the roundtable as Billy begins his recitation. When he is done, Uncle Adrian pulls out a Swiss Army knife, and opens the blade. "We must each cut our hands and mix the blood together, the blood of real brothers, the blood which makes us blood brothers," and he hands the knife to me.

"Oh darn, do I have to go first?" I blurt out.

"Philly, it's really no problem with the palms of your hand; there are very few nerves there. You'll barely feel it. The tips of the fingers have all the nerves. It would be painful if you cut there." I grab the knife with my right hand and lightly jab the blade into the meaty part of my left palm. Nothing happens.

"Sissy pants," Billy yells, "You've got to poke it harder than that."

"Shut up, Billy, I know how to do it." I swallow hard this time slowly pressing the tip of the blade into my left palm until I see the skin sever. I pull it out and feel a sharp stinging sensation, no pain, and then a lot of blood pours forth.

"Brave one, Philly. Your turn, Billy," Uncle Adrian says.

Billy grabs the knife from my right hand with his right hand and plunges it into his left palm, blood immediately oozes out and runs on the ground. He winces, though with a half laugh.

"Okay, Billy, but maybe a little too hard," Uncle Adrian advises and raises his right eyebrow, a gesture he often makes.

Uncle Adrian takes the knife from Billy and starts to cut his right hand, when I say, "Hey, you haven't sworn on the Bible yet. You have to do it too for it to count," I emphatically add as I hold my bleeding hand. I take the Bible in my bleeding hand and hold it out to Uncle Adrian who solemnly recites the pledge. He then takes the knife and cuts a small slit in his right palm as if he were opening a package. The blood flows quickly and he states, "Dear noble comrades we rub our blood together to create a power larger than each of us, larger than the sum of the three of us. Henceforth, the tenets, beliefs, rights, rituals, and practices that we may conduct as men will remain forever consecrated and shall remain secret until eternity within the confines of our group, The Blood Brothers. Death shall result to any one who betrays or interferes with this pact. This is the Word of our Supreme Master, his ancient spirit watches over us and knows all and sees all and will follow us throughout our lives."

Uncle Adrian takes our bleeding hands and rubs them together with his. Then, we each put a bloody thumbprint by our name printed on a proclamation Uncle Adrian pulls from the case. The proclamation has a big gold seal on it, and I recognize Uncle Adrian's perfectly neat handwriting on it. He puts the proclamation back in his case and says it is time to disrobe and enter the holy waters. Billy and I immediately

"Suck off?" I ask.

"Yes, that's what you call what I just did to you."

To my surprise, Billy falls down to his knees and takes my todger in his mouth and begins to suck. The feeling is indeed pleasant, and I soon feel a warm burning climbing through my rear end and balls up through my todger and before I know it, my todger is throbbing violently in Billy's mouth and Billy pulls off, spits and says, "Yuk, what's that salty stuff coming out of your todger?"

"That, my boys, is sperm. Congratulations, Philip, you have just ejaculated, probably for the first time in your life."

"Nirvana?"

"Yes, Nirvana. Now, you two take turns stroking my todger, and I'll demonstrate how a grown man reaches Nirvana."

We each take turns stroking Uncle Adrian's long penis. After a while he asks Billy to rub his balls and asks me to rub his nipples. We do and Uncle Adrian rapidly rubs his todger up and down with his left hand until he groans like an animal and white sperm shoots like a fountain out of his todger, spraying warm stickiness all over us.

"How perfectly wonderful," he says. "Don't forget boys, all this is top secret. No one must ever know."

"Okay," I say.

"Scouts honor. No, Blood Brothers honor," Billy states.

"Very good. Let's swim now. We've got the rest of the summer to have more Blood Brothers meetings."

Billy makes a perfect cannon ball entry into the swimming hole, splashing Uncle Adrian and me with cold water. I look up at Uncle Adrian, the semen and water droplets on his face and chest glisten, and even though he is smiling at me, his pale blue wolf-like eyes peering into mine frighten me. I turn around and dive into the cool, dark deepness of the pool.

I pick up the canvas, letting my eyes flow over it. The three figures are holding hands, I'm certain of that. Billy holds my left hand with his right hand, but there is something else in his right hand. I look closer, squinting my eyes a bit until it comes into focus—the Swiss army knife we used to cut ourselves in the ceremony. A wave of repulsion, then nausea sweeps over me. The blade of the knife is pointed straight toward the heart of Adrian. I pick up the canvas and slide it back into one of the storage bins. I need some air, so I walk out through the French doors in the studio to the terrace.

The mist has burned off completely, the temperature is climbing to a pleasant level, and I turn my face toward the sun closing my eyes. Billy loved the sun, and he loved the water. Memories from all the good times we have spent together at creeks, lakes, and beaches spill through my mind. I am still holding the plastic bag. I smile and open my eyes, looking down at a big pile of dog shit already covered with several flies, their shiny black-green and violet bodies glimmering as they crawl.

CHAPTER 4

Sitting at Billy's desk in the large room that serves as his office and studio, I click his Address Book icon to scan the contacts. With a few clicks of the mouse I determine that he has 512 contacts noted as Friends, Family and Business Associates—most of the contacts are in the Friends and Business Associates

categories. I wonder who are all the people who are not classified at all. My shoulders are arched up and tight. I heave a large sigh slumping back into the chair.

"Dear God, are we gonna have five hundred people here on Friday?" I ask out loud. Clark, sprawled out on his belly in his large suede dog bed, with his hind legs sticking straight back and the rawhide bone held between his front paws, interrupts his rhythmic gnawing to look up at me. He sighs as if to answer in the affirmative, and then resumes his bone chewing. I peer out into the room, my brother's inner sanctum, where he spent innumerable hours intensely focused on his creations. His desk is a large, beautiful, nineteenth century Boule desk with bronze doré. The doré includes Cardinals or popes on the cabriole legs and the top of the desk is inlaid with leather. His desk chair is a high back leather office chair, of the same deep burgundy as the leather in the desk, with bronze button tufting. The only items on the desk are the screen and keyboard of his Mac, a telephone, and a Tiffany desk lamp with a bronze base shaped like a tree trunk and an intricately designed stained-glass shade covered with leaves in varying shades of green and violet. The room is rectangular and larger than the living room and is arranged into two sections: a study/library section and a working studio that is specifically designed to admit sunlight. The ceiling is high, slanted, ribbed with huge oak beams and contains four large skylights. The long eastern facing wall is covered with floor to ceiling windows and three separate sets of French doors leading to the terrace. A large fireplace and a massive fieldstone chimney, rising up to the highest point of the sloped ceiling, bisect the western wall. A large, ornate wooden chandelier, finished in antique blue with speckles of gold leafing, hangs from the ceiling in front of the fireplace. Billy told me the chandelier came from an old hotel in Havana. Zone controlled recessed lighting covers the ceiling. The northern half of the room comprises the study/library, richly paneled in warm English Oak, with floor to ceiling bookcases and a large, wooden, library ladder. The floors are twenty-four-inch wide heart of pine planks stained a rich dark brown. The planks were cut from logs from virgin pine forests felled in the mid-1800's that sank to the bottom of the Cape Fear River in North Carolina. An entrepreneur recovered the perfectly preserved logs in the early 1990's. Billy could not resist them for his studio floor. There are three groupings of furniture in this area: one surrounding his desk which sits in the northeast corner, one in front of the large fireplace, and one facing the windows to the east. The furniture consists of an eclectic mix of American, English, and French antiques mixed with sumptuous upholstered chairs and sofas dispersed over three large oriental rugs. The south half of the room is his studio where he has three large easels in front of the windows. Storage bins constructed of the same oak as the bookshelves line the western wall and built-in storage cabinets are located in front of the bins. Several large pieces of sculpture are dispersed throughout the room. The room contains two large ficus trees, a couple of large false aralias, and two tall Palmetto trees, the state tree of our home state. A large guest suite, complete with its own kitchenette, is located off of the south end of the room.

"Billy has a good friend who always caters his parties. Shit, what's his name, hickamagig—Ricky. Ricky what? What's the name of his firm?"

I type in Ricky in the search box in the Address Book and five Ricky's pop up. Immediately, I spot Ricky Wallitsch and Upper Crust Events, LLC.

"Bingo Clark, we're saved!" I shout.

Clark drops his bone, hops up, trots over to me, jumps up into my lap and licks my face. I laugh and hug him. "Goddamit Clark!" I gasp in pain as he pushes his right front paw into my left nut. I push him to the floor. His tail goes between his legs; he lowers his head, looking at me with big, sad eyes.

"It's okay, boy," I whisper. His head lifts and his tail slowly begins to wag. Still reeling in pain I dial Ricky's cell phone number.

"Hey Billy, how are you?" Ricky answers his phone with an energetic, high tenor.

"Uhm, uhm, Ricky, this is Philip Hampton, Billy's brother," I deliver and swallow hard.

"Hi Philip. Are you doing well?" he cheerfully asks.

"Yes, nice to speak to you again," I return, thinking how stupid this sounds.

"What's up Philip? You visiting your brother?" He sounds confused at this point.

"Ricky, Billy died this morning at St. Vincent's," I reply flatly.

"Dear God, what? How can that be? I just saw him last week. I mean—"

"He somehow ingested an overdose of a drug called GHB Saturday night at Splash."

"Oh, my God—"

"Yes, he was found unconscious in a bathroom stall and by the time they got him to the hospital he was brain dead. He died around ten-thirty this morning after suffering a round of bad seizures."

"I'm so sorry, Philip. I don't know what to say—"

"You don't need to say anything, but you can help me out."

"Of course, I'll do whatever you need."

"Billy's last wishes were to be cremated and to have a very large wake slash cocktail buffet with his remains in one of our Mother's old Chinese urns."

"I see—"

"That wake needs to happen this Friday, and I think we'll be inviting upwards of five hundred and fifty people. Can we make this happen on such short notice?"

"Not a problem. You leave it to me. I'll take care of everything."

"You sure it can be done?"

"Philip, this is what I get paid the big bucks for. Oh shit, I didn't mean it like that. I won't charge you for my time or any mark up at all for this—"

"No, no! Ricky, Billy has explicitly requested that this be the mother of wakes, so I want you to go all out with food, drinks, champagne, flowers. Yes, yes, the best flowers you can find. You know how much Billy loved flowers, especially white orchids."

"Right—"

"And staff, as much as you need. It will all be covered by Billy's estate. And Ricky, I absolutely insist that you not work for free and that you put in your normal mark-ups. And, I don't mind if you charge a premium. I mean, gee, look at the short notice."

"Okay, Philip. I am happy to do this for Billy. Do you need anyone to help you contact people or make any other arrangements?"

"No thanks. I have a good friend coming into town tonight. She's a pro at all that. In fact, I'll have her call you tomorrow to firm up the number and go over everything you're planning."

"Great, just have her call me before ten in the morning. Okay?"

"Okay! You're a great help."

"Sure thing. Oh, what's you friend's name?"

"Oh yeah, it's Luscious."

"Oh, I've met Lush before, at one of Billy's openings—attractive woman, and of course, you don't forget a name like that. Well, I'll look forward to talking to her in the morning. And Philip, I'm so sorry about Billy. It just doesn't seem possible."

"Thank you."

"Oh, is it okay if I pass the news along to some of our friends?"

"Yes, in fact, I'd appreciate that."

"Right. I'm glad to do it. He is loved by so many people."

"Thanks, Ricky."

"You bet, bye."

"Good bye."

I hang up the phone feeling great relief. "Now I have to get out the news and invitations, but by what method? Luscious will be able to help out with that. And then there's the obituary that has to be written. I'm sure his death will make the evening news and the papers tomorrow." The telephone rings.

"Mr. Hampton, your father is here to see you," Rodney, one of the daytime doormen, states peremptorily in his Bostonian accent.

"Thank you. Please let them up." I hang up and head out into the living room and into the foyer. Clark sits in front of the elevator door, wagging his tale, and intermittently turning his head to look up at me. I look at myself in the mirrored walls and realize that I have not changed clothes, shaved or bathed since early Sunday morning. I'm a wreck, and I can smell my own body odor. The door opens and Brenda and Dad emerge. Clark immediately jumps up to greet Brenda.

"Oh, oh my," she says.

"Clark, no, boy, down, down," I say as I grab his collar, pulling him down off Brenda.

"Sit Clark, you stay down." He obeys.

"Sorry Brenda. Hello. Hi Dad," I say looking back and forth between Brenda's and Dad's faces. Dad's face is puffy and red. The lines in his forehead seem more pronounced than I remember; his eyelids are heavy, partially concealing his blue eyes, the whites streaked with red. His black hair has become completely flecked with grey, and he is wearing it longer than I ever remember. His dark complexion appears faded, splotched. I feel awkward. Brenda senses this and moves forward to hug me.

"Philip honey, we're so sorry," she says as she hugs me tightly. I bend down to embrace her and am enveloped in her softness and her appealing floral perfume. Clark lets out two rapid barks, followed by a short growl.

"Hush, Clark, it's okay. Sit!" I say in a firm tone. He whines and obeys. I turn to look at Dad. I recognize the same lost, hopeless look he expressed after we learned of Mother's death—the look I always associated with his withdrawal into himself and away from Billy and me, sporadically during the first year after Mother's death, then permanently after he turned us over completely to Fatgram. My emotions toward Dad are mixed, but I sense that I have the advantage of strength at this point, so I embrace him. He embraces me back. We are the same height and he leans his head over my left shoulder and weeps. Tears begin to fall from Brenda's eyes, and she opens her purse to retrieve a Kleenex.

"Dad, I'm sorry. It's okay. Come on in and sit down," I offer in a soft voice. I guide Dad into the living room with my right arm around his waist. Brenda and Clark follow. I steer him onto one of the large sofas and sit down beside him. Brenda sits on the other side. Clark lies down at our feet. Dad says nothing, staring down at the floor. A tear runs down to the tip of his nose and jiggles. Brenda gently dabs it with a Kleenex. I know she deeply loves my Dad, and I am remorseful that I have never been able to accept it or to accept her.

"Dad? Billy and I both have had our estates planned and our wills done for quite some time now. I guess I pushed it because we've had so much loss in our family, and our trust officer certainly encouraged it."

He doesn't seem to acknowledge what I'm saying, but I decide to go on.

"Well, it was Billy's desire to be cremated and then to have a wake here. I'm in the process of arranging the wake for this Friday. Luscious, you know my friend Sarah Richardson from Louisville, is coming up this evening to help out."

Dad turns his face toward mine and looks into my eyes and turns up the corners of his mouth in a slight smile. He takes my left hand in both of his and squeezes it slightly.

"Son, you're the best brother Billy could have ever asked for," he says. I see his eyes are filling up with tears.

"When you were just a little tot, maybe four years old, Billy fell against a chest of drawers and hit his head hard. He screamed and cried and cried and wouldn't stop. A big red bump popped up on his forehead. You were so concerned and wanted to make the pain stop for him. You promised your mother and me that you would take care of him, always. And you have." He looks at me with a kind of smiling frown, and I feel my eyes welling up with tears.

"Philly, I just can't believe our little Billy's gone—my pretty little boy, fearless, tough, determined, talented, who grew up to accomplish so much." He lets go of my hand and puts both hands on his knees, weeping. Clark stands up and sticks his head into Dad's lap. Dad strokes his head. Brenda is weeping audibly.

"You know Philip. Brenda met me in those years I was tortured after your Mother's death—staying on the road working, running away from everything, from the pain, from my children, relying on alcohol to get me by." Dad speaks slowly and deliberately, occasionally repeating words when the tears get in the way.

"She pulled me out of my gloom, got me on my feet again, married me, gave me hope and now we have a beautiful family…. But…. But, I didn't listen to the one thing she pleaded with me to do over and over…. Get right with my boys…" I am stunned listening to Dad.

"I tried many times, son, but it's a simple truth: I was never man enough to do it. I, I felt so at fault for your Mother's death. I felt that I had driven her to suicide. I just couldn't face you and your brother feeling that way. Fatgram made it easy for me too. You know what a strong willed woman she was. She always thought Eva had married beneath her. She never said it, but I sensed it, everyone knew that was what she felt, and she was especially happy to take you guys in. God knows she was a much better parent than I could ever have been at that point."

"Dad, it's all right, you don't have to get into this now," I interject, not wanting to be put on the spot, not wanting to feel compelled to forgive him at this moment.

"No son, I have to finish this. Your mother loved you boys more than you know, and I love you and Billy so very, very much. And now, I'll never be able to say that to Billy. But, I will say it to you. I have never stopped loving you for one minute, and I never will stop loving you." I give in completely and hug my Dad, putting my face against his, crying. Clark whimpers and tries to climb into Dad's lap. We all laugh even though we are crying.

"Stay down, Clark," I say, gently pushing him back. We all sit without speaking for a while.

I stand up and say, "Look, we're all emotional wrecks and tired. I need a shower and a shave in the worst way. I'm going to send down for your bags, and y'all are gonna stay here with me."

"Oh Philip, that's sweet of you, but maybe we better stay in a hotel. We don't want to be in the way of all you have to do," Brenda says in a conciliatory tone.

"Nonsense, y'all are staying here, there're five bedrooms, and you can help me and Luscious get Billy's wake together. You know Billy would want this to be a splendid affair and a splendid affair it shall be. Why, he's having over five hundred people to this wake."

"Good heavens," Brenda exclaims as she stands up, "We've got work to do, gentlemen."

Spontaneously Brenda grabs Dad's right hand, and I grab his left hand and we pull him up off the sofa.

"Follow me, let me give you a refresher tour of the place and show you your room. I want you to make yourselves completely at home. Y'all can have the guest suite off the studio, and I'll put Luscious in one of the bedrooms down the hall from Billy's. Just keep your door closed if you don't want Clark nosing around." We follow Clark through the living room into the kitchen.

"My, I forgot how exquisite this place is," Brenda observes, and I regret that in fifteen years I have never given this woman the time of day.

CHAPTER 5

After making certain Dad and Brenda have their luggage and are settled in the guest suite, I excuse myself to get a shower and shave. My little shadow Clark trails me, and I wonder what the future holds for both of us. As I take off my clothes down to my boxers, I realize I have only brought a couple of pair of jeans, one pair of khakis and a few shirts. I go into Billy's huge walk-in closet and turn on the lights—everything is in perfect order. Overcoats, jackets, suits, sport coats, dress shirts, casual shirts, dress slacks, and casual slacks are arranged by color and hang in neat rows. Belts and ties are arranged in the same manner. Custom made shelves contain dozens of pairs of shoes. Built-in drawers hide everything else. Billy and I are virtually the same size, even in shoes, and I know all these clothes are now mine—I wonder if I will be able to wear any of them and what shall I do with all the rest. My taste in clothes is simple—Billy possesses the wardrobe of a supermodel. I approach the rows of hanging suits, sport coats, and shirts. I touch the fabrics and think about him wearing the clothes I recognize. I gently grab the sleeve of a white dress shirt and pull it to my nose—no scent of Billy, just a fresh starch smell. I remember the white bag from the hospital containing his clothes, and I go back to the bedroom to get it. Clark beats me to the bag and sticks his head in and sniffs vigorously—my intentions exactly. I pull out the white shirt which has a few flecks of dried yellow vomit on the front and breath into it deeply, immediately recognizing Billy's scent, a subtle earthy smell with a distinctive tinge, like a wood fire on a crisp autumn day. I take the shirt back into the closet and place it on a hanger and zip it up in a plastic garment bag. I pick out a pair of khaki pants and a white button down collar dress shirt along with a brown pair of Cole Hahn loafers and a brown belt, place them on the bed, and I smile as I recall how Billy always said that my sense of fashion in clothes was perpetually stuck in the preppy mode. I grab my toilet kit and head in the bathroom. A cell phone begins to ring. I realize it's coming from the closet. I go back in and see Billy's cell phone in a charger on one of the shelves. I wonder why he didn't take it with him Saturday night. The caller ID shows a blocked number. I answer the phone. No one responds, and I hear a click. I shut the phone and take it with me to the bathroom and set it on the counter.

I adjust the dimmer so the lights are not too bright as I gaze at myself in the mirror.

"How fast life can change—two days ago I was getting ready to leave for a month long trip to China for research; now I'm standing in my dead brother's bathroom in my underwear having just reconciled with Dad. How does this make me feel? How the hell do you think it makes you feel Hampton? I feel wasted, almost used by Dad to ease his own pain, and my soul hurts." I look into my eyes. All at once I feel as if I'm about to cry, then I laugh, then I scream out, "Goddamn you Billy, Goddamn you." Clark nudges my left leg.

"It's okay boy. I'm just venting and wondering what fucked up your daddy enough to make him kill himself or get in the position to be killed by someone. Oh, God Clark, he's really gone. He's left us, boy." Clark quizzically cocks his head, sticks out his tongue, pants a bit, then turns around, walks into the bedroom, jumps up on the bed, lies down beside the clothes I placed there, sighs, moans, and stares into the bathroom.

"I'm going to shower, you stay there," I say as I shut the door to the bathroom. The truth is I do not feel comfortable masturbating in front of Clark. By the time I turn back to the mirror, my cock is hard and throbbing through the boxers. I drop the boxers and look at my naked body in Billy's mirror.

"Not bad for thirty-three." I grab my cock with my left hand and begin to stroke it. I close my eyes and focus on the pleasure of the sensation and let my mind wander. I picture a slim oriental beauty riding my cock with her head thrown back in ecstasy, long silky black hair whipping through the air as I fondle her firm breasts and drive my cock up into her. Usually, when I'm in Hong Kong, I'll hire just this sort of

prostitute for an hour or two of fun. My cock is slippery with pre-cum, but I spit on it anyway to increase the wetness and warmth. As I get closer to ejaculation, I picture myself rolling the beauty on her back, spreading her legs wide and thrusting my cock in her. She begs for more, screams for me to fuck her harder. As I pump furiously she grabs hold of my throat, screaming with pleasure. As I ram her, she chokes me, begging me to blow my load into her. My left hand pumps wildly, and I moan and stand on my tiptoes as I shoot all over the counter and onto the mirror as a vision of me, Billy, and Uncle Adrian—Blood Brothers—standing in a circle naked with erect cocks at the swimming hole, precipitates in my mind, calming me like the serenity of a first snowfall. Exhausted and relieved I open my eyes to see myself holding my cock with my left hand and holding my throat with my right hand.

"Way to go, Hampton, you're as fucked up as anybody." I begin to cry as the truth oozes forth like blood from a bad cut. Billy and I were victims of our beloved Uncle Adrian. It has always been a part of me, and Billy too, I think, but unavailable, only pulled out in dreams, and contorted into unusual sexual behavior. I'm overcome with guilt, dread, and a futile hollowness in my chest as memories of that night in St. Barts, eight years ago, spread through my mind and body like an evil, verdant, voracious kudzu, feeding on my soul, choking my essence until I'm completely covered and unrecognizable as myself. And now I can feel his touch, his hot breath smelling of cigarettes, gin and marijuana, the woodland, musky smell of his body pressing into mine.

"Come on, Philly, you know you want it as much as I," his right arm is around my waist as we stumble from the cab and up the walk to the villa he has rented in Anse de Gouverneur. I hear the pound of the surf as I glance down at something small moving, illuminated in the landscape lighting, in front of us on the walk.

"Oh my God, look, Billy, it's a scorpion," I say as I stop, stooping over to observe the inch long yellowish creature. Billy reaches for it, and I pull him back abruptly.

"Billy, don't, you fool, it will sting you," I exclaim as the little creature faces us with its quivering tail raised.

"Sting, schming," he quips, "that little stinger couldn't hurt a flea," he looks at me and smiles, "But I bet yours could."

"You're crazy, drunk, and stoned. That little stinger can probably deliver a nasty poison. Let's give him room. Just let him alone." I laugh, trying to bear Billy's weight and keep my balance as I move him forward around the scorpion and guide him up the stairs past a long stucco wall with a recessed planting area in which a carved stone Buddha, his blind eyes staring into infinity, sits among various types of succulents.

He puts his mouth on my neck and blows out a hot stream and rubs his face against my neck while emitting a soft guttural moan. I pull back a bit and say, "Hey, get off bro. I'm not one of your pretty boys here."

"Get off. Yes, just what I had in mind, brother." He hesitates a moment then strokes my cheek with his left hand, "But you are, Philly, you are. You were always the prettiest, and the nicest to me, and you always took the best care of me," he replies with a gentle whine in his voice.

"Geez, I haven't seen you this drunk in a long time," I say as I punch in the code to the electronic lock. Nothing happens.

"Shit, I thought the code was 464646."

"No, you ninny, it's 484848 pound," he says, quickly pulls me around into him, presses his groin into mine, looks into my eyes, smiles, and while I focus on his beautiful white teeth, he lightly kisses me on my lips.

"Now you're the ninny. Move aside and let me get this lock open," I say as I withdraw from his embrace and punch in the number. The lock releases making the sound of a camera shutter.

"No more photos today, I'm off work now," Billy laughs, and leans toward me. The long gold chain with a big gold charm, which he says symbolizes 'man and woman', slips out of his white shirt and hits my chest.

"Let's get inside. We both need sleep. You worked all day, and I traveled all day," I say as I pull open the glass door and direct him inside.

The sprawling villa is large and secluded, precariously hanging off the steep mountainside overlooking Gouverneur Bay. The house is shaped like a segmented crescent framing a large infinity pool that appears to meld into the ocean. The main living room overlooks the pool and is filled with large overstuffed sectionals and sofas, all covered in fabrics in shades of white and off white. The Polynesian style roof slants up sharply culminating in ceilings that must be at least twenty feet tall. The wall facing the pool and bay is comprised of a series of large sliding glass doors, mounted in between round white columns, leading onto a covered porch that runs the length of the house. Electronic shades hang on top of each door. Dark, tropical hardwood coffee tables, designed in a Ming Dynasty style are scattered about the groupings of the white furniture. Behind the living room is a large eating area with an immense wooden dining table surrounded with oval-back wooden chairs upholstered in zebra skin. Directly behind the dining room is a large kitchen with stainless steel appliances and darkly stained mahogany cabinets and woodwork with a mirror glazed finish. A long bar separates the kitchen from the dining area. The bar counter is a highly polished white granite with grey veining, in sharp contrast to the shiny, dark cabinetry. Eight stainless bar stools with white leather cushioned seats line the bar. "Oh come on, Philly. Let's have a nightcap on the porch. I mean, look at the moon on the water. It's a shame to waste that view."

"Okay, but maybe you should have water instead. Don't you have another shoot tomorrow?"

"Yes, last day, but it's not until late afternoon. Nigel wants the golden light at Rockefeller's Beach for the shoot. We can sleep in."

"I see. How are you and Nigel getting along these days?"

He sighs, rolling his eyes, "As well as can be expected."

I laugh, "Who would have ever thought your college roomie would become the hottest fashion photographer going?"

He laughs, "Yes, but would you have ever thought I'd become one of the hottest fashion models?"

"Little brother, with your looks, I don't think that surprised anyone," I reply and pat him on the right shoulder.

He smiles and heads to the wet bar, opens a cabinet and pulls out a bottle of 30 year old Macallan Single Malt.

"Let's finish off with a bit of this, Philly?" Billy says as he grabs two crystal glasses.

"Damn, that's got to be five-hundred dollars a bottle," I exclaim.

"More like six," he replies as he pours two drinks, neat, and hands me a glass.

"Cheers, Philly, and welcome. Here's to a week of solitude in paradise. Just you and me, brother."

I smile at him and we clink glasses and each take a sip. He gives me a look that lets me know he has something on his mind—God only knows what, I think to myself as we walk out to the porch and sit on two cushioned lounges.

"Oh my God, Philly, look out there, it's a moon bow, how beautiful."

I look out over the infinity pool and out over Gouverneur Bay. Mist is rising up off the hillsides sloping into the water and the moonlight filtering through has created the faintest of rainbows, arching over the bay.

"Wow. That's magnificent, Billy. It doesn't look real."

"No it doesn't. I wonder how you could capture that on canvas?"

"Have you done any painting lately?" I ask.

"Just a little. Too much travel. But some day," he says. I hear the longing in his voice.

"Yes, you'll get there when the time comes," I add.

"I suppose so," he says, pulls out a joint from his silver cigarette case, lights it, and inhales deeply. He looks over to me and offers the joint.

"What the hell, I'm on vacation," I say, take the joint and inhale. The weed is smooth but strong. Almost immediately I feel the slight pressure behind my eyeballs that always tells me I'm going to get really stoned.

"Good, isn't it?"

"Whew," I sigh as I blow out a stream of smoke and begin to cough in short fits at first, but quickly escalating into a guttural, deep-lung cough. I feel my face burning as I gasp for air, so I take a sip of the warm scotch. The mellow oak flavor warms my throat and quells the cough. "Yes, damn good I'd say. A toke or two of that and I'll be wasted," I add.

"That's the idea, isn't it?"

"Well, I suppose. Where did you get this?"

"The bartender, Alejandrao, at LaTi."

"So that's where you disappeared during dinner for such a long time?"

"Yes, sampling his goodies. He keeps me well supplied whenever I'm in St. Barts."

"And what else did you sample tonight, hum?"

"Just a little coke, but I know you don't approve of that, so I didn't buy any."

"So I thought. No wonder you were in such a dancing mood after dinner. You had those girls from Seattle drooling all over you."

"Yeah, well you know good and well you could have laid anyone of them, Philly."

"So, I've fallen to the level of your sloppy seconds?" I ask with a smile.

"Yeah, right. Like hell. It didn't take them too long to figure out that I'm more interested in pretty men than pretty women. They could tell you're straight from a mile away."

"Am I that obvious?"

"Oh, go to hell. You probably have twice as much sex as I do."

"Yeah right. And when is the last time you had sex?"

"Well, as best as I can remember, last night."

"A ha, just what I speculated. Well, I haven't had sex in, geez, well, well."

"Well when, Philly?"

"I'm ashamed to admit it, but about six weeks ago in Hong Kong."

"You're still into those oriental hookers?"

"Don't knock it unless you've tried it."

"I have."

"I figured as much, and…."

"Well, it was okay, but nothing I'd write home about."

"And who would you write to?"

"Fatgram, of course, if she were still alive."

"Yes, dearest Fatgram," I say taking in the beauty of the night as I ascend further into a stoned blissfulness, and I find myself desiring to go higher and higher.

Billy takes a couple of drags off the joint and passes it back to me. This time I take it without hesitation, and I inhale as deeply as I can, inviting the smoke to carry me into a world of no worries or inner-demons.

"I hope this shit is not the kind that makes you paranoid?"

"I can assure you it's not. Alejandrao knows my tastes."

"So I suppose you know how he tastes?"

"Philly, this pot brings out your true colors!"

"Well, I saw how he looked at you. He's straight isn't he, yet you seduced him?"

"Okay, he's basically straight, but bi-curious. Anyway, I went to his pad last week to pick up some coke. What the fuck, you caught me. It's hard to get through this goddamned high fashioned life without it. Anyway, his girlfriend was there, a slim, brown babe from Paris, and we all had a few drinks, smoked some pot and snorted a bit of coke. Before I know it, she is all over me. I think to myself, Holy shit, Alejandrao is a hot-blooded Mexican. He's going to pull out a machete and cut off my pecker. Wrongo was I. It totally turned him on. You should've seen the major hard-on showing through his balloon pants. I was sucking his beautiful cock in a flash. Well, that just turned on his girlfriend even more. The next thing I remember is that I was eating his ass out, he was moaning like a French whore, and she was riding my cock. My God she screamed louder than he did as she came, really quickly too. Then, after a while, he let me fuck him while he ate her pussy. This turned her on so much she came again. Then I asked him if he would like to try fucking me. He said that would be nice, so I let him fuck me while she masturbated me. Boy did I shoot a load. Our petite orgy went on for quite some time. I woke up entwined with their bodies the next morning. We've all been on the best of speaking terms since."

The mental picture of the orgy, combined with the pot, is making me exceedingly horny, and my cock is throbbing against the baggy, white linen pants tied at the waist with a drawstring that Billy gave me and insisted I wear tonight. I see him looking at my crotch with a grin on his face, and I start to turn my pelvis away from him, but before I can he reaches over and starts rubbing my cock through the pants.

"Hey Billy, this is not a good idea. You better stop."

"Oh what's the big deal, Philly? It's just a little sex," he says as he presses his hand harder against my cock. "I mean, it's not like we've never done it together before. You used to really like it," he adds.

"Yeah, but that was a long time ago, in a far away place."

"This is a far away place, brother. And it's just you and me, and I want to make you feel things tonight no hooker in Hong Kong or Thailand can make you feel."

"You're forgetting I'm straight, Billy," I say as he sits on the side of my lounge and begins untying the drawstring on my pants.

"Not forgetting, Philly. But remembering, remembering how good we used to make each other feel." My cock throbs intensely as he finishes the sentence, pulls down my pants and boxers, and puts his mouth on my cock. At first he licks it like an ice cream cone, playing with the head with his tongue and sucking up my pre-cum. Then, he runs his nose up and down the shaft and then down into my balls while he moans and says, "God, Philly, I've always loved the way you smell—so rich, so manly, it drives me wild. Sometimes I jerk off remembering your smell."

I'm overcome with uneasiness and guilt. I do the same thing, but I'd never have the courage to admit it to him. After all, I'm straight. He's the gay brother. Nonetheless, I am totally overcome by him as he presses his chest into mine, his shirt now open, exposing the incredible pectorals and abdominals, covered in short brown hair, revealed to so many people around the world in magazines and on billboards. His job requires him to maintain an absurd body building work out schedule, and I can feel the sinewy muscles in his legs as he kisses me deeply, his own hard cock pulsing within his pants. After a while he sits up, smiles, takes the last sip of his drink and says, "Just sleep in my room tonight, Philly. It'll be like old times."

I nod okay and he grabs my hands, pulls me up, and leads me into one of the two identical king suites which flank the kitchen and dining area. The room is spacious with a hand carved mahogany four-poster bed as the focal point. Two overstuffed chairs with ottomans face the sliding doors offering a splendid view of the bay and moon bow. White fabrics adorn the furniture in this room also, along with several plush white rugs of varying shapes, which look like the hide of some mythical sheep only tended for the wealthy, strategically scattered along the logical pathways from the bed to the bathroom, from the bed to the porch and from the bed to the bedroom entrance to protect bare feet from the cold stone floors. A large flat screen TV is mounted on the wall facing the bed. Graphite works of nudes hang behind the bed. The bathroom is large with his and hers sinks, two commodes in separate closets, and a bidet. The shower is

constructed of white marble tiles with swirls of grey veins laid from floor to ceiling in a recessed area of the room that is completely open. An array of brushed nickel sprayers, nozzles, and overhead fixtures that mimic rainfall protrude from the marble tiles like sculpture. A large sunken tub, more like a small pool, with Jacuzzis, is installed in front of glass doors overlooking the bay.

Billy leads me into the bathroom and says, "Let's take a bath. We're both sweaty, it'll make us sleep better." At this point, I'm so stoned that I'm putty in his hands, so I shake my head in agreement.

"I gotta pee," I say.

"Well, go ahead, there's the john. I'll run the water."

I go into one of the closets, turn on the light, pull out my cock, and try to pee, but I can't because my cock is still too hard. "Fuck, my bladder is about to burst," I say out loud.

"What's that?" Billy asks over the sound of water running into the tub.

"Nothing," I say as I pull down my pants, turn around and sit down on the john to try to think of anything but sex so my cock will go down allowing me to release my bladder. I notice magazines on a small chest beside the toilet, so I grab one and start thumbing through the pages. It's amazing how enjoyable a magazine can be when you are stoned. I seem to notice more details about photographs and even nuances in the text that I would never otherwise uncover. This particular magazine is rather touristy in that it is exclusively about St. Barts. Nevertheless, before long I am engrossed in an article about a woman from Paris who has recently opened a modern art gallery in Gustavia. The woman's name is Isabella de la Croix. She is the daughter of the famous Parisian avant-garde painter, Janine de la Croix, who died in a car crash in Paris in the 1970's. Isabella operates a gallery in Gustavia during the season from Thanksgiving until March. From April until Thanksgiving she operates a gallery in Santa Fe. "This chick has got it down, and she's a babe to boot," I say as I observe the photograph of her in front of one of her mother's paintings. She has an oval face with sharp features and thick, straight brown hair that hangs to her shoulders. She has on a light blue dress with a white shawl over her shoulders. Her arms are crossed just under her breasts forming a modest and lovely cleavage. The slight smile does little to cover the sadness emanating from her large brown eyes. "Damn, I'd like to meet her. I mean we both have mothers who were famous artists and are now deceased. I bet we'd hit it off," I think to myself. I am in the middle of perusing Isabella's life story when Billy raps loudly on the door.

"Damn, Philly. What are you doing in there? Taking a big girl sit-down?"

I laugh. I haven't heard this particular expression of Fatgram's for a bowel movement in a long time. It was a term she used to toilet train Mother, and I guess it just got carried over to us, although Mother changed it to big boy sit-down. "No, just reading a magazine. I'll be right out." I realize that I have completely emptied my bladder while reading, so I put the magazine on the table, stand up, pull up my pants, flush the toilet and head out. Billy is standing by the tub wearing a white terry cloth bathrobe made of a luxurious Egyptian cotton. He is taking a toke from another joint. I notice a crystal champagne bucket full of ice covering a bottle of Cristal. The lights in the room are very dim, and he has lit pillar candles and placed them around the tub. Two tall crystal champagne flutes sit beside the bucket. He smiles at me, and his robe falls open revealing his beautiful body. His cock is half hard and I think it really doesn't bother me that I'm the older brother and that his cock is longer and fatter than mine. I apprehensively approach him and sigh.

"I think I'll just turn in. I'm really tired."

"Oh, no you don't. I mean, please, Philly. Just take a bath with me. Come on."

He grabs my hand and pulls me toward the tub. He lets his robe fall from his shoulders and off. Then he reaches over and begins unbuttoning my shirt. Each time he unfastens one button he kisses a part of my face. On the last button, he slips my shirt off and kisses me on the lips. Then he pulls off my pants and squats down as I step out of them. He reaches over, grabs the joint he put in a marble ashtray beside the ice bucket, stands up, puts the burning end of the joint in his mouth, aims the other end toward my

lips, and gives me a major shotgun. The strong stream of smoke rushes into my lungs, and even though I'm already stoned, I feel my eyes bulging again. I hold the smoke in as long as I can, then blow it over his right shoulder. I realize that I am holding on to his waist. He smiles, takes the joint out if his mouth, turns it around, inhales deeply, all the while staring into my eyes with his deep green eyes. He has released his long hair from a ponytail, and it cascades about his shoulders. His face is covered with a perfectly manicured three days growth of beard, and I know he knows I'm thinking how beautiful he is. He turns around and bends over to put the joint down. Even his ass is perfect, well muscled, covered in brown down, transitioning into large sinewy hamstrings. The hair covering his legs is thick, but light brown from the sun. His balls hang low and appear through the backs of his legs as he bends over. His waist seems so tiny, almost like a woman's, yet it angles up dramatically into the perfect masculine chest and back. I think to myself, I am a similar, but less perfect version of him, and I look down and feel ashamed that I'm starting to get a small accumulation of fat around my own belly. "More running and weights from now on," I think to myself. Billy turns around, stands up, takes my hands and leads me into the warmth of the churning waters. At first we just stand there looking into each other's eyes. Then he takes our cocks in his hands and rubs them together. The physical sensation, the sound of the churning water, the smell of my brother take me back. I give in to him completely. I almost expect to look up to see Uncle Adrian descending into the tub with his white, skinny body covered in reddish-brown hair, his cold blue eyes peering into mine, the smile showing his crooked teeth, the large white cock with the red-purple head throbbing. Then I look down at the beauty of my brother as he sucks my cock, and I wonder what Uncle Adrian would say, would feel, and would do, if he could see us now. I close my eyes and am lost in the sensation and the spontaneity of passion—he runs his tongue up to my navel, then up my chest and softly bites my right nipple sending a wave of pleasure through my groin. I moan. He growls softly, then bites my other nipple. I grab his hard cock, he grabs mine, and we kiss deeply, running our tongues over each other's. The sensation of having sex with someone who is stronger, more powerful, more forceful than I am is new to me, but intriguing, and I wonder fearfully if he will try to fuck me. I begin to explore, so I bend over and bite his left nipple. He immediately flexes his chest out to meet my bite and says, "Oh God that feels so good."

I bite his other nipple and stroke his rock hard cock, pulling it horizontal from its vertical stance. He moans loudly and reaches down and grabs me below my ass and picks me up out of the water, holding me up as he sucks my cock like a glutton with a juicy turkey leg.

"Shit, you are strong," I laugh as he slides me down his chest, bringing my mouth to his. He kisses me lightly, brushes the sweat off my face, and backs me up to the side of the tub beside a big stack of fluffy white towels. He arranges a thick layer of towels on the tile floor, grabs hold of my thighs, and lifts me to the side of the tub on top of the towels. He spreads my legs a bit and goes down on my cock. A few times he grabs the shaft, squeezing it with his right hand as he sucks. Mostly, he just sucks it, his mouth going all the way down to my balls. After a while he works my legs over his shoulders and begins licking my shaft and balls. I lay back resting on my elbows watching him. Gradually, he works his mouth and tongue under my balls and pushes my legs back, exposing my asshole. His tongue flicks around the outside, slightly grazing my asshole. I haven't been rimmed in a long time and the sensation is wonderful. I moan as his tongue pushes into my asshole. He has managed to open a bottle of oil, pours some into his hands, and begins stroking my cock as he continues to tongue my asshole. The feeling is wonderful, and I think to myself maybe this means he doesn't want to fuck me after all because he is definitely going to make me cum.

"Oh shit, Billy, I'm gonna shoot," I say as I lean back in ecstasy. He immediately pulls his tongue out and stops stroking my cock. He pulls me up to him in the water and thrusts his tongue into my mouth and kisses me deeply for a while.

"That's what you taste like, big brother."

"Hmmp, well, that's a first for me."

"Oh, no it's not," he says."

"What do you mean?"

He gives me a strange, hurt look, starts to say something, stops, and then asks, "No women have ever given you a decent rim job?"

"Never."

"You're just not moving in the right crowds."

"Guess not. But why did you stop? I was just about to blow?"

"Because, it's my turn now."

"Oh, geez, uhm, I can suck your cock, Billy, but, I don't think I want to rim you."

"That's fine. No use traveling down memory lane, brother, I'll take what I can get," he says as he gets out of the tub and sits his butt down on the towels. I push his legs open, take his cock into my right hand, and start to suck it.

"Jesus," he pulls back quickly, "Watch those teeth, brother! It's like you still have braces on."

"Sorry, it's been a long time since I've done this." I pull my lips over my teeth and start again. He bursts out laughing.

"Don't do that. Just purse your lips a bit and your teeth will stay out of the way."

I lick my lips, smile at him and try again. This time he groans giving me more confidence in my blowjob skills. His cock must be at least eight and one-half inches long because mine is seven. I'll never be able to get it all the way into my mouth, but I continue to try because he is enjoying it so much. Finally, I hit my limit, and I spontaneously gag. Billy is laughing as I bend over, coughing into the water.

"Good try, Philly. Here, sit up here beside me," he pats the layer of towels. I push up out of the water onto the soft towels. He grabs more towels and drapes them over our bodies, drying us off. There are so many towels on the floor that it feels like a soft mattress. He scoots back to lean his back against the window so I do the same. He takes the oil, pours some into his right hand and puts it on his cock. He hands me the bottle, and I put some on my cock, then turn around to face him, putting my legs over his. We stroke our own cocks, looking at each other.

"Just like we used to do at Fatgram's, todger to todger."

"Yeah," I say, a bit embarrassed, remembering how we did this just about every day for most of our early teenage years.

"Feels so good to be here with you like this," he says. I smile at him. We each continue to masturbate, looking into each other's eyes.

"You close, Philly?"

"Yeah, I'm close."

He scoots up closer to me until our balls are touching. He begins rubbing his balls into mine as we continue jacking our cocks.

"It feels really good, doesn't it?"

"Yeah, Billy, it does." He leans back a little, pulls his balls up with his left hand and starts playing with his asshole.

"Try doing this, Philly," he directs. I do. It feels really good. We continue this for a while, then Billy lays on his back, pulls his legs back, exposing his asshole to me.

"Philly, just rub my asshole with your fingers." I hesitate, then oblige. He moans loudly.

"Oh yeah man, now just stick your index finger in my ass." I do.

"Yeah, now fuck me with your finger."

I begin finger fucking him. His asshole grips my finger tightly, and he begins to thrust into my finger, moving his ass around as he alternately jacks himself and pinches his nipples. His cock gets even bigger, and I notice his balls begin to climb up toward his cock. I become very aroused and stand on my knees as I insert my middle finger alongside my index finger.

"Fuck yeah," he screams out as I fuck him with two fingers. My cock is throbbing and dripping pre-cum. He grabs the head of it with his right hand and starts rubbing it. He looks up at me with an expression of passionate desire, neediness, and begging all rolled into one.

"Philly, just stick your cock in me. Just stick it in." I pull my fingers out of his ass, and he grabs the back of his thighs with his hands and offers his asshole up to me. I push the head of my cock on it and rub it around. His eyes roll back in his head, and he says, "Oh yeah, Goddamn, that feels good."

I push my cock head into his ass and am amazed, "Damn, your ass is so tight. Am I hurting you?"

"Fuck no, brother. Stick it in." I lean forward, planting my hands on either side of his chest, push up off my toes and slide my whole cock into his ass. His head rolls back.

"Fuck, yeah." I watch his face and begin pumping slowly. The tightness, warmth, and slippery feeling are intoxicating. I begin pumping harder.

"Oh shit, Philly, fuck my ass, brother. Yeah, fuck me harder."

I pump harder. I kiss him. I bite his nipples. I jack his cock. I rub our sweaty, hairy chests together, and I fuck him harder and harder. I pin his arms down, growl at him like a deranged animal fucking him harder. He succumbs to my cock, gives himself to me completely, as much as any woman ever has. He senses I am close, and he begins beating his cock. I fuck him harder. I feel and hear my balls slapping his ass. He begins to grunt with each stroke of my cock into him. I hear myself yelling, "Yeah, little brother. Big brother is fucking the shit out of you."

"You like it?" I scream.

"Yes, fuck yeah," he screams back.

"Fuck yeah, you do," I say as I let it all go, nailing him with all my strength. I feel the semen rising through my shaft. I begin shooting off uncontrollably into his ass. He groans as his own cock goes into spasms. He shoots cum everywhere on his chest, my chest, his face, my face, and into my panting mouth. The saltiness surprises me, disgusts me, and I instinctively spit it out over his left shoulder. I collapse onto his chest. We are a heaving, sweaty, clump of sticky, hairy flesh. I roll onto my side withdrawing my still pounding cock from his ass. I see that it is covered in a liquid brown substance. The unmistakable odor of shit fills the room.

"Oh shit, how fucking gross," I say and roll into the warm waters of the Jacuzzi and put my cock in front of one of the jets to clean it off. Billy is laughing his ass off. He rolls into the water, pulls me up close to him, and says, "Thanks, Philly. I really needed that."

I look at him, and he adds, "You okay?"

"Yeah," I say, "just spent."

"Relax, I'm gonna clean you up."

"No, that's okay."

"No, I know you just want to run away from me as far as you can go right now, but, please, please let me bathe you."

I am overcome with shame, guilt, and fear—all those things that caused me to stop beating off with him so long ago. I just want to get the hell out of there, out of St. Barts, right now. I look into his eyes, and I see Mother. It's almost as if she is there asking me to stay. I'm emotionally torn. He senses this. I freeze, looking down into the water. He walks behind me, puts his strong arms around me, and hugs me tightly. Tears seep from my eyes. He takes a sponge, puts some bath gel that smells like the peaches from Fatgram's orchards, and begins to bathe my chest very gently. Images of Mother, Dad, Uncle Adrian, Billy, and Fatgram churn through my mind. I am overcome with exhaustion. I cannot focus on any one thing, and I am almost oblivious as Billy tenderly bathes my entire body. After a while I hear Billy singing, and I realize I am floating on my back.

"Hush little Philly, don't say a word, Billy's gonna buy you a Mocking Bird, and if that Mockingbird don't sing, Billy's gonna buy you a...."

Billy is singing softly to me as he holds me up in the water with his hands under my back, slowly spinning me around.

"Now that we're all fresh and clean, let's dry off and get to bed," he whispers as he leans over me letting his long wet hair brush my face. I smile and nod. We get out of the tub. Billy hands me a large, white, fluffy towel. I rub my hair and face, then work my way down my body. Billy smiles as he does the same. He pours the remaining champagne in our glasses then takes them to one of the vanities made of black granite streaked with white veins. He motions for me to join him. I do. He faces us toward the mirror, picks up an electric blow dryer and begins to alternately blow my hair and his hair, all the while looking at me in the mirror. My short hair dries quickly so he puts his left arm around my waist as he continues to dry his hair until the long locks release the dampness and began to blow wildly around his face and mine. He turns the blow dryer off, puts it down, picks up the flutes, hands me one, smiles, and says, "Here's to brotherly love."

We clink flutes, and I follow his lead as he guzzles the entire glass. We put our glasses on the vanity and turn to go into the bedroom. The lights are very low, and I hear soft music playing which sounds familiar to me, so I ask, "What is that playing?"

"Julee Cruise," he replies.

He sees the quizzical look on my face, "Remember, it's from the series Twin Peaks? It's called *Falling.*"

"Yeah, I do."

"Go to sleep now," he says.

An ethereal voice sings in echoes, "Don't let yourself get hurt this time." I crawl into the soft mass of whiteness and quickly fall asleep. During the night I dream that the dancing midget from "Twin Peaks" is dancing around Uncle Adrian, Billy and me as we jack off at Fatgram's swimming hole. When I wake up in the morning, Billy is not around. I put on one of the white terry cloth robes and go into the kitchen. A beautiful young woman with long brown hair and dark complexion mops the floor.

I clear my throat, "Good morning."

"Oh, good morning sir. Your brother has gone wind surfing. He says he'll be back for lunch. Can I fix you some breakfast?" Her accent is thick, but not French. I cannot place it.

"No thank you. I've received a call—business emergency. I must get back to Atlanta today. Could you get me a cab to the airport?"

Her brow wrinkles. "Now?"

"Yes, please. I didn't even unpack. I'm ready, just have to get dressed."

"Yes sir, I'll call now."

Twelve hours later, I'm sitting at the Oak Bar at the Plaza in New York, nursing a bourbon, which is as close to Atlanta as I could get today, when my cell phone rings.

"Mr. Hampton?"

Cold chills run up my spine as I discern a French accent.

"Mr. Philip Hampton?"

"Yes. This is he."

"This is Inspector Girard Dupris with the national police in St. Bartholomy. Mr. Hampton, there's been an accident. Your brother, well, he is in the hospital in Gustavia."

"What? Is he alright?"

"The doctors say he will recover fully."

"What happened? Wind surfing?"

"No. You see. I'm sorry to say, we believe he tried to commit suicide by hanging himself."

"Oh my God."

"Can you come down here?"

"Yes. I can get there tomorrow. I'm in New York."

"Yes. That's good. We'll see you tomorrow at the hospital."

I grab some Kleenex, wipe up my semen, flush it, grab my razor, and head into the shower feeling more alone than I can ever remember feeling. I have another crying spell as I soap up all over and scrub my body with a washcloth. I put shampoo in my hair, lather up, rinse, and repeat while Billy's cell phone begins to ring again.

"Why the hell do I always repeat?" I ask myself and answer. "Because it says so on the damned shampoo bottle, another way to sell more shampoo."

I look into the shaving mirror and cover my face and neck with shaving gel that does not lather up the way I'm used to. I shave automatically, watching my eyes in the mirror. I'm haunted by the image of Billy's painting and the memories from St. Barts, but I force my thoughts away from them. I rinse off, turn off the shower, take one of the luxurious bath sheets folded on the counter, dry off and head back into the bedroom.

"Nothing like a good hot shower to revive a man's soul, Clark," I say to him as I stand by the bed. Clark immediately stands up and sniffs my penis.

"Hey boy, I'm not a dog. Next thing you know, you'll be wanting to sniff my ass." He wags his tail, sits down, looking up at me in anticipation. "Not on your life, you trashy street dog," I joke as I plop down on the bed and roll Clark onto his back and rub his tummy vigorously. He play bites my hands and pushes at them with all four feet as he growls in his playful tone. I decrease the rubbing to gentle strokes; he relaxes completely; his hind legs splay out; he closes his eyes and sticks out his tongue. A chunk the size of a pea is missing from the left side of his tongue. That must have been a horrible fight. When Clark first went home to live with Luscious after she had rescued him, she hired a canine behavior specialist to assist her in Clark's transition from street dog to country club dog. The specialist told Luscious that Clark had most certainly been bred for fighting—a common but illegal parimutuel sport throughout rural Kentucky and in the projects of Louisville—as evidenced by the large scars on his legs, his head, the relaxed ear which had resulted from torn ligaments, and the tear in his tongue. The specialist classified Clark as a pit bull mix, but said he was extremely intelligent, willing to please humans, and would make a fantastic pet. Luscious was delighted, but her husband David was appalled. His exact words were, "I'm not having some goddamn project nigger's pit bull in my house. Out he goes to the pound, immediately." Luscious was devastated because she had already fallen in love with Clark who had become house broken on his first day at her house. She demanded that David let her keep him until she found a suitable home. He, in turn, gave her exactly two weeks and insisted that the dog be crated whenever he was at home. She called me; I called Billy who had told me he wanted to get a dog. Billy flew to Louisville, rented a car, and made a new friend as he drove Clark back to New York. Before Billy's arrival to pick up Clark, Luscious was so intent on finding out more about Clark's origins that she took him to a psychic specializing in dogs who informed her that Clark had been the runt of a litter of fighting dogs. He had been used as a bait dog to teach other larger pups how to fight. She said people who train these dogs use runts, kittens, and other stray pups to throw into a pen of aggressive fighting puppies who are encouraged to rip the bait animal to shreds. She said though severely wounded, Clark survived several of these bait sessions by holding his own through sheer courage and a superior intellect. One day while being the bait dog to a group of pit bull pups from a line of champion fighters, Clark severed the throat of the pick of the litter while defending himself. The owner was so mad at losing the prize pup that he went after Clark with an axe. Clark narrowly escaped and eked out a life on the streets, mainly taking handouts from the homeless. He survived this way from six months of age until Luscious coaxed him into her car when he was just a year old. The psychic said that Clark wanted Luscious to know all that he had been through and that he pledged to protect her and be

47

a very good dog, but that he understood if she didn't want to keep a street mongrel like himself, but could she find it in her heart to help him find a good home. I was skeptical about the whole psychic thing, but I'm a dog lover, Clark turned out to be an incredibly smart and loving dog, and the psychic's story does seem to explain everything. Maybe I should do an article on psychics who specialize in animals—I can see Florence's expression when I pitch that one, but as any good agent knows, animal stories sell lots of newspapers and magazines.

Clark is fast asleep now and I can see his eyeballs rapidly moving from side to side under his eyelids. I quietly get up, put on the pair of boxers and proceed to put on Billy's clothes, which fit me perfectly, but I'm uncomfortable in a shirt and pants that have been starched and ironed to perfection. I twist and beat on the shirt with my hands and do a couple of deep knee bends to relax the fabrics, movements which resurrect Clark from his deep sleep and he rolls onto his left side and looks at me as if I am deranged.

"Yoga, I need to get to yoga, more than ever now," I tell myself. I started doing Bikram Yoga five years ago after developing severe pain in my left knee as a result of years of running and one too many marathons. After two months of doing this yoga four to five times a week, my knee pain subsided. I became a devotee to the 26 poses done in an exact sequence in 90 minutes in 105°F heat and high humidity. I also began doing another type of hot yoga called the Barkan Method that is more of a flow of postures and includes postures great for upper body strength that allowed me to tone and develop my upper body without having to lift weights. Another unexpected but extremely pleasant side benefit of these types of yoga for me was a large and varied supply of women willing to go from the yoga room to the bedroom—I estimate the ratio of men (especially fit, somewhat attractive men) to women is about 1 to 15. Of course when one is bedding more than one woman in the same yoga class, complications may arise from time to time. My mood brightens as I think about the many good yoga studios in New York, and then my stomach growls audibly.

"Clark, I bet Dad and Brenda are starving too. Let's go see what we can find to eat."

I enter the kitchen to find Brenda in complete control of the lunch preparation.

"I hope you don't mind Philip. I know everyone is hungry," she smiles at me.

"Not at all. I see it doesn't take you any time to find your way around a kitchen. My culinary skills peaked with mastering peanut butter and grape jelly on white bread."

"Well, with three children, kitchen skills are a necessity." She pauses and looks up from tossing a large bowl of mixed salad greens with an expression that reveals she senses that the subject of my half brothers and sisters should probably be avoided. I feel a knot in my throat.

"It's alright, Brenda." She smiles as I look into her blue eyes and take in her entire petite frame that reeks with sophistication.

"I barely know their names. I'm so ashamed."

"According to your father Peter is a lot like you; Andrew's got Billy's temper and 'joie de vivre'; and little Emma is the spitting image of your father. Not to worry though, I see plenty of my side mixed in them too." Brenda finishes tossing the salad, grabbing a bit to taste as she talks.

"How old are they now?"

"Peter is twelve—on the brink of puberty," she rolls her eyes. "Andrew, we call him Drew, is ten, wishing he were thirteen," she chuckles. "And sweet Emma is eight, a perfect little lady, unless you get on her bad side," she chuckles, and I notice her small, delicate ears, each lobe pierced and sparkling with a diamond stud.

"Brenda, let them come for the wake. I'm sure Billy would want them here," I interject.

She hesitates a moment, smiles, and says, "It's fine by me, but we better see what your father thinks about this—"

"Thinks about what?" Dad is staring at us like he just caught us sticking our fingers in the icing bowl. Brenda and I look at each other with eyes agape.

"Dad, let the kids fly up for the wake. Let them come up tomorrow, there's plenty of room here. I know a wake is a morbid way to spend spring break, but y'all can do other things in the city, and—"

"Son, I don't think it's such a good idea—"

"Dad, I'll pay for their tickets."

"It's not that son, I just don't know, they barely knew Billy and—"

"Dad they're Billy's blood, they're my blood, they're your blood and Brenda's blood. Shouldn't we all be together as a family to say goodbye to Billy?"

We all look at each other, tears welling in our eyes, the agreement unspoken.

"I'll call my sister-in-law after lunch, but first you gents are going to eat this divine meal I've prepared," Brenda wipes away a tear and directs us to help her carry out the food and heads out to the terrace. "It's a lovely afternoon, let's enjoy the terrace. Billy has a wonderfully stocked Sub-Zero."

We take the bowl of salad, a large plate of fruit and cheeses, and a large platter of sandwiches Brenda has neatly prepared from chicken salad, ham salad, and pimento cheese. We walk out to the terrace to find that Brenda has set one of the wrought iron tables with crisp pastel linens and sterling, an arrangement of fresh tulips in the center, and a bottle of Chardonnay chilling in a silver ice bucket.

"Wow, this is beautiful Brenda," I say.

"It's a simple task with the plethora of beautiful things your brother has. Look at this view. What a glorious spring day." She smiles at Dad and me as we sit down. Clark sits down beside my chair and begins to patiently wait, never begging.

"I have to say Clark is one of the most well behaved dogs I've ever seen." Brenda blows him an air kiss followed by "Sweet, sweet, Clark." His tail wags.

"Y'all know his story don't you?"

"Didn't Luscious find him starving on the street?" she asks.

"Pretty much, and she never even had to train him. He's just that smart."

"Amazing, isn't it, Charles? I never would have thought a pit bull could be so charming and such a good pet. Does he like children?"

"Loves them. The family on the floor below has a boy and a girl and they spend as much time as their parents will let them with Clark. They even keep him when Billy goes on trips."

Dad opens the wine and pours everyone a glass. They see the puzzled look on my face.

"AA saved me, son. Well, of course that and Brenda. I've arrived at a point in my life where I am comfortable with moderation."

"That's cool Dad, I just haven't seen you with a drink for years."

Dad smiles and holds up his wine glass, "I propose a toast. To our family—to those with us and to those we have lost—long may we remain a family! And that includes you too, Clark."

"Elegant Charles," Brenda adds.

"Indeed," I say.

CHAPTER 6

"My, Philip, and I thought my Peter could eat," Brenda laughs as I devour my fifth sandwich.

"Sorry," smacking my lips, "no food in my tummy since Saturday night."

"You poor dear, no wonder."

"Darling, you and Philly stay out here and enjoy this sunshine. I'll go in and make travel arrangements for the kids."

"Splendid Charles. I'd love to visit with Philip. I'm sure the two of us can polish off this wonderful Chardonnay?" She looks at me with a mischievous, girlish expression.

"Perhaps we'll open another?" I add. "Oh dear, well, being the light weight drinker I am," Dad says as he stands up, "I shall now leave you two to the company of yourselves." He takes the last sip of his one glass of wine and walks away.

"What'da ya say, Clark? Wanna come with me boy?" Clark jumps up, tail swinging in anticipation.

"Is it alright if I take him for a W-A-L-K after I make the travel plans?" Clark immediately starts a chirping sort of bark and stamps his front feet, looking up at Dad.

"Well I see he can spell too. Come on boy." They trail off in to the kitchen while Brenda refills our wine glasses.

"You bring out the best in Dad. I mean that's the Dad I remember and loved."

"Charles brings out the best in me too."

"Until Mother's death," I say, "Dad was the best Dad you could imagine, that is, when he was at home. He traveled most of the time. Mother was certainly a challenge for Dad. Does it bother you if I talk about her?"

"No, Philip, not at all. Eva was a remarkable and gifted woman, and I know she must have loved you and Billy a great deal."

"She did. But she wasn't the glue in our family; it was Dad and Ala Mary. I've come to realize that Mother most probably suffered from depression and some kind of bipolar disorder."

"Yes, Charles has said the same thing."

"When she was up she was up—sometimes she would paint for three weeks straight, hardly coming out of her studio. Other times, she'd sink into an alcohol induced rage, followed by deep depression, after which she might go to bed for three weeks."

"I'm sorry you had to experience that; it must've been extraordinarily difficult for you and Billy."

"It was, but you know we stuck together. We managed. Ala Mary was always there, Dad on many weekends, and, for several years, Uncle Adrian," I say and lapse into thought. "Shit, why did I mention his name? Did he really love Billy and me or did he just use us for sex? Fuck, how can I sort this all out now? Is that really why I spent so much time covering the sex trade in Thailand? Could I have been trying to subconsciously justify Uncle Adrian's actions? My God, it took Billy's painting to bring all this to the surface. Billy went to his death with this on his mind. I wonder what all he knew about this?"

"Philip? Philip, dear, are you alright?" Brenda's soft voice alarms me.

"What? Yes, I'm sorry. Just thinking. I'm fine."

"I was just asking you about Adrian. Charles doesn't have a lot to say about him. I believe he thinks he somehow contributed to Eva's use of drugs and alcohol."

"It's hard for me to say, but he was the one person on earth Mother would listen to. They were like two magnets, not sexually, but creatively. I believe he encouraged some of her greatest paintings."

"Yes, I've read that too."

"I always thought Dad and Fatgram were a little bit jealous of Adrian because he was so close to Mother and because…."

"Because what Philip?"

"Because Billy and I adored him so."

"Really, Philip?"

"Oh yes. He was the ultimate 'Uncle'. There was nothing he wouldn't do for us—not just toys, treats, and such, he spent real quality time with us and took a great interest in everything we did. He was also one of the most intelligent people I've ever met, and it seemed important to him to make sure Billy and

50

I understood things. He knew a lot about a lot of things, yet he could break it down simply enough for a child to understand. It was uncanny. Dad was great with helping me with homework, but when Adrian did it, I always caught on much faster."

"Interesting," Brenda says, moving her wine glass toward her lips, so attractive in their fullness, their deep pink shade, their shape as she speaks.

"Ala Mary always said it wasn't natural for a 'full growed' man to act like a little boy. But, really that's what he was like at times. He played our games, took us to movies, did our homework with us, and took us to friends' birthday parties."

"I didn't realize he spent so much time with you all."

"Well, when he visited, it always coincided with Mother preparing for an opening or some large commission, so he often stayed for weeks. Mother even let us come to New York alone to stay with him several times. He took us to museums, shows, and concerts. Really, any culture that sticks with me today is due to him."

"Oh, but your Mother and Grandmother were extremely cultured women."

"Absolutely, but Uncle Adrian could relate art to us on our level."

"Fascinating."

"Yes, but then Mother killed herself in France while on that painting trip with Uncle Adrian. I've always believed that he felt so bad about that that he could never face Billy and me. There was this giant guilt like a noose around his neck. After Mother's funeral we saw him only a couple of times and that was it—gone. It was as if he died along with Mother. He abandoned us kids when we needed him the most. I always meant to go see him in New York, sort of confront him about the whole thing, but, I guess Dad told you how he died?"

"Yes, in a fire?"

"Yes, he was agent and mentor to Dyanne O'Bryan. They both died in a house fire at her farm in Bardstown, outside of Louisville."

"That's right. Isn't she the one who outraged the Catholic Church with her paintings?"

"Yes, very famous, and a great artist. MOMA paid twenty five million dollars for three of her religious paintings, including the famous *The Crucifixion of the Madonna*, in the late nineties—an extremely controversial purchase, but a brilliant sale by Uncle Adrian."

"When did they die?"

"Well, it wasn't long after Adrian sold the paintings to MOMA. It must have been in the summer of 1998. Billy's art was just getting attention then. He told me he had visited with Uncle Adrian a few times. Adrian was taking an interest in his work, and then he died."

While I'm wondering if Billy ever confronted Uncle Adrian before he died, Brenda reaches over and gently puts her right hand on top of my left hand, "You and Billy experienced horrible losses as children. I can't even imagine it. But somehow you both survived and became successful men."

"Yeah, but look where it's taken Billy," I say, thinking that he surely would have confided in me anything he discussed with Uncle Adrian, but I don't remember anything significant besides art talk.

She sighs. "I suppose." She squeezes my hand. "You are a good brother, Philip."

I smile at Brenda, "Care for a cigarette?"

"Why yes. How did you know I might want one? I so seldom smoke nowadays—certainly never in front of the kids."

"I remember when Dad brought you to Billy's first big opening—I would barely speak to you. Forgive me?"

"That's in the past. It is okay Philip," she replies, smiling.

"No, it's not. Really, it's not. Billy and I did our best to make you feel unwelcome and uncomfortable."

"Yes, I remember a few snide comments."

"More than a few. And then at some point during the evening I noticed you standing alone on the terrace at the gallery, holding a glass of champagne, and smoking. You looked like a million dollars—smart, black cocktail dress, pearls—a bit bored, undaunted by our juvenile jealousies, reeking of a privileged upbringing. And I thought to myself, 'There's a woman Mother would've liked, no wonder Dad married her'."

"Really?" Her eyes widen, the corners of her lips turn up into a smile.

I stand up to go get the cigarettes, "Yes. Another bottle?"

"Let's," she says, smiling as she rearranges the tulips.

I return with cigarettes and more wine and pull out two cigarettes from the package and hand one to Brenda. She takes it, places it between her lips, and I light it with the onyx lighter.

"Thank you," she says after I light it and she exhales her first puff. Then, she tilts her head back, shakes back her shoulder length blonde hair, and inhales deeply. I see the tip of the cigarette glow bright red against slender, manicured fingers, and I focus on her profile—porcelain skin, blue eyes, perfect nose, and lovely smooth throat.

Aware of my stare, she exhales the smoke straight up into the air and turns to face me, "Shall we have more wine?"

"Of course." I pick up the bottle, twist the metal foil off with my hands, grab the corkscrew and begin to open it. Suddenly I hear the hissing of the onyx lighter and turn to see Brenda holding the flame toward the unlit cigarette hanging from my mouth. I smile as she lights my cigarette. I pull out the cork.

"Thank you." I pour each of us another glass.

"Philip, you really are a lot like your father."

"I've heard that all my life. But I believe there's greater similarity between Billy and Mother," I say trying to divert her attention away from the fact that I'm thinking how nice it would be to lean over and blow into her ear and gently caress her right breast which is creating the most beautiful mound in her pink cashmere sweater. I wonder if she is attracted to me, and I surmise the answer must be yes because, after all, I'm a younger version of my father.

"Yes, Charles says the same thing. He never talked much about Eva when we first starting dating and early in our marriage. But, as the years have passed, he talks about her more."

"Really?"

"Yes. I think as our relationship has become stronger, more secure, and the children have grown, he's better able to process his tumultuous relationship with Eva."

"That makes sense," I respond, disguising my crestfallen mood.

"Well, it has also been easier for me to talk about my first marriage as time has passed."

"I had no idea you were married before meeting Dad."

"Oh yes, at twenty-one, just graduated from Sweet Briar."

"Hah!"

"What?"

"I knew you were a spoiled rich kid!"

She raises her eyebrows and replies, "As if you weren't also. Spoiled, well, I was a Daddy's girl." She inhales again, and I focus on the large canary diamond on her right hand.

"Humph, I bet you are," I reply, my enthusiastic tone tinged with sarcasm.

"Now, now, what are you implying?"

"Nothing, I'm just teasing you. How long did your first marriage last?"

"Only two years."

"Well?"

"Well, what?"

"Why did it end?"

"Talk about spoiled brats. Darren's family owned one of the largest rubber gasket businesses in the world. He was the handsome, party loving, Kappa Sig from UVa. I fell for him completely. After we were married, he continued the partying, and never reported to work at his Dad's business. This suited his Dad, because an older brother already had the reins of the business. So, Dad kept the money coming, and Darren kept partying. After the first year, he started beating me. I put up with it for another year until he broke my left arm one night. That was it."

"My God, I'm so sorry."

"Thank you. I came from such a loving family. I was pretty sheltered, so when the beatings started, I was so embarrassed I wouldn't tell anyone, not even my mother or my best friends. But it all came out with the broken arm. My brother Harry confronted Darren. Darren has four false teeth as a result of that meeting."

"Good for Harry," I say.

"Anyway, after that, I poured my efforts into the family furniture business, and that's how I met your Dad in High Point."

"Yes, I remember, I was just a freshman at Chapel Hill."

"It's hard to believe we've been married for fifteen years."

Dad comes back onto the terrace with Clark on a leash.

"Oops, you caught us smoking, darling. Going for your walk?" Brenda smiles at Dad.

"I was, dear. Philip, I ran into two detectives from the police department in the lobby. They talked to me a bit, now they want to ask you some questions about Billy. They're waiting in the living room."

"I see." Startled, I'm knocked back into reality once again. "Okay."

"Brenda, why don't you join Clark and me for a stroll?" Dad asks.

"That would be lovely, dear. Let's go. I'll clean all this up when we get back."

We walk out into the living room and two plain-clothes detectives, a young female with brown hair and olive skin and a middle-aged African American man with closely cropped, graying hair, stand to greet me.

"Mr. Philip Hampton?"

"Yes."

"I'm detective Frederick Johnson, New York City Police Department," he says and extends his right hand. I shake it. He adds, "This is my partner, detective Bren Bell." Detective Bell extends her slender right hand, and I shake it. She is a young, attractive woman. Her clothes surprise me—a highly tailored, double-breasted wool jacket in light blue and brown houndstooth pattern, dark brown slacks, expensive shoes and a large brown leather purse. She looks as if she is headed to Barney's or Bergdorf Goodman for lunch and shopping. Detective Johnson wears an off the rack grey, pen-stripe suit. I introduce them to Brenda, and Brenda and Dad excuse themselves to walk Clark.

"Sorry to intrude at such a time, Mr. Hampton, but we are doing a routine investigation of your brother's death," Detective Johnson, a tall man, looks down into my eyes, stretching his lips out horizontally after he speaks.

"No problem, detective."

"Thank you, sir." He replies.

"Mr. Hampton," Detective Bell asks in a smooth, forceful voice, "Was your brother a habitual drug user?"

"Good heavens, let's jump right in," I reply noticing that Detective Bell is as sleek and muscular as a cheetah.

"Your brother is very high profile; we just need to get to the bottom of his death, sir," she says.

"Well, mostly he used alcohol and drugs in moderation. At times, he partied a bit too hard, but not often," I reply, feeling my shoulders tightening, and a dull pain awakens somewhere in my cervical spine.

"I see," she replies, "What sorts of drugs did he use?"

"He smoked pot, probably a couple of times a month, and snorted a little cocaine every now and then, every other month or so."

"Anything else?" Detective Johnson asks in a baritone voice.

"I'm pretty sure he tried ecstasy before and crystal meth, but I don't think he used them much."

"You're describing a pretty calm existence for a super model, A-party list guy," Detective Bell interjects with a sneer.

"Ex-supermodel who had calmed down a lot in order to pursue his art," I return with a stern tone.

They say nothing and look at each other.

"Mr. Hampton, do you think your brother committed suicide?" Detective Bell abruptly asks.

"Absolutely not!"

"Why not? He's tried at least twice before," she throws out.

"I don't think he was really trying to kill himself those times," I offer.

"Oh, just the 'cry for help' type of thing from a rich kid and a supermodel?" she lobs back.

"Jesus Christ, who the hell do you think you are talking to me like that?" I ask, turning my body directly toward her.

"I think I'm a detective with the New York City Police Department trying to determine if your brother overdosed himself, purposely killed himself, or if we have a homicide here," she states like a drill sergeant, not backing down one bit. Detective Johnson is stretching his lips again so much that his ears wiggle. I break out in a cold sweat.

"Look, my brother is dead. I knew him better than anybody. He didn't kill himself. He wasn't experimenting with GHB. He was pulling his life together, and creating great works of art." I realize I'm crying again as I am speaking.

They seemed stunned by my outburst of tears. I sniff hard and wipe my face with my left sleeve.

"Mr. Hampton, we're sorry to upset you, just doing our job," Detective Johnson says in a gentler voice. "Who were your brother's closest associates?"

"Well, other than myself. There's Julianna Morgan—the gallery owner who reps his work."

"Yes, we plan to talk to her," Detective Bell states.

"She's Billy's closest friend, besides me," I reply, trying to hold back my tears.

"Do you think you really know your brother that well, Mr. Hampton?" Detective Bell questions me as though she doesn't believe a thing I'm telling her.

"To his core," I reply, blinking through my tears, trying to stare back at her. She blinks, and the corners of her lips turn up, almost imperceptibly.

"Elliott Fields?" Detective Johnson booms out again.

"Never met him. They'd only been dating a couple of months. I talked to him quite a while this morning. He told me everything that happened at the bar. I have his cell number—"

"We have it," he states.

"Mr. Hampton, was your brother sexually promiscuous?" Detective Bell asks.

"What do you mean?"

"I mean did he have a multiplicity of sexual partners?" She stares at me with a slight furrow in her brow.

"I don't see what his sex life has to do with this."

"Mr. Hampton, just answer my question."

"You just have to know Billy. I wouldn't call him promiscuous. He never really had a steady partner and sometimes, when he was down or when he was totally absorbed in his work, he wouldn't have sex for long stretches—months, even. You all know he has the looks, but when he's on, his personality is mesmerizing. He could usually get anyone he wanted in bed, gay men, straight women, even straight men and gay women."

"I see," Detective Bell says, and I can sense her mentally comparing me to my brother. "I'll take that to mean he had a lot of sexual partners."

Detective Johnson rubs his chin and adds, "Mr. Hampton, I would appreciate it if you could take some time and provide us with a list of everyone you know or suspect your brother may have been intimate with."

"Now?"

"No, not now, but in the next couple of days. I'm sorry, but it could really be useful to us," he replies, crossing both his arms in front of his chest.

"Right, but do you all know something about my brother's death you aren't telling me?"

Detective Johnson grimaces, shakes his head, and replies, "As I said earlier, this is routine on very high profile people."

"Mr. Hampton. Does your brother have a will?" Detective Bell asks.

"Yes."

"Do you have a copy of it?" she asks.

"Yes, I do."

"Who's the primary beneficiary of his estate?" She looks directly into my eyes. I bristle when I realize what she's implying.

"I am, but if you think for one minute that I had anything—."

"Mr. Hampton, Mr. Hampton, please calm down," Detective Johnson says in a demanding tone. "These are routine questions, and you are in an extremely stressed state. Please, just try to answer our questions without supposing anything. Our job is to determine who and what caused your brother's death."

"You're the only beneficiary aren't you?" she asks.

"Yes I am," I say and swallow hard. "Would you like me to make you a copy of it?"

"That won't be necessary, we'll get an official copy from his attorney or trust company," Detective Johnson snaps. I am amazed, but not surprised, at how much these people already know about my brother. He's only been dead a little over five hours.

"Mr. Hampton, do you know of anyone who would want to harm your brother?" Detective Bell asks.

"No."

She looks at me dead on and asks, "Was he in any kind of trouble at all?"

"Not that I know of."

She looks up at Detective Johnson who says, "We let the hospital have his organs as you requested, but we are going to perform a routine autopsy."

"I see. How long will that take?"

"The body should be released by tomorrow afternoon. We'll contact the funeral home. Your dad told us about the wake on Friday, so we'll get this done fast," he replies, studying me carefully.

"Thanks." I reply.

They give each other a quick glance, and Detective Bell says, "Thanks for your time, Mr. Hampton. We'll let you know what we find."

"Yes," adds Detective Johnson, "Here are our cards. Call us if you think of anything else you feel we might need to know and you can email that list to us when you complete it."

"I will," I say and I escort them to the elevator and press the button. The door opens, they walk in, turn around, saying nothing. Detective Johnson pushes the button, looks down at Detective Bell, and the door closes.

"Dear God," I say out loud, rubbing my temples with both hands.

CHAPTER 7

I head through the living room out to the terrace to start clearing up the lunch dishes and am overcome with a confusing state of weariness—I feel some sort of gnawing bleakness inside, part of me wants to get drunk or stoned, the other part wants to curl up in a corner and hide and cry. I sigh at the lunch table and walk back through the kitchen and into Billy's studio. A large sofa covered in beige silk embroidered in white silk thread with delicate, intricate designs of Chinese fishermen invites me. I slip off the loafers and lie on my back letting the softness of the cushions absorb me. I study the volumes of books in the cases attempting to clear my mind of all thoughts. I drift off to sleep. At some point I'm aware of something licking my face and then a warm, furry presence settles against me, and I instinctively cuddle around it. I sleep soundly, void of thoughts and nightmares.A sharp bark, followed by a thud awakens me as Clark jumps down off the sofa. I crave him back with me, back into my arms into the sweet, painless world.

"Clark, come back up here, buddy?" I weakly call out. I hear his barks in the living room heading to the foyer. The sky has dulled and the light entering the study is indirect and diffuse.

"I see you're awake," Brenda says as she comes into the studio from the kitchen.

"Yeah, what time is it?"

"It's almost seven o'clock. You were sleeping so soundly; we thought it best to leave you alone. Luscious is on the way up now."

"Oh." I put my feet on the floor, rub my eyes, comb my fingers through my hair, slip on the loafers and stand up.

"Can you tell I've been napping?"

Brenda laughs, "Well yes I can, but I'm glad you have. You need the rest." Clark's barks rise in pitch and frequency, so I know Luscious has ascended.

"Let's go greet her," I say to Brenda.

"Certainly, your dad's already there."

We walk down the hall into the foyer where Luscious is sitting on the floor hugging Clark. He licks her face and ears, displaying his biggest smile and most fervent tail wagging.

"Lush," I say with my arms outstretched. I pull her up off the floor, embrace her tightly and start convulsing with sobs.

"Oh, don't cry, baby, I'm so, so sorry," she replies, and I feel her beginning to cry. We just hold each other for a while.

Clark sits down and whines loudly, then starts pawing my right leg with his right paw.

"It's okay boy," I push away from Lush, looking down at Clark.

"Darling, I just don't know what to say." Luscious squeezes both my hands and looks up into my eyes. Tears, with a slight tinge of mascara, are running down her face.

"I know Lush. Thanks for coming up."

"Don't even think about it," she replies.

"Luscious, this is Brenda Hamp—."

"Yes, of course, we met several years ago at one of Billy's openings," Lush quickly replies and extends her right hand to Brenda. They shake and Brenda offers her a tissue from a box she is holding.

"Thank you so much," Luscious smiles at Brenda, takes a couple of tissues, dabs her eyes, and gently blows her nose. Lush is dressed in a black sweater dress with a dark green silk jacket. A lovely jade buckle clasps together the black belt that encircles her slim waist. Her auburn hair is pulled back and up and fastened by some sort of tortoise shell clip—it has always fascinated me how she handles her long hair without even looking at it, just twirling it around with her hands up and behind her head, securing it with

strange looking clasps, sometimes sticking in a few bobby pins or whatever type of fastener she holds between her teeth as she continues whatever conversation she's having. She wears thin black hose and black leather shoes with flat heels, at five feet, ten inches she avoids high heels. She carries a black Hermes Birkin bag. Dad holds on to two large black suitcases on rollers and a computer case.

"Lush, I'm in Billy's room. I'll put you in the guest room next to his. Dad and Brenda are in the suite. Their kids are coming up tomorrow—Peter and Andrew can share a guest room and Emma can have her own."

She gives me a quizzical look that resolves into a smile, then she says, "Great, we've a full house, and we're going to need all the help we can get to pull this wake off by Friday. Charles tells me we're inviting five hundred and fifty people."

"That's what Billy wants," I add.

"Then, he shall have it," Lush states and looks at me. "Well Todge, who's in charge of this show?" Dad and Brenda give me a surprised look.

"Uhm, that's Lush's nickname for me. It kinda got started the same time I came up with Luscious," I explain. No one says anything.

"Anyway, Luscious is the ultimate organizer, so I hope I'm not offending anyone by putting her in charge?" I ask.

"Certainly not, I'll do whatever I can," Brenda responds. Dad just smiles shaking, his head signaling that it's all right by him.

"Wonderful! Brenda, I'll bet you cold cash you know your way around caterers and party set up," Lush beams at her.

"As a matter of fact, I do—" she replies.

"I've already hired the caterer, he's the best, he's a good friend of Billy's—Ricky Wallitsch with Upper Crust Catering," I interject.

"Yes, he telephoned while you were napping, Philip. He is so kind. He's delivering dinner to us tonight at seven-thirty. I told him there would be four of us," Brenda says.

"That's great," I reply.

"Perfect," says Lush.

"Brenda, you handle all the food, drinks, set-up and flowers with Ricky," Lush directs.

"Philip, you finalize the guest list in the morning. We'll send out email invitations along with personal phone calls. Charles, you and the kids can split up the list and make the calls tomorrow. Is that okay?"

"That's fine, Sarah, the kids will want to help," he replies.

"Charles, call me Luscious or Lush or I'll start calling you Mr. Hampton," she returns, smiling and arching her eyebrows.

"Of course, Lush."

Luscious clasps her hands and looks at me. "Have you issued any kind of press statement yet?"

"Well, no, I was waiting for you," I reply.

"Oh dear, where's the closest TV. Turn it on, quick!"

"In the kitchen, but why?" I ask.

"Honey, this is the kind of thing those vultures just love. We need to release a statement from the family immediately. Where's my laptop?" Dad hands Luscious her computer case, she grabs it, hurrying into the kitchen, motioning us to follow.

"I'll put Luscious's bags in the bedroom," Dad offers.

"Thanks Dad," I reply as Clark, Brenda, and I follow Lush into the kitchen. I find the clicker and direct it to a large plasma TV on the wall. CNN is on.

"Turn it to local news," Luscious orders. I do so and the local weather report comes on.

"Just leave it there, hon, and we'll see what comes on," Luscious says as she puts her computer on the counter, sits on a bar stool and starts looking through her purse. She pulls out a pack of her trademark Treasurer Black cigarettes and a slim, gold lighter on which her initials are engraved and puts them on the counter.

"As I recall, Billy doesn't mind if I smoke in here, do y'all?" she asks as she adjusts the tortoise shell clip holding back her hair.

Brenda and I both break out laughing.

"What?" Lush looks at us both.

"Nothing, it's just that Philip and I have been sneaking Billy's cigarettes today," Brenda explains.

"Well, I wish I could get by with just sneaking. I've never been able to quit, but at least these Treasurers come in slim now, and if I'm going to smoke, it might as well be the best damned tobacco money can buy." Lush replies.

She pulls out one of the elegant, long cigarettes with a gold tipped filter, lights it and inhales. I get a heavy pink marble ashtray from a cabinet and put it on the counter.

"Oh damn!" Luscious screams out pointing at the TV.

A full color headshot of Billy is on the screen. Yellow script scrolls on the bottom of the screen, flashing 'Breaking news, ex-Supermodel and artist Billy Hampton is dead at 31 years of age'. The camera zooms in on a pretty blonde reporter in a business suit.

"We have breaking news from our city reporters. It has been confirmed this evening that former Supermodel and current well known artist, Billy Hampton, died this morning at St. Vincent's Hospital from an apparent drug overdose," she delivers with a bit of urgency. We are glued to the screen as we watch famous pictures of my brother in everything from white briefs to tuxedos flash on the screen.

"News Alive's sources tell us that Hampton, who frequently appeared at A-list parties in New York, was seen celebrating with Supermodel Elliott Fields (a headshot of a wide grinning Elliott Fields flashes up) Saturday night at Splash, a well known Gay Bar in the West Village. Hampton was found unconscious in a stall in the Men's Room around 3 am Sunday morning when he was taken to St. Vincent's. He died sometime before noon today. Authorities are not yet confirming the exact cause of death."

"Okay, not to worry. Have a seat, Philly and let's write a statement for the press," Lush motions for me to sit down.

Brenda sighs, "I think I'll go find Billy's cigarettes. Anyone want a drink?"

"Can you make a perfect Manhattan, Brenda?" Luscious asks.

"Certainly, dear," Brenda returns with a smile.

"Divine, straight up with a twist, please. And you are welcome to these Treasurers, Brenda."

"Oh, let's not waste that expensive tobacco on me. I just need the nicotine high. Philip, what would you like?" Brenda looks my way.

"Well, how 'bout a Grey Goose on the rocks with a twist, please."

"I'll be right back," Brenda turns to leave. Clark follows her.

"Okay Philip, I think we need a short, straight forward statement from you concerning Billy's death. I'll email it to the Associated Press. We'll deal with the rest of the press tomorrow."

"Fine. Just write it, Lush, I'm drained to the bone. You're the better writer anyway," I say rubbing my forehead with my fingers.

Her fingers dart over the keyboard, and I watch her face as she types, taking breaks every thirty seconds or so to take a drag off her cigarette and review what she's written. Brenda returns with a tray with Lush's and my drinks and what appears to be a dirty martini. She sets the tray down, passes around the drinks and hands me the Marlboros and the onyx lighter.

"May I propose a toast?" Brenda asks. "To old friends and new friends and all those in between." We clink our glasses together and take a sip.

"Mmmm, Brenda, you make a damn good drink, girl!" Luscious looks at Brenda who soaks up the compliment with a smile.

"Thanks."

"All right, I'm done," Luscious states. "Listen, tell me what you think." She sits up straight, wiggles her bottom on the stool and begins, "The family of William B. Hampton is saddened to announce his death. Billy died unexpectedly this morning, April 7, 2006. Although he leaves us so soon at 31 years of age, he touched many of our lives during his career as a model and, afterwards, as a renowned artist. The family asks that any expressions of remembrance or sympathy be made to the Humane Society of New York City in care of the Clark Hampton Fund for Animal Rescue."

"That's great, Luscious. How did you know about the Clark Hampton fund?" I ask.

"Billy sent me a note when he endowed it a couple of years ago. I've contributed to it, rather generously, I'll have you know."

"Hmm, I bet David had a thing or two to say about that," I add.

"Fuckwad?" She asks. "He can go to hell," her eyes narrow as she says this and Brenda's eyebrows raise.

"Oh, don't mind me, Brenda. I'm just in a marriage that has seen its better days, and I just haven't had the strength to get out of it. But that's going to change and soon." She takes a drag, blows out a stream of smoke and grinds out the cigarette in the ashtray.

"Dear, sorry to hear that," Brenda replies as she takes a Marlboro and lights it.

"Well, it's just a vestige from my twenties. Mother was dying from breast cancer and really wanted to see her only child married before she died. David had the prerequisite pedigree but no money. That was fine by mother because my father was running her family's drug store business and she wanted my future husband to relieve Dad. It all seemed so simple." Luscious sighs then sips her Manhattan.

"Do you have any children, Luscious?" Brenda asks.

"No," she sighs, her eyes cast down. "David's sperm count is extremely low, and he would never consider adoption. He wouldn't even let me keep Clark."

"Yes, I've heard about Clark," Brenda responds with a look of concern. Clark lets out a couple of attention seeking whines and then two alert barks.

"It's turned out to be a blessing in disguise. I mean, if I had his children, I'd be tied to him in some regard for the rest of my life."

"Why haven't you divorced him?" Brenda asks.

"I ask myself that every day. I'm not codependent. It's just that everything is so easy this way. I mean, we're accepted everywhere: church, country club, parties, charity events, business circles, you name it. I will say David is one for keeping up the appearance of the perfect husband and wife. He is also a hard worker and led the takeover of the drug stores by a big national chain." Luscious looks dejected as she delivers this soliloquy I've heard so many times before and starts pecking at her keyboard with her fingers.

"Don't roll your eyes at me, Todge," Luscious exclaims as she looks up at me.

"I'm not rolling my eyes, it's just that you've said for years you're going to end this and you never do," I reply, reaching for a cigarette.

"Now that Dad's gone, it's going to end soon. I'm sure David senses this," she replies to me.

"Oh, did your father die recently?" Brenda asks.

"Yes, unfortunately last year. He seemed to be in good health, but one day he just slumped out of the golf cart at the country club—massive coronary, dead almost instantly. The sad thing is it was just two years to the day from the closing of the sell of the stores and Dad's official entry into retirement. He had planned to play golf, go on a couple of world cruises, even learn Spanish," she wiggles again as she speaks. I observe Luscious. She is still the slender, firm, ball of fire whom I met at freshman orientation in college. My mind drifts and I picture us having sex the first week of classes—I was in heaven. This bold

southern beauty was as horny and as sexually curious as I was. We tried everything in bed. I'll never forget the Friday night, about two weeks after we had first slept together, I got off seven times and she got off nine times. I still get a hard on just thinking about that night. We were inseparable until mid-term. As the newness of the sex wore down, she began talking about a long-term relationship and how we might spend our lives together. The more she talked along these lines, the more I found myself withdrawing from her. I felt trapped, I couldn't explain it to her, but that's the way I felt. I didn't know what to do, so I finally made out with another girl in front of her as she walked out of the bathroom one night at a pub. She didn't speak to me again for three years. We were both journalism majors and ended up in a senior seminar together in the same work group. Over the course of that semester, working together in the group, we began speaking and communicating again. By the end of the semester, we were friends, not lovers. We each decided to stay on and get our masters during which time we became close friends and confidants.

"Well, I want to know where Todge comes from. I can guess Luscious by simply looking at Sarah, but Todge?" Brenda directs the question to me.

"It's British slang for penis, Brenda. Billy and I called our penises Todgers when we were kids. I guess we picked it up from Uncle Adrian," I reply feeling heat shoot up my neck into my face.

"I see," says Brenda and she gives Luscious a questioning look.

"I'm afraid the nickname was my doing. Philip was the first man I ever slept with, and I became quite enamored, even to the point of fascination, with his penis. So when I heard him call it his Todger, the name just stuck. Besides, he was already calling me Luscious in front of my friends and it stuck with them, so I just had to have a nickname for him," Luscious explains this as if she is a defendant on the stand.

Brenda laughs and says, "And I thought the UVA coeds were the sexperts."

"All coeds wanna be sexperts, Brenda," Luscious replies, "Just wait until your boys hit high school."

"Yes, I know we have quite the road ahead of us," she replies.

"Any idea what Billy's password is into his wireless?" Luscious looks my way.

"Yes, it's Clarkham2, altogether," I reply.

"Great. Philip, I'm sending this statement out, and I'm instructing the press that I am the contact point for all communications concerning Billy's death. I hope that's okay with you," Luscious sees me shake my head. "Good, I'll give them my mobile number and email, so I expect the onslaught to begin soon. I hope the food comes and we can eat first though, I'm starved."

"Did I hear someone say food?" Dad asks as he walks in with two young men from the Upper Crust Catering Company who roll in a cart wafting wonderful smells.

"Perfect timing," Luscious exclaims. Clark walks over and starts sniffing the skinny, Asian guy's shoes who immediately freezes, a look of terror pasted on his face.

"Oh, he don't like Benny," the guy with the nametag Luka smiles. "Come here Clark," he says. Clark looks at Luka, but continues sniffing Benny's shoes and legs.

"We know Clark. He don't like Benny. We verked for Mr. Billy before. I sorry to hear he died," Luka directs his comments to me.

"Thank you. Clark, get over here. Leave him alone," I direct. Clark turns around, looks at me, turns back for one more quick sniff and then comes to me wagging his tail. He sits down, turns his head back toward the man, yawns, pulling his lips back revealing an intimidating set of sharp, shiny white teeth and four, inch and one-half, dagger-like canines. He emits a high pitch whine as he yawns. He turns his head back toward me looking into my eyes.

"What all do we have here?" Brenda asks Luka, who has cropped black hair, a couple of days of beard growth, and a pierced left eyebrow.

"Madam, they are the appetizers, they are caviar toasts wid cream fraiche, fried chili won ton wid motzrella cheese, and cold shrimps cocktail. For your zoup, we have chanterelle mushroom wid chicken stock, then freezay salad with herbs and creamy saysar dressing. For main coarse they are feelet minon

wid béarnaise sauce, they are sallmon feelets with dill sauce, and they are baked chicken with curry sauce and basmati rice. Ve have assorted steamed vegetables and roasted potatoes wid the rosemerry. Three pies for desert. They are bananna crème, dutch apple, and chocolate decadence." He proudly points to each container as he speaks, thick accent revealing his newness in America from, my guess is, somewhere in Croatia. They are smartly dressed in black slacks, white shirts, black bow ties and vests with rich burgundy brocade.

"Thank you, my, how nice. Just put them here on the counter and we'll take care of the rest," Brenda directs.

"Madame, Mr. Ricky say we stay to serve you and clean up," he replies to her with a puzzled look.

"Oh, I see, well, in that case, Philip, what do you think?" Brenda looks at me.

Luscious chimes in, "Why that's divine. These fine gents can serve us, clean up, which will give us more time to get caught up and plan."

"Yes, that's fine," I say, "Let's eat in the dining room. Brenda, can you show them where everything is here in the kitchen, and I'll go set the dining room table?"

"Certainly," she says, "Charles, can you help me in here?"

"Dad, would you mind feeding Clark? There's his bowl. He gets one large scoop of dry food kept in that concealed pantry over there by the entrance to the studio." Clark looks up at me with a hopeful expression wagging his tail. "Clark, go follow Dad, he's gonna feed you." I point to Dad. Clark immediately follows him to the pantry.

Luscious closes her laptop, and we take our drinks into the large dining room that is adjacent to the north side of the kitchen. This room has the same heart of pine floors as the study, but is a smaller room. Its west entrance is into the living room and the eastern side is comprised of floor to ceiling windows and French doors leading out to the terrace. The northern wall contains a large fireplace. The fireplace is faced with pink marble with a black granite threshold. The mantel is wooden with pairs of fluted columns on each side that run through the mantel up to an intricate cornice. This structure is built around a large, old pier mirror from Fatgram's foyer in Union. Two large candelabra in the shape of trees—the trunk and limbs are made of sterling silver and the tiny leaves are gold—flank the mantel. Each candelabrum holds six slender white candles. There is a pair of Kangxi period Blue and White baluster vases on the mantel with scenes of small deer Mother called the '100 deer design'. Fatgram's large mahogany dining room table with inlaid bands of rosewood is centered in the rectangular room, surrounded by twenty-four matching ribbon back chairs with large saddle seats covered in a soft grey leather. The table sits on an immense Tabriz rug with curvilinear floral designs in orange, grey, and tan on a cream background. This too came from Fatgram's front foyer. A large oval, mirrored, sterling plateau is centered in the table. It contains two large sterling candelabra, each with three arms, a sterling silver coffee and tea set, and several pairs of sterling salt and pepper shakers. The large bohemian crystal chandelier from Fatgram's dining room remains above this table where it has hung for the past one hundred and fifty years. No one in our family ever wanted this electrified, so it still holds forty-five small candles. Billy has dripless candles custom made for it. The walls and ceiling of the room are the same oak used in the studio, stained a lighter shade of brown and contain more ornate moldings and facings. The ceiling is divided into eight equal rectangular sections each of which has rectangular sections of molding ascending and decreasing in size giving an appearance of looking up inside a pyramid. Recessed halogen lights are symmetrically dispersed in the uppermost panels as well as sprinkler heads and security devices. Gilded French sconces in the shape of robed cherubs holding torches flank the French doors of the south and west entrances to the room. The room contains two paintings by Mother as well as a Picasso and a Klimt. Hidden paneled doors, built in the western and northern walls, cover cabinets containing silverware, china, crystal and table linens. One of the doors leads to a private powder room, another leads to the hallway containing Billy's bedroom. I bring the lights up and head toward the door where the silverware is located. We set our drinks down on the table.

"Let's see, there are four of us, let's eat with something plain," I say to Luscious.

"My dear, there's nothing plain in this place. Plain was not a word in your brother's vocabulary," she replies.

"I reckon you're right, Lush."

"Reckon? Don't hear that word much anymore," she smiles.

"I know. Fatgram used it a lot, and Billy loved it." I open a silver drawer. Everything in it is ornate. I open another and find something fairly simple. "Here, this looks good." I get out four place settings and hand them to Lush.

"You wanna do two facing each other at one end of the table?" she asks.

"Sure that's fine. Let's do the end closest to the kitchen."

"Let me find some placemats and napkins," I say and begin opening other drawers. I spot some light yellow linen placemats and grab four. I can't find matching napkins, so I settle for plain white linen. I walk back to Lush.

"Two for you and two for me," I say as I reach across to hand her two placemats and napkins. We each start setting the table.

"Todge, what do you think really happened to Billy?"

"I wish I knew, but I know he didn't deliberately overdose. GHB is not the kind of drug he used for partying. The police were here earlier this afternoon."

"You're kidding. Do they think it's a homicide?"

"Pretty tight lipped they were—an older black man and a sexy little vixen type—both rather rude."

"Dear, don't tell me you're after a police woman now."

"Whatever," I deliver back.

"Sorry, you know me, always trying to keep tabs on your love life."

"It's okay, what would I do without you to look out for me?" I walk over and give Lush a bear hug, lifting her off the floor. She laughs.

"What's going on in here?" Brenda asks, smiling, as she enters the room.

"Just two old friends glad to be together," I offer.

"Philip, I wondered what kind of wine you wanted for dinner? Billy has an incredible selection. He must have five hundred bottles in those coolers in here."

"Pick out whatever you like, Brenda. Do a white and a red, I guess."

"Brenda, get a Zinfandel. I'm craving a good Zin," Luscious coos.

"Yes mam, you got it." She turns back into the kitchen. Lush watches her walking away.

"She is certainly put together well and in great shape. How old is she, Todge?"

"I believe she is around forty-two."

"Looks more like thirty-two to me. My God, our age," she replies.

"I know. She's a good person, too. Loves Dad, their kids. At first she insisted they not stay here. She knew my feelings about Dad and her were strained. She gave me plenty of room."

"But you asked them to stay here and bring their kids?"

"Yeah, Dad kind of broke down when he got here today. Treated me in a way like he used to before Mother died and he started drinking so much. Told me how much he loves Billy and me. Somehow all those years of bad feelings melted away."

"That's great, Philip."

I feel myself getting teary and I say, "I know, but it's just so awful that it took Billy's death to make it happen." We look at each other, sigh, and take a sip from our drinks which both have left little wet rings on the table.

"Damn, let me get some cocktail napkins. Billy would cuss a blue streak if we leave rings on Fatgram's table," I smile at Lush and she smiles back with full red lips and dazzling white teeth.

I find the cocktail napkins while Luscious chooses the crystal. We are both silent with our own thoughts for a while as we finish setting the table. Dad and Brenda enter the dining room with the wine, followed by Luka and Benny carrying trays with the food. Clark scurries through and disappears under the table.

"I thought we'd start with the soup and a little white wine, then just pass around everything else," Brenda says.

"Sounds great. Lush and I will sit on this side and you and Dad sit on that side," I say and motion to Brenda. Luka pulls out Brenda's chair, gives Benny a stern stare causing him to quickly pull out Luscious's chair. We all sit down and Luka serves us the mushroom soup while Benny pours the Sauvignon Blanc Brenda selected. We begin eating without a toast. Luka and Benny station themselves on either side of the kitchen door and freeze with their arms behind their backs. I notice that Benny is extremely handsome, with a fragile, boyish, feminine appearance. He wears white gloves, Luka doesn't. I think how much Billy would enjoy this scene. He'd say to Luka and Benny, 'Hum, I think I'll gild you both and add you to my collection, but only after I've had each of you, or maybe the both of you together.' My ears feel heavy and hot as an image of Benny, Luka, and Billy, naked limbs entwined into a lecherous tangle, Billy eating the young Asian's ass who is licking the thick cock of Luka who, in turn, is sucking Billy's cock. I hear the moans of pleasure emanating from the trio, and I feel my cock growing. I shift in my chair, stretch my legs out under the table, smile, and look over at Lush as she tastes her soup.

"Mmm, this soup is excellent," Lush exclaims.

"Yes it is," Brenda says as she takes another spoonful.

"Son, have you heard from the man who took Billy to the hospital?"

"Yes, I called him today. He's still in Bermuda at a photo shoot."

I continue to tell everyone about my conversation with Elliott Fields after which they are all curious about my conversation with the two detectives. At this point, we are well into the main courses and are drinking the Zinfandel. Luscious graciously changes the subject for a while and asks about Dad and Brenda's furniture stores in Iowa. Dad, in turn, is curious about the sale of Lush's family drug stores.

"The sale was completed two years ago, and as I was telling Brenda earlier, Dad finally was able to retire completely and he had planned to do nothing but play golf and go on some world cruises in the winter. He poured himself into that business after Mom died, spent all his time grooming David and expanding the stores. We had seventy-five stores in Kentucky and Indiana by the time of the sale. Then dad died two years later, on the anniversary of the closing."

"Oh, how awful, Luscious," he replies, "Did you ever work in the business?"

"No, Charles. I know this may sound strange, but the business came to us through the maternal side of my family. My great grandmother's father started it right after the Civil War. There were never any male children born in that line, so husbands always ran the business. My parents encouraged me to follow suit."

"How interesting," Dad replies.

"Anyhow, as you know, I wanted to pursue a career in journalism, but after I got my Masters, mother got breast cancer. I married David, mother died, and the next thing I knew, I was a bored country-club housewife who couldn't get pregnant. I couldn't get a job in journalism in Louisville, so one day I decided to take a real estate course, and I ended up getting my license. The next thing I knew I was selling the homes of my parents' friends, and then finding houses for my friends. It's been a great career for me. I am my own boss, and, thanks to your lovely son here, I've even managed to get a few essays and articles published over the years."

"You're being modest. She's the queen of high end residential in Louisville," I add with a big smile.

"Oh, Todge, you are so full of you know what—"

"Oh my, I apologize everyone—that horrible smell. It must be Clark," I say as I stick my head under the table where the smell is so awful I can't breath. The offender just lies there with sad eyes, slowly wagging his tail.

"Rank. That's some real ghetto gas, Clark boy," Luscious says, "Let's open these French doors up."

She stands but Luka, who is trying his best not to laugh, runs over and says, "Allow me, madam." Lush sits back down. Luka unlocks and opens the set of French doors nearest to us. A cool breeze rushes in, and Clark heads out on the terrace to his grassy spot.

"Well, I guess he was just trying to tell us something," Dad offers. We all laugh, except for Benny, whom I guess doesn't understand much English.

Billy's telephone begins to ring. There is a portable unit on one of the kitchen counters, and Luka asks me if he should bring it in. I hesitate, and then tell him to get it. He does and I answer it.

"Hello. Yes, this is Philip Hampton." I sense everyone watching me carefully. I listen to the caller, but can hardly believe what he's saying to me.

"I see. No, I haven't noticed anything out of the ordinary here. Is there anything else I need to do tonight? Right. Well, I suppose that's okay. Thank you. Goodnight."

I click the phone off, put it on the table and look at everyone. I feel the tears pressing from inside my eyeballs as I say, "That was Detective Johnson. The hospital notified him that when they tested Billy's blood prior to releasing his organs for donations they found extremely high levels of GHB. He said low levels of GHB naturally occur in everyone's blood, and that the higher levels Billy ingested yesterday would have been fully metabolized. The only explanation is that someone injected a concentrated solution of GHB into his bloodstream this morning. Someone murdered Billy in the hospital this morning."

CHAPTER 8

Everyone is shocked into silence for a few moments, then Dad says, "Who could have done this? Why would anyone possibly want to kill Billy? Philip, is there anything you haven't told us?"

I hesitate and start to get angry thinking to myself, "There's a helluva lot I haven't told you Dad. Where the hell have you been since I was thirteen?" But, I manage to push back the emotion and reply, "No there isn't. I have no idea why anyone would want to harm Billy."

"Well, you can bet the police have already crawled all over St. Vincent's," Lush makes a sweeping motion with her left hand and takes a sip of Zinfandel.

"Tragic, I can't imagine. It seems unreal," Brenda says, staring at her plate with a blank look on her face.

"Detective Johnson asked if they could bring in an investigative unit for a couple of hours in the morning," I say. "He asked if we could vacate the condo during this time."

"Absolutely not!" Lush loudly interjects. "Christ, you can't turn loose a bunch of nitwits in here. Philip, think of how many priceless objects Billy has here."

I sigh, "You've got a point. I guess I better give Billy's attorney a call tonight."

"Good idea, son."

"Philip, now that this is a murder investigation, do you think we should cancel the kids?" Brenda looks up from her plate at me.

"No, I still feel Billy would want them here. I know it will be difficult to explain this all to them, but—."

"They're really perceptive, son, they'll handle it all right," Dad offers.

"Yes, I suppose you're right, Charles." Brenda reaches over and touches Dad's left hand. He turns to her and puts her hand in both of his and smiles at her.

"Philip, someone was hell-bent to see Billy dead. I mean, they tried to drug him and when that failed, they risked sneaking into St. Vincent's ICU to finish him off." Lush's brow wrinkles while she's talking.

"I know, Lush, you're reading my mind."

"I figured as much. You're Billy's closest confidant. Right?" Lush opens her right hand and points to me with her index finger. She always gesticulates with her hands as she speaks, some sort of hidden sign language I've often thought.

"I have always thought so. Ever since he started seeing that psychiatrist, I believe his name is Dr. Gerard—sounds French—he's been a bit remote. But even so, he spoke to me about some of his sessions."

"Hmmn," Lush replies, and I know her brain is churning out endless possibilities.

I slam my right hand down on the table, startling everyone, and spit out, "Whoever did this will pay. They'll pay the same price Billy paid. I'll see to it or die trying."

Brenda and Dad look frightened. Lush smiles, raises her glass, and says, "I'm with you all the way, darling." I smile at her and we toast.

"Anyone care for dessert?" Brenda meekly asks. No one does.

"I bet your kids will make short work of these pies, anyway," Lush says.

"Yes, Lush, you're right, especially the boys. It's amazing the quantities they put away," Brenda replies.

"I suggest we let these fellows cleanup here. Let's all go out on the terrace for a nightcap and a cigarette," Lush claps her hands and folds her fingers, looking at everyone.

"Yes, why don't we? You all go on. I'll show Luka and Benny where everything goes. I'll join you shortly," Brenda starts to get up as she speaks. Luka immediately moves to pull out her chair. He again motions for Benny to assist Luscious.

"Honey, could you see if Billy has any decaf?" Dad asks as he gets up.

"He does, I noticed this afternoon. Anyone else care for coffee?"

"No thanks, Brenda, I'm after some brandy or B&B," Lush replies.

"Billy's got anything you want. I'll get you a B&B, Lush. Brenda, what will you have?" I ask.

"Put out some Bailey's please, and I'll get some on the rocks when I join you all," she replies.

Clark hears the movement of chairs and comes back inside from the terrace. He disappears under the table and emerges at Benny's feet, sniffing again. Benny immediately stiffens and Clark, with his tail rigid and perpendicular to his back, begins to growl.

"Clark, what is with you, boy? Leave him alone!" I sharply command. Clark pulls his ears back close to his head, walks over to Luscious and nudges her left leg.

She bends over to stroke his head and says to Benny, "He's really such a sweet dog. He just smells something on your shoes."

Benny stares at Lush, unresponsive to her assurances, apparently only taking direction from Luka.

"Speaking of smells, I bet you left us something on the terrace," I say to Clark. "I better get a plastic bag to clean it up before we go out there."

"Show me where the bags are, and I'll do it, son. You can fix drinks for you and Luscious."

"You sure?"

"Yes, yes."

Dad and I head into the kitchen. Lush follows and turns toward the wet bar, I go for the bags. Brenda, Luka, and Benny enter carrying dishes.

"We're going to have plenty of left-overs," Brenda remarks.

"I'm sure none of it will go to waste," I reply. "Here are the bags, Dad," I say and hand him a bag.

"Come on, Clark, let's go clean up your mess." Dad and Clark leave the kitchen. Brenda is pulling out Saran wrap and directing Luka and Benny. I walk over to the wet bar where Lush is fixing her B&B.

"What'll you have, Todge?"

"B&B sounds good."

She gets another brandy snifter and pours me a generous drink. I grab Billy's Marlboros and the onyx lighter.

"Let's go outside," I say.

"After you, dear," Lush replies.

We head out and meet Dad at the French doors in the dining room. He is holding the plastic bag full of Clark's poop.

"A lot of poop for a dog his size," Dad smiles.

"Yeah, I've noticed that. I guess he's healthy though," I reply.

"I'll be right back. It's a little chilly out here," he says.

"Oh, it feels divine, Charles," Lush says. "Philip, why don't you light some of these candles?"

"Sure," I reply. Billy has numerous mosaic candle holders sitting on walls and tables on the terrace. I set my drink and cigarettes on a table, take the lighter and begin lighting the candles. Lush sits down, sighs, and lights one of her own cigarettes. We are quiet, listening to the night sounds of the city. The terrace takes on a warm glow as I light all the candles, reflecting shimmering light off of sculpture, wrought iron, boxwood, and brickwork. The breeze is slight and cool.

"Todge, you must be a wreck inside," Lush looks up at me as I pull out a chair next to her.

"I suppose I am. These past two days seem like two months of unending pure hell."

"You're strong, darling, it'll get better in time," she puts her left hand on my hands.

"One can hope, but right now I keep slipping from sadness to despair to anger. I swear to God, Lush if whoever did this to Billy were sitting here in front of me, I'd take my bare hands and choke the life out of them."

"I'd help you do it," she replies, releases my hands and takes a deep drag off her cigarette. "Once we get through the wake, I think we should do some investigation of our own. I'm here for as long as you need me, and I'll bet you we can find out a thing or two the police can't."

"I'm all for that, and, once again, I'm glad to be on your team."

"Our team," she smiles and turns her head toward Dad and Clark who emerge from the dining room. Dad is carrying a glass of water. Clark trots over to me, and I pat his head. Dad sits down.

"Dad, we were talking about our exposé of Senator Beckman. You know, we really made history at UNC. I don't think the graduate program in journalism was ever the same after we left."

"That must have been exhilarating for you both, sort of like winning the journalism Power Ball. I know you worked very hard for it. I wish I had been around to, to…."

"We blew them away, didn't we?" smiling, Lush interjects and leans back in her chair and looks up at the sky.

"Yes, and as I've said a thousand times before, Lush, it was mainly your doing. It was your idea to pursue Beckman, all your hunches and your leads. I was just the worker bee," I say while I study Dad's sad expression as he looks down into his glass of water.

"You mean the writer bee and a damn good one at that," Lush smacks the table and laughs.

"Why thank you, dear. Whoever would have thought two graduate students working on an investigative journalism project would bring down a United States senator for corruption in the swine industry?"

"'Pork Producers Funnel Millions to Beckman's Offshore Account—Environmental Disasters Overlooked'," Lush proudly states.

"By Sarah Richardson and Philip Hampton," I add. "Sid Hollingsworth sure had balls to let the *News and Observer* run our piece."

"What a great editor. He's still there, isn't he?"

"Oh, yes. He emails me from time to time. I don't think he ever got over you not taking the job at *The Washington Post*."

"I know, but at least you took the position at *The Constitution*."

"Funny, I never thought I'd stay in Atlanta," I say and reach for a cigarette. Dad's expression has changed from melancholy to emotionless. He is still staring into his glass of water as if it were a crystal ball or an oracle of some sort, and I want badly to ask him if he's alright, but I can't bring myself to do it—I still feel the sting of his never having acknowledged my and Lush's extraordinary early success with journalism.

"Do you have any idea what you will do, Philip? This is all yours now," Lush asks, sweeping her right hand around.

"Not a clue. But I will stay here until we find out who murdered Billy."

"Goodness, I'm glad I have on cashmere. I think I'll shut these doors so you won't waste heat, Philip," Brenda closes the French doors, walks over with her drink and sits down beside Dad who seems to come out of his trance and smiles at her. She pats his right hand. Clark goes off on a sniffing expedition of the terrace.

"That Luka knows where everything is. He's worked here several times. He's got everything under control and will come out here when they've finished cleaning up," Brenda states as she goes for a Marlboro that I light for her. "Benny never says a word—strange, but what a beautiful boy. How old do you think he is?"

"Late teens, early twenties," I reply. "I'll bet he's Thai. Sometimes it's hard to tell their ages."

"You should know, as much as you've traveled over there," Lush offers.

"I've always wanted to go to Bangkok," Brenda says, ice tinkling in her glass as she takes a sip of Bailey's.

"Fascinating city," I add, "Be sure to stay at the Shangri La Hotel when you go. It sits on the Chao Phraya River and is beautiful. The lobby is famous for its orchid displays and there is a great Thai restaurant with outdoor dining right on the river."

"Sounds lovely," Brenda replies.

"How long were you in Thailand when you were doing the article on the sex trade, son?"

"Wow, that's been a while back. Off and on maybe six or seven months," I reply.

"Great article!"

"Thanks Lush," I reply, and I change the subject, "What time are the kids arriving tomorrow?" Lush knots her forehead in response. "Ten thirty in the morning, son. We'll take a cab out to meet them and get a van back."

"Good, y'all can come back, get settled, and have lunch here," I reply.

"That sounds nice. I think you'll enjoy the children," Brenda smiles.

"I'm looking forward to getting to know them," I reply and light my cigarette. We hear an ambulance siren in the distance, and I think how Billy was in just such an ambulance two nights ago, and I wonder who in this great city heard his siren. Clark is over by the doors into the studio and he starts to whine.

"Philip. I'd like to create a slide, video presentation of Billy's life for the wake." Lush sits up straight in her chair peering at me with her large brown eyes, lit up by the flickering candles on the table.

"I think that would be awesome, Lush. You know how much he loved photos. He's got Mother's photo albums here, so you can scan some of those in, too," I reply, so thankful that she is here to direct things, make them happen.

"Great. I'll need his iPod too. I want to set it all to his favorite music."

"Boy, he liked so many different kinds of music. This could take a while," I reply.

"No problem. I'll get to work on that as soon as we write the obituary in the morning," she replies, sits back and takes a sip of B&B. Clark begins to bark.

"What's he barking at?" Dad asks.

"Oh, probably that siren," I reply. "Clark, come on over here boy, come on." He looks at me, whines again, then trots over and sits beside me. I pat his head. He wags his tail and whimpers.

"I think he's waiting for Billy to get home," Lush says.

"I don't know," I reply. "Poor boy. He really seemed to sense it when the nurse called this morning to tell me about Billy."

"Dogs are awfully intuitive," Lush says, takes a drag and begins to speak as the smoke streams from her beautiful mouth, "Mamma's little Shih Tzu, Mei Ling, grieved herself to death after Mamma died. She literally had no will to live and was dead within six months."

"How terribly sad, Lush," Brenda says.

"Yes. I for one, think animals feel emotions and have souls, the same as us," Lush states. Clark lets out a whimper and gets up and runs over to the studio windows again and starts barking furiously.

"What on earth is he barking at?" Lush asks.

"I'll check," I say as I get up and put my cigarette out in an ashtray. "Shouldn't those fellows be done by now?" I ask as I walk over to Clark who is now barking and scratching on one of the French doors trying to get in the study. At first glance, everything appears normal. Then something catches my eye. One of the oak panels on the library side is open revealing Billy's large safe. It is wide open. I grab the door handle and turn it. It is locked.

"Oh, my God, someone has broken into Billy's safe. It has to be those kids," I shout as I run toward the dining room doors, Clark right on my heels.

"What?" I hear Lush ask.

I open the dining room doors and run into the kitchen. Everyone follows me. We are stunned. Luka is lying on the floor on his right side unconscious in a pool of blood. Duct tape is wrapped around his mouth, hands, and feet. I bend down, turn him on his back, and see that he has sustained a nasty blow to the right side of his head. He groans and opens his eyes.

"Quick, get some scissors," I direct.

Brenda runs over and starts opening drawers. "Here are some kitchen shears."

"Dad, check the study and the rest of the house. See if you can find Benny."

"I'll go with you, Charles," Brenda says and moves into the studio with Dad. Clark follows them after he sniffs the blood on the floor.

Lush and I carefully remove all the duct tape from Luka. Lush hands me a wet cloth, and I gently wipe the blood from his face. I am sitting on the floor with his head in my lap.

"Vat happened?" he asks in a state of grogginess.

"We don't know. Someone knocked you out and taped you up. Do you remember who did it? Did Benny do it?" I ask.

"I didn't see nobody. One minute I'm vorking in the kitchen, the next I wake up here."

"Lush, stay with him. I'm gonna look around."

Dad and Brenda return and Dad says, "There's no one else here. The safe is open, but there seems to be a lot of stuff in there still."

"Philip, I'll call the ambulance, you call downstairs to see if Benny left, then call the detectives," Lush directs.

"Good idea," I say. I run to the foyer and press the intercom.

"Good evening Mr. Hampton," Timmy says.

"Timmy, did an Asian waiter leave here?"

"Yes he did. About five minutes ago," he stutters.

"Was he carrying anything?"

"Yes, a brown envelop. Boy, was he ever in a hurry. Ran out the door and jumped in a car that pulled up right as he hit the sidewalk."

"Damn," I say.

"What's the matter, Mr. Hampton, I mean, Philip?"

"That kid knocked out the other waiter and broke into Billy's safe."

"Oh my God. Shall I call the police?"

"No Timmy. I'm going to call them right now. That kid is on tape leaving isn't he?"

"Yes sir."

"Good, get that ready for the police please, Timmy."

"Yes sir. Philip?"

"Yes, Timmy."

"I'm really sorry about Billy. I mean, I just don't know what to say."

"Thanks, Timmy. Just so you know. He didn't overdose. Somebody murdered him in the hospital this morning."

"Oh my God," Timmy stutters as I turn back into the living room to find Detective Bell's card.

CHAPTER 9

The paramedics, two younger men dressed in blue jumpsuits, are observing Luka and questioning him in the living room where we have moved him to a sofa when Timmy phones that the detectives have arrived.

"Send them up, Timmy, thanks," I say and click off Billy's telephone. A minute later the elevator door opens and out steps Detective Johnson followed by Detective Bell. Clark approaches them warily.

"It's okay, Clark. Good evening detectives," I say, "I never expected we'd meet again tonight."

"Nor did we, Mr. Hampton," Detective Johnson states. He has on the same grey pinstripe suit he had on earlier. Detective Bell has changed clothes. She is wearing a black wool overcoat that is opened in the front revealing a black cocktail dress. She and Detective Johnson observe me as my eyes travel down the front of her dress.

"The injured waiter is still here. Everyone's in the living room," I quickly turn and motion them to follow me.

"You all met my Dad and his wife, Brenda, earlier. This is my friend Sarah Richardson from Louisville," I say. "Lu—Sarah, this is Detective Johnson and Detective Bell."

"Pleased to meet you both," Lush says as she shakes hands with them both. She widens her eyes at me after she shakes hands with Detective Bell.

The paramedics are taking Luka's blood pressure. One of them says, "He seems okay, his pupils are normal and his reflexes are okay. From the look of the blow to the right side of his head, he may have sustained a concussion. We're gonna take him in."

"Blood pressure is okay," the other paramedic states.

"Mind if we ask him a few quick questions?" Detective Bell asks.

"Should be fine if he feels up to it," the paramedic who took the blood pressure reading says.

"Sure, it's okay," Luka says.

"What's your full name, son?" Detective Johnson asks.

"Luka Stojanovic."

"And where are you from, Luka?"

"Zagreb, Croatia," he replies.

"How long have you lived here?" Detective Johnson continues.

"For four years now."

"Do you remember who hit you?" Detective Bell asks.

"No, no thing. I vas standing in the kitchen wrapping the food and the next thing I know I wake up on the floor wid my head hurting and mouth taped shut."

"How long did the other waiter work for your firm?" Detective Johnson asks.

"Benny, he's new. He been here just since January. He don't talk much. I feel sorry for him, so I try to help him out," Luka says then touches the right side of his head with his right hand. "Ouch!"

"Do you know much about him? Where he lives? Where he comes from? What's his last name?" Detective Bell asks.

"He told me he lives in Morningside Heights. Like I say, he don't talk much, just listen. His last name is something like Boonmay."

"He must not speak English very well," Detective Johnson states.

"No, he speak it very well, better than me," Luka states.

"Really?" Detective Johnson asks.

"Yes, well, I heared him to talk on his mobile phone sometimes. He speak very good English. English English."

"You mean with a British accent?" Detective Bell asks.

"Yes, British accent, no Asian accent. He also speak very good French. I heared him."

"Hmmm, do you have his mobile phone number?" Detective Johnson asks, rubbing his chin.

Luka pulls out his mobile from his pants pocket, flips it open, and retrieves Benny's number and hands the phone to Detective Johnson, "That's it there."

"Thank you," Detective Johnson says as he pulls out a small notebook and a pen and writes the number down, then hands the phone back to Luka.

"Detectives," I look back and forth at each detective as I speak. "I called the owner of the catering company, Ricky Wallitsch. He is a good friend of my brother's. I told him what happened. He said Benny has only been with him for a couple of months. His name is Benny Boonmee."

"Anything else, Mr. Hampton?" Detective Bell's dark brown eyes engage mine.

I hesitate to respond. "Yes, well, he said that Billy had introduced Benny to him as a friend of a friend who needed a job. He said that was why he hired him."

"Well I'll be damned," Luscious quickly injects as everyone looks at me as if I'm guilty of withholding evidence or something.

"Are you aware of any relationship your brother may have had with Benny?" Detective Bell directs to me.

"None, he never mentioned him to me."

She turns toward Luka, "Mr. Stojanovic, when was the last time you served here?"

"Two weeks ago, on a Friday, mam. Mr. Hampton had a dinner party for twelve people."

"Did Benny serve with you?"

"Yes mam, he did."

"Anyone else?"

"Yes mam, Adam, he vas bartender."

"I see. And before that?"

"Yes, that would be Mr. Hampton's big Valentine's Day party. Maybe hundred peoples. We had staff of ten here."

"Was Benny here then?"

"Yes mam. That's right after he first started working for Mr. Ricky. That was his first big party."

"Were you aware that Benny knew Mr. Hampton?"

Luka blushes and replies, "Yes mam."

"Hmmn," Detective Bell lifts the slender index finger of her right hand, gently presses her mouth, and I notice the tip of her tongue touch the finger for just an instance. She pulls the finger away and abruptly asks, "Mr. Stojanovic, did you or Benny ever have a sexual relationship with Billy Hampton?"

Luka hesitates, bends his head toward the floor and replies, "Yes mam, we both did after that last dinner party."

"Damn, the plot thickens," Lush looks up at me, arms akimbo, waiting for some sort of action or explanation from me. I don't have one, but my earlier presentiment about the three-way was on target.

"You say you don't know Benny that well, yet you've had sex with him?" Detective Bell moves closer to Luka.

"Not really with him, more with Mr. Hampton. We had three way," Luka responds as a wave of red color shoots up his neck and over his face.

"Were any drugs involved?" she asks.

"We smoked pot. Well Mr. Hampton and I did. Benny don't do no drugs or alcohol."

"Anything else?"

"No, just pot."

Refocusing my senses back to the present, I feel the thickness of tension and smell the spread of anxiety in the room. Brenda is staring out of the windows, zombie-like, her right hand, knuckles white and rigid, crowned with the canary diamond sparkling like a big dew drop in the sun, tightly clasping Dad's left hand. "Breathe Brenda, breathe," I think to myself. Dad sits motionless, with the same weary look he always had on his face after ten days on his feet at the High Point furniture market. The paramedics seem stunned. Luka begins to cry profusely, heaving. Snot drips from his nose onto an Oushak. Clark moves over and starts licking up the snot.

"Mr. Billy, he vas so nice. He vas good man. I'm so sorry he dead," Luka struggles to deliver this through undulating sobs. His emotions resurrect Brenda. She quickly releases Dad's hand, stands up, walks over to Luka, sits beside him, puts her left arm around him, and her right hand on his right thigh. She asks one of the paramedics for a tissue and hands it to Luka who blows his nose.

No one says anything for a while as Luka's crying subsides, but plenty of looks are exchanged and a few sighs are muffled. Clark comes over to me, sits, looks up wagging his tail as if he is about to whine, but doesn't. I bend down to pat him without saying a word. Detective Johnson's baritone mars the silence.

"Mr. Stojanovic, I'm not going to question you here and now about your sex life, but we are going to need to question you at length after the doctors have checked your injuries. I plan to do it tomorrow morning."

"Yes sir, will be fine," he looks embarrassed as he speaks.

"Do you have a green card, son?"

"No sir, just verk Visa."

"Well, don't get any ideas about leaving. I'm assigning two officers to you until we can fully question you."

"You don't think I had anything to do with Mr. Hampton's death?"

"Right now son, it doesn't matter what I think."

"Excuse me sir," one of the paramedics looks up at Detective Johnson, "We'd like to take him in now."

"Luka, please write your mobile number and address down for us," Detective Johnson directs.

"Yes," he says and sighs. I can see he is in pain. Detective Johnson walks over and hands him a small note pad and a pen. Luka takes them and quickly writes down the information and hands the note pad back to Detective Johnson.

"Luka, can I have my pen back, too?"

"Oh, sorry, here."

"Thanks."

Brenda and one of the paramedics help Luka up. The other paramedic rolls over a wheel chair. Luka is led to the chair and sits down. As the paramedics begin to roll him to the foyer he looks up at me and says, "Mr. Billy, he vas always very nice to me." Clark guards the foyer as they wait for the elevator.

"If you gentlemen wouldn't mind waiting down in the lobby for five minutes until the officers arrive to escort you, I'd appreciate it," Detective Johnson directs.

"Yes sir," one of the paramedics responds.

"Mr. Hampton," Detective Johnson delivers with a bit of irritation in his voice as the elevator door opens and the paramedics get in pushing Luka, "Our investigative team is on the way here now. We will need a couple of hours in here. Is that okay?"

"I suppose it is. Should we all just stay here?" I ask.

"Yes, that will be fine," he replies. "Detective Bell, call Filiatro and Compton to cover Mr. Stojanovic. Then call Peters and find out what's taking his crew so long." Detective Bell walks over to the far side of the room where a Picasso oil painting hangs and stares at it as she holds her cell phone to her left ear. She starts to talk, almost in a whisper.

The phone rings and I answer it.

"Okay, send them up. Thanks, Timmy."

"The CSI are here," I say to Detective Johnson.

"Good, Mr. Hampton, could you leash the dog or put him up somewhere while the investigative crew is here? I don't want him contaminating any evidence."

"He has a crate in Billy's closet, but I'd prefer to keep him with me on a leash," I reply. Clark knows we are talking about him and he comes over to me and rears up. I catch his front paws on my right wrist.

"Smart dog, you, go get your leash," I say. He yelps because he thinks he is going for a walk and starts out toward the kitchen.

"No, stop him!" Detective Johnson shouts. "Contamination, Mr. Hampton."

"Clark, stop. Come here boy," I immediately shout. He stops, gives me a quizzical look and trots back over.

"Philip, I put the leash on that chest over there when I came back from walking him today," Dad interjects. "Sorry, I meant to ask you where it belongs."

"Oh, that's okay," I say as I walk over to the diminutive early American serpentine, bow front chest of drawers which Fatgram always said was her best piece and pick up the brown leather leash. Clark jumps up to me again, panting and wagging his tail, and I clasp the leash to his red leather collar that is festooned with tiny silver rivets. The elevator door opens and Clark rushes forward pulling the leash out of my hands. He sees an elevator full of strangers and begins growling furiously, contracting the muscles in his face and lips revealing his large canines.

"Holy shit," I hear a man shout from the elevator.

"No, Clark, it's okay," I shout and run over to him, grabbing his collar. There are four men in defensive postures in the elevator, two uniformed officers with batons drawn like swords and two others in plain clothes with aluminum carrying cases held out to protect themselves.

"Sorry, officers, it's okay, he's just startled," I offer as I pull Clark away from the elevator. "Please, come in, it's okay, I've got him," I add as Detective Johnson approaches me.

"Mr. Hampton, perhaps you should put him in his crate?"

"I can control him Detective Johnson, really, he was just surprised. He thought he was going for a walk, and the elevator opened with strangers in it."

"Fine, but could you get someone else to hold him. I'd like you to show us the lay of the land here. Peters, guys, come on in," he gestures to the men in the elevator. They enter the foyer and follow us into the living room. I observe the men taking in the grandeur of the room as one of the guys in uniform remarks to the other, "You don't expect to run into a pit bull in a pad like this."

Clark is wagging his tail as I hand off the leash to Lush.

Detective Bell, who has completed her phone call, crosses the room and asks, "What sort of security system is in operation here?"

Muffled chuckles come from the officers and one with a thick Jersey accent says, "The kind with fangs, Bell." Laughter erupts from the four men.

"Funny, Peters," she glares at him, then turns to me, "I'm sure your brother's insurance company must require an extensive security system."

"Well, there are motion detectors everywhere, and sensors on the terrace windows and doors," I offer. "But since he's had Clark, he doesn't arm it because Clark kept setting it off and he just never had it adjusted for a dog. I do know he sets it when he travels and leaves Clark with the neighbors."

"I see, what about cameras?"

"Only in the elevator itself and outside the stairwell door. Those are monitored at the front desk."

"Detectives, you won't find any fingerprints from the Thai waiter. He wore white gloves the entire evening. The doorman told me he had them on when he fled the premises," Lush states flatly.

Detective Bell turns toward Lush. "And how do you know the suspect is Thai?"

"Well, Philip has spent a lot of time in Thailand and he says the kid looks Thai. And isn't Boonmee a Thai name, Philip?" Lush replies. "By the way, I think you'll see from the lobby video that this kid has an extraordinarily beautiful face."

"Hmmm and what has that got to do with this investigation, Mam?" Detective Bell delivers the question in a sneering tone.

"Oh please, Detective Bell, call me Lush, not Mam." Detective Bell does not speak but responds with a confused look on her face. Lush laughs, "Oh dear, it's just a nickname that has stuck with me. Anyway, my point is that a beautiful young Thai man in New York could possibly be kept by someone. Perhaps that someone is whom you need to locate. My hunch is that someone is Billy's murderer."

"Miss Richardson, what do you do for a living?" Detective Bell asks.

"I'm a real estate agent."

"Well, Miss Richardson, I suggest you stick to real estate and let us handle murder investigations," Detective Bell delivers this with condescension.

"Just trying to give y'all a leg up," Lush smirks back at her.

"That won't be necessary, Mam—"

"Has anyone touched the safe or anything in it?" Detective Johnson interjects.

"No Detective, we all figured you'd be dusting it, so we let it alone. However, Lush found this list of items in the safe on Billy's hard drive." Detective Johnson looks at Lush then takes the printout and peruses it.

"It appears the most valuable items in the safe are jewelry," he says and hands the paper to Detective Bell. "Yes, Billy kept all the jewelry he and I inherited from my late Mother and Grandmother here. He wanted it near all their other things."

"So some of this jewelry and maybe some of the antiques and artwork in here are yours too?" Detective Bell asks.

"Yes, Billy and I inherited everything equally. When he purchased this place we decided to consolidate everything here. I travel constantly and just didn't want to leave valuable antiques and jewelry in my house in Atlanta."

"And now it's all yours, including this condo?" Detective Bell asks raising her eyebrows.

"I thought we covered that earlier today," I reply.

"Mr. Hampton." Detective Johnson states.

"Yes." Dad and I answer Detective Johnson simultaneously because he is not looking at either of us, but up at Mother's painting of Billy and me on Pawley's.

"I'm sorry," he replies, "Mr. Philip Hampton. You tell us that this happened while you, Mr. and Mrs. Hampton and Miss Richardson were all outside on the terrace?"

"Correct."

"Who was the last person or persons to see Mr. Stojanovic and Mr. Boonmee?"

"Well, I suppose it was I," Brenda says looking up at Detective Johnson. "I remained in the kitchen to help them clean up while all the others went to the terrace to have a nightcap."

"Did you notice anything unusual about either waiter? Funny eye contact? Signals of any sort?" Detective Johnson asks.

"No, not at all. Luka was very friendly and talked quite a bit. The other boy, Benny, never said a word. When it became apparent that they knew where everything was, I left them to finish and joined the others on the terrace."

"How long were you with them in the kitchen?"

"Oh, not more than ten minutes."

"And you're sure you observed nothing out of the ordinary?"

Brenda looks at me, then at Clark and says, "I did notice during dinner how tense Benny seemed around Clark. Clark kept sniffing Benny's shoes. I got the impression he didn't like Benny. Maybe he just sensed that Benny was afraid of him."

Clark is wagging his tail, and Lush pats him on the back and says, "Good watch dog, good boy, you can smell a crook a mile away."

Detective Johnson turns to me and says, "Would you please give us a tour of the unit? Let's start in the kitchen where you found the injured waiter. Haley, Washburn, come with me. Detective Bell, take officer Vance with you and inspect this other wing. Who can show them?"

"I can, I know it well," Lush says. "Here, Brenda would you mind taking Clark. I can tell he likes you."

Detective Johnson turns and looks at everyone else. "If you all wouldn't mind waiting in here. I know it's late and you've all had a stressful day, but we'll be as quick as we can. Carter, you stay in here with everyone. If anyone needs a drink or the restroom, Officer Carter will accompany you."

"To the bathroom too?" Lush asks Detective Johnson.

"Mam, he'll wait outside the door," he replies with a slight grin and motions for me to lead the way while Lush, Detective Bell, and Officer Vance head off down the hall to the bedrooms.

I take them into the dining room, show them the doors to the terrace, and then we make our way into the kitchen. The CSI guys start opening their cases and putting on latex gloves. One of them pulls out a camera and starts taking pictures of the blood on the floor and the general kitchen area. The other starts taking samples of the blood. Detective Johnson grabs a pair of latex gloves, puts them on, walks over and turns up the lights, then walks over to one of the counters and carefully picks up the heavy pink marble ashtray I had been using. There's blood on the bottom of it.

"This must be the weapon used on Mr. Stojanovic. Process it, Detective Haley," Detective Johnson says.

A roll of silver duct tape sits by the ashtray. "Check out this roll of duct tape, too," he adds.

"Yes sir," Detective Haley replies. He is a stocky, handsome young man with closely cropped light brown hair with long side burns that, in the bright kitchen light, are flecked with light grey patches resembling the shiny, flakey morsels of mica we used to pull out of the red clay on Fatgram's farm and pretend were flakes of gold.

"Where's the duct tape you pulled off the victim?" Detective Johnson asks me.

"I put it in the trash, in this closet over here," I answer as I walk over, open the closet, and point out the stainless trashcan.

"Haley, get this too," Detective Johnson directs.

"Yes sir."

"You guys continue on in here. Let's go to the safe, Mr. Hampton," Detective Johnson says. He certainly knows his way around a crime scene I think to myself.

I lead the way into Billy's studio.

"My goodness. What a beautiful room," Detective Johnson exclaims as his eyes move over the room.

"Billy designed it all and decorated it himself," I say and I feel the pain of losing him engulf me again as I recall how excited and involved he was in building and decorating all of this. "Here's the safe," I say as I walk over to it.

Detective Johnson looks up from where he is standing looking at the Tiffany lamp on Billy's desk. "Yes, I see it. Mr. Hampton, we're going to have to take the computer hard drive with us."

"Yes, I thought you might, that's fine," I say as I silently thank Lush for being brilliant and a whiz with computers. After we found Luka, she immediately went to Billy's computer and starting looking at various files and programs. She quickly found out that Billy uses a remote service to back-up everything on his system and that he uses the Clarkham2 password for everything. She backed-up everything on the remote system and transferred all his files, email files, and Address Book files to her own laptop before the detectives arrived. She then asked me for his cell phone, which just happened to be the same models as hers. She quickly attached a cable to it and downloaded all of its information onto her hard drive.

Detective Johnson walks over and looks into the safe, and says to himself, "I wonder how the kid got the combination to the safe."

"Billy was never good with numbers. He keeps all his PIN's, passwords, security codes, and combinations on a card in his desk over there," I remark.

Detective Johnson is examining the bookshelves surrounding the safe and points to an index card laying on one shelf. "Would that be it?" he asks.

I look at the card without picking it up. "Yes, that is it."

Detective Johnson looks directly into my eyes and asks, "Mr. Hampton, think carefully. Whatever was in that brown envelope probably caused your brother to be murdered. Do you have any idea whatsoever it might be?"

"I have no idea at all, Detective Johnson," I reply returning his stare.

"Well, could you show me the rest of the place?" I lead him toward the guest suite. I cannot help but feel apprehensive.

CHAPTER 10

I wake up to a throbbing headache thinking, "Damn, I hope I'm not getting a sinus infection." I reach my hands down into my boxers and grab my hard cock, and begin gently stroking it while I imagine unzipping the back of Detective Bell's black dress, lighting kissing the back of her neck, teasing her with my stubble. This image morphs into the swimming hole with Billy, me, and Uncle Adrian, and then

transforms into fresh sexual images of the three of us in New York at his apartment and at our beach house on Pawley's Island. My throat tightens and my ears begin to burn, and I am overcome with dread.

I hear a soft knock on my door, and I expect Clark to bark, then I notice he's not in bed with me.

"Philip, it's me. I think you better wake up, it's 10 am," Lush says.

Damn, I jump out of bed and walk over and open the door. Clark barrels in and jumps up on the bed, turns toward me wagging his tail.

"I hope you don't mind, he bunked with me last night," Lush smiles, and I see her eyes travel down my bare chest to the bulge in my boxers.

"Oh shit, I'm sorry. I'm so used to living alone, I didn't think to—"

"Mmm, still looks good to me," she laughs, "It's not like I haven't seen it before."

"Hang on a second," I say, "I'll be right back."

I run into Billy's closet and grab a fluffy white bathrobe and put it on as I walk back into the bedroom. Lush is standing by the bed petting Clark.

"Your dad and Brenda are at the airport picking up the kids. I asked him to stop on the way back and get you a replacement phone. I hope you don't mind, but I thought you might be getting some important calls as the news of Billy's death gets out."

"Right. Yes, thanks. I can't believe I slept so late."

"Honey, you needed it. Listen, get yourself together and come into the kitchen, and I'll fix you some breakfast."

"Okay, give me ten minutes."

She turns and walks out. Clark turns his head, looks at me, and jumps off the bed to follow Lush. I head into the bathroom, peel off the robe and boxers, turn on the shower and walk over to the toilet to pee. My cock is only half hard now as I watch the strong yellow stream arch into the commode. It's been several weeks since I've had sex with anyone other than myself, and I'm feeling horny. "Think with the head on your neck, not the one in your trousers," I smile as I recall Fatgram's blunt advice to her adolescent grandsons, and I wonder what she would have done had she known about Adrian. I finish peeing, flush the toilet, realize I need to crap, sit down, do my business, wipe, flush, walk over to the shower, and stick my hand in to see if the water temperature is right. It is perfect. I step in, close my eyes, turn my face up toward the showerhead, letting the warmth of the cascading water envelop me. I wish I had Fatgram here to deal with Billy's murder. She'd know exactly what to do. She's the last person on earth I'd want coming after me, especially if I had murdered one of her own. The warm water comforts my senses, but inside I feel despair and hopelessness, and I ask myself how could it be possible that my brother was murdered. My stomach growls. I grab the soap and begin to lather my arms, chest, back, as well as I can reach it, then my groin, ass, asshole, and finally legs and feet. As I rinse off, I wonder why I always bathe in this ritualistic manner. I make a mental note to do it differently next time. I close my eyes, lather my hair with shampoo, massage my scalp a bit, and run the lather over my face, ears and neck, after which I rinse my hair and face, then one final body rinse. I turn off the water, step out, grab a towel, dry off, and head into Billy's closet for more khakis and a blue, oxford cloth shirt. After putting on the clothes and shoes and socks, I head back into the bathroom, quickly comb back my wet hair, brush my teeth, and head out to the kitchen.

Lush hears me coming and is pouring a cup of coffee for me out of a French press pitcher. "That was fast. You have always amazed me at how quickly you can shower and dress. Remember how impatient you used to get with me. I believe you referred to my getting dressed as occurring at 'a glacial pace.'" She smiles and hands me a cup of black coffee. I take a big sniff from the cup, then take a sip.

"God, he always has good coffee," I say. "I bet this will stop my headache."

"Yeah, I found Costa Rican beans and ground them this morning. Want some ibuprofen, Todge?"

"No thanks, Lush." I put the cup down, walk over and embrace her and say while I'm holding her, "It means so much to me that you are here. It would be so hard without you." She doesn't say anything, but

I know her eyes are tearing up. I let go of her and go back to my coffee cup. She grabs a paper towel and starts dabbing her eyes. She smiles at me and we both laugh a little.

"What would you like for breakfast?" she asks.

"Gosh. One of your fried egg sandwiches would be wonderful."

"I thought that might be what you wanted. Today's your lucky day because I've already checked and your brother does have bacon. Two graduate school hangover cures on the way."

"Great, let me help you."

"No, you sit there and enjoy that coffee. I'll take care of the sandwiches."

"You haven't eaten yet?"

"No, just coffee and cigarettes. I've been working on more press releases, and I made a stab at the obituary."

"Do you feel like looking over these while I cook?" She hands me a few sheets of paper.

"Sure, but I think I'll need a cigarette myself first."

"Here are your Marlboros. I straightened up the living room this morning and found them."

"Jesus, I thought the detectives would never leave last night," I exclaim as I light a cigarette and inhale deeply.

"I know," Luscious replies, "Two a.m. was pushing it a bit. They seemed thorough though."

"Yes," I reply, "I'm okay with that Johnson fellow, but Detective Bell is always so confrontational toward me. I think she believes I am involved in Billy's murder."

"Well, I think maybe they are just doing the good guy-bad guy routine," she says as she puts four strips of bacon into a cast iron frying pan.

"Maybe you're right, but I don't know. I think she's out to get me for some reason."

"You'd like to get her. That is, in bed," Lush says as she turns on the flame.

"Now Lush. I'm not that bad. Am I?"

"I saw how you looked at her. I mean she is a beautiful woman, and she looked great in that black cocktail dress."

"Well, I admit she does look great. You can tell she's in great shape too."

"Okay, so I'm right. You'd like to have your way with her."

"Christ, Lush, a man would have to be a zombie or totally gay not to want that. But I can't believe we're sitting here talking about sex now."

"Why not Todge? There's a thin line between love and hate and life and death. Horribly emotional events bring out the extremes in us. Don't they?" She glares at me, and I recognize that look of hers that precedes an outburst. "So why is it so damn unusual to think that you might want to fuck a beautiful detective who happens to be investigating your brother's murder? Shit, I bet you want to fuck Brenda too!"

"Lush," I put my cigarette down, then stand up and walk over to her. "You know me too well. Yes, I admit Detective Bell turns me on, but you do too. My God, think of all the great sex, I mean really hot, knock down, drag out fucking we used to do. We fucked in elevators, bathrooms, cars, and stairwells. Where haven't we fucked, Lush? Even in a Goddamned airplane bathroom at thirty thousand fucking feet." My voice is loud; I am grabbing her shoulders. I feel my armpits sweating and my cock is getting hard. I press her into my body. I can tell she is holding her breath. Clark is at our feet barking furiously.

"It's okay, boy, it's okay, we're just communicating here." I suddenly release her. She gasps. I look into her eyes, and then walk back to my seat at the bar.

She sighs and says, "I knew we wouldn't be together long before we flashed." The smell of frying bacon fills the kitchen. "How the hell do you turn on this hood?" she asks as she pushes white and red buttons on the hood. She hits a black one and the roar of a strong fan resounds. "Good."

She turns around towards me, "Todge, that was all my fault."

"No it wasn't."

"Yes, listen. I can't help myself, but I've told you this before, and you know that I'll always be a little jealous of you and other women. It's not fair, but I can't help what I feel. Nonetheless, although it's tempting, we've come so far in our relationship. Sex would only ruin it, not reinforce it. This time, it's me. I'm just so fucking miserable in my marriage, and I feel like a Goddamned failure because I haven't gotten out of it after all these years." She talks loudly as she focuses on turning the bacon.

"You'll get out when you're ready to get out, Lush. I mean you've always been saddled with family responsibilities way more than a lot of people, and you were an only child to boot."

"That's no excuse. You've had as many family responsibilities as I have, even more. I, I just want to be loved by a man with a compassionate heart—someone who is always glad to see me, someone who loves me without conditions."

"And you would be describing a dog, my dear. Voila, monsieur Clark, " I can't help but interject. We both break out in laughter.

"Seriously, Todge. Affairs don't work for me either. God knows I've had my share of them. I hate all the sneaking around and pretending. I just won't do that for sex anymore."

"I know what you mean," I reply. "One night stands and casual affairs seem less satisfying to me than they used to be."

"By God, I just don't want to waste any more of my youth, or what's left of it. I want to get it right this time," she stresses her syllables with urgency as she removes the bacon to drain on folded paper towels, turns down the flame, then turns off the hood. "Todge, I can't talk to anyone else in the world the way I talk to you. Not even with my closest girlfriends at home."

"I'm the same with you, Lush. Now that Billy's gone, you're all I've got."

"You've got your Dad and Brenda and their kids."

"Yeah, but they're practically strangers."

"We're both of us broken souls," she says, "Maybe we can help each other mend?" Lush puts an oven mitt on her right hand, picks up the pan and pours off the bacon grease into a mug. The stream of golden, molten fat fills half the mug and tapers into a brown bits-laced trickle. She puts the pan back on the burner, pulls off the mitt, and reaches for the eggs.

"I'm willing to try, if you are," I say to her as she cracks open an egg. The smell of bacon and the sound of eggs sizzling in the grease take me back to Sunday mornings in Lush's apartment at Chapel Hill. I am overcome with a pulse of sadness, so I take a deep drag on my cigarette to numb it away.

"Well, for me, that's a given. I promise I'll work through this sexual energy-jealousy thing with you," she says and cracks another egg into the grease.

"Lush, that's just part of us, part of our relationship. I mean you were my first love, the love of my life. Remember how delicious it was teaching each other about sex, exploring every part of each other's body. My God, how could you ever expect to get over that? I mean I still masturbate thinking about us having sex."

Her eyes are tearing up again and she says softly, "I know, I do too."

I get up and tenderly embrace her, "Lush, move up here with me for a while. You can have the guest suite once Dad and Brenda leave. Get away from Louisville, from David. File for divorce if you want. Get a job here. Help me find Billy's murderer. Help me take care of Clark. Help me take care of myself, and I'll help you take care of yourself. I don't know how it will turn out, but maybe, just maybe, we'll each find our own way."

She looks up at me and asks, "What about us?"

"You mean us as a couple?"

"Yes."

"Honest to God truth?"

"Yes, honest to God truth," she replies.

"You go first, Lush."

"Why is that fair?"

"Because of chivalry and because you are more level headed in these matters than I."

"Bullshit to both of those, but I'll go first anyway. You broke my heart at Chapel Hill. You were my knight in shining armor and everything I'd ever hoped for in a man. Having said that, I have come to recognize and accept over the years that my main reason for wanting to possess you so was because if I didn't or couldn't make it happen, I'd be a failure to my parents. This is the truth. I fucked us up by wanting to possess you so. Now, I have no desire to possess you, just to know you for yourself as my closest, most compassionate friend. Honest to God."

"Wow," I say. "Thanks for being so honest. Okay, here I go. To begin with, you were the hottest babe I'd ever laid eyes on. Not only were you hot, you were smart, very smart, like Mother. I just had to have you, but on my personal condition that I wouldn't fall for you completely. I had to maintain a comfortable distance because I knew in my heart that you would end up leaving me like everyone else I had ever loved, except Billy, and now he's gone," my voice cracks, so I take another deep drag and exhale slowly before I resume speaking. "So when I did fall for you completely, I just couldn't stand it. I would lie awake at night fantasizing how you would finally dump me or how a truck on campus would mow you down, and then I'd lose someone I loved again. I had to spread myself out for protection. So, I did that with other girls. You see, Lush, from my perspective, I'm really the one who fucked it up. But after we starting connecting again in graduate school and as we have remained so close over the years, I find myself thanking God that I have such a close connection with you. Honest to God, that's how I feel."Tears are running down my cheeks and down hers. We embrace once more and she says, "I accept your invitation to move up here. Oh my God, let me get these eggs out."

My cigarette has burned down to the filter. I pick up the pack, there are only two left. "My God, did Brenda and I smoke a whole pack yesterday? No wonder I feel like I'm getting a sinus infection," I mumble as I light another one, take a draw and add, "I can't keep this up for long. It'll tear my lungs up for yoga." A twinge of guilt flushes through my body as I think of how I'm polluting it and how anti-yoga this is. Another twinge lights up as I think about how I've used yoga to meet women for sex. For some inexplicable reason, the more I've done yoga over the years, the more spiritual I feel. My investigative proclivities led me to do extensive research on yoga, and I discovered Patanjali and the Eight-fold path—a system of principles and practices for moral and spiritual living dating back thousands of years and codified by Patanjali somewhere around the time of the birth of Christ. During the past year I have tried to incorporate some of these guidelines into my life: some such as honesty are easy for me, others like moderation in sex for pleasure are more of a challenge. I've even tried to meditate—the ultimate goal of yoga, to quiet the mind to allow for meditation. "Oh well, once I get through this week, I'll try to refocus on my yoga," I tell myself as I twirl the lit cigarette between my right thumb and index finger.

"God, Todge, I forgot to tell you. I tried Bikram in Louisville a couple of months ago. It damn near killed me. I barely made it through. I just don't see how you do it so much. I'll stick to my Pilates and morning walks in the park."

"Yes, it's torture at first, but after the first ten or so classes, you get used to the heat. You'd do fine if you'd just—"

"Just quit smoking, I know, nag, nag, nag."

"Come on, you know I do it out of love."

"Right, I know, but right now I'd say we have the classic case of the pot calling the kettle black, my dear."

"Bee--itch," I shout. "Maybe you should consider converting to one of those hard core diesel dykes."

We both laugh and she replies, "Don't think it hasn't crossed my mind, darling. I'd never have to worry about how I looked. I wouldn't have to waste time putting on my face. I could eat anything I wanted.

Think of the money I'd save on my wardrobe—just some blue jeans, a few flannel shirts and a leather jacket or two. And what's best, I could have my pussy eaten out anytime I wanted."

"Yes, but you'd have to return that favor."

"Uhn un, won't happen. There you have it. I can suck a dick all day long, but I just can't bring myself to go down on a muff. I'd be a failure as a lesbian."

"What if it's shaved?" I ask.

"Oh, for God's sakes, Todge! Do shaved twats turn you on?"

"Not really. I mean they don't turn me off either. By the way, I remember you even let me fuck you in the ass. Can you believe that's all the rage now?"

"Nothing about sex surprises me, Todge. I mean, considering that we tried almost everything we could imagine. I'll have to say, you're the only man I've ever fucked in the ass with a strap-on and choked at the same time while you jacked yourself off."

That sudden image sends a wave of guilt through my soul and my expression drops.

"What's the matter, darling? Too graphic for breakfast conversation?" she asks as she spreads mayonnaise on slices of toast.

"No, I just can't believe how openly we can talk about anything."

"I know what you mean. Whenever I'm around you, Todge, all the forbidden and hurtful topics seem to well up inside me and come gushing out. I wonder why that is?"

"It seems to me it's because we have been about as close as two people could possibly be."

"That feels right, at least, I think it does," she replies as she put slices of American cheese on the toast and then adds the fried eggs and bacon slices.

"God, that looks delicious," I say and take a drag on the cigarette.

She puts the sandwiches on white porcelain salad plates and places them on the bar. "Freshly squeezed OJ? I made it this morning for Brenda and Charles."

"Yes, please."

She pours two glasses of orange juice from a glass pitcher and joins me on the bar stools. We begin to eat.

"This is so good Lush. Thank you."

"My pleasure, darling."

"You can cram more into a unit of time than any person I know, Lush. I used to be so envious of that in school. What's your secret?"

"A proverb."

"What?"

"You know the one 'Never put off till tomorrow what you can do today.'"

"You're kidding," I reply while I'm taking a last drag off my cigarette.

"No I'm not. When I was a little girl, seven or eight years old, my great grandfather on my mother's side was still alive. He lived in one of those big old houses on Cherokee Road in the Highlands, which he had built in the early 1900's. By the time I was born, he was pretty much wheel chair bound. He had a sweet, old black woman named Cora who lived there and took care of him. When I'd visit him with Mom, he'd light up and seem so glad to see me. Every time he'd recite a proverb to me and then explained it to me in terms so that I could understand what it meant. That one stuck above all the others, and I've just sort of made it a life tenet—something I practice and try to live by each day. I know at times I might have been a bit anal about it, but it's always served me well, and it always makes me feel good about myself and gives me comfort—guardian angel type comfort, as if great grandpa Kendrick is watching over me, protecting me."

"That's really nice, Lush," I say and then I take a big bite of my sandwhich. "Oh my, this is so good, Lush," I state with my mouth full.

"Don't you sort of feel that way about your Fatgram?"

"I guess in a way I do," trying to simultaneously swallow and talk, "But Fatgram was more like a general commanding troops—a witty and loving general, but a general none-the-less. Mother was the only person I ever remember who crossed Fatgram. My God did they ever have some rows, and they didn't care who witnessed them. It used to embarrass me to death. Billy always thought they were funny. He always wanted to bet a quarter on who would win. Ala Mary always said they carried on like two cats thrown into a potato sack."

"Who would usually win?"

"I'd say all in all it was about a fifty-fifty split."

"They must have been a lot alike."

"In a lot of ways they were, but Mother had that dark side I never witnessed in Fatgram."

"Dark side?"

"Yeah, you know, spells of depression, turning in on herself and away from us. I'd try to comfort her, but it was no use. She'd say, Mother still loves you Philly, and Billy too. It's not your fault I'm so blue. There's nothing you can do, darling, but I just feel like crawling into a hole and dying. That would scare the shit out of me, Billy too, but he just wouldn't show it. And the funny thing is that's what she ended up doing in France. I remember overhearing Fatgram talking to someone on the phone a couple of months after Mother's suicide." Tears are falling from my eyes onto my sandwich as I look at the bright yellow yoke oozing onto the harsh white plate. My appetite is gone. I sniff and look up at Lush, "I overheard Fatgram say to someone. I heard her say. And she was crying too. Yes, that's the only time I ever remember hearing her really crying. Not even crying, more like moaning or wailing—like that tortured sound a cow makes who's lost her calf. The calf may be dead or lost or taken away, but it's all the same to the cow. She roams the fields searching for her baby and nothing else matters to her and she cries and wails and you say to yourself that's the sound of a broken heart. And Fatgram must have surely thought we were out somewhere because, unlike that mother cow, she'd never let us see her carry on like that. No. No. No. Not Fatgram. And then she said to someone. And I've thought and thought and thought who that someone could have been who could draw out such emotion from her. And to this day I don't know who it was, I just could never figure it out. She said to that person. She said, 'Goddammit. Goddammit, you listen to me and you listen to me good. A French housemaid found my baby girl curled up in a wool blanket in a fetal position under the bed in her room. My sweet, precious, baby girl died all alone.' And then I ran and I ran until I was out of breath and couldn't run anymore. I suppose I'm still running."

Lush just looks at me with pure compassion as her tears stream down her face, then she whispers to me as she stands up, "I'm so sorry, Philip. I'm so sorry." She grabs both of my hands and sort of shakes them and says through smiles and tears, "It's a privilege to be your friend and to witness these overwhelming feelings. Thank you so much. I'll be right back. I need a Xanax. You want one, sugar?"

"Luscious", I say as I wipe my eyes and nose on my sleeve, "You are my Xanax."

Clark is looking up at me, and I stare into his dark, unblinking eyes to see all the sadness in my soul reflected back at me, and my gut feeling is that if I could vaporize my body and pour my essence into his eyes, I would reunite with everything I crave, canceling out all the sadness. His tail wags once. I interpret that as a signal that he has read my thoughts, and, from my right hand, I reverently offer him the remainder of my fried egg sandwich. The gentle wizard dog instantaneously morphs into a lunging, furry, red reptilian as it snags the sandwich with sharp white fangs and swallows it in a gulp. I recoil in disbelief at Clark's speed and ferocity, and I'm left with an aftershock of the same disturbing feeling caused by my dream about Mother.

"Shit, maybe I do need a Xanax," I say out loud as I watch Clark sit back down, wagging his tale, panting. He whines and sits up on his hind legs with his front paws hanging in the air.

"I suppose you want what's left of Lush's sandwich too?"

This time I toss the sandwich in the air and Clark gracefully leaps up to catch it. It disappears in one bite.

"Little bear, no telling what you ate or how you got food on the streets," I say in a gentle tone. He smiles, jumps up to put his front legs on my lap, so I can pat his head. I oblige. I peer into his dark brown eyes and think about how much Billy loved this dog, and then I remember the obituary Lush has begun to write. It lies there on the black granite counter top, so I muster all the energy I can to reach over and grab it.

CHAPTER 11

Clark and I pass through the living room into the kitchen to observe Lush typing in the final additions I've left her for Billy's obituary. She turns toward me, smiles, and asks, "Philip, do you want to do a final read?"

"No, Lush, I know it is fine. You've done a great job. Billy would be happy with this. Go ahead and send the file."

"Okay, let's see," she says as her fingers skate over the keyboard, "Final spell check, save the file, attached to email to the *Times*, AP and *The Union Daily Times*. I thought you still might have relatives or family friends in Union. Is that okay?"

"That's fine. I suppose there are lots of people who were close to our family still living there."

She executes a few more keystrokes and says, "Voila, it's done." She shuts her laptop and grabs her cigarettes.

I unleash Clark who trots up to Lush. She pats his head, "Did you have a nice walk, boy?" He wags his tail as she rubs under his chin, stretching his neck up revealing a white strip of fur that emanates from his black muzzle and runs under his chin opening into a star pattern on his chest.

"Lush, there's something I need to show you. It's a painting. Billy's last painting."

"Of course, I'd love to see it," she says as she gets up from the stool and follows me into the studio.

I go over to the storage bins and pull out Blood Brothers and put it onto the center easel. She observes me, holding her right elbow in her left hand, while taking drags from a Treasurer. Her eyes widen when she sees the painting. She moves closer, studying the faces in the painting, takes another deep drag off her cigarette, fully exhales a stream of blue smoke and fastens her eyes to mine. "Extraordinary, I've never seen anything like it. It looks as if everything is moving in the painting. I recognize you and Billy, but who is the man?"

"Uncle Adrian."

"I see. Philip, this painting really bothers you, doesn't it?"

"Yes it does, Lush."

"Why."

"Because it tells the truth."

"Truth? About what?"

"Sex."

"Well, I see the penises."

"Elliott Fields told me Billy named this painting Blood Brothers. Blood Brothers is the name of the secret club Uncle Adrian formed with Billy and me when I was just a kid, ten or eleven." I sigh, looking down at the floor.

"Well, lots of kids have secret clubs, darling. Maybe not with adults though."

Still looking at the floor, I say, "Our club was a sex club—a club where Uncle Adrian had sex with us and made us have sex with each other."

"Dear God, Philip. I'm so sorry."

I take her cigarette from her hand, take a long drag on it, and walk over to a work desk, snuff it out in an ashtray, sit on a stool and put my head in my hands. Lush and Clark walk over. Lush puts her left hand on my back and gently pats me.

"Philip, you and Billy were innocent children, victims, it's not your fault," she softly says, her pats turning into rubs.

"I'm just a bit surprised you've never said anything about this before."

"I can't explain why. It's always been with me, inside me. Billy, too, but we never spoke about it. I guess I was ashamed, afraid, embarrassed, I just don't know why, Lush."

I'm crying again into my hands. My entire body is heaving, almost violently.

"Oh darling, honey," Lush says and puts her hands on my shoulders and lays her head against the back of my neck. Clark whimpers and jumps up, puts his front paws in my lap, nudging my belly.

"Lush, everything's so fucked up now. I miss Billy. I miss him so much," I say through heaves and sniffles.

"Darling," Lush says and holds me tighter.

"I know he went to sex clubs sometimes. Maybe he got mixed up with some weirdo? Maybe that's why he's dead?" I raise my face.

"We will find out, Philip."

"Goddamn you, Adrian. Goddamn you for screwing us up," I shout, looking up, shaking my right fist toward the blue sky visible through the skylights.

Clark lets out a loud, rolling, alarm bark and runs toward the kitchen. We look up to see Dad, Brenda and their three children standing at the entrance to the studio, all holding hands with anxious expressions on their faces. Dad quickly bends down to intercept Clark.

"Hey boy, it's just me. Come say hello to everybody." Clark melts into a puppy as Dad hugs him. The boys immediately kneel beside their father and start petting Clark who sniffs them both, then starts licking their faces. They burst out in laughter. The girl holds on tightly to her mother's hand, observing her brothers. The youngest boy's physical resemblance to Billy as a boy unsettles me for a moment as I force myself to withdraw from my emotional state.

My face feels as swollen as my nasal passages, and I know it is red from crying and sudden embarrassment. "Hello everyone. Welcome. I'm sorry you caught me like this. It's just, it's just. Well you know, losing Billy and all," I manage to say, sniffing, trying to smile, looking at Lush for guidance and wondering how much they witnessed.

Lush lifts her chin, smiles, hands me part of the wad of Kleenex she has grabbed, pulls me up off the stool and guides me over to the group, "Yes, yes, we both were just having a good cry."

Brenda puts her arms on the girl's shoulders, pulling her in closer, bends her head down and says, "Children, this is your brother Philip Hampton and his friend from Louisville, Mrs. Richardson." She smiles at Lush and me and says, "This is Peter, Andrew, and Emma." She directs her right hand towards each child as she makes the introductions, and I silently thank her for her graciousness as I quickly dab my eyes and nose with the Kleenex and stuff them into my right pocket.

Peter and Andrew both stand up and extend their hands. "Hello, Peter," I shake his hand. "Hello, Andrew, nice to meet you," I shake his hand. I take Emma's frail right hand in mine and pat it with my left hand. "Emma, very nice to meet you." Lush shakes their hands too and exclaims to Emma, "My, you are a beautiful girl."

"Thank you," she softly says, looking up at her mother.

"I like your dog, Mr. Hampton," Andrew says to me.

"Thank you, Andrew. Clark is actually Billy's dog. Our brother, Billy, I say, my eyes tearing again. I clear my throat loudly, "Please children, just call me Philip. I know I'm a grown up and all, but we are brothers and sisters, aren't we?"

Peter, who is obviously in the middle of a growth spurt, is taller than Brenda, and is lanky with big feet, curly blond hair of medium length, pulled back and combed behind his ears, and has a line of thick blond fuzz over his upper lip. He looks at me, then at his Dad, then back at me and says, "Well, I guess so."

"You look more like an uncle than a brother," Andrew blurts out with a defiant expression beneath his wavy auburn hair—green eyes peer at me and surprise me. He is a good half-foot shorter than Peter, but is stocky and appears to be strong.

I chuckle. "Well, I understand how you could make that association, Andrew."

"Let's all go to the kitchen, get something to drink, and sit outside; it's such a wonderful day," Lush interjects.

"Yes, what a good idea, Lush. Then perhaps we can serve some of the leftovers from last night for lunch?" Brenda adds, turning the kids toward the kitchen. Lush, Brenda and the kids move toward the kitchen, but Dad lingers. Brenda looks back over her left shoulder at Dad, and I see her eyes dart to Blood Brothers for an instant.

"I'm right behind y'all," I say, "I just need to get something in here."

Dad looks me in the eyes, hesitates and then asks, "Son, is there something I need to know about Adrian?"

"Uhm, no Dad. I mean, I don't think this is a good time to get into this with the kids here and everything," I say almost in a whisper.

"Philip, I know this is difficult for you. It's just as difficult for me, but I want to be here for you now— now and in the future." As he moves his right hand toward my shoulder, I wince, my pain reflecting on him as he quickly withdraws his hand to his mouth, bites his knuckles, grimacing.

"Dad, I'm sorry. This is all happening so fast. Just give me a little time."

"Right, right. I understand."

"Dad, I'm really glad you all are here. Thank you." I smile at him and fold my hands under my underarms.

He smiles back, "You always stood that way when you were unsure of something. I love you, Philip." He looks over at Blood Brothers, looks at me and then turns to go into the kitchen. I walk over, grab the painting and push it back into a storage slot.

"We're certainly fortunate to have this streak of warm weather so early in spring," Brenda smiles, the diamonds on her fingers and ear lobes capture the oblique spring sunlight accenting the turn of her head and the sweep of her hands with fiery sparkles. The effect is mesmerizing as I observe her, noticing the many varied hues of the strands of her luxurious blonde hair. She adds, "Emma, dear, aren't you getting warm in that sweater?"

"No, I'm fine, mom," she looks up at Brenda and makes a half-hearted attempt to cut a piece of cold salmon with her fork. Everything about her is delicate and frail. The round shape of her face and her dark, auburn hair are definitely Dad's, but her clear, blue eyes, pale skin and perfect nose are Brenda's.

"Emma's always cold, and she eats like a bird," Andrew says with a defiant tone. She cuts him a cold look and then sticks her tongue out at him. Lush and I laugh out loud.

"Drew, that's not a nice way to speak about your sister," Dad turns to his youngest son.

"But it's true, Dad. Right, Peter?" Andrew looks at his brother for a response.

"Well, I guess it's because she's so small," Peter replies. "Papa says she'll get her growth when the time's right," Peter looks at Andrew, then at me as he speaks."Is Papa your mother's dad?" I ask.

"Yes sir, he is," I notice Peter is sitting on his hands as he talks to me, looking back and forth from his Dad's eyes to mine.

"Peter, Drew, Emma, no 'yes sir' and 'no sirs' with me. I may look very old and grown up to you all, but I am your half-brother. Please, let's be casual with one another, if that's alright with your parents." Everyone looks at Brenda and Dad. Their eyes meet scanning one another for signals of approval or disapproval. Brenda is the first to visibly respond with a slight smile, and I notice the faint smile lines that form cute and sexy parentheses at the corners of her lips. As my attraction to her intensifies, I feel Lush's eyes reading me, so I quickly turn my gaze towards Dad.

"So, whaddaya say, Dad?"

"I say it's fine, son. Children, just try to call your brother by his name, Philip. Or you can even call him by his nickname, Philly."

The children giggle, and Emma says, "That rhymes with Billy. Is that why they call you Philly?" Her voice is soft and high pitched, but tender and charming.

"Dad? I think you know the answer to that better than I," I reply.

"Yes. Actually, it was Billy who coined it when he was about eighteen months old. He couldn't say Philip, but he could say Philly. I guess because it was so close to his own name, Billy. Since then, everyone just started calling Philip, Philly. Billy also coined 'Fatgram' for Eva's mother. She wanted to be called gram, so when she was around when Billy was a toddler we'd say that's gram and somehow he turned that into 'Fatgram'. Eva's mother was always a slim woman, never a bit overweight, but she cherished the nickname all the same. Anyway, you're right, Emma, the rhyme was easy for little Billy."

Emma beams at her father and then looks at me smiling. Andrew's dark green eyes narrow, and his lips poke out as if he is about to pout as he states emphatically to Dad, "Yes, but now he is dead. How did he die, Philip? Dad and Mom won't tell us."

Lush's eyes widen as she looks at Andrew and then at me. Dad shifts in his seat, and Brenda appears to be holding her breath.

"Aunt Pam says it was an accident, but Randy told me and Peter he took a drug overdose," Andrew defiantly states. Emma looks worried and leans toward her mother. Brenda pulls her close and strokes her hair.

"Who is Randy, Andrew?" I ask.

"Our cousin. He's fourteen and real smart," he replies.

"I see," I say looking once again at Dad and Brenda for assistance. I am not used to being around children, and I have no idea what sort of boundaries, particularly relating to sensitive topics, Dad and Brenda have set for theirs.

"Children," Dad's face is sad but serious, "Your mother and I have told you that your brother Billy was a famous fashion model and becoming a famous artist, just like his mother. He was well respected and had many, many friends. But it appears that someone, for some unknown reason, wanted to harm him and in fact did kill him with drugs."

The children appear stunned. Lush looks at me with her eyebrows raised.

"Maybe it was because he was a faggot," Andrew blurts out.

"Drew, what a terrible, utterly disgusting thing to say about your brother," Brenda exclaims with an angry tone. "You are never to use that term again in my presence. Do you understand me?"

"Yes mam," he reluctantly replies.

"Who told you that?" Brenda's lovely visage now appears stone-like, her jaws tense, her gaze sharp and penetrating, like a hawk, at the nadir of a mid-air dive, reaching for a mouse with its talons.

"Randy did. He pulled all this stuff up about Billy on the internet last night," he says defensively, glaring at Lush and me.

"Andrew, dear," Lush places her hands on the table as she speaks. "I knew Billy very well, and I know your brother Philip very well. They are devoted brothers who love each other very much and care for each other a great deal. They accept one another for who they are: all their strengths, weaknesses, good points, and bad points. It really is insignificant if someone is gay or not, if someone is black or white, if someone is poor or rich or famous or unknown, or fat or slim. Now we are all here as a family, and even though I'm not a blood relative, I feel as if I'm a part of this family and we all are here to celebrate your brother's life, the time he spent enriching our lives, the time we spent loving him and will always to continue to love him. And we have a huge celebration planned for this Friday night and we just can't get it all done by ourselves. So we all thought, and your parents agreed, that if you all came here, you could help us with all the arrangements we have to make before Friday. For instance, we have to get in touch with over five hundred people to invite them to the memorial ceremony. We plan to email announcements, but we'd also like to personally telephone all these people. Your Dad and I have prepared little phone scripts for you to use and the three of you and your Dad are going to call all these people in the next twenty-four hours." Lush is animated, but smooth. The mood has changed from tense to excitement and the children are clearly pleased to be involved.

"Wow, we can do that," Peter states, sitting erect in his chair, "Do we get paid, Dad?"

Lush and I laugh while Brenda shakes her head back and forth, sighs, and replies, "No Peter, we're not going to pay you to help with the party for your brother, but if you all get finished in a timely fashion, we are going to take you to a splendid musical tomorrow and the Museum of Natural History. Alright?"

"I wanna see Lion King, Mamma," Emma says, clutching her sweater, pulling it tight around her chest.

"Well, we were going to surprise you all, but that is what we plan to see," Brenda replies, smiling.

"Yes, yes, yes," says Andrew as he jumps up out of his chair while Emma lets go of her sweater and claps her hands in delight.

I watch, with amazement, this scene unfold. Dad, Brenda, and the children are animated as Lush passes out the telephone scripts, the assigned numbers, and a schedule of events for the next five days. Brenda brings out the banana, apple, and chocolate pies from last night and begins cutting slices for everyone. A wave of profound peace and happiness rolls through me as I watch everyone interacting, laughing, and planning. Then I think how much Billy would have engaged these kids, how easily he would have turned around Andrew's "faggot" comment, and I feel deep in my soul for an instant that it should be Billy here planning my wake. It certainly would be an easier task because I doubt my death would even draw one hundred people. I look back and forth across the table at Andrew and Peter and my heart feels heavy as surges of remorse, sadness, regret, longing, guilt, despair, trust, betrayal, loyalty, and love fan themselves across my psyche like the multitude of colors my brother splashed across his canvas in creating Blood Brothers. Peter becomes me and Andrew becomes Billy. I recognize that I am jealous of my half brothers for two reasons: because Dad created a new Philip and a new Billy, Peter with my curly blond hair and blue eyes, and Andrew with Billy's thick auburn hair and green eyes and because they have been spared, to my knowledge, the wickedness of an Uncle Adrian. An image of Billy and me taking turns choking each other with a pink and black striped silk tie as we masturbate in our bedroom at Fatgram's pierces my internal vision. This strange procedure which produces explosive orgasms and feelings of utter euphoria was taught to us by Uncle Adrian during our Blood Brothers initiation ceremony in New York City, complete with the gift of matching pink and black striped silk ties, the spring break I was twelve and Mother let Billy and me spend it in New York with Uncle Adrian. My groin area and armpits were becoming covered by dark blonde hair by then. Billy was just starting to get any hairs at all. It seemed to me that Uncle Adrian gave him much more attention, especially during the Blood Brothers ceremonies, and I recall feeling rejected and jealous. I finally learned during my early twenties that owning feelings of jealousy is the key to mitigating them. This works in this instance as the jealousy transforms into anger

against Adrian and whatever bastard killed Billy. Clark has sensed my unrest and has laid his head in my lap, and I am conscious that I am stroking his head with my right hand and looking at the long black whiskers on his muzzle when I hear a faint voice of a girl child.

"Philip, Philip." I look up across the table and focus on Emma, trying to form a pleasant look on my face.

"Yes, Emma."

"Will you go to the musical and museum with us tomorrow?"

"Yes Emma, I'd love to. Thank you for inviting me," I say as I stand up looking at the uneaten piece of banana crème pie at my place. I feel the love of little Emma reaching out to me, but I desperately need to be alone.

"Will you all please excuse me for a while? I have thirty-one new messages on my mobile. I really need to retrieve them and return the calls. I'm sure they concern Billy. Please, make yourselves at home, children. Lush and your parents will show you where your bedrooms are and where everything else is. I'll be in Billy's room if you need anything. Maybe after we all do some of the work Lush has laid out for us, you guys can help me take C-L-A-R-K to the dog park," I add, as I turn to leave.

"Who's Lush?" Andrew asks.

"That's me. That's my nickname, kids. Just like your brother's is Philly and Andrew's is Drew," she quickly replies.

"Where's that from, Mrs. Richardson?" I hear Peter ask as I walk inside, Clark trailing me, and I laugh to myself as I try to guess how Lush will explain this one.

I go into Billy's room, into his closet and start rummaging through drawers until I find two unopened packs of Marlboro reds, another lighter, and an ashtray. I glance up to the shelf where Billy's cell phone was before the police took it and silently say, "Thank you, God, for Lush's keen intellect, swiftness to act, and plain old street smarts." I take a pack of cigarettes, the lighter, and ashtray and walk back into the bedroom over to the chaise lounge where Clark is stretched out.

"Over boy," I say as I sit down, pushing him over so I can stretch out beside him. I open the cigarettes, light one, and put the package down on a small tray table beside the chaise lounge where I set the ashtray. The tray table is a hunt scene that Mother painted. It depicts Mother on her bay gelding, Picasso, and Fatgram on her old mare, Whinny, jumping a stone fence in pursuit of a pack of foxhounds. I clearly hear Whinny's long, shrill neigh that sounds like a whine to Billy and me, so we always refer to her as Whiney, which makes Fatgram mad as hell. The setting is Tryon, North Carolina, in the rolling foothills adjacent to the Blue Ridge Mountains where Fatgram and Mother belonged to The Tryon Riding and Hunt Club and cherished fox hunting in the fall and early winter. We also attended the Blockhouse Steeplechase in Tryon every April. Dad would take us to observe the hunts on crisp fall mornings. Excitement filled the air at the chaotic pre-hunt breakfasts. Long tables, covered with white table clothes, held an array of sausages, bacon, scrambled and poached eggs, grits, French toast, waffles, sweet breads, muffins, tarts, Danish, and fruit. Adults huddled in groups, punctuated by the scarlet hunt coats of the men, sipped steaming coffee and hot apple cider with rum or eggnog. Some preferred Bloody Marys, though. Children gorged on sweets and ran about like nervous chickens amid the cacophony of bays and barks of the anxious caged hounds as anticipation advanced and the time neared for the blowing of the bugle and the call for "riders up." Mother and Fatgram always looked so grand in their black hunt coats and polished black boots. A few times, Dad took Fatgram's old jeep and we followed the hunt as hill toppers along roads and trails. Fatgram was an accomplished equestrienne, maintained lovely stables at her Buffalo, South Carolina farm, and passed her skill and love of horses along to Mother. Many of Mother's early commissions were for horse people in Kentucky and Florida. Those commissions gave her the confidence to pursue her art full time. Billy and I were taught to ride and had our own ponies and eventually horses, but we never progressed after Mother's death because Fatgram didn't encourage it. I think it must have been too painful for her because it was

something she and Mother always did together. We did go on a few trail rides the first couple of years we lived with her, but she finally said both she and Whinny needed to be put out to pasture to retire and that Picasso needed a skilled rider to challenge him, so she sold him and all her other horses except for Whinny and a couple of companion ponies who enjoyed their final years out to pasture.

My cigarette has grown long; I flick it in the ashtray and fish out the new cell phone from my pocket. Dad was able to finesse a fully charged battery from the phone store, so I punch in my voice mail number and begin to listen to messages. This is a daunting task, and I do not enjoy it, though I am surprised by how sincere and heartfelt most of the callers are, most are friends of mine, but several are celebrity friends of Billy's from fashion, film, and art. Strangely enough, only a couple of people request a return call, most just need to put their shock and grief into audible words. I have taken a legal pad and a red pen and made a list of everyone who called to cross check it against the Address Book list to make sure we do not exclude anyone close to Billy from the memorial ceremony. I then see that I have four text messages. The first two were sent last night from Atlanta friends who sent their condolences, the fourth is from the phone company this morning when this phone was activated, but the third is from a number that looks vaguely familiar and was sent at four this morning. It has a photo attachment. I click on it. It opens. The photo is dim and blurry, but I clearly make out who it is. It is Benny, the waiter. He has a slight smile on his face, his chest is bare, he is wearing white gloves, and he is holding a rope. I feel nauseated. I run to my backpack and fish out the letter from Fields. The number on my phone with the photograph of Benny is Elliott Fields's mobile number. I stumble into the bathroom holding the phone and Elliott's letter, fall on my knees in front of the toilet and begin to vomit violently until there is nothing left but dry heaves and a few tears. The smell is sickening, but Clark tries to stick his head in the toilet.

"No, boy, that's nasty, get back." He obeys. I flush the toilet, stand up, go to the sink, turn on the faucet, cup my right hand under, suck water into my mouth, rinse, and spit it out. I rinse a couple of times and look at my face in the mirror and ask out loud in a trembling voice, "Dear God, why is this all happening to me?"

I can't focus my thoughts, which flash across my mind in no order. Is it too late to save Elliott? Should I dial his cell number? Should I notify Detectives Johnson and Bell this minute? Is Benny the murderer or someone's pawn? Why didn't I tell the police everything I knew? Was it a mistake to try to bond with Dad, Brenda, and their kids during all this? Am I a deviant for being sexually attracted to Brenda? Was Billy involved in some weird sexual cult? Did he pull Elliott into it? Does Timmy know something about all this? Why have I lost the two people I have loved most in this world? Will I have panic attacks like I did after Mother's death? Can Lush and I really coexist without getting sexual again? Should I sell my house in Atlanta? Will I stay here permanently? I have Clark to look after now. How will I be able to travel weeks at a time for a story? I wonder if the police interviewed that Nurse Ostro; she must have been there when someone slipped in and injected the GHB into Billy's IV. How sick but clever was Adrian that he went to such extremes to seduce Billy and me and kept it all hidden from Mother, Dad, Fatgram, and Ala Mary? Did Adrian have any other victims? He must have. I need to find that out. Lush will help me. I need to find Lush, and I crave an icy ginger ale now, a remedy Fatgram used for unsettled or upset stomachs. I head down the hall to the kitchen. Lush is sitting on a bar stool looking at her computer. CNN is on the television and a young male reporter is reporting on Billy's death.

"Hi, Todge," she smiles at me, then says quickly in a soft voice, "Maybe you'd prefer that I don't call you that anymore?"

"Thanks Lush, but I associate that name a lot more with you than I do Uncle Adrian. It's okay."

"Good. Listen, the press has already picked up that Billy's death is now a suspected murder," she says and points toward the television.

"Sources within the New York Police Department have confirmed that the death of top fashion model and artist, Billy Hampton, is being investigated as a homicide. Hampton was discovered unconscious at the popular disco…."

"Lush."

"Shhh," she puts her right index finger to her mouth, pursing her lips and knotting her forehead then points to the television.

I hold up the picture of Benny with the rope on my phone. She quickly glances at it, wrinkles her forehead again, looks back at the television, then looks back at my phone with her mouth agape.

"Oh my God, Todge, it's Benny. What's he holding, a rope? And he has on white gloves."

"Shhh," I do the index finger quieting gesture to Lush and whisper, "Where is everyone?"

"They are all in the guest suite making phone calls for the memorial service," she whispers back.

"Good. Let's keep our voices down."

"Fine," she whispers.

"This picture was sent to me at four this morning from Elliott Fields mobile phone."

"He's in Bermuda, right?" she asks as she takes the clicker and turns down the sound on the television as pictures of Billy appear.

"Yes, he's not due back in town until Thursday."

"Crap. That little S.O.B. How did he get to Bermuda so quickly?" she scoops a big handful of her thick hair behind her right ear and peers at my phone closer.

"Lush, I think he went there to kill Elliott Fields."

"What do you mean? Why?"

"Dunno. But I suspect Elliott must have known the same thing Billy knew—information someone is willing to commit murder to suppress."

"Of course," she replies and I can see her eyes moving rapidly back and forth, and I know her brain is working in overdrive.

"Lush, I'm guessing that someone, probably a maid, found Elliott in his hotel room this morning, naked and hanged, made to look like an accidental death from a self induced episode of autoerotic asphyxiation," I state quietly and plainly.

"Please tell me what you are talking about, Todge?" She rubs her forehead, and I can see she's looking for her cigarettes.

"Okay, but let me get a ginger ale, and let's go out on the terrace to talk."

"Alright. Where's Clark?" she asks.

"He was following me. I bet he went to see where everyone else is."

"You fix your ginger ale. I'd love one too, with a shot of bourbon. I'll tiptoe into the studio and see if he's in there," she says and moves through the kitchen toward the studio, then freezes in front of the television.

"Quick Todge, turn the sound back up."

I grab the remote and increase the volume while a picture of a smiling Elliott Fields appears on the screen and the voice of the young male reporter is saying, "Fields was found hanged in his hotel room in Bermuda this morning. The Bermuda Police Service says it is too early in their investigation to determine if the death was a result of suicide, homicide, or an accident. Fields was a rising star in the international fashion scene and was with ex-model and artist Billy Hampton this past Saturday night when Hampton was found unconscious in a bathroom stall at the popular gay discotheque, Splash, in New York. As we just revealed, the New York City Police Department has issued a statement that Hampton's death is now being investigated as a homicide. We now go live to Bermuda when CNN reporter Sylvia Pound is reporting from the Fairmont Hotel in Southampton, Bermuda."

"Thank you, Rick." An attractive blonde woman with a British accent appears on the screen in front of a beautiful pink building surrounded by palm trees. A steady breeze is blowing the palm fronds and the reporter's hair. "It's another lovely day in paradise here with the exception of the somber mood set upon these luxurious surroundings by the discovery of Elliott Field's body this morning at about eleven, Atlantic Time Zone, by a hotel staff member. The Bermuda Police Service has restricted access to several areas in the hotel and is revealing little about their investigation to the media. Rick, as you know, news travels rapidly through hotel staff, and I've talk to several of the staff this morning who tell me essentially the same story. A young woman from the cleaning staff entered the room this morning after knocking and receiving no answer. She has indicated the 'Do Not Disturb' sign was not displayed. She started her cleaning routine when she went to open the draperies to discover the largely nude body of Mr. Fields on the floor in front of the window. She described a white rope that had been fashioned into a noose around Mr. Field's neck. The rope was long enough that it passed up over the cornice board and down to the floor. Rick, I heard mentioned by several staff members that Mr. Fields was wearing a pair of black patent leather ladies stiletto shoes as well as a pair of black fish net hose."

"Sylvia, given the bizarre nature of the dress, has there been any mention that this could have been a botched sexual act?" the male reporter asks.

"Yes, Rick. I feel certain the Police are considering this scenario, as well as suicide."

"Has there been any talk of a possible connection of Elliott Field's death with that of Billy Hampton?"

"Again Rick, the Bermuda Police will only say that its investigation is progressing rapidly, but I'm sure they must be communicating with the New York Police Department as well."

I've heard enough, so I turn the television off. Lush fires a questioning glance at me, then says, "You were one hundred percent right, Todge. Benny must've done it. How the hell did he get to Bermuda so fast? I mean he was out of here at what, ten pm?"

"I've been wondering that too," I say rubbing my jaw.

"I'll check on-line, but I bet there were no commercial flights that late. Had to be private jet," she states, then adds, "Still want to go outside?"

"Yeah, I'll make the drinks, you check on Clark."

"Be right back," she smiles and tiptoes out again.

I go to the pantry and find two cans of Canada Dry, then go to the wet bar for glasses, ice, and bourbon. I fill the glasses with ice from the icemaker and then pour Woodford Reserve in the bottom quarter of each glass. "What the hell. I don't care if I burn a hole in my guts," I say to myself as I pour ginger ale to fill each glass. I take a stainless bar spoon and stir each glass. I look into a cabinet and grab two linen cocktail napkins with a palmetto tree and a crescent moon embroidered with blue thread on each napkin. 'No Goddamn paper napkins for little brother,' I whisper as I wrap the bottom of the glasses with the napkins and turn to go onto the terrace. Lush is tiptoeing towards me.

"Clark is asleep in his bed in the study. Little guy must be worn out from all the commotion. I sense that he's grieving for Billy too," she whispers.

"Aren't we all?" I snap back. She shoots me a quizzical look.

"Why the sarcasm, Todge?"

I sigh deeply, looking down at the floor, biting the inside of my lips. I look up at her and motion for her to follow me. I take the drinks, she grabs her lighter and cigarettes and we head for the terrace. I become cognizant of the sound of the streets as a steady breeze hits my face. A lone small brown bird chirps from one of the budding serviceberry trees in a raised planter. I walk over to the outside wall of the terrace which is red brick capped with limestone blocks. The height of the wall is at my chest level. An ornate wrought iron fence is mounted on the limestone cap and extends to a height of over seven feet. Billy designed the wall so that you could see out, but you couldn't fall off and down twenty stories if you had a few too many martinis. I take a sip of the drink. It goes down easily. Lush takes a

sip, sets her drink down, and I cup my hands around her lighter as she lights a cigarette. She inhales, then offers it to me.

"No thanks. Lush, I need to come clean with you. I know more about this than I've let on."

"What are you saying, Philip? You know why Billy and Elliott were murdered?"

"No, it's not that. I mean. I mean I know more about Billy's sexual life—the deviancy of it all."

She shrugs her shoulders, tosses her hair back over her shoulders and says, "Darling, we are all deviant in our own ways when it comes to sex. Do you really think Billy's and Elliott's sexual practices had something to do with their deaths?"

"I don't know for sure, but I think that photograph of Benny is a big clue, and I think, Elliott, in desperation, must have sent it to me as a last resort. I mean, Benny doesn't appear that he minds or even knows that he's being photographed."

She wears Prada sunglasses with dark lenses, but I make out that she is squinting her eyes at me. Her necklace, alternating beads of white pearls and golden grains of rice, hangs down toward her lovely chest, framed by an off white silk blouse through which I can barely discern a lacey bra of the same color holding her beautiful breasts. I think about her perfectly formed nipples, and how I used to lick them and suck them. Her gold and stainless Rolex flashes on her left wrist as do two gold and diamond tennis bracelets on her right wrist. An intricately woven belt fashioned from a variety of green glass beads and fastened with a gold buckle sets off her slim waist and the hunter green linen slacks she wears. David is a damned fool, I think to myself.

"What are you trying to say, Todge?"

"What I'm trying to say is that because of Uncle Adrian, Billy and I learned all sorts of deviant sexual practices, one of which is autoerotic asphyxiation. He showed us how to do that right here in New York. God, I must have been only twelve," I shake my head looking at her for help.

"Philip, that's horrible. That guy was sick, a pervert, a pedophile. You know that, honey. You can't take responsibility for what he did to you and Billy."

"I know, Lush. It's just that, just that, I think I was able to get out of all those practices and lead a pretty normal heterosexual life. I don't think Billy ever did."

"Do you think that confused Billy? That maybe he wasn't gay, just mixed up from Adrian's sexual abuse?"

"No, I think Billy was born gay. I feel certain, but I think he enjoyed a lot of those sexual practices and abused them, especially whenever he had emotional setbacks."

We take sips from our drinks and look out over the city. Lush smokes her cigarette, plays with her hair, and adjusts her sunglasses.

"Philip, what does all this sexual stuff have to do with Billy's murder?"

"I'm not exactly sure, Lush, but I believe there's a connection. I've got something to show you. Let's go into the studio."

We take our drinks and walk back into the kitchen and into the studio. Clark senses our presence, yawns, and stretches his body before he stands up. Wagging his tail, he walks over to greet us. I pat his head and motion for Lush to follow me. We walk through the study toward the foyer leading into the guest suite. On the right side of the foyer is a large guest bathroom. I enter. Lush and Clark follow. I switch on the light and shut the door. On the far wall of the bathroom, opposite the door, is a series of shelves from the floor to the ceiling which contain folded bath towels, hand towels, wash cloths, assorted fancy, hard milled soaps, and containers of fancy bath gels, all interspersed with framed black and white photos of Billy with other celebrities, all autographed by the celebrities. I walk over and give a hard push to the molding on the right side of the shelving, and the entire structure of shelving revolves out toward me. Lush gasps. Clark, tail at attention, moves in sniffing. Behind the shelving is a small, dark area leading to a door. We set our drinks on the bathroom counter, and I turn on a light switch in the area and pull open

the hidden door revealing a large sort of closet with mirrors on all four sides and the ceiling. In the middle of this small chamber two sturdy square wooden posts are bolted to the floor. A large crossbeam connects the top of the posts. Wooden peg handles are arranged on each post, facing inward toward each other, from the floor to the crossbeam and are evenly spaced about a foot and a half apart. A pink and black striped silk noose and several stainless steel hooks hang from the crossbeam. A pile of chains and what appears to be a leather body harness are in a pile at the bottom of the scaffold beside several folded towels and a plastic bottle of lube.

"Oh my God," Lush exclaims.

Clark moves over to where there is some sort of residue on one of the lower mirrors and begins to lick it.

"Clark, don't do that. Come back here," I whisper as loud as I can. He looks up at me and moves toward me.

"I'm afraid to ask what that stain is," Lush directs to me.

"I'm thinking it's dried semen," I reply, then add, "Lush, this is Billy's specially designed room for choking yourself while you masturbate. It has extra thick walls and is totally sound-proof."

"Well, I'm amazed," she replies, then quickly adds, "Is it that good, Todge?"

"Is what that good?"

"Oh, gimme a break. Is jerking off while practically choking yourself to death that big of a turn on?"

"It's pretty strong, if the timing is just right."

"So, that explains why you wanted me to choke you when you were fucking me," she says as if she were talking about better ways to fold laundry.

"That's true, now you know."

"So piece together this puzzle for me, Philip."

"Okay, see when Billy finished building out this condo and showed me this secret closet, I was so pissed, I didn't talk to him for weeks. I told him he had to give this practice up because one day he'd go too far and kill himself. He'd just laugh and say, 'but what a good fucking way to die.'"

"How often did he do this?"

"I'm not sure, Lush," I hesitate and I feel my eyes darting, "But, but I do know he had to be hospitalized twice for it, and each time it was after major emotional events in his life. The first time he was still in college in Syracuse. He had fallen in love with his roommate from St. Andrew's School. They were inseparable during the last couple of years of boarding school. His name was Victor Magiolo. Anyway, Billy went to Syracuse to study fine art while Vic went to Vanderbilt for pre-med. They visited each other several times during their first year at college and shared an apartment in Provincetown that summer where they both worked as waiters in a restaurant. Billy really wanted to transfer to Vanderbilt after his first year, but I encouraged him to stay at Syracuse and pursue his talent. During their sophomore year Vic started dating a girl, but didn't tell Billy. One weekend when Billy was in Nashville visiting Vic, they both got blasted, but separated, at a bar. Billy finally wandered back to Vic's apartment in the wee hours of the morning to discover Vic and his girlfriend having sex. Billy was devastated and immediately left and checked into the Marriott Courtyard on West End. I was a senior at Chapel Hill; you and I weren't on speaking terms again yet. So I get a call from a hospital in Nashville that they found Billy in his hotel room, naked and unconscious on the floor with his leather belt around his neck. Apparently, after he made a noose with the belt through the buckle he had tied it to a hinge on the armoire. Fortunately for him, his weight had snapped the hinge releasing the noose before he killed himself."

"Dear God, Todge. Why didn't you ever tell me this?" Her expression reveals worry, and I look into her eyes, then at the sunglasses she has pushed up on her head.

"Well, by the time we reconnected, I didn't want to do anything to fuck it up again, especially with stories about my brother's screwed up sexual habits. I think his practice of autoerotic asphyxiation was

a cry for help and an attempt to regain closeness to someone or something. I know that may be hard to believe, but after Mother died and Dad left us with Fatgram, Billy and I were all each other had and those sick sexual rituals Uncle Adrian drilled into us just brought us closer to one another. So, we practiced them almost religiously until I got old enough to realize that they were not normal. Most people didn't behave that way and we had to stop it. I never was able at the age of fifteen to convince a thirteen-year-old Billy why this was the right thing to do, but as I withdrew from him in these sexual practices, it just made him withdraw into himself. I mean, I know he was hurting over it, but I just couldn't explain it at the time. I just had to do it, and I made Fatgram give me my own bedroom. It still breaks my heart when I think of the look he gave me when I told him I wanted my own bedroom. Even that didn't work, so I finally convinced Fatgram to let me go to boarding school. That's how I ended up at the Asheville School and Billy at St. Andrew's. I was the one who did that."

Lush reaches over and grabs my hands, "Oh, honey, that is so sad. I don't know what to say."

"Thanks, but there's nothing to say. It is as it is. The second time he almost died from this practice was six years ago in St. Barts, about a year before 9/11. Remember, I told you and everyone else that he was injured in a wind surfing accident."

"Yes, I remember. You both invited me on that trip, but I had a couple of big closings that week."

"I'm sorry I lied to you, but I didn't want any of this to get out."

"Don't apologize, Todge, I understand."

"He was at the top of his modeling career and doing a shoot down there. He invited me to spend a week at a posh villa he had rented. I had been working really hard on a story about al-Qaeda terrorist cells in the U.S. and U.K., and I was spent. The first night I arrived we went out to dinner at this restaurant call La-Ti that turns into a disco-nightclub at midnight. We both drank a lot and Billy got some coke form the bartender. We got back to the villa at about two in the morning. Billy wants to have a nightcap, so we drink some really good scotch and smoke some killer weed. You know me; I'm a lightweight when it comes to booze and drugs. Well, Billy keeps trying to seduce me. I resist, but finally we end up in this incredible Jacuzzi pool in his room, drinking Cristal and smoking more pot. We have sex. I mean, not only do we have sex, but he gets me to fuck him. I do and actually come inside him as he jerks off. I still can't believe I did that. Anyway, the next morning I wake up in his bed and he's gone windsurfing. I feel so Goddamned bad—ashamed, mad and guilty—that I leave without saying anything to him. Didn't even leave him a note. I fly from St. Barts to St. Marten. I miss the flight to Atlanta, so I get on a plane to New York and go straight to the Plaza and check in. I'm sitting at the Oak Bar that night when I get a call from the police in St. Barts telling me that Billy has tried to commit suicide by hanging himself. I fly back down there the next day to be with him in the hospital. Lush, he's the perfect gentleman and tells me it's not my fault, but his for getting carried away with his ravenous sexual appetite. All I can do is hold his hand and weep as I look at the purple bruises on his neck. But after that, he stopped modeling altogether and poured himself into his art. You see, I thought, I guessed, I hoped and I prayed that he'd grown stronger and didn't have to fall back on all this, but when I saw the photo of Benny and the rope, and we know from Luka that he had sex with Benny, well it's easy to put two and two together to know why Benny has that rope in his hands."

"Philip, we need to call those detectives right now," Lush states emphatically.

"Yes, I know."

"Wait, Philip, you didn't show this room to them, did you?"

"No."

"They could get you for withholding evidence and for interfering with an investigation. What were you thinking, Philip?"

"I was thinking I didn't want those pushy detectives, especially that hard ass Detective Bell, to know all the sordid details about my brother and for some dumb, blonde reporter to relish in the news as she spreads it all over the world," I reply in an irritated tone.

"What do we do now?" she asks in a voice that lets me know she is completely on my side.

"Let's go down to the police station, after we stop at the phone store, so I can get another phone. I'm sure the police will want this one. I don't want to tell Dad, Brenda, and the kids about this. It's just too much."

"I agree," she replies, "But, what about this room?"

"I'm gonna tell the detectives because there may be clues in here, but beg that they come to examine it while everyone is gone to the show and museum tomorrow."

"Good idea, I hope they will agree. Philip, do you think you should get an attorney's help?"

"Probably, I meant to call Billy's attorney, but haven't yet. I just do not feel like going through everything with somebody else. I'm willing to take my chances with the police at this point."

"We'll get through it okay," she replies, smiles, and turns to go back into the bathroom.

I turn and shut the door, turn off the light, and carefully push the wall of shelving back into place. We take our drinks, leave the bathroom and move quietly through the studio back into the kitchen. Lush takes my cell phone and downloads everything to her computer and makes a few phone calls while I go knock on the door to the suite to let everyone know that Lush and I have a few errands to run. Dad, Brenda and the kids have called a hundred and seventy eight people already and are ready for a break. They agree to take Clark to the dog park while Lush and I are gone.

CHAPTER 12

"Good afternoon Mr. Hampton, Miss Richardson. I'm not surprised to see you here," Detective Johnson states, holding a clip board in his left hand and a ballpoint pen in his right hand. "I guess you've heard the news about Elliott Fields?"

"Yes, Detective, we have," I reply. "I'd like to discuss that and a few other things with you."

"Fine, follow me. We'll go into one of our small conference rooms. Detective Bell should be here in a few minutes." We follow Detective Johnson down a hallway to an internal bank of elevators. He pushes the up button and the door opens immediately.

"Must be my lucky day," he smiles and motions with his right hand for us to go in. He pushes number 5 and states, "As you can imagine, Elliott Field's death has broadened our investigation a great deal. I was just getting ready to give you a call when I was told you were in the lobby." He looks at me directly and holds my gaze for a moment before looking at Lush.

"Is there anything you've discovered that you can share with us, Detective?" Lush calmly asks.

"Perhaps, but I need to hear what you all have to say first."

"I see," Lush replies and looks over at me. The elevator door opens and Detective Johnson holds it with his left hand, "After you." We step out and he says, "Follow me, please. Can I get you some coffee? Water?"

"No thanks," I reply.

"Coffee, black, would be great," Lush replies.

We arrive at a door marked 2C-1 and Detective Johnson opens it. We go inside. There is a small conference table with four chairs around it, two on one side and two on the other.

"Please have a seat. I'll be right back with the coffee." He walks out and shuts the door.

"Christ, this looks like a police interrogation room to me, Lush," I say, feeling anxiety crawling up my spine.

"I think you're right," she replies.

"I suppose we're being watched and taped this very moment?" I ask. "Right again, Todge."

"Oh well, I've got nothing to hide. I may as well strip naked and walk down the Goddamn streets of New York City reciting every dark secret I harbor." Lush breaks out in laughter.

"You poor dear, you're already portraying yourself as the martyr."

"I can always count on you to put me in my place," I snap back.

"Darling, it's a messy job, but someone's got to do it." She smiles at me.

"Yeah, you and Florence," I smile and reply.

"How is Florence?" Lush asks.

"Fine. Same as ever, always trying to fix me up with one of her girlfriends anytime I'm here."

"Agent and match maker? Not a bad combination when you think about it. Have you talked to her since Billy's death?"

"No, she's in London this week, but she left me a nice message yesterday. Which reminds me, I need to call her to tell her about the memorial service. I hope she can make it."

The door opens abruptly. Detectives Johnson and Bell enter the room and shut the door. Detective Johnson sets a Styrofoam cup of coffee down in front of Lush.

"Thank you, Detective Johnson," Lush smiles at him and then looks at Detective Bell.

"So, we all meet again so soon, Mr. Hampton, Mrs. Richardson," she glares at us as she pulls out the chair directly across from me and sits down. She is dressed in what Lush would describe as a "smart outfit"—hip hugging black skirt with tight fitting white jacket with large, pointed lapels, and what I think must be a Hermes silk scarf wrapped around her neck and stuffed into the jacket. Detective Johnson sits down beside her.

"Mr. Hampton, what is it you want to talk to us about?" Detective Johnson gently slaps the surface of the table with both hands and looks at me. I pull out my cell phone, locate the message from Elliott Fields, click open the photograph of Benny, and turn it around toward their faces.

"This photograph was sent to me at about four this morning from Elliott Field's phone," I state as I look at their faces, absent of any emotional response.

"Interesting. So why has it taken until three-thirty pm for you to bring this to our attention?" Detective Bell's eyes narrow as she focuses on me.

"Well, I dropped my phone at the hospital Sunday and broke it. My father got me this new one this morning. I only had a chance to retrieve messages after lunch today, so I've only known this for a couple of hours. By that time, we'd already learned about Elliott's death from CNN."

"I see," Detective Johnson states. "I'll need to take this phone for evidence."

"Fine, we figured that, so we stopped by the phone store on the way here, and I purchased another one. The one you're keeping has already been deactivated."

"Okay. Is there anything else you want to tell us or need to show us?" Detective Johnson asks.

"Well, yes there is," I say and look at Lush who gives me a slight smile. "You see, this has been very hard for me. My brother is so important to me, I mean, after our Mother died and my Dad practically abandoned us, I always felt I had to look out after Billy because he was younger than I. I promised my Mother and Dad I would always do that." I look at the detectives' faces and realize this is not the kind of thing they want or need to hear. "So, anyway, because Billy is so famous, I just didn't want the press to get wind of any peculiar sexual proclivities he might have."

"Such as autoerotic asphyxiation?" Detective Bell asks in a harsh, flat, sarcastic tone.

"Detectives," Lush can't hold back any longer, "Philip and his brother, Billy, were childhood victims of a shrewd and polished pedophile, who happened to be one of their Mother's closest confidants as well as her agent."

"So you're accusing Adrian McWhorter of being a pedophile?" Detective Bell snaps at Lush.

"No, I'm not accusing him, Detective Bell, I'm telling you a factual story," Lush replies.

"Perhaps it's best, Mrs. Richardson, if we hear this story from one of the victims himself?" She raises her eyebrows at Lush, then looks at me.

"So Detective Bell, is there anything about my life and my family you don't know?"

"I'm hoping you might enlighten me along those lines, Mr. Hampton."

"By all means, call me Philip since you are so familiar with me."

"Very well, Philip, we're not here to listen to a sob story about victims of pedophilia, we're here to solve a murder. And now, two murders, the second one of which may very well have been prevented if you had put aside your elitist pride and told us the entire truth about your brother yesterday and last night." She leans over toward me and bangs her fist on the table.

"Darling, why don't you save your intimidation tactics and diaphanous good guy, bad guy routine for the unwashed mob with which I'm sure you're more comfortable dealing?" Lush slams back at her.

Detective Bell's eyes sparkle as she asks, "Mrs. Richardson, is there really any reason for your presence here, other than as a crutch for Philip?"

"I believe my observations could be extremely useful to your investigation."

"Well, that's so kind of you to offer, but let us be the judge of that," Detective Bell delivers with all the sarcasm she can muster.

Detective Johnson sits up erect in his chair, clears his throat loudly, and asks, "Why don't we get back to Mr. Hampton's story?"

My right leg is crossed over my left leg and my left leg has gone completely to sleep. I uncross my legs, lean forward in my chair and begin to speak, "To make a long story short, Adrian, or, as Billy and I called him, Uncle Adrian, managed to make us believe as kids from the time Billy was nine until I turned thirteen that sex with grown men was a 'right of passage' for all boys. He formed a secret club with us called Blood Brothers and we experimented with him in many different sexual situations. One of the most bizarre was choking yourself while you achieved orgasm. This is where Billy learned that, and I know he practiced it throughout his life. I tried my best to discourage him, but, whenever something didn't go right for him, he'd fall back on this."

"So, are you saying he practiced this with Elliott Fields and Benny Boonmee?" Detective Johnson asks.

"I don't know for sure, but after receiving that photograph from Elliott, I suspect that's the case. I think Benny must have somehow gotten to Bermuda quickly after he left Billy's last night, probably by private jet, met up with Elliott, perhaps seduced him, and then killed him by strangulation."

"And what do you think his motive would have been?" Detective Bell asks.

"Whatever was in that brown envelope he took from Billy's safe."

"And, today, Mr. Hampton, do you have any ideas as to what might be in that envelope?" Detective Bell points her hand at me as she questions me.

"No, not really. Something to do with sex? I mean, I dunno. Billy knew a lot of very rich and powerful people. Maybe he was doing something weird sexually with someone who didn't want that information exposed. Maybe that was what was in that envelope. I mean, don't get me wrong, Billy would never blackmail anyone. He's not that type, and he didn't need or crave money, he had enough to last a dozen lifetimes. Benny must be just someone's pawn or a hired killer."

Detective Johnson rubs his moustache with his right hand, leans back in his chair and asks, "What else do you have to tell us, Mr. Hampton?"

"Well, just one thing. I couldn't bring myself to show you one room in the condo last night. You see, Billy has a hidden room, covered in mirrors, that contains a sort of wooden gallows where he could practice autoerotic asphyxiation in somewhat of a controlled setting. I think you need to send your investigation team back to cover that room. It probably holds some secrets."

Detective Bell slams both hands down on the table, stands up, and says, "Can you tell me any reason why we shouldn't book you right now for withholding evidence from and interfering in a murder investigation?"

"Well, I certainly can, Detective Bell," Lush smugly replies, "You won't have a snowball's chance in hell of penetrating Billy's social circles, even with your NYPD badge. You're going to need our help, starting with Billy's memorial Friday night at which there will be a few hundred of his closest contacts. You arrest Philip and none of that will happen."

The two detectives look at one another; Detective Johnson smiles, revealing a full set of straight, white teeth, and, to my complete surprise, Detective Bell leans her head back and laughs.

"Pardon our moment of humor," Detective Johnson, still smiling, turns toward me, "Yes, Detective Bell and I would like your help a great deal. We fully expected that you had not revealed the, the, let's just call it, the full range of your brother's sexual activities. Now that you have, and now that Detective Bell has completed a detailed examination of your past through resources at our disposal, we have no reason to believe that you are involved in these murders in any way."

"Well that's a relief," I reply and look at Lush.

"Yes, you're squeaky clean, Mr. Hampton," Detective Bell says to me and then begins to recite: "You have no debt, a credit rating as high as I've ever seen, solid earnings, strong assets, no IRS problems, great work references, great personal references, reasonable personal expenditures, especially for a multi-millionaire, and not even a traffic ticket. Yes, you will inherit many more millions from your brother, but it's obvious money is not what motivates you."

"You've done your homework," I reply. She looks at me without replying.

"We have completed extensive questioning with the hospital staff at St. Vincent's who were on duty during the shift when Billy was murdered. Staff there, particularly a Miss Ostro, identified a photograph of Benny Boonmee we took from the security disks in your brother's building as a computer technician who was in the IC unit working on components in the system near the time your brother started convulsions again. Naturally, the hospital has no record of any request from the IC unit for computer assistance, nor was any routine maintenance scheduled."

"So the little bastard did kill Billy," I angrily state. "God, what I wouldn't give for the chance to be alone with him for just thirty seconds."

"That might be your last thirty seconds, Mr. Hampton," Detective Johnson says in a serious tone, "This 'little bastard' is a highly trained killer. Not just the shoot them and run type, but one who has great skill with computers, electronics, and drugs."

"What do you know about him?" Lush asks Detective Johnson.

"Unfortunately, very little beyond what he looks like. It seems he is fastidiously clean. People at the catering company say he was never without latex or white serving gloves, which means we can't get any fingerprints, not even from his locker. All of his information is phony: New York driver's license and social security number; he probably has several phony passports. He must live somewhere in the city, but no one is familiar with him at the address he listed in Morningside Heights."

Detective Bell adjusts the scarf around her neck and says, "Luka has had the most contact with him of anyone we know so far. But, he basically just saw him at work. He's sticking to his story that he only had sex with him as part of a three way with your brother that one time."

"Did Luka say whether Benny had any distinguishing features, Detective Bell?" Lush asks.

"Well, of course, we asked him that—you know a birth mark, noticeable mole, or tattoo. Luka says he can't recall anything." Her tone is becoming warm and friendly now.

"I see," Lush replies.

"Why do you ask?" Detective Bell looks at Lush.

"Well, there were no commercial flights into Bermuda last night that Benny could have possibly made. I called the executive jet service at L.F. Wade International Airport this afternoon and managed to find out that only two private plans landed last night—one at 11:30 pm and one at 4:30 am. So, neither of those are possibilities. Perhaps he could have arrived via a seaplane of some sort, but I suspect we may have a pair of twin assassins here."

"What? Siamese twin assassins?" I ask incredulously. Everyone immediately laughs.

"Geez," I say, "I mean Thai twin assassins."

Detective Johnson leans back in his chair and looks over at Detective Bell, and states, "Not a bad deduction, Mrs. Richardson. Now I understand the reason you wanted to know about any distinguishing features. We can have an expert compare this photograph with those we have from the security cameras from the building last night. We'll also check with the Bermuda Police Department. They may have security photographs showing Benny, or as you speculate, his twin in the hotel. They may also have access to additional airport information that could corroborate or disprove your twin theory."

"Mr. Hampton," Detective Bell addresses me, "I believe there is sufficient cause to believe that you may be in danger as well. Whoever is orchestrating these murders may have reason to believe that you know something too. It is widely known that you maintained a close relationship with your brother. It's reasonable to suspect that he might confide in you. Also, Elliott Fields' apartment was completely ransacked when we checked it today. Someone is still looking for something—something they want badly, badly enough to have killed two people so far."

It's difficult for me to adjust to a caring attitude from her, but I reply, "I see your point but wouldn't they have already tried to kill me?"

"Perhaps they have, and you just don't know it," she returns, "I mean, you've been surrounded by friends and family and that formidable dog."

"Good ole Clark. He'd never let anyone hurt me. I just wish he'd been with Billy at the disco. He was certainly right about Benny," I say with a weary sigh.

"Dog or no dog, I want to keep a pair of plain clothes detectives outside your building, 24/7 and one inside your condo until at least after the memorial service," Detective Johnson says in a tone that gives me little choice.

"Todge, I think it's a good idea, especially with the children there," Lush says.

"What children?" Detective Johnson asks.

"My dad's three kids have arrived from St. Louis for the memorial service. They are all staying with us at Billy's."

"I see," he replies, "All the more reason for security. If you could, try to limit your outings the next few days. Go in a group when you have to go out, and we'll have a team flank you. Just give the detective stationed inside fifteen or so minutes' notice. Agreed?"

"Okay, that's fine."

"Are you both headed back home now?" he asks.

"Yes," I reply.

"Fine. Wait here just a few minutes and we'll have the first watch escort you back. I'll also send over an investigative unit immediately to go over the hidden room," Detective Johnson states as he stands up. Then he says, "Thank you both for your time, and you, Mrs. Richardson, for your investigative input."

Lush beams at him and replies, "You're quite welcome. I've always liked a good puzzle."

"Detective Johnson?" I ask.

"Yes, Mr. Hampton."

"I have a gut feeling that somehow all this is a result of what Billy and I went through with Uncle Adrian. I mean all the weird sexual stuff. I know he's dead, but I need to know if Adrian did this sort of thing to any other children. Could you possibly check into that?"

"We'll see what we can find. The answer is most likely yes, though. Pedophiles move from one victim to the next as the current victim matures and is no longer a sexual attraction. I'll let you know what we find."

"Mrs. Richardson, Mr. Hampton thank you for your time. We'll do everything we can to find the killer or killers and bring them to justice," Detective Bell states as she stands up and straightens her skirt. Lush and I stand and shake hands with them and they turn and leave. We sit back down, look at each other, and wait.

It takes longer than the detectives anticipated to get together the first shift of officers to guard us, so they let Lush and me take a cab home so we can have time to explain to Dad, Brenda, and the kids what is happening. The streets are crowded so it takes me a few minutes to get a cab to stop. We get into the back seat and the cab proceeds at a slow pace.

"Lush, that Nurse Ostro the detectives mentioned was very nice to me. She was the one who called to tell me of Billy's death. She also told me she studies art and knows Mother's and Billy's work. Do you think she'd think I'm strange if I called and invited her to the memorial service?"

"Not at all. I think that would be a nice gesture and perhaps we could find out more about Benny from her?"

"I thought you might be thinking that. How did you come up with the twin theory so quickly?"

"Well, after I talked to the airport and saw on-line there were no commercial flights he could have taken to get there in time to be in that photo Elliott sent to you, it just made sense."

"Yeah, it really does. I feel really bad about Elliott. Dear God, what a way to die. He must have let Benny in his room. He must have been participating voluntarily until he realized he was in danger. Why did he send the photo to me? I only talked to him one time. How would he have known I would know who Benny is?"

"I've been running the same questions over and over in my mind, too. If Benny, or his twin, realized Elliott took that photo and determined that he sent it to your mobile phone, I'd say you are in danger."

"Yeah, but how would Benny, or his twin, know what my mobile is?"

"Well, for one thing, your mobile has a 404 area code. They could easily see that's from Atlanta. I'm sure they know that's where you live."

"You're right. Especially with the internet, it's so easy to find out practically anything about anyone."

"True, but we can use that to our advantage, too, Todge." She smiles and raises her right eyebrow.

"You really are determined to solve this, aren't you?"

"Not me, we. And, yes, we really will solve this. How could it be much more difficult than flushing out Senator Beckman?"

"I suppose you've got a point, but that took us almost a year."

"So, I've got at least a year to spare. What about you?"

"I suppose I won't be able to concentrate on anything else until I know exactly who did this to my brother and why."

"Go ahead and phone that nurse."

I call information and get connected to the neurological intensive care unit at St. Vincent's. I ask to speak to Miss Ostro and am informed she works third shift and will not arrive until ten pm. I leave a message for her to call me on my mobile number and hang up.

"I was thinking, Philip, perhaps you should invite Nurse Ostro over before the party. It would be a lot easier to talk to her without all those hundreds of people around," Lush says as she looks at her face in the mirror of a small compact and applies a coat of fresh lipstick.

"That's a good idea. I'll see if she can come over sometime tomorrow afternoon," I reply, observing her blotting her lips on a tissue.

"What about the show and the museum? You promised Emma," she folds the tissue, puts it in her purse and looks at me.

"Oh dear. I forgot. I'll just have to explain to her that with everything that's going on, I've just got too much to do. I'll make it up to her somehow."

"She's a darling child. She certainly holds her own with her brothers. When she stuck her tongue out at Andrew, I thought I'd die."

I laugh at her remark and add, "I think that spunk must come from Brenda's side of the family."

"I'm certain of that," she replies, shuts her compact and puts it back into her purse. "Todge, who does Billy use to clean his place?"

"A woman named Lois. She does several units in his building. I believe she comes to Billy's on Monday, Wednesday, and Friday. Though, she didn't come by or call yesterday as far as I know."

"Well, I'll find her number and call her when we get back. I think we're going to need someone everyday until your family leaves."

"Yeah, you're right. Brenda will kill herself trying to keep everything just perfect."

"I know what you mean. I think she's the glue in that family, and what a handsome family it is."

"Yes, Dad said as much to me when they first arrived."

"Your father works in her family's furniture business, doesn't he?"

"Yes, they have a chain of furniture stores throughout the Midwest. It's a fairly large operation, maybe twenty or thirty stores. Brenda and her brother pretty much run it. Dad has told me that they get along extremely well, which I'm sure contributes to the company's success. Dad knows the furniture market inside and out, so I think he brought a new dimension to the company when he became their buyer. That's been about fifteen years now."

"He doesn't mind having his wife as his boss?"

"I think you can see from Brenda, she's not the type to hold anything over anyone. I don't know exactly what their business arrangement is, but I know they do very well. It seems obvious to me how much she loves Dad."

"Oh, I agree. She certainly does love Charles. He's a lucky man to have such a woman."

"Yes, he is."

"Charles must have qualities, besides his good looks, which attract strong women. Look at how strong willed your Mother was. And, I, for one, wouldn't cherish going head to head with Brenda."

I laugh and say, "Well, until Mother committed suicide, I think Dad had high self esteem; and he's always been level-headed and fair."

"Those things would certainly attract strong women."

"But with Mother's death he went into a tailspin. Well, you know the rest of that story."

"Yes. Do you think your parents were faithful to one another?"

"I always have believed that Dad was even though he spent so much time on the road and would have had ample opportunities. I guess I could just ask him, though."

"Hmmn, but what about your Mother?"

I sigh, asking myself how many more memories are going to be dragged from places where I've so painstakingly kept them buried all these years.

"Are you okay, Todge? I didn't mean to pry."

"No, it's all right. Well, we were talking about strong women. But, I think every strong woman has her weaker side, too."

"You're right about that, Todge."

"Brenda told me yesterday that her first husband abused her, actually physically abused her to the point of breaking her left arm."

"Dear God, that surprises me. I never would have guessed she'd been married before."

"Well, it was right out of college and only lasted two years."

"I see. Do you think it's my weaker side that puts up with all of David's emotional abuse?"

"Geez, Lush. That's hard to say. I guess I don't really think it's your weaker side. I just think you have built a life with David that must satisfy your needs enough so that you haven't had to make a change."

I catch her gaze and see that she is considering what I've just said. After a while she replies, "I think you've pretty much hit the nail on the head. My relationship with David was stable enough to get me through to this point in my life, but it's just no longer enough. I've been on the precipice of change for such a long time, though. It's kind of like I have a fault line running through my soul, and Billy's murder and being here with you in New York has caused a magnitude nine quake. I will never go back to David. I know that now. I need so much more in my life. Honestly, Todge, I don't even know if it's in Louisville. I'm going to take it a day at a time, and as we uncover clues to Billy's murder, I think I may uncover clues to where I'm going in my life."

I take her hands in mind and gently squeeze them and say, "Lush, that's wonderful. I think you are doing the right thing, and I'm glad to be a part of it." I put her hands back in her lap and say, "Now back to your question about Mother's fidelity. No, I think she had more than one affair, several most likely. This is a story I've never told anyone. One summer day when I was ten, Billy and I were at Fatgram's while she and Ala Mary were busy in the kitchen putting up jars of pickled peaches. God, I loved those spicy pickled peaches. Anyway, Mother was working on a commission and Dad was on the road, so Fatgram was keeping us for the day since she was using Ala Mary in the kitchen. Billy and I were outside building a fort out of dirt and sticks that we were going to have attacked by aliens. We needed our walkie-talkies to expedite this, but we had left them at home, so we decided to hop on our bikes and ride back home to get them. After we got the walkie-talkies and were getting ready to bike back to Fatgram's house, I was overcome with a strong urge to spy on Mother. She would have skinned us alive had she ever caught us spying on her, so we were very careful. Bonnie Belle, Mother's beagle, was sound asleep on the walkway to Mother's studio. We tiptoed back into the kitchen and got a big Milkbone. When we went back to the cottage I whispered for Bonnie and immediately gave her the Milkbone. This kept her from barking. Mother had vertical blinds installed in all the windows in the cottage so she could precisely control the amount of light coming in. They were all closed, so we couldn't see anything. When she redid the cottage she had the ceiling taken out so that when you walked inside you were exposed to beams and rafters all of which were painted white. She also had small Palladian type windows installed up high, just under the roof, at either end of the cottage to let in sunlight. These two windows did not have blinds on them. One of our favorite trees for climbing, a big old, live oak, grew to the west of Mother's cottage. We found out that if we climbed high enough, we could look directly in the western Palladian window and watch Mother paint. Mother used a lot of nude models and that's how we saw our first fully naked woman. I thought that day that I might get to see another naked lady. Instead, when we reached the vantage point and peered in we saw a naked man kissing Mother, who was also naked. We watched them for a while and realized that the man was Darrell Coots, a guy who lived in the remnants of the mill village our great grandfather built, a guy most people referred to as white trash. That's how I figured out the facts of life, watching Darrell fuck Mother. I think Billy was just a little too young to get it at the time."

Lush has a worried expression on her face, "Do you remember how you felt, Todge?"

"Yeah, I do. Scared at first, then mad, and then horny. That's the first time I recall feeling horny. I also think that set up some of the distrust I have with women and relationships."

"That's certainly not a surprise, darling. I know how much you loved your mother. You must have been able to forgive her for cheating on your dad."

"Now, as an adult, I have. Back then it was harder, more confusing. I mean, I was so devoted to her. But, she was, after all, Mother—it was all part of the tumultuous emotional cycles she experienced and we endured."

"Endured you have, and rather well, I'd say," she pats my hands.

"Lush?"

"Yes, Philip."

"I know we've got a lot to do before Friday, but I think we should shut ourselves in the studio, maybe tomorrow when everyone is gone to the show and go through Billy's new paintings. I've only seen Blood Brothers, but I think since they all deal with sex, we may find some clues or answers in some of the others."

"Absolutely," she smiles at me.

"Damn, I need to call Julianna Morgan. She's left three messages for me. We probably should have her over to view the collection with us, after all, she'll know more about it than anyone."

I dial Julianna's number. A young woman answers.

"Good afternoon. Morgan Fine Art Galleries, may I help you."

"Yes, this is Philip Hampton for Julianna," I say.

"Yes, just a moment, sir." I pull the phone away from my ear a bit, so Lush can hear, too. She leans closer in towards me.

"Oh Philip, I'm shattered. I just can't believe this has happened to Billy," Julianna says, on the verge of tears.

"It's unthinkable, Julianna, but it's now our reality."

She is crying now. "Yes, but why him? He was working on his greatest works ever, Philip. He was so thrilled, so motivated. I've never seen him in a better place."

"At least he was in a good place when he was taken from us," I reply. "Julianna, have the police talked to you yet?"

"Yes, twice, Philip. I'm so glad you called. I need to talk to you. They are really pushing me into revealing very personal things about Billy. Things he told me in confidence. I just don't know what to do. I can tell they know I'm withholding things. I certainly don't want to impede their investigation. Whoever did this will pay, but I can't betray Billy either."

"Julianna, can you come by tomorrow afternoon, say around two o'clock to help us go through Billy's latest works? I think they may offer some clues. You remember my friend Lush?"

"Oh yes."

"She's here to help with everything for the memorial. But Lush and I also intend to conduct our own personal investigation into Billy's and now Elliott's murders."

"Yes, the detectives, a Detective Johnson and a Detective Bell, came back again this morning. They told me about Elliott Fields. Philip, they told me they think Billy's sexual practices may have been what led to his murder."

"That appears to be the case, Julianna."

"Philip, Billy was very serious about keeping his latest collection a secret until he was ready to show it. He's been developing it and working on it for over two years now. It encompasses fifty four paintings, the last of which he finished the day he was murdered."

"I saw the painting Blood Brothers," I add.

"Philip, the name of this showing was going to be Rapture," she states, then adds, "It's about pushing the limits of sexuality, and I can assure you it does just that."

"Christ. Julianna, I need to know everything. Please come tomorrow."

"I'll be there, Philip. Can I help out in any other way?"

"Thanks, I think we're managing okay. See you tomorrow, Julianna."

"Two pm tomorrow. Bye, Philip."

I flip my phone shut. Lush looks at me and asks, "Philip, do you trust Julianna?"

"Yes I do. I have no reason not to. She's been with Billy every step of the way with his art. She practically discovered him, gave him his first showing, guided him artistically, and helped establish him as the important artist he is. I will say she is a shrewd business woman."

I look at Lush and can tell my answer is not good enough. She sighs and adds, "I know all that, Philip. I mean do you trust her deep down inside, in your gut?"

I lean back, rub my forehead with my right hand, sigh, and look back at Lush and say, "I really do. But I think she'll tell us more, more than she's told the police."

"Fine," she replies. "It's important to establish whom we trust and whom we don't. I'm afraid this all could get rather messy in a hurry."

"I agree, Lush."

We both sit back, watching the city through the windows as the car moves on towards Billy's.

CHAPTER 13

We arrive back at Billy's building and enter the lobby. Timmy is at the front desk.

"You're here early today, Timmy," I remark.

"Doing double shift. Need the money," he stutters.

"Timmy, have the police talked to you yet?"

"Yes, last night. And, I got a call they're coming by here again tonight. Guess it has to do with Mr. Fields."

"Probably. Timmy, they're really going to be focusing on Billy's sex life. I provided your name to them as someone I know had sex with Billy."

"Okay," he replies, stuttering, with an uncertain look on his face.

"Just tell them the truth," I add.

"Okay."

"Timmy, did you ever do any weird or kinky sexual stuff with Billy?"

He looks surprised but asks, "Like what?"

"Like strangulation while achieving orgasm," I offer.

"Yes."

"Really? So you've been in his hidden room?" I ask.

"Yes, a couple of times."

"With other people or alone with Billy?" Lush asks.

"Just Billy."

"What did you do in there?" she quickly asks.

A bright pink color runs up Timmy's neck and covers his face and he looks down at the desk.

"Timmy, I know this is embarrassing, and I'm sorry to put you on the spot like this, but I have to know. It might help find Billy's killer. Please?" I plead.

"Well, well, he told me how good," he takes a deep breath, "Good it feels to cum while you choke yourself. We got stoned. He took me in the room. We started having sex. I was afraid, but I trusted Billy. He put the noose around my neck and told me to hold on to the handles and lower myself untill I felt choking. He stood behind me and jacked me off." He finishes, takes a deep breath, and I see a tear run out of his left eye. A man and a woman, arm in arm, enter from the street. Billy quickly wipes his face, stands up straight and smiles.

"Good afternoon, Timmy," the woman smiles as she speaks. She wears Versace sunglasses with large dark lenses and thick black frames and does not remove them. She is elegantly dressed in a camel colored

pants suit and beige silk blouse. Her purse and shoes are matching brown ostrich skin and her jewelry and watch look expensive. The man is tall with thinning gray hair and a dour expression on his face. He does not speak or take notice of anyone in the lobby. They both have dark tans.

"Good afternoon Mrs. Dillman, Mr. Dillman," he struggles to get out.

"Horrible news about Billy Hampton," she says and looks in my direction.

"Yes mam, it is," Timmy replies.

The elevator door opens as they walk toward it, get in and the door closes. We resume our conversation.

"Is it really that pleasurable to go through all that and risk choking yourself to death?" Lush asks.

"It felt really really good. Billy calls it his rapture room. I only did it twice. The second time I passed out so I don't remember much. That was it for me though, too scared of it."

Lush and I look at each other, and I turn to Timmy and ask, "Timmy, any other types of strange sex with Billy?"

"No not really. Some three ways, sometimes more than three."

"How many?" Lush asks.

"As many as a dozen or so."

"Good God!" I exclaim.

"Oh, that didn't happen much," he replies.

"Timmy, do you know if he arranged for sex on-line, you know chat rooms and such?" Lush asks.

"Maybe a little bit, but you know how good looking he was. He didn't have to look very far for sex."

"Anything else?" I ask.

He pauses, lifts his head, then looks at me and says, "He told me the best sex he ever had was with you."

Now my face and ears are burning, and I know I'm completely red. I look at Lush, back at Timmy and say, "Timmy, let me know if you come up with anything at all that might help us find the murderer. Also, please tell the police everything you know."

"Yes sir, I will."

"Thanks," I take Lush's right arm and we walk to the elevator. On the way up she holds onto my arm.

"Are you okay, Philip?"

"I'm okay."

"You know," she looks at me as if she is frightened, "I'm afraid we're in for a lot of shocking news about Billy before we get to the bottom of this."

"How could it be any more shocking than what we know already?"

"I think we may find that out when we review his collection tomorrow."

The elevator stops, the door opens and Emma, Peter, and Andrew are standing in the foyer with Clark sitting in front of them waiting for us with smiles on their faces.

"Philip, Philip, we've finished with all the calls," Emma exclaims.

"Yep, we just finished about five minutes ago," Andrew adds with his hands in his pockets.

"How wonderful," I reply, "I knew I could count on my little brothers and sister to get things done."

"That's great children, I'm impressed," Lush adds.

"Well, Mom made it go faster, by getting four of her office ladies to help out from St. Louis," Peter admits shyly.

"Perfect," I say, "Now you guys will have plenty of time to sightsee here in New York."

Emma claps her hands and jumps up and down. Clark barks in excitement and jumps up on Lush.

"I see you, baby. How's my little boy dog doing?" She leans over and kisses his nose and face.

"Dad took Clark to the dog park," Peter says, "We stayed and helped mom with the calls."

"Yeah, mom made him go because he kept crying when he got someone on the phone," Andrew says.

"Oh, poor Charles," Lush says, looking at me.

"Oh, poor Charles is fine now," Dad states and walks into the foyer. "Clark and I had a grand time together. He and I agreed to celebrate Billy's life, not mourn it. Isn't that right Clark, ole boy?" Clark, panting, turns his head toward Dad, gets up and walks over to him. Dad bends over and pets him.

"Let's go in and get something to drink," Lush says, "It's cocktail hour anyway, isn't it?"

"Close enough," I add. "Kids, get your mother. Lush and I have some news for you."

They all take off running down the limestone hallway, the sound of their shoes hitting the stone echoes through the hallway reminding me of my dream night before last. Clark runs after them barking.

"Children, children! Slow down. Don't run in here, you may break something," Dad shouts as he runs after them.

Lush and I laugh.

"How 'bout a smoke and a drink, Lush?"

"Sounds good to me, darling."

"Perfect Manhattan, up with a twist?" I ask Lush as we walk to the bar.

"Divine. I'll get a lemon from the kitchen," she says and heads to the kitchen.

I go to the wet bar, get two martini glasses, put ice and water in them, get out a shaker and a bottle of Old Forester, Lush's preferred bourbon. I look in a drawer for a knife for the lemon and my eye catches a slender, Tiffany-blue case. I pull it out as Lush arrives with the lemon.

"Oh, Tiffany, what's in there?" she asks.

"It's a sterling silver straw with a little monkey climbing up it. I gave it to Billy for Christmas five or six years ago."

I pull the straw out; it is pristine, not tarnished at all.

"How adorable," Lush says.

"Yeah, Billy always loved drinking icy Pepsi with a straw. Never Coke. Not sweet enough for him. So, what do you get a man that has everything? How 'bout a sterling silver straw? I think he liked this better than any other gift I ever gave him."

I put the monkey straw back in its case and back in the drawer. I hand Lush a paring knife and a small cutting board. "You cut the twists, and I'll mix the drinks."

"Okay, but let's put one twist in the shaker. It's better that way," she says as she begins to cut the lemon.

"Okay," I say.

She works quickly with the knife so that before I've poured any bourbon or vermouth, she's cut four long strips of lemon. "Here you go," she says. "I'll be right back. I want to see if I can connect with the housekeeper, Lois. How do I call the front desk?"

"Just dial star 10 and you'll ring Timmy," I reply as I scoop ice into the shaker. "Hurry back. I'll have these ready in a jiff."

"Be right back," she says and she heads down the hall toward her bedroom.

I hear someone in the kitchen, so I put the bourbon bottle down and walk into the kitchen to see Brenda pouring three glasses of milk. She looks up and smiles, "Well, hello, Philip. I'm just fixing a snack for the kids. They are going to watch a movie in our suite while we have cocktails. I hope that's all right with you. They'll charge Billy's cable five dollars and ninety-nine cents for the movie, but I'll pay for it."

"Don't be ridiculous, Brenda. They may watch as many movies as they please," I smile, observing her demeanor. She has pulled back her hair into a ponytail and is wearing a short sleeve, pink polo shirt with khakis and burgundy penny loafers. She looks lovely, even younger than I thought earlier. I just want to walk over, take her into my arms, pull her into me and kiss her. We stand there looking into each other's eyes until she must sense what I'm thinking. I wonder if she wants the same thing from me. She turns around abruptly and reaches for a white bag setting on the counter.

"There was an adorable bakery beside the phone store we went into this morning. While Charles dealt with the phone people, I went next door, picked out a beautiful coffee cake and kuchen for breakfast in the morning and bought these exquisitely decorated sugar cookies for the children." She holds up a cookie that is decorated as a tulip; it is beautiful and looks as if it would taste wonderful. "I'm going to fix up a tray for the kids, get the movie started, and Charles and I will be back in to join you and Lush for a drink," she says as she arranges cookies on a plate. "That's great," I say. I can barely resist the temptation to walk over to her, hold her, smell her, and let her run her hands down my chest. I think how incredibly sexy she is, and I want to see her naked more than anything else at this moment. She must know I'm undressing her with my eyes, but I keep on, until I sense someone watching me. I look up to see Dad standing in the doorway from the studio.

"The troops are getting restless, dear. They want to start the movie."

Brenda turns to her husband, smiling, "Go ahead, honey. Let them begin. I'll be right in with the milk and cookies."

"I'll let them know." He glances at me before he turns to go. I feel like a total lecher, and I say to myself, "Goddamn, Hampton. Put a lid on your pecker. You're as fucked up as Billy ever had time to be. Wanting to screw your own Dad's wife."

"Brenda, I guess Dad will want a glass of white wine. What will you have?"

"Hmm, vodka martini, up, slightly dirty. Thanks. We'll be right back." She has the cookies and glasses of milk on a tray and is heading out to the studio. I can't take my eyes off her slim waist and sexy ass as she walks.

I head back to the wet bar, ice another martini glass, and begin mixing the drinks. I sigh and begin to think about my sex drive—a force at times so strong, I'm compelled to do things I'd never do in a normal situation. I know Billy had this too, and I know he acted out on his sex drive much more than I. But, isn't this just a normal male thing? I mean I know guys who are totally driven in the hunt for pussy—would do almost anything to get laid. But did they begin as young as Billy and I? We've got Uncle Adrian to thank for that. No, it's not normal, by any stretch of the imagination, for a grown man to have sex with boys, particularly prepubescent boys. I've known this always, I think, but certainly by the time I became a teenager and knew that having sex with Billy wasn't right either. Why did it take Billy's death to make this crystal clear to me? Why did Billy and I keep this hidden? Was it because we lost Mother at such a young age? My God, what would she have done if she had discovered what her beloved Adrian was doing to us? Goddamn, I hate to even ask this, but did she, in fact, know and let it happen? No, I can't go there. That's not Mother, she had a strong sense of right and wrong. Or did she? I can still see Mother lying back on the sofa in her studio, opening her legs for Darrell's cock, which I remember as looking almost like a fist protruding from a black, hairy bush. I can see the rapture on her face as he fucked her hard, his hairy ass pumping into her. I can see her grabbing his ass, pulling him into her; I can hear her rhythmic moaning, then the crescendo of two voices in rapture. I remember my own cock getting hard, uncomfortable in my Wranglers. I look down and see my cock is starting to push against my khakis. Shit. Does this mean I would fuck my own Mother? Freud says we all have feelings of the Oedipus complex hidden deep within us. Fuck Freud, Fuck Mother, Fuck Uncle Adrian. I just want my brother back. That's why I'm feeling this way; that's why I have no limits at this time— feelings cycling to extremes.

"You look as if you're about to cut the world's largest diamond, or something." I hear Lush's voice, and realize I'm holding the sweet vermouth, aiming the top of the bottle into the shaker, my hand unsteady.

"I think I'm losing it, Lush. I feel out of control, completely." I set the bottle down.

"Allow me, honey. What you need is a stiff drink." She takes the bottle from me and pours some vermouth in the shaker, looks up and says, "Have you put the dry in yet?"

"No, just bourbon and sweet."

"What's Brenda having?"

"Vodka martini, slightly dirty."

She pours in the dry vermouth, drops in a twist, puts the top on the shaker and hands it to me. "You shake this while I mix Brenda's."

I grab the cold shaker with both hands, hold it over my right shoulder and shake it as hard as I can, watching Lush prepare Brenda's drink, until Lush turns around to stop me.

"Damn, Todge, that ought to be good and icy by now."

I set the shaker down. She hands me the other one; I take it and begin to shake again. She empties the ice water out of all the martini glasses and pours the two Manhattans. She takes a twist, twists it hard with her fingers, rubs the skin of the lemon on the rim of the glass, then drops it in. I look at her lovely hands, long slim fingers, nails done in a French manicure, and a big marquise-cut diamond on her left ring finger. She repeats the procedure with the twist for the other Manhattan and looks at me. I stop shaking the shaker and set it down. She pours Brenda's drink and gigs two large pimento stuffed olives with a small, sterling silver pitchfork and puts this in the drink. Brenda and Dad walk in.

"Oh, looks yummy," Brenda exclaims.

"Dad, what sort of wine would you like?"

"Chardonnay would be fine, son."

I bend down, open the wine cooler and pull out a couple of bottles until I find a Chardonnay.

"Has anyone thought about dinner tonight?" Brenda asks.

"I thought it might be nice if we all just walked somewhere," Lush responds. "I talked to Timmy downstairs. He recommended several good restaurants within walking distance—a couple he thought would be good for the kids, too."

"That sounds good to me," I say as I uncork the wine with a wine key, inlaid with lapis lazuli and opals, I purchased in Hong Kong for Billy for his twenty-fifth birthday. I pour the wine in a large wine glass and hand it to Dad. We all take our drinks and look at each other.

"Well, I propose a toast," Lush states with a smile, "To the murderers. May the gods of misery and despair descend upon you until we catch up with you. And catch up with you we will. And when we do, you'll regret the day you ever fucked with us. And once you are dead, may you rot in hell for eternity."

"Cheers, well stated, Lush," I say and clink her glass.

"Well, I must say, I've never heard a toast like that, but I'm with you, Lush," Brenda says and clinks our glasses. Dad just looks sad as he holds his wine glass up to clink with the others. I put the martini glass to my lips, tilt it up, and gulp. It goes down smooth, and I immediately feel better. Everyone is staring at me.

"Damn, Todge, I've never seen you do that before," Lush says.

I laugh and reply, "I know, but it just felt like the thing to do after a toast like that. Now, I'm gonna mix myself another, which I promise to sip. After all, as Fatgram always said, 'You can't fly with just one wing'." Everyone laughs.

"Philip, let me mix it. You know I mix great Manhattans, darling. Lots of experience, you know," Lush picks up the Manhattan shaker. "This shaker is already seasoned, it'll be an even better drink than the first one."

"Of course, Lush," I reply and smile. "Dad, Brenda, there's more I need to tell you. Have you all watched any television today?"

"No, we focused on getting the calls made," Brenda replies.

"Well, if you had, you would have learned that Elliot Fields, Billy's boyfriend who was with him at Splash and who is in Bermuda doing a shoot for Ralph Lauren, was murdered in his hotel room early this morning."

"Dear God," Brenda says. Dad looks stunned.

"I thought it best to keep it from you for a while until Lush and I talked to the police again. That's where we were this afternoon."

"I see," Dad says. "Did you find out anything?"

"Well, we went to the police because when I was checking my phone messages after lunch today I discovered that I had a message from Elliott Fields. It was sent at around four o'clock this morning. It was just a photo—a photo of Benny with a rope in his hands."

"What?" Brenda asks. "The waiter Benny?"

"Yes, that's the one," I reply.

"But how did he get to Bermuda so quickly?" Dad sets his wine glass on the counter and folds his arms.

"I dunno. Lush thinks maybe he, the guy in the photo, is actually Benny's identical twin."

"How was Elliott Fields murdered?" Brenda asks as she takes a sip of her martini.

"Strangulation, made to look like a sexual act," I reply.

"Sexual act, son?"

"Yes, it's called autoerotic asphyxiation. You strangle yourself while you are having an orgasm to get a euphoric effect."

"Yes, I've heard of that. A friend of my sister-in-law had a son who died that way. At first they thought it was suicide until they looked at his emails to friends and discovered that it was sort of a form of masturbation that went terribly wrong," Brenda states.

"Listen, let's go outside and sit down. I want to smoke. I have more to tell you both," I say. Lush has made my second drink and hands it to me. I grab my Marlboros, the onyx lighter, and head out. I head to a small wrought iron table on the far north side of the terrace that is hidden behind a raised bed of boxwoods. Everyone follows and we sit down. Lush, Brenda, and I all take cigarettes, and I light them all.

"We'll have ample warning if the kids come out here," I say as I light Brenda's cigarette.

"Thanks," she smiles as she replies.

I get a vision that I'm on a ten meter platform preparing to execute an incredibly difficult dive when I suddenly realize I know nothing about diving, I'm afraid of heights, and I don't even know how to swim. I look at Lush for strength. I sense she knows what I'm about to do. She nods her head, almost imperceptibly, then smiles. I take a drag off my cigarette, blow it out, and turn toward my father.

"Dad, what I have to tell you is not pleasant. But, but, considering what has happened to Billy, and now Elliot Fields, I really think I need to tell you now."

"Go ahead, I'm listening, son," he looks at me with his blue-grey eyes, the same as mine, and I feel like a little boy again, afraid to tell my dad I broke something of his.

"Dad, Billy and I, from the time I was ten until I was thirteen, were sexually abused by Uncle Adrian. Abused a lot and badly."

Dad frowns, shake his head back and forth sideways, sighs, then looks up into the sky as his eyes tear up and says, "Please tell me about it, Philip."

"Well, Dad, I've suppressed so much of it for so long, and I think Billy must have too. It took his death and seeing that painting you all saw today to make me face it—to give me the courage to admit that someone I loved so much was really doing bad things to me."

Tears are running down Dad's cheeks. Brenda reaches over and pats his right knee.

"I'm so sorry, son. I had no idea, and I know your mother didn't either. You have to know neither one of us would have ever let that happen had we known," he says with the saddest expression I can ever remember seeing on his face. "What exactly did Adrian do to you and Billy?"

"Well, first of all he spent the first couple of years becoming our best friends, especially when you were on the road and Mother was shut in painting. You remember all the gifts he gave us, GI Joes, Star Wars figures, walkie talkies, magic sets, I mean he was always bringing us fantastic things. He took us

to movies, introduced us to art on our level, listened to us, played with us, and took care of us. Dad, we trusted him completely. The summer I turned eleven, Billy was just nine, Mother was working on getting ready for a fall show in New York—you were on the road a lot that summer—is when the sexual abuse started. Uncle Adrian came in July and didn't leave until Labor Day. He got us all excited about a secret club that was supposed to be formed between fathers and sons, but since you were on the road so much, he told us you asked him to do it in your absence. The club was called the Blood Brothers club. We all had to cut our hands, mix the blood together, mark the blood on a secret document, and swear to never tell anyone. It thrilled us; we were so excited. He conducted the ceremony at Fatgram's swimming hole. Well it turned out the club was a ruse to teach us how to masturbate and to have sex with him. We would all get naked at the swimming hole, masturbate each other, suck each other, and basically have sex with Uncle Adrian. He even photographed a lot of it with his Hasselblad. He convinced us it was natural. It was not until I was about fifteen that I realized something had gone wrong. That painting you saw today was Billy's last painting—he calls it Blood Brothers."

"Dear God, Philip. I'm so sorry for you and Billy. You both were the same ages as Peter and Andrew. I'd kill anyone that did that to them." Brenda looks at me and then at Dad as she speaks. She shakes her blonde hair back and inhales deeply from her cigarette.

"Amen, sister," says Lush. "Fortunately the bastard already got his by burning to death. Serves him right."

"What else, son?"

"The else is a lot Dad, and I do not feel like going into it all now. In a nutshell, after the initiation, whenever we were around Uncle Adrian, at home or in New York, we'd have sex, and lots of it. He taught us how to choke ourselves to create an extremely euphoric feeling during orgasm. So you see how this could connect with Elliott Fields and Benny. Billy and I continued having sex with each other until I began to really feel guilty about it, when I was about fifteen, and I finally convinced Fatgram that I needed my own bedroom."

"Good heavens," Brenda almost gasps.

Dad appears to be turning white and green around the eyes. All at once he gets up, leans over the raised bed containing small boxwoods and begins to vomit. Brenda snuffs her cigarette out, looks at me and then Lush, gets up, stands behind Dad, and pats him on the back while he continues to vomit. I realize my own feelings of nausea when I'm under extreme stress must have come from Dad. I read a deep compassion for Dad in Lush's eyes. After a couple of minutes, Dad stops. Brenda hands him a cocktail napkin that he takes to wipe off his mouth and chin. He seems to be crying and laughing at the same time, but I realize he is starting to hyperventilate.

"Brenda, sit him down now. I'll run get a paper bag." I sprint in to the kitchen and start opening cabinets and drawers, looking for a bag. Finally I find some gallon plastic storage bags and I grab one and run back to the terrace. Dad is worse and is barely able to catch his breath.

"Here, Dad, blow into this." I bunch up the opening of the bag and put it over his mouth and nose. "Blow into it and inhale from it." He does. "Good, keep doing this. Slowly, good. Breathe in deeply." As he follows my instructions, I can tell he is calming and resuming normal breathing. I take the fog filled bag away. "Lush, would you mind getting Dad a glass of water?"

"I'll be right back," she says, gets up, and quickly walks to the kitchen.

Dad is leaning back in his chair, breathing heavily, with his eyes closed. His face is sweaty and Brenda is patting it with a napkin.

"Dear, are you okay? You still feel sort of clammy. Should we call a doctor?"

"No, no. I'm fine. I'm better. Thank you. Just let me get my breath back."

Brenda sits down beside Dad and we sit in silence until I hear toenails clinking on the slate terrace. Clark runs up to me, wags his tail, sniffs, then immediately goes to Dad, puts his front legs on Dad's lap

and vigorously sniffs toward his face. Dad opens his eyes, smiles, and leans forward. Clark immediately licks Dad's entire face.

"Clark, don't do that. Get down," I demand.

Dad is laughing now and he says, as he leans forward to embrace Clark, "It's okay son. He's just worried about me."

"What a sweet dog," Brenda says and pats Clark's head. He gives her one of his biggest dog smiles, trots under the table, jumps up into the raised bed and gulps up Dad's vomit before I can stop him.

"Gross, Clark, don't do that," I shout. He ignores me and completes his meal.

"Is he doing what I think he's doing?" Lush says as she returns with a glass of water. She hands the glass to Dad. He takes it.

"Thanks so much, Lush." He takes a couple of sips.

Clark jumps down, prances around the table twice, sits down, grunts, then bends over and starts thoroughly licking his asshole and penis.

"Oh well, dogs will be dogs," Lush says. "How ya feeling, Charles?"

"Much better, thank you. I apologize for getting sick in front of you all. Just the thought of Adrian having, I mean, abusing, well, sexually abusing my sons. Well, it just turned my stomach."

"I'd say that's a pretty normal reaction, Charles," Lush says. "I've known Philip and Billy all these years, and I just learned about it today, too."

"Dad. I need to say that I do not think Uncle Adrian's abuse of us had anything to do with Billy's sexuality. I think he was born gay. I really do."

"You're probably right, son. Your Mother always thought that."

"Really, Dad?"

"Oh yes. She always told me she thought Billy tried to cover his sensitivity and femininity with his 'he man, I don't give a shit attitude'. She said, 'Charles, you mark my words, our pretty little boy will turn out to like pretty boys himself.'"

"Damn, what did she say about me, Dad?"

"She said you were a little me, and that knowing you was like knowing me as a little boy which made her love us both just that much more."

"Wow, did Mother care that Billy was gay or going to be gay?"

"Absolutely not. She embraced it and Billy. It just gave her another dimension of him to love. She knew that he would grow up to be about as handsome as a man can get. She would tell him in private that he must never let his good looks get in the way of being a good person—good to himself and to others."

"Eva must have been incredibly intuitive," Brenda states. I look at her to see if this conversation is causing her discomfort. It appears to me that it is not.

"She was, dear. But, as Philly and I know, that gift and all her great, extraordinary gifts were given, I've always felt, with a twin dark side. Please, don't take this the wrong way. Not a bad, dark side, but a side that inflicted her with internal demons. Things she couldn't control, things that made her feel desperate, alone, hopeless, depressed, and anxious—all these things and more combined to create what she called the 'mean blues'. I never fully understood that. I guess I never will. I guess I finally resolved that it was the 'mean blues' that caused her to take her own life."

"Did she ever seek professional treatment, Charles?" Lush asks.

"Oh yes. She didn't really want to. She was, like her mother, a very self-reliant woman. She thought she could control it. But she couldn't. Ina knew this."

"Ina is the one and only Fatgram, isn't she?" Lush lights another cigarette as she looks at Dad.

"Oh yes. Ina was so close to Eva. Ina was relentless in trying to help her only child. She forced her to go to all kinds of doctors and psychiatrists, the best in the country, but nothing ever worked for long. When we were first married, I was convinced that I could help her. I tried everything I could, but to no

avail. One day after Eva and I had a heated argument over her condition, Ala Mary took me aside and told me that she had raised Miss Eva from the cradle to a full womanhood and that she knew her better than anybody. Well, I believed that to be true. She went on to say Miss Eva had this demon in her from the time she was a little tot and there was nothing anybody, except the good Lord, could do about it. She said she had come to believe that God had put half of a demon in Eva so that she could know how bad bad can be so that the other half could paint pure beauty for the rest of us to see. You know, after all these years, Ala Mary's theory still gets my vote."

"Amazing," Lush says and takes the final sip of her Manhattan.

"Dad, there's so much I want to know about Mother, our family back then and why you..." I stop speaking because I realize I do not want to get into all this now. He smiles at me and shakes his head.

"It's okay, son. There's a lot I want and need to know from you too." He looks into my eyes as he says this, and we exchange the unspoken knowledge that we will indeed be there for one another in the years to come. I reach over to him. He hands me his right hand, I take it in mine, and we hold each other's hands, squeezing firmly, but not shaking at all. After a moment, I let go and sit back.

"The police are stationing an officer inside the condo and two out front of the building until after Billy's memorial," I state. "They think I might be in danger if the killer thinks I possess whatever knowledge Billy, and apparently Elliot Fields, had."

"Oh my God," Brenda sits erect in her chair, "Charles, what about the children?"

"I know, dear. I think we should send them back home immediately," he replies.

"Do you really thinks that's the thing to do, Brenda?" Lush asks. "I mean, this is a very secure building, we have police protection, and they'll always be with us. What could the killer possibly want with them?"

"Well, I don't know. But, he could kidnap one of them in order to force Philip to deliver whatever knowledge or thing he's after," she replies.

"I see your point, that's a possibility, but I think a very slim one," Lush replies. "Philip thinks this all has to do with sex in some regard. I just don't think that will impact the kids in any way." Lush looks back and forth from Brenda to Dad as she talks.

"Sex, Lush?" Dad looks puzzled.

"Yes, Dad," I say. "I've gotten a bit off track, but that was why I wanted to tell you about Uncle Adrian. Another thing Billy and I kept hidden from you was that Billy almost killed himself twice, close enough that he was hospitalized twice, once when he was nineteen in college and once at St. Barts when he was winding down his modeling career."

"What?" He looks at me, and I see a flash of anger in his face.

"Well, the hospitals and police classified both episodes as attempted suicide, and I sort of let everyone believe that, but I know they were just sessions of autoerotic asphyxiation gone too far—just like your sister-in-law's friend's son, Brenda. You see, Billy hung on, so to speak, to Uncle Adrian's sexual practices. I think they offered him some kind of internal solace whenever things got really bad for him, you know, emotionally. I begged and chastised him for years to stop. I tried to convince him to seek psychiatric help, but he wouldn't, at least until a couple of years ago. He is so much like Mother. Anyway, you know Billy; he would only pursue something if he thought he could achieve perfection. I think he was that way with sex also." I stand up. "Follow me, I have to show you something. Let's go quietly. I don't want the kids to hear us."

I lead them into the kitchen and through the study to the guest bathroom. We can hear the sound of the television in the guest suite, but no kids are in sight. Clark trots into the guest suite. I lead them into the bathroom and shut the door. I go over, push the shelving unit, and watch the expressions on Dad and Brenda's faces as the unit revolves outward, revealing the secret chamber. I reach in, turn on the light,

open the door, and admonish, "Please, do not touch anything. The police are coming over to go over this room for any fingerprints or other clues."

"Is this what I think it is?" Dad whispers.

"Yes, it is. Billy's elaborate toy for self-strangulation. I found out about it only after he had completed construction and moved in," I whisper back. I let everyone look for a minute. Brenda is speechless. I motion for everyone to withdraw; I shut the door, turn off the light, and push the shelving unit back into place. We leave the bathroom and walk back into the study.

"I'm going to check on the kids," Brenda says in a low voice and walks back toward the guest suite.

"Let's go make more drinks," Lush says and we head to the wet bar.

"Well, I usually only have one glass of wine, but today I think I'll have another," Dad says reaching up in the cabinet for another wine glass.

"Todge, can you handle another Manhattan?" Lush asks.

"Yes. Strangely enough, I don't even feel a buzz from the first two. So you see Dad, the police are thinking that perhaps Billy might have engaged in some sexual acts with one or more high profile people who didn't want it revealed. At least that's one theory they are pursuing."

"Yes, I see," he replies.

The phone rings. I answer the unit on the bar. It's Timmy.

"Mr. Hampton? Philip?"

"Yes, Timmy."

"Detectives Johnson and Bell are down here with three officers. Shall I let them up?"

"Fine Timmy."

Lush motions for me to hand her the phone. "Timmy, it's Lush. Could you make a reservation for seven of us at seven thirty at the Landmark?"

"Of course. I'll call you back if there's a problem."

"Thanks, Timmy." Lush puts the phone down. "Still want the drinks with the cops on the way?"

"Sure," I reply.

"The kids are engrossed in one of those Harry Potter movies. It's got about an hour to go," Brenda states as she walks into the bar with Clark trailing behind her.

"Good. I got dinner reservations at seven thirty at the Landmark. We can walk there, and Timmy says they have a great kids menu. Oh, I almost forgot. I got a hold of Lois, Billy's housekeeper. She has been out of town for a long weekend—devastated by the news when she heard about it. She didn't know whom to contact. She agreed to come tomorrow and Thursday and she can bring a friend to help on Friday and Saturday."

"Great. Thanks, Lush," I say.

"No problem. I also told her the police would probably want to talk to her. She didn't have a problem with that. She said they knew where to find her. I just let that one rest."

"Hmmm. Wonder what that means? Any ideas, Lush?" I ask.

"No, but I bet Timmy knows. My guess would be a drug connection, but I'll check it out," she replies, then asks, "Want another drink, Brenda?"

"Sure, thanks, Lush."

"Brenda, the detectives as well as some officers are on the way up," I turn to her, "I'll take Clark and meet them. I'm sure they will want to see the 'secret room'. Why don't you all take your drinks back on the terrace and I'll meet you there?"

"Fine, son," Dad replies. "Would you mind if Brenda and I speak with the detectives before they leave? We'd really like their opinion as to whether or not we let the kids stay for the memorial."

"Of course, Dad. I'll bring them out. Lush, make me a great one."

"Coming right up, darling."

"Come on, Clark. We're the welcome wagon."

Chapter 14

I'm sound asleep; I must be dreaming. I hear a child's voice calling my name.

"Philip, Philip, wake up, we're scared."

As I brace myself for the onslaught of another nightmare, I become conscious of Clark's cold, wet nose, nudging against my neck, and I hear him whimpering. Something is also tapping my left arm. I pat Clark's head with my right hand and open my eyes to see Emma poking my arm and her two brothers standing behind her.

"Philip, we're scared. We're afraid someone is going to murder us, too," she says as she pulls back her right hand, clutching a Teddy bear with her left hand.

"I'm not afraid," Drew says defiantly.

"You are too," Emma replies, "or you would have stayed in bed instead of coming in here with us."

"Scaredy pants, scaredy pants," Drew taunts her.

"Uncle Philip, I mean Philip," Peter says in a whisper, "I think we're just not used to this place yet. And with all that's happened to Billy and now that other man, his boyfriend getting murdered."

"Who told you that?" I sit up in bed and notice that all three children look quite frightened. "Here, you all hop up in bed with me and the Clarkster." I pat the bed. They all immediately climb on the bed. Emma wedges herself between Clark and me. I put my right arm around her.

"Peter got a text from Randy," Drew states.

"Aw, good ole cousin Randy. He certainly keeps you kids well informed."

"Please don't tell Mom and Dad, Philip. We know they want to send us home, but we want to stay here with you for Billy's memorial?" Peter pleads.

"Well, of course I won't tell. I'm no snitch." They all smile. I smile back thinking that they really are scared out of their wits. "Do you all have mobile phones?"

"No, we just have one we share, but Peter has it most of the time 'cause he's the oldest," Emma replies.

"I'm glad we can stay, Philip. Randy says we'll see a bunch of famous people at the memorial service. Is that true?" Drew asks as he sits Indian style by my legs.

"Well, it is true, Andrew. But you know famous people are just like you and me, they put one pants leg on at a time." The kids laugh. Peter is stretched out, stomach down, beside his brother, leaning on his elbows watching me. I am touched by their trust in me, a man they have never met before, and I get a lump in my throat as I become a part of their innocence, an innocence I remember well with my brother before Uncle Adrian changed our lives.

"Will Harry Potter be there?" Emma asks.

"No, Emma, Harry won't be there. There'll probably be some celebrities you'll recognize, though," I reply.

"Like who?" Drew demands.

"Well, I don't know for sure, we'll just have to wait and see. It's all such short notice and we aren't asking for RSVP's."

"What's RSVP?" Emma asks.

"Respondez, s'il vous plait," Peter replies. "It means please respond, to an invitation."

"That's right, Peter. Do you take French?"

"Yes sir, since third grade."

"Cool, but no yes sir to me, remember?"

"Yes sir, I mean, yes, well, okay," he says, embarrassed.

"Philip, do you think the murderer will try to come here to kill us?" Drew asks matter-of-factly.

"No, Drew, I do not. I don't know why anyone would have wanted to murder our brother or Elliott Fields. I do know for sure that it has nothing to do with all of us here. We're as safe and as snug as a bug in a rug."

"A bug in a rug! That's funny," Emma replies and laughs out loud.

"Shhhhh, Emma," Peter warns. "You don't want to wake up Dad and Mom."

I smile at them all. "It's okay, this is an awfully big place. I don't think they'll hear us all the way in here."

"Well, she might wake Mrs. Richardson," he adds.

"What? Lush? She could sleep through a hurricane," I state. They all giggle. Clark moans loudly, stretches his body out as long as he can get it, raises his head, glances around, puts his head back down, moans again, and shuts his eyes. We all giggle.

"I think he's telling us to go to sleep," I say.

"Yeah, he's probably tired from all that going back and forth," Peter says.

"What do you mean?" I ask.

"Well, you know Mom said for us to leave our doors open in case we need anything, we could yell for you or for Officer Kelly in the foyer," Peter explains. "Clark keeps coming into our room, sleeping for a bit, then going into Emma's room, sleeping for a bit, then going out into the foyer to check on Officer Kelly, then back to our room. He's been doing this all night long. That's one reason we're all awake. We're not used to having dogs in our beds. Mom won't allow Henry in our beds."

"Henry?"

"Our dog—a boxer," Peter says.

"That's funny," I say.

"Why is it funny? Henry's the best. We love him." Emma looks puzzled.

"Oh, I guess I don't mean funny. It's just that. Well, did you know your Dad had a boxer named Henry, actually three boxers named Henry when he was growing up?"

"Yeah, we know. That's why Henry's real name is Henry the fourth," Drew says.

"Well, that makes sense. Where does Henry the fourth sleep?"

"In his dog bed in Mom and Dad's bedroom," Peter replies. I remember that Dad always wanted a boxer but Mother wouldn't hear of it because she didn't want to upset dear old Bonnie Belle who died at sixteen years of age right after Mother killed herself. Somehow Bonnie sensed Mother would never return. The old dog couldn't bear living without Mother.

"Well, I think Clark did tire himself out watching over you guys. What a great dog he is."

"Yeah, we like him," Drew says, "But Randy says he's the kind of dog that kills people, a pit bull dog."

"Let me guess, you guys sent Randy a photo of Clark from your mobile?"

"Uhmm, yes, just a couple of photos," Peter admits.

"Well, it's true. He's part pit bull—a mix. Lush found him starving on the streets in downtown Louisville where she lives. She rescued him and Billy was wanting to get a dog, so Clark ended up here."

"Wow, he's a lucky dog," Peter says.

"He is a lucky dog, and a very smart dog. He loves kids, as you can tell. I think your cousin Randy might change his mind about pit bulls if he met Clark."

"Yeah, Clark's great," Andrew says and bends over and hugs him. He moans again and wedges his muzzle under Emma's legs. I look over at the clock; it is 3:30 am.

"Okay kids, are you ready to go to sleep now? Do you feel safe enough?"

"Yes, if we can sleep in here with you, Philip?" Emma says. I can see from all their faces, they want this to happen.

"Fine by me. It's a great big king size bed anyway. Boys crawl up and get under the covers. Emma, I'm gonna slide down a bit. I'm going to sleep on my left side so I won't snore. You can snuggle up against my back if you like?" She does. Everyone says goodnight. I'm not used to sleeping with anyone, especially three kids and a dog, but I'm happy, almost grateful to share the bed with my siblings and Clark.

I lay awake thinking about the events of the day. Within minutes the children's rhythmic breathing lets me know they are asleep. I silently chuckle as I remember the look on Detective Johnson's face when I showed him and Detective Bell Billy's secret room. He's seen a lot in New York, but I don't think he's ever seen anything quite like that. A vision flashes through my mind of a nude Detective Bell, strapped in one of Billy's leather harnesses with me entering her doggie style while we watch each other in all those mirrors. I want to follow this fantasy, but I quickly quell it because of the presence of my bedmates, one of who is snoring a soft child's snore. I think it must be Andrew. Dinner was great tonight—almost an adventure for the kids. It was exciting to have an unidentified police officer trailing us, guarding us. Officer Kelly is an extremely friendly man. You can tell he loves children, which is good since he has four little ones of his own. He is a perfect choice to guard my little brothers and sister. Strange, I think of them as my full brothers and sisters, even though I know they are only half. Brenda's great. What an ass I am to lust after her. I wish Billy could have known Peter, Andrew, and Emma. Shit, I'm getting hard again. Not now, asshole. I'll never get to sleep, but does it really matter? How fortunate I am to be surrounded by these great kids and Clark too. What would you say, Billy, if you could see us now, all piled up in your bed? Lord, if this bed could talk. Who knows what it has witnessed? What did you do Billy? Who did you screw that would kill you over it? Politician? Movie star? Wall Street mogul? Famous heir or heiress? Who was it? Was it over sex? What else could it be? Not drugs. They were only a crutch for you, at times. Not a way of life. I just can't figure it out. Who would want to kill you, someone so physically beautiful, so immensely talented, so fun to be with? I wonder if your psychiatrist knows anything? What's his name? I guess they invited him to the wake? Lush and I will definitely corner him. I wonder what he's legally obliged to tell the police? I gave them his name, what the hell is it? Goddamn Adrian! I really loved you so much. Why the hell did you do that to us? Billy and me. What sickness made you do it? Did someone do that to you? I don't know anything about you, other than interacting with you. You were raised in England I know, but where? How? Who fucked you up? Someone must have. Who else did you prey on besides Billy and me? There had to be others. Lush will find this out. She's so good with all that. I can't believe she came back after dinner and started creating the video presentation for the memorial. How did she get so proficient with computers? She can do anything. I should get her to show me some things while she's here. Damn, she looks better than ever. What a dick I was to fuck up that relationship. I wonder how long she'll stay? I wonder if we can really solve this crime? Especially before the police? They have so many more resources. Or do they? I don't think I'll ever find a wife now. Do I really want a wife? Do I want kids? I've always thought I might. Christ, I'd better hurry. Who wants a father that looks like a grandfather? God, I'm fortunate as far as money goes. How did I end up with all this? All of Fatgram's wealth, all of Mother's, all of Billy's, and everything I've made? Geez, it was never my goal to be rich, but I am. What the fuck do I need all this money for? Fatgram always drilled into me that you have to live off the interest and dividends. Preserve the 'nut' for those coming after you. Who's coming after me? Emma? Andrew? Peter? I know Brenda and Dad must be worth a wad. These kids aren't wanting for anything. Good for them. God knows they have to be experiencing a better life than I did at their age. Always worrying

about Dad and Mother. Trying to please Ala Mary and Fatgram. Always trying to look after Billy. In a lot of ways, I think I see Billy as my child. Then why did I fuck him? That was all his doing. He really coerced me. Or did he? I mean, I think I enjoyed it. Well, as much as I could. Men just do not turn me on that much. I crave pussy. But Billy was so damn perfect physically. So perfect. What a fucking idiot he was. I don't think he ever really knew what a perfect physical specimen he was. Well, you'd think it would have sunk in. I mean, people lined up to pay him twenty thousand dollars a day to stand around, look pretty, and have his photo taken. Give me a break. He had to know. But that didn't matter to him. I think it was almost a chore. He was happiest painting, like Mother. Shit, I'm never going back to sleep now. I'm afraid to turn over. I might crush Emma, she's so tiny. Damn, what if Brenda and Dad walk in and see me in bed with their kids. They'll probably think I'm a pedophile like Uncle Adrian. After all isn't it a vicious cycle that's hard to break? Don't be a fucking idiot, Hampton. You know children do not turn you on sexually in the least little bit. I just don't think I can go back to Atlanta now. I'm hardly there anyway and New York has more convenient flights everywhere than Hartsfield. I'll just move my stuff up here, sell the house and poof, I'm outta there. That Nurse Ostro knows something. I don't know what, but, at least I have a good feeling about her. I hope she returns my call. I'm sure the detectives will shit a brick if she shows up Friday. I don't give a damn. I'm willing to bet Lush and I solve this before they do. I can't keep smoking and drinking so much. I know it's the pain now, but I need to get back to yoga. I'll promise myself I'll do it Sunday, not Saturday. I'm sure the memorial will take a lot out of me. My God, who will show up? I bet a lot of people will. It will be great publicity for the celebrities. Going to a memorial with an aura of suspense, mystery—yes, even murder hanging in the air. Christ, I can't wait to meet with Julianna tomorrow. No telling what going over Billy's paintings will reveal. I know one thing for sure, Julianna knows more than she's letting on to me or to the police. She a savvy woman, she's invested a lot in Billy and his work, she's not going to let anything fuck that up. Of course I'll let her go on with his last show. I'll bet his prices will skyrocket since he's gone. I know Mother's did. It absolutely amazed Fatgram. She always thought it would be her burden to provide for Billy and me since our Dad was just a traveling furniture salesman. I think it surprised her completely that Uncle Adrian managed to sell off Mother's final works at such exorbitant prices in the years after Mother's death, leaving us a 'nut' almost as big as what Fatgram left us. Funny, now I feel as if some of that money from Mother should have gone to Dad. He never asked for a penny, yet he loved and nurtured Mother all those years. Fatgram must have communicated with Adrian after he stopped seeing us. I know he was totally smitten by Billy, especially right as Billy started to hit puberty at eleven. Was Mother's suicide really enough to keep him away from us? Especially Billy? I just think Fatgram had something to do with it. I wonder if she somehow found out what he was doing to us? Ala Mary certainly never trusted Adrian and he knew that. Although he tried to ingratiate himself to her, she wouldn't give him an inch. Behind her back he called her 'the meddling negro'. I wonder if that was Adrian Fatgram was talking to on the phone that time I overheard her crying about how the maid found Mother? But Adrian was there; he would have known that. I wonder if Fatgram had a lover we didn't know about. She was so full of life I can't imagine she wasn't interested in sex even as she got older. I wonder if she had a vibrator? I'll bet she did. She was the only female in a fourteen piece traveling band during the roaring twenties. God, could she ever play the piano. Billy and I used to sit for hours listening to her play rags, jazz pieces, and classical pieces. Her dad, Great Grandpa Robertson, President and Owner of Union Cotton Mills—an empire started by his own father, must have about lost it when his only child and daughter left home as soon as she graduated from Converse College with a degree in music to play in joints all over the south. Fatgram must have been a total wild hair. Think of the sex she had. No wonder Billy was the way he was. I bet that gene came from Fatgram. I wish I knew more about Fatgram's life. I can't believe I never interviewed her about it. I was into journalism at boarding school, what a great project that would have been. What a woman of fortitude. How she must have

suffered that last year. I guess she knew it was her time, but what a shock to come home for Christmas break to find out she was terminally ill. 1992 was the worst Christmas ever. She made it through Christmas though and died on Tuesday the 29th. We buried her on that Friday, a frigid, gray, New Year's day. She had to know something was seriously wrong. You don't just get diagnosed with colon cancer, then die three weeks later. Billy, Billy, Billy, there's so much I want to say to you, to ask you. I'm just not ready for you to be gone. How will I get through each day knowing I'll never hear your warm voice again calling up saying, 'How ya doing, big brother? Why don't ya come up for the weekend? I'm having a dinner party Saturday. It'll be fun. There's a pretty lady I want you to meet. Please, oh please, oh please.' My eyes well up with tears. Why do I feel so alone with a house full of people? Time won't cure this heartache. I know that well from Mother's death. You just go on. That's all, you have no other choice but to go on and you carry that heartache with you, but it never gets less of a burden, never. I'm never going to get back to sleep now. My stomach hurts, I need to fart, but I can't with these kids in bed. Okay, I'm going to get up quietly, go pee, and find one of those Ambien Timmy gave me Monday night. That'll make me sleep. I slowly slide out of bed and tiptoe to the bathroom. To my surprise, Clark doesn't even stir. Poor guy, he must really be fatigued from all that is going on. I shut the door, turn on the light, and pull down my boxers, and sit on the toilet to pee and fart so I won't make much noise. I pee and reach around to flush the toilet. Shit, that noise may wake them. Oh well. I get up, pull up my boxers and open the medicine cabinet. There are a lot of prescription drugs in there, a couple of antidepressants, I think, yes that the shrink's name, Dr. Gerard. I find a bottle that says Ambien. I open it, pull out a small blue pill, pop it in my mouth, get a handful of water from the faucet, and swallow. I wipe my mouth on a towel, turn off the bathroom light, open the door and carefully walk back to bed. Everyone is sleeping so peacefully; I don't want to disturb them. I walk over to the chaise lounge, lie down, pulling a big, fluffy chenille throw over my body. I curl up, pretending that I'm behind a big waterfall in a tropical jungle somewhere. I'm in a dry cave behind the waterfall on a bed of soft dry straw. All the jungle animals rest in friendly peace at the mouth of the cave—lions, wolves, elephants, tigers, jaguars, giant snakes, eagles, bears, wolverines, cheetahs, hyenas, rhinoceros, giant moose, huge condors, and cougars all standing guard—protecting me from any harm, from Uncle Adrian, from doing things with him and Billy I really don't want to do, from Mother and Dad screaming at each other, from visions of Mother taking her own life. I hear the sound of the waterfall. I pull the throw down a bit to let the fresh wind from the waterfall stir up a slight chill on my skin so I know the waterfall is really there. This is the place I feel safest. No one can harm me here—my own 'Peaceable Kingdom', one of my favorite paintings I remember from childhood. I wonder why I associate safeness with waterfalls? The only waterfall I remember from childhood is Pearson's Falls near Saluda. Mother's best friend, Carol, had a house at Lake Summit. Sometimes we'd go there during really hot spells in the summer if we weren't at Pawleys. Now, it's coming back. I must have been eight or nine and Mother wanted to start a painting of Pearson's Falls. I remember hiking up to the falls; it seemed like a long way: a damp, rocky path, closed in with steep hills covered in rhododendron, ferns, and trees. We passed granite outcrops, seeping water, covered in lichens and slime molds, gooey and cold to the touch. Dad carried Mother's easel and a cooler; Mother carried a folding stool, her painting supplies in a case that looked like a tackle box, and some blankets. The sound of rushing water filled the air as the large creek tumbled through the gorge over granite rocks and boulders worn smooth over the millennia. Billy and I kept thinking that each rushing sound of water would be from the falls, but Dad kept saying we weren't there yet. Then finally, we crossed a stone bridge, ascended a bit more and the sound of the water intensified and the path spilled into a large piece of granite, like a giant table, the forest opened up, and the falls, framed by the tall trees, rose up before us, a giant monument of sound and milky white, rushing water, cascading down from where the trees opened up to blue sky and sunlight poured in illuminating the rocks and water. Mother exclaimed that

the light was perfect and immediately set up her easel and started sketching. Dad spread the blankets out on the large rock and set out our lunch of cold fried chicken, potato salad, deviled eggs, iced tea and chocolate cake. Mother was so focused she barely ate, and I watched Dad take her a chicken leg, her favorite part, a deviled egg, a glass of tea. He walked over and fed her a bite of his cake at one point. She looked up at him, smiling, taking the cake in her mouth, returning quickly to the canvas. I felt so happy to see them like this, happy together, not fighting. I wished it could always be like this. The only distraction that day were the yellow jackets trying to land on our food, but we batted them away. Billy took a rock and smashed one that landed on a chicken leg bone. After lunch we explored the margins of the creek, poking at minnows, searching for crawdads, looking for snakes. The afternoon wore on and Mother was so engrossed in her painting, that Dad took us on a hike so we wouldn't bother her. Dad loved the outdoors and knew a lot about plants because he majored in biology at Chapel Hill so he pointed out all kinds of ferns and orchids to us. After our hike, he piled the blankets in a dry spot on the granite and the three of us lay down on our backs looking up at the forest canopy. I felt so content, so safe. We fell asleep and slept until Mother woke us up in a frenzy telling us to hurry because she heard thunder and wanted to get back to the car before it rained. We quickly packed up and made our way down the trail back to the parking lot as fast as we could as the sound of the thunder moved closer and closer, reverberating through the gorge. Just as we got to the parking area, it began to rain. The canopy shielded us at first, and Billy and I jumped into the back seat while Dad and Mother hurriedly put everything in the back. But the heavens opened up, Mother screamed with laughter, and by the time they closed the back and ran to get in the front, they were both drenched. We all laughed and laughed and I reached over the back and grabbed a blanket to hand to Mother and Dad, so they could dry off. The three Manhattans, two glasses of wine with dinner, and the Ambien begin to take over now. I surrender to the comforting sound of the waterfall. I make a mental note to instruct my younger brothers and sister of the benefits and safety of secret caves behind waterfalls. As I drift off to sleep I realize that they probably don't have the need for such apparitions.

CHAPTER 15

"Philip, wake up. Wake up, darling."

I hear Lush's voice, and I open my eyes. I realize I must have been sleeping a long time. My lower back aches from sleeping on the soft chaise.

"What time is it?"

"It's almost eleven o'clock," she says, peering at me from the doorway. Clark runs in and jumps up on the chaise with me.

"Hey boy, good morning. Why did you all let me sleep for so long?"

"Because you must need it," Lush says.

"I guess so. Boy, I feel like I could go back to sleep right now."

"Well, honey, if you think you need to, go ahead. You know Julianna is coming at two, and I thought you might want to check to see if Nurse Ostro has called you."

Everything rushes back at me, and my head is pounding again. I need a pseudoephedrine tablet. These damn sinuses. "You're right, Lush. Let me shower, and I'll be out in a minute. I need some coffee bad. I'm groggy from that Ambien."

"I wondered if you'd been having to take sleeping pills," she states. "I was gonna offer you some of mine. I didn't know you had any."

"I don't. Found some in Billy's medicine cabinet. I'm just not used to taking them. Knocked me out cold, I guess."

"Did you take it when we all went to bed? That was about eleven thirty. My, you've been asleep almost twelve hours."

"No, it was about three thirty." I put my feet over the side, using the throw to conceal my morning wood and rub my eyes. "The kids came in and woke me up. They were afraid of murderers. They ended up sleeping in here. That's why I'm on the chaise."

"Yeah, I tiptoed past when I got up this morning. What a sweet scene that was. All the kids and Clark piled into bed asleep. And you on the chaise, snoring away."

"Was I really snoring?"

"Yes, you were, but it didn't seem to bother anyone. Clark didn't even hear me tiptoe by."

"What time did you get up?"

"Hmmm, about six-thirty."

"Damn, Lush, you've never been able to sleep past eight o'clock in your life, have you?"

"Rarely, darling. Anyway, I've been through all the family photo albums you gave me, and a shitload of photos from Billy's hard drive. I've put them to the list of favorite songs you provided, but I also looked at his iPod and pulled off the top twenty-five songs he played, so there are some surprises, but I think you're gonna really like it."

"You're done already?"

"Yep."

"I wish I had one half your energy."

"Darling, you do, it just manifests itself in other ways besides getting things done quickly."

"You're an angel," I look up and smile at her.

She smiles back. "Go shower, Todge, your hair's a mess. Oh, we've had a changing of the guard. It's an Officer Graham now. I gave her a tour of the place."

"Her?"

"Yeah, her."

"What's she look like?"

"Do you ever have anything but sex on your mind, Todge?" she asks in a teasing manner.

"What else is there to think about?" I fire back.

"You're hopeless. Now get ready, I'll make you some coffee. Brenda cooked a big breakfast for everyone and there's bacon and sweet rolls left," she says as she starts to pull the door closed.

"Hey, let Clark go with you. I'm sure he'd rather be out there with the kids."

"Okay. Come on Clark, let's go."

He jumps down, runs out the door and Lush closes it. I hear her walking down the hall. I feel a bowel movement coming on, so I grab my phone from the bedside table and head for the toilet. I pull down my boxers and sit down carefully, aiming my boner down and pushing it down toward the water with my left hand so I won't piss out through the seat. I flick open my phone with my right hand and see that I have twelve new messages. Damn, now I've got to listen to all of these. I go through them as I take a dump. Most of them are from concerned friends expressing their condolences and one is from Detective Bell saying that they will be sending the crime scene investigation team over promptly at two pm to check out the secret room. The final message, which came at ten am, is from Janet Ostro. She has returned my call and has left me her mobile number. I shut the phone, put it on the counter, wipe, flush and head for the shower. I look in the mirror as I pass, one day's growth of beard. Hell, I won't bother to shave today. I wonder if Detective Bell likes that look. I wonder what Officer Graham looks like. I turn on the water and

start counting tile squares in the shower until the water warms. Today, I jump in and put a larger quantity of shampoo in my hands. I start soaping my head, work down to my face and neck, then chest, back, stomach, cock, ass, legs, and feet—all in one continuous sweep. I rinse thoroughly and, voila, I'm done. I have to remember to instruct Lush in the right way to take a two-minute shower. I grab a towel, dry off, put on deodorant, brush my teeth, comb my hair and head for the closet for yet another pair of khakis and a button down oxford-cloth shirt. Today I choose a pink striped shirt and burgundy weejuns with a matching belt; screw the socks. I go back into the bathroom, grab my phone and press the call back button for Janet Ostro's number. I look at myself in the mirror as the phone rings.

"Hello."

"Miss Ostro?"

"Yes."

"This is Philip Hampton."

"Yes, Mr. Hampton?"

"Well, thanks so much for returning my call, I really appreciate it."

"Of course, glad to."

"Well, hmm, they're a couple of things I want to ask you. First off, I would like to invite you to Billy's memorial service or wake, if you will, here at his condo. It will start at six pm this Friday. Do you think you could attend?"

"Why Mr. Hampton. It's so nice of you to invite me. I'd love to attend. It works fine because I don't work on Wednesdays, Thursdays, and Fridays."

"Really? That's great. Let's see. His condo is the penthouse at 15 and one-half Warren Street. Just come into the lobby and the doorman will direct you."

"Fine. Well again, I'm so sorry about your brother, Mr. Hampton, and I'll see you Friday evening."

"Thank you Miss Ostro. Uhh, there is one other thing. You see. Well, because we know someone murdered Billy. Well, I just wondered if we could meet before Friday. I'd like to hear from you what all transpired that morning. I'd like to ask you some questions, if you wouldn't mind?"

"I see. Well, I've gave an extensive statement to two detectives yesterday. I got the impression they didn't want me to talk about it to anyone, at least until they have a suspect."

"I'm sure they don't want you to talk about it. Miss Ostro, I'm not trying to inhibit the police investigation at all. My background and livelihood is investigative journalism. My closest friend, who is also trained in that field, is here and we are going to do everything in our power to find Billy's murderer. I just don't want to leave it entirely to the police. I feel like I owe that to my brother."

"I see. Well, I suppose I can help you some. When would you like to meet?"

"Is today possible? This afternoon?"

"Well, I have an art class at four o'clock. How about two?"

"Would one thirty work?

"Yes, I suppose that will work. Where would you like to meet?"

"Here, at Billy's. I'm happy to send a car for you."

"Thanks, but that won't be necessary. I'll see you at one thirty, Mr. Hampton."

"Thank you so much, Miss Ostro. I really appreciate it."

"Goodbye, Mr. Hampton."

"Goodbye."

"Hallelujah!" I shout out loud. I run out of the bathroom, down the hall, and into the kitchen to find Lush.

"Damn, that was fast. Record time for a shower I'd say, but no shave I see."

"Fast, right, remind me to tell you how to take a two-minute shower. But, Lush, Janet Ostro will be here at one thirty today."

"You're kidding," she says as she pours a cup of freshly pressed coffee for me, "How did you manage that?"

"Don't know. Did I tell you she's an art student in her spare time?"

"Yeah."

"Well, maybe she just wants to take a gander at how Billy lived. I don't know; I'm just glad she's coming. And, she's also going to attend the service Friday."

"That's fantastic, Todge. Johnson and Bell will have a cow when they see her here."

"I know. Hey, where is everyone?"

"They're in the studio looking at a city map. I found one for them. They're planning their afternoon. Oh, I already did your dirty work for you."

"What do you mean?"

"Well, there's no way you can go to the matinee and museum today. We've got Julianna at two and now, Nurse Ostro at one thirty."

"Shit, you're right. What did you tell them?"

"I told them that because of everything we have to do to get ready for Friday, we just couldn't possibly take that much time today. But, I extended to them, on your behalf, an open invitation to come back for a week when you would spend the whole week with them showing them the city."

"Thanks, Lush. How did they take it?"

"The boys, fine. But little Emma seemed a bit disappointed. She's really getting attached to you."

"I know. She crawled in bed right beside me last night, even nudged in between Clark and me."

"Oh, how sweet. I think they are planning to leave in just a bit, get some lunch, then go to the matinee. I think they'll save the Metropolitan Museum for tomorrow."

"Good."

"Well hi, Mr. Hampton," Lois smiles as she walks in from the study carrying a rectangular plastic container by its handle. The container holds all sorts of cleaning agents, sponges, clothes, and feather dusters. She sets the container down on a counter and says, "I just don't know what to say. I'm so sorry. I can't believe he's really gone. It sure seems real unfair."

"Thanks Lois, I can't believe it either. I just don't know why anyone would want to kill Billy."

She looks down at the floor and shakes her head in agreement. Lois is one of those women who, just by looking at them—the way their skin appears rougher than most women's; the way their hair is often just pulled back, without much thought, into a ponytail with a rubber band; the way they hold a glass of whiskey or a longneck; the way they hold themselves, rigid, as if they are about to be hit and hit hard; the way they light a cigarette, take a drag, flick at their unpolished finger nails; and the way they gaze out at the world like they just don't give a shit anymore—you know they've led a hard life. The grey dress with white collar and apron—a uniform I'm certain she must be required to wear—doesn't suit her demeanor. Tight frayed jeans, a tube top under a leather jacket, and leather boots are more her style, yet if Lush were to ask me if I trust Lois on a gut level, I'd say yes in a snap.

Lois is also the type of person you don't beat around the bush with, so I just ask her what's on my mind, "Look Lois, I don't mean to be pushy or prying, but you were around Billy a lot. Is there anything you know that might shed some light on his murder?"

She hesitates a moment, looks down at the floor, then asks, "Mind if we go out on the terrace?"

"Not at all. Let's go. Lush, come with us."

"Lois, wanna a cup of coffee? I just made it," Lush holds up the French press.

"Sure, Miss Richardson. I like it black."

I take my cup as Lush pours out two more cups of coffee, hands one to Lois, and takes the other. We proceed out to the private table on the north side of the terrace. We all sit down. Lush is carrying a packet of Treasurers and pulls out one.

"Anyone care for one?"

"Thanks, but those look a little too fancy for me," Lois says with a half grin and pulls out a packet of Camels. She sees me looking at them.

"Have one, Mr. Hampton," she says as she hands the pack to me.

"Thanks, Lois, I will. Please, just call me Philip."

"Okay, Philip."

Lush lights her cigarette and passes the lighter to Lois who picks it up, observes it, and says as she lights her cigarette, "Nice lighter, Miss Richardson. Never seen one so pretty as this." She passes the lighter to me.

"Thanks, Lois. It was a gift. Please, just call me Lush. It's a nickname, but it's what I prefer." Lois smiles at her, shaking her head and blows out a stream of smoke. I light my Camel and inhale deeply.

"Well, what kind of information are you looking for?" She sits back in her chair, picks up her cup and takes a sip of coffee.

"Lois, I won't rest until I find out who did this to Billy. I just can't sit around waiting for the police. I just can't. Lush and I both are investigative journalists. It's sorta in our blood to find things out."

"Well, I can't blame you for that. You get tangled up with the police, you never know how things will turn out," she says, eyes downcast toward her cigarette.

"Lois, do you know anything about Billy's drug use or sexual habits?" Lush leans over toward her.

"Wow. I sorta figured you might be asking that," she replies, still looking down.

"Well, do you Lois?" Lush asks again. "We need to know. Information about either one could help us find the murderer."

Lois sighs, sets her cigarette in an ashtray, pulls at the side seams of the grey dress and says, "Look, I've had my run-ins with the police before, but I've never been charged with a felony, never done time. I know where to get just about any drug you want, but I sure as hell ain't revealing my sources to you all or anybody else, especially the police. Of course, I won't be telling them any of this either. Billy asked me to get stuff for him sometimes. He was mainly interested in real good pot, hashish and good coke, nothing else. I know he was gay and everything, but I don't think he did all those fag drugs: Tina, Special K, G, and Ecstasy. He was the best dude. Whenever I'd get him anything, he'd always give me part of it as a tip, along with a couple of one hundred dollar bills."

"Thanks Lois. We certainly will not tell anyone, especially the police about this," I say. "So, you don't think there's a drug connection in all this?"

"Other than some bastard used a drug to kill him. No, Billy was always far away from the big dealers and suppliers. Besides, he wasn't that big of a user anyway. He never sold anything. Shit, he'd usually end up giving most of it away. I've helped out at parties here where he'd spend a couple of thousand on coke and never even have one snort."

I take a sip of coffee and take another drag. Lush studies me, then Lois, and asks. "Lois, what about his sexual behavior? Can you think of anything along those lines? Maybe somebody really famous he was fooling around with or some public official?"

"Gee, Lush, there were a lot of those. I never knew who might be walking around here bare ass naked in the morning. I mean rich and famous people like sex just like the rest of the world. Billy trusted me and compensated me real good to keep those things private. You know, he really trusted me. I never let him down, not once. If I had noticed anything strange, like someone angry with him when I saw them, or whatever, I'd tell you. Mostly those people, you know, they're usually very used to servants. I was nothing more than a wall figure or a body to 'do this', 'do that', 'get me this', or 'get me that'. Billy wasn't that way, but most of the famous ones were. The other ones, the ones not rich or famous, were just usually overwhelmed by the digs here. I mean, how many people in the world get to screw in a place like this?"

Lois is laughing now. Lush looks confused and ask, "What's so funny, Lois?"

"Oh, Lordy, I'm sorry mam, I mean, Lush. Billy is such a sweetheart. He let me bring my old man here. We had the place for almost a whole week. We were 'house sitting' for him." She chuckles and stubs out her cigarette in the ashtray. "Well, it was mainly to keep Clark company. Man, I love that dog. I kept telling him, I'd say, 'Billy you ever get tired of Mister Clark, you just send him my way. Yes siree. I need a dog like that in my neighborhood. Dog's got the heart of a lion and the soul of an angel.' He'd laugh and say, that's why I'm never gonna get rid of him, Lois."

"When did you house sit, Lois?" I ask because I don't remember Billy going anywhere for a week, especially since he'd been working so hard on this collection for the past two years.

"Well, it was last year, second week of March, I believe. You know, that is kind of a strange thing. Billy didn't want a soul to know about this trip. That's why he didn't leave Clark with the Gustersons downstairs. I had to promise to only use the service elevator to his unit. He gave all the doormen big, big tips to keep their mouths shut, too. He especially didn't want Miss Morgan to know."

I'm stunned. I look at Lois and ask, "Do you know where he went, Lois?"

She looks down at her feet and lets out a big sigh. "Philip, he gave me a thousand dollars to keep it a secret." She looks up at me, then says, "But I guess I better tell you. He went to Dubai. He said he wanted someone to know in case someone needed to get in touch with him. All the doormen knew I could get a hold of him. I don't know the name of the place he was staying, but it's that big hotel that looks like a sailboat. He showed me a picture when he got back."

"The Burj Al Arab," Lush says.

"Yeah, that's it," Lois says as she lights another cigarette.

"What the hell was he doing in Dubai?" Lush squints her eyes as she looks up toward the sun. "At least he picked the best place to stay."

"I'll be damned," I add, "He never said a word to me about Dubai, and he knew I'd been there several times. That's really strange. Lois, did he tell you why he was going?"

"Yeah. He said it was private research for these paintings he was working on."

"Private research, what kind?" I ask.

"Dunno, that's all he told me."

Lush looks at me, then asks Lois, "How long was he gone?"

"Well, he left on a Sunday and got back on that Friday. He had to be back by that weekend for some function of some sort."

"So strange," I say. "Lois, have you seen any of his new works?"

"Yes, but I never bothered him much when he was working. They are mostly paintings of naked people. That's all I could make of them. I'm not really into art."

"Did you see any of the models?" Lush asks.

"No, he used them mainly at night, then worked from photographs or sketches."

Lush lights another Treasurer, stares into Lois's brown eyes and asks, "So Lois, how long have you known about Billy's secret room?"

"Oh Lord, Rocky, my old man. Me and him had us a good ole time in there," she looks down laughing and stretches her feet out. She has on white hose and white work shoes. "But, no, seriously, he showed it to me about a year after I started working here, after he got to know me a bit. Just wanted me to clean it good once a week."

"Did you ever find anything unusual or out of the ordinary in there?" I ask.

"Uh, well I'd say the whole damn thing is pretty unusual and out of the ordinary," she laughs hard, a deep, gravelly laugh, followed by a smoker's cough. "Excuse me, but, not really, just towels, a couple of times a little blood or shit stains on them, not much, you know, spooge on the mirror sometimes, that's all."

Lush's attention is fixed on Lois and she asks, "Lois, I'm dying to know. What exactly did you and Rocky do in there?"

"Oh honey, you never tried it hanging in a harness? It's just one a those things you need to do before you die."

"I'll keep that in mind, thanks."

"Lois, do you know anything else about this trip or anything else at all that seemed strange or odd?" I ask.

"Honestly, Philip, I can't think of anything. I mean when Rocky and me was driving back from Atlantic City yesterday and heard the news on the radio, well Rocky, he said, 'Well I'll be Goddamned', and me, well I was just shocked."

"Yes, all of us were. Well, Lois, Lush and I greatly appreciate you being so truthful with us. You can count on us to keep everything on the hush. I'm pretty sure you know how to handle the police. I expect they'll want to talk to you today. They're coming here at two.""It's all fine. You know, I'd do anything for Billy. I can tell you and him are from the same mold—decent men. They broke most of them molds, I tell you."

"Thanks Lois. You're a life saver for us, agreeing to work through Saturday, and getting a friend to help."

"Shoot. I wouldn't miss that wake for the world."

"Lois, you and your friend bring your street clothes. When it's time for the wake to start, I want you there as a guest, not as a worker. The caterer can handle the wake. I know that's what Billy would want."

"Oh, that's really nice Philip. I'll do that. But don't you worry any. We'll have this place shining like a new nickel before the wake and clean enough to eat off the floor come Saturday. Lord knows your Fatgram would have it that way."

"Fatgram?" I ask.

"I feel like I know that woman. What a character she was. Me and her woulda got alone mighty fine. Billy used to tell me stories about her all the time. Cracked me up. Like the time she caught you and Billy sneaking in the liquor cabinet. And she says, 'Well that's just fine, you all are big boys, so we're just gonna have us our own little cocktail party. Go get the Monopoly board.' And then she set you all down, and made you both drink bourbon and play Monopoly with her until you both started puking."

Lois starts laughing and smacking her thighs with her hands. Lush can't help but join her, so I give in and laugh too and say, "Well, that's a true story. I was just fourteen, but I was always careful with booze after that. Hardly ever touched it until college. No wonder I'm only good for about three drinks. Fatgram's discipline methods might not set well with today's child rearing standards, but, I'll have to say, they worked on us."

"I hear you," Lois says, "Yeah, whenever Billy wanted something looking really good, like me polishing Fatgram's antique furniture that time he was expecting to 'receive' members of the royal family, he'd say with a phony British accent, 'Now me lady, let's see if your efforts of servitude pass the Ina B. Robertson white glove inspection'. That would always tickle me to death. Anyway, I'm sure he's with her now. I know they'll both be here in spirit on Friday, so you can count on me to make it right."

"Lois, thanks so much. Thanks for everything." I feel like giving her a hug, but she doesn't seem the hugging type, or the handshake type either, so I just smile.

"Well, I better get on the bedrooms now. Thanks for the coffee, Lush."

"You're welcome, Lois. Thanks for all your help."

Lois takes her coffee cup, gets up, and heads back inside.

"We're on our way, Todge," Lush smiles at me.

"Yeah, Lois was a gold mine. Will you check all his credit cards, Lush?"

"Did it this morning, nothing about a trip to Dubai—unless he has a credit card we don't know about."

"Not likely. I suppose he could have done the whole thing with cash or travelers checks?"

"True, but he was really going out of his way to keep it a secret then. Does that sound like Billy, Todge?"

"No, it doesn't. Well, maybe someone else footed the bill?"

"I think you're on to something, but who?"

"Don't have a clue, Lush. Maybe a member of the royal family?"

"Yeah, right. Well, at least we have a beginning. I have a feeling our meetings this afternoon will reveal more."

"Me too. Who knows, we may be headed for Dubai soon."

Lush gives me her biggest smile. "How thrilling, Todge, I've wanted to go there for some time now. I suppose we will have to stay at the Burj Al Arab, since it would be central to the investigation?"

"Suppose you're right, dear." She claps her hands, and I can clearly see the little girl in her, and for a brief moment, I feel good and warm inside.

Clark comes running up to us. In his wake the children, Emma, followed by Andrew, followed by Peter, converge upon us.

"Philip, you sure you can't go to the Lion King with us?" Emma asks in a pouting tone and touches my right knee.

"Darling, nothing would make me happier. But, as you know, we're going to have over five hundred people here in two days. I just want to make sure everything is perfect for Billy's wake. You can understand that, can't you?"

"Yes, I suppose so," and she runs over to Lush who pulls her up in her lap. "Lush says you invited us back and that you promise to show us everything in New York."

"That's one hundred percent true. We just need to talk it over with your parents and decide when the best time is. Maybe later this summer or in the early fall before it gets too cold," I reply.

"Yippee," Emma claps her hands and then says, "Philip, don't you and Lush know smoking is bad for you?"

"Yes, Emma, we do. And we both are trying to quit. I think we will be able to soon." Lush smiles and hugs Emma.

"Are you guys excited about the show today?" I ask.

"Yeah, I know all the music already. I can even play some of it on the piano," Peter proudly states.

"I didn't know you played piano, Peter. Surely, you noticed the beautiful grand in the living room?" I ask.

"Well, yeah, but Mom told me not to disturb anyone, considering what happened to Billy and all," he replies patting Clark on the head who is panting and wagging his tail, waiting for attention.

"Maybe you can play a song for us before you leave today?" Lush asks.

"Uhmm, well, let me go ask Mom," and he takes off back to the kitchen. Clark runs after him.

"Drew, do you play anything?" I ask.

"Yeah, soccer."

"Oh. I see. You're the family athlete?"

"Well. Peter's bigger and he can run faster, but I can handle a soccer ball better."

"Are you in a league?"

"Well, yeah. Dad's the coach of our team."

"He is? Wow. I knew he liked soccer, but I never knew he played it."

"Sure he did, when he was a kid. He's good." Andrew moves all around as he talks, full of nervous energy.

"Do you kids go to the same school?" Lush asks.

"Yes," Emma replies, "We all go to the Mary Institute and St. Louis Country Day School."

"Oh, do you like it?" Lush asks and opens her eyes wide toward me and mouths the word 'money.'

"I like school a lot," Emma says.

"Yeah, it's okay," Drew says and pulls a blue Yo Yo out of his pocket, puts the string loop on the middle finger of his left hand and starts to play with it. To my surprise, the Yo Yo lights up with blinking lights as it spins.

"I know Dad taught you how to do that, didn't he Drew?"

"Yeah, he's good with Yo Yo's. He can do all sorts of things with them."

"So you're left handed, Drew?" I ask.

"Yes."

"What about Emma and Peter?" I ask looking at Emma.

"No, they both are right handed," he replies.

Peter comes running back, breathing heavily, "Mom says I can play one song for you guys. I'm gonna play, 'Can You Feel the Love Tonight'."

"Great," I say, "Let's go inside."

We all walk into the living room and sit down on a big sofa near the piano. Clark walks over with Peter. Peter looks at the large grand piano and says, "We've got a couple like this at school." He pulls out the bench, sits down, and opens the lid. Clark lies down near him. Peter looks at the keys and begins to play. I'm really surprised because he plays very well and what sounds to me like an intricate version. I look at Lush and whisper, "He's quite good." Then, I'm astonished as he begins to sing the piece. His voice has not yet started to change, so it is the clear soprano of a child, and it is strong and on perfect pitch. Emma and Andrew watch their brother with what appears to me to be admiration. Lush is clearly pleased. His manner around me has been the most reserved of the children, even bordering on shyness, but not now. Peter is an animated and gifted performer, his hands move over the keys in fluid, sweeping motions, and he fearlessly soars into the high notes. He is definitely in his element. I am suddenly struck by the thought that Fatgram would love to see this performance. She always encouraged Billy and me to play the piano, but neither one of us ever got past simple pieces. It even sounds to me as if he embellishes the piano part somewhat. He delivers a beautiful ending to the song and we all jump up and clap. I look behind me and see Brenda and Dad and a young woman with short brown hair in grey pin stripe slacks and jacket with a white blouse clapping. I didn't hear them arrive during the performance.

"Peter, I'm overwhelmed. I had no idea you were so talented. That was really, really good. Thank you so much," I say as I walk over and pat him on the back. He smiles up at me and says, "Thanks," in a soft voice which is the antithesis of his powerful singing voice.

"Peter, you belong on Broadway, dear," Lush says. "That was just remarkable."

"Yes, he can even play by his ears," Emma adds.

"Darling, you mean, 'play by ear'," Brenda says.

I look at Dad and see the happiest expression on his face I've seen in years. He really loves these children, and I can tell his care and nurturing of them, along with Brenda's, is paying off. The children get along with each other, they are polite, they converse easily with adults, they dress themselves well, and they respect their parents. I am thankful for them all, and I'm glad I told Dad and Brenda about Adrian so that they will even be better able to protect these great kids. I walk over to the officer and shake hands.

"Hello, I'm Philip Hampton."

"Officer Peggy Graham, NYPD," she replies as she firmly shakes my hand and says, "Pleased to meet you." She looks around me toward Peter and says, "Very nice performance, Peter."

"Thank you."

"I have a seven year old son who has just started taking piano lessons. I hope he'll be as good as you someday," she says.

"Well, if he practices everyday, he'll be good, well pretty good after, well, after maybe three or four years," he replies. The adults all laugh.

"Well, Peter, I'll make sure he does. Thanks for the advice," Officer Graham says.

"Alright children," Brenda says, "Go to the restroom if you need to, grab a jacket, and let's get going." The children disperse with Clark trailing after them.

"Son, Officer Graham says we are all fine by ourselves so long as we stay together. So, I've hired a car to drive us up to the theatre district. We're going to walk around a bit, find a place for lunch, then go to the show. The driver will pick us up after the show and bring us back."

"Great, Dad. You sure you feel comfortable with this?"

"I do. Brenda does too."

"Okay, what time will you be back?" Lush asks.

"By five thirty at the latest," Brenda says. "Philip, if it's alright with you, I'd love to cook dinner tonight. I thought tomorrow night we'd be too busy getting ready for Friday."

"That would be great. Are you sure?"

"I would love to. I already ordered all the groceries this morning. They'll deliver them by three pm. We're having a Bibb lettuce salad with pears and stilton; pan roasted, free range chicken breasts with a sage, shallot, vermouth sauce; a wild and long grain white rice pilaf; an assortment of roasted vegetables; and New York style cheesecake with fresh strawberries."

"Geez, Brenda, that sounds great. Is there anything we can do to help?" Lush asks.

"No thanks, Lush, I know you all have a million things to do in preparation for Friday. Charles and the kids are great sous chefs. We all work well together in the kitchen, and we'd like to do this for you all."

"Where did Peter get his talent?" I direct to Brenda.

"We have no idea, no one on my side is musical and Charles says no one on his side is either. But, I'll tell you this Philip, Peter was able to whistle melodies before he could talk. I have no idea how he learned that; he just started doing it one day. I thought there was a bird loose in the nursery, and to my amazement, it was little Peter."

"Extraordinary," I reply. "Does he read music too?"

"Oh yes, quite well. He's made it clear, he intends to pursue this for a career. But I really think he's a lucky boy, because it really is his passion," she replies.

"Son, he's already written orchestral pieces," Dad proudly states.

"Good Heavens," Lush says and turns to Dad and Brenda. "He belongs at Julliard." Dad and Brenda look at each other and smile. "What are you two thinking?" Lush asks.

"Well, it's just that Peter knew he has a half brother in Manhattan, and he's been fantasizing for the past couple of years that he could come live with Billy, go to a school in Manhattan and enroll in the pre-College department of Julliard which meets on weekends from September through May," Dad says.

"Lord," I reply, "Would you all even consider that?"

"It would be a difficult thing for us all, but you heard him playing and singing. He is gifted and they're not that many people in St. Louis capable of teaching him a lot at this point," Brenda says.

"I've pretty much made up my mind to relocate here, Dad. Let's talk about this some more. Lush has also decided she needs a change and she's moving up here, too. Maybe we can work something out."

"Thanks, son. I appreciate it. Maybe we can explore this a little later on."

"Right, I mean, good. Okay you guys, go see the city and have a good time," I say as the kids come back in ready to go.

"Let's go," Dad says. Clark's ears perk up and he wags his tail in anticipation of going out and he runs to the elevator door and sits, turning his head back to look at everyone approaching.

"Hey, little guy," I say and bend over him, "You're gonna stay here with Lush and me and Officer Graham. Okay?" His good ear folds against his head and he begins to whine.

"What time is it?" I ask, realizing I haven't worn my watch since Sunday.

"Twelve o'clock," Lush states.

"Good," I reply, "I've got time to take C-L-A-R-K to the D-O-G R-U-N," I say. Clark immediately lets out a shrill bark and jumps up, putting his front paws on my waist. "I guess he really can spell," I say as everyone laughs.

Dad pushes the elevator call button and the door opens. "Is your car already downstairs?" I ask.

"Yes, they rang while Peter was playing."

"Okay, have fun, everyone," I say.

"Enjoy your afternoon," Lush says.

"Remember, stay together, and use the buddy system when going to the restroom," Officer Graham admonishes.

The door starts to close once my Dad's family is inside, and, at the last minute before the doors close completely, Clark rushes in. The door shuts. Lush, Officer Graham, and I break out laughing. The door opens immediately and Clark is sitting down in front of everyone. He looks at me with a canine guilty expression like I've just caught him taking a bite out of the Thanksgiving turkey. Everyone laughs. I bend over and pull him into the foyer by his collar.

"I know you want to go with them, buddy, but just wait a minute, and I'm gonna take you out," I say. He looks happy again.

"Bye, bye, goodbye," several voices converge as the elevator door shuts again.

"Todge, I'll go with you and Clark. I need some fresh air. Then we can come back and have a sandwich before Nurse Ostro and Julianna get here," Lush says.

"Great, I'll go get some treats, his leash and some poop bags," I say. Then, I look at Officer Graham, "Guess you'll be coming along, too?"

"Yes sir, but don't mind me, I'll just tag along behind. You'll never even know I'm there."

I smile at her and say, "Thanks, it's good to know. With an undercover officer packing a piece and a fearless pit bull, I think we'll be about as safe as one can be in this city."

"Amen," Lush says. "I'll be right back. I wanna put on a pair of jeans and some comfortable walking shoes"

"Good idea, I better put on some tennis shoes too," I say and head to Billy's room as Clark trails behind me whimpering in high tones of anticipation.

Today is another beautiful day but a few degrees cooler. A cold front passed through during the night, rinsed the city with showers and moved out to sea. Clark leads the way with determination and a prancing gait as we head toward the Hudson River Park. He is completely street savvy—stopping at the appropriate times at cross walks, nonchalantly weaving among pedestrians, and turning his full attention to other dogs passing by.

"Lush, look at the muscles in Clark's hind legs," I say, "They're rock hard and big."

"I know; he's compact, but he's a tank," she replies.

"I bet he could jump over something six or seven feet high."

"Oh, I'm sure he could, Todge."

"Have you seen Officer Graham, Lush?"

She pauses, turns around to look back, and says, "I don't see her at all, but I bet she's looking at us right this minute."

"Yeah, you're probably right. Do you think the murderer would really come after me, Lush?"

"I can't imagine why. Unless there's more you haven't told me yet." She pulls her sunglasses down and gives me a serious stare.

"I've told you everything. At least everything I can think of. I just can't figure out what Benny took out of the safe. Elliott Fields must have known what it was. Otherwise why did they kill him, too?"

"Yes, I'm been pondering the same thing. It could have been photographs, letters, receipts, recordings, who knows? The only thing is though, with today's technology, everything digital and the Internet, it seems to me it couldn't have been any of those things, because it would have been so easy to copy them."

"That's a good point. I'm stuck on this one. I do hope Billy's psychiatrist, Dr. Gerard, comes Friday. I'd like to chat with him a bit. If he doesn't, I'm going to make an appointment with him."

"Good, Todge, although I'm sure the police have already talked to him. I know the general consensus of courts and liability insurance carriers is that psychiatrists have a 'duty to warn' victims or potential victims of possible violent acts by patients. In this case, if Billy knew he was in danger or that Elliott Fields was, surely Dr. Gerard would have done something?"

"I dunno, but we're gonna find out."

"Todge, I've opened dozens of Billy's files, emails, photos, letters, spreadsheets, you name it. I haven't found anything that would give us a clue yet."

"Thanks, Lush, we'll just have to keep searching."

We stop at another crosswalk. Clark is happily panting. He turns around to check on us, then moves to the curb to wait. I scan the streets looking for Officer Graham, but I do not see her.

"Boy, I just don't understand why we don't see Officer Graham. She made us tell her our exact route, but you'd think we'd a least get a glimpse of her," I remark to Lush.

"Yeah, she's the amazing invisible detective." We both laugh.

We walk for thirty minutes, decide to get hot dogs and Cokes from a street vendor for lunch, cigarettes for dessert, and make our way back to Billy's. We window shop, look at restaurant menus, chat about nothing in particular with no mention of Billy, but underlying all our thoughts and actions, the hunt for the truth pushes us and several others forward.

CHAPTER 16

We return to Billy's building with our minds clearer and Clark satisfied, although I promise him I'll take him as soon as I can to Central Park where he can run off lead. Even though he is so obedient, I sense he craves the chance to run at will—all of us deserve this.

I notice there is no doorman at the front desk. Nurse Ostro sits on one of the leather sofas in the lobby clutching a black leather purse in her lap. She does not appear as obese as I recall, and I mentally attribute this to her outfit—a dark brown pants suit and a white blouse with a ruffled front. I approach her and extend my hand.

"Miss Ostro, thank you so much for coming. I hope we haven't kept you waiting long?"

She stands up, shakes my hand and replies, "Oh no, Mr. Hampton. I'm early, it's just one fifteen now."

"Good. Miss Ostro, this is my good friend Sarah Richardson from Louisville."

"Pleased to meet you, Miss Richardson."

"Nice to meet you, too, Miss Ostro."

Clark walks over to her, sniffs her feet, sniffs her purse, and wags his tail inviting her to pet him as she tugs at the tail of her blouse, making sure it is straight and even around her girth.

"And who is this lovely creature?" she asks and leans over to pat his head.

"This is Billy's dog, Clark." I say.

"Well hello, Clark. Mind if I give him a treat?""Not at all," I reply. She opens her purse, pulls out a plastic bag containing small dog biscuits in a variety of colors, opens the bag, and pulls out one.

"Can you sit, Clark?" He immediately sits, and she feeds him the treat.

"What a good boy you are. I can tell you're a smart dog." He holds up his right paw for her to shake. "Oh, you wanna shake hands? Well that deserves another treat." She gives him another treat, pats his head and puts the treats back into her purse.

"Appears you are a dog lover, Miss Ostro," Lush says.

"Oh yes, I have Harry and Sally, two mixed breeds I got from the pound about eight years ago. They're a little smaller than Clark. Love them dearly." She opens her purse again, pulls out a slim leather case, and opens it to reveal two pictures of the dogs, both shaggy long hair mixes with pointy noses and big ears sticking straight up.

"How adorable," Lush remarks.

"Cute dogs. They look like good companions," I say smiling.

"The best," she smiles as she puts the pictures back in her purse.

"Well, Miss Ostro, let's go on up," I say pointing toward the elevator.

"Fine. But please just call me Janet."

"Agreed, so long as you call me Philip."

"Okay, Philip, it's a deal."

"Well, I want in on this too. Janet, call me Lush."

"Lush, of course, what an unusual name?" She smiles at Lush.

"Yes, it's a nickname Philip started in college. It spread like wildfire among my friends and has stuck. I rather like it now. You'll observe I call him Todge quite often, a reciprocal nickname I gave him in college."

"Well, I guess you all go way back?" We walk into the elevator and as the door closes I see Officer Graham talking on her mobile phone as she enters the lobby. I wonder if she knows who Nurse Ostro is.

"Yes, we met as freshmen at the University of North Carolina. We were both journalism majors, and we both ended up staying on after graduating and getting our Masters in journalism," Lush replies.

"Oh, so you're a journalist too, Lush?"

"Only by education. I've spent most of my career as a residential real estate agent in Louisville. But if I had it all to do again, I definitely would have pursued a career in journalism."

"Well, I know how you feel, but you're a young woman, and you know it's never too late to change."

"Well, as a matter of fact, I've begun to give that serious thought lately."

"Although I truly enjoy being a nurse, I'm much more passionate about art, but nursing has always enabled me to have a livelihood."

"Yes, Philip told me you're also an artist."

"Well, I wouldn't say that, but I am studying and practicing." She smiles as the elevator stops. "Some day I'll get there."

We walk into the foyer and into the living room.

"Oh my," Janet gasps. "Please forgive me. This is. Well this has to be the most beautiful room I've ever been in. My Lord, look at the paintings." Janet rotates her entire body as she takes in the room and its bounty of art.

"Please feel free to examine anything," I offer.

"Thank you, Philip. I'm overwhelmed. It's so beautiful. But, well I'm here to answer your questions, not to ogle your brother's wonderful art." Lush and I laugh.

"Ogle it all you desire, Janet. It's meant to be enjoyed." Lush says. "Can I get you anything to drink?"

"Thank you so much. I'm fine."

"Please, have a seat, Janet," I say as I direct her to a large wingback chair facing a sofa. She sits down and Lush and I settle on the sofa.

"Mr. Hamp..., excuse me, Philip. Again, I am so sorry about your brother." That expression of concern and compassion she portrayed in the hospital shapes her face again, and I think how much I really like this woman. "As you know, when he came to us, he was in a particularly dire condition from which there was little or no hope of recovery. My heart just melted when I found out who he was—such a beautiful and talented young man. It just never occurred to me in a million years that someone might enter the unit to harm him." Her eyes are tearing up. "Excuse me, please," she says and opens her purse and pulls out a tissue. As she dabs her eyes she says, "I thought it odd that that computer technician came in with a work request. None of us remember requesting it, and there were no notes about it on the schedule. Nothing was on the blink. All systems were go," she says and looks up smiling through her tears. "Anyway, it appeared to be a valid work order to update some of the software on our system. He told us we might lose video surveillance for a minute or two on some cameras, but not to worry they'd come back on after a minute."

"What did he look like?" I ask in an urgent tone.

"Well, he was a young Asian man. He looked more like a teenager. Extremely nice looking, and had a lovely British accent. He joked around with us. Very pleasant."

"Have you identified him to the police?"

"Why yes I have."

"Did they tell you his name?" Lush asks.

"No, I just identified him from a photo. He told me his name was Meng and he was Chinese but had been raised in Singapore."

I flip open my newest phone on which we downloaded everything before going to the police yesterday and find the photo from Elliott Fields. I show it to Janet.

"Yes, that's the young man," she says. What's he doing with that rope?"

"Getting ready to murder Elliott Fields," I reply.

She gasps and puts her right hand on her chest, "Oh my, yes, I heard he'd been murdered, too. That just goes to show. It's so hard to read people. Although I was suspicious of the work order, I never would have pegged him for a murderer. He was so friendly."

"Interesting," Lush states. "He wasn't that way around us. Not at all."

"Oh, you've met him, too?"

"Well, he was employed by the caterer Billy uses who sent us dinner Monday night. He never said a word. Clark certainly didn't like him. While we were all out on the terrace after dinner, he knocked out the other waiter, broke into Billy's safe and stole something," I explain.

"Dear Lord," Janet exclaims, "What kind of criminal is this?"

"The kind working for someone else. At least that's our theory," Lush replies. "How did he manage to get into Billy's cubicle to inject the GHB?"

"Well, a little before ten o'clock he was working and said he had to use the rest room and that he'd be right back. I had just completed rounds and was making notes in the system. He didn't return after about five minutes so I looked up and noticed that Billy's camera was off. I looked at the screen, saw that it had been turned off, you know on the software, and I clicked it back on. It immediately turned on. To my horror, I saw Billy was in convulsions," She pauses a moment and her eyes fill with tears.

"It's okay, Janet. I know you did everything in your power to save Billy," I say. "He must have just started the convulsions when the camera came back on because none of the other alarms had gone off yet. We spent the next thirty minutes with Billy. I totally forgot about Meng until the police contacted me."

"Did the police dust for finger prints on the keyboards or anywhere?" I ask.

"No, Meng, or whoever he is, put on latex gloves. I didn't think anything of it. You know, that's not unusual in a hospital."

"Of course," I reply, "Did he say anything else about himself, anything that could give us a clue at all who he really is?"

"No. He just said he felt sorry for all the patients in the unit. He said he'd lived in New York for two years to attend a computer school and had just started at St. Vincent's."

"Did he seem to know what he was doing on the computer system?" Lush asks.

"Oh yes, he had to have an administrative password to get in. I have no idea how someone outside the hospital could get that." Janet replies.

"It's amazing how resourceful high tech criminals can be," Lush says.

"Well, I don't think I've been much help to you, but everything happened so fast that morning," Janet says and sighs.

"Janet, you've been very helpful, and I can not thank you enough for taking time to come here," I say to her. She smiles and I see her eyes moving toward the paintings.

"Listen, let me fix you something to drink, and I'll show you around. I think you'll enjoy the art," Lush says.

"Well, if it wouldn't be an inconvenience, I'd love a cup of hot tea."

"Good. What do you take in it?"

"A little cream and sugar."

"I'll be back in a minute. Philip, care for anything?"

"Hot tea would be great, Lush. Cream and sugar, also."

As Lush leaves the room, the phone rings. It's the doorman notifying me that Officer Graham wants to come up. I tell him it's okay.

"Janet, have a look around at the art in here, then go into the dining room through there. We have an officer who's keeping an eye on the place because of the two murders. I'm gonna go meet her."

"Thanks, Philip," she says as she pulls a case containing reading glasses from her purse. "I'll be very careful. I know these are masterpieces."

I laugh, "Please enjoy them. If you have any questions, I'll try to answer them."

"Thank you," she stands and heads for the fireplace.

Clark and I head to the foyer as the elevator door opens and Officer Graham steps out.

"Hello, Mr. Hampton. Did you all enjoy your walk?" Clark tries to jump up on her. She bends over to pet him.

"We did, thank you. We looked for you, but never saw you. Were you trailing us?"

She smiles. "I was. I remained in the background, taking photos. Already sent them to an analyst."

"What are you looking for?"

"Well, mainly if anyone, besides me, was following or observing you."

"Did you see anyone?"

"I didn't, but if there was someone, I'm hoping the camera caught them."

"Interesting. Will you let me know if you find anyone?"

"Of course. Why is Nurse Ostro here?"

"Oh, well, I invited her to look at Billy's art. I found out that she's an artist herself. She was so good to Billy and me at the hospital. Well, I just thought it was a nice thing to do."

"I see. So it has nothing to do with your own investigation?" She smiles as she asks this.

"I'm not sure I follow you, Officer Graham."

"Oh please, Mr. Hampton. We are aware that you and Mrs. Richardson are trying to solve these murders yourselves. That's a very risky business. We advise against it. You may unknowingly interfere with our investigation process. Detectives Johnson and Bell asked me to bring this up with you."

"Officer Graham. I've been an investigative journalist my entire career. Never once, have I interfered with a police investigation and I do not intend to now, even though it involves the murders of my brother

and his boyfriend. I do, however, intend to collect any information I can to satisfy my need to know exactly why this happened. I don't see any harm in that."

"Well, Mr. Hampton. We are aware of your expertise and ability in your field. We fully expect you to share any information you obtain that affects this case."

"Absolutely, you'll be the first to know."

"Good. Is the housekeeper, Lois Macpherson, here?"

"Yes she is. You want me to get her?"

"No. Detective Johnson and Detective Bell want to interview her when they arrive with the investigation unit at two."

"That's fine. I'll let her know. Can I get you anything to drink?"

"No thank you. I'll sit out here and work on my laptop."

"Alright, but please make yourself at home."

"Thank you."

Clark and I walk down the hall into the kitchen where Lush is making tea.

"They're on to us," I whisper.

"Who, the cops?" she whispers back.

"Yeah, Officer Graham just told me they know we are conducting our own investigation. She politely told me that we'd better not interfere with theirs, but that they expected us to share any and all information."

"Imagine that," she whispers in a sarcastic tone.

"Lush, I don't think Julianna should be here when the police are here. What do you think?"

"My first reaction is to agree with you. But on second thought…" she pauses.

"Yes," I say.

"On second thought, what's keeping them from confiscating all of Billy's paintings if they think they may provide clues? Maybe it's better to let them hear the story Julianna has to tell through his art?"

"True, but if she reveals something, they might take it anyway. I can't bear the thought of them taking his paintings," I reply.

"Well then, you better get on the phone to her and postpone the meeting."

"Do you think the police have bugged this place?"

"No, we're not suspects."

"They seem to know an awful lot about us."

"Well, Todge, that is their job, now, isn't it?"

"Shit!" I say.

"What?" Lush asks.

"I'm not gonna postpone the meeting. Officer Graham will tell Johnson and Bell in a heartbeat when Julianna arrives. She knew exactly who Nurse Ostro was."

"You're right. I suppose we have to let the chips fall where they may."

"Right. We'll just say Julianna is here to help us plan for Billy's posthumous showing of his last works."

"Sounds good," Lush says and pours boiling water into three teacups and puts in the teabags.

"Billy really has the best of everything," Lush states. "These are PG Tips tea bags from England."

"Oh, we've been using those for years," I reply.

"What?"

"You know how southerners like their sweet iced tea. Well, Uncle Adrian challenged Mother and Ala Mary to a sweet tea making contest years ago. He loathed iced tea, would only drink hot tea. Anyway, Ala Mary and Mother used their Tetley tea bags and Uncle Adrian pulled out PG Tips from his suitcase, only

it was loose tea. They each made a gallon of iced tea. Uncle Adrian won, hands down. Even Ala Mary conceded. We've been using PG Tips ever since."

"Amazing." She looks up at me, examining my face.

"What?" I ask.

"Well, Todge. I guess you have good memories of Uncle Adrian, too?"

I feel my stomach wrench and I grimace. "Lush, this all has just torn me up: inside and out. Yeah, I have good memories, great memories in fact." A vision of Billy, Uncle Adrian, and me sitting at the movies, sharing popcorn, and having a great time, just three best buddies, flashes through my mind. We're watching Indiana Jones and the Temple of Doom for the third time this summer. Billy is enthralled with Indiana Jones's kid sidekick, Short Round. That summer, Uncle Adrian dreamed up amazing stories based on the Indiana Jones character and would design and orchestrate elaborate treasure hunts for us. We would set off on these expeditions with Billy and me on our ponies and Uncle Adrian on Fatgram's horse, Whinny. Uncle Adrian had gone to great extremes to plant secret clues and maps revealing hidden treasurers. He must have given the farm workers money, including the regulars and migrant workers at peach harvest, because they were often involved and could reveal important clues. We would spend a whole day, sometimes two days doing this. We were always rewarded with something special, like real gold coins or jewelry we'd give to Mother or Fatgram. At some point along the way, the quest would involve a Blood Brothers ritual. Even in his big dark New York apartment, stuffed with all types of religious art and relics, he'd mastermind treasure hunts for us. We had our own bedroom there with bunk beds he had built into a tall wooden structure that resembled a tree house with decking around both beds—Billy and I would alternate nights in the top bunk. He also gave each of us our own beautiful, wooden treasure chests, each with a bottom drawer to hold the secret maps and messages he'd leave for us and a top compartment with a rotary lock which we could set for our own personal combination so no one else, not even Uncle Adrian, could get inside. Billy and I never told Adrian, but we knew each other's codes—mine was 4444 and his was 8888."

"Philip, Philip. Are you okay?" Lush asks.

"Fine, fine. Just remembering. I need a smoke. Let's take our tea outside. I'll let Janet know."

"Okay, I'll meet you outside."

I head into the dining room and find Janet observing the Klimt.

"I've only seen Klimt's works in books and museums; never in a private home. I'm overwhelmed. What a genius he was."

"Yes, it's a wonderful painting; one of Billy's favorites. Lush and I thought it might be nice to have our tea on the terrace. Is that alright with you?"

"Of course. That's fine with me."

We go out on the terrace where Lush and Clark are waiting.

"It's warmed up a bit. Sit down and have some tea. Mind if we smoke, Janet?" Lush asks.

"Not at all. In fact, I'll join you." She sits down, opens her purse and pulls out a package of Dunhill International Lights.

"Nice cigarettes, Janet," Lush smiles and pulls out a Treasurer.

"Yes, but not quite as nice as yours, Lush," she smiles.

"I'll just stick to my Marlboros," I say. "I just can't compete with you ladies."

Janet laughs in a warm rich, infectious tone. Lush reaches over and lights Janet's cigarette, then mine. We all take drags and sip our tea. I feel very much at ease with Janet.

"Janet, how did you get to be both a nurse and an artist?" I ask.

"Oh dear. Well, I'm from a very large family, three brothers and four sisters. I'm the oldest, so by the time I was in first grade I was used to taking care of others. When I was twelve, my father's parents, who were elderly and in poor health, moved in with us. It was pretty much my responsibility to take care of

them when I wasn't in school because both my parents worked—had to in order to keep food on the table for twelve mouths."

"My goodness, that's a lot of people in one house," Lush says. "I hope you all got along?"

"Fortunately we did. We lived in a big, old, row house in Locust Point in Baltimore. It had four bedrooms: one for my parents, one for my grandparents, one for the boys and one for the girls. My parents were pretty strict and demanded order—an advantage in a house with only one bathroom. They're Polish Catholics. My grandparents spoke very little English."

"Is Ostro your family name?" Lush asks.

"Yes, but it's short for Ostrowski. My parents thought it would be easier on their kids to do that."

"So, taking care of your little brothers and sisters and your grandparents led you to a career in nursing?" I ask. Clark is stretched out on the slate patio by my feet. He groans loudly, stretches his legs, lifts his head, sneezes, then returns to his nap.

"Pretty much. My grades were okay in high school. I was accepted into a local junior college that had a pre-med program. At the time, medical school seemed like an unattainable goal for a fat Polish girl from a poor family. But nursing seemed within my reach. And really, caring for others is what attracted me most to the medical field. Lord knows nurses do this far better than most doctors. Some of my most satisfying moments in nursing have been in a volunteer program I participate in every other year which provides health care services to some of the poorest parts of Appalachia."

"How wonderful," Lush says. "But what about painting? Your love of art?"

"Well, I fell in love with the religious paintings in our Cathedral. I would sit at mass when I was a little girl and just study the artwork. I really wanted to paint, become an artist, but my father wouldn't allow it. Papa would say, 'No vay for my girl to make a living with painting.'"

"So you waited to pursue it after you left your family?" I ask.

"No. After I became a RN, I began working in Baltimore, still living at home. My brothers and sisters all grew up, and one by one got married and flew the coop. It was pretty obvious that I was destined to live my life out there caring for my parents as they aged. Don't get me wrong, I loved them very much, and I was glad to do it, but I had to have an outlet, so I started taking drawing classes at night and progressed into painting. I even set up a studio in what had been my brothers' bedroom."

"How long did you live there?" Lush asks, "I mean, I assume your grandparents and parents have passed away?"

"Yes, they have. Mama was the last to go. I had just turned thirty-five. I had saved practically every cent I had ever made and my siblings insisted that I take everything my parents had left, which wasn't a lot besides the house. Anyway, I decided I had to live in Manhattan to seriously pursue art, so I got a job at St. Vincent's and moved here. That was twelve years ago."

"So you really are pursuing your passion," Lush states.

"Yes I am. It has enabled me to learn so much and to realize I have so much more to learn." Janet smiles, sighs, and takes a sip of tea. "Well, I feel as if I've told you my life's story. I apologize. I really didn't mean to be so long-winded."

"Janet, please, don't apologize. I really enjoyed learning more about you. You were so kind to me and to Billy. I knew you had to be a really good person."

"Ditto for me," Lush says. "I liked you as soon as I laid eyes on you. I'm so glad you came by today, Janet, and I hope to see more of you while I'm in New York."

Janet beams and says, "Why that's so kind of you both. How long will you be staying in New York, Lush?"

"I think it's going to be a while, Janet. At least until we find Billy's murderer or murderers."

"Really. Well, if there's anything at all I can do to help out, please let me know. I really didn't know him, although I did meet him at one of his showings a couple of years ago. I just feel connected to him in some way now."

"Well, that's because you are, Janet," I say. "You cared for him, and you held his hand while he died. I just have to believe he knew and sensed that he had a person imbued with an essential goodness holding his hand as he died, indeed, an angel." I reach over and clasp Janet's left hand as my eyes filll with tears. She looks into my eyes and I feel her goodness and her pain pour into me, and, in this instance, I know what I can do for her. "Janet, Billy's friend and art representative Julianna Morgan is on the way here to walk us through his latest works. There are over fifty paintings. She tells me they are masterpieces. Please, stay with us for this?"

"Oh, Philip. I'd be honored. You are so kind. Thank you," she says as tears runs from the corners of her eyes and down her cheeks. I let go of her hand and she fishes in her purse for a tissue. She pulls out a small package, takes one, and offers Lush and me one.

"Well, I think we're building an invincible team, Todge," Lush says, wiping her own eyes. She looks over at Janet and asks, "That is, if now we have Janet on board?"

"Oh yes, Lush," Janet replies smiling, "Janet is on board."

"Great, more tea anyone?" Lush asks. Janet and I shake our heads. "No, well then, how about a swig of sherry as we review Billy's masterpieces?"

"Yes," I say, "Billy would certainly approve. What do you say, Janet?"

"Well, I'm sure it's cocktail hour somewhere on this planet."

"That-a-girl," I reply, "You sound like Fatgram, my grandmother. She definitely would approve. Let's go in."

We all stand up to go inside. Clark gets up, trots over to the grassy section and squats like a bitch to pee.

"When his bladder is really full, he pees like a female dog," I say. "Let's wait a minute until he finishes. He'll stop midstream if he sees us go inside."

"Speaking of which," Janet says, "may I use the facilities?"

"Certainly," Lush says. "When we go into the kitchen, there's a powder room right outside the door into the hallway."

Lois walks out onto the terrace as Clark finishes peeing. "Philip, Miss Morgan is on the way up."

"Thanks, Lois. Lois, this is Janet Ostro. Janet, this is Lois Macpherson." They exchange greetings and we head into the kitchen. Lois slips beside me and whispers, "Those detectives just grilled me for twenty minutes. Everything is A okay." She winks at me. I stop while Lush and Janet move on into the kitchen.

"Thanks, Lois."

"No problem. Also, the crime unit is in the 'secret room' right this minute."

"How long have they been in there?"

"They came with the detectives, so about twenty minutes."

"Thanks. I better leash Clark. No telling what he might do with so many unannounced strangers in the house."

"Good idea, Philip. I wouldn't want to be on that dog's bad side."

"Why? Have you ever seen him be real aggressive toward anyone?"

"No, but me and him are sorta the same, we got it in us if we need it."

I smile and say, "I don't doubt it one bit, Lois," and head in to get Clark's leash.

Lush is hand washing the teacups as I walk in. Lois follows me in, sees Lush and says, "Oh Lush, let me do that, honey."

"Thanks, Lois, I don't mind, I'm just about finished anyway. You can dry them and put them away, while I go get the sherry and glasses."

"Sure," Lois replies as she opens a drawer and takes out a dish towel.

I get Clark's leash and hook his collar to it. He prances all around, thinking he's going out for another walk.

"Not right now, boy. After dinner, maybe. Let's go see who's here."

Julianna sweeps into the kitchen with a dramatic entrance; attired in a beautiful light green cashmere sweater dress with matching jacket; a dazzling, large, silver necklace, which resembles a rope with a big knot tied in it, with matching bangles and earrings—I'm certain these have been created especially for her by some aspiring jewelry designer because Julianna can wear someone's design to just one party and put that designer on the map—high heel, leather pumps, the exact shade of green as her dress, and a large, darker green, crocodile leather purse which she pitches on the counter as she strides over to me and says as she embraces me, "Oh, Philip, darling. Whatever is the world coming to? Our darling, Billy. Now, Elliott Fields. What or who next?"

"I know, Julianna. Thanks for coming," I say as I embrace her, smelling some divine perfume she wears.

Clark knows her well and waits patiently for her to acknowledge him, which she does in one quick bend of her knees. I'm always amazed by her agility and gracefulness—unexpected characteristics of a woman who stands six feet one inch on her bare feet. She lets Clark lick her face and says to him, "Oh poor little pookie bear. I know you miss your daddy. So do I."

She gets up as quickly as she stoops down, turns around, sees Lois, and says, "Lois dear. Are you holding up all right?"

"Oh, Miss Morgan, I'm okay. I'm just gonna miss him so is all. That and I'd like to get my hands on the bastard that did this."

"As would I, Lois. Justice will prevail. I just have to believe that."

"Yes mam, I suppose, justice in some shape, form, or fashion," Lois replies looking at me.

Lush walks in carrying a tray with a bottle of sherry and four crystal glasses and says, "Julianna, dear, I thought I heard your voice. It's so good to see you again. I just wish it wasn't under these circumstances."

"You too, Lush, darling. You always manage to look marvelous. How are you?"

"Sad as hell, dear. And you?"

"The same."

"Well, as usual, you look like a million bucks, Julianna. That's an incredibly beautiful necklace."

"Thanks. It's a creation by a young Czech designer named Merick Skala. I adore his masculine designs, especially on women. His last name means 'strong as a rock'. I assure you he is."

"Well you certainly have the knack of really getting to know your artists, dear," Lush fires back with a tad of sarcasm that always flavors the verbal exchange between these two bona fide debutantes, one from the south and the other from the north.

"I ran into those two detectives in the lobby," Julianna turns toward me. "They were with several other plain clothes officers. They wanted to know when I could talk to them again. I told them tomorrow. They seemed really in a rush. I wonder if they have a lead on the case?"

"Interesting. I certainly hope so," I reply. "I guess the investigative team is finished in here then?"

"I guess they are. I'll go check," Lois says and heads out to the study. Everyone looks up as Janet walks into the kitchen.

"Janet Ostro, this is Julianna Morgan," I say.

"Nice to see you, Miss Morgan," Janet says.

"Likewise Miss Ostro. You look familiar," Julianna replies.

"Well, I've been to your gallery several times," Janet replies, clutching her purse tightly and appearing uncomfortable. I wonder if she is self-conscious about her weight when she is around slim, attractive women like Lush and Julianna.

"Of course, I remember you, and I know your name from our mailing list. How nice to see you again." Julianna's tone transforms from rather cold to conciliatory. Janet responds with a smile.

"I've been to some wonderful showings at your gallery, Miss Morgan. I always look forward to receiving your catalogs."

"Thank you. Please call me Julianna. Okay if I call you Janet?"

"Please do."

"Are you a collector, Janet? I don't recall," Julianna studies Janet for clues to her purchasing potential.

"Well, I would like to be, but no. I am, well I am. You see, I study painting," Janet replies.

"Oh, you're an artist. Well you must invite me to see your work."

"Well, I don't think. You see, I'm still developing, trying, well trying to be a real painter."

"Nonsense, all artists are continually learning and improving and increasing their skills," Julianna flips her right hand up and down as she talks. "Besides, since you're a friend of Billy's, I must see your work."

"Well, you see. You see, Julianna. I'm not really a friend of Billy's, but I'm very familiar with his work. I just love it." Janet looks my way for help.

"Julianna, Janet is the nurse from St. Vincent's who attended Billy. She held his hand as he died, and she treated me very kindly Monday. She is one of the few eyewitnesses to the killer who was disguised as a computer technician. She is indeed an artist, at least with the human spirit. That I know for certain. I've asked her to be with us today as you go over Billy's latest works."

"I see. Well, I think that's wonderful, Philip. And, Janet, God bless you for being there for Billy. I wish you had been able to get to know him. He was a wonderful man, and a truly gifted artist. You are in for an exceptional art experience today."

"Alright, everyone. Please take a glass of sherry and let's go into the studio," Lush says as she passes around the glasses.

"Excuse me, Mr. Hampton," Officer Graham and Lois walk into the kitchen. "The crime unit has finished their inspections and has left," Officer Graham says. "I'll be leaving at six pm. Officer Kelly will replace me."

"Thanks," I reply. "Can I get you anything to drink?"

"No thank you. I have some coffee in the living room."

"Well, if you'll excuse us, Officer Graham, these lovely ladies and I have some work to do in the studio."

"Certainly. Mr. Hampton, the photo lab has determined that someone other than myself was following you and Mrs. Richardson today. They are trying to determine who it is. Detectives Johnson and Bell are on the way to talk to the analysts right now."

"Shit. I can't believe it. What the hell do they think I know? Lush?"

"Philip," Lush replies, "Whatever it was in that safe would be my guess. What if what they took is not what they really wanted?"

"Oh dear, this is really getting to be a nightmare," Julianna says taking a sip of her sherry.

"The detectives have asked me to ask all of you here to think again carefully about anything at all you might have overlooked or forgotten that may help this investigation." Officer Graham looks at each one of us individually as she says this.

"Thank you," I reply, "We will certainly contact the detectives if anything comes up." I turn to walk into the study and Clark gets up from where he's been sleeping in front of the Sub-Zero to follow me.

"Oh excuse me, Mr. Hampton," Officer Graham says holding up her right index finger, "There is just one more thing. Detective Bell told me to tell you and Mrs. Morgan that if you don't fully disclose everything you discuss today as you're going over your brother's new paintings, she intends to confiscate every piece of it for evidence."

"Is that a threat, Officer Graham?" I ask as my face reddens with anger.

"Oh no sir. It's not a threat at all. It's a fact," she replies with a smile, clearly enjoying her display of power. "Detective Bell already has a warrant for Judge Reinhold to sign. Why, she told me that the judge encouraged her to go ahead and do it now, but she wouldn't before you all had a chance to at least look

at them. I suppose out of respect for your brother or maybe you all; I'm not sure who." She smiles, turns around and walks back into the living room.

"Well I'll be damned," Lush whispers, "If that's not a threat, I don't know what the hell is."

"Let's just get started," Julianna says, brushing past me into the study. Janet looks worried and puzzled as she follows Julianna. Lois is furiously polishing the granite countertops in a futile attempt to dispel her anger toward the police. Lush walks over, hooks her right arm through my left arm, and we enter the studio, followed by Clark.

"Please, everyone sit down and get comfortable," Julianna instructs. "I'd like to familiarize you with the intent, purpose, and structure of this collection of Billy's—this final collection of Billy's, his greatest works by far, works which I'm certain will propel him to be among the most important artists in the past twenty years."

She takes another sip of sherry and sets the glass down on the coffee table in front of the sofa on which Janet, Lush, and I sit. Clark walks over and gets into his bed, and I smile as I observe Julianna in her element and remember the countless stories about her Billy has told me. She is an eloquent speaker, and the passion she possesses for art, especially contemporary art, exudes as she speaks. She rarely publicizes the fact that she is incredibly educated in her field. Her passion for art began as a young girl when her mother, Regina, a New York socialite, who traced her roots back to one of the original Dutch families in Manhattan, would painstakingly educate her only child about the family's vast art collection, a great part of which was passed down from previous generations and is displayed in their large upper east side townhouse. After the obligatory social marriage, which ended childless and in divorce in its third year, Regina met and married a young, handsome, struggling attorney, Raymond Morgan, from Toledo, who became a shrewd investment banker and made his own fortune during the nineteen sixties and seventies. This fortune allowed Regina to substantially augment the family's aging collection with contemporary works. By ten years of age, Julianna felt comfortable in all the art museums and important galleries in New York and could discuss art with any adult. In this regard she was a precocious student at the exclusive, all girls, Brearley School. As a teenager, she spent most of her spare time from school, and most holidays and summer breaks assisting her mother in buying important contemporary works of art. She worked with many art dealers, and attended all the important actions at Christies and Sotheby's, where, whenever her mother would tap Julianna's thigh, she would hold up her bid number to place a bid on her mother's behalf. By the time Julianna reached fifteen, Regina realized the thigh tapping was no longer necessary. It was no surprise to anyone in her set when Julianna entered Columbia University at the age of seventeen to pursue a Bachelors of Art with a focus in Art History. It was quite a surprise when she emerged from Columbia six years later with a BA, MFA, and Ph.D. in contemporary art. She immediately opened her first gallery in Soho in 1982 in the height of a recession, and, much to the delight of her father, turned a profit the first year, and has expanded her business each year since. Today her clients include important museums worldwide, mega-wealthy collectors, corporations, rock stars, movie stars, and royalty. I sit back prepared for Julianna's presentation and feel good that I have been able to share this with Janet.

"Everything I am about to tell you is of an extreme personal nature concerning Billy. Of course, all art, that is, all good and relevant art, is of an extreme personal nature. I believe I am one of Billy's closest friends, and probably, excluding you, Philip, his closet friend and confidant." She pauses a moment, cups her hands and pulls them up to her lips, then continues. "For the past couple of years, Billy has been on a mission to resolve in his mind what he called 'the human condition of sexuality' and where he saw himself fitting into it. A condition because it is both inherited through the mixing and perhaps mutating of our parents' chromosomes and impressed upon us, like an ink stamp, by ourselves, through experimentation and by other humans. Pertaining to the former condition Billy believed we leave our mothers' wombs programmed as completely heterosexual or homosexual or anywhere on the spectrum between the two. He also recognized other branches of the result of human copulation including, but not

limited to, transsexuals, hermaphrodites, and asexual persons. Picture in your mind models sought and retained for study and painting from these diverse groups. Now, if you will, consider the latter condition: what has been imprinted upon us sexually. For example, the toddler learns that rubbing his erection produces a pleasurable reaction, much to the concern of his young mother; a newly pubescent girl finds out that massaging her clitoris gives her great pleasure and causes orgasms; and a twelve-year-old boy locks himself in the bathroom, secretly masturbating to purloined issues of his father's Playboy magazine. Think about and go back in your mind to your first memorable sexual awareness of your own body as a child." She pauses a moment; I take a sip of the sweet, sticky sherry and glance at Lush and Janet. They appear glued to Julianna's words, as am I, but my underarms are beginning to perspire, and I bite my cheeks to prevent an embarrassing hard on, because I think I know where Julianna is headed. She walks back and forth in front of us, deep in thought, almost as if she were an attorney, delivering a closing argument to a jury, an argument upon which some defendant's life hinges, and, I realize, although it is most likely unknown to her, she may, in fact, be doing this. "Now, let's take this a step further to a side of the human sexual condition which at one end of the spectrum is among the most pleasurable experiences known—that would be consensual sex among two adults who are in love, well, at the least, in lust—to the other end of the spectrum where one person physically and violently forces another person to have sex—the most familiar example of this is probably the brutal rape of a woman or girl by a man. Other, less familiar examples of this include things like pedophilia." She pauses and looks directly at me, and I realize she knows about Billy, me, and Uncle Adrian. She continues, "Now blend in other paraphilia like incest, sadomasochism, asphyxiation techniques, role playing, fetishes, and, well, I think you can see, the list goes on and on and on." She pauses again and looks at me point blank and asks, "Philip, in order for me to continue, some of what I must say is about you in a personal and private way. Would you like for me to stop here or explain the truth of this exhibition?"

"Julianna, even though I now own every one of these paintings, and have every right legally under Billy's contract with you to prevent any of this from ever coming out, do I really have a choice?"

"I certainly don't think you do," she replies.

"Then, why did you even bother to ask me?"

"Philip, in many ways you are like your brother, but in many ways you are not. He's the one I can speak for when it comes to his art. I cannot do this for you. Well, at least until I get to know you better and you give me permission to."

I hold my glass up to her in a mock toast, take a sip, and say, "By all means, please continue, Julianna." And I think to myself, I bet she's a helluva fuck.

"Billy's main purpose for creating this collection of paintings was to place himself, his own unique sexual condition, among the colors of this sexual spectrum I've been describing. In short, he needed to know and feel good about where he fit in. It was a physical and spiritual maturation he desperately wanted in order to lead a happier life and continue to pursue his passion and his gift. Billy was born gay, but he was manipulated, as was Philip, by their mother's art representative, Adrian McWhorter, to engage in dozens and dozens of abnormal sex acts with Adrian and Philip from the time he was nine years old until his mother died when he was eleven, after which he only felt 'normal or at peace' when he had sex with you, Philip. A practice you justifiably stopped when you realized at around fifteen years old that it was not normal or right. Billy could never fully relinquish this practice, so he hung on to vestiges of it, such as autoerotic asphyxiation in order to get what he called 'his sexual fix' and as he matured into the drop dead gorgeous man he was and had people of both sexes, from all ranges of the human sexual spectrum, literally lining up to have sex with him, he pursued this relentlessly, largely to no avail, that is never really being satisfied sexually. The seminal point in his life, no pun intended, was the night in St. Barts, about eight years ago when he seduced you, Philip, and he manipulated you sexually until you fucked him hard in his ass in missionary style and came inside him. After his botched episode of autoerotic asphyxiation

the next day and his full realization of the horrible thing he did to you, Philip, a brother he loved more than anything or anybody, he realized that his art, his true calling would be his only chance at self-salvation and happiness. That's when he gave up modeling entirely and pursued his passion. These new paintings, several of which he never let even me see, are the culmination of that journey which began that night at St. Barts." Her face takes on a look of intense sorrow and tears begin to stream from her eyes and she continues as her voice cracks with sobs, "And now, when he was so close to attaining the self-acceptance and happiness he so desperately sought, and I have to believe, Dear God I just have to believe, and I keep telling myself that with the completion of the last work on Saturday, he must have indeed felt the serenity he was seeking, if only for a few hours. Philip, you've lost your darling brother, I've lost my best friend, but the real crime is that the world has lost the genius of all the great works, I know in my heart, in my soul, in my bones, that he would have created." She walks over weeping and sits in a Regency style armchair upholstered in silver and grey Fortuny. Lush and Janet are softly crying. I just don't have any tears left at this point. Oddly enough, I don't feel embarrassed or exposed at all in front of Janet. I get up, grab a pewter tissue holder from the bookshelves and offer a tissue to each woman. They all dab their eyes and blow their noses without saying anything. I just stand and look at these three women, all of whom are strong and intelligent, loving, compassionate, and in their own ways beautiful and driven, and I feel blessed to have them around me, even though it is more likely than not, that Benny, or someone is waiting out there, for the right moment to murder me.

CHAPTER 17

Julianna stands up, straightens her dress, smiles, and says, "Lush, would you be so kind as to refill our glasses? I believe we could all use another drink."

"Of course, Julianna. That was so powerful and moving. Thank you for sharing it with us."

"This is the audience for whom it was meant. I realized that as I was speaking. Janet, would you mind helping me pull all these paintings? I know an artist will know how to handle the canvasses, and I have, in my mind, how I want to arrange them in here."

"I'm going to step outside to smoke," I say. "Lush, want to join me?"

"Love to," she replies as she refills the sherry glasses.

"Come on Clark," I say. He jumps up from his bed and trots over. We get our glasses and head into the kitchen for our cigarettes, then out onto the terrace to one of the wrought iron tables. Clark heads off for a sniffing expedition around the terrace.

"That was quite an introduction, Todge. Julianna is mesmerizing when she wants to be," Lush says and lights a cigarette.

"Yes, she is. You know, it's evident to me that she was closer to Billy than I thought."

"Does that bother you?"

"No. Well, yes. Well, I know it shouldn't but it does." I pull out a cigarette, light it, and take a deep drag, blow out the smoke and take a sip of sherry.

"Why does it bother you?" Lush asks and I can tell she is reading my body language.

"You know how close I was to Billy, and I know he felt the same. We always got along better than most brothers I know. And with Mother's death and Dad's abandonment, we grew to rely more and more on each other. The sexual bond introduced by Uncle Adrian and all our incestuous sexual acts thereafter

were also a strong bond—one that I always thought we were in agreement to suppress; I certainly could not repress it. And even though I cut that bond by orchestrating our enrollments in different boarding schools, it was still a strong unspoken bond. I never divulged it to anyone, not you, Lush, not anyone, until his death. Knowing that Julianna knows all about this from Billy, well, I know it's unhealthy, but it does make me feel a bit betrayed."

"Darling, I see your point. But I think that what Billy came to realize is that that bond you speak about is in itself wrong and as unhealthy as the incest was. He had to break it in order to heal and move on. Does that make sense?"

"Yes, it does. At least, it does now," I sigh, take another drag and say, "I couldn't have admitted that a week ago."

"Todge, this has to be a healing process for you, too. It's a horrible thing to think that Billy had to die for this to happen, but I think you need to take care of yourself. The grief won't ever stop. You know that better than anyone. Maybe if you think of this as a gift from Billy to you, it might be easier to accept."

"I suppose you're right, Lush. But, I just need some time to sort all this out."

"And there will be time, Todge, but not just yet. We have to find out why all this happened and that's going to take every ounce of energy and mental acumen we've got. My God, we're up against some very sophisticated killers. This Benny, and if my hunch is right, and his twin brother, are professionals. Think about what they had to do to get into St. Vincent's and in such a short time frame."

"It's a bit scary. I suppose you're going to tell me next that that was Benny trailing us today?"

"That's where I put my money. I bet our two detective friends are making that determination right about now."

"What the hell can this all be about, Lush? I just can't imagine how bad it must really be for someone to want to murder him. I just can't grasp that."

She inhales and exhales a steady stream of silky smoke and says, "I know. I feel the same. But sometimes analyzing what is not there, say in a great painting, or a wonderful dialogue, can really give more information than the obvious."

"Oh shit, Lush, you're getting way over my head now. What the fuck are you talking about?"

"Well, look at it this way. Julianna has no idea Billy was in Dubai. Does she? At least, according to Lois. And I for one don't think Lois is giving us any bullshit."

"Damn, I see. You're good, Lush. Why the hell do you let that dickhead, David, control your life? For God's sake, you've got so much more to offer. Get out of that town. It's like you've got a fucking umbilical cord connected to Louisville. They don't deserve you. What the hell is there anyway besides the Kentucky Derby?"

"What's all this anger about, Philip? I'm just trying to help you find Billy's killer."

"Hell, I dunno. Christ. I mean. Life is so fucking unfair. Billy's dead; you're rotting in Louisville; I don't know what the fuck I'm gonna do." Clark hears my emotional outburst and trots over, sits down in front of me and stares at me. "Look at him, Lush. He can read my mind. What I wouldn't give to be a damn dog like you, Clark." He raises his right paw and motions at me with it.

"Todge, you're just feeling stress. It makes you feel things you normally wouldn't. I told you, I'm using this opportunity to get away from Louisville for a while. I mean it. I mean to get a divorce from David. He's probably ecstatic that I'm gone—probably screwing some young, dumb, social climbing bitch's brains out while I'm gone. I don't care. But I do care about you, and Clark, and Billy, and Brenda, and your dad and their kids. I do care, and I feel a great need to help you solve this. I need this as much as you do, Todge. That's a selfish thing to say, but it's the truth. I know we can do this if we just don't let our emotions get in the way and if we follow the truth."

"The truth, the truth. What the fuck is the truth, Lush? I always thought I was following some truth, but now, that seems like a bunch of bullshit. The only real truth that speaks to me right now is that all people are fucked up in their own ways and that you're born and then you die. It's as simple as that."

"Philip, indulge me a second. What are three of your favorite memories? I mean all time best memories—things you remember and reflect on from time to time."

"Well, I remember waking up on summer mornings at Pawley's Island with the smell of bacon and coffee throughout the house and thinking that Ala Mary had a wonderful breakfast waiting for us and that Billy and I had the whole day ahead of us to do whatever we wanted, fishing, swimming, crabbing, seining for shrimp, clam digging, building sandcastles, and riding our bicycles on the beach. That's one for sure. Another is the first time, when I was twenty-six, that Time published my article on horrible working conditions in cottage industries in China, and I opened the magazine and saw my name in print. That was a great feeling. Another is most definitely the first time you and I ever made love. That's the first time I ever made love to a woman. I'll never forget that; we were just eighteen."

"Wonderful memories, Todge. Those memories are yours forever; you can summons them at will."

"Yeah, so what?"

"So what? So, those memories are truths for you. Truths that mean a hell of a lot more than just living and dying."

"Okay, so I'm just pissed about everything that has happened. I do get your point—it's the journey, not the start and finish."

"That seems like a good way to look at it to me, Todge—not that I'm the omniscient one or anything."

"But you are, Lush. You're way far ahead of me when it comes to being connected to what you really feel."

"Well, I've paid my dues in therapy—twice a week for five years."

"Wow. That's a lot, Lush. Maybe I should go see a therapist."

"Philip, you're way ahead of most people. You're so intuitive. Sometimes, I need a set of instructions in front of me. That's kinda what therapy has been for me, especially group therapy."

"How's that?"

"Well, you've got several other people trying to connect with you, as best as they can, giving you real time feed back about how they feel about you and how they perceive you feel about them. It's pretty powerful stuff."

"I wonder if Billy was getting that much out of his therapy?"

"I dunno, but maybe we'll find out Friday if Dr. Gerard shows up."

"Lush, you think the detectives have talked to him?"

"I would think so."

"Yeah, me too."

Julianna opens a French door from the studio and walks toward us. I see her eyes are red and her face is puffy. "Well, we're ready for you all now. Please come in."

"Julianna, what's wrong, dear?" Lush asks.

"Nothing, Lush. Nothing's wrong. Just come observe the power of this collection."

Clark leads the way in, and we follow. Janet is sitting on a stool at one of Billy's tables weeping audibly. Lush rushes to her and says, "Janet, are you alright?"

"Yes, yes, Lush. Thank you. Excuse me." She takes a tissue, wipes her eyes and blows her nose. "It's these paintings. I'm. Well, I'm just overwhelmed." She makes a sweeping motion around the room with her right hand. My eyes follow her hand, and I quickly take in the array of paintings. My eyes fall on one painting in particular, and I become aware of the aroma of linseed oil like Ala Mary used to condition the knotty pine paneling in our bedroom. I feel tightness in my throat and tingling sensations in my hands, arms, feet and legs, and everything fades into darkness.

"Philip, Philip, are you okay? Can you hear me? Give him some room, ladies. He's just passed put. He's okay." I hear Janet's voice.

"Todge, honey, wake up. Wake up."

Suddenly I feel a great wet tongue on my face.

"Oh dear, I'm not sure we should let Clark lick him that way," I hear Julianna say.

"Probably good for him. Whatdaya think, Janet? You're the nurse," I hear Lush say.

I try to open my eyes. At first I see nothing but darkness. Then slowly, I discern images, forms moving, then colors appear, and I see the faces of Lush, Janet, Julianna and Clark all peering down at me. Clark's tongue is hanging out and he is panting with a curious, worried look on his face. The image of these three women with Clark in the middle of them seems hilarious to me, and I start laughing and continue laughing, almost uncontrollably.

"Todge, what are you laughing at? Were you faking? Were you?" Lush asks with a perturbed look on her face.

"Oh no, Lush," Janet responds, "He was not faking. He most definitely fainted."

I try to take slow breaths and quell the laughter. After a while, I feel I can speak. "Lush, I'm sorry. I just woke up to three women with very worried faces peering into my eyes alongside that of Clark with his worried face and eight inch long tongue hanging out. And, it was funny to see. It was," I start laughing again, "It was one of the funniest things I've ever seen." I roll over and continue to laugh. I feel Clark pawing my back.

"Well I don't know whether to laugh or smack the shit out of you," Lush says. "I'm just glad you're awake. Are you alright, Todge?"

"I'm fine. I guess I just fainted. I know I fainted."

"You certainly did," Julianna says, "And I think I know why."

"Why, Julianna?" Janet asks.

"Well, his eyes were glued to that painting when he fainted. It's a painting of a teenage Billy, choking Philip with a neck tie as they are masturbating."

It all hits me like a ton of bricks and I moan, "Oh shit, you're right. Why in hell did he paint that? Why? I guess he needed to. Dear God, please help me." I plead. Everyone is silent for a long while. I roll over, open my eyes and push up from my elbows and look at the painting. There we are, Billy and I. I'm fifteen; he's thirteen. Dear God, he's got it just right. That's exactly what we looked like at those ages. That's exactly what we did. We would take turns choking each other, to the point of blacking out, right as we reached orgasm. In the painting, Billy has the pink and black noose around my neck, pulling it tight. The view is down and in front of us looking up. He has painted our upper torsos and faces, but it is obvious that I'm masturbating with my left hand and just at the point of ejaculation and my eyes are half shut, in ecstasy and I'm blacking out from the noose which Billy is carefully regulating. He is behind me, nude, watching me and regulating the noose. The lighting on our faces is shocking to me, very Dutch School, Vermeer-like, while the juxtaposition of our bodies reminds me of Winslow Homer's paintings. Billy has painted each of us almost like a photograph, yet the background, which is most definitely our bedroom in Fatgram's house, is much more abstract. I recognize the knotty pine paneling, but everything is blended together. It's almost as if everything in the room is being stirred in a large mixer and the only things painted with definite clarity are Billy and me. I'm amazed and confounded. I realize that my fainting must be my body remembering that scene, that specific time and place that happened to me and happened to my brother. I am speechless. I sit up and put my head between my knees and begin a tearless weep. Clark pushes his nose between my arm and face, sniffs hard and tries to lick my face. I throw my arms around him, burying my face into his neck. I feel hands stroking my back. We stay this way for a while.

"Come on, Todge, get up. Get up. We've got work to do." Lush's sensible voice encourages me, and I do as she says.

"I'm sorry, ladies," I say. "Julianna, please go ahead with your presentation."

"Are you certain you are ready for this, Philip?" Julianna asks with her hands clasped as if she were about to pray.

"Yes, thank you, I'm ready. Please go ahead."

"Alright. There are a total of sixty paintings now. Several of these I've never seen before. Janet and I have arranged them in the following fashion: from so called 'normal' acts of love and sex by heterosexuals to 'abnormal' or violent acts involving sex. I've transitioned from heterosexual to homosexual and then into the sexual aberrations involving all types of sexuality. You'll notice from a sweeping glance at the paintings that we do not have an array of pornographic works, but works portraying incredibly intense emotions and feelings."

As I scan the paintings, I'm relieved to see that they are indeed not a collection of just raw sex acts with hard cocks, vaginas, and tits everywhere. Billy has focused on facial expressions and body language to convey his story. You do see genitals, but they are not the main focus of the paintings and they are not, at least to me, offensive. I notice Lush walking up to a painting of two young men, their bodies entwined, facing each other in a sitting position, deeply kissing and masturbating each other. As I get closer, I notice they are Asian.

"This is it," Lush says in an alarming, loud tone. "Sorry, Julianna, but this is a painting of Benny, and I bet you a thousand dollars, his twin brother."

I approach the painting and look at it closely. Lush is right. The view of the faces is a side view and it is clearly a painting of two young Asian men who are twins having sex. "You're right Lush, it is Benny. That has to be his twin."

"Yes, that's Meng from the hospital," Janet says.

"Julianna, do you know anything about this painting?" I ask.

"No, I've never seen it until today. Turn it around, he usually tapes notes to me to the back of his canvases."

Lush picks up the painting and turns it around. There's a piece of yellow, lined legal paper taped to the back with the following written in Billy's neat print:

Benny and Bernie. They showed up at the West Side Club in October of 2005.

"Well, your twin theory was right, Lush," I say. "The detectives will definitely want to see this. So he met his murderer in a bathhouse. Julianna, did Billy ever keep notes about any of his paintings on his computer?"

"Not that I'm aware of. He usually hand wrote them like this or just told me about the paintings and we, of course, would publish the information in our catalogs."

"What about photographs?" Lush asks. "Did he ever photograph his models in preparation for a painting?"

"Oh yes, almost always," Julianna replies.

"Strange," Lush says, "I've been through all the photos from his hard drive, and I didn't see any that looked like set ups for paintings."

"That's because he didn't want to take a chance that they would get into someone else's hands. As you'll soon see, some of the people in these paintings are very high profile. He has another MacBook with nothing but photographs on it. He keeps that over here in this cabinet with his digital camera." Julianna walks over to one of the large storage cabinets and opens it. There appears to be nothing but art supplies in it. "Billy was clever. This one has a false front." She pushes at the top of the cabinet and the shelves rotate out, revealing another set of shelves. She pulls out a white MacBook and a digital camera and hands them to me.

"Damn, Billy loves his secret chambers and rooms," Lush says.

"Here, Lush, you know what to do with these before we give them to the detectives," I say as I hand the computer and camera to her.

"Right. I'll go through them before dinner and copy all the files."

"Excuse me, Philip," Lois says as she walks into the room. "There's a man here from Riverside Mortuary. He's delivering, well, he's got Billy's remains."

"Oh, yes, well. Ladies, let's take a break for a few minutes," I say.

"Okay everyone," Lush says, "I'm gonna fix some hors d'oeuvres to go with this sherry."

"I need to make a few phone calls," Julianna says as she looks at her watch. "Goodness, it's almost three o'clock."

"Lush, can I help you in the kitchen?" Janet asks.

"Sure, let's go."

Clark and I head out in front of the women and go through the kitchen and down the hall into the foyer. Clarks walks up to a tall man with grey hair wearing a black suit, black horn rimmed glasses and a grave expression on his face. Clark sniffs his shoes, wags his tail, sits down and looks up at the man. The man is holding a black plastic box in his left arm and hand. He looks down at Clark, then looks up at me and says, "Mr. Hampton, I presume?"

"Yes," I reply.

"I'm Mr. Bailey from Riverside. I have your brother's remains here. May I express my condolences for the loss of your loved one." He hands me the box. I take it. It's heavier than I thought, maybe five or six pounds.

"Thank you, Mr. Bailey."

"Mr. Hampton, would you mind signing this release form? Please press down hard. The form is in triplicate." He slowly reaches into his lapel pocket and pulls out a form and a gold pen. I set the box down on a hand painted, antique, Italian demilune table, take the form and pen and sign my name with great force on the pen.

"Thank you, sir," Mr. Bailey says, takes the form and pen, tears off the back copy, hands it to me, and turns toward the elevator. I walk over, press the button, and the door opens. Mr. Bailey walks inside, turns around, nods his head, and as the door closes, says, "Again, may I express my condolences for the loss of your loved one."

"Jeez, what a creepy fellow, Clark," I say, walk over, pick up the box and take it in the kitchen. Lush and Janet have prepared a platter with brie, a blue cheese, and a Swiss cheese, along with white and red grapes, sliced Granny Smith apples, and strawberries. Another tray has an array of crackers on it. I walk over to one of the granite counters and set the box down. Lush and Janet look up at me.

"Here's Billy," I sigh and look at them. I guess I'll go get the Chinese jar he requested his remains go in. It's in the living room.

"Okay," Lush says. "Todge, I'm tired of sherry, is it okay if I open a good bottle of chardonnay to go with the cheese and fruit?"

"Of course, Lush. You know you don't have to ask. I'll be right back."

Officer Graham is sitting on a sofa that gives her a clear view of the foyer, and I realize she witnessed the delivery of Billy's ashes. Clark trots up to her and jumps up beside her in the sofa.

"Hello Clark," she says and pets him. "Is he allowed on the furniture?"

"Yes, he's allowed to go anywhere he pleases in this house," I say, still perturbed at her bitchy attitude over Billy's new paintings.

"How's the review of the new paintings going?" "It's going just fine," I reply and walk over to a long, narrow, hall table near the entrance of the living room that has four intricately carved Doric columns for legs, supporting two slabs of white marble with black and grey veins. One slab rests a few inches off the

floor and the other serves as the top of the table. The paint on the columns is very old and crackled, and is a mixture of antique white, red and gilding. Two large matching lamps flank the top of the table. They have been fashioned from large, hand carved wooden candleholders with a patina of faded shades of blue with traces of silver leaf and are fitted with leather half shades. In the center of the table the large Kangxi ginger jar sits with pots of live white phaelanopsis orchids, Billy's favorite, on either side of it. I pick up the jar and walk back into the kitchen. Clark jumps off the sofa and follows me. I put the jar down beside the box containing Billy's ashes.

"What a beautiful jar, Philip," Janet says and walks over to examine it.

"Thank you. Both my mother and grandmother were avid collectors of blue and white Chinese porcelain. This jar is from the Kangxi period which I believe is the late sixteen hundreds and early seventeen hundreds. It depicts what is called 'The Three Friends of Winter' which are the pine tree, the prunus tree, and the bamboo tree—you see they endure the winter and even flourish, like the prunus here which evens blooms in the winter and together they symbolize longevity, perseverance, and integrity which are the virtues of the ideal scholar-gentleman, and also the three main religions of China--Buddhism, Daoism and Confucianism. These crosshatched areas represent ice."

"My, you know a lot about Chinese porcelain," Janet says.

"Well, I know a lot about the pieces Mother and Fatgram left us. They wanted us to appreciate the beauty and purpose of each piece. This piece would have probably been given as a gift in celebration of the Chinese New Year."

"I see," Janet says. "That must be a museum quality piece. The blue is so vivid and the painting is exquisite."

"Yes, it is. And it has always been Billy's favorite piece. He especially loved the blooming prunus painted here."

Julianna walks in from the study and says, "Oh, that exquisite blue and white piece. I can't think of a better vessel for Billy's remains."

"Okay, everyone, I changed my mind when I realized we have to make a toast to Billy when Philip transfers his ashes into the Chinese jar. It's Cristal; his favorite." Lush brings over a silver tray with five crystal flutes of champagne. She looks back over her shoulder at Lois who is washing the sherry glasses. "Lois, get over here girl. You're in on this, too." Lois smiles, wipes her hands on a dishtowel and walks over.

"Thanks, Lush. Well, here it goes." I open the plastic box and pull out a plastic bag containing Billy's ashes. I hold it up for everyone to see. I observe what appears to be ground up bones near the top of the bag and I wince a little. Julianna walks over and carefully takes the lid off the jar. I turn and put the plastic bag down into the jar and put the lid back on. Lush passes a glass of champagne to everyone. Everyone looks at me.

"Yes. Well, this is to you, Billy, my dearest, darling brother. I promise, you will rest in peace—that is, as soon as we find the evil bastards who killed you. This toast is my promise to you that I will not rest, no, we will not rest," I pause and look at each of the women, "until we solve this horrible crime and expose the killers for the devils they are. Then, you will rest little brother. Then you will rest." I hold my glass up and we all clink our glasses together and take a sip.

"Well said, Todge," Lush says.

"Indeed," Julianna adds.

"Oh my this is delicious champagne," Janet says, "I've never had this before."

"Yes, dear, Cristal is one of the best," Julianna says, "I love the honey and white chocolate notes in it."

Janet takes another sip and says, "Yes, I taste them, Julianna. How wonderful. Perhaps a little apple flavor, too?"

"Yes, yes, there's definitely apple on the palette," Julianna replies, then asks, "Lois, do you like it?"

"Oh, yes mam, I do. I'm definitely more of a beer drinker, and I never did get into champagne much, but Billy has given this to me a few times before, and well, hell, what's not to like about this stuff?" She laughs her rough laugh. We all laugh and clink our glasses one more time. Lush divides up the rest of the bottle.

"Well, let's finish going over the exhibition," Julianna says.

"Yes, we need to get finished and put everything back before Dad, Brenda and the kids get back from the theatre," I say.

"Oh, your Dad and his wife and their children are staying here with you, Philip?" Julianna asks.

"They are. This surprises you, doesn't it, Julianna?"

"Well, forgive me, Philip. I just thought you and Billy were rather estranged from your father. He has only been to one of Billy's openings. As I recall, he just showed up, he wasn't invited."

"That's true, Julianna. But he and I have had a sort of reconciliation since Billy's death. It's a beginning anyway. His wife and my little brothers and sister are really wonderful."

She touches my right arm and says, "That's good, Philip. I'm happy for you."

"Thanks."

We take our glasses into the study and Lois follows with the cheese tray and puts it down on one of Billy's worktables. Clark jumps up, puts his front paws on the side of the table and sniffs, but he's too short to snatch anything off the tray. Lush has the tray with crackers in one hand and her champagne flute in the other. She sets the crackers down by the cheese and fruit.

"Philip, I've got some sweeping and cleaning to do on the terrace," Lois says, "Is it okay to take Clark with me? He usually keeps me company out there."

"Sure, Lois. I know he'll love that."

"Clark, come on boy. Let's go out," Lois says. Clark runs over to her and they turn and go back into the kitchen.

Julianna begins again and continues for the next hour. We do not discover any other paintings of Benny or anything really obvious that might give us a clue about Billy's murder. There are several paintings of famous and high profile people in a variety of sexual situations, but Julianna knows most of these people well, and she has seen all these particular paintings before and does not feel that any of the people involved would harm Billy in any way. There is one painting of Billy making love to a handsome, young Arab man who wears nothing but a white Keffiyea with a black band. No one recognizes this man. The two men rest in each other's arms on a sumptuous oriental rug and on large silk pillows with jeweled tassels. The painting is clearly inside a white tent of some sort and the shadow of a grazing camel is visible on the left side of the tent. Billy and the handsome Arab are lying on their sides, embracing, legs entwined, gazing into each other's eyes. The painting is beautiful and it evokes the feeling of love in exotic lands. Lush remarks, "Well, I suppose there's a daddy sheikh somewhere that would pay a king's ransom to keep that one out of public view?"

"You may have a point, Lush," Julianna replies. "I can't imagine who that is? Billy's certainly never been over to the Middle East, and he's left no notes about this painting. It's obviously a fresh one too, only a couple of weeks old. It's extraordinarily beautiful though, one of his best works of realism. Don't you feel as if you could just crawl up there with them? Look at the bowl of fruit, dates, and cheese, and the shadow of the camel, and the faint shadow of the palm trees. Remarkable. I hope we find more information about this on his other computer."

Lush and I exchange glances, but remain silent. The only painting of Billy and Elliott together makes the hairs on the back of my neck stand up, for it foreshadows how each man was murdered. The painting shows a smiling Billy holding a martini in his right hand and playfully grabbing the tie Elliott wears and is pulling it up behind his neck to cause a gentle choke while he whispers something into Elliott's right ear. Benny or Bernie or someone slipped a large dose of GHB in Billy's martini at Splash. Bernie must have

somehow seduced Elliott into having sex with him and participating in the choking game. Julianna says this is a painting of Billy introducing the erotic possibilities of choking to Elliott. She also says Billy told her Elliott liked it a lot when he finally experienced it with Billy.

There are a few more surprises. One of the larger paintings is of Julianna and Billy, just after they had made love for the first time. Julianna is sitting on the edge of her bed, staring out, with an intensely serious expression on her face, as if she is trying to figure out something. Her breasts sag a bit, but she is in good shape for a middle-aged woman. Yet, when you see Billy's image, it is clear he is a much younger man. Billy is standing on the other side of the bed with his back to Julianna, beginning to walk away. His left leg is bent back and is still on the bed, and he is clutching the edge of the bed sheet in his left hand. There is a large mirror hanging over a low dresser and you see Billy's full frontal image in it. He is smiling and he is half erect. The painting shows how beautiful he is from both the front and back. Lush, Janet, and I are shocked when we observe red lines and droplets of blood running down Billy's upper back. Julianna admits she lost control when they first made love and unconsciously clawed his back with her fingernails as they both reached orgasm.

Another painting that catches me off guard is a highly detailed execution of Billy and myself up in the big live oak peeping in through the Palladian window in Mother's studio watching Darrell Coots fuck her. Even though there is nothing cartoon-like about the painting, it reminds me of a Norman Rockwell painting—an X-rated version. When Lush sees this she says, "Well, Todge, I guess your little brother knew more than you thought." You see mainly the back of Darrell's head, his broad back, hairy butt and legs on top of Mother, but Mother's face is turned over her right shoulder and her eyes are closed. She almost appears asleep. And strangest of all, and I suppose this is how it really was, but something I never would have noticed, the reflection of our faces appear like ghosts in the window glass. I look surprised; Billy looks as if he were taking notes for an important exam. Just as it did twenty-three years ago, this image is giving me a hard-on as the painting comes to life in my mind and I can hear Darrell fucking Mother, the smell of sex and perspiration surround me, my ears burn as I fall into the sexual abyss once again, so I walk back to the table to eat some cheese and fruit.

As I take a bite of blue cheese on a cracker I turn around to scan several paintings resting along the French doors of the studio. I suspected it might exist and here it is: a painting of me fucking Billy in St. Barts. Strangely, in my opinion, it is one of the least erotic in the entire collection because of the perspective of the painting—it is what Billy saw with his own eyes. The central focus of the painting is my face—it holds a look approaching agony or pain, my chest—chest hair is matted with sweat, and my arms—bulging biceps and triceps with elbows locked to provide my body leverage. My mouth is slightly open as if I'm saying something. Again, Billy uses reflections in glass to tell a story. His face is peering up at mine with a serene happy look. His long hair is spread out over the white towels and he holds his bent legs up with his hands on his thighs. In the reflection you see my entire body, but it is quite vague, and you can barely make out my balls on his ass as my cock is fully inserted at the instance this painting depicts. The moon on the water is lovely and you can see the faintest trace of a moon bow hanging over Gouverneur Bay.

The painting that is most remarkable to me is the only painting of Dad, and it brings back a memory I had completely forgotten—the swimming lessons at Fatgram's swimming hole Dad gave Billy and me the summer I was six and Billy was four. One day Dad left the bag containing our swimsuits and towels on the front porch, so when we arrived at the swimming hole, he said we'd just have to skinny dip that day. Billy and I thought this was great fun and we practiced swimming on top of the water and under water with Dad. To teach us to swim underwater he would tell us to take a breath, keep our eyes open, since the water was clear and fresh, and swim through his legs which he spread apart a bit. We did this several times each. After we were finished, we sat on the rocks to let the sun dry us as we ate juicy peaches. The painting is a phenomenon of perspective, especially from four-year-old Billy who is underwater looking up at Dad's

legs and penis in the water. He sees his little hands out front, Dad smiling down through the rippling water with a halo of light and tree branches surrounding his head, and my feet and legs kicking as I pass through Dad's legs ahead of Billy. The central focus of the painting is Dad's penis, and I suppose Billy remembered this as perhaps his first sexual experience. He always told me that he knew he liked men from as far back as he could remember. I was always amazed by Dad's penis because it seemed so much bigger than mine and it was so hairy, but I never thought of that as sexual, at least not until Uncle Adrian showed me otherwise. I blush all over when I imagine what Dad's reaction will be when he sees this painting. I truly love this painting for two reasons: it brings back a lovely moment in time when I was truly bonded with my Dad and my brother, and it shows the extraordinary talent of my brother. I will keep this one.

Julianna goes into great detail about each painting, pointing out its singularities but also illustrating how it is a part of the continuum of the entire collection. She tells us the collection is brilliant because Billy has taken characteristics of many great artists he loved, including Mother, incorporated them into his work, yet broadcasts them in a contemporary style all his own. She points out specific artists and specific examples in each painting. Janet is clearly taking in everything Julianna is saying—I imagine it must be the most enjoyable art lecture she's ever experienced. Lush is also listening carefully, but I know she is listening for clues, bits of information, anything that may help her make an association or piece together some pathway leading to the motives of the murderers. I am not able to focus on what she is saying as my eyes move over the many canvases which I know he toiled over, sometimes days at a time, with little rest, and only enough food to keep his brush moving. My mind wanders and a multitude of memories tumble through my mind as I sip my champagne and stare at the paintings.

I realize Julianna is winding up her presentation and she is finishing with Blood Brothers, which she has displayed on an easel. Suddenly, I am overcome with a great desire to see if Billy taped any notes on the back of the canvas; I didn't think to look before. I walk over, pick up the painting, turn it around, and set it back on the easel. To my surprise a brown envelope is taped securely, on all sides, to the back of the painting.

"Shit, there's something in here," I say as I grab at the tape trying to pull it off, but my fingernails are too short.

"Wait, please, Philip. We need to be gentle; this painting is not even dry yet. We shouldn't poke the canvas," Julianna says.

"Allow me," Janet says and she applies her perfectly manicured red nails to the tape and it peels off easily. She hands me the envelope. I run my finger under the sealed flap, pull up the metal clasp, reach in and pull out a piece of paper.

"Where the hell did he get this?" I ask.

"What is it, some kind of old award or certificate?" Lush asks.

"It's the Blood Brother's Proclamation Uncle Adrian created for us. See these brown thumbprints. Those are each of ours done in our blood we mixed together from cutting our hands with a pocketknife, a red Swiss Army knife, in fact. I haven't seen this since the day when we did this. See, July 2, 1982. Where the hell did Billy get this? I wonder if Adrian gave it to him before he died? It just seems as if Billy would have told me."

"My God, look at the precision of his printing, the layout, and the gold seal. What an elaborate deception aimed at you and your brother. Goddamn Adrian McWhorter. I'm glad he's dead. I never liked the man anyway," Julianna says with a disgusted look on her face.

"Did you know him well, Julianna?" Lush asks.

"Yes, quite well, but strictly on a business basis. I thought he was a great prick, always condescending to me, always offering pieces of advice, which he made sure to point out that an inexperienced young dealer and gallery operator like myself could benefit from greatly, but in reality only offered in an attempt to extract from me information about what was happening in the more cutting edge circles of art. Don't get

me wrong, he had great vision and was a major influence on some great artists, like your Mother, Philip. But I never trusted him. My mother, who tended to focus on the positive aspects of people, referred to him in private as odd and fastidious to an extreme."

"Interesting," Lush replies. "So you transacted business with him?"

"Oh my, yes. It was hard to get around him in the art world during the seventies, eighties, and nineties. Well, he represented some of the greatest women artists in the past thirty years."

"Women artists?" Lush asks.

"Why yes," Julianna replies, "Some of the greatest. He mentored and guided Hi Lu Zeng, the talented young Chinese artist who defected to the states in the early nineteen seventies. She painted the emotional face of China—its real people, you know—and Adrian made it possible for the world to see this. She was brilliant, but troubled, caught in the Studio 54 scene in the late seventies and ended up overdosing on heroine. Then, there was your Mother whom he brought to international prominence in the early eighties. Eva was one of my mother's favorites and Mother commissioned her to do six paintings. I cherish each one of them. Eva was always so kind to me. She always encouraged me to pursue my dream of being a dealer and gallery owner. She told me how important it was for a woman to have confidence in what was most assuredly at the time, a man's world. Mother and I were devastated when she died. After your mother, he introduced Janine de la Croix, the extremely talented and passionate contemporary abstract artist, to the world. Janine was tempestuous, feisty, and driven to produce great art. She was, at times, ill tempered, irascible and obstinate, but she always listened to Adrian. He literally plucked her from the streets of Paris, where she spent her days and nights, sketching her abstracts, and selling them to tourists for pennies in an attempt to feed herself and her two children. She was homeless and supplemented her art sales by turning tricks. The father of the children was a drug addict who abandoned them soon after the son was born. Adrian told me that when he discovered Janine as he sat having coffee at a café, two filthy children approached him begging. Well, the children turned out to be Andre and Isabella, Janine's two children. I will have to say, Adrian did a noble thing, taking them in immediately, renting them a flat and giving Janine an income until her works began to sell."

"That's right," I say. "I remember reading an article about Isabella. She now has galleries in St. Barts, Paris, and Sante Fe."

"She does indeed and she is a talented woman in her own right—great gallery operator, artist representative, and gifted still life painter," Julianna says. "I know her and do business with her. In fact, Billy and I were discussing with her details for making her his west coast representative. She is a delightful, caring, and compassionate person, which amazes me considering the life she's experienced, starting out as a child begging in the streets of Paris, transitioning into the lap of luxury with her mother's great success, then losing both her mother and her brother."

"Oh dear," Janet says, "What happened to them?"

"Well, one rainy night Adrian and Janine were driving back to Paris from the country estate of one of Janine's patrons. Something ran out in the road in front of them, Adrian swerved to miss it, ran off the road and hit a tree. Janine's airbag failed to deploy and she was killed instantly. Adrian broke a leg and lost a few teeth, but survived. After Janine's death, Adrian pretty much took care of the children. Isabella flourished, but Andre sank into a world of drugs and crime. He hanged himself in a Paris prison when he was twenty-three."

"My, how sad," Janet says.

Lush's eyeballs keep darting about and she unconsciously begins to bite her nails, a trait she despises in herself, but I know this usually heralds some sort of epiphany.

"Okay, so I know he fashioned Dyanne O'Bryan's career, too, because she came from Bardstown, Kentucky which is right outside of Louisville," Lush directs to Julianna.

"Yes, indeed. I used to tell Mother that Adrian hit the jackpot with Dyanne. Such an immense talent and courage enough to take on the Catholic Church and other institutions that were, at least in her mind, oppressive. The Museum of Modern Art paid twenty five million dollars in 1999 for her three provocative paintings that slammed the Catholic Church, *The Crucifixion of the Madonna*, *The Rape of the Rosary*, and *The Hanging of St. John Houghton*, at the time, a record for a work by a living woman artist acquired by a museum. Of course, as you all know, she and Adrian were both killed in a fire at her farmhouse near Bardstown."

"Julianna," Lush approaches her like a cat stalking a mouse, "Think carefully. Did Adrian ever represent any male artists?"

"Hmmn. Let me think. Well, I know he bought and sold paintings by male artists. But, now that you mention it, I am not aware of any male artist he actually represented."

"A ha!" Lush shouts. "Did Hi Lu Zeng have a young son?"

"Yes, Jonathan. He's a banker in Hong Kong now."

"Did she have a husband or long term boyfriend?" Lush asks.

"Oh no. She played the field for years. I don't know if she even knew who Jonathan's father was," Julianna replies with a smirk.

"Just as I thought," Lush says, her eyes again moving back and forth, rapidly. "Eva had Billy and Philip. Janine had Andre. Dyanne had twin sons, I know because I met them at one of her Louisville showings. I remember they were hanging close to Adrian."

"Yes, she did have two sons, Noel and Christopher. Noel committed suicide when he was fifteen. But what are you saying, Lush?" Julianna asks.

"Don't you all see? It's as plain as day."

"My God, Lush," I say, "He's been targeting female artists with young sons who don't have father figures or, in our case, who have fathers that travel most of the time, so he can prey off their sons, feeding his pedophilia. The fucking bastard. I'm so glad he's dead—except that I regret not having the opportunity to confront him, then punch his lights out."

Lush is pacing back and forth now. She picks up Julianna's glass of champagne that is still full and kills it in one gulp. She is breathing heavy. I begin to worry about her. Clark, sensing tension in the air, trots back in from the kitchen, observes all of us, then walks up to Lush, who stops pacing to pat his head.

"Julianna. I suspect that Adrian McWhorter is the person who found the body of Hi Lu Zeng. Am I right?"

"You are right, Lush."

I feel overwhelmed and dizzy, and I feel tears pushing at my eyes again, and I say in what I think must sound like the voice of a child, "Lush, what are you saying? What are you saying?" The tears stream down. I know deep in my heart what she is about to say.

"Philly, my dear sweet, Philly, I'm saying Adrian McWhorter murdered all of these women, including your mother. He killed them because the women eventually found out that he was sexually abusing their sons. He killed them because he knew he would also make a fortune from their works in his control once they were dead and no new works would ever be created."

I look up at Lush, and I walk over and sit on one of the luxurious sofas. My ears are burning and suddenly I'm thirteen again and all of the rage and fear and hopelessness and loss of control I felt then courses through my veins and I cry and I howl and I moan and I wail for my Mother, snot drips from my nose and drool from my mouth but as I feel the loving arms of three women encircling me, wiping my face, holding me and the head of a red-brown dog resting in my lap watching my face with eyes full of compassionate worry, I realize, even as I am convulsing with tears and pain, that I am a lucky man.

Chapter 18

The women remain silent, letting me cry until I begin to regain my composure, which I do as I stroke Clark's head. The salutary outcome of the three women and the dog silently witnessing as I relive the emotional pain and suffering of my mother's death is extraordinary—it is as if a great, pus-filled boil on my soul, my core self, my essential goodness has been lanced and all the deleterious fluids of the infection have been sucked out, neutralized, and dispersed, leaving only a shallow but tender scar. Although I am emotionally and physically exhausted, I begin to feel a slight awareness of a nascent inner-strength, one that my gut tells me that, for the first time in my life, will set me out beyond the rifts and chasms of fear and despair forged into the fabric of my life by Adrian.

"Thank you all for just being here. I'm a bit embarrassed by all this gushing of emotion, but thank you for seeing me through it," I say, trying to smile.

"Please, Philip. You're the one we should thank for trusting us and honoring us to bear witness to your pain. It's as healing for me, I think, as it is for you," Julianna says, smiling back at me. Lush and Janet nod their heads in agreement. Clark rises up and licks my wet face, causing me to laugh. I hug him, pat his belly, and ask, "Where do we go from here?"

"Todge, we have to substantiate my theories about Adrian, don't you think?" Lush asks.

"I certainly do. I definitely want to talk to Jonathan, Isabella, and Christopher about Adrian. And I want to find a way to solidly connect him to the deaths, well, murders, of all these women. But how?"

"Don't you worry, we'll put those puzzles together in due time," Lush replies. "But what I'm wondering at this point is what do we tell the police? I'm beginning to think we should tell them everything, Philip."

"That may be the thing to do. I mean, if your theories are right, and I think they are, I know, I just know, then the police will have far more available avenues than we will have to get information," I say.

"I don't mean to intrude," Janet says hesitantly, "But won't the police be focusing on Billy and Elliott's murders, rather than on older cases?"

"One would think that," Julianna replies, "Unless, of course, they're connected."

"Hmmm," Lush says, standing with arms akimbo, observing Julianna, "I think you may be on to something, Julianna."

"Really, such as?" I ask.

"Such as this. What if Adrian faked his death at Dyanne O'Bryan's farm?"

"That seems implausible, Lush," Julianna replies.

"Does it? Just think about it a moment. We've already established that he is a very clever bastard whose modus operandi involve carefully manipulating people over long periods of time, gaining immense sexual and financial rewards, then killing them. Why wouldn't he apply this same technique to himself?"

"But whatever for, Lush?" Julianna asks.

"Well, I'm not certain. But just suppose he knew he was on the verge of being caught, by the police, in his pedophilia schemes. By faking his death, he could avoid the police and perhaps even been rewarded greater than ever financially."

"How is that?" I ask.

"Well, life insurance, for one," Lush replies.

"How would we ever prove this?" Janet asks.

Lush is pacing again, but more slowly this time, and she says, "I remember reading an article about Dyanne and Adrian's deaths in the *Courier-Journal* shortly after they occurred. The article said that the fire was so bad that the bodies had to be identified from dental records. Julianna, didn't you say Adrian lost some teeth in the auto wreck with Janine?"

"Yes, several of his front teeth, as I recall."

"There you have it. He could have easily had a full set of dentures by the time of the fire at Dyanne's. He could have bonked some poor migrant tobacco worker in the head, pulled out his teeth with a set of pliers, stuck in his own dentures, and voila, Adrian McWhorter is dead."

"Well, I certainly wouldn't put that past him. I think we all realize he's capable of something like that," I say.

"Precisely," Lush says, "And just suppose that Billy discovered this somehow. Let's imagine that he was ready to expose Adrian and his thirty years of evil doing. My God, what better motive than that would Adrian have for murdering Billy? And it would make complete sense that his lover might know, so he kills Elliott, too."

"Well, if that's the case," Julianna interjects, "Then you really are next, Philip. Perhaps me as well? Adrian certainly would suppose that Billy would have confided in us."

"Yes, you're right, Julianna. But just let the bastard try. Let him send his little Thai twinkies after me, I'll gut them like a catfish, and then, when I do get my hands on Adrian, I'll take the greatest pleasure in my life choking him with my bare hands and watching the life fade from those cold blue eyes. That's it. We cannot tell the police anything. If we do, I may never get the chance to kill him."

"Dear God, Philip. I know how you must feel, but you can't go after him, especially to kill him. That would put you on his level," Julianna says with a look of alarm in her eyes.

"Fuck it. He's forced me to be on his level for most of my life. He's taken my mother and now my brother from me. Why is it not completely rational and sane for me to want to take his life, that is, if he is, in fact, still alive?"

"Well, it is rational, Todge," Lush says, "Completely rational. But I don't want you serving time for a murder. We'll just have to find another way."

"So you agree with me, Lush, that he should be dead?"

"Of course I do, but I don't think we'll have to worry about planning his murder. By the time we find him, I think it'll be a simple act of self defense," she says, smiling a big smile, then adds, "Ladies, do you all agree with me?" Julianna and Janet nod their heads in agreement. "Good, there you have it, Todge: A team of three savvy broads and a pit bull to boot. What more could you ask for?"

"Nothing. I am blessed," I say and smile.

Lush claps her hands, startling Clark, who jumps up on all fours, "Sorry, puppy. This is all coming together in my brain. It just makes perfect sense. The smoking gun is the Blood Brothers Proclamation. That has to be what Benny was after Monday night. God, how obvious is this? It has Adrian's thumb print on it. It will prove he's alive somewhere."

"Oh Lush, that does make perfect sense," Janet adds enthusiastically. I look at Janet and feel glad she's here. I get the sense that she's glad, too.

"Yes, Janet it does. Okay, here's another question for you, Julianna. Adrian must have been worth a fortune; he must have had significant assets. Who did he leave them to?"

"That's simple. His cousin, Julian. Julian Ainsworth," she replies.

"What?" I ask incredulously. "You know his cousin?"

"Well, I've never met him, but I've talked to him on the telephone several times. You see, he resided in Amsterdam and always ran the European side of Adrian's business. It's pretty well known that Adrian left everything to him, including his business. A few years ago, he shut his operation in Amsterdam and moved everything to Dubai. He's a major force now in attracting great works of art there for the wealthy Arabs and the newly formed art museums in the gulf area."

"Well I'll be damned," Lush says. "That explains why Billy went to Dubai for a week in March, last year."

"Did what?" Julianna asks. "He did not. Why, he was getting ready for this opening. I talked to him every day."

"Yes, but did you see him every day?" Lush asks.

"Well, no. But you're mistaken, I know he was here."

"No, he wasn't, Julianna," Lush replies, "Lois has already confirmed it. He paid her a thousand dollars to keep it on the Q T that he was in Dubai. He stayed at the Burj Al Arab. Must have paid cash for everything or was on someone else's nickel."

"Well, that's shocking news to me. I wonder why he hid it from me?"

"My hunch is that he had already figured out everything we have today and he didn't want to endanger anyone else," Lush replies. "Okay, back to the trail, the scent is strong now! Julianna, what does Julian look like?"

"Well, I've never seen him in person, but he is blind in one eye. I can't remember which one, but he wears a black eye patch. He's known to be fairly reclusive and sees few people, only his wealthiest clients. Much of his transactions are done through staff."

"Yes, I bet he does," Lush says. "Let's see. Adrian fakes his death, flies to Argentina for a little plastic surgery, and now he's Julian Ainsworth, a character he developed and sustained for years."

"You think Adrian is Julian?" I ask.

"Of course he is. It explains everything," Lush says and clasps her hands together in a triumphant gesture.

"Lush, you missed your calling, dear, you should've been a detective or at least a private investigator," Julianna says.

"Thanks, Julianna. By the way, do you, or you, Todge, ever recall Adrian traveling to Thailand?"

"No, I don't know that he did," Julianna replies.

"Well, I do," I reply, "He sent Billy and me these fantastic masks and costumes for Halloween one year. He said they were from Bangkok. No one in Union had ever seen anything like them. We won the costume contest at the country club that year."

"Bingo!" Lush states and shakes her right fist up in the air. "I'll bet he even has a residence there. Philip, you know from your research how Thailand is a known source of children for the sex trade, a haven for wealthy pedophiles, I suppose. That's where he got Benny and Bernie. I bet he adopted them, abused them, too, and carefully fashioned them into his pawns to do his dirty work from afar. I bet you he planted them at that bathhouse for the sole purpose of getting them close to Billy."

"You are on a roll, Lush," Julianna says, "And Billy would have come to trust these two."

"Precisely. And they were, or are, the eyes, ears, and even hands of Adrian. Billy must have made contact with Adrian, I mean Julian before last fall when they appeared," Lush knots her brow and pauses.

"What are you thinking now, Lush?" I ask.

"Well, I'm thinking we need to do a strip search on Julian," she replies.

I blush and she knows I follow her. "I see your point," I say.

"Well, I don't," Julianna says, "Would you mind enlightening Janet and me?"

"Certainly," Lush replies. "You see, I doubt Adrian would have gone to the extreme extent to burn off his finger prints, you know, scar them for life. I wouldn't put it past him, though, but if he was so fastidious, I don't think he would have done that. Yet, I wonder if he had any other distinguishing physical features underneath his clothes? Say, a mole on his penis or something? Philip has certainly seen him naked enough times. He should know." They all look at me.

"Well, there is. He has a distinctive birthmark right above his right hip. And if we could find all those pornographic photographs he took with his Hasselblad, I could show you."

"Well, maybe we will find them," Lush says, "But it'll probably be easier to get you to Dubai and in a steam room, for instance, with a naked Julian. Then, we'll know for sure."

"Shouldn't we just tell the police and let them do all of this?" Julianna asks.

"Well, I vote no on that, but I think it should be Philip's call," Lush replies and turns to me. I sigh and right as I'm about to speak, Lois walks in from the kitchen.

"Excuse me. Sorry to interrupt. Timmy called up, Philip. He says there's a gentleman waiting who would like a minute with you. Says his name is Julian Ainsworth."

"For crying out loud…." Lush says.

"Do you think he's here to kill us all?" I ask.

"I doubt it," Lois replies. "He'll have to do it with his bare hands. Officer Graham is already down there checking him out. Told me she's been instructed to go over everyone coming up here with a metal detector and a thorough pat down."

"I bet she has," I reply. "Tell Timmy to send him up, Lois. Then, bring him in here."

"Okay," she turns to leave and Clark follows her.

"Make sure Clark behaves, Lois. But, let him have a good sniffing."

"Will do," she says and walks out.

"'Comme c'est bizarre. Comme qu'elle coincidence'," I quote from *The Bald Soprano*, a favorite quote of Lush's and mine from a French literature class we both took our freshman year at Chapel Hill.

"Indeed it is, Todge. I smell a skunk. I mean, why the hell has this guy jetted over here from Dubai after Billy's murder when you say he's a virtual recluse, Julianna?"

"I haven't a clue, dear, but I think we'll know soon."

"Good heavens," Janet says, "I'm exhausted, emotionally, that is. I've experience more emotional ups and downs this afternoon than I have in my previous forty-seven years of living," she laughs as she says this.

"I believe we all have," I reply.

"Oh honey, stick around, we're just getting started," Lush says and winks at her.

"Philip, I think we should go meet him in the living room. I don't think it would be a good idea for him to see this collection," Julianna says.

"Good point, Julianna, you're absolutely right. Let's go."

We all get up, head into the kitchen and out into the living room. Lois and Clark are waiting in the foyer.

"Lois, we've decided to meet in here," I yell out.

"Okay," she replies just as I hear the elevator door opening.

"Hello, oh! What sort of fine animal specimen do we have here? My goodness, such a robust dog," we hear the somewhat jovial voice of a man who speaks with the accent of the British upper classes.

"Excuse me sir," Lois says, "he just wants to be friendly."

"Oh, not a problem, madam. I'm a lover of hounds of all types. Will he let me pet him?"

"Sure," Lois says.

"Lois," Officer Graham says, "This is Mr. Julian Ainsworth, from Dubai. He's here to pay condolences to Mr. Hampton."

"Yes, well, please come into the living room," Lois instructs. He walks in, Officer Graham remains in the foyer, and Lois walks into the kitchen.

I am filled with anxiety and anticipation, but as soon as I see Julian, I realize that this couldn't be Adrian because no amount of plastic surgery could create such differences. Julian is old; he must be at least seventy. Adrian would be in his mid-fifties. Julian is a plump man, impeccably dressed in an elegant grey suit with a matching vest, and he limps along slowly with the aid of a black cane, its silver handle shaped like the head of an eagle. He is completely bald, a black patch covers his right eye, and his skin is extremely pale. He proceeds toward us with an air of confidence, walks right up to me, and says, "My dear, Mr. Hampton, please forgive my unannounced intrusion. My name is Julian Ainsworth," he bows his head as he says this.

"Pleased to make your acquaintance, Mr. Ainsworth," I reply and put forth my right hand. He quickly moves his cane from his right hand, which I notice trembles, to his left hand, grasps my hand, and shakes it firmly. Clark walks over, bites the end of the cane and tries to start a game of tug of war with Julian.

"My goodness. Playful fellow you have here, Mr. Hampton," Mr. Ainsworth says as he tries to pull his cane back from Clark. Clark growls and wags his tail.

"No Clark. No. Spit it out," I say in a forceful voice. Clark drops it immediately, turns toward me, and sits down. "Good boy, thank you, Clark," I say as I pat his head.

"Yes, well, where were we?" Mr. Ainsworth scratches his head with his right hand. "Oh, I've been in New York this week handling some affairs of business, and I was shocked and devastated to hear the news of your brother. Please, sir, I would like to express my deepest sympathies and heartfelt condolences to you and your family," he says looking into my eyes with his left eye that is a hazel green color. I glance at Lush who is eyeing Julian with a great deal of suspicion. "Thank you, Mr. Ainsworth, how kind of you. Allow me to introduce you to my friends. This is Sarah Richardson, from Louisville, Kentucky."

"Miss Richardson, my pleasure, madam," he says, nods his head, adding, "Several of my associates travel to the bluegrass frequently in search of the perfect equine specimen."

"I'm sure they do, Mr. Ainsworth. Nice to meet you," she replies.

"This is Janet Ostro who resides here in New York."

"Enchanté, Miss Ostro, I'm so pleased to make your acquaintance," he smiles, bowing again.

"Thank you, Mr. Ainsworth. I'm delighted to meet you as well," she replies with a bit of an affected accent that almost makes me laugh out loud.

"Please excuse me sir, but there's no need for an introduction to this lovely lady, for her elegant visage is more famous, I dare say, than the many talented artists she represents. Miss Julianna Morgan, what a great privilege and pleasure it is to finally meet you."

Julianna extends her right hand, he takes it, and gently kisses it as she says, "How marvelous to finally meet you, Mr. Ainsworth, after all these years we've talked over the telephone. I was beginning to wonder if you were a real person."

"Yes, indeed. I'm rather a recluse. That is, I much prefer to spend my time in study and observation of fine art. I'm not the social one. Adrian always took care of that. Even so, after his tragic death, I only make public appearances when absolutely necessary, as is the case here this week."

"Please, Mr. Ainsworth, won't you take a seat?" I ask.

"Thank you sir, at my age, my legs just are not as dependable as they used to be." He slowly backs up and sits in an upholstered high back armchair, observes us all for a moment, then says. "I arrived here on Monday. You see, I'm finally disposing of Adrian's properties here, and it is just much less complicated if I do it in person, rather than establishing power of attorneys and proxies and overnight deliveries of documents and such. What a complicated world we live in these days? Right? Yes, well, there's also the matter of the artwork in his flat. He has some exquisite pieces, as you might certainly imagine, and I felt it absolutely necessary that I supervise the packing personally." He clears his throat, smiles, looks at us over his hands that are both holding the handle of his cane, and then pauses. "Let's see, where was I?" He laughs again, causing his big belly to shake, and I cannot help but like this man. I notice the women are looking at him attentively, and I think they must be falling for his charm, too. "Dear me, another problem with aging is that you are right in the middle of delivering some important point or observation, or whatever else it is which is of concern to one. That is, something worthy of some sort of comment, and blasted, well, there you have it. You forget about what you were speaking. Confounded! Yes, well, that's it. I heard the disturbing news concerning Billy on the BBC. Contacts in the business told me you were here, Mr. Hampton, and I thought, that, well that since your family and mine have been engaged together in the business of art for so many years, well, I thought it was my rightful duty to call upon you and pay

my respects. There you have it!" He starts to chuckle, but emits a loud and guttural throat clearing sound and assumes a somber look on his face.

"That's very kind of you, Mr. Ainsworth. As strange as this may seem to you, we all were just discussing you and your cousin, Adrian, when we were informed of your arrival here," I look at him straight in his eye.

"Really? How extraordinary! Things can be so unexpected at times." He clears his throat loudly again and says, "Please forgive all this noise. I've become quite accustomed to the dry air of Dubai—a blessing for the sinuses. I fear a pestilence from this soggy, chilled, New England air. By the way, not cousin, he's really my brother."

"Brother?" I ask.

"Indeed, brother. Adrian and I were not cousins, but truly, we both started life as mere foundlings, taken in by a clergyman, a rector, in fact, Rector Ainsworth, and his wife in the little village of Ecton in Northhamptonshire. I was a boy of ten when they brought in little Adrian in a basket with the name Adrian McWhorter on a bit of paper pinned to the blanket, so they kept his name. No names were found on my basket, so the rector gave me the name Julian Ainsworth. Life at the rectory in such a small village was hard, especially after dear Mrs. Ainsworth passed away from a horrible cancer when I was twelve and Adrian just a tot. The rector was a stern, cold man who basically used us as slave labor for completing tasks around the church and the rectory. He schooled us himself, allowed us very little interaction with the children of the village, and regularly abused us."

"Abused you? How?" I ask.

"Well. This is a difficult subject, especially in the presence of ladies. Do you mind if I speak frankly, Mr. Hampton?"

"Mr. Ainsworth, you may."

"Yes, very well, then. I'm speaking about sexual abuse. You see, the most Reverend Mr. Ainsworth was nothing more than a pedophile walking around in priest robes. Most unpleasant topic, but it is the truth. Of course, I've heard about all that sort of thing happening over here in the Catholic Church, so I suppose it's not so uncommon a thing."

"Mr. Ainsworth, are you telling us this, in an attempt to make us forgive Adrian for his extreme and long term acts of pedophilia against Billy and Philip Hampton, and quite possibly many other sons of his women clients?" Lush asks him point blank.

"Oh no, dear lady. No indeed. It never occurred to me that Adrian could possibly be a pedophile himself until Billy Hampton started contacting me last year wanting to discuss this matter. I was reluctant to get into such conversation, what with Adrian dead and gone, but Billy was persistent, and I could tell he needed resolution on this matter in order to move on with his work and his life."

"So, it was you he visited in Dubai last year?" I ask.

"Yes, it was."

"So he was in the Middle East last year?" Julianna asks.

"Yes, we found out from Lois. We have no records of him spending anything on that trip. Did you pay for it, Julian?" I ask.

"Well, in a way, I did. My closest friends in Dubai are members of the ruling family of the United Arab Emirates as well as rulers in Saudi Arabia, Kuwait, Oman, and several other oil nations. We share an intense desire to introduce and establish the great art of these countries on the world stage and to acquire great examples of world art to house in all the new museums being built in the Middle East. My friends in these countries have a strong desire to use the huge surplus of disposable income they have from oil production to build, maintain, and endow world-class art institutions. So you see, I rarely have to travel by commercial airline. I simply make a call and there is always someone going to New York, Geneva, Hong Kong, wherever. Billy flew over on a close friend of mine's Airbus and back on the 777 of a prince. Of

course his stay at Burj Al Arab was complimentary. Several of my clients already own works from Billy and from his Mother and they are excited about the possibilities of his new collection. Billy and I met on two occasions while he was there. I introduced him to one of the crown princes of a neighboring oil producing country who has admired his work. The two of them became friends and spent a good deal of time together. "

"Yes, I see, but may we get back to Adrian, a bit?" Lush says.

"Of course, madam."

"So you were not aware Adrian was a pedophile?" Lush directs to Mr. Ainsworth.

"Dear lady," he replies as a red blush runs over his face and head, "I, myself, was subjected to the evil invasions of a sexual nature by the very Reverend Ainsworth from the time I was seven until I went away to Amsterdam when I was seventeen to study architecture. I remained in close contact with Adrian, whom I loved as my brother. I was very aware that Reverend Ainsworth perpetrated sexual abuse on Adrian, the same as he did on me, but I was helpless to aid Adrian until Adrian got older and I had somewhat established myself. When Adrian turned fifteen, I arranged for him to come live with me in Amsterdam. That's where Adrian started his life long love of the Dutch Masters and his life's work in fine arts."

"And whatever became of Reverend Ainsworth?" Lush asks.

"I don't know. Once Adrian joined me, I never had any more contact with Ecton or anyone from there. If he's still alive, he'd be a very old man by now."

"Well, thank you for sharing that with us Mr. Ainsworth. I do have another question concerning Adrian," Lush peers at him and her eyes narrow.

"In going through his belongings in the years since his death, did you not discover the photographs he made of himself and his victims? I am referring to explicit photographs showing Adrian having sex with little boys."

"Dear God, no, madam. I've never seen anything like that. I just can't believe Adrian could have ever done something that horrible."

"It's true, Mr. Ainsworth," I say. "I am a survivor of Adrian's filthy acts toward little boys. He photographed my brother and me on many occasions at my hometown and in his apartment here in New York. He always used his old Hasselblad. Why, Billy and I even helped him develop some of the photos in his dark room here. Something must exist—negatives, something, there were so many of them."

Mr. Ainsworth's face has become beaded with perspiration and his breathing is a bit labored. He pulls out a linen handkerchief from his lapel pocket and begins to dab his face. "Please excuse me. I'm afraid all of this horrible news is just a bit much for me. My dear Adrian, so kind, so gentle, this is all so unexpected." He sighs and continues to wipe his face. I really begin to feel sorry for this old man.

"Mr. Ainsworth, might I offer you some cold water or tea?" I ask.

"Thank you, Mr. Hampton, you're so kind to offer. I would so love a glass of cold water, no ice please, and, if it would not be any trouble, a nice shot of scotch, neat, on the side."

"Certainly," I say. I see Lush smiling.

"Todge, I'll get it, does anyone else care for a libation?" Lush asks. I notice when Lush calls me Todge, Mr. Ainsworth seems alarmed, but only for a brief moment.

"No thank you, Lush. I need to be going soon, but first I want to put everything back in the studio," Julianna says, and stands up. Everyone stands up, and Mr. Ainsworth grabs hold of the arms of the chair and tries to stand, gets half way up, then falls back into the chair. His cane falls on the rug.

"Oh, please, Mr. Ainsworth. There's no need to get up," Julianna walks over to him and takes both his hands in hers. "It's been delightful meeting you, even though the circumstances are of a difficult nature. I do hope to see you again. Perhaps we can get together or have lunch while you're in town?"

He seems visibly pleased by Julianna's remarks and he smiles and says, "Dear lady, there's nothing I'd like better than to have luncheon with you. It is my great misfortune that I will be engaged at the

barrister's, rather, attorney's offices for most of the day tomorrow and my friend's plane leaves tomorrow evening."

"Well, it's my loss, too, Mr. Ainsworth. Perhaps another time?"

"Yes, indeed madam."

"Mr. Ainsworth," Janet walks up to him, "I've greatly enjoyed making your acquaintance as well. I'm afraid I have to take my leave as soon as I finish helping Julianna in the studio."

"Well, thank you madam. I'm most delighted to have made your acquaintance as well. By the way, could I be so presumptuous to ask if you all are previewing Billy's latest works in the studio?"

Janet's mouth falls open and Julianna immediately responds, "Mr. Ainsworth, if I had not had the pleasure of seeing what a gentleman you are with my own eyes, I might be forced to think that you were here not only to pay your condolences to Philip, but to sneak a preview of Billy's final works."

"Good heavens, Miss Morgan, never would I stoop to such. Billy did give me a brief description of the overall theme of these works. Why he even showed me a few digital photographs. I just thought it might be possible for me to take a quick peek at some of the actual paintings," he says, smiling at Julianna.

"Well, if it were up to me, Mr. Ainsworth, I'd show them to you in an instant, because I know you have clients who would probably buy every one of the paintings prior to my exhibition of them. Sadly, though, it's completely out of my control and out of the control of their new owner, Philip. You see, the police came in this morning and confiscated every single piece as evidence in the murder of Billy Hampton."

Lush does a double take, and I have to bite my tongue hard. I would never have guessed that Julianna was such a skilled liar.

"Evidence?" Mr. Ainsworth asks in a weak voice and looks down at the floor.

"Yes, indeed. You see, the police think these paintings tell a story—a story that will lead them straight to the killers," Julianna responds, smiles, then says, "Come along, Janet, dear, let's go clean up the mess the police made." They walk out into the kitchen and Clark trots behind them.

"Todge, I'm going to make an Old Fashioned, you want one?" Lush asks.

"What time is it?" I ask

"Four thirty."

"Sure." She walks over to the wet bar and starts to make the drinks.

"Mr. Ainsworth, my brother means more to me than anything. I will not rest until I find the persons responsible for his murder. He went to great extremes to hide his trip to Dubai last March. Please tell me anything you can about the trip or any conversations you had with him before or after the trip." I look at him straight in his eye.

"Yes, well, of course, certainly." He clears his throat loudly. "Well, this has all happened so quickly. You see, I received a telephone call from your brother near the end of February a year ago. He said he would really appreciate visiting with me in person to discuss a matter of a personal nature that he was uncomfortable discussing over phone lines. I told him that I had plans to be in New York during the first part of April, but he was quick to reply that that wasn't soon enough. I told him that he could come to Dubai any time, and I would be willing to meet with him. He said that, because of the sensitive nature of his latest works and because of what he needed to discuss with me that would pertain to those works, it was important that this trip to Dubai be of a clandestine nature. Well, given our long association with your family, Mr. Hampton, and the fact that I have many clients willing to pay vast sums for your brother's best works, I told him that I could arrange for his travel and stay in Dubai without him having to spend anything, thus leaving not a trace. He acquiesced and the trip was set—I believe he arrived on the twelfth and left on the seventeenth, March, a year ago."

"Yes, that's what his housekeeper, Lois has told us. Please, continue."

"Well, I met him at the Burj Al Arab on Sunday evening and we dined in his suite. He informed me about Adrian's acts of pedophilia on himself and you. I, of course, truthfully told him I had no knowledge

160

of this, but that it was not out of the realm of possibilities because of what Adrian and I had experienced ourselves as children at the hand of Reverend Ainsworth. Billy told me that he had, I believe he phrased it, 'worked through' this childhood abuse with the aide of a competent psychiatrist, but that he just needed to get closure from someone close to Adrian—someone who might corroborate the abuse. Obviously, I was closer to Adrian than anyone, I believe, but I was not able to corroborate for certain the episodes of pedophilia."

"Episodes of pedophilia?" I ask.

"Yes, indeed. Is that not the correct phrase for his accusations?"

"Mr. Ainsworth. You have told me today that you yourself were a victim of sexual abuse from an adult when you were a child. Do you really think of that as 'episodes of pedophilia'?" I ask.

"Yes, well, sir, I do see your point. Rather, well, in my case, I always assumed it was just something I had to endure, being a foundling and all. For heavens sake, I realized I was lucky too have been taken in at all."

"Mr. Ainsworth, in my view, all children deserve to be taken in, and no child deserves to endure any abuse, no, sir, no abuse of any kind, at any time."

"Well, I quite agree with you, sir," he replies.

"I explained to Billy that I had no knowledge of Adrian's sexual proclivities—I just always assumed Adrian's love of art and his business prevented him from ever having any sort of long-term relationship."

"Excuse me, Mr. Ainsworth, didn't you ever think that strange? I mean—well are you married?"

"I am a widower, Mr. Hampton. My wife and my young son died over forty years ago—they both drowned on a ferry boat that capsized in a storm while visiting her parents in North Holland on holiday."

"I'm so sorry, Mr. Ainsworth," I reply, "I don't mean to cause you to suffer. I just have to find out all I can about Billy's death."

"Please, Mr. Hampton, it's no intrusion at all. I'll help you any way I can. It's just that, I'm afraid there's not much left to tell you. I invited your brother for luncheon the next day, Monday, at my house. I invited several of my clients and friends who knew his work or your mother's work. My guests included a sheikh of a small oil-producing nation and his son. Your brother and the son took an instant liking to one another. After that luncheon, I never saw or talked to your brother again. He sent me a most marvelous arrangement of white orchids that Friday, and I learned from my friend, the sheikh, that his son had spent the week giving your brother a complete tour of the royal palace and other wonderful features of that particular country. The son personally delivered your brother back to New York on the new Boeing 777 the son received for his twenty-first birthday last year. I imagine they had a grand time, but I assure you, Mr. Hampton, that's all I know to tell you."

"But can't you tell me who this sheikh and his son are?" I ask.

"Mr. Hampton, please do not take this as condescension. My friends and clients in the Middle East remain my friends and clients because I respect and honor their need for privacy. In that regard I honored your brother's need of privacy in his visit to me. However, he did reveal to me the nature of his latest works, and I would be a dishonest man if I did not reveal to you that it is of great concern to me and my friend, the sheikh, that your brother may have included a painting of his son in, well let's just say, in a position which would not be advantageous at all for a future leader of a nation." He lets out a great sigh as Lush arrives with the drinks.

"And how in God's name would you know about any such work?" I snap back.

"Well, it seems as if the son bragged about posing in the nude with nothing on but his Keffiyea to one of his sisters, who, in turn, betrayed her brother's confidence, to their father, when the brother refused to let the her borrow his 777 for a trip to Paris. Subsequently I received a call from the sheikh."

"I see. Thanks for the drinks, Lush," I say as she sets the water and scotch on a small table beside Mr. Ainsworth's chair and then hands me an Old Fashioned.

"Mr. Ainsworth, is that really why you came here today?" I ask.

"Certainly not. As I indicated previously, this trip has been scheduled for some months now. The sheikh had only called me last week, he was so kind to offer his plane for my trip, so I told him I would get in touch with Billy to talk about any paintings of his son. Naturally, when I heard the news of Billy's murder, I was shocked and wanted to come pay my respects when I learned of your arrival."

"I wonder if the New York City police would consider this sheikh of this small oil producing nation a suspect in my brother's murder? What do you think, Lush?"

"Sounds like a reasonable motive to me." She replies.

"Oh my, oh my. This is not good, no, no. Not good at all. I assure you, the sheikh is a most benevolent and gentle man and would never have anything to do with any murder. He has authorized me to pay a handsome sum for any painting or paintings that your brother might have done of his son."

"Oh he has, has he? Well here's a toast to the sheikh, the sheikh of some small oil producing nation who doesn't want the world to know that his son had sex with my brother." I hold up my glass to toast.

"I'll drink to that," Lush says and clinks her glass to mine, then she turns to Mr. Ainsworth and says, "Well, Mr. Ainsworth?"

"Oh dear me, do you really think they slept together? Perhaps it was just a case of normal male camaraderie. I assured the sheikh that was probably all it was. Dear me, yes I do need this drink." He forces a quick smile, puts the scotch glass to his lips and imbibes the drink in one gulp.

"Delightful," he says. Lush laughs.

"How about another?"

"Yes, please madam." She walks over, gets the bottle of scotch and fills his glass.

"Thank you, Miss Richardson, you are most generous." He takes a large gulp, then sets the glass down on the side table. "Mr. Hampton, the sheikh has authorized me to offer the sum of five million dollars for the painting or paintings of his son we have discussed. This, of course, must all be done in secrecy and the existence of such painting or paintings must never be disclosed."

"Mr. Ainsworth, I only got the most cursory of looks at some of my brother's works today before the situation with the police Miss Morgan described to you transpired. As you are aware, this condominium is under twenty-four-hour surveillance by the police with armed officers inside and outside. The police believe that the killer or killers may try to murder me as well. I am not familiar with this royal family about whom you've spoken today, and I cannot recall seeing anyone in my brother's paintings who resembled a crown prince. However, since most of the subjects were indeed nude and engaged in a variety of sexual acts, it would be hard for me to differentiate a crowned prince from a street hustler."

Mr. Ainsworth's mouth falls open at this statement and he retrieves the scotch for another healthy sip. "Furthermore, my brother has left me specific instructions about what to do with his remaining paintings. We do plan to have a posthumous exhibition of these works when and if they are returned to us and they will be offered for sale. I'm sure Julianna will keep you informed as to the date of the exhibition."

"Oh yes, I'm sure she will," he replies and lets out a big sigh. "Well, I've taken enough of your time today, Mr. Hampton." He grabs the arms of the chair and gives a mighty heave. This time he manages to stand, but nearly falls forward. Lush and I both rush toward him to steady him.

"Thank you both. I apologize, my balance just is not that good anymore."

I bend down, pick up his cane, hand it to him, and say, "Mr. Ainsworth, I really appreciate your coming by today to pay your respects to Billy. It means a great deal to me."

"It is my honor, sir." He takes his cane and bows his head again.

"Madam, delightful meeting you," he says to Lush.

"And you as well, Mr. Ainsworth," she nods back. We escort him to the elevator. Officer Graham gets up from the upholstered bench where she has been waiting and says, "I'll be happy to escort Mr. Ainsworth down."

"Thank you, Officer Graham," I say. The elevator door opens and Officer Graham gets in and holds the door open. Mr. Ainsworth enters, turns around, reaches into his lapel pocket, pulls out a card, and hands it to me.

"There you go, my dear boy. That's my contact information. Please let me know if you ever have plans to be in Dubai. I think I could introduce you to a side of the Middle East that might interest a fine journalist such as yourself a great deal. Good day." He nods his head as the door closes.

I look at Lush, shake my head and ask, "What the fuck was that all about?"

"I'm not sure, Todge, but I'm thinking a visit to Ecton is in order, and soon," she replies.

"I'm in total agreement. Let's go regroup with Julianna and Janet. We need to set forth a unified plan of action."

"Great, let's go."

CHAPTER 19

We enter the studio as Julianna and Janet are finishing returning the paintings to the storage slots. Clark, who is stretched out asleep in his bed, hears us, opens his eyes, and jumps up to greet us. I stop, bend over, rub his back, pat his head, and say, "Well, ladies, our surprise visitor has left us. I thought we might have a quick meeting to summarize and figure out where we're going from here."

"Good idea," Julianna says as she walks over to us, wiping her hands with a cloth. "As careful as we tried to be, some of these paintings are still wet, but we just touched the edges, no damage. I brought my digital camera and we've photographed each painting and any comments Billy posted on the backs."

"That's good, ladies," Lush says.

"Listen, Philip," Julianna stops wiping her hands and looks at me, "I was thinking. I have an idea for the police. The value of these paintings is easily in the tens of millions of dollars."

"Yes, I know. Mr. Ainsworth just offered me five million dollars for the painting of Billy and the young Arab. It seems the young man is the son of a sheikh of a small oil producing country."

Julianna's mouth falls open, "Goodness, I was going to start pricing at one half million, but if we already have an offer of five million, there's no telling what this collection will bring."

"Well, not to disrupt your marketing plans for the exhibition, but I told him I was unaware of any such painting. I thought it better to keep these paintings on as low profile as possible until this murder is solved."

"Yes, of course, you're right about that. I hadn't considered that, but this whole aura of murder and sex around these paintings should make their prices skyrocket," she replies.

"Yes, I agree with that," I reply.

"Oh, how did Julian know about the painting?" Julianna asks.

"It seems the crown prince bragged about it to one of the princesses who ratted on her brother to the king who is a friend and client of Julian's," I reply.

"I see. Well, back to what I was saying, Philip. I bet you can reason with the police to leave the paintings here, for the time being, anyway. They can send over their ace photographers and take as many photos as they please. Then, they'll have all the evidence they need, and digitally, at their fingertips."

"Good thinking, Julianna," Lush says.

"Yes, I agree," I say, "I'll talk to the detectives. Speaking of them, what do you all think we should reveal to them this point?"

"Well, they're going to see the paintings, so they'll know about Benny and Bernie. I don't think we should share my theory about Adrian at this point, and I don't think you should give them the Blood Brother's Proclamation," Lush says.

"But hasn't Julian's visit pretty much undermined your theory that Adrian committed the murders and is still alive?" Julianna asks.

"Oh no, not in my mind. I don't buy one bit of Julian's story. I'm certain his presence here is somehow connected to Billy's murder. What I wouldn't give to have someone follow him?" Lush says, clasping her hands together to keep from biting her nails.

"Yes, Lush," Julianna says. "Listen, I use a private investigator from time to time. You can imagine the situations that occur when you are buying, selling, transporting, displaying, and conserving paintings worth big dollars. His name is Jonas Grey. He's an ex-NYPD detective and ex-Navy Seal. He's one of the best in town; all the big insurers use him. I'm sure if I give him a call, he or one of his associates could squeeze us in."

"I think we ought to do it," I say. "For instance, I'd like to have Adrian's fingerprint from the proclamation checked out to see if it matches anything in the FBI's database. He could do, that couldn't he?"

"Oh yes, quite easily, I think," Julianna replies.

"I think we should save Julian's scotch glass and have that checked, too," Lush says.

"Good idea," I reply, "Listen, Julianna, it's hard for me to make a move without the police knowing everything I do. Could you call up Mr. Grey, maybe even meet him as soon as you leave here and engage him? I don't care what it costs. I don't know where Julian is staying, but give him Adrian's address. Have him start there to see if Julian is, in fact, packing paintings and closing on the property. You can fill him in on as many of the details as you see fit."

"Absolutely," she replies.

"I don't mean to butt in," Janet says who has been blotting perspiration from her face with a white handkerchief, "But maybe they should also check the airports to find out what private planes are here from the Middle East. Mr. Ainsworth did say his friend's plane was leaving tomorrow evening."

"Brilliant, Janet," Lush says, "And, honey, you're not butting in at all. Keep those ideas coming. We need all the help we can get."

"Just want to pull my weight," Janet smiles and adds, "And, there's plenty of it to pull."

"Oh, Janet, dear", Julianna quickly throws a sharp glance of disapproval at Janet like a dart hitting the bull's-eye, then looks at Lush and me, then back at Janet, "Please don't poke fun at yourself like that. You're among people who accept you the way you are. I can't tell you how much I've enjoyed our conversation this afternoon—you're extremely intelligent, sensitive, compassionate, easy going, and a good conversationalist, and I feel fortunate to have made your acquaintance and hope we can become friends."

Janet begins to blush, her brow tightens, and she seems to stop breathing.

"Good heavens," Julianna says, "I don't mean to be critical, Janet. It's just that making fun of one's self is a sore spot with me. I used to be the same way as a younger person. I was always so much taller than all the other girls and many of the boys, for that matter. Some mean girls at prep school nicknamed me "stretch" so I began to cope with the pain of it all by making fun of my height in front of them and others. My mother witnessed this one day. I could tell by her expressions that she was extremely bothered by my statements. That evening before bed as I was sitting at my vanity brushing my hair, she came in, put her hands on my shoulders and told me that I may not be able to understand it then, but that the key to happiness in life is to accept yourself for what you truly are and turn what you perceive as your

weaknesses and bad points into strengths. I listened to my mother and you know what I found out? That it works, at least in my case. A tall woman has an advantage in dealing with men in business situations in a man's world. My mother was a very clever woman."

"Thank you, Julianna," Janet replies, then sighs. "It's just that I've been overweight my entire life. I've tried just about everything to lose weight, but nothing has worked. My family was terrific—they all loved me and never made fun of me, but, of course, the kids at school always did. I guess I've just coped with it by showing other people that I can laugh at it too. Deep down inside, I know you are right. I hope I can get there someday, and I'm sorry to have upset you."

Julianna walks over and hugs Janet and says, "Dear, I'm not upset. You'll find that I don't beat around the bush with my feelings, particularly with people who I sense have a lot to offer to others and me. Isn't that right, Philip?"

"Quite right, Julianna," I reply. "But a warning, Janet. Don't ever make her mad or…." I let out a long whistle and smile.

"You devious bastard," Julianna fires back.

"See, what did I tell you, Janet?"

We all laugh.

"Alright," Julianna says, "Is there anything else I need to know before I go?"

"I think we all agree on what to say to the police," Lush replies.

"Yes, basically just about seeing the paintings, but no mention of the proclamation," Julianna replies.

"Yes, let's keep them on the trail of Benny and now Bernie. We can always pitch them a bone later if we need their help," Lush states.

"That sounds good to me," I say. "Julianna, thanks so much for the wonderful and moving explanation of Billy's work. It's just so sad that he will not be here to see his wonderful collection unfold upon the world."

"You're welcome and well said, Philip darling," Julianna replies.

"Janet, I can't thank you enough for coming here today. I know it's probably been sort of a weird experience for you, but I just can't thank you enough for coming and for everything you did for my brother."

"Philip, it's been my pleasure, and I'll do everything I can to help solve this crime. And I can't thank you enough for including me and introducing me to Julianna and Lush." Clark walks over and nudges her right leg. She leans over to pet him. "And of course, Mr. Clark. He's just the best dog. Yes he is."

Lush walks over to Janet and gives her a hug. "Janet, I'm so glad you came today. Here's my card with all my contact information. I got your mobile number from Philip. I'll be in touch."

"Lush, thank you. I'm really glad I got to meet you," Janet replies, smiling with a look of true joy on her face. It always amazes me how quickly women can bond. Here they are acting like sorority sisters after just a short afternoon together. Even Lush and Julianna have withdrawn their claws usually aimed at one another. Well, perhaps there's a lesson for me to learn here, but I am thankful I have these women on my side. I'm certain it will make this journey on which we all are about to embark a much richer experience. And, I for one, would not want the three of them coming after me. Damn, I wish Fatgram were here, she'd love these women.

"Janet, I insist," Julianna says as we walk to the foyer. "You've already missed your art lesson. My car is waiting downstairs. You can accompany me to Jonas's office, then we'll pop by the gallery so I can wrap things up there for the day, and then, you're just going to love this, we'll go to my house for a little dinner, and I want to show you my family's art collection."

"Oh, Julianna, I'd love to but, my dogs, they need to go outside and I have to feed them," she replies.

"Isn't there someone you can call, a neighbor, perhaps, who can do that for you?" Julianna asks.

"Normally, yes, but both of my standbys are out of town this week, and I need to give my dog sitter advanced notice," she replies.

"Not a problem, we'll just swing by your place, after we stop at the gallery. Do your dogs travel well?"

"What do you mean?"

"Well, just feed them and then we'll put them in the car with us and take them to my place. I have a lovely little garden, all enclosed; they can have the run of it. My cat, Esmeralda, is fine with dogs. Do they mind cats?"

"Oh dear, that's too much of an imposition, Julianna."

"Not at all. It'll be fun. My driver can take you home when you're ready."

"Well, okay. Harry and Sally love to ride in cars and they'll be fine with Esmeralda. Several friends in my building have cats and the dogs are used to them."

"Wonderful. Philip, Lush, I'll call you and let you know what Jonas says," Julianna says as we arrive in the foyer. Officer Graham stands up and smiles at us.

"Miss Morgan and Miss Ostro are leaving," I say and push the button for the elevator. A moment later the door opens and Dad, Brenda, and the kids are in the elevators. Clark is so happy to see them, he runs into the elevator and starts jumping up on the kids.

"Hello everyone," I say, "Clark, stop jumping, get back in here." They all move into the foyer, and I hold the elevator door open and say, as quickly as I can, "This is my Dad and his wife Brenda. And these are their children Peter, Andrew, and Emma. This is Julianna Morgan, Billy's art representative. And this is Janet Ostro, the nurse who took care of Billy this week." Everyone exchanges greetings and Julianna and Janet get in the elevator and say goodbye as the door closes.

"Sorry for the rush, you guys," I say shrugging my shoulders, "But they've been here all afternoon and they really needed to get going. How was 'The Lion King'?"

"It was great, Philip. Nala is my favorite, I wanna be just like her," Emma says and runs over to me. I instantly pick her up. She is carrying a stuffed animal.

"What's that?" I ask.

"It's Nala, silly. Haven't you seen 'The Lion King'?"

"Well, as a matter of fact I have, missy, but I'm old and I just can't remember it as well as you can." She laughs and gives me a kiss on my cheek.

"Yuk, prickly, you need to shave, Philip."

"You're right, I let it go today, but I will tomorrow, I promise. Here you go, honey." I set her down. Clark immediately walks up and tries to pull Nala from her grasp.

"No Clark, you mustn't hurt Nala, she's a good lion cub. You need to go after the hyenas," she says loudly. Clark immediately lets go and looks up to me for support.

"That's right, boy," I say and I bend down to hug him, "I'll get you an old hyena stuffed toy to play with. But a Greenie first." He wags his tail and licks my face. I stand back up. "Did you boys like the show?"

"Awesome," Peter says. "The music rocked."

"Yeah, I liked all the costumes and the dancers," Andrew says as he rocks on his feet, fidgeting.

"It was marvelous," Brenda says. "The children were enthralled—their first Broadway musical. Now kids, run along and change into your play clothes. Put these clothes away neatly, you may have to wear them again. I'll be checking." They run down the hall into the bedrooms, Clark in pursuit.

"I'm so glad you all got to go," Lush says, "Your children will never forget this."

"You're right, Lush," Dad replies. "It's a marvelous thing for children to see a Broadway play, especially one geared toward children." He turns to me. "Do you remember when your mother and I took you and your brother to see 'Cats' in 1983?"

"I do, Dad, very well." I reply, but I think my expression must give away my surprise that he remembers this at all. He was in New York working at some furniture or gift show and we hardly saw him. We spent all our time with Mother and Uncle Adrian and we were all surprised when Dad showed up, in the darkened theatre, after the show had begun.

"I hope they delivered the groceries I ordered," Brenda quickly interjects.

"Oh dear, we've been so busy with Billy's new works, I didn't even notice," Lush says. "I'm sure Lois took care of them. Is she still here?"

"I'm still here, Miss Richardson," Lois says walking into the foyer, "But I'm on the way home now. The groceries all came, Mrs. Hampton. I checked everything against your list. They forgot the shallots and strawberries, so I made them go back and bring them."

"Splendid, Lois," Brenda says, "Thank you so much for doing that."

"Not a problem, mam. Well, I'll be back at nine in the morning with my friend Tammy. We'll be doing deep cleaning tomorrow and we'll stay as long as it takes."

"Thanks Lois," I say, "We'll see you in the morning."

She gets into the elevator and says, "Now, listen, you all enjoy yourselves tonight. Don't worry about cleaning up the kitchen. Leave everything for me and Tammy. I know where everything goes so it don't matter what you dirty up." She smiles at us as the door closes.

"Thanks, Lois," Brenda says, "What a perfect housekeeper. I wish she'd move to St. Louis. Well, I better go change and start cooking. Lord, it's a quarter to six. Anyone for a cocktail?"

"I'll fix drinks while you all change," Lush says. "What are you having? The usual?"

"Suits me," Brenda says. "Charles?"

Dad looks at me with a bit of a sad expression and says, "Just a glass of ginger ale for me, Lush, thanks."

They walk away and Lush and I start to move into the living room.

"Mr. Hampton," Officer Graham says, "Officer Kelly will be replacing me at six pm. Do you think anyone will be going out tonight?"

"No, Officer Graham, I don't think so."

"Good. Officer Kelly and I are dividing the watch up into two twelve-hour shifts to make it easier on you all. I mean, I know it's difficult having strangers in your house and all.""Thank you," I say and think to myself that this woman is wishy-washy: ready to stab us on reviewing Billy's collection and now apologizing for the inconveniences of her presence.

"Detective Bell called and asked me to tell you and Miss Richardson that they've determined that that Benny fellow was indeed following you all today. It seems he was taking photographs of you. He's very good. Two other officers were trailing me. None of us saw him. Thank goodness for our own photographers."

"I'm not really worried about him in here, Officer Graham. Clark will rip his throat out."

"Really?"

"Oh yes, really. It was all we could do to keep Clark off him the other night. It was obvious Clark scared Benny shitless," Lush replies flippantly.

"I see," Officer Graham replies. "Well, that's a dog I'd want on my side."

"Well, have a good evening, Officer Graham. I suppose we'll see you in the morning," I say.

"Yes, have a nice dinner," she replies.

"Thanks," I say and Lush and I walk into the living room.

"I'll get Julian's glass and put it in a plastic bag," I say as I walk over to where he sat. "Damn, Lois beat me to it. I bet she's already washed it and put it up."

"Shoot," Lush says, "Well, let's hope this Jonas guy comes up with something."

"Yes, if he's as good as Julianna says, I expect he will," I reply.

"Listen, Todge. Julian is lying. His expressions don't read right to me. I mean, he tries to cover everything up with that 'old man senile routine' but he's as sharp as a tack. I know it."

"I feel the same, something's not right."

"Do you think that king or sheikh or whatever he is could have had Billy and Elliott killed to cover up the affair between Billy and the crowned prince?" Lush asks.

"It's possible, but somehow that doesn't play right with me. Perhaps we should tell the police about Billy's visit to Dubai and ask them to check his phone to see if there were any calls made to or received from the Middle East recently?"

"I think they have already done that. And I looked through his calls; several of them were unidentified international numbers. I'm sure the police have checked with immigration and found out he went to Dubai, unless he was traveling under an alias."

"That just doesn't sound like Billy. I know he tried to keep the trip a secret, but I can't imagine him going to such an extreme," I reply.

"Right. I'm thinking Benny and Bernie were planted at that bathhouse on purpose to lure Billy in. I had it in my mind that Adrian did that," Lush says, folding her arms.

"We've got some traveling to do, Lush. As I see it, we're going to have to go to Ecton, Amsterdam, and Dubai to research Adrian and Julian. And I really want to talk to Hi Lu Zeng's son and Dyanne O'Bryan's son. And, of course, Isabella de la Croix."

"Right, well, I know from my Catholic friends in Louisville that Dyanne's son, Christopher, is a monk or is becoming a monk at St. Meinrad's near Louisville."

"You're kidding me, right?" I ask in disbelief.

"No, why?"

"Well, she was such an extremist revealing the horrors of the Catholic Church in her paintings; it just surprises me her son would choose to be a monk, a disciple of the very thing she despised." I reply.

"Does it really, Todge? You know human nature better than that. There's a fine line between love and hate. Who knows what's going on in that kid's head?"

"Well, I intend to find out if Adrian had anything to do with it," I reply.

"Good, we can stay at my house when we go. St. Meinrad's is only an hour away from Louisville, over in southern Indiana."

"Sounds good. I'm sure David will welcome me with open arms." Lush rolls her eyes and furrows her brow.

"Isabella will be in Sante Fe for the summer, I would suppose. And according to Julianna, Hi Lu's son is in Hong Kong. Plus you have to go to South Carolina, Key West and St. Barts to spread Billy's ashes," Lush states as she runs her right hand along the silk cording on the chair where Julian sat.

"A lot of travel, but that's pretty much what I do anyway. Listen, let's digest all this overnight and try to come up with a plan tomorrow. I don't know about you, but my brain is tired. Let's go have a drink and a smoke. I've got to pee first," I say.

"Good idea. Pit stop for me, too, then I'll meet you at the wet bar. What do you want? Perfect Manhattan?

"Sounds good," I say and head to the guest bathroom in the hall. Lush walks down the hall to her bedroom.

I enter the bathroom and turn up the lights. It is a large bathroom, with intricately paneled walls and ceiling in the same dark-stained oak as the dining room, which gives me the feeling of a men's room in a private club. There are two full size urinals, side by side on the wall to the right as you enter and two toilets contained in separate closets with paneled doors at the back of the room. The urinals are spaced close together so that if two men were relieving themselves at the same time, their shoulders would probably touch. On the left are two sinks sunken in a granite countertop with swirls and veins

of a dark red-brown color similar to the stain of the oak paneling. The sink faucets are bronze cherub heads mounted on the granite backsplash. When you turn on the faucets, water pours from the cherubs' mouths. The wall over the sink is mirrored with crystal sconces mounted high above each sink. Dozens of white linen hand towels, monogrammed with Billy's initials in dark brown thread, are neatly folded and stacked in a dark brown, lacquered, woven basket sitting on the countertop between the two sinks. Two pewter liquid soap dispensers are beside each sink. Paneled cabinets flank the sinks with a bronze plaque inscribed 'ladies' mounted on the left cabinet door and 'gentlemen' on the right cabinet door. Each cabinet is stocked with toiletries either sex might require from tampons to after-shave. Nineteenth century pencil drawings of nudes from art schools in Paris adorn the walls. I walk over to the closest urinal, unzip my pants, pull out my penis, and pee. The nude over this urinal is of a young man, sitting on a stool, holding his left leg with both hands clasped just below the knee. He is fit, and I notice how the artist has used varying shades of grey to define the sleek muscles. His right foot rests on two wooden blocks. I am amazed at the detail of the feet and toes, veins, skin folds, hair, and nails clearly drawn. I glance at the lower left of the drawing and see the name Rene Chaquet penciled in with a date of 1892. I've seen this drawing many times before, but I look at the young man today and wonder who he was— probably just some guy on the streets of Paris who was happy to sit naked for a couple of hours for a few francs, or maybe he was just one of the art students. His eyes are almost shut, in what appears to me as an expression of sadness as he peers down at the floor. His right arm covers most of his genitals, but you can just make out part of his bush and the bottom of his scrotum. His hair is rather short—his ears are visible and he has short bangs combed down over his forehead and short sideburns. I think about how modern this dude looks; it's hard for me to believe this drawing was done one hundred and fourteen years ago. I wonder what Billy thought when he looked at this drawing. This guy and my brother are both dead. I sigh, shake my penis, zip up, and flush and turn around to see Emma and Clark both staring at me.

"Emma! Oh my, I guess I forgot to shut the door. I'm sorry," I say thinking I hope she doesn't tell Dad and Brenda she watched me pee, then they'll really think Adrian rubbed off on me.

"It's okay, I see Drew and Peter pee all the time. All boys have penises."

"Yes, well, let me wash my hands and we'll go see what everyone is doing."

I walk over, turn on one of the faucets, and soap up my hands.

"Look, Philip, all these pictures are of naked men and women," she says as she points to a drawing of a nude female.

"Yes, Emma. These are all old drawings from art schools in Paris. This is how they taught students to draw the human body. You see, they used real live models, nude models, and the students would draw them. They are all over one hundred years old."

"Oh, they don't look that old. My great grandmother is ninety-nine years old. She's almost one hundred and she's all wrinkled and bent over."

"Oh, no, these are all young models. But the drawings were done over a hundred years ago," I reply.

"Oh." She says and twirls around on her toes like a ballerina.

"Are you going to help your mother cook tonight?"

"No, I'm going to draw, Peter's going to practice the piano, and Drew's going to play a video game."

"Oh you like to draw, Emma?" I ask as I wipe my hands with a towel and then throw it in a basket in the cabinet under the sinks.

"Uh huh. I'm going to be an artist like Billy when I grow up."

"I think that's wonderful. What are you going to draw tonight?"

"Clark. And he won't even have to take off his clothes," she replies, turns around and walks out the door. Clark follows her. I look at myself in the mirror, shake my head back and forth, smile and walk out. Emma has run ahead into the kitchen, and I can hear her talking to Brenda. I head over to the wet bar and

get out three martini glasses and ice them up. I take out the Woodford, the vermouths, and a bottle of Grey Goose.

"I'll make them, if you like Philip," Lush says as she walks up.

"I like," I say noticing that she has brushed her hair and reapplied lipstick.

"Todge, I was thinking. I really want to get a massage. I'm sure you could use one, too. I phoned down and talked to Timmy to see if he knew anyone. Turns out he's a licensed massage therapist, so I booked him for four ninety minute sessions Friday."

"Four?" I ask.

"Why yes, one for me, one for you and one for Brenda and one for Charles. All my treat."

"How thoughtful, Lush. Yes, we all could use them. Timmy is very good. I've used him before. He can do deep tissue if you like it."

"Yes, he told me all he can do. He's such a little stud; too bad he's gay," she replies.

"Hah," I laugh, "Are you feeling a little horny, darling?"

"Well, as a matter of fact I am. Anything wrong with that?"

"Not at all. I'm sure for the right tip, Timmy would oblige you. I'm pretty sure he can go both ways."

"Really? Well, we'll just see how it goes," she smiles and reaches in the cabinet for a shaker.

"I'll go feed Clark while you make the drinks. Then, let's go out for a smoke. Geez, you haven't had a cigarette in hours. That's unusual. Are you trying to quit?"

"Well, no. Well, yes. Hell, maybe. It's just that I was looking at Lois's skin today. You know, you can tell a woman who has smoked a couple of packs a day for years. The skin on their face is always wrinkled with thousands of little wrinkles. Lois is well on the way to that. And how old do you think she is? Forty, at the most, but she looks closer to fifty."

"Well, Saturday will be my last day to smoke. Why don't you try to quit with me?" I ask.

"Maybe, but I can't do it without patches. Let me think about it," she says with a frightened look.

"No pressure, Lush. You'll quit when and if you are ready."

"Thanks, Todge."

I walk into the kitchen where Brenda is chopping squash, eggplant, and peppers. Emma has disappeared, but Clark is sitting at Brenda's feet watching her. She looks up and back at me, smiles, turns back to the cutting board, and says, "He's sitting here waiting for anything that falls on the floor. He even gobbled up a piece of eggplant."

I just want to walk over, wrap my arms around her waist, gently kiss the back of her neck, and pull her into me. She has changed into khaki slacks, loafers, a white blouse with large blue stripes and a big collar which lays atop a thin, light blue V-neck cashmere sweater. The blouse has large cuffs that she has rolled up over the sleeves of the sweater. She wears a beige linen apron with "Queen of the Kitchen" embroidered in big pink letters across the front. She turns around to find me staring at her and says, "Somehow I don't think this apron was meant for a woman."

"I'm sure it wasn't but it looks better on you than it would any man," I reply, wishing I hadn't said that.

"Oh, thank you, Philip. How sweet. Charles is watching the news. He'll be in a minute to help out. He's always so helpful in the kitchen."

She would have to bring up Dad right when I'm fantasizing about taking her, wearing only that apron, on one of the large granite counters. I feel so depraved. I can't put my finger on what it is about Brenda that is so attractive to me. Is it that my father has her? Is it that she bore my half siblings? Maybe, but I really think it is that she is just about the perfect size and shape for my taste in women, plus she is so damned good looking for a women in her early forties. Some of the best sex I have had in recent years is with women in their forties—my sexual stamina and energy seems so well aligned with theirs. I feel my cock begin to get hard, so I walk toward the pantry.

"Come on, Clarkus, dinner time." He stands up and follows me, and I can feel Brenda's eyes on me now. I pick up Clark's bowl, put in a cup of the dry kibble and put it back on the mat. He immediately begins to eat it as fast as he can.

"Wow, this must be heaven for him after living on the streets," Brenda says, and I turn around to see her standing in front of me with a red bell pepper in one hand and a butcher knife in the other. As her eyes travel from Clark to my face, they pause, just for a second, at my crotch, and I have the sudden impulse to grab both her wrists, pull them over her head and back against the wall, kiss her passionately, and push my half hard cock into her groin area. Instead, our eyes lock together, and we arrive at an unspoken understanding—there exists between us a strong sexual attraction, one upon which we will never act.

"Philip, when I came into the kitchen earlier I noticed that lovely blue Chinese jar sitting on the counter. I remembered it had been in the living room. I took the lid off and looked in and realized that it contained Billy's ashes. I hope you don't mind, but I put it back on the table where it was in the living room."

"Oh no, that's fine, thank you. I meant to put it back and just got busy with everything going on this afternoon."

"Sous chef to your rescue, madam," Dad says, startling Brenda and me.

"Oh, Charles, I didn't hear you come in the kitchen," Brenda says turning around to face him.

"Sorry, dear. I should know better than to sneak up on a woman wielding a ten-inch butcher knife."

"You're just in time, Charles. I've cut up most of the vegetables. If you would please chop that red onion in large slices for roasting and then mince these three shallots, that would be grand," she says as she points toward the cutting board and hands Dad the knife and the pepper.

"Want me to chop this pepper, too?" he asks.

"Yes, please," she turns back toward me. "Charles is a life-saver in the kitchen. My eyes are particularly sensitive to onions and shallots, so he always chops them for me if he's around. I saw some candles in one of these cabinets. I'll light one for him. It really helps reduce the burning sensation in your eyes when you're chopping onions."

"Really? I didn't know that," I reply.

"Oh yes, it works very well," she says as she opens several cabinets until she finds one which contains several candles in glass holders painted with traditional landscape designs of Chinese paintings. She chooses a lovely one painted with a mountain scene with a waterfall, pine trees and deer. I have the onyx lighter in my pants pocket, so I pull it out and light the candle for her and steal a quick look into her eyes. They tell me the same thing—attraction duly noted and filed away in a file marked 'No Further Action'. She takes the candle from me, walks over to Dad, sets it on the counter near him, pats him on the back and says, "Here, darling, this will help. Thanks for saving me from the onions. I'm going to brine the chicken breasts now." Dad looks at her and smiles and a wave of guilt and remorse crash through me as I think that, given the right circumstances, I might actually try to make love to Brenda. What the fuck is wrong with me? How could I do that to either one of them? They clearly love each other a great deal. I feel certain Brenda would never let it go that far, even if I pressed her with as much charm and sex appeal as I could muster. I resolve to push these feelings back to the farthest corners of my being, to no longer acknowledge them, to render them sterile. I don't know how the hell I'll manage to do this, but I'm going to try. I really need to have sex with someone other than myself. Why do I feel so horny right in the midst of all my grief of losing Billy? I need to go see a shrink. I really need help. I hear Dad's voice.

"What, Dad?"

"I said are you okay, son?"

"Sure, fine. Just thinking, that's all."

"Anything you want to talk about?"

"Well, no. It's just I'm still a bit overwhelmed with everything that's happened in the last few days." And I think to myself, yes, I want to talk about it. About what a freak I am for wanting to fuck your wife right under your nose. Maybe it's what you deserve for abandoning Billy and me all those years.

"Yes, I understand." He stops chopping the onion, looks over his reading glasses at me, and sighs. "Well, maybe I don't really understand, son, but I'd sure like to try. I mean, the bond you had with your brother. Well, I know how much he meant, means to you. And you to him. I feel so bad I wasn't there for you both all those years. I, well I just wish I could make it up to you somehow." His eyes are tearing up, and I think to myself how convenient it is to get emotional while you're chopping onions.

"Dad, I'm okay. It's okay. You don't have to bring all that up."

"But I want to bring it up son. I need to," he replies with an urgent tone.

"Well, right now, I need for you to not bring it up," I reply sharply. Brenda is pretending to be fully absorbed in washing chicken breasts.

"Yes, whatever you want, son." I know I have a disgusted look on my face, and I can't think of anything else to say, so I walk out of the room to find Lush at the wet bar.

"All the drinks are ready," she turns and looks at me. "What's wrong?"

"Nothing, I just need a drink and a smoke. Wanna join me on the terrace?"

"Sure, but let's take Brenda and Charles their drinks."

"They're both in the kitchen. Would you mind taking them?"

"Not at all."

"Bring Clark back with you, please. He just ate. He probably needs to relieve himself."

"Sure. You take my drink. I'll meet you outside." She looks at me, trying to discern my feelings, picks up the martini and ginger ale and heads into the kitchen. I put her cigarettes in my pocket, pick up the Manhattans and head out to the terrace.

The sun has settled low on the horizon over New Jersey and a stiff, cool breeze rustles the plants on the terrace, but I can not make out from which direction it is blowing because it seems to be rushing in from all sides of the building. I set the drinks down on a table, walk over, grab the railings and look down at the street below. I shouldn't have stormed out on Dad and Brenda. How fucking immature is that? I've got to get a grip. He's really trying. I just get so angry with him. God, how it tore Billy and me up when he left us with Fatgram and we knew it was for good. Traffic is crawling and suited men and women are making their way home from work. Most of these people probably work in the financial district, I think. What a boring life that would be, relentlessly chasing numbers, forever depending on the whim of the market for your next dollar. Granted, people make fortunes here, but I just don't see how it could be fulfilling unless the only thing you care about is money. I hear Clark's tags clinking and his toenails clipping on the slate as he trots over to me and jumps up to greet me. I bend over and he licks my face.

"Hey, Clark, buddy. I'm glad to see you, too."

"Well," Lush says as she walks over to talk to me, "Charles and Brenda really seemed grateful of my offer for massages on Friday." The wind blows her long brown hair about her face and she clasps her arms below her bosom and shivers.

"Good," I reply. "Too cold out here to smoke?"

"No, but let's sit over there behind that wall; it's less windy there."

"Okay, I'll get the drinks," I reply.

"Did you pick up my cigarettes?" she asks, still studying my face.

"Yes, here they are," I say as I pull them out of my pocket and hand them to her.

"Thanks," she says as she takes them, turns, and scurries toward the sheltered table. I go get the drinks from a table by the door and return to Lush, who has lit up a cigarette.

"Boy, you could have cut the air with a knife in the kitchen; the pent up emotion was so thick between Brenda and Charles," she says, bats her long lashes at me, then takes a long draw.

172

"May I have one of your smokes, please? I'm all out of Billy's."

"Certainly." She hands me the pack. I take one out and light it with the onyx lighter from my pocket.

"It's nothing really, Lush. Dad is just trying too hard and too fast to make amends. I know he regrets leaving us with Fatgram, but what's done is done. And, every time he gets that sad look on his face and starts apologizing to me, and tries to get closer to me, I just end up getting angry." I sigh and pick up my martini glass. "Here's to those of us who are fucked up." Lush picks up her glass and we toast.

"That would be a rather large group of people, Todge."

"Yes, it would, but right now, I feel like I'm at the top of that heap."

She smiles at me and says, "Honey, just give yourself some time. Surely Charles understands that he can't just waltz in and make everything perfect after all these years have passed?"

"No, I think he knows that. I just think that since Billy is dead, he feels he doesn't have any time to lose. And that just makes me feel that much more of a bastard for not being able to open up to him as fast as he wants me to."

"Time, time, time," she reiterates, "It's going to take time."

I nod my head in agreement and start singing, "But it's going to take some time this time, no matter what I've planned. And, like the young trees in the winter time, I'll learn how to bend."

Lush laughs out loud and says, you must be feeling better, you're singing on demand again. I join her laugh and say, "God, did Mother love the Carpenters or what? She played them all the time. She used to sing 'Close to You' to me and run her fingers through my hair. 'On the day that you were born the angels got together and decided to create a dream come true. So they sprinkled moon dust in your hair of gold and starlight in your eyes of blue.'"

"You have a pretty voice, Philip," she says.

"Thanks, that song always made me feel so special."

"Well, you are special—special to me and to a lot of other people." She reaches over and grabs my left hand with her right hand.

"You know, back then, back when Mother would sing that song to me, I had a real family—a mother, a father, and a little brother." My eyes well up with tears, and I look at Lush and smile through the tears.

"Oh, Todge, you still have a family. You've got me, you've got Clark, you've got Charles and Brenda and their kids now."

"Yeah, thanks Lush." We sip our drinks in silence for a while. Clark has gone over to his little lawn and has taken a big dump. I put a plastic dog poop bag in my pocket when I got his dinner, so I pull it out. "Listen, I'm going to clean up his poop and go in and listen to voice mails before dinner."

"Okay," Lush replies. I'm dying to take a look at Billy's other computer. I noticed there were some disks in that compartment, I got those too."

"Great, I'll be in Billy's room. Let me know if you find anything."

"Will do. I'll take the glasses in." She stands up, takes the glasses and heads back into the kitchen. I get up, walk over, pick up the poop with the plastic bag, tie it off, and put it in a trashcan on the terrace.

"Come on Clarkster, let's go in."

I head inside the dining room and immediately hear the sound of someone playing the piano in the living room—it must be Peter. Clark and I enter the living room and see Peter absorbed in playing. It is a beautiful classical piece I've never heard before, quick in pace and upbeat. His hands and fingers race up and down the keyboard. I am amazed at his performance, his skill, the rhythmic, fluid movements his body makes as he sways back and forth and side to side—he must be a sort of child prodigy, there is not even music on the piano, he's playing all of this from memory. I notice Officer Kelly sitting on a sofa, completely mesmerized by Peter. I start to go up to the piano, then stop because I get a sudden feeling that I should not disturb them. I turn around, and head down the hall, unnoticed. Clark follows me into Billy's bedroom. I pick up my cell phone off the bedside table, sit on the bed, flip open the phone, and see that

I have eleven new messages. Clark jumps up on the bed beside me as I begin listening to the messages. My agent Florence has left a message saying she will be back in town in time for the memorial service. Mr. Barksdale, the trust officer Fatgram appointed for Billy and me, phoned from Spartanburg to give his condolences and to pass on condolences from several people in Union, including Newt and Brooker T, Ala Mary's husband and son, who still live on Fatgram's farm in Buffalo. She left them the twelve hundred acre farm in her will for the years of service their family had given to her family. The rest of the calls are from friends expressing sympathy and from people who are unable to attend the memorial service. I jot the callers' names down on the legal pad containing my list of previous callers. I wonder if the police are answering Billy's phone or are they letting everything go to voice mail. I'll have to get Lush on that. I'll bet he has received dozens of calls on his mobile. I put the list and phone on the table and lie back on the sumptuous pillows, sigh, and begin to wonder how all this will end. I feel so tired. Clark sniffs at the pillows and wedges himself among them so that just his head is sticking out and resting on a beautiful, blue and green silk pillow with braided cording and bushy tassels. I laugh and close my eyes. I focus on the far away sound of Peter playing beautiful music, and I catch a faint smell of roasting chicken and I feel grateful for having these special people around me, and I drift off to sleep.

"Philip, honey. Philip, wake up."

"Humm? What?" I feel someone shaking my shoulders, and I open my eyes to see a blurred visage of Lush looking down at me.

"Wake up, Philip. I've got something you must see," Lush says with an extremely urgent tone in her voice.

"Yes, what. I'm awake. I guess I just nodded off for a minute," I respond, rubbing my eyes and trying to adjust to the light in the room.

"More like an hour, dear. It's seven o'clock and Brenda says dinner will be served in fifteen minutes. Oh my God, I had no idea she is such a good cook. It smells absolutely wonderful in the kitchen. I can't wait to eat." Lush peers down at me, holding a silver package.

"What's that?" I ask.

"It's Billy's hidden computer. You're not gonna believe what I found on it. Sit up, Todge. You must see this before dinner."

I struggle up and push a few pillows behind me to support my back. I see Clark has emerged from his cocoon of pillows and is stretched out, unconcerned, along the foot of the bed. My shirt has pulled out of my pants and has come unbuttoned halfway up my chest, exposing my navel and lower abdomen. I see Lush focusing on it, and I think to myself, "Should I just pull her into my arms now?" But then I reverse and think, "You fucking idiot, life's not all about sex and she has something important to tell you." I smile, look at her, and say, "Well, let's see what you've found, Lush."

"Well, it's clear to me that Billy used this computer for research for his current works. He's bookmarked numerous erotic and pornographic sites, many for which he's paying monthly fees on a credit card. So, I figure the police know all about those. By the way, I'll be happy to cancel all these if you want me to."

"Yes, when you get time, please do," I say.

"Anyway," she continues, "There are also all types of scholarly articles on pedophilia and a host of other aberrant sexual behavior. But the most interesting discovery so far is that he uses this computer for his confidential emails. He really should have used a different password, but he didn't and I got in. For instance, he first contacted Julian Ainsworth about two years ago. It seems Billy had been having discussions with an avant garde artist named Dominick Montaigne who lives here in New York and whose paintings and sculptures many critics have characterized as child pornography. Dominick lived in Amsterdam for several years and was able to obtain what he called high quality child pornography there. Billy found out from Dominick that the photographs of a particular pedophile named Nairda are the most sought after by those with the means to afford them. No one knows who Nairda is but his work started

174

appearing in the nineteen seventies and continues today. Nairda appears in some of the pornographic shots himself, but never shows his face. Brace yourself, Todge. Dominick had only two examples of Nairda's work to show Billy, and here they are."

She pushes her index finger around the cursor pad, clicks a few keys and a black and white photograph appears on the screen. My mouth falls open; it is a picture of Billy sucking my cock. This picture was taken the day Adrian initiated us into the Blood Brothers.

"Nairda, N-A-I-R-D-A," Lush says, "Is simply Adrian spelled backwards. Now look at this one."

She pushes the right arrow key and another black and white photograph appears. This one is of two little Asian boys, both licking a grown man's erect cock.

"Recognize anyone?" Lush asks.

"That's definitely Benny and Bernie. And that is definitely Adrian's cock."

"I never thought I'd be saying this to you, but I thought you might recognize that cock," Lush says with her eyebrows arching up.

"Oh it's definitely Adrian. See the little birthmark below the right hip? It's shaped like Italy—definitely Adrian. Damn, so Billy knew a year ago that Adrian is alive."

"That's right," Lush says, "And he also must have known that Benny and Bernie were sent to watch him."

"Why the fuck didn't he confide any of this to me? I just don't understand that."

"Maybe he was protecting you."

"From what, Lush?"

"Well, from being murdered, for one."

"I dunno. This is so unlike him."

"Well, there's more to all this than we've figured out. I haven't yet gone through all the emails, but I focused on ones from the past month and there are several with Najeed, who is the sheikh's son in the painting. Look at this one in particular, sent two weeks ago.

Billy. Your suspicions are right. My friends made contact with Julian Ainsworth's Indian housekeeper. She was terrified to talk, but did so after my friends gave her a large sum of money. Claude Blakemore is still there and he is in fact Adrian McWhorter just as we thought. Except for the housekeeper, all the other servants are young men and boys from Thailand. You are right—two of the young Thai men are identical twins. Adrian rarely goes out or travels, but he receives many Arab visitors, often late at night. The housekeeper says there are areas of the compound that remain under lock and key and in which she is forbidden to go. You'll be proud of my friends for what they obtained for you. It's clear she's motivated by money because she offered to sell my friends a disk she claims fell out of a case of one of Adrian's Arab visitors. She saw the disk fall in between two sofa cushions and retrieved it after the visitors left. Julian and Claude asked her several times if she had found any type of disk a guest had lost. They searched and searched for it. She kept it because she thought it might be valuable some day. My friends paid her the equivalent of a thousand dollars for it. I hope you don't mind. I looked at the disk, but was unable to open any of the files. Anyway, I tried to copy it, but it won't copy so I'll have the original sent to you by air express. I hope this helps you. I can hardly wait to see you again which I sincerely hope will be in two weeks when I arrive in New York. I hope you will accept my invitation to go to Keeneland with me for the two-year-old-in-training sales. It will be a lot of fun. I want to show you the horses I hope to purchase. We should have a lot to celebrate by the time I arrive. Please feel free to invite your friend to join us. Najeed.

"Oh shit. I can't believe this. That mother fucker Julian was here scoping out the place, looking for that disk, I'll bet. And Claude Blackmore is Adrian McWhorter," I say.

"Todge, this may be getting too deep for us. Do you think we should get the police involved?"

"My gut says no, but my brain says yes. Gut wins—we won't tell, not just yet."

"You sure?" Lush asks with a tone of uncertainty in her voice.

"Yes," I reply with certainty in my voice. "Were any of those disks what Najeed sent?"

"No, not that I could tell. They contained all the photographs Billy took of his subjects."

"Okay. Well, he must have received it last week. We'll ask Timmy. I'm sure they keep a log of all the packages received at the front desk."

"Good thinking, Todge. But, if he did receive it, where would it be? Holy shit, I'm such a dumbass." She quickly executes a few keystrokes on the computer and says, "Yes, yes, yes, yes. This has to be it! It's in this disk drive. It was right here all the time. You see, I used my laptop to look at the other disks, and I hadn't gotten around to check to see if this computer had a disk in it."

"Wow, what luck," I say, "Let's see what is on there."

"Well, there seems to be a lot of picture files and some text files and some other types I am not familiar with. Let's see if I can get the picture files to open. Here we go. Damn, I can't get anything to open. Here's an executable file; I'll try that. Shit, it's asking for a password. Shit. I'll try administrator. Well, what do you know?"

The picture files open into an array of thumbnails on the screen, and I am sickened to my core by what I see—explicit photographs depicting young boys being sexually abused by men armed with weapons. At first glance, all the men are bearded, wearing turbans, and appear filthy. Weapons used are machine guns, other types of guns, knifes, machetes, chains, whips, and ropes. The backdrops are dingy rooms, building rubble, and outdoor shots. The things these vile men are doing to the boys and making the boys do are horrifying to view: sodomy, oral sex, insertion of weapons in the anus, strangulation, copulation with sheep, self mutilation, and a host of other abusive, inimical sexual acts.

"Dear God in heaven, how could this be? How could you let this happen?" Lush says slowly as her eyes well up with tears. She pushes a key and another page of thumbnails appears, then another, and another.

"I don't think I can look at anymore of these. Those goddamned dirty bastards. Who the fuck are they? They definitely look Muslim. Do you think they are Taliban, maybe, or al-Qaeda?" I ask, still looking at the images.

"Could be either," Lush replies, "Whoever they are, it's pretty clear that they have some sort of large scale sexual abuse of boys going on here. Do you think this is how they control and brainwash these kids?"

"It wouldn't surprise me. I mean if a boy is subjected to this long enough, imagine what psychological damage would be done? Hell, strapping a bomb on yourself with a free ticket to heaven would be an easy alternative for them," I say.

"Yes, it would explain a lot. These people must use sexual abuse as a way to shape and control the boys, a way to manipulate them into accepting beliefs and executing destructive actions. If these photographs got out to the media, can you imagine the backlash? Dear God, no wonder they are killing for it. Todge, I think we are in really grave danger. I mean, they're liable to blow this place up," Lush says in an urgent manner as she continues to scroll through the pictures, her eyes scanning the pages.

"Philip, Lush, dinner is ready," Emma yells as she comes running into the room. I immediately slam the laptop shut.

"Hi Emma," Lush says and smiles sweetly.

"What are you all doing on the laptop? Playing games?" Emma asks. "Can I see?"

"Oh darling, we were just working on some pictures for Billy, for the service," I say, "Just old family photos. You'll get to see them on Friday."

"Okay. Mom says dinner is ready. I helped Dad set the table."

"You did?" Lush asks.

"Uh huh," she says as she pets Clark causing his tail to start thumping on the bed.

"I bet it looks great," Lush says. "Run back, dear and tell your mother we are on our way. We're just going to wash our hands and we'll be right in."

"Okay." She turns and runs out of the room. Clark jumps off the bed and runs after her.

"Wow, that was close," I say.

"Thank goodness you shut it. I don't think she saw a thing," Lush says.

"Listen, Lush. Save that photo of Adrian on the hard drive. Also mark where it was. I want to see if there are others of him."

"Sure. We can continue this after dinner," she replies as she opens the laptop and starts clicking the keys.

"I think I will wash my hands. I feel dirty after looking at those photos," I say.

"I think I'll do the same. What are we going to do?"

"Dunno. Let's talk about it after dinner," I reply.

"See you at the table," she says carrying the laptop out of the room with her.

CHAPTER 20

I walk into the dining room to see the children sitting at their places, talking to each other and patiently waiting for everyone to sit down. Brenda's dinner looks divine, and she has arranged everything on the table on platters and dishes for family-style dining. The platter of roasted chicken breasts is garnished with sprigs of sage and sends out a rich aroma of chicken, shallots and sage. Beside it a large dish is filled with roasted vegetables marked with charred, diagonal, grill marks. The peppers, onions, eggplant, squash, and whole green beans glisten with olive oil and are sprinkled with a variety of spices. The rice pilaf is steaming and I notice bits of red, orange, and green dispersed throughout the long grains of black and white rice. The Bibb lettuce salad is a work of art with rich green lettuce leaves covered in dressing with sliced pears, chucks of Stilton and roasted pecans tossed throughout the salad. The children all have glasses of milk and water, and I notice a bottle of pinot noir and chardonnay on the table.

"Philip, I found these large buffet plates and thought it would be fun just to pass everything around and pile it all on one plate for dinner. I hope that's okay with you?" Brenda asks as she pours water from a crystal pitcher into the adults' water glasses.

"Oh yes, anything's fine. This looks fantastic and it smells even better," I reply.

"Brenda, what a sumptuous feast; the smell is intoxicating," Lush exclaims as she enters the dining room.

"Thank you, Lush," Brenda replies smiling, looking pleased and content.

"Where should we sit?" Lush asks.

"Anywhere you like. I'll sit beside Emma because we'll share a chicken breast," Brenda replies, sets the water pitcher down on a towel, and pulls out the chair beside Emma. Dad and Emma set seven places on the south end of the large dining room table using the end seat and three seats on each side. Drew, Brenda, and Emma have the eastern side with Brenda in the middle and Emma beside the end. Peter is sitting in the middle of the western side.

"Dad, you take the end," I say, "Lush, you sit there beside Dad, and I'll sit here beside Peter and across from Drew."

"Philip, if it's okay with you, I'd like to say grace," Dad says as he sits down. "Of course," I say. I remember now that Dad became a Catholic before he married Brenda. Peter grabs my right hand with his left, and I realize they pray holding hands. We bow our heads and Dad begins.

"Dear Heavenly Father, we are grateful to be here together tonight to enjoy this marvelous dinner prepared by my lovely wife. Please give us all the strength and courage to face the coming days as we say goodbye to Billy. We are comforted in the knowledge that he and his friend, Elliott Fields, are in your presence now. Please be with the family and friends of Elliott. Please aid the police in their search to bring to justice the perpetrators of these heinous crimes. Please keep us safe and healthy dear Lord. Lead, guide, and direct us all to be more loving and compassionate toward others. In Christ's name we pray. Amen."

Everyone but I says, "Amen." I wonder why Dad said 'safe and healthy'. If he only knew what Lush and I have discovered, I don't think he'd leave his family here. Maybe I should tell him. Maybe that private detective will have some advice. I'm going to call Julianna after dinner. The extreme cruelty in those pictures haunts me. How could anyone do such horrible things to other humans, especially children? Adrian did horrible things to Billy and me. What is the basis of such cruelty? Julian claims Adrian was abused by the Rector who took him in. No one with any trust in people could be so cruel. This chain of cruelty depicted in those photographs must end. I have to get in touch with Najeed. Maybe he'll be willing to help.

"I put everything on towels so we can just slide it all around to each other," Brenda says, "Some of these dishes are pretty heavy."

Everyone begins serving, except for Emma. Brenda puts small portions on Emma's plate before serving her own plate.

"Lush, would you like pinot or chardonnay?" Dad asks.

"Pinot, please." He pours the burgundy wine in her glass.

"Thanks, Charles," she says.

"Son? Which would you like?"

"Pinot, too, Dad."

Dad gets up, walks over and pours wine in my glass. He then sets the bottle down on a wine coaster near my plate. He walks back to his place, picks up the chardonnay, walks over to Brenda's seat and pours it into her wine glass.

"Thank you, dear," she says. Dad takes his seat and pours chardonnay into his glass.

"Dad, I'll have a little chardonnay, too," Andrew says.

"Yes, I bet you will," Dad replies.

"Why do adults always get to have all the fun stuff?" Andrew asks.

"Son, wine and alcohol are not for children," Dad replies.

"Why not?" Andrew asks.

"Because, alcohol or drinks containing alcohol are harmful to growing children," Dad replies.

"If it's harmful to growing children, how come it's not harmful to adults," Peter asks.

"Yeah, dad, how come?" Andrew asks.

"Well, it can be," Dad replies. "Excessive drinking can kill you."

"Then why do you drink it?" Emma asks.

Dad looks at her and smiles. "Good question, Emma. In the right combinations, wine and food enhance each other. In other words they go well together, just like Oreos and milk. And some people enjoy the taste of other types of alcohol. For instance, your mother likes her martinis. But, even adults must drink all alcohol in moderation or it can be poisonous to us, too."

"Is that why you always have just one glass of wine, Dad?" Andrew asks.

"Well, the truth is son, that a long time ago, before I met your mother, I got in the habit of drinking too much alcohol and it was slowly poisoning me. I had to get help from other people, including your mother, to stop. I didn't drink any alcohol for many years, and now I only drink it in moderation."

"So, it's bad for you, like smoking is," Emma states, looks at Lush and says, "Lush, I think you should stop smoking because it's bad for you."

"Darling, you are quite right. I should quit, and I am going to try really hard this time. I've tried before and just never have been successful," Lush replies.

"Why not?" Emma asks.

"Well, you see, Emma," Lush replies in a soothing tone, "cigarettes contain a substance called nicotine. Nicotine is addictive. That means once you get used to it, your body craves it, thinks it has to have it. Because of that, it's hard to quit."

Emma looks at Lush with a puzzled look on her face, turns to her mother and asks, "Mom, is strawberry ice cream addictive?"

Brenda chuckles, "No dear, not in your case anyhow. I suppose food, in general, can be addictive to certain people, but you don't have to worry about strawberry ice cream. You can eat as much as you like."

I look down at the meager portions of food Brenda has placed on Emma's plate, and I understand she is encouraging Emma to eat almost anything. Emma does appear frail and fragile and I know Dad and Brenda must constantly worry about this.

"Uhmm, Brenda, this food looks and smells divine," I say in exaggerated tones. "I could eat a mountain of it." I cut into my deeply browned chicken breast with my knife and juices and steam pour out, which surprises me because I'm used to dryer white meat, which is why I prefer the juicy thighs. I put a bite of the breast in my mouth and am rewarded with a tender, juicy piece of chicken with a rich roasted flavor with a hint of salt and sage. "My Lord, this is the best roasted chicken I've ever had, Brenda."

"Thank you, Philip," she responds.

"Wait until you put some of the pan sauce on it, son," Dad adds, "It'll put your taste buds in overdrive." He hands the pewter sauce dish to Lush, who pours a stream over her breast and passes it to Peter who passes it directly to me.

"Don't you want some sauce, Peter?" I ask.

"No thanks, I like it plain."

I pour some sauce over my breast and cut another piece and taste it. "Yum. I taste some shallots, sage, maybe some white wine? How did you prepare this chicken, Brenda?"

"It's really simple, Philip. First brine the breast in a cup of kosher salt dissolved in two quarts of water for about twenty minutes. Then, brown the breast in a little oil on top of the stove on medium high heat, then roast them in the same pan used for browning for fifteen minutes in a hot oven, about four hundred and fifty degrees. Then take the breasts out, sauté some shallots, deglaze with some vermouth, add a little chicken stock and a little white wine, some fresh sage, reduce it and add a little butter, and that's it."

"It's extraordinary," Lush says, "I never would have guessed it was such a simple recipe. It's so juicy and complex. This pan sauce is to die for, Brenda."

"Thanks, Lush. It's easy and you can change it around by using onions and mushrooms, cognac and red wine, garlic and rosemary, almost any type of spice or herb you like," Brenda replies.

"Mom, can I have more chicken breast?" Emma asks.

"Why certainly, darling," she replies and carves off a large piece of the breast on her plate and puts it on Emma's plate. "Here you go."

"Thank you," Emma replies and starts to cut the piece of meat into little pieces with her knife and fork.

Peter and Andrew have helped themselves to rather large servings and they are both consuming the food at a rapid pace. I'm amazed that they are eating everything: salad, wild rice pilaf, roasted vegetables, and chicken. Andrew even douses his chicken breast with the pan sauce and rubs a speared piece of chicken breast in the sauce before he eats it. Billy and I would have turned up our noses at this fancy food when we were boys. Ala Mary did the majority of the cooking and it was mainly simple, but always wonderful to eat. Her dinner meats included fried chicken, pot roasts, beef stew, chicken and dumplings, country fried steak, meatloaf, country ham, roast beef, chili, pork chops, and ribs. Her mainstay vegetable

dishes were stewed green beans with country ham, black eyed peas, fried green tomatoes, corn pudding, cream style corn, glazed carrots, greens (turnips, mustard, kale, and collards), lima beans, crowder peas, mashed potatoes, baked potatoes, candied yams, sweet potato casserole, and baked beans. Her biscuits and yeast rolls are, to this day, some of the best I've ever had. As far as I know, she took those bread-making skills to the grave with her. Her own three children were all boys, and I don't think they were much interested in cooking. God, and her desserts, from the best imaginable peach cobbler to a superb chocolate cake, I can still taste and smell them. But I think my favorite thing about her cooking was waking up every morning to the smells of bacon, sausage, coffee, baking biscuits, and sitting down to a big breakfast. My favorite was country ham with red eye gravy on steaming grits, eggs sunny side up, and biscuits with butter, honey, and peach jam. I always felt so safe and secure going into the kitchen in the morning with Ala Mary standing over the hot stove in her white dress, humming what she called 'gospels' to herself while Dad, when he was home, sat at the table, drinking coffee and reading the paper while he waited for Billy and me to join him. Sometimes Mother would be there, but her sleep patterns were so erratic that often she would sleep until noon, or she might be out in her studio so engrossed in her painting that she worked through the night, requiring no sleep at all. Sometimes Dad would grill steaks, hamburgers, or hotdogs if he was home on weekends and he could make a great grilled cheese sandwich. Mother almost never cooked. She said she hated it and claimed it was Fatgram's and Ala Mary's fault for forcing culinary skills upon her during the better part of her girlhood. The first instance I recall of Fatgram 'raising hell', as Mother referred to it, with Mother was over food, or the lack of preparation of it. I know I was in first grade, so I was six and Billy would have been four. Dad was on the road, and for some reason Ala Mary left after breakfast that morning. When I walked home from school that day Mother was not there to walk me home as she promised she would be since Ala Mary couldn't do it that day. When I got home, Billy was sitting in the kitchen crying because he was hungry. I knew how to make a peanut butter and jelly sandwich, so I made him one. He immediately ate it and stopped crying. I went upstairs to find Mother and found her lying in bed asleep, I thought. All the curtains were closed. I was scared. I tried to wake her, but she just mumbled something and ignored me. I went back downstairs and Billy and I played together until dinnertime. I went upstairs again to ask Mother to make dinner for us. The same thing happened again; her speech was slurred, drawn out, incomprehensible to me. I was afraid, so I called Fatgram's house, but no one answered. So I got out more white bread and made peanut butter and jelly sandwiches for Billy and me for dinner. While we were eating our sandwiches in front of the television in the den, Fatgram walked in.

"What are you boys doing in here eating peanut butter and jelly sandwiches and watching T.V.?" I look at the black purse, one of her church purses, hanging from her right wrist.

"Fatgram!" Billy screams and runs to her arms. She picks him up and kisses him, then puts him down.

"Fatgram, I called you but no one answered. Why are you all dressed up in your church clothes?" I ask.

"Sweet heart, Fatgram had to go to a funeral this afternoon and then to a gathering," she replies. "Where is your Mother?"

"She's upstairs sleeping," I reply. "I tried to wake her, but she wouldn't get up and she's talking funny."

"Dear God," Fatgram says. "You boys go watch T.V. while I deal with your Mother. Then I'll make sure you get a decent dinner." She looks worried or mad and that frightens me.

"Okay," I say.

"Okie dokie," Billy says.

We go back to the television and start watching "Little House on the Prairie" which means it is Monday evening. Mother lets us stay up until nine o'clock on Mondays to watch this show. I love it and fantasize that Billy and I could become members of the Ingalls's family who always stay together and never fight, well, at least not like Mother and Dad do. I hear Fatgram screaming at Mother upstairs, but

we just keep watching the television. I hear Fatgram shouting the words drunk, drug addict, unfit mother, and unstable.

"I think Fatgram is mad at Mother, Philly," Billy says to me as he scoots closer to me. Something breaks upstairs and we hear a wailing sound coming from the room—something unearthly, something scary. We hold each other as tightly as we can.

Fatgram comes down the stairs quickly and comes toward us with a furious expression on her face, but she says in her kindest voice, "Come on boys, you all are going to spend the night with me tonight and we're going to have a ball."

"Yay!" Billy says, turning loose of me and clapping his little hands.

"That's right. No school tomorrow for you, Philip. We're going to have fun all day," she says smiling so wide that I can see the silver fillings in her back teeth.

"What about Mother?" I ask.

She lets out a big sigh and says, "Boys, your Mother is not feeling well. What she needs is an extended period of rest to get better. Fatgram is going to make sure she gets that so she can come back soon and be the good mother to you boys I know she can be."

"How long will she be gone?" I ask, suddenly frightened at the prospect of not having Mother around, especially since Dad is gone.

"Oh, not long at all, dear. You fellows will stay with me until your father gets back. We'll have a grand 'ole time. I promise. Now let's go."

And so we went to Fatgram's that night and remained there until Christmas. Dad spent the weekends with us there, only six blocks away from our own house. It seemed he didn't want us back at home until Mother returned from her "rest" somewhere out west in the desert, Fatgram told us.

"Son, son, are you okay?" Dad says to me. I look up to see everyone has just about finished eating and I look down at my plate and see most of the food still there.

"Fine. I'm fine, Dad. Just thinking, that's all. Hey, I need to catch up with you guys." I start eating as fast as I can without being crude, but the taste and smell of the food have lost their appeal as everything seems to collapse in on me at once as visions of Mother in a mental ward, Billy gaunt on his death bed, and Adrian standing in front of Billy and me at the swimming hole with his cock throbbing in my face fill my head.

"Philip, no need to eat it all now. I'll wrap your plate up and you can eat it later tonight if you get hungry. With everything that's happened this week, I'm surprised you have any appetite at all," Brenda says.

"Well, I suppose you're right. Thanks, Brenda, I'll just sip some wine. Sometimes that settles my stomach."

I realize the children are looking at me as if a grotesque eruption of pustules has transformed my face into a turgid horror, and I think to myself that's exactly what I feel like on the inside which for some strange reason makes me start laughing. I shake my head, look down, and rub my forehead and say, "Kids, I'm sorry to be so ill mannered this evening. I'm just a little under the weather with the stress, I suppose. But, I'm okay. Why don't we have some of that cheesecake, now?" I force a big grin at my half-siblings.

"It's okay, Philip. It would really stress me out, too if someone murdered my brother or sister," Peter says with a confused look on his face which lights up with a blush as he quickly and awkwardly adds, "And you, too. I mean if they murdered you, I'd feel bad."

"That's kind of you to say, Peter. By the way, I heard you practicing the piano this afternoon. It was lovely. Would it be an imposition to ask you to play some during Billy's wake?"

"Oh," he gasps, "I'd like that very much. Is that alright, Mother, Dad?" His face lights up with pure joy now, and I feel certain this kid is lucky enough to have discovered his passion in life at an early age.

"Of course it's alright," Brenda says.

"Yes, it's an honor, thank you, son," Dad says.

Andrew looks agitated and says, "Well, if Peter gets to play for everyone, what do Emma and I get to do?"

"Well, Drew, you like Clark, don't you?" I ask. Clark hears his name and emerges from under the table, where he has been patiently resting, looks up at me and whimpers.

"You can be the keeper of Clark," I say. "We'll put on his fanciest collar and lead and you can keep him with you. I know Billy would want him here, but, with so many people in the place, I don't want him running loose."

"That's so cool. Thanks, Philip. I can't wait to tell Randy."

"And Emma. I want you to put on your prettiest dress. In fact, I think your Mother should take you shopping tomorrow for a special dress, and I want you to greet everyone as they come in and hand all the women a Tropicana rose. That was Billy's favorite color of rose, and it just sounds like something he would do."

She wiggles in her seat and smiles at me and says, "Oh Mother, won't that be fun? What's a Tropicana rose?"

"It's a rose with a beautiful orange color with a pinkish tint on the ends of the petals," Brenda smiles down at her, "What a grand idea for an angel like you. Especially since you ate such a big dinner tonight, you'll have plenty of energy to hand out all those roses."

"These are all splendid touches to the wake," Lush says. I am aware that she, too, has been rather quiet and subdued during dinner, and I suppose it's because her mind is working on overdrive trying to piece together our new discoveries. "Peter, perhaps tomorrow you can give me a list of the music you want to play, and I can coordinate some of the slideshows and videos with that. I also have a list of Billy's favorite songs. Would you mind looking over it to see if you know any of them?"

"Sure, Lush," he replies enthusiastically.

"Andrew, in addition to handling Clark, I think you should give each guest as they arrive an orange ribbon. It signifies humane treatment of animals and prevention of cruelty to animals. That's something Billy cared about immensely," Lush says.

"Okay, I can do that, too," he states and sits up in a proud posture in his chair.

"Good. Children, please help your father and me clear the table. Then we'll bring out the dessert in a few minutes," Brenda says as she gets up. "Coffee, anyone?"

"I'd love some, Brenda," Lush says, "I can make it."

"Oh, keep Philip company, dear, I'm glad to make it. Regular or decaf?"

"Regular for me," Lush replies.

"Me, too. Thanks, Brenda," I add.

Within a few minutes, the Hampton family has removed everything from the table except the water glasses, my and Lush's wine glasses, and the half bottle of pinot remaining. They are all in the kitchen scraping dishes, wrapping food, and rinsing. Clark is with them, and I hear the kitchen door to the terrace open, and Clark's toenails clinking outside on the slate terrace.

"Todge, I'm frightened," Lush says to me as she moves to the chair beside mine and pours more wine in my glass. I meet her eyes without responding.

"I mean, really," she continues, undaunted by my steadfast gaze, "If we have some crazed Muslin sect or the Taliban or worse, al-Qaeda after us, we don't have a snowball's chance in hell."

"Oh, don't we?" I ask with a supercilious tone I know she despises.

Unabashed, she fires back at me, "And we have what advantage?"

"The advantage of poker, my dear."

She laughs, shaking her thick hair back, basking in the temptation to take on my challenge, loving every second of it. "You know that's why I've always loved you so, Todge. At the most unexpected moments, your genius shines through and lights up my world."

182

At this point, I realize she is on to me, and I laugh and take a sip of wine.

"I had forgotten about your brilliant article for *The Los Angeles Times*. Let's see what was it, 'The Western World Finances Islamic Terrorism Through Its Addiction To Oil'. Yes, that's it, and you won some little award for that—A National Press Club Award?" She beams at me and continues, "So, let's see, your ace in this hand of poker would be Najeed?"

"Well, the way I see it is that Julian Ainsworth is the ace. If we expose him, we're liable to flush out all sorts of royals," I reply, smiling.

"This could get extremely messy and dangerous," Lush says and takes a sip of wine.

"I believe it already has, my dear. The more I think about it, the more I want to get that private detective involved. I hope Julianna calls with some news. I'd just love to get inside Adrian's condominium here."

"Where is it?" Lush asks.

"Oh, Upper East Side, around the East Seventies and Third Avenue. It's one of those older buildings. His unit is on the tenth floor, a corner unit, and it is really large, as I recall. But I haven't been there for twenty years."

"What are you hoping to find in there, Todge?"

"God, only knows, but I'm willing to bet Benny and Bernie stayed there while they were here infiltrating Billy's life," I say and twirl the red wine in my glass.

"You're exactly right. I wonder if private detectives will do illegal things for us, like a break-in?"

"I suppose they'll do most anything if you pay them enough," I reply.

Brenda walks back in with a tray containing a French press and two coffee cups with saucers and says, "If it is okay with you all, we're going to retire to the suite and watch a movie with the children. They are a little tired, and I know you both have a lot to do before Friday. We'll have dessert in front of the television."

"That's fine, Brenda. I hope I haven't scared you all away with my bad manners at dinner," I say.

"Nonsense, Philip. We are so grateful just to be here and we want to support you in any way we can," she replies as she pours out the coffee.

"Thanks," I reply.

"Do you all need cream or sugar?" Brenda asks.

"Black is fine," Lush says. "I think I'll go outside for a cigarette, y'all want to join me?"

"Sure," I reply.

"Let me cut the cheesecake for Charles and the kids, and I'll pop out for a quick one. Do you want some cheesecake?"

"Maybe later, Brenda," Lush replies. "Sometimes I get a sweet tooth before turning in."

"I know what you mean, I'm the same way," Brenda smiles. "I'll see you outside in a minute." She turns and walks back into the kitchen.

"What a wonderful woman, Todge. Charles is a lucky man to have hooked her."

"Yes, I know. And to think I have resented her all these years. I could just kick myself in the ass for that."

"Well, it's not like you really had the chance to get to know her until this tragedy happened," Lush says and takes a sip of the coffee.

"Yeah, but I could have taken the initiative, but I was just too angry at Dad. I really dread revealing this whole story to him and who knows where it is going. More and more I feel like he was just an innocent by-stander in events that shaped his life."

"That's true, Philip, but look where it has taken him. Look at the wonderful, loving family he has now. Excluding rebuilding his relationship with you and the loss of Billy, I believe Charles must be a very happy man."

"I suppose you're right, Lush," I say as I stand up. "Let's take our coffee and go smoke. I have to bum off you. I'll get my own tomorrow."

CHAPTER 21

I hear an alarm clock beeping and I open my eyes and look over at Billy's clock. It is seven am, so I reach over and turn the alarm off. Clark yawns with a slight screeching sound and stretches his front and back legs out as far as he can; his front paws dig into my side with great force.

"Ouch, boy, that hurts," I say with a little laugh and roll him on his back and start stroking his tummy. He moans, sighs, licks his lips, and his eyes close into narrow slits.

"Okay, boy. We have to get up! We've got a whole lot to do today."

My cell phone rings. I pick it up off the bedside table and see that it is Julianna calling.

"Hello."

"Philip, it's Julianna. I know you tried to call me last night. Sorry, I didn't pick up, but Janet and I were really connecting, and I didn't have any news from Jonas yet."

"That's fine, but what did he say when you talked to him yesterday?"

"Well, we're in luck. His caseload was very light, so he started immediately. He's here at my house right now. Philip, he photographed Julian getting onto a private jumbo jet at Newark last night around ten pm. The Sheikh of one of the United Arab Emirates owns it. His name is Sheikh Abbas and he is Najeed's father."

"Holy shit," I say, "Julian said he wasn't leaving until this evening. Something we said spooked him."

"Listen, Philip. Can you meet us at my gallery in say, thirty minutes? I'll have some breakfast brought in and we can meet back in my office. Your police escort will never know Jonas is there."

"Right, Lush and I will be there."

"Good. See you soon, Philip."

I hop out of bed, go into the closet to get a bathrobe, put it on and head out to the kitchen where I know I'll find Lush. Clark follows me. Lush is sitting at the counter with two laptops open, drinking a cup of coffee and looking intently at the screens.

"Good morning, Lush," I say.

"Well, good morning, so you did set your alarm for seven?" She looks up at me, smiling.

"Yes. Listen, we've got to hurry. Julianna just phoned. She wants us to meet her and Jonas, the private detective, at her office in thirty minutes. He got photographs of Julian boarding Najeed's father's jet at Newark last night at midnight."

"Wow," she exclaims, "This is beginning to coalesce, Todge."

"Yes, it is. I'm going to take a really quick shower. Would you mind feeding Clark?"

"Of course not, I know where his food is. How much food does he get?"

"About a cup. Is anyone else up yet?"

"Your Dad came in earlier and made some coffee to take to Brenda. I haven't heard a peep out of the kids yet," she says.

"Maybe you could leave them a note that we had to go to a breakfast meeting at Julianna's gallery. Also, why don't you give Julianna a call and see if she can get you Dominick Montaigne's phone number? Maybe we should pay him a visit today, too."

"Okay, I'll write the note. I already pulled Dominick's number from one of his emails to Billy. Want me to call him?"

"Sure, but don't you think it's a bit early?"

"Well, yes maybe, but that never stopped me," she replies.

I giggle. "So go ahead and wake him up."

"Done," she says. "Come on, Clark. You want your breakfast?"

He pants, wags his tail and follows Lush to the food pantry. I head back to Billy's bathroom where I shower quickly without shaving, brush my teeth and go in Billy's closet looking for clothes. I recall that Lush said last night that it was going to be quite a bit cooler today, so I choose a pair of tightly ribbed, hunter green corduroy pants with pleats and cuffs, a burgundy cotton turtle neck shirt, and a beige, crew neck, cable-knit sweater which feels very soft. Today I put on a pair of navy blue and green argyle socks and slip on a pair of Billy's Gucci loafers. They fit me like a glove. I find a matching Gucci belt and put it on. The entire time I'm showering and dressing I keep thinking about Ala Mary and her sons. I was so tired last night that as soon as Lush and I had finished a cigarette after dinner, I went to bed. I slept great all night, not getting up even once to pee, but I do remember a series of dreams all involving Ala Mary's husband, Newt, and their three sons, Willie B, Clevis, and Little Man. Mother sent us on an expedition to find the reddest clay on Fatgram's farm. She wanted to make red paint out of it to paint a landscape. Throughout the dream, which seemed to last a long time Billy and I would be digging in creek banks and ravines and gullies alongside Newt, Willie B, Clevis, and Little Man. Mother had given us fancy sterling silver teaspoons from one of Fatgram's sets and told us that the clay had to be dug with the finest silver, but that we had to take extreme care not to bend the spoons. Willie B and Clevis, big, strong men in their prime, Newt, Billy and I could not get the clay out without ruining the spoons. They would contort and twist as we tried to dig out the stiff clay. Newt would chuckle and say we all were just expecting too much from our spoons and needed to have more patience to get the clay out without bending them. He would take the dainty, twisted spoons and with his rough, black fingers, gently stroke them, and they would straighten out good as new. We would try again and the same thing would happen. But Little Man, barely a teenager, with astonishing, cat-like, hazel eyes and much lighter skin and smaller build than his brothers could easily get the clay out without bending the spoons. He would put the tip of the spoon in the clay, twirl it around like a drill and a perfect red cone of clay would come out every time. He would laugh and say to me, "I sure don't wanna disappoint yo momma, Miss Eva. She trusts me with her prize Camelias same as she trusts me with her clay." I cannot decipher the meaning of the dream. Why did I dream about red clay? Clay is what killed Willie B and Clevis. Willie B lost his footing and fell into a giant open vat of slip, or powdered clay, used in the manufacture of porcelain bathroom fixtures. Clevis jumped in, thinking he could pull his brother out, and they both suffocated. Little Man never worked at that factory, so he did not perish in the clay, so maybe that's why he could get it out in the dream. But that doesn't make sense because, Newt, Billy, and I couldn't get the clay out either. Little Man, whose real name is Brooker T, is not actually Newt and Ala Mary's real son, but the baby of one of Ala Mary's sisters who died in childbirth. Ala Mary and Newt took him in and raised him as their own. Could this be why he could get the red clay out?

Clark trots back into the closet to find me. As I pet him I hear Lush walking into the bedroom.

"You ready, Todge? I fed Clark and let him out. He did his business."

"I'm ready," I say as I walk out of the closet.

"My, you look nice in those clothes," she says.

"Thanks, I didn't bring much, so I have to wear Billy's."

"Well, those certainly suit you. I already informed Officer Graham about our plans. One of the officers downstairs will drive us over and accompany us."

"Good. Let's go. Did you get in touch with Dominick?"

"Yes, I did. He was very nice. Said he's an early bird and was already up working out. He said he would be willing to meet us today, so I tentatively set it for ten o'clock at his place. His studio is in Soho. I have the address."

"Great, Lush. We'll go there after Julianna's."

"Good morning Mr. Hampton," Officer Graham says as we enter the foyer.

"Good morning, Officer Graham."

"Will you all be out long?" she asks.

"Probably, a couple of hours. We'll be back by lunch at the latest," I reply and push the elevator button.

"Fine. Officer O'Daniel is waiting in a car out front. He'll drive you and accompany you," she says.

"Thank you," I say. The elevator door opens, and Lush and I get in. "You stay here Clark and help Officer Graham guard the house," I say. He pastes his ears back against his head, sits down, licks his muzzle and whines.

"Oh, he looks so pitiful," Lush says as the door closes. She sets her computer case down on the floor and says, "It's heavy today with two computers in it."

I reach over and take the shoulder strap from her. "Please let me carry it. I'm pretty used to schlepping heavy cases."

"Thanks, Todge."

"You're welcome. By the way, you look nice today, too."

"Why thank you," she says, smiling her biggest smile which generates cute little dimples in her cheeks. She is wearing an outfit—a light grey, cowl-neck sweater dress with a black belt with a large silver buckle around her waist and black leather boots—that accentuates her curvaceous body in a manner I find most pleasing. The dress is long, covering the boots at about her mid-calf, and she wears a long, black, camelhair coat over the dress. Her earrings are inch long platinum bars that dangle from her lobes—I know they are platinum, or white gold, because I learned when I gave her a sterling silver bracelet back in college that she can not wear silver because it reacts with her skin and stains it green. She reaches into her black Hermes bag and pulls out a pair of big, black oval, Chanel sun glasses and puts them on. The elevator stops, the door opens and we walk into the lobby.

"Mr. Hampton, it's so good to see you. I was so sorry to hear about Billy," Henry, an elderly, gentle, pleasant, white haired African American man, who fills in for the regular doormen, pats me on the left shoulder and bows his head.

"Thank you, Henry. I appreciate your concern," I say as I take his right hand and shake it. "Billy thought very highly of you, Henry."

"Yes sir, and I felt the same about him. He was a good and generous man. This past fall I was talking to him about how I couldn't think of a thing to get my wife for Christmas. A couple of weeks later, he asks me to come up to his place after my shift ended. Well, what do you know, but he had painted a picture of me sitting down here at this desk reading the paper. He says, 'Henry, here's what you can give your wife for Christmas.' Now, he didn't have to do that. What a kind man he was. And my wife, she cried when she looked at that picture on Christmas morning. I was so proud. And, thanks to your brother."

"What a sweet story, Henry," Lush says.

"Henry, this is my friend from Louisville, Sarah Richardson," I add in quickly.

"Oh, yes, I remember Miss Richardson, nice to see you again," he says.

"Thank you, Henry. It's good to see you again," Lush replies.

"We'll see you in a few hours, Henry," I say as we walk to the door.

"Yes sir, have a nice day," he replies.

"You, too, Henry," I say and push open the door. The wind whips around us with pulses of cold against my face and ears.

"My goodness," Lush says, "It feels like it may snow."

"I sure hope not," I say as put my right arm around Lush's back and pull her close to me as we walk down the stairs toward a navy blue sedan with a young man with a buzz cut holding open the back door of the car for us.

"Me too," Lush replies.

"Spring is the most beautiful season, I think, but it can also be the cruelest when a late freeze blasts through killing all the buds and blossoms," I say as we reach the car.

"Good morning Mr. Hampton, Mrs. Richardson," the Officer says and motions for us to get in the back seat. I help Lush in, and then I get in.

"I remember back in the late eighties, all the peach trees on Fatgram's orchards were in full bloom. What a beautiful site that is. She had over sixty thousand peach trees on four hundred acres. The temperature was forecast to get into the teens that night. In order to save the crop, she had huge fans, powered by generators, placed strategically throughout the orchards. Bales of hay were placed around the orchards and set on fire. The fans blew the warm air into the orchards through the night. She was able to save most of the crop. That was one of the eeriest sites I've ever seen, ribbons of fire burning all night long through the orchards and the collective hum of dozens of large generators. Billy and I stayed up half the night watching those fires. But everything else was ruined. Even the young, green leaves on trees froze making them look like they were covered with ugly brown cornflakes until new leaves reformed a few weeks later."

"Good Lord, that must have taken a lot of labor," Lush says.

"I suppose it did, but Fatgram could pull off most anything," I reply.

Officer O'Daniel gets in and looks at us through the rear view mirror and says, "Let's see, we're going Uptown to Morgan Galleries, nine-hundred block of Madison Avenue?"

"Yes, that's correct," I reply.

As we start off through the traffic, Lush pulls out a black notebook and opens it. It's a list of things to do before the wake tomorrow and a list of how she anticipates the event will unfold. She wants my input and agreement on every detail which I greatly appreciate but feel is unnecessary because her planning and organizing skills far exceed mine, so I endure her dissection of the event but offer many affirmative nods and spoken expressions of praise and thanks for her thoroughness and creativity in planning. As she covers the final topics on her list, we pull in front of Julianna's gallery, Morgan Fine Art, that occupies one half of the ground floor of a relatively new, mixed use building on Madison Avenue. Four large plate glass windows provide excellent display area for her storefront and she uses the space to promote upcoming and ongoing shows, artist retrospectives, samplings of artists she represents, and special events she organizes. Today the windows show several of her artists, including Billy, whose representative painting is of Clark on a walk painted from the perspective of Billy walking Clark. Clark has turned around and is looking up at Billy whose left arm and hand, holding the leash, are seen, as well as his left leg and foot as he takes a step forward. The painting is full of motion and portrays Clark's enthusiasm for the walk and the unspoken bond between him and his master.

"Oh my God, what a great painting of Clark," Lush says as I help her out of the car.

"Yes, he did several from the perspective of the person walking the dog," I reply.

"I really cherish the one he sent me last Christmas of Clark smiling up at him when he sees the leash in Billy's hand," she says.

"Yeah, that's a great one, too," I reply.

We approach the door and Officer O'Daniel opens it for us.

"Thanks," Lush says, "Are you coming in with us?"

"Yes mam," he replies, "I've been instructed to stick with you all."

"I see, but don't you have to park the car?" Lush asks.

He laughs. "Let's just say we're exempt from parking tickets."

"Yes, I suppose," Lush says, "But we anticipate our meeting with Miss Morgan to be of a private nature concerning Mr. Hampton's plans for his brother's posthumous exhibition. Surely you can wait outside Julianna's office for us?"

"That's not a problem, mam," he replies.

We walk into the central foyer of the building with its dazzling marble floor comprised of black, grey, and white marble tiles arranged in a massive star medallion in the center surrounded by hundreds of squares done in a parquet pattern. The entrance to Morgan Galleries is the first on the left of the foyer as you walk in the building and resembles the façade of a Greek temple, except that the columns and pediment are constructed of shining black marble veined with narrow streaks of white. 'Morgan Fine Art Galleries' is chiseled in the marble of the pediment facing and covered with gold leaf. The imposing entrance always surprises me and makes me speculate that Julianna's rent must be exorbitant. Although Julianna comes from great wealth, I imagine she has to sell several six-figure paintings a quarter to make this a profitable enterprise. Perhaps her father owns this building. I make a mental note to check that out. Through the large, glass double doors, there is a curved wall, painted a dark grey, with three large, exceedingly colorful paintings, each framed in simple gold frames, hanging above a reception desk faced with the same black marble as the entranceway. Officer O'Daniel tries to open the door, but it is locked. I see an intercom to the right of the doors and I push the button on it. I notice that the gallery hours are painted at the bottom of the right door in gold calligraphy, 'Hours – Tuesday through Saturday, Eleven am until Five pm or by Appointment'.

"Hello, is that you, Philip?" Julianna's rich voice resounds through the intercom, and I imagine, if she sings, she must be a contralto.

"Yes, we're here," I reply.

"Okay, come on in," she says as we hear the magnetic locks release.

Officer O'Daniel pushes the door open and motions for us to enter. We enter and as we walk toward the reception desk, I hear the locks engage. The floor of the gallery is also marble, but solid white, and I suppose that Julianna chose this color for its light reflecting properties. The large painting over the desk is a group of people selling produce at a market place. The people are dressed in brightly colored robes and all are wearing turbans or kerchiefs. Halogen lights suspended from the ceiling illuminate the paintings, revealing the many layers of thickly applied paint and varnish that create texture and movement in these paintings. The painting to the left is of a worker in a vineyard carrying an open barrel of grapes on his back and the painting to the right is of a standing saxophone player. "These paintings are wonderful," Lush says.

"Yes, I like them a lot," I add, "I wonder who the artist is." The sound of a woman walking in heels fills the gallery, and I turn to my right to see a young woman approaching us with an air of confidence and a beautiful smile. She reaches us, and I am shocked by her beauty—rich brown skin; a huge volume of mahogany hair, pulled back and braided into an immense single braid hanging over her right shoulder and down below her breasts, which I know just from seeing them, are full and firm, covered by the dark green wrap dress; big, pale green eyes the color of shallow tropical waters; long, lean, limbs; hips with just the right amount of curves; a slender neck with a beautiful necklace which appears to be made from pieces of blue, green, and lavender sea glass and terminating in a gold cross riding the precipice of her perfect cleavage; full lips; and near perfect facial features. This young woman is as beautiful as any of the female models who were friends and coworkers of Billy. I sense that her beauty overwhelms Lush and Officer O'Daniel, too.

"Good morning, I'm Alejandraia Espinoza," she says in a smooth voice tinged with a hint of a Spanish accent. "Miss Morgan is expecting you, Mrs. Richardson and," she looks back and forth between me and Officer O'Daniel and says, "Mr. Hampton?"

"I'm Philip Hampton and this is Officer O'Daniel," I say smiling at her, hoping she likes my looks more than Officer O'Daniel's, who is a little shorter than I, compact, with sharp facial features, dark eyes,

and a shaved head covered with dark stubble that blends seamlessly through his sideburns onto his cheeks, chin, and neck, and powerfully built—I would not care to sustain a punch from his fists—and probably the same age as Alejandraia.

"Pleased to meet you all. Aren't these paintings wonderful?"

"They're really beautiful," Lush says, "Who is the artist?"

"Her name is Monique Retailleau. She is from Nice. She travels the world, painting scenes of everyday life. Her medium is acrylic. As you can see from the built up layers of paint—impasto—she applies the paint thickly, with knifes, no brushes. That's why the faces don't have a lot of detail. She also paints very fast. These paintings have many layers of paint and many layers of varnish."

"Fascinating," Lush says.

"Yes," Alejandraia replies, "Please follow me. I'll take you to Miss Morgan's office." She turns to lead the way, and the first thing I notice is that she has a splendid ass, too. Officer O'Daniel has not said a word and has been unable to take his eyes off her. We walk along the front of the gallery and then turn left and proceed toward the back. The gallery is large by New York standards—probably over twenty thousand square feet. We proceed to a lounge area that resembles the first class lounge of an international airline replete with sumptuous leather chairs and sofas, groupings of marble tables with leather club chairs, and a shiny, black, grand piano. A smaller scale replica of the entrance façade of the gallery surrounds a beautiful bar with black marble facing and a stainless steel bar top, rimmed with a black leather armrest. A large plasma television hangs above and behind the bar and below the marble pediment.

"Please have a seat. I'll go get Miss Morgan," Alejandraia says. "She just received a call from a client in Asia, but she shouldn't be long." She smiles, quickly turning around, causing her long braid to bounce back over her right shoulder, hang down her back, and swing like a pendulum in cadence with the motion of her hips.

"Thank you, Alejandraia," I say, watching her walk away. Lush widens her eyes at me in a dismissive gesture of my ogling. We sit down on a sofa and Officer O'Daniel sits near us in a leather chair.

"Officer O'Daniel, do you know if Detectives Bell and Johnson have made any headway on the case since yesterday?" Lush asks as she crosses her legs and adjusts the bottom of her dress.

"Mrs. Richardson, I know they are working around the clock on this case. I am briefed on the case and given instructions about my specific duties, but I don't know details on breaking discoveries."

"I see, well I'm sure they'll phone us if anything significant is uncovered," Lush replies.

"Yes mam, I'm sure they will," Officer O'Daniel replies and looks up at the bar as one of the swinging doors flanking the plasma television swings open and a waiter, a middle aged Asian woman wearing black pants, a white shirt with a black bow tie and a vest made out of a royal blue, heavy brocade, rolls in a cart covered with a white linen tablecloth carrying a large silver tray with a complete sterling tea and coffee set, several china cups, and a platter of pastries.

"Good morning, may I offer you some coffee, tea, fresh squeezed orange juice, and pastries?" she asks with a thick accent and a smile.

"Thank you. Black coffee for me," Lush replies.

"Regular or decaf, madam?"

"Regular, please."

"I'll have the same, please," I add.

"You sir?" She looks at Officer O'Daniel.

"The same also, thanks."

She takes three coffee cups and saucers and places them on a marble table, picks up a sterling coffee pot and begins pouring. She fills each cup by positioning the spout of the pot near the cup and pulls it up over two feet as a pencil thin stream of brown, steaming liquid fills the cup without one drop splashing. She smiles and hands each of us a saucer and cup with steady hands.

"Orange juice?" She points to a crystal carafe full of orange juice.

"I'll have some, please," Lush says.

"Anyone, else?"

"No thanks," I reply.

"None for me," Officer O'Daniel replies.

She pours juice into a beautiful, intricately carved, crystal juice glass and hands it to Lush.

"Thank you."

"Pastry, Danish?" She asks as she picks up a pair of silver tongs and points to the pastry. Everyone declines.

"Anything else I can get for you? Mimosa? Bloody Mary? Champagne?"

Again, we all decline.

"Thank you." She says and rolls the cart over to the bar and goes back through the swinging door.

Lush and I have been to several openings here before and are used to the lavish surroundings and high level of personal service, but I sense from the way Officer O'Daniel gawks at the surroundings that he is a bit uncomfortable. He appears to be in his early twenties, and I conjecture that he has probably spent most of his time on the police force on a beat on the streets of the city. We sit a while without speaking, sipping our coffee and listening to piano music playing softly from speakers in the ceiling. The music is somewhat familiar, but I have no idea what it is.

"That's a lovely piece," Officer O'Daniel says to Lush and me.

"What piece are you looking at?" I ask.

"Oh, I was referring to the piano sonata. It is the Adagio cantabile from Beethoven's Piano Sonata No. 8 in C minor," he says, looks up, closes his eyes, and seems to absorb the music into every pore in his skin. Lush and I look at each other in total surprise, and she breaks into a big smile.

"You'll have to excuse me, Officer O'Daniel, but I never would have guessed that you would be into classical music, much less knowing the name of this song playing," Lush states.

"Why is that Mrs. Richardson?" He asks with an element of challenge in his voice.

"Oh, well, I thought, you just, just appear to be the tough street cop type. I mean, well. Well, how stupid of me. I apologize if I have offended you," she says with a red flush in her cheeks.

He laughs, smiles at us, gets up, walks over to the piano, sits down and begins to play the same piece we've been listening to. Lush and I get up and walk over to the piano. He plays beautifully, swaying with emotion, his eyes closed. I watch Lush observe him, and I realize she and I have both envisioned sexual conquests this morning, and I smile. Officer O'Daniel's hands slow down and he softly lifts them from the keys and the music stops. He looks up directly into Lush's eyes and says, "I studied at Julliard before entering the police force."

"That was lovely, Officer O'Daniel," Lush says.

"Very nice," I add, "And how did you get from Julliard to the NYPD?"

He smiles, sighs, and says, "It's a long story."

"Good morning all!" Julianna says in a cheery tone, making her way toward the piano with long elegant strides, presenting a striking image in a white pantsuit trimmed in black—immediately bringing to mind the beautiful red-crowned cranes I observed on the cold island of Hokkaido in northern Japan for a week early in my free-lance career for a story which ended up in the *New York Times*. The cranes are magnificent with their white plumage with black secondary and tertiary feathers as they execute intricate dances of bonding and courtship.

"Good morning, Julianna," I say.

"Who is this talented young man?" she asks.

"Julianna, this is Officer O'Daniel. He's been assigned to us today," Lush says.

Julianna walks over, extends her hand, and says, "Pleased to meet you Officer O'Daniel. I'm Julianna Morgan. You play that Beethoven Sonata beautifully."

He lightly shakes her hand, smiling, obviously pleased that she recognizes the piece, and says, "Thank you, Miss Morgan."

"Well, perhaps you'd like to stay out here and play while Mrs. Richardson, Mr. Hampton, and I have our meeting in my office?"

"Thank you, that would be nice. It's not often I get to play while on duty," he says, smiling up at us.

"Good. I don't expect we'll be more than half an hour or so," Julianna states.

We follow Julianna back to her office as Officer O'Daniel begins playing again, but this piece is much faster, aggressive, much more masculine than the Beethoven—I perceive it as a conscious statement to us—and Julianna says, as if thinking out loud, "My, from Beethoven's Piano Sonata No. 8 in C minor to Chopin's Polonaise No. 6 in A flat major, what a surprise"

"Yes, indeed," Lush says, but all I am thinking is how the hell does Julianna know all these exact pieces. I suppose her vast knowledge of art encompasses music as well. She opens the tall door, covered with intricate recessed panels, to her office and motions for us to enter. Lush goes in, and I follow her, and I look up to see two men and Janet Ostro sitting around the library table in Julianna's office.

"Janet, I didn't expect to see you this morning." Lush says, "But what a nice surprise."

"Good morning, nice to see you too, Lush, Philip," Janet says smiling. "Yes, I'm surprised to be here, too."

"I insisted she come," Julianna says as she shuts the door and walks over to the library table. "I kept her up most of the night going through her paintings. She's phenomenal—my newest discovery, and I have you two to thank for it. Picture this, 'a twenty-first century Mary Cassatt', that's as close as I can come to describing her talent. Major. Major. Major. So you see, I can't lose sight of her until she signs my contract!" Julianna laughs, then quickly adds, "No, seriously, I think you both know Janet can provide a lot of useful information to Jonas, and she has graciously agreed to meet with us."

"Well, that's great news, Janet," I say and notice she seems to be leaning to her left side moving her left arm in a strange way. I walk over and see that she is petting two dogs. "Well, this must be Harry and Sally?"

"Yes, the tan one is Harry and the brown one is Sally. Julianna insisted I bring them today since I had previously made plans to spend my day off with the dogs."

"Well, they are beautiful and are so well behaved," I say. Both dogs remain seated, wagging their shaggy tails, peering up at me. Lush peers over at the dogs and smiles.

"Oh, they are adorable, Janet. May I pet them?"

"Certainly." Lush bends down and gives each dog a pat on the head and a rub under the chin.

"Lush, Philip, allow me to present Mr. Jonas Grey and his associate, Mr. Mabry Whittaker," Julianna says standing behind the two men. "Janet and I visited with Jonas for over an hour last night. When I received your email on my Blackberry late last night, Lush, that you think you found some sort of code on a disk from Julian's compound in Dubai, I emailed Jonas. He brought along Mabry who is an expert in cracking codes."

"Nice to meet you both," I say. "I appreciate you helping out at such short notice, Mr. Grey."

"Please, call me, Jonas," he says in a deep, but remarkably gentle voice.

"Please, take a seat," Julianna says to Lush and me as she pulls out a chair beside Jonas and sits down. Her office is spacious with two walls of floor to ceiling book cases containing hundreds of books and leather bound volumes, most of which I assume are art reference books. Another wall has two large bay windows, each containing upholstered sofas and chairs, facing out to a small courtyard garden—I can see the faint green-gold first leaves on several small trees. A large Regency style desk sits in front of the fourth wall upon which several paintings hang. All the furniture in the office is Regency, and I am certain

all the pieces are authentic antiques. The room has wall-to-wall carpet of a deep tan color with small back diamonds uniformly dispersed through it with a reversed color pattern in a foot wide border. The carpet is lush with thick padding underneath and I wonder how Julianna navigates it in high heels.

"Jonas, I guess you know by now that this is a pretty contorted case. I'm afraid it is becoming more bizarre by the day," I add as I look into Jonas's blue-grey eyes and begin forming my first impressions of him. His countenance clearly reads, 'Don't fuck with me or you'll live to regret it'. I suspect he must be in his early forties because his thick, short, light brown hair is graying at his temples and sideburns. I discern an incredibly well built but lean body through the blue blazer and white shirt with open collar he wears. His facial features are sharp, well defined; yet, the overall hardness he exudes prevents him from being truly handsome.

"Yes, complicated, interesting, and challenging, Philip. May I call you, Philip?"

"Of course," I reply.

"Philip, I know a lot about this case already, but what I need to know from you is exactly what it is you want and how far are you willing to go to get it?" He maintains his gaze into my eyes.

"Fair enough," I reply. "Jonas, I want you to help me determine exactly why my brother was murdered and exactly who is responsible for it. Also, I want to determine if Adrian McWhorter murdered my mother. Finally, I want to know these things as quickly as is humanly possible. I'm willing to commit significant resources to it."

"I can help you, Philip. Here's my contract. I require a ten thousand dollar retainer. I bill out at five hundred dollars an hour, plus all expenses. Mabry will be billed out at two hundred and twenty-five dollars per hour." He slides the contract toward me. I look at him and make the decision that I trust him and do believe he will help me. I pull out a blank check from my wallet, write in ten thousand dollars, sign it, and hand it to him.

"Jonas, you can fill out the payable to line," I say as I sign the contract without reading a word of it.

"Good, now that formalities are out of the way, what can you tell us so far, Jonas?" Lush asks.

Jonas smiles, turning to look at Lush. "Well, Lush, at this point, I suspect you know quite a bit more than I. As you know, I was able to confirm Julian Ainsworth's departure last night, about ten thirty from Newark aboard Sheik Abbas's jet. I also know they loaded several containers and crates of 'artworks' into the main cabin. My suspicion is that Benny Boonmee was in one of these containers."

"Yes, that would make sense," Lush says as someone knocks on the door. Julianna walks over and opens it.

"Oh, please come in, Jiao," Julianna says as she opens the door and the Asian woman rolls in the breakfast cart. Piano music filters into the room. "He's still playing Chopin," Julianna says as she shuts the door.

Jiao makes her way to the library table and begins offering everyone coffee, juice and pastries. It is clear that Jonas does not intend to pursue his line of questioning in front of Jiao, so he remains silent until she finishes serving and leaves the room.

"Philip," Jonas says as he reaches for a cup of black coffee, "I'm interested in knowing more about this disk from Dubai Julianna says you found in your brother's computer."

"Yes, it's disgusting—a collection of hundreds of photographs of child pornography, mostly of little boys being cruelly sexually abused by men, all of middle eastern extraction," I explain.

"Did you bring it and your brother's laptop?" he asks.

"Yes, I have them," Lush says.

"Would you mind if Mabry has a look at them while we talk?"

"No, not at all." She reaches in her case and pulls out the laptop and the disk and hands them to Mabry who has not spoken one word during the meeting. He looks very young, as if he were still in high school with a mass of curly, brown hair hanging over his ears and around his face, which has traces of acne

dispersed over his cheeks and running down both jaw lines. His skin is pasty white and his brown eyes are set deeply in his face and are separated by a large, over-projected nose supporting a pair of wire rimmed, John Lennon-type glasses. He is lanky and tall and the sleeves of his blue blazer appear too short as his hairy wrists protrude from them as reaches for the laptop and disk. He quickly puts the disk into his own laptop and starts pecking at the keyboard with long fingers.

Jonas begins to thoroughly and methodically question each of us. I keep looking over at Mabry to see if he shows any expressions or emotions from viewing the pictures, but he continues to punch keys as his eyes move back and forth rapidly from the screen to the keyboard, revealing nothing. His left ear contains an earphone connected to his laptop. I respond to Jonas when he asks questions and I listen to the responses of Julianna, Janet, and Lush. The events I've lived through the past several days unfold themselves again, and I begin to wonder how all this will ever end. I feel hollow, void, and empty of meaning—the only real comfort seems to come when my mind lapses into a hot sexual fantasy and I feel the burning in my ears and the beginning of an erection and all I want to do is pull down my pants and beat off violently. I would just love to have Alejandraia bend over the piano bench, and I would pull down my pants, lift up her skirt over her ass and take her from behind. O'Daniel is still playing away. It must be Chopin. It sounds like Chopin. Fatgram loved Chopin and played it quite a bit, but I never could remember the complicated names of the pieces. Hell, at this point, I wouldn't even mind watching O'Daniel fuck Alejandraia. I imagine that we are having Billy's posthumous exhibition, and I take a break to go pee. As I walk back toward the bathrooms, I hear a sound in Julianna's office. The door is slightly cracked and I peer through the crack. Alejandraia is up on the library table with her dress pulled up around her torso and her legs spread wide. O'Daniel's shirt is unbuttoned and his pants are down around his ankles and he is driving his cock into Alejandraia. Their faces hold expressions of extreme lustful need as their bodies meld.

"So, Philip, Lush says it's important to you to get into Adrian's apartment. What are you expecting to find there?" Jonas asks me.

"Pictures," I reply as my cheeks flush. "Pictures of a pornographic nature Adrian took of Billy and me when we were kids."

"We can definitely get in there, but I strongly suspect anything which might incriminate Adrian or Julian is on that plane to Dubai right now," Jonas replies.

"You're probably right about that," I reply.

Mabry looks up at Jonas and says in a soft nasal voice, "I've made some interesting preliminary findings."

"Let's hear them, Mabry," Jonas replies, leans back, puts his hand in a prayer position and rests his chin on them.

"Uhmm, well, dude, what we have is, all these, uhmmn, picture files are in fact, well they make up a steganographic catalog—actually a steganographic catalog containing intricate cryptograms. You see, in applications requiring extreme security, cryptographic methods are ineffective and susceptible to rapid and complete decoding. I can easily break those even though I don't read or speak Pashtu, but through word positioning software. And after applying my own fractal decoding program to several of the steganographs, I am convinced this in fact a detailed compilation of SOP's and contingency plans." He smiles, and then looks back down at the keyboard of his laptop.

Lush's eyes are as big as saucers and she says, "Mabry, hon, I'm assuming that wasn't just bombast?"

"Uhh, no, it wasn't," he replies stealing a couple of quick looks at Lush and turning very red.

"Good. Could you please repeat that at a level, well, let's see, that maybe a sixth grader could understand?"

"Sixth grader?" Mabry asks with a surprised look on his face. Jonas chuckles.

"Yes, dear. I think if you try to get down to that level, the rest of us might be able to comprehend what you just said," Lush says and leans forward in her chair.

"Well, okay, I suppose?" He looks at Jonas.

"It's fine Mabry. You've done a great job, just simplify it for us all," Jonas says, smiling.

"Uhmn, these pictures, these dirty, uhm, pornographic, well, pedophile, well, these pictures form the basis of a website for groups of terrorist operatives. Each picture contains information about standard operating procedures, protocols, strategies, plans, and directions. By having a 'key' in the form of software, a person accessing this website can decode the pictures. This site probably has dozens of different keys, depending on who has access to what information. It is one of the most complex and sophisticated I've ever seen. It is probably updated daily or at least weekly. This disk is used to update a user's personal computer to the site; I'm sure for control purposes." He pauses and looks at Lush.

"Well, do you know which terrorist group it is?" Lush asks.

"I've decoded the words 'International Islamic Front for Jihad Against Jews and Crusaders'—al-Qaeda. I don't think they would want us to have this, especially since I'm probably one of a handful of people on earth who can crack this. This disk was meant to go to cells in Madrid and Jakarta."

"Oh my God. We're doomed," Lush says. "It's true, our worst fears, Todge."

Janet and Julianna have worried looks on their faces. One of Janet's dogs whimpers.

"No, maybe not, Lush," Jonas says. "Scotland Yard has discovered this type of coded information involving pornographic websites from computers confiscated from busted al-Qaeda cells in London, just last year. Who would ever suspect that a group, even a terrorist group, with such strong religious views would use pornography to send coded messages? Anyway, I doubt seriously that Scotland Yard could decode it as well as Mabry can. You see, he wrote his doctoral thesis at MIT on fractal encoding. He's pretty much the world's authority on the subject. These codes evolve quickly and the keys can be changed instantly as well as any plans or procedures on a given disk. I believe Najeed unknowingly exposed Billy to this through Billy's quest to make contact with Adrian. If Claude is in fact Adrian, then he must be involved in the production and distribution of this code for al-Qaeda. From the standpoint of a career pedophile like Adrian, producing these disks with their filthy photographs must be a dream job, and immensely profitable one I suspect. Someone close to Najeed obviously leaked back to Julian and Adrian that Najeed's friends had purchased the disk from the housekeeper. I imagine that housekeeper is no longer alive."

"Yes, that explains a lot," Lush says.

"You sound as if you know a lot about al-Qaeda, Jonas," I say.

"Well, I've been on the ground in Afghanistan and Pakistan over a dozen of times in the past ten years with the Navy Seals and on special assignment with our government," he replies.

"Thank God we hired you," Lush says.

"I believe Benny did not intend to kill your brother, at least not right away," Jonas says.

"What do you mean?" I ask. "He even went back to the hospital to finish him off," I add, feeling anger surge within my body.

"Hear me out, Philip," Jonas says. "You see, I believe Benny's job was to retrieve the disk taken by Julian's housekeeper. If he killed Billy, how would Benny ever be certain he could find the disk? No, I think he used GHB to drug Billy so he could get him back to his home, and get him to reveal the whereabouts of the disk. But he must have overestimated the amount of GHB needed, probably because Billy had been drinking a lot that night."

"Well, if that's the case, why did Benny return to the hospital Monday morning to kill Billy?" I ask.

"Janet tells me that Benny, disguised as the computer technician, Meng, was talkative as he worked and asked questions about the young man in the unit—questions like why was the man there and was he going to be alright. When he learned from Janet of Billy's dire prognosis, that he wasn't going to improve, that he'd be no use in providing information concerning the disk's whereabouts, he finished him off. He must have been instructed to do this. Plus, I imagine anyone wanting to keep

194

the knowledge of Billy and Najeed's affair from the world would find Billy's death a benefit. Elliott was murdered as a safeguard, in case he knew too much and as a diversion to create a 'sex scandal' associated with Billy."

"Well, I guess that's plausible," I say, "but, it still seems as if something is missing."

"That may well be, and I may not have it exactly right, but I think we're getting very close," Jonas says.

"How important is that disk?" Lush asks. "I mean is it irreplaceable?"

"Mabry, what do you think?" Jonas says then bites his bottom lip.

"Uhmm, the disk is copy protected with an advanced algorithm, but I'm certain I can break that, too. I've been looking for information on the disk's creator that has been left out on purpose, but a lot of times it gets attached to a file without the creator realizing it. I'm scanning the disk right now for it."

"So, as I understand it, the main threat, excluding revealing all the secret al-Qaeda information, is revealing the creator of this disk?" Lush asks.

"Exactly," Jonas replies, "The creator would have the motive to kill most anyone who possesses the knowledge or has the potential to have the knowledge of what's on the disk and who created it."

"But obviously, Benny never got the disk," Lush says.

"That's right," Jonas says. "And, I also found out that Sheikh Abbass's plane landed in Newark on Tuesday afternoon. So Julian lied to you all, he hadn't been in New York on business, but arrived after Benny had been unable to retrieve the disk."

"I knew I didn't trust that patch-eyed old bastard," Lush says. "What the hell did he think he was going to do, find the disk himself? He could barely walk."

"Well, he may well have implanted a listening device," Jonas says.

"That's a good point," I say.

"Wow, dude," Mabry says as he looks at his screen. "I found one file which is not encoded at all. It's just a picture file, a black and white picture file. It's pretty gross looking. The creator is called Nairda and this was created on the third of June, 2005."

We all get up to look at the screen. It is a photograph of a naked boy sucking the cock of a grown man. The man is holding a noose made of leather around the boy's neck. The boy's eyes are closed and he is masturbating himself with his left hand. Only the man's torso and upper legs are visible.

"Oh my God, Lush. Look," I say, "That's Adrian. That's fucking Adrian McWhorter."

"Are you certain, Philip?" she asks and grabs my left arm.

"Oh, I'm certain. See the birthmark on his right hip. It's the same one we saw last night on that photo of our Blood Brothers initiation. See how it is shaped like Italy, that's Adrian. And look what he's doing to that kid. He's strangling him while the kid masturbates. That's Adrian's favorite thing, that's exactly the way he taught Billy and me."

"Well, everything is falling into place now, Todge," Lush says. "Adrian has to be the mastermind of all this, he just has to."

"Now we know why that disk is so important—it proves he's alive, it identifies him as the pedophile pornographer, Nairda, and it links him with al-Qaeda," I say.

"Plus we have his thumbprint and a dried blood sample from the 'Blood Brothers' certificate we found on the back of Billy's last painting," Julianna adds.

"Yes, his last painting," I say. "All because of Adrian. I'll kill the bastard with my bare hands." I slam my right hand down on the table and turn away. No one says anything for a moment, and I walk over to Julianna's desk and pick up a picture in a pewter frame of Billy and Julianna taken six years ago at his first opening at her gallery. I look at his beautiful smiling face, and I realize what I have to do. I take the picture and walk back to the library table.

"I know how to resolve this. I know what has to be done. I must finish what my brother Billy started and was close to realizing: I must confront Adrian McWhorter, face to face. I must do it for Billy, for Mother, for the other women artists and their children, for all the other boys he's abused, and for me."

"But Philip, how can you? Imagine the protection, the resources he has? He's portrayed himself for dead for years. How would you ever confront him?" Lush asks and I look into her eyes and see fear.

"It's simple, I think," I reply, still looking at Billy's photograph. "If he wants to keep his anonymity and wants this disk back, then the only way he will get it is by meeting me, face to face, and taking it from my hand. As we know, a simple email or phone call to Najeed should be sufficient to transmit that information to Adrian. But he must come to me, to Billy, to Billy's house to get it, on my turf, not his. And he must give me some time."

"Time?" Lush asks.

"Yes, time to talk to Jonathan Zeng, Isabella de la Croix, and Christopher O'Bryan. Time to know the truth of their stories. Even though I can only imagine it to be pure evil, to try to know the truth of Adrian's story. There has to be some meaning in all this for me, for all of us." I pause, and as I look at Billy's smile, my eyes fill with tears. "Billy wants me to spread his ashes in his favorite places within six months of his death. This has to be completed by then."

Everyone stares at me.

"Well, are you all with me or not?" I ask.

Lush sighs, crosses her arms, smiles and says, "I'm with you."

"I'm with you as well, Philip," Julianna says.

"Me too," Janet says.

"Well, considering you've signed my contract and paid me a retainer, Mabry and I are in," Jonas says. "But I must warn you, what you are planning is dangerous and could result in your death, but it makes good sense to get him in this country. You do intend to turn him over to authorities once you have your say with him. Don't you, Philip?"

"I suppose so. As much as I'd like to strangle him, I'd rather expose him to the world."

"Good. The message you transmit should be concise but thorough. It must let him know you are dead serious and that this disk and everything you know about him will be exposed to the world should so much as a hair be harmed on you or anyone close to you before the meeting."

"Yeah," Mabry says, "Wouldn't it be cool if we sent the message to him in a picture encoded with his own methods?"

"Brilliant, Mabry," Lush says. "That would give him a good idea of our own resources."

"Sweet," Mabry adds and smiles for the first time this morning.

"And, Jonas," I say, "I'd like to have Mabry go through everything on that disk as soon as possible to determine if it reveals any sort of imminent danger to anyone from these terrorist cells. I don't care how much it costs, I want it done."

"Certainly. I think you'll find Mabry most efficient," Jonas says.

"Todge, what are we going to tell the police?" Lush asks.

"Nothing. We'll try our best not to impede their investigation, but I think they'll be hitting dead ends quickly," I reply.

Mabry's computer makes a siren sound and he reaches over, puts the cursor on a blinking symbol and clicks on it. An email appears and he reads it and says, "Wow, dude!"

"What Mabry? Is that from Sheila?" Jonas asks.

"Yea, she just picked up that two bodies have been discovered in an air cargo container at Newark airport. They are young Asian men—twins."

"Benny and Bernie," Lush says. "That wicked Adrian. Boy, this will preoccupy the police for a while."

"Philip, the sooner we transmit that message to Adrian, the better," Jonas says.

196

"Alright," I reply, "Let's set up Billy's computer and I'll compose a little epistle for Adrian—special delivery, compliments of Najeed."

Mabry focuses on Billy's computer for a few seconds and says, "Here, Mr. Hampton. I need the body of the message you want to send to Najeed—just type in what you want."

"Thanks, Mabry. Please, just call me Philip." I sit down. The message comes out quickly and easily:

Najeed, I'm Philip Hampton, Billy's brother. I'm sure you have heard of his death by now. I'm certain Adrian McWhorter, who is masquerading as Claude Blackmore, is responsible. Adrian had Billy murdered for two reasons: 1) Billy was in possession of the disk that your associates obtained from the housekeeper and 2) Billy was in a position to expose Adrian and his long list of villainous, wicked, and despicable deeds to the world. I would greatly appreciate it if you would make certain Adrian receives the following communication from me as quickly as possible:

Adrian:

If you want your disk back, you must come in person to New York and get it from me. I've had it decoded by an expert, and I know everything it says. It is in a safe deposit box. As you can see from this picture we are well aware of your fractal encoding techniques. I have to tell you we are way ahead of you in this technology. You may want to invest in better technical help. If anything happens to me, or anyone close to me, the disk, as well as its decoded content, will be delivered directly to the New York City Police Department. Come and meet me, Adrian and I promise I will never reveal all I know about you. Don't come and I will reveal everything I know to the authorities in the United States and Dubai. You have until Saturday, April 13 to let me know. Please contact me through Najeed. Philip.

"Okay, Mabry. This is what I want to say," I say as I turn the laptop toward him. "Lush, you've got all the pictures for the wake on your laptop here, don't you?"

"Yes, they are all on the hard disk," she replies.

"Good. Do you have any of Billy, Adrian, and me?"

"I do. And, as a matter of fact, I was going to delete them in light of our discoveries about Adrian."

"No, don't delete them. They're a part of our life. Could I look at them now?"

"Sure," she replies and gets out her laptop and opens it up. "Give me a second."

"Everyone, come read what I wrote to Adrian," I direct. "Mabry, can you take this passage to Adrian and encode it in a picture I choose?"

"No problem, dude. I mean, Philip," he replies.

"Great. That will be the perfect message to him."

"Here you go, Todge," Lush says and turns her laptop toward me. "Look at these. This one is adorable." She pulls up a photograph of Adrian, Mother, Billy and me sitting in the seat of a double Ferris wheel. The picture was taken at an amusement park in Myrtle Beach. Dad took the photograph. He never liked heights and wouldn't ride it. Billy and I are smiling. Mom is laughing and Uncle Adrian is smiling with his left arm around Billy and me. We look like the perfect happy family on vacation. I feel my heart in my throat as I look at the picture.

"Perfect," I say. "Use that one, please, Mabry."

"It's done," he replies. "This will take me about fifteen minutes to do. Can I see your computer a moment, Miss Richardson? I need to email that photo to my computer."

"Sure," she says and hands him her laptop.

"Great," I say. "Jonas, how fast can you get us into Adrian's apartment?"

"Today, if it's that urgent," he replies.

"No, we've got so much to do before tomorrow," I reply. "What about Saturday?"

"No problem. Let me get back to you on the best time," he says, rubbing his chin with his right hand.

"Well, I appreciate all your help, Jonas. I think you should definitely come to the wake tomorrow night," I say and reach over to take a sip of coffee.

"Yes, of course. I plan to be there," he replies.

"Mabry, your skills are amazing. Thanks for cracking those codes," I say.

"Oh man, no prob. That's what I do," he replies without looking at me, fingers moving rapidly over his keyboard.

"Jonas, I'll call you after our visit with Dominick Montaigne to fill you in," I say.

"That's fine. Meanwhile, I'll be doing research on Mr. McWhorter," he replies.

"Great," I say. "Julianna. Thanks so much for arranging all this and introducing us to these fine detectives."

"My pleasure, Philip. Perhaps Janet and I should arrive early tomorrow to help with any last minute details?"

"That would be great," Lush says. "It's going to be a monumental effort to pull this off smoothly and we could use all the help we can get."

"Fine," Julianna replies. "Janet, do you think we could arrange to get there by five?"

"Of course," Janet replies getting up out of her seat and disturbing Harry and Sally from their slumber.

Lush and I shake hands with Jonas and Mabry and embrace Julianna and Janet. I open the door and the sound of Officer O'Daniel playing the piano rushes in.

CHAPTER 22

My mind races as Officer O'Daniel drives us to Montaigne's Soho apartment. It's hard for me to believe how much my life has changed this week—everything spins through my head like a Rolodex containing snapshots from the past evoking a range of emotion from happiness to despair but all underlain with dull, gnawing feelings toward Adrian of contempt, disgust, revulsion, and abhorrence. Adrian is the pestilence of my life and he must be eradicated. Lush is being chatty with Officer O'Daniel which pisses me off. It seems insignificant to me that he joined the police force, dropping out of Julliard, after his father, a NYPD narcotics officer, was killed in a drug raid. I am surprised that he is twenty-eight years old because he looks younger, and I am irritated because it is obvious to me that he likes Lush and the attention he is getting from her. I sigh a couple of times and give her looks of disapproval, but she continues her chat with O'Daniel, so I resign myself to sit back and wallow in my shitty feelings alone.

We finally pull up in front of an apartment building with a limestone and red brick façade in need of a thorough steam cleaning. Officer O'Daniel looks at it, grimaces, and says, "I think I should go up with you all. Fourth floor, right?"

"Yes," Lush replies with a slight smile. "Dominick said to ring the bell and he'd buzz us up." She turns to look at me, "You okay, Todge?"

"I'm fine," I reply, opening the car door.

I help Lush out, and we walk up to the entrance followed by Officer O'Daniel. Lush reaches up and pushes the white button beside Unit 4.

"Yes, may I help you," a male voice, thick with a French-Caribbean accent, responds.

"Dominick, it's Sarah Richardson and Philip Hampton," Lush replies.

"Oh, yes, please come up," he says as we hear a buzzer indicating the door is unlocked. Officer O'Daniel opens the door and we walk into an entrance hall onto faded and worn squares of black and white marble. The hall is bare except for a line of sturdy metal mailboxes hanging from one wall and two

wall lanterns emitting dim light. The smell of the place is musty with a high note of curry. A large, ornate, darkly stained wooden staircase dominates the foyer, ascending for six stories with stairs covered in a dark grey, thick, worn carpet revealing an intricate grey and black pattern. There is no elevator.

"Well, at least I'll get some exercise today," Lush says as she looks up the staircase and we begin our silent climb, Lush leading and Officer O'Daniel following behind me. I let my left hand glide along the banister, polished smooth by thousands of hands over the years and I wonder who all the people are. What did they do? Where did they come from? Did they have fulfilled lives? Did they achieve their goals? Did they have goals? Did they give a damn? Did anyone give a damn about them? Half way up Lush begins to breathe heavily and she stops.

"Lord, I'm almost out of breath," she says. "I really do need to stop smoking.""Are you okay, Mrs. Richardson?" Officer O'Daniel asks with a look of concern.

"Yes, thank you. Just give me a second," she replies.

I, too, notice a slight shortness in my own breathing as a result of a week of heavy smoking, and I vow to myself to quit on Saturday. Lush begins to climb again, this time with the watchful O'Daniel behind her. As I climb, his ass is at my face level and I watch his powerful gluteus muscles contract through his navy slacks as they lift his stocky frame up the stairs. As we reach the fourth landing, a very tall, twelve paneled door opens and out walks a man dressed in a white wife beater shirt with army combat uniform cargo pants and black lace-up boots. He smiles, extending his right hand to Lush, "Hello, Dominick Montaigne. Good exercise for you, these stairs."

"Yes, yes," Lush says, trying to catch her breath. She shakes his hand. "I'm Sarah Richardson. This is Officer O'Daniel." They shake hands and then she says, "And this is Philip Hampton, Billy's brother."

"Pleased to meet you," I say as I shake his hand and become aware of his strong body odor. Dominick is in outstanding physical shape. His arms are powerful, muscled, with intricate tattoos circling the bulging biceps and triceps and running down his massive forearms. I see well-defined pectorals beneath the wife beater that exposes thick patches of hair from under his arms and at the top of his chest. He is clean-shaven, including his head and adorned with piercings on both ears, both eyebrows, the right side of his nose, and his tongue. A green Chinese dragon is tattooed around his neck; its fierce head and front claws peering from the left side of his throat chasing two pearls in clouds on the right side of his throat. His waist is small, his belly is flat and hard, and his muscular ass fills out the army pants he wears. Both wrists are covered in metal bracelets. His skin is a light café au lait color. His body odor embraces me again, this time it's not as offensive, and I detect a hint of patchouli over the heavy musk smell.

"Please come in. I'm having some green tea. Can I fix you some?" he asks. We all decline. The beauty of the apartment stuns me—it appears to be a black and white photograph, almost monochromatic. All the furniture is black or dark grey leather. The walls are painted light grey and with dark grey and black rugs dispersed over the walnut stained wooden floors. The walls are adorned with large black and white photographs of fit nude people. They are provocative, not pornographic. A big horizontal photograph of a nude man and woman embracing in a prone position hangs over a sofa. The woman is arched up into the arms of the man. Even though they are both naked and presumably in the middle of coitus, you do not see any genitalia, not even the nipples on the woman's breast. His face looks down at her with vivid concentration. Her face is turned out toward the viewer and shows both agony and pleasure. Her skin is black and in sharp contrast to the lighter color of the man's skin. It's obvious from the tattoos on the man that it is Dominick and the picture reveals the outstanding physical shape he is in. Another large square photograph hanging over a grouping of leather chairs is a shot of the chest of a man. The photographer had to be right at the man's groin to get that shot. The body is beautiful. The man's arms are held straight up and apart and his head is thrown back so that all you see is under his chin and long, dark, hair cascading down.

"Oh my God. That photograph is Billy, isn't it?" I ask.

"Yes it is," Dominick smiles. "That's one of my favorite shots. Is it not wonderful?"

"Yes it is," Lush says. Officer O'Daniel is staring at the picture.

"Yes, your brother let me photograph him after he became my student. What a model he is. It causes me great pain to learn of his death." Dominick looks into my eyes as he says this, but I'm not sure how to reply.

"Student? Did you teach him art, photography?" I say with a puzzled look.

"No, no. I don't think there's much about art I could teach Billy. Now, he did give me some extremely good points of criticism on my work," he laughs a bold, deep, powerful laugh. "You see, I'm a Jiu-Jitsu Master. Billy became my student; he was proceeding quite well."

I look at Lush, "Wow, I never knew Billy was into Jiu-Jitsu," I say. She shrugs her shoulders.

"Well," Dominick says directing us with his right hand, "Please come into the kitchen and take a seat. Are you sure you don't want any green tea?"

"Well, maybe I'll have some if you're already making it," Lush says.

"Very good, madam," Dominick replies, smiling at Lush.

"I'll just wait in here for you all to have your meeting," Officer O'Daniel states abruptly.

Lush studies him a moment, smiles and replies, "Thank you, that's fine, we won't be long." She turns around and walks into the kitchen area. I follow her.

"Officer, please sit down and make yourself comfortable while we talk," Dominick says and turns to follow us. I turn my head back and glance at O'Daniel as he sits down in a chair that gives him a good view of all the evocative art in the room.

The kitchen area is an extension of the living room, which makes it rather large by New York apartment standards and the monochrome theme is continued with stainless steel appliances and black granite counter tops. The sinks, stoves, refrigerator, in fact everything, even the knives neatly arranged side by side, according to length, on a magnetic bar fastened to the wall, seem to be of a professional grade. This could be the kitchen of a small restaurant. A black metal pot rack hangs from the ceiling containing many aluminum pots and pans with the dark burn marks seen on cookware in restaurants. He directs us to sit on metal bar stools with black leather cushions at the bar which is a large black granite counter top containing a large sink and a small sink, each with large, curved neck, commercial grade faucets.

"Looks as if some one knows their way around a kitchen in here," Lush says in a flirty tone to Dominick. Damn, she needs to get laid, I think to myself, wondering what sensual effects Dominick's great body and heavy odor have on her.

"Guilty, madam," Dominick says and laughs in a deep voice. "You see, I was trained at the Cordon Bleu and worked several years in Europe and in the Caribbean as a chef."

"Well that certainly explains this kitchen," she replies. "But tell me, Dominick, how did you go from chef to artist?"

"Aw my dear Madam Richardson," he replies, "Cooking is an art, so the transition is quite easy."

Lush seems satisfied with his answer and observes him as he delicately pours a steaming, dark, emerald green tea from a small, terra cotta teapot into three tiny terra cotta teacups. He hands us both one, looks at me and says, "Drink this, you need it. This I know. It is very strong, but will help you with all the stress you face." I take the teacup and raise it to my lips and start to take a sip.

"Wait, wait, Mr. Hampton. It's too hot. Let it cool a couple of minutes, then drink it," Dominick directs.

"Yes, of course. Thank you," I reply.

"So, you're interested in my connection with your brother? But more specifically my connection with the photographs of a pornographic nature I supplied to him?" He looks back and forth from Lush to me as he speaks.

"Yes, that's right," Lush replies.

"I'm happy to help," he smiles. "Please allow me to make a long story short. Your brother and I, as I'm certain you and I would, Mr. Hampton—"

"Please, call me Philip," I interject.

"Certainly, Philip. We are connected because we are both victims of pedophiles. I ran away from extreme poverty, violence and drugs as a twelve year old in the Dominican Republic. A very wealthy man took me in. A man who had, well, let's call it, a craving for young mulatto boys. I found out quickly that all I had to do was to allow him to play with my penis, and the money flowed." He laughs with vigor.

"I'm so sorry that happened to you," Lush says with a look of concern.

"Sorry? No, madam, don't feel sorry. It was the best thing that ever happened to me. It was my way out of the Caribbean ghetto into a world of very fine things. He would dress me in silk loincloths, paint my face with make-up, put silver bells on golden chains around my ankles, fancy Venetian collars around my neck and parade me around his yacht on a leash made of golden chain. I thought it was the best thing. Total luxury and all the money I could spend, just for letting the old booger suck my cock?"

"So that's where your paintings of children dressed in outrageous, but sexually provocative costumes come from?" Lush asks.

"Exactement, madam. They are not creations of a deranged pedophile, but only memories of what it was like to be me at twelve."

I feel sick to my stomach. "Are you telling me that some sick bastard actually dressed you up like a circus monkey, paraded you around his friends on his yacht for their enjoyment, and then had sex with you?" I ask.

"Yes, that's what I'm saying, monsieur. Not only me, but other boys and girls. There was a group of wealthy men who had their 'pets' and who enjoyed the photography of Nairda. And you, monsieur, and your beautiful brother, were some of the celebrated stars. What some of those men would have given to dress you and your brother up and parade you around on their yachts."

"How old are you, Dominick?" I ask.

"Twenty-six," he replies.

"So when I was nineteen, a freshman in college, you were a twelve year old sex slave on a yacht in the Caribbean who saw pornographic photographs of Billy and me and Adrian when I was twelve?"

"That's right. Very good, sir. You made my long story short for us all," he replies.

"Who is the bastard that abused you?"

"It does not matter. I knew what I was doing," he replies. "It was a, how do you say, a mutually beneficial relationship."

"Oh Dominick, no twelve year old should be put in that position. You were just too young to know any better," Lush says.

"No madam. I saw my mamma sell herself to sailors and worthless men, just to get money for her drug habit. I don't know who my daddy is other than he had to be a white man, probably some sailor. I know what it's like to go hungry and dig through garbage piles and beg for food on the streets. I knew quite well what I was doing." He stops, picks up his little teacup, tilts his head back and pours the green liquid into his mouth and swallows in one motion.

"You see, I was always so envious of you and your brother—rich, white Americans I imagined, and as it turned out, I was right. I saw the beautiful photographs of you two having sex with each other and that white man, and I wished that I could join you. I saw people pay thousands of dollars for those photographs. The only ones more valuable than yours were of two monozygotic white boys having sex with one another. My master cherished the arrival of them from Holland. I asked him if he couldn't photograph me and maybe let me have the money he got from selling them so I could send it back to my mother and little sister. He laughed and said it would be a waste of time. I was only good for live action,

because no body would pay much at all for a photograph of a little nigger boy with a big cock, those were too easy to come by."

"Dominick," I say, bothered that he still refers to the rich pedophile as "Master", holding his gaze with mine, "You must believe that whoever that man was took advantage of you despite the fact of your poverty."

He smiles. "I do know that. My art is my therapy, and I have come to realize that he stole something from me that all the money he had could never replace. As worldly and corrupt as I was at twelve, he fed upon the security, stability, and comfort that I had always craved from adults, but never had."

"Exactly," Lush replies, "That's how pedophiles operate by satisfying unmet emotional needs of children and often, material and emotional needs of the parents."

"But I have to tell you truthfully, I don't hate the man, I still love him—he has been the biggest supporter of my life and he never abandoned me, except sexually, as I matured. He put me through Cordon Bleu. We are still very close to this day."

Dominick's words drive deep into my heart where there remains a boy who unconditionally loves his Uncle Adrian and whose sadness bursts forth like water from a fractured dam and overflows into the room. Dominick watches me for a moment and then pours more tea into my cup. Lush reaches over, gently cupping her right hand over mine.

I blink several times, trying to keep in the tears, and I look at Dominick and say, "So, you and Billy obviously figured out that Adrian is Nairda."

"Oh yes, with the first picture I showed him."

"And how did he react?" I ask.

"He gave a little laugh and said, 'It's no big surprise. After all, Uncle Adrian taught me everything I know about making love to the camera shutter.'"

I smile and look at Lush, "That's my brother."

"Your brother's quest allowed me to meet him. And for that I'm grateful. We were becoming close, in our friendship, in our art, in our views."

"What about sexually?" I ask.

"Yes, like yourself, I like women, but I could not resist his sexual allure. We were together a few times." He smiles, leans back in his chair, stretches out his legs, crosses his arms and says, "And I especially liked his secret room." Lush and I look at each other.

"Dominick, when was the last time you saw Billy?" Lush asks.

"Well, it was a couple of Saturdays ago. He came by to pick up all the photographs I got for him."

"What photographs?" she asks.

"After I got to know Billy, I thought that he should be the rightful owner of my Master's Nairda collection. He's dying of colon cancer now. I phoned him and he graciously sent the original photos to me. There were about twenty-five of them—exceptionally well done black and white eight by tens."

Lush looks at me and I know she is thinking that that must be what Benny stole from Billy's safe.

"Do you have copies of those photographs, Dominick?" I ask.

"Certainly, I do," he replies.

"Could I get a set?" I ask, swallowing hard.

"But, of course. I'll get you a set before you all leave. Well, would you all like to come into my studio and see some of my work? Then you can decide for yourselves if I'm a pedophile or not."

We get up and follow him into the studio area of his apartment, my heart thumping hard with dread.

CHAPTER 23

On the drive back to Billy's, Lush resumes her flirty chatting with Officer O'Daniel. She is really hitting it off with him, and I am somewhat surprised that he does not maintain more of a professional distance. She must be intoxicating to him. I'm jealous, sure. But at the same time I'm glad for both of them. I hope they manage to find a way to get together at some point. Dominick's paintings disturbed me, at least the ones of children. I loved the bold strokes and vivid colors in his Caribbean landscapes and seascapes and his paintings of Paris, but the children, well, they haunt me, their expressions most of all. They were all oil paintings of individual children, some dressed in outlandish circus costumes, some dressed in play clothes, some in nightclothes, and some dressed in no clothes. Some had exposed genitalia and breasts; some did not. The ages ranged from very small children to pre-teens with budding breasts and nascent pubic hair. Their faces, whether happy, sad, angry or indifferent, expressed an aura of sexuality—innocent sexuality, but nonetheless, provocative, inviting, and enticing. That's what really bothers me the most—his paintings depict these children as sexual objects—premature sex symbols. I cannot and do not want to connect with this even though I know I did with Uncle Adrian and Billy. My first impulse was to grab a rag and some mineral spirits and rub out all the faces of those children—I didn't want to see them, and I didn't want them to see me looking at them. I made Lush take the envelope of photographs made by Adrian. I told her to keep them until after the wake. I do not want to see them—yet. I just want to go back to Billy's, shut myself in his room and curl up on the bed with Clark and go to sleep and wake up and find out that all this is just an elaborate dream, and know that I'll be coming to New York soon to be with my brother.

My cell phone rings. I fish it from my left pocket and flip it open.

"Hello."

"Philip, it's Brenda."

"Hi Brenda. Is everything okay?"

"Oh, yes. We are all well underway cleaning for tomorrow. Lois is doing a superb job giving us all tasks. She really knows this place, inside and out."

"Good, but don't work too hard."

"Oh, the children love it. It's funny how competitive they are to see who can win Lois's approval, which I assure you is not easily obtained. She has strict standards. This place will be spotless by tomorrow."

"That's great," I say chuckling.

"Well, sorry to bother you, I just wanted to check in with you and Lush to talk about lunch and dinner plans."

"Oh, that's fine, Brenda. In fact, we are on the way back now."

"Good. We had a lot of chicken left over so I threw together a chicken, wild rice, and sausage casserole. Billy had some canned fruit, so I made curried fruit. And we have plenty of asparagus, so I've poached it. I thought we could have this for lunch."

"Gosh, Brenda. That sounds great. Thanks for doing that."

"Good, I didn't know if you and Lush planned to be here or not for lunch."

"No, we plan to be there."

"Your father wants me to ask you if it would be okay for him to grill out steaks tonight for dinner. Even though it's cold and the weather forecasts flurries tonight, he likes cooking outside and often does it at home in the winter."

"Gee, I think that would be fine, Brenda."

"Good. It will be simple—just steaks, baked potatoes, steamed broccoli with Hollandaise, and a Caesar salad. I'll throw together Bananas Foster for dessert. The kids love the flaming part and it's easy to make."

"Sounds great."

"I talked to Ricky Wallitsch concerning tomorrow. He's sending his set-up crew at eleven tomorrow. Detective Bell called here and said that they would like to scan all the crew and guests tomorrow with metal detectors."

"Shit," I say. "I think that is ridiculous and totally unnecessary."

"Well, it does seem a bit extreme, but you probably should call her."

"I will, thanks."

"Good. Ricky said he will send plenty of lunch for all of us and his set up crew if that is okay with you."

"That's fine."

"Okay, we'll see you in a bit. Thanks, Philip."

"And thank you, Brenda, for all your help."

"Well, I'm thankful you invited us all to be a part of this. It's times like these families should pull together, help and support each other."

"You're an angel, Brenda."

"No, just someone who cares about you a great deal."

"That's very kind. We'll see you in a few minutes. Bye."

"Goodbye."

Lush has temporarily slackened her conversation with Officer O'Daniel to eavesdrop on my conversation. I put my phone on vibrate and slip it back into the right front pocket of my pants.

"Has Brenda got everything under control?" She turns toward me and asks.

"Yes, it certainly seems that way. She is so kind."

"Yes she is. And what a great mother she is," Lush replies as she opens her purse, rummaging around inside the purse with her hands while looking at me.

"Yeah. Well she has made lunch for us from leftovers—a chicken, sausage, wild rice casserole; poached asparagus; and curried fruit."

"Yum," Lush replies.

"Dad also wants to grill steaks for us tonight, and Ricky is sending over lunch tomorrow with his set-up staff."

"Great. We won't have to go out again until Saturday," Lush replies. "What else did she say?"

"That's about it."

"Really? I thought I heard you say 'shit' about something."

"Oh yeah. We can discuss that later." I observe Officer O'Daniel looking at us from the rear view mirror.

"Right. Officer O'Daniel, is it okay to smoke in a police car?" Lush bats her eyelids as she asks this. "I can crack my window."

"It's against departmental policy, but it is not enforced. Go ahead, Mrs. Richardson," he replies.

Sure, I think. He'd let her light up a joint buck-naked in here if she wanted. She pulls out her Treasurers from her purse, picks out one, cracks her window, lights it, and takes a deep drag, exhaling toward the cracked window which sucks out the blue-grey smoke as we drive along.

"Care for one, darling?" she asks.

At first I'm not certain whether she is addressing me or Officer O'Daniel, but I look up to see her looking at me. "No thanks, maybe just one drag off of yours." She hands me the cigarette. I crack my window, take a puff, and blow it out the window, as I watch Officer O'Daniel glance up at me several times

in the rear view mirror. Now I'm making him jealous I think. That's good. I hand Lush her cigarette, and as I settle back into my seat, I feel my cell phone vibrating in my pocket. I reach in, grab it, flip it open, and answer.

"Hello."

"Philip, it's Brooker T," I hear a soft voice say.

"Little Man?" I respond in surprise.

"Yeah," he laughs, "Ain't nobody called me that in a long time."

"Oh, sorry, Brooker T. I'm just so used to calling you that."

"It's alright, Philip. It's just after Momma died and you guys went off to college, seemed everyone just switched back to calling me Brooker T." The fluid cadence of his voice fills me with comfort, yet stirs a feeling of sadness as a wave of homesickness washes over me.

"Well, it's good to hear your voice, Brooker T."

"Thank you, Philip. It sho is good to hear yorn, too," he says and I can picture his startling hazel eyes. "I, I wanted to tell you how sorry I am about Billy. Sho don't seem right."

"Thanks, Brooker T. I know you know what it's like to lose a brother."

"Yes sir, hardly a day goes by, I don't think about them. Wish they were on the farm working with me." He pauses for a moment. "Well, I got the call from your Dad inviting me and Dad to the wake."

"Oh, good, Brooker T. I'm glad he called you, but, listen, I don't expect you to come up here. I know how busy April is on the farm."

"Oh, daddy, he's slowing down—been a bad winter for him, ain't fit to travel."

"I'm sorry to hear that. I need to call him. Give him my regards. I'll be down there sometime this summer. You see, Billy has requested that some of his ashes be spread in the swimming hole on your farm. I was going to call you to ask if it would be okay."

"Course it's okay and you know you don't have to ask for that."

"Thanks, Brooker T. I knew you'd understand."

"Yes sir, I do. Philip, I decided to come pay my respects to Billy. I got here this morning."

"Oh, you're in New York, Brooker T?"

"Yes sir. First time I ever flew on a jet plane. Gotta say I liked it. It was fun."

"That's great. I'm really glad you came."

"Thanks, Philip. This is some city, makes Atlanta look small."

"That it does. Do you have a place to stay?"

"Yes. Got a travel agent friend in Union who fixed it all up for me. Got me a good rate at the Waldorf. Said if I was going to New York, that's where I had to stay."

"Well that's great. How long are you going to stay?"

"Oh, just 'till Saturday. Don't wanna be away from Daddy too long and it is about planting time."

"Wow, it really means a lot to me that you came up here, Brooker T. I just wish Billy were here to see you."

"Yes sir. I do, too. But, he'll be smiling down from heaven, and I'll be smiling right back up at him."

"That's right, Brooker T. We'll both be smiling up at him, together."

"Philip, I was wondering if you had a few minutes to see me today. There's something on my mind. Well, I just need to talk to you about it, and I didn't think tomorrow would be a good time. What with the wake going on and all."

"Of course, of course. Listen, I don't know if you've heard, but Billy was murdered, and there's a police investigation going on. It's probably better if you come down to Billy's. Is that okay?"

"That's fine. I hate to be a bother, but, what with Billy's murder. Yes sir, it's all over the news. You see, I just need to talk to you for a little bit."

"I'm glad to do it, Brooker T. Can you come down around two this afternoon?"

"Yes sir. That'll be fine."

"Do you know how to get there? It's probably easiest just to take a cab."

"Well, I got me a subway map. I'll figure it out."

"I'm sure you will. You were always the best tracker around."

He laughs. "Yes sir. We sho had some good times running all over Miss Ina's farm."

"Yes we did. And it's your farm now, Brooker T."

"Yes sir, it is, but it will always be Miss Ina's in my mind. I'm just taking good care of it for her."

"I'm looking forward to seeing you this afternoon, Brooker T. It's been a long time."

"Me too, Philip. I'll be there at two. Bye, bye."

"Bye, Brooker T."

I close the phone and look at Lush, her eyes demanding a full account of my conversation.

"Well, I'll be damned. That was Brooker T, Ala Mary's boy. He's come up for the service tomorrow. Says he wants to see me today—got something on his mind he wants to talk about," I say, mitigating her curiosity.

"Really. He's the one y'all called Little Man?"

"Yes, that's the nickname his older brothers Willie Bee and Clevis gave him. They were big, strapping fellows and it was obvious Brooker T would never grow to their sizes. Of course, he was really their first cousin that Ala Mary and Newt adopted when his mother died in childbirth."

"Hmmm," she says, brushing long hair back behind her right ear with her right hand, "I wonder what he wants. Any idea?"

"Not a clue, but it must be important for him to come here. I mean, it's the first time he's ever flown in his life and he's got to be pushing forty."

"Strange," she says picking a piece of white lint off the front of her dress. "So he's the one who ended up with all that land your grandmother left her maid?"

"Well, yes. Fatgram always made it known to us that she intended to leave the farm to Ala Mary and Newt. I mean they worked for her and us for over fifty years."

"Good Lord," Lush says.

"I don't know what they were paid in wages, but I'm sure that big farm is worth a lot today. But, they deserve it. Strange, though, that land had been in our family since the mid-1700's, part of a grant from the British government to my great, great, great, great, great grandfather."

"Damn, Todge, that's five greats. Haven't you ever thought it strange that your grandmother let that land get out of the family after owning it for over two centuries?"

"Yes, but Newt, Ala Mary, and Brooker T always seemed like family. Fatgram told me that both Newt and Ala Mary's ancestors had once been slaves owned by our family. I think this caused her a lot of pain and guilt. She always felt responsible for them and their children. Anyway, I think she sensed that Billy and I would never settle there. We're sort of the end of the line. That's turning out to be true."

"Now, wait a minute, Todge. You're still young. You may have a family yet," she states in a tone that is almost a question.

"Yeah, who knows, we'll see," I say with a big sigh. "For the life of me, I can't think what it is he wants to talk about."

"Well, if Billy's death precipitated his visit, it must be something he wished Billy had known too before he was murdered," Lush says, looking at me with eyes reeking of raw intelligence.

"I'd say you're right, Lush. You're always right about things like that." Officer O'Daniel looks up at me in the rearview mirror as I speak, and I hold his gaze for a moment, mentally transmitting to him that if he's lucky enough to catch hold of Lush's interest, he better grab it, because he may never find such a wonderful woman again. We pull up to the curb in front of Billy's building. Officer O'Daniel turns off the car, jumps out, and immediately opens Lush's door. She grabs her purse with her left hand, swings her

legs out, and offers her right hand to Officer O'Daniel who flashes a smile of contentment as her gently takes her hand with his right hand and takes hold of her right elbow with his left hand, helping her out of the car. I sigh again, slide over, get out, shut the door, and follow them as he escorts her up the stairs. And I thought I was the one in danger of being murdered.

Henry sees us coming up to the front door and clicks the lock open. Officer O'Daniel pulls the door open and we enter to find Detectives Johnson and Bell sitting on a sofa in the lobby.

"Welcome back Mr. Hampton, Mrs. Richardson," Henry smiles and nods his head to us as we enter. "These two detectives are here to see you both," he says and motions toward them.

"Thank you, Henry," I say and turn to greet the detectives. "Well, Detective Bell, Detective Johnson, I guess you've found some more information."

"We have," Detective Bell says flatly. Today she wears a tan Burberry trench coat, revealing a light green V-neck sweater and white blouse and grey wool slacks, attire which, in my opinion, is more fitting for a detective's routine than her previous outfits. Her expression transmits dissatisfaction, frustration, and anger. "Mr. Hampton, might we go somewhere private to speak with you and Mrs. Richardson?"

"Yes of course. Henry, may we use one of the meeting rooms down here for a while?" I turn and ask Henry.

"Oh, yes sir. Nothing is going on today. Take any room you like," he replies, smiling at me.

"Thank you, Henry. Detectives, follow me, we can talk in one of these rooms," I say and start to walk.

"O'Daniel, you can wait out here," Detective Johnson directs.

"Yes sir," he replies and looks at Lush who smiles at him as she turns toward me.

"Please, follow me," I say and walk through the loggia that leads into a large courtyard and a hallway with various public rooms branching from it. I push the door open into a sitting room with several dark brown, leather chairs, of a modern design, arranged with a coffee table, several stainless steel side tables, and lamps made from chrome with black silk shades. "We can talk in here," I say.

Detective Bell and Detective Johnson sit facing each other and Lush and I take chairs across the coffee table from them.

"Well, let's see," Detective Johnson, wearing a grey suit with a tie with grey and black stripes in a diagonal pattern, says clasping his hands. "A lot has happened since we last met. The bodies of two young Asian twins were discovered early this morning in a cargo container at the executive terminal at Newark airport. It is apparent that they are Benny and Bernie Boonmee."

"Oh. How were they killed?" Lush asks as if she's surprised by the news.

"Execution style. Bullet in the temple," he replies.

"Mr. Hampton," Detective Bell says, "Did you know your brother had been in Dubai in March of last year?"

Shit, I thought she was going to ask me if I knew about the twin's deaths, so I reply, "Well, I just found that out yesterday. You see, a Mr. Julian Ainsworth dropped by to pay his respects. He told me Billy had visited him in Dubai last year."

"And were you planning on sharing that information with us?" Detective Bell asks.

"Of course," I lie, "I was planning to contact you all today. We've really been terribly busy trying to get ready for the wake tomorrow."

"Too busy to help solve your brother's murder?" Detective Bell asks in a sarcastic tone.

"Absolutely not," I reply, trying to impart a tone of concern. "Billy made the trip to Dubai as a guest of Mr. Ainsworth. You see, Mr. Ainsworth is an art dealer who supplies wealthy Arabs with art from around the world. He wanted to discuss potential commissions for Billy."

"Didn't you think it odd Billy never told you about this trip, or did he?" Detective Bell asks.

"Well, in February I was in Panama doing research on how rain forests are reclaiming abandoned farm land, and when I got back to Atlanta in March, I had a deadline to meet, not to mention having to

get ready for a trip to China. If he mentioned it to me, I guess I forgot about it. But, I really don't think he mentioned it to me."

"Hmmmn," she says and glances at Lush.

"Mr. Hampton, Mrs. Richardson," Detective Johnsons looks at each of us as he speaks, "Do either of you think there could be an association between the Boonmee twins and Julian Ainsworth?"

"That seems rather odd," Lush replies. "I suppose anything is possible, but he seemed like such a nice old gentleman. And the only thing he really talked about was art," she adds.

"Why do you ask, Detective Johnson?" I ask.

"Well, Mr. Ainsworth departed from Newark last night on a private jumbo jet owned by a sheikh who rules one of the United Arab Emirates," Detective Johnson replies.

"Oh, well," I say crossing my left leg over my right, exposing part of my left calf which catches the eye of Detective Bell, "I suppose that sheikh must be one of Mr. Ainsworth's clients. He did mention that he was in New York finalizing some major purchases for clients and escorting the works back to Dubai. When he learned about Billy, he took it upon himself to pay me a visit."

"Don't you think it too coincidental that the Boonmee twins were found murdered in the same hanger where the sheikh's plane was parked?" Detective Johnson asks bending forward toward Lush and me.

"It does seem rather odd," I reply.

"But didn't you all determine that Benny was following Philip and me on our walk yesterday?" Lush sits upright in her chair and shifts her weight to her left buttocks.

"Yes he was. Following you and photographing you," Detective Bell replies.

"Well perhaps, for whatever reason," Lush continues, "He followed Mr. Ainsworth from Billy's. Perhaps he and his brother followed him. Maybe they knew he represented clients with great wealth. Maybe they knew he would be transporting artworks of immense value. Maybe they tried to rob him. Maybe whoever was guarding the artworks just killed Benny and Bernie. Maybe they just decided to take justice into their own hands."

"Mrs. Richardson, you have a vivid imagination," Detective Bell says, "And is that what you and Mr. Hampton intend to do?"

"Excuse me," Lush replies.

"Take justice into your own hands, you and Mr. Hampton?" She glares at Lush.

"Really, Detective Bell, you're presuming a lot," Lush replies.

"Are we, Mrs. Richardson?" Detective Bell asks and fires off in rapid succession: "You didn't come forth in a timely manner with the information on Julian Ainsworth and Billy's visit to Dubai; we know you've retained Jonas Grey; and we know you visited Dominick Montaigne this morning. Where is your investigation going from here, Mrs. Richardson?"

"Now wait a minute Detective Bell," I interject, "I have every right to hire a private investigator to answer questions I have about my brother and about who may have murdered him."

"Yes, you do, Mr. Hampton," Detective Johnson says, his deep baritone filling up the sitting room, "But you do not have the right to withhold important information or evidence from the police in a murder investigation."

"Detective Johnson, we are not withholding anything from you all. Besides, with all the surveillance you have on us, we can barely go to the bathroom without you all knowing," I reply in a frustrated tone.

"Mr. Hampton," he replies, "We are doing this for your safety and the safety of your friends and family."

"I understand, but now that the Boonmees are dead, is all this necessary?" I ask.

"Probably more than ever," he replies. "There's a good chance that the Boonmee twins didn't complete their tasks as requested. As a result, they paid with their lives. Do you want that outcome for you or Mrs. Richardson here?"

"Certainly not," I reply, "But don't you think if Billy is harboring something that important, they would have gotten to us by now, Detective?"

"It would be difficult with all the surveillance and manpower we have around you," he replies.

"Well, now that the Boonmees are dead, I feel much safer," I repeat.

"Do you know something about them you are not sharing with us, Mr. Hampton?" Detective Bell asks.

"No, but I do know they were the killers of Billy and Elliott Fields, so I just feel safer now that they are out of the picture," I reply and uncross my legs wondering if she liked looking at my hairy left calf.

"Has Jonas Grey found out anything we should know about?" Detective Johnson asks.

"Not in my opinion. And just for the record, I hired him to find out anything he could about Billy's murder, but also to check into Adrian McWhorter and his appetite for little boys," I reply.

"Well, Grey's good, and usually cooperative with us. But we'll subpoena him if we have to," Detective Johnson states.

"Mr. Hampton, we would like to screen all of the guests tomorrow night," Detective Bell states.

"And how do you intend to screen them, Detective Bell?" I ask.

"With metal detectors and a portable X-ray machine for purses," she replies.

"Do you really think that is necessary?" Lush asks.

"We most definitely do, Mrs. Richardson," Detective Bell replies. "Mrs. Hampton says that she and the caterer are estimating around four hundred people here, a good number of them celebrities and high profile people. It's as much for their safety as it is yours."

"Very well," I say, "Where do you intend to do it?"

"Down here in the lobby, Mr. Hampton," Detective Johnson says, "Don't you worry; we'll take care of everything and make sure it all goes smoothly. We'll be set up by nine in the morning. We'll also cover the service entrance and will be most definitely carefully screening any employees from the caterer and examining every cart that goes up with them."

"Alright," I reply. "Have you all found out anything else?"

"Actually, Mrs. Richardson," Detective Bell begins, "Your art theory may hold water, after all. Benny didn't need the money from working at Upper Crust Catering. Their bookkeeper told us he never has cashed a single paycheck. Upper Crust does a lot of work for galleries and Benny's schedule shows he was frequently assigned to those as well as parties and dinners of clients known to have valuable collections."

"Interesting," Lush states.

"Yes, and now it seems the Boonmees may have been connected, in some way, with Julian Ainsworth," Detective Bell replies, adjusts the belt on her trench coat, and looks up at me. "Mr. Hampton, do you know anything about the relationship between your brother and Mr. Ainsworth?"

"Well, to my knowledge, Billy never transacted business with him. I'm sure Julianna could tell you for sure. However, Julian Ainsworth is Adrian McWhorter's older brother, both boys were foundlings. Julian took over Adrian's business when Adrian died. Adrian never represented Billy, to my knowledge, but he did represent my mother. I suppose there could have been some crossover. I don't know. Again, Julianna could fill you in on all this."

"Yes, well, we'll certainly cover this with Miss Morgan," Detective Bell says as she opens a Louis Vuitton purse and pulls out a large white envelope folded over and wrapped with a rubber band. She pulls off the rubber band, unfolds the envelope, which has 'NYCP Evidence' stamped on it with some other illegible writing on it, reaches in and pulls out a plastic bag containing a small brown furry object, hands the bag to me, and says, "Mr. Hampton, do you recognize this object?"

I take the bag and my mouth falls open. "I do, I do."

"I thought you might," Detective Bell says and reaches to take it back from me, but I pull it away, my eyes fixed on it.

"What the hell is that, Todge?" Lush says.

"It's Billy's lucky rabbit foot. It's capped in gold with a small gold chain and a gold charm with his initials, WRH. I have one just like it, except with my initials. My grandmother gave them to us as part of a Christmas gift one year. Billy and I used to carry them all the time when we were boys. Fatgram had Newt, her gardener, shoot two rabbits in our family's graveyard to get two left hind feet for these charms. The bearer of a rabbit's foot obtained in such a way could supposedly control other people, even control life and death—it's folklore brought to America by Africans. Fatgram was an educated, liberated woman for her time, but she wasn't the type to scoff at traditional means to stack the cards in her favor, so to speak. Very strange, I haven't carried mine in years, but when I got the call that Billy was in a coma, I just grabbed it and stuck it in my pocket. It's back at his place."

Detective Bell abruptly takes the bag from me. "I had to twist the rules to get this piece of evidence from headquarters. It was found in Benny's left front pants pocket. It was the only thing found on him besides his clothing. Any idea how he got it, Mr. Hampton?"

"None. He could have stolen it from Billy. Or, I guess Billy could have even given it to him. Who knows?"

"When was the last time you saw this?" she asks.

"Gosh, had to be before we went to boarding school. Maybe when I was fourteen."

She studies my face for a moment and then says, "There's a nice thumb print on the cap. It's not Benny's, Bernie's, or Billy's. It matches nothing we can pull up. Not even yours, Mr. Hampton," she says slowly.

"My prints are on file somewhere?" I ask.

"Oh yes, you must know that—all the high risk countries you've visited, for work, I suppose?" She raises her eyebrows as she speaks to me.

"Yeah, right. I vaguely remember getting my prints done before," I reply.

"Mr. Hampton, we're going to find clues to help us solve this crime in your brother's new paintings, aren't we?" She leans towards me as she speaks.

"Perhaps, I mean, I don't know." I reply, glancing at Lush.

"Detectives," Lush says in a stern voice, "Billy's last paintings are complex sexual studies involving dozens of people, many quite famous. I'm sure you could weave a motive for murder into almost any one of those paintings."

"Mrs. Richardson," Detective Johnson says, then sighs and looks at the floor, "We're not interested in weaving anything. All we aim to do is find the truth." He pauses a moment and rubs his chin. "I thought after our meeting yesterday, you all would help us in this search, but it seems to me you are running your own investigation, covering up things, or intentionally not revealing them to us. Perhaps even throwing us a bone when you think it's appropriate?"

Lush's eyes dart towards mine. Crap, I think, these cops must have a wire in Billy's place, too, along with Adrian and God knows who else. I've got to get Jonas over there to scan the place for bugs.

Detective Johnson stands up and leans toward me, "Mr. Hampton, you are, I'm told, a skilled investigative journalist, and I know Mrs. Richardson is trained in that field also. But, but, I know you are in over your heads in this matter. Detective Bell, let's have the photographs."

She pulls out a brown envelope from her purse and hands it to Detective Johnson. He pulls out what appear to be glossy photographs and hands them to me. "Take a look at those Mr. Hampton, Mrs. Richardson."

I take the photographs as Lush stands up, walks over and sits on the arm of my chair. I thumb through the photos as we both look. They are gruesome images of Elliott Fields, dead, hanging from a cornice in his hotel room. His head droops down toward his shoulder, blonde hair cascading down, tongue protruding from his mouth, and eyes fixed on the floor. He is nude except for a pair of black fishnet stockings and a

pair of black patent leather stilettos—both feet rest on the floor, but the right foot is bent in an awkward angle with the weight of his body resting on the top outside of the foot. His knees are slightly bent. His penis and balls hang perpendicular to the floor, and it is obvious from the lush white carpet that he excreted both urine and feces as the noose constricted. Bernie must have been strong; he must have thrown his weight into the rope, or even routed it around something heavy for leverage and support. The rope is tied off on the handle of a French door leading out onto a balcony. A braided leather riding crop rests on the floor beside Elliott's feet. I wonder if Elliott sensed he was in danger? Why else would he have sent me the photo of Bernie?

"How awful," Lush says, "He must have been drugged, too?"

"Yes he was," Detective Johnson says, "GHB, same as Billy Hampton."

"Ratty little bastards, I'm glad they got executed," I say and hand the pictures back to Detective Bell.

"Please, Mr. Hampton, Mrs. Richardson," Detective Johnsons says, "Include us. Let us drive this investigation. We'll get to the bottom of it, and you'll both live to see the perpetrators brought to justice."

"Detective Johnson," I reply, "I've given you everything I can. I don't know what else you want me to say?"

He and Detective Bell look at each other and he says, "Very well, then, we'll keep in touch. Detective Bell and I along with two other detectives will attend the wake tomorrow."

"That's fine," I reply.

"Will Jonas Grey attend the wake?" Detective Bell asks.

"Yes, he will," I reply. "I asked him to come—for added security he's coming and bringing a couple of his associates."

"I thought so," she replies.

I stand up and say, "If there's nothing else detectives, Mrs. Richardson and I have a lot to do."

"That's all for now, I suppose," Detective Bell says.

"Goodbye, then," I say.

"Good day, detectives," Lush says and we both walk out ahead of them to the lobby. Officer O'Daniel gets up out of an armchair when he sees us approaching.

"Nice talking to you, and I really enjoyed your piano performance," Lush says, extending her hand to him.

"Oh, thank you, Mrs. Richardson," he replies, and I see a tint of pink flash through his cheeks.

"Thanks for driving us, Officer O'Daniel," I add and Lush and I walk into the elevator which Henry has open for us.

"Thank you, Henry," I say. "Oh, has anyone been out with Clark today, Henry?"

"Yes sir. Your father has, twice," he replies.

"Thanks, Henry," I say, smiling, as the elevator door closes.

I turn to Lush and say, "Well, I think Officer O'Daniel appeals to you."

"He's very sweet and sensitive, for a police officer," she replies, smiling. "Besides, he's a hunk and he's obviously talented and cultured."

"Yes, all that's true," I reply, "But isn't there some sort of rule against bedding officers assigned to provide protection?"

She laughs. "Well, I'm sure there is, Todge. But, he's rather insignificant to this investigation. I'm sure he could find a way to be excused from it in exchange for a date with me."

"Oh? You don't say, you evil vixen. It's no wonder your sex succumbed to the serpent before us gents."

"Ha!" she shouts. "I'm going to smack your handsome cheeks for that," she says and plants a light smack with her right hand on my right cheek. I grab her hand with my right hand, look into her eyes, really

wanting to make love to her right now in the elevator and say, "I think you should go for him, Lush. I think he may be just what you need. At least for a while anyway."

The elevator door opens and Clark rushes in with a shrill bark of joy, jumping up on us both, panting, with his tongue hanging out, and an expression of happiness on his face.

"Oh, we're glad to see you, too, precious," Lush says, bending over so he can lick her face.

"Come on, you two," I say, laughing, immediately feeling a sensation of happiness and satisfaction as I watch Clark's exuberant display of affection. The feeling flickers as I escort Clark and Lush out of the elevator, pondering the immense attachment between Clark and Billy, and fades into despair. Clark's emotional sensory is as acute as his olfactory. Sensing my swift change of mood, he lets out a small whine, flattening his ears back against his head as he lowers it and his tail.

"What's wrong, boy?" Lush says and bends down to hug him. He wags his tail as she hugs him. Lush looks up at me, examines my face, and says, "How touching; he's picked up on your sadness. What are you thinking about, Philip?"

"Just about how much Billy loved him and he loved Billy and how that will never be again. Do you think Clark understands Billy's gone for good?" My eyes are welling up.

"Yes, I do. But you're wrong about something—that love you mentioned; it's not gone for good—it was and it will always be. I think Clark understands that."

"Well, Lush, that's a good way to look at it," I reply.

"It's the only way, Todge."

CHAPTER 24

I am unable to shake the intense feelings of melancholy and sadness the rest of the morning. Lois's friend Tammy, who has come along to help out, appears physically to be a more petite version of Lois but with dirty blonde hair. They, Brenda, Lush, and the kids dash about Billy's place like bees in a hive. I can't decide if the queen bee is Brenda, Lush, or Lois, but whoever it is, everyone seems to be executing assigned tasks by rote, while carefully avoiding entwining me in any chore, leaving me to my own endeavors which include going through my emails for the first time in nearly a week, calling Jonas to discuss our meeting with Dominique, and smoking on the terrace. Dad is mysteriously absent; I suspect he's nursing his own pain under the guise of catching up with business matters back in the guest suite. The truth is the only company I desire is Clark's. He senses this, never leaving my side, even during the delicious buffet lunch Brenda has prepared. She has laid out the chicken casserole, the curried fruit, and poached asparagus in a beautiful presentation on one of the granite counters in the kitchen. I am surprised to see her remove two cookie sheets of homemade biscuits from the oven. She insists that we all squeeze in together at the breakfast table located in a large bay window that overlooks the terrace. It is cozy, but we all fit in comfortably, even Lois and Tammy join in at Brenda's insistence. The food tastes great and the warm biscuits smothered in butter and honey lift my spirits and take me back to our own kitchen table in Union where Billy and I would anxiously watch Ala Mary mix up a batch of flakey buttermilk biscuits which she would deliver to us straight out of the oven. We would grab the hot biscuits, tossing them back and forth between our hands to prevent burns, then we would split them open with our fingers and coat them with butter and honey from hives on Fatgram's farm before devouring them. On Sundays, Ala Mary would make delicious white sausage gravy we would pour over the biscuits and eat along with

hard-boiled eggs. Emma, Peter, and Drew are animated at lunch, effusive in their descriptions of their morning accomplishments for the benefit of Lois and Tammy who seem delighted to be included. I cannot help but smile as I watch these interactions, and I feel thankful that they are here. Dad tries to get in on the conversation, despite his moroseness; the dark crescents underneath his eyes amplify his despair. I notice him looking at me several times during lunch, and I sense he has something on his mind he wants to discuss with me. Lush and Brenda chat about final details for the wake and what Lush's plans are for the coming weeks.

"Hey, Dad," I say, "I got a call from Brooker T this morning. He's coming up to New York for the wake."

"Little Man's here?" he asks with a surprised expression.

"Yes," I reply, "And he's coming here in about fifteen minutes. Says there's something on his mind he wants to talk to me about." I carefully examine Dad's face and to my astonishment he smiles slightly, shakes his head up and down once, and sighs.

"Dad, do you have any idea what he wants?"

"Son, I think I may, but hear him out and then we can discuss it—old family business, I suspect."

"Old family business?" I ask, feeling the heat rising up my chest into my face. "Shouldn't I have been made aware of that? I mean, shouldn't Billy have had the chance to know about it too?"

"Philip," Dad says in a deliberate, calm voice, "There are a lot of things that I should have told you and Billy and vice versa. I have great hope that you and I can change all that." As he looks at me, the sadness in his soul pours out and envelops me and I feel compassion for him. My anger subsides, and I do not want to make a scene in front of my new family members.

"That's my hope too, Dad." I wink and smile at Emma who is sitting across from me. In this instance, the collective tension at the table crescendos and collapses, and everyone begins to chatter again. Lush and Brenda both look at me and smile. I get up, walk behind Dad, put my arms around him, bend over, place my face against his, and hug him. He takes hold of my arms with his hands and pulls them in close to his chest. My half brothers and sister stare in amazement at their father and me.

"I love you, Dad," I say in a low voice.

"I love you, Philip, so much," he replies.

We hold each other for a second longer.

"Well, Brenda, that was absolutely a delicious lunch," I say as I straighten up, noticing the tears in Brenda's and Lush's eyes.

"Yes, Mrs. Hampton, it was mighty good food," Lois adds.

"Oh, thank you, my pleasure," Brenda says, dabbing the corners of her eyes with her napkin.

"Well, if you all will please excuse me, I'm going to go downstairs and meet Brooker T for a while. I'll bring him up here when we've finished our talk." I smile at everyone as I walk away. "Emma, Drew, Peter, thanks for your help and keep up the good work. Lois tells me she may have to recruit y'all to help her on some other big jobs." The children smile and wiggle in their seats.

"Oh, we love helping out, Philip," Emma says, sitting on her hands, swinging her legs from the knees down. "And Dad is paying us a lot of money, too," she adds.

Everyone laughs and I say, "Well, that's great, Emma. Thanks for the help. Come on Clark, I'll let you go outside before we go downstairs."

I go out through the kitchen, past the wet bar, and pick up a pack of Marlboros I had Lois pick up for me. I grab the onyx lighter and head out to the terrace. A gray, thick, homogenous layer of clouds fills the sky preventing me from spotting the position of the sun. A chilly, damp breeze brushes my cheeks and chin, and I'm glad I have on the turtleneck and sweater. I open the Marlboros, pull out one, light it, and take a deep drag. Damn, so Dad knows what's up with Little Man. I can't imagine what it is. I guess I'm making headway on forgiving Dad for the years of abandonment. It feels pretty good to me. I wish Billy

213

could have felt this, too. Maybe he did. From what I can piece together, it seems like his last collection was the culmination of quite an emotional journey—one of deep and intense self-examination. I take another drag. I, on the other hand, I've been running, running since the day Mother died, Saturday, August 2, 1986.

"Dad, this Zebco spinner is the best. I'm going to catch a big boy today," I say as I examine the green and black fishing reel. I'm sitting in the back seat of Dad's big, blue Mercedes station wagon, the back of which is loaded with furniture catalogs and fabric samples. We have just visited the Farm, Feed, and Field store where Dad let me pick out a new spinner for my birthday that is coming up on Thursday. Billy is in the front seat examining the packets of new rubber worms we purchased for bass fishing. It's Saturday morning and Dad is home from the road and we are planning to camp out tonight at the swimming hole on Fatgram's farm. We'll fish for catfish until we're sleepy and get up before dawn to fish for the big bass that feed in the shallows of the river in the early morning.

"These are the best ones," Billy says as he pulls a long black worm, dappled, with white spots from the package.

Dad smiles, looking down at Billy as he turns off the highway onto the road we call the 'back way' to our house. "Well, son, those black worms with white dots resemble spring salamanders. You may not have much luck with them this late in the summer."

"Oh, I dunno know, Dad," he replies and flings the worm over the back seat, hitting me in the face.

"You little turd," I say, grab the worm, reach over the seat, and try to push it into Billy's left ear canal. He grabs my hands with his, pushes them away from his head, then starts to punch my arms.

"Boys, boys. Stop it right now. I'm trying to drive."

"He started it, Dad," I reply.

"He started it, Dad," Billy mocks me.

"I said cut it out, or I'll cancel the campout," Dad's voice booms out.

"Oh, Dad we're just playing," Billy says, turning back around in his seat.

"Well, playing or not, I don't need all that commotion while I'm trying to drive," he replies.

I carefully put the spinner back into its styrofoam packing container and into the box. I can't wait to try it out.

"Dad, are you going to make your special catfish bait for tonight?" I ask.

"Yep, I am. That is if Ala Mary will let me in the kitchen. You know how she hates the smell of my catfish hushpuppies."

"Pew wee, they do stink," Billy says as he opens a package of brown and green worms.

"Those will be the ones that will work, son. The fish will think they're baby water snakes and gobble them right up," he says.

"Water moccasins, Dad?" I ask.

"Oh, any type of water snake, son."

"Won't cottonmouths bite the fish and kill them, Dad?" Billy asks.

"No, son. A swimming snake, especially a baby, will never see what hit him. That big old bass will just ambush the snake from underneath and, before he knows it, he's in the fish's belly, breakfast." He makes a gobble sound with his mouth wide open. Billy and I laugh.

"Hey, Dad. If we catch any bluegill, can me and Philly filet them?"

"Sure, son, so long as you promise to be careful with the knife."

"Cool," I say.

"No, real cool," Billy says. For years, Billy and I have carefully observed Dad as he takes a bluegill, runs a teaspoon over its body, removing the scales in a flash, and in a few swift, confidant motions with his knife, produce two perfect, boneless filets. There's no better eating than dosing them in a special, spicy, corn meal and Corn Flakes mix Ala Mary fixes, and frying them in hot Crisco. Dad will make this for us

for breakfast in the morning at our campsite. This summer Dad has begun teaching us how to filet. The scaling is easy, but the filleting is going to take a lot of practice. Dad said his father taught him and that he could do it pretty well by my age, and I'm excited to be turning thirteen this summer—finally a teenager. Dad's parents were killed in a head-on collision in their hometown of Raleigh, North Carolina right before I was born. I can tell he misses them a lot. The song "Rock Me Amadeus" comes on the radio.

"Dad, can I turn it up some?" Billy eagerly asks.

"Sure, son."

Billy turns the volume up and starts to try to sing the German words. When Falco sings the word 'Superstar' Billy says, "Superstar, that's what I'm going to be someday."

Dad smiles, looks at him and says, "You already are my little Superstar." Then he looks up at me through the rear view mirror and says, "And, you Philly are my teenage Superstar." We all laugh and start singing along with the radio. As we pull up into our driveway, I sense something is wrong, bad wrong. The front door is wide open. Fatgram, Ala Mary and Bonnie Bell are standing there waiting for us. Ala Mary has her right arm around Fatgram's waist. She appears to be holding Fatgram up.

"What's wrong with Fatgram, Dad? Is she sick?" Billy asks.

Dad doesn't say a word, but quickly stops the car, shifts into park, leaves the engine running, opens the door and runs toward Fatgram and Ala Mary. Billy and I sit in the car watching. Fatgram's lips move and then Dad takes both of his hands and covers his face and bends over and moves in a slow circle. He appears to be heaving or convulsing. We can see both Fatgram and Ala Mary are crying.

"Philly. Philly, what's wrong? Why is Dad doing that?" Billy looks at me. I can tell he's scared out of his wits. I feel the same way.

"Dunno. Come on." I put aside my spinner on the seat and open my door and stand on the ground. My knees buckle; I feel weak. Billy gets out and grabs my left hand and we turn and start walking toward the house. Dad, weeping out loud, is sitting on the steps of the front porch. Fatgram and Ala Mary are standing over him, their hands on his shoulders. As Billy and I slowly approach, Bonnie Bell waddles toward us, sniffs the air as if she searching for something or someone, then turns around and goes back to the adults. We reach Dad who looks up at us with tears running down his face and says, "I'm so sorry, boys. I'm so sorry. Your Mother died early this morning in France. I'm so sorry." Billy's hand tightens in mine as Dad reaches out and pulls us into his arms. At that moment I become frozen. I hear Falco singing 'Rock Me Amadeus' punctuated with the dinging of the Mercedes key indicator, the sobs of Fatgram and Ala Mary, the violent, shaking sobs of Dad, and the mournful whimper of Bonnie Bell.

Something nudges my right leg. I hear whimpering. I look down through tears to see Clark nudging me with his nose. My cigarette has burned down to the filter. I push the cigarette butt into one of the raised beds into some ivy and turn around.

"Come on, Clark, let's go see what Little Man wants." We walk through the dining room and living room to avoid encountering anyone, but I forgot about Officer Graham who is sitting in the living room reading a magazine.

"Going out for a walk with Clark, Mr. Hampton?" she inquires.

"No, I'm not. A friend of the family's is coming over and we want privacy, so I'm going to meet him in one of the meeting rooms downstairs."

"Oh. Is this a trusted friend of yours, Mr. Hampton?" she asks looking up from her magazine.

"Yes, Officer Graham. It's someone from our hometown. So, I don't think there's any danger of concealed weapons or anything."

"I see," she replies, "Well, I'll let O'Daniel know just the same."

"Oh, is Officer O'Daniel still downstairs?" I ask.

"Yes, he's on building lookout today," she replies.

"Well, I'll be back after a while. Mr. Finch, my guest, he may be with me. I plan to ask him to dinner."

"Have a nice meeting, Mr. Hampton."

"Thank you. Come on, Clark."

We go to the elevator, get on, and ride downstairs. I realize I forgot Clark's leash. "Clark, you stay right by me. Don't go off sniffing anyone unless you're invited."

The door opens, and I see Brooker T talking to Henry. Officer O'Daniel is walking out of the front door. Clark begins to trot toward Brooker T.

"Clark, get back here, right now," I say forcefully. He obeys. Brooker T is watching Clark as I walk up to him and extend my right hand. "Brooker T, it's great to see you. I hope you didn't have to undergo interrogation and a strip search by Officer O'Daniel." Brooker T laughs.

"No, nothing like that. Good to see you, too, Philip," he says as he shakes my hand, and I am surprised by the rough, callous feel of his hand in mine. I lean forward and embrace him. It's been over ten years since I've seen him. He's filled out a bit, but appears to be in good physical shape. We give each other a squeeze and step back. His hazel eyes dazzle against his light brown skin, and I think to myself his father must have been a white man.

"That's a fine looking pit bull you got there," he says.

"This is Clark. He's Billy's dog. A friend of mine rescued him from the streets in Louisville. He's a great dog."

"He sure looks like a fine dog," Brooker T says, "A real fine dog. One you'd want on your side in a bad situation." Clark wags his tail, sniffs Brooker T's shoes, and trots over behind the reception counter to visit with Henry.

"Henry, may Brooker T and I use one of the meeting rooms?" I ask.

"Sure, Mr. Hampton, they're all available."

"Thanks. Let's go in here Brooker T," I say and begin to lead the way. "Come on, Clark." He trots over to me.

"Mr. Hampton, I'm happy to visit here with Mr. Clark while you gentlemen have your meeting. Billy leaves him down here with me sometimes. He obeys and just loves to watch the people come and go."

"Oh, well, sure, Henry, that's fine. Clark, you be good now." He wags his tail, turns around, and goes back to Henry.

"That's one smart dog," Brooker T says.

"Yes he is. Come on this way Brooker T," I say and walk towards the loggia.

"New York sho' is a big town. Never thought I'd see anything like it," he says as we walk through the loggia and into the same room where Lush and I met with Detectives Bell and Johnson this morning.

"Yes, it is," I reply, "Did you have any trouble finding the Waldorf or getting down here?"

"Nope. People sho' been nice, here. Fast talking, but nice," he replies looking around the room.

"Please, have a seat, Brooker T," I say, noticing that he has dressed for the cooler New York weather. He wears a green, wool, V-neck sweater and a yellow, oxford cloth, button down collar shirt, khaki trousers, and brown Oxfords. At first glance, he could easily be mistaken for a software engineer who resides in the city. That is, until he speaks, his drawl accented with tones and phrases from southern, African American vernacular, immediately placing him geographically. Closer inspection reveals rough, cracked hands, and skin, although uniform in its light brown color and tone, possessing the kind of hardened veneer of people who have spent most of their lives outdoors. His hair, a dark red brown, lacking the intense tight curls of many blacks, would be luxurious and wavy were he to let it grow. But he has always kept it closely cropped. His facial features are neither dull nor sharp, and on first acquaintance, many people assume he is of Hispanic origin. When I think back, I can hardly ever remember seeing Brooker T indoors unless he slipped inside the kitchen through the back door to deliver a string of fish or a dozen quail to Ala Mary. I've always associated Brooker T with the land, the red earth of Union County and its beautiful forests of pine and hardwood. By the time he was fourteen, Brooker T replaced Newt as the primary gardener for

Mother and Fatgram. Accompanied by his beloved Max and Hedda—a pair of pure-bred Weimaraners Fatgram purchased from a man who operated a bird hunting operation in south Georgia in hopes of installing them as bird dogs on her farm for hunting parties in the fall and winter, but the pair grew up to be so high strung and aloof towards most people, that they would only respond to their caretaker, Brooker T, and would only hunt or retrieve at his command, so Fatgram ended up giving him the pair outright which she said must have been destiny because they all shared the same astonishing yellow-hazel eyes. He patrolled Fatgram's vast landholdings along the Tyger River and the thousands of acres in the adjacent Sumter National Forest, discovering the secrets of the forests, rivers, and creeks, including the best spots for hunting deer, turkey, and quail. He understood the ways of the more illusive creatures: fox, coyotes, beavers, otters, wild European boar and even the big cats, bobcat and puma, thought to be extirpated, but well known to Brooker T. Max and Hedda accompanied Little Man almost everywhere, and the townspeople of Union became accustomed to seeing him walking along the street flanked by the big grey dogs with yellow eyes, and someone remarked one day that those dogs were called grey ghosts, and someone else added that Brooker T and those dogs could appear and disappear in the woods like ghosts, so the threesome became well known around town as Little Man and the grey ghosts. Mother's painting of them in a field on a misty autumn morning, framed by the woods, with Max and Hedda on either side of Brooker T, who is kneeling down putting quail into a bird bag, Max and Brooker T looking out at the painter, their ethereal yellow eyes glowing and Hedda focusing intently on her master's face, entitled "Little Man and the Grey Ghosts," became Fatgram's favorite painting of Mother's. Fatgram hung the painting in the study off of her bedroom where she spent a great deal of time reading and conducting business. She bequeathed the painting to the Spartanburg Art Museum where, along with Robert Henri's "The Girl with the Red Hair," it is one of the museum's most popular and best-known paintings. From the dogs, Brooker T learned how scents carry in the air and lie on the land; he learned how to track by the signs, both obvious and subtle, animals and humans leave behind. He alone knew where to harvest the best, tender asparagus shoots in the spring and where the bucks shed their antlers in the winter. Although gentle, friendly, and kind to us, Billy and I always viewed Little Man as mysterious. It was not uncommon for him to appear out of nowhere just to say hello when we were on trail rides deep in the forest, only to disappear into the dense growth without a trace. Sometimes we'd be galloping our ponies through a remote pasture and Max and Hedda would emerge from a thicket and gallop with us for a while before retreating back into the woods. Brooker T must be nearby we'd say to each other. We often accused him of spying on us, or sending out his ghostly sentinels to monitor us, but he'd just laugh and say he had better things to find in the woods than two white boys. We speculated that Fatgram paid him to keep an eye on us. His love and compassion for his dogs was obvious; but it always startled me to happen upon him field dressing a deer or capping a raccoon with a few quick strokes of a sharp, flashing blade. His woodland senses were so acute, he could discern from the bark of a squirrel what animal or bird was instigating its distress and because of the feel of the breeze on his upturned face whether or not deer would move along a certain hillside. A few times while we were growing up, he'd come find Billy and me and ask us if we wanted to see something special, which of course we always did. On one such occasion on a lovely spring day in March, he took us to a beautiful little creek fed from a small spring bubbling up from the red earth in a dense growth of hardwoods. We lay down prone on a bed of soft green moss and stuck our heads out over the bank of a crevice eroded by the stream. Max and Hedda lay beside us motionless at Brooker T's command. At some point in time, this area must have been a homestead because thousands of daffodils were in bloom throughout the forest. He pointed to a large oak tree growing near the stream down the creek from us and told us to stay quiet and keep our eyes on the base of the old oak. After a while, a red fox popped up from under the tree, went to the creek, lapped up some water, turned around and emitted a sharp bark. Soon four little kits emerged, greeted the vixen and began playing like puppies beside the creek. After a few minutes, another fox appeared with a baby rabbit in its mouth. Little Man said this was

the father or dog and that he was bringing food home for his family. He dropped the rabbit and the kits began playing tug of war with it like puppies do with toys. The vixen walked over, took it from them, held it down with one paw, and ripped it open with her sharp, shiny, white teeth, revealing a pink, slimy interior. The kits made yapping noises and began licking the pink tissue. Finally, they began tearing apart and eating little chunks of the rabbit. After the meal, the dog trotted away with the carcass, the vixen licked the kits clean and returned to the den. The kits followed. We got up and quietly walked away. Little Man said the wind was blowing in the right direction. If the vixen caught our scent, even hours after we were there, she would relocate her kits immediately to another den. He told us red fox pair off for life, but only live together to raise the kits, then go their separate ways in the summer. He also said our woods contained as many gray fox as red.

I look into Brooker T's yellow eyes, trying to reestablish my childhood trust in him—his eyes convey wildness, but not the wolf-like, predatory, coldness I always sensed from Adrian's eyes, but more of a desire to be in the wild, to be free—definitely the eyes of Max and Hedda. I was never afraid of Max and Hedda, though Uncle Adrian was, especially after Hedda bit him once when he tried to pet her, but I did respect their great skill as hunters, their speed in the field, and their insatiable desire to please Brooker T, and yet I knew they descended from wolves—at some level, I believe, we all have a bit of wolf in us, that primordial, innate desire to pursue prey, to fill our bellies, satisfy our needs, procreate, an instinct intensely shocking to me when I have witnessed its manifestations unexpectedly like the time Fatgram, Billy and I were riding on horseback the perimeter of the peach orchards on a warm April morning when the peach trees were in full bloom—the undulating red hills shrouded in intense pink so beautiful against the blue sky. We pulled the horses up at a high point, observing the pink vista from our mounts, disturbed only by the nickering of the horses. Fatgram was remarking that with any luck this could well be a bumper year for peach production when a faint sound arrived on the wind—all the horses ears stood forward and erect— Whinny snorted, shook her head, pawing the ground with her front right foot. Fatgram patted her neck.

"Steady, girl, it's okay." Fatgram turns her head so that her good ear, the right one, faces into the breeze. We wait a bit and the sound comes again, louder this time—it is an urgent, high-pitched, bleating.

"Damn, Fatgram," Billy says, "Sounds like a lamb crying."

"No, no, it's a fawn bleating, calling for its mother. It's lost or hurt."

"Let's go see if we can help it, Fatgram," I add standing up in my stirrups to stretch out my calf muscles because we had been riding for over an hour.

"No, Philly. Wild things are better left alone to take care of themselves. You know that, son," she replies. "Let's head on up to the shed. You boys can have a cold Coca Cola, and I'll have some of Newt's black mud." The shed is actually a vast, open, barnlike structure where all the peach processing takes place during the harvest in July. Newt has an office there where he always keeps a pot of the strong, black coffee he sips all day long. Fatgram calls it black mud and adores it for its 'pick me up' effects and 'hangover curative properties.' Newt also keeps an old chest-type, red Coca Cola machine filled with icy glass bottles of Cokes for the peach workers, Billy and me.

"Great," Billy says, turning his fat pony Peanuts toward the shed, urging him on with a click of his tongue and a couple of kicks with his brown field boots. The bleating sound becomes much louder, much more frantic. Fatgram looks down at me with a worried expression.

"Oh come on, Fatgram," I urge, "let's at least go check it out."

"Well, alright. It sounds like it's coming from the northeast side of the orchard. You boys follow me. Be careful, we're going to gallop."

"Yippee!" Billy yells.

"Okay," I say.

Fatgram gathers up the reins, turns Whinny's head toward the fence, shifts her weight forward a bit in the saddle and breaks into a brisk trot. Billy follows on Peanuts and I ask my own pony, Noodles, to trot.

We trot briskly for a few hundred feet to where a dirt service road bisects part of the orchard. I can hear the bleating of the fawn over the sound of the trotting horses. Fatgram breaks into a canter on Whinny, then urges her into a full gallop. Noodles is larger and faster than Peanuts so I have caught up with Billy by now and we gallop our ponies side by side in Whinny's dust. Peanuts farts loudly which makes Billy laugh, but I'm too worried about the distressed fawn. We gallop for a few hundred yards, and I am glad when Fatgram slows Whinny to a trot because my legs are tired from holding my weight up in the saddle during the gallop. The bleating is really loud and close by.

"It's over there on that side of the cow pasture," Fatgram says. "Billy, hop down and open this gate for us, dear."

Billy jumps off Peanuts in one quick motion, throws his reins over Peanut's head, walks to the metal gate, unlatches it, opening it for us to pass through. Fatgram and I walk our mounts through; Billy follows, leading Peanuts, latches the gate and hops back up in the saddle. The bleating is almost overwhelming as we look to our left along the wire fencerow. My mouth falls open as we coax our nervous steeds toward the noise. A fawn is hanging head down on the fence, its back legs entangled in the top of the wire fence. Max and Hedda are ferociously attacking the fawn, tearing open its stomach and pulling out long strands of intestines. They don't even seem to notice us as I start shouting, "Max, Hedda, get away, get away, leave it alone, leave it alone."

The dogs appear wild, shaking their heads, growling, tugging ropes of intestines from each other's mouths. I look into the fawn's big brown eyes and feel the terror as its little mouth opens emitting its death call. I start to jump down.

"Stay put boys," Fatgram screams at us. I watch her take off her brown leather riding gloves, reach over, pull from her saddle bag the ivory handled, engraved nickel plated Colt Cobra .38 Special her father gave her on her twenty first birthday, raise the pistol, aim, and fire one shot. In that instance it is all over. The fawn hangs motionless with a bullet through its brain, Max and Hedda, momentarily startled out of their feeding frenzy, look up into the air, thinking since they heard gunfire there must be a bird to retrieve, but quickly refocus their jaws on the dead fawn which they now succeed to rip in half off the fence, the fawn's back legs, rump and groin area remain hanging on the fence, guts spilling forth. Max has part of the fawn's rib cage in his mouth and Hedda has its spine. They shake their heads, growling again, tugging furiously until the rib cage tears away from the spine, Max trots away with the abdomen in his mouth and Hedda heads in an opposite direction with the fawn's spine, its front legs and head, brown eyes open, staring into nothing. Brooker T is running up from the peach shed at full sprint yelling, "Miss Ina, Miss Ina, y'all okay? Y'all okay?"

He arrives out of breath. "Everything's fine, Brooker T," Fatgram calmly says as she puts the snub-nose pistol back into her saddlebag and pulls on her riding gloves. "We heard a fawn bleating and found it tangled in the fence here. The doe must have jumped over and the fawn tried to follow and went through it instead of over it. Probably broke its back legs in the process. Hedda and Max were putting it out of its misery. I just sped things up a bit."

Brooker T glances at the fence, grimaces, then sights both his dogs who are each lying down in the field gnawing on fawn parts. "I'm sho' glad everything's okay. Daddy and me was fixing to drive into town when we heard that gunfire. 'Bout scared us to death."

"Everything's fine Brooker T. Those dogs of yours disemboweled the poor thing. I've never seen that before. Wished I'd had the guts to do that to my husband when I caught him with the widow Lampton." Billy laughs, picking his noise as Fatgram fires me a look of disapproval indicating to me she sees the tear trails on my face.

"Come on boys, let's head to the shed for drinks. Brooker T, you get back to work and leave these dogs to their lunch." She trots off toward the shed on Whinny. Brooker T looks into my eyes, "It's okay Philip. It's okay—it's jes Mother Nature."

"Yeah, come on, Philly," Billy says, "It's just Mother Nature, and I wanna cold Coca Cola."

"This sho' looks like a nice building Billy lives in here," he says as he sits down in one of the leather chairs.

"It is, Brooker T," I reply, "Do you still have Weimaraners?"

"Oh yes," he says rubbing his knees with his hands, "On the sixth generation now from Max and Hedda, had a litter last month, nine of the cutest pups you've ever seen."

"Wow, sixth generation. That's a lot of dogs," I reply.

"A whole lot of dogs, good bird hunting dogs, which is what I breed for, you know. Though some of the pups I sold to people who turned em into show dog champions. Now wouldn't Miss Ina be proud of that?"

"Yes, she would. She sure would," I reply remembering how Fatgram carried on about the fine pedigrees of Max and Hedda. "After we have our talk, Brooker T, you'll have to come upstairs and see Billy's place. I'm sure Dad wants to see you, and I'd like you to meet his wife and children and my friend, Sarah Richardson."

"You look good, Philip," he says, "Ain't change much at all in, what's it been, ten or twelve years since I last seen you?"

"Yeah, it was right after I finished up at UNC. About eleven years," I reply, "And you're looking good, too, Brooker T."

"Well, thank you, sir. Lot a hard work 'round that farm, you know. Daddy, he'll be eighty-one in June. He's slowing down some, but still got his mind."

"Isn't it about time for the peach trees to bloom?" I ask.

"Yes sir, they be blooming right now. We ain't in danger of no freeze, so it was okay for me to come on up here."

"Is everything okay on the farm?" I ask.

"Oh, price of fuel keeps rising faster than the price of peaches and corn, but it's getting along just fine. A few years back, we started putting in strawberries, tomatoes, beans, peppers, and pumpkins and started one of them u-pick businesses. It's doing right well. Helps us offset them fuel prices."

"That sounds like a good plan, Brooker T. Sounds like something Fatgram would've come up with," I reply.

He laughs a little, "Yes, it sho' do. Your grandmamma was one right smart woman." He pauses a bit, looking down at the floor.

"Brooker T, what is it you want to talk about?" I ask, gently.

"Well, Philip. It sho' has been a bad week, a strange week, what with Billy getting murdered and all," he moves his beautiful eyes back and forth from my eyes to the floor, and he rubs his hands together as if he is washing them. "Well sir, I may as well get on with it. Daddy says he has something he has to tell me after supper on Monday. He says he ain't never promised nobody not to tell, but Momma and your Grandmama, always said it wasn't nobody else's business, and it was just best for everyone and the whole town if we all just pretended it never happened." He pauses and looks down at the floor.

"Pretended what never happened, Brooker T?" I ask as I feel my heart thumping faster.

"Well sir, pretended that I ain't the child of your Momma, Miss Eva, and Willie B," he replies, widening his cat eyes as he looks at me.

My mouth falls open, and I stare at his face, his hazel eyes, his light skin, his features, the dark redness in his hair, and I clearly see it. I see traces of Mother in him. I see the blending of her delicate features with the strong, hard features of Willie B. I see where the astonishing eye color come from: her vivid green with his dark brown. I see it all, and it has all been right in front of me my entire life. No wonder Fatgram

220

left Newt and Brooker T the farm; she didn't let land that had been in our family since the 1700's get out of the family, after all.

"Well, I don't know what to say Brooker T," I reply. "I mean, I mean, I believe you. I can see it's true just by looking at you. That means we're half brothers: you and I, and you and Billy."

"That's right," he replies with a slight smile.

"Well, I'm fine with this Brooker T. I can't think of a better person to be related to than you or any member of your family."

He sighs, smiles, and says, "Philip, that about the nicest thing anybody's said to me in a long time."

"Well, it's the truth. It's the way I feel. I'm sure Billy would have felt the same, too."

"Yes, I 'spect he would. But that's why Daddy told me. He said it ain't right Billy done gone to his grave without knowing we was half-brothers. That's what made him tell me."

"Well, Newt did the right thing. I wish he would have told us all after Ala Mary and Fatgram died," I say clasping my hands and resting my chin on them.

"Yes sir, but he just couldn't bring himself to do it."

"Well, I can understand now why you made the trip up here, and I am thankful you did," I add.

"Well, Philip, the truth is that I wasn't planning on it. I mean, I wasn't planning on ever telling you. I figured if your Grandmama, who was so good to me and my family, and my Momma—I mean the woman I knew as my Momma and you know there ain't never been no better woman on God's earth than her—didn't want us to know, then it wasn't my place to be running around telling anyone." He looks into my face for a moment, then continues, "But when your daddy done called me Tuesday night, well, I changed my mind."

"What did Dad say, Brooker T?"

"He said it was important for him to know if I knew who my real mother was. And when I told him I did, but only since the day before, he said good 'cause he was fixing to tell me if I still thought my real momma was Ala Mary's baby sister. Then, he said he thought it was important for all of us to be together to see Billy off, and he told me he was going to arrange for me and Daddy to come up here."

"Well I'll be damned," I respond, "So, Dad knew about this all these years?"

"I reckon he did. He said your Momma done told him before they was married," he replies.

"You mean our Momma, don't you, Brooker T?" A flood of questions rushes through my mind, and I realize there's probably a plethora of information Dad and I are withholding from each other.

"Reckon so, Philip. Miss Eva was always so good to me. But don't take this the wrong way. I know she bore me, but my real Momma will always be my sweet Momma Ala Mary." I can see the big hazel eyes begin to water.

"You know, Brooker T, Ala Mary was often more of a mother to me and Billy than Mother was." He shakes his head up and down. "I mean, I loved Mother dearly, but sometimes she was so unapproachable, and Ala Mary was always there with her arms open to us." He shakes his head again.

"Tell me, Brooker T, how did all this happen?"

"Well, Daddy say Miss Eva was a feisty, independent young gal, the way Miss Ina was. Take right after her momma. Daddy say they be two peas in a pod. Well, the summer she turned fifteen was a mighty hot one and Miss Eva spent a lot of time down at the swimming hole with girlfriends, but sometimes alone. Daddy says she and Willie B, who was helping Daddy in Miss Ina's garden, started making eyes at each other that summer. Daddy say he done told Willie B, 'Willie B, don't you be messing 'round wid no white gal, 'specially Miss Eva.' Daddy say he reckon they must have started meeting secretly at the swimming hole. Well, I guess I'm the result of them secret meetings. Anyway, when Miss Ina found out Miss Eva was with child, Miss Eva say to her she going to marry Willie B. Well, Miss Ina wasn't going to have none of that. No sir. She done planned a yearlong trip to Europe and told everyone Miss Eva was going to finishing school in Switzerland. And Miss Ina

would stay in Europe to be close to Miss Eva. Come to find out, they took a secluded villa in Italy, where Miss Eva did nothing but read and paint, and when her time came, I was born in a Catholic hospital in Florence."

"What a story," I say. " So I guess Fatgram and Ala Mary made up the story about you being Ala Mary's sister's child?"

"That's right, they did. That's also when your Fatgram set up in her will to leave the big farm to Momma, but when Momma died before her, she left it to Daddy and me."

"Do you think she would have left Ala Mary and Newt the farm if you had never been born?" I ask, not really believing I've had the nerve to ask this.

"Well, I don't rightly know, Philip. That's a hard question." He rubs his forehead with his right hand and looks down.

"Fatgram always told us that your family had served our family for over a hundred and fifty years and that you all deserved that land," I say.

"Uhmm, I remember hearing that and believing it. I reckon Miss Ina would've given it to Momma, even if I hadn't been born. Daddy says this isn't the first time that your family and his family have mixed blood. He said it happened a few times with your great great grandpa while we was still slaves."

"That doesn't surprise me, Brooker T. I don't think anything surprises me anymore, not after this week," I say, sighing. "Mother must have really loved Willie B."

"How you know that? Could've just been young people and puppy love," he says.

"Well, it all makes sense to me now," I say, the pieces falling together in my mind like a puzzle, "I remember Mother's first nervous breakdown. I was in the first grade. It was the day Fatgram sent her away to Arizona. It was also the day of the funeral for Willie B and Clevis."

"Lord-a-mercy. I'm sorry to add to your worries with this news, Philip. I don't mean no harm to you."

"Oh, Brooker T, I know that. Please don't apologize. I've just learned so much about Mother, Billy, and myself this week. And now this news about you, well, it's good news to me, not bad."

"Yes sir, it's been a rough week for us all," he replies.

"Remember Uncle Adrian?" I ask.

He makes a slight scowl and replies, "Yeah, I remember him."

"What's wrong, Brooker T? Did he ever do anything bad to you?"

"No sir, but I reckon he done did bad to you and Billy," he replies.

"What do you mean?"

"Well sir, I hate to admit it, but I spied on you and Billy. I did. And Miss Ina always told me to keep an eye on you young uns, especially when you were on the horses in the woods."

"Yeah, Billy and I sort of figured that out. But what about Uncle Adrian?"

He shifts his weight in the chair and leans over with his elbows on his knees and looks me right in the eyes, "Mister Philip, I seen all those sexual things he made you and Billy do down at the swimming hole. I seen it all and him taking pictures of it all."

"Brooker T, we're brothers for God's sake. Don't ever call me Mister Philip again," I flash. He sits back and sighs.

"I'm sorry, Brooker T, I didn't mean to speak to you in that tone."

"It's okay, Philip."

"Listen, after all these years, I'm just coming to grips with what Adrian did to Billy and me. I'm just so damned angry about it. Why didn't you ever tell anyone what you saw, Brooker T?"

He looks down, his countenance transforms into an image of desolation. He says nothing. I see tears fall on the marble floor.

"Brooker T, what's wrong, why are you so sad?"

He looks up, a single tear inches down his face. He wipes it away with his jacket sleeve and sniffs. "Philip, I ain't never told anyone. I should've; but I ain't. I'm so ashamed, don't know if the Lord will ever forgive me."

I stand up and put my right hand on his right shoulder. "Brooker T, it's alright. I mean you were just a teenager, a young man, when you witnessed that. None of it was your fault. I'm sure you didn't know what to do or think."

"No, no, no," he shakes his head and puts his face in his hands, "It ain't that. It ain't that. You see, you see, the truth is, the truth is, I liked it. I liked watching it."

"Brooker T, are you saying you like little boys in a sexual way?"

"No, no that ain't what I'm saying. I don't like boys; I like men."

"You mean you're gay?"

"Yes, I am," he replies, looking up at me with wet eyes and a pink tint on his cheeks.

"So seeing Adrian naked and having sex with us turned you on, Brooker T?"

"It did. I'd watch you guys, hidden where you'd never see me. Just sitting there, playing with myself, thinking Mr. Adrian outta be messing with me, instead of you young uns." He looks down and sighs. "I'm so ashamed of myself. I know I should've told Momma or Miss Ina. I know I should've. I felt so guilty about it all. It just froze me all over."

"Listen, Brooker T, none of this was your fault. Adrian is an evil, corrupt, pedophile who feeds off of vulnerable women and their little boys. In fact, he did the same thing to a lot of other boys and worse to several other people over the years."

"Lord God Almighty, Philip. Is that so?"

"I believe it to be, Brooker T, but I'll fill you in on more of that later. What's important now is for you to know that you did nothing wrong," I say, standing over him like an authoritative parent.

"But it was wrong, Philip. I should've told someone," he replies looking even more despondent.

"No, no Brooker T. You can't think that way. It's not your fault. Just like it's not your fault you were born gay. Look at Billy; he's gay and he got along okay that way. You were just a young man yourself, discovering your own sexuality when you saw us with Adrian at the swimming hole. No one can ever blame you for the way you reacted. Please, please don't put all this on your shoulders."

"But Philip, ain't you gay, too. I mean. Well, I seen you and Billy carrying on with each other for years after Mr. Adrian was gone," he says.

I can feel myself blushing all over; my neck is red hot. "No, Brooker T, I'm not gay. I don't have anything against gays whatsoever. I'm just straight. I can't really explain why I did what I did with Billy until I was about fifteen. I'm sure it had a lot to do with Adrian's molestation of us. I'm sure it had to do with losing Mother. It kept us close—we sorta felt like all we had was each other. But, but, I grew out of it. I really knew all along that I liked women, sexually."

"Can you ever forgive me, Philip? For the spying and the not telling."

"Brooker T, I forgive you, but there's nothing to forgive. You've got to believe me on this," I reply.

"Philip, it just don't seem fair—all that's happened to us, but Momma always said God has his reasons for what happens to us all, black or white."

"Ala Mary was a wise woman. Are you religious, Brooker T?"

"I try to be. I mean, I take Daddy to church every Sunday. But so much of it just don't seem right to me."

"I know what you mean. I'm not religious, but I'm spiritual, and I know the difference between good and evil," I reply.

"Well, when I'm out roaming in the woods, seeing all the thangs nature gives us, that's when I see God, that's when I feel spiritual."

"That's a beautiful way to look at it, Brooker T. You seem to me to be true to yourself. I mean, you never got married which, in my opinion, wouldn't have been a true choice for you."

"That's right. I done told everybody I ain't have no time to marry a woman and raise a family 'cause I got Daddy and this big farm to care for. Truth is though, I knew no woman could ever make me happy or me her."

"Do you have anyone back there, Brooker T? Anyone who does make you happy?"

He shrugs his shoulders and smiles, "Well, yes, there's Landrum Sims, he's the foreman on our farm."

"Really? I remember Landrum. He was a couple of years ahead of me in grade school. He was always quiet, never said much."

"Well, he ain't changed much, but he sure know the peach and corn business and he gets thangs done. He's really getting us into organic farming, some of the peaches and vegetables; we get more money for those. He lives in the old caretaker's cottage down by the peach sheds."

"So you guys are boyfriends?"

"I guess you could say so, but ain't nobody in Union knows about it. We been seeing each other for ten years now, after his wife run off to California."

"Well, I imagine it would cause quite a stir in Union if everyone knew you had a white boyfriend," I say.

"Sho' enough would," Brooker T replies, then stands up.

"So Newt doesn't know about Landrum?"

"Daddy ain't no fool. I spect he knows everything, but he ain't never said so to me. But he loves me same no matter what, and I'll do everything in my power to take care of him every day of his life."

"Newt's a fine man and a lucky man to have you for a son—grandson. And now I'm lucky to have you as a brother." I embrace him and he jerks back, just for an instant, then embraces me back.

"Let's go upstairs. I want you to meet the rest of the family," I say.

"Okay, Philip."

As we are walking through the loggia I ask, "Brooker T, do you drink?"

"Well, Landrum likes a little whiskey on Saturday nights. And I'll have to say, most times I join him. Sometimes Daddy do too, for medicinal purposes, you know, to ease the pain in his joints."

"Yes, indeed. So, good, let's go toast to being brothers."

We walk into the lobby to find Henry seated, bifocals pulled down near the tip of his nose, reading a book while Clark, sound asleep, legs dream-twitching, lies stretched out, his belly, covered in soft reddish blonde fur, touching Henry's feet.

"You gentlemen finished down here?" Henry looks up form his book, smiling.

"Yes we are. Thanks, Henry. Let's go, Clarkus, you little bear," I say.

Clark's eyes pop open and he is on all fours within a second. He trots over to us with his tail wagging. We all laugh.

Brooker T, Clark and I get on the elevator, and I slide the plastic card into the slot and the elevator lifts us to the twentieth floor.

"Seems strange to get into an elevator and go up to get to your house," Brooker T says.

"Yeah, it is. But Billy's got a lot of room and a big terrace up here, so it's not too bad," I reply.

"Brooker T, does anyone else in Union know about your true origin?"

"Not that I know of. I 'spect Miss Ina's lawyer, Mr. Dunvegan, might. He's got Alzheimer's real bad, but maybe his son, James, who took over the practice might know."

"I bet he does," I reply.

"And Landrum. I told Lannie, but he won't ever tell nobody."

"Brooker T, I want the whole world to know. It's nothing I'm ashamed of or feel I have to hide."

224

"Well, that's a good way to be Philip, but I don't think most folks in Union will take too kindly to the news."

"Well, pardon the expression, but fuck most folks in Union. Sometimes I believe Mother did."

Brooker T looks surprised and says, "Philip, why you say that 'bout your momma?"

"Oh, I'm sorry Brooker T. I just get so angry about all the secrets and deceptions started by people in our family and then passed on down the line. It just makes me mad."

"I guess sometimes people feel they ain't got no other choice," he replies.

"Yeah, but it just keeps bad energy flowing," I reply.

"Well, I hear you, but it sho' would be hard for me to live in Union with folks knowing who my real momma is," he replies.

"I see your point. You don't have to worry about me telling anyone down there. If you want people to know, that's entirely up to you, Brooker T."

"Thanks, Philip," he says as the elevator door opens. Clarks hears the voices of the children and trots off to find them. We walk through the foyer and into the living room. I see Brooker T's eyes moving over everything.

"Mmmm, mmm. All Miss Ina's and Miss Eva's thangs ended up here," he says.

"Yes, Billy made this place an homage to them and their antiques," I reply.

"Well, it sho' do look nice in here," he says.

"Thanks, it's all Billy's doing."

Officer Graham, sitting in the same chair as when I left, stands up when she sees us enter the room. Lush must have seen Clark come in because she walks in from the kitchen and says, "You're back," and walks over to us.

"Officer Graham, Sarah Richardson, I'd like you to meet my half-brother, Brooker T. Finch," I say. Brooker T gives me a questioning look and turns toward Officer Graham.

"Pleased to meet you, Mr. Finch," Officer Graham says, extending her right hand. I glance at Lush who looks as if someone just told her that her husband has been run over by a freight train.

"Good to meet you, mam," Brooker T says as he shakes Officer Graham's hand.

"Brooker T, it's so nice to finally meet you. I've heard a lot of good stories about you," Lush says, extending her right hand. "But, please just call me Lush, that's the nickname I prefer."

"Nice to meet you too, Miss Lush," he says and shakes her hand. She smiles at him and says, "Well, Philip never told me you all were half-brothers," and gives me her most serious look to cover up the hurt she must feel from thinking I've deceived her.

"Well, mam, that would be because he didn't know about it until today. It may be old news to a few people, but it's new news to Philip and me. My Daddy just told me on Monday," he replies and shifts his weight from one foot to the other and looks a bit embarrassed.

"Well," I say, "We're going to the bar to have a toast to being brothers. Will you please excuse us, Officer Graham?"

"Certainly," she says. I wonder how long it will take her to pass this piece of news along to the detectives.

"The bar's in through here, Brooker T," I say.

"Well, it's almost three o'clock and we're all done with our work here, so I'm all for cocktails," Lush says, hooks her left arm through Brooker T's right arm and says, "Brooker T, you've simply got to fill me in. I've known Philip for fifteen years and every day we seem to find out new things about his family."

They start walking behind me, and I wonder if Brooker T will be able to handle Lush, and then I change my mind to wonder if Lush will be able to handle Brooker T.

I've always mentally placed predicting the weather and Mother's moods in the same category, and, to my complete surprise, the cloudy, breezy, cold midday which threatened snow has transformed

into a clear afternoon with a temperature approaching fifty degrees. I walk around the terrace to view the setting sun over New Jersey and offer it my thanks where I see Dad grilling New York strips on the elaborate gas grill Billy has in the outdoor kitchen area of his terrace, which wraps behind the guest suite. It is the first time I've seen any semblance of contentment on my father's face since he arrived on Tuesday and quite possibly, I think, since before Mother's death. His eyes focus on the steaks as he flips them and his lips are drawn up at the corners, ever so slightly, into the beginning of a smile that always signaled to me when I was a child that he was in the best of moods. Clark is sitting beside him, occasionally wagging his tail, watching every movement of Dad's hands, taking in the delicious aromas emanating from the grill. I take a sip of my Old Fashioned followed by a drag off my cigarette, nursing the deepest urge to go up and embrace my Dad, tell him how much I've missed him, needed him, loved him all these years. I still remember the comfort of his strong arms when I was a child. Mother would be in one of her moods, or Billy would have broken something of mine, or I, on the verge of tears, would have failed solving an impossible word problem in math homework. He'd take me in his arms, sit me in his lap, hug me, whispering in his low voice into my ears, "Listen here, Philly, you can solve any problem or conquer any bad situation. Just think it through carefully, and give it your best shot." He'd hug me, kiss me, his stubble tickling my face and neck. I would laugh, feeling better while he'd say, "And I'm always here to help you out, little buddy." Well, that was a lie, but I'm glad he's back in my life. I am beginning to understand the depth of the profound torment he must have experienced in his years with Mother, the years after her death, the years of our abandonment. My throat catches forcing an involuntary cough. Simultaneously, Dad and Clark turn their heads toward me.

"Hi son, don't these steaks look great," he smiles.

"Yes, they do, and you look like one happy cook."

He chuckles. "Well, I love grilling outdoors, even in New York City."

"You always have been a master chef on the grill," I reply.

"Thanks," he replies. "I think Clark is sitting here willing that I drop one of these babies when I turn them."

"I'm sure he is. I expect it would be down his gullet in one big gulp if you did," I reply.

"I'm sure you're right, son."

"Hey, Dad, I just wanna tell you that I thought that was a really generous, heartfelt, and touching way you introduced Brooker T to everyone this afternoon."

"Oh, well, it's nothing, Philip, just the way I really feel," he looks into my eyes briefly before focusing back on the steaks.

"Yes it was something—it was eloquent, it was wonderful, Dad. You really have a way with words. You made it sound as if Mother was the fair maiden and Willie B the handsome prince, who fell in love despite all odds, producing a beautiful baby never to be acknowledged by his true parents because of the warped code of ethics of their society. Although they lived out their lives in close contact, they carried the secret of their love and their child to the grave."

"Well, son. That's the truth. That's the way your Mother explained it to me."

"Yet you still married her knowing she was in love with Willie B?"

"Oh, by the time we met, seven years after the birth of Brooker T, she had long since fallen out of love with Willie B. Although I suspect Willie B never stopped loving your Mother because he never married, never even dated as I remember."

"So you and Mother were really in love with each other?"

"Deeply, son. I think it sort of swept both of us off our feet—we were best friends, fervent lovers; we craved one another. I don't think I've ever felt the passion I felt during our first few years together." I see the sadness creep into his eyes as he speaks.

"Well, then what happened, Dad? I grew up petrified you two would divorce or kill each other. I mean the fights, especially when you both were drinking."

"I think you just answered your own question, son. Don't get me wrong, your mother and I always enjoyed partying and cocktails as much as anyone. But it was always pretty much in moderation, especially when she was pregnant with you and Billy and when you boys were toddlers. But then, as she became increasingly more renowned in the art world, and we attended more parties and more openings, we both began to drink more. In her late twenties and early thirties, she began experiencing bouts of deep depression and periods of extreme highs and lows. Despite all the doctors, psychiatrists, treatments, and medicines Fatgram got for her, nothing seemed to work, nothing except alcohol."

"Shit, Dad, I can't imagine how stressful it had to be on all of you having Brooker T under your nose every day knowing that Willie B and Mother had once been lovers."

"Well, as I just told you, your Mother was completely honest with me about all that. And you know how prejudiced people are in small southern towns. You know the duplicities, the deceptions, the compromises that are part of the daily routine down there."

"Wait a minute, Dad. I know all that goes on. I suspect the whole situation about concealing Brooker T's identity was Fatgram's doing, but that doesn't mean it made accepting it and living with it easy."

"Well, I see your point, son. And I can't deny your Mother had real regrets about that every day of her life, but I do not think that is what caused her sickness, her depressions, her lack of self esteem and self assurance, her inability to hold on to reality at times. I think that was something in her brain. I really do. I think that's what drove her to suicide. I was helpless to guide her away from it. I really believe I unknowingly made it worse for her with my own drinking and my own emotional unavailability to her in retaliation of hers toward me."

"But, Dad," I say, stopping in midsentence. I want to tell him the truth about Mother's death and Uncle Adrian, but I fear too much of losing my chance to get to Adrian if I tell Dad or the police what I know. No, I must wait. Patience must prevail. I have to hold on to this until I get Adrian where I want him.

"But what, son?" I look at him, and I see in his face my chance to go deeper.

"But why did you really leave me and Billy? Why, Dad?"

He sighs, looks at the steaks, and shuts the grill cover. "These need one more searing burst of heat before I take them off." He turns toward me, his face gaunt, his eyes sunken, dark, hollow. "Because your Mother was five months pregnant with our third child when she took her life, and I just couldn't look you boys in the eye every day knowing that I was a failure in our relationship, in saving her, in saving our child." His face contorts with sadness, with pain; he kicks at the terrace with his right foot, lifts his heel, rotating the ball of his foot in a grinding motion, extinguishing some imaginary cigarette. He looks up at me with tears in his eyes, "I mean, for God's sake, Philip, I was so unobserving I allowed fucking Adrian McWhorter to sexually abuse you boys right under my Goddamned nose."

"Oh Dad. Shit. Fuck. I'm so sorry." I put my drink down on a table, throw the cigarette on the terrace, put it out with my right foot, reach out my arms and pull him into me.

He cries like a little boy. Now I feel like the father even though I feel his stubble on my neck, and he keeps whispering through his sobs, "I'm so sorry, Philly. I'm so sorry I gave up. I'm so sorry."

I hold him in my arms, grateful, willing to support the weight of his sorrow, "Dad, you didn't give up. You just took a break when you didn't know what else to do. But you are here now. That's all that matters. And Dad, from looking at Billy's last painting of you, I know he would feel the same."

Dad pulls back and with a combination of laughing and crying says, "Thanks, son. I was afraid I'd lost you forever. Now, if I don't get these steaks off, we will lose them forever." He opens the lid of the grill and picks up a long pair of tongs.

"You haven't lost me, Dad. I haven't lost you," I say and reach for the platter.

"Thank you, son."

"Here's the platter," I say, holding it out as he places each sizzling steak on it. I keep thinking about Mother and her unborn child—my unborn sibling. I wonder if the child was a boy or girl. My hatred for Adrian erupts anew, spawning a rebellion in my soul I presume will only be quelled when I clasp my bare hands around his throat and, with glee, feel his life drain from his body, watch it fade from his eyes.

CHAPTER 25

"Okay you two, do I have a surprise for you," Lush says, grinning slyly, as she sets a tray with three mugs of coffee and Amarula down on the wrought iron coffee table. Brenda and I are sitting on cushioned chairs in front of the brick fireplace on Billy's terrace, yellow and orange flames shuffle and sputter over gas logs, throwing off bits of heat, but not enough to overcome the chill of the night, so I have lit two propane patio heaters, glowing orange under cone reflectors, radiating circles of warmth, melting the sprinkling of snowflakes falling within their domain. Clark, curled up on a thick sheep's fleece pad I put on the hearth, lifts his head, looks up at Lush, tiny flames flickering in his dark eyes, sniffs the air, sighing as he curls back into himself like a pill bug.

"When I opened a drawer in the bar to get a spoon, I noticed a small silver box. I opened it and voila, I discovered Billy's pot stash. Look at these two perfectly rolled joints—even designer papers." She passes a joint to each of us. I turn mine over and over, observing tiny green marijuana leaves printed on yellow rolling paper.

"Yep, I remember these papers. He buys them at a head shop on Duval Street in Key West," I say and put the joint back on the tray. "Billy must have rolled these. He does it so perfectly with a dollar bill."

Brenda runs the joint under her nose, "Goodness, I haven't smelled that in a long time."

"Well, I don't know about y'all, but I intend to light up one of these babies," Lush says as she hands hot mugs to Brenda and me. "Do you mind, Brenda? Charles and the children are tucked in watching a movie, aren't they?"

"No, Lush, I don't mind. I think you're okay out here. I wouldn't want the children to see, though."

"Certainly. I'll keep watch," Lush replies, sits down, picks up a joint, takes her gold lighter, puts the flame to the joint and sucks on it several times until the end of the joint glows. She takes a couple of big tokes, holding them in, but only for a few seconds. A blast of blue smoke erupts from her mouth, followed by a fit of convulsive coughing. Brenda and I smile at each other.

"Oh, pardon me," Lush says between coughs, "Geez, this is really strong shit." She hands the joint to me.

"Don't mind if I do." I take two small drags from the joint, holding the smoke in my lungs, suppressing the urge to cough. I offer the joint to Brenda. She hesitates, looks down, takes it from my hand, and says, "Well, maybe just one little puff. I haven't smoked pot in years." I start to cough as she takes a toke.

"Be careful, Brenda, it's strong, but good." I feel the tell tale pressure behind my eyeballs that signals strong marijuana. I notice a stream of smoke coming out of Brenda's nose, enabling her to survive the first round without coughing. Lush and I each take several more tokes between sips of coffee. Brenda declines more pot. By the time the joint is barely half gone, I am pleasantly stoned. I zip up the front of my jacket over my sweater, lean my head back, sticking out my tongue, aiming for snowflakes. Lush laughs.

"If it weren't for the city noise, I'd swear we were at a ski lodge," she says.

"I wanted to go skiing this year, just didn't have the time," I say.

"Well, next year, you'll both have to come out to my parents' place in Aspen," Brenda says, smiling and leaning forward.

"Aspen!" Lush says, "Lord, Brenda how may furniture stores do y'all have?"

Brenda laughs, "Well, thirty-eight at last count, but my father was a developer also. He got into Aspen about thirty years ago and did well there. He bought a ranch and developed it before the zoning got so tight. They kept a big log A-frame with seven bedrooms."

"Damn, Brenda. How nice. Do you all use it much?" Lush asks.

"We go out a couple of times a year. The kids love snowboarding. We've spent a few Christmases there." She sits up, clasps her hands, smiling with excitement, "In fact, why don't we plan next Christmas there? You all could come out. It would be such fun."

I smile, "Hey, sounds great to me. You really mean it, Brenda?"

"Of course I mean it. Lush, you in for Christmas?"

"It sounds lovely, Brenda. I've just got to deal with David before then, but I'm in."

"Great, I'll tell Charles. We'll start the wheels in motion," she says.

"What about your parents, Brenda? Will they be there?" Lush asks.

"Not this year. They go on a world cruise every other year and this year they'll be on one during Christmas. I believe Mom said they'll be in Rio for Christmas."

Brenda giggles like a girl, "I just love planning fun trips. It so nice to have something special to look forward to."

"Yes it is," Lush replies, "Especially when there are great cooks like you and Charles in the group. Dinner and lunch today were just outstanding, Brenda. Thanks again."

"Oh, Lush, you're most welcome. I really enjoy cooking, especially for loved ones." She reaches over and pats Lush's left knee.

"How sweet, Brenda, thank you," Lush replies.

"I wish we could have persuaded Brooker T to stay for dinner," Brenda says as she reaches for her mug.

"Yes, that would have been nice," I reply. "But, I think he really wanted to see some of the city before he leaves Saturday morning."

"He certainly seems to have no fear about being in New York, flying for the first time, and meeting all of us," Brenda says.

"Yes, he's definitely self-confidant," Lush adds, "Even with such an obvious accent, which might hold some people back from expressing themselves in unfamiliar surroundings, he plows ahead in conversation."

"Brooker T has always been a bit of an enigma," I say. "On the one hand he was always outgoing, always willing to lend a hand, and, on the other hand, he was an elusive forest creature, spending countless hours roaming the woods with his bird dogs. I don't think I've ever seen anyone so attached to the earth. I'm willing to bet, he ends up walking all over Central Park in order to get connected to the city."

"How interesting," Brenda says. "He really got on well with the kids. Did you notice how they were transfixed by his description of his farm operations?"

"Yes, especially Andrew," I remark, "He ate it up. You may have to find him a 4-H club to join back in St. Louis."

"Well, that probably wouldn't be a bad thing," Brenda says, "Sometimes it's a challenge to focus all his energy."

"Brenda, I think you and Charles have done a fine job with your children," Lush says, "My God, they're well behaved, polite, comfortable around adults. What more could you ask for?"

"Thanks, Lush. You're nice to say that. I know I'm lucky so far, but I do worry about the teenage years. Things can happen. A perfectly sweet, loving, and well-mannered child can turn into a hellion. I've seen it happen with some of my friends' kids. Drugs, sex, more drugs—even in the early teens. Sometimes

I worry so." She folds her legs up in the chair underneath her body, crossing her arms, rubbing her thick, burgundy cable knit, ski sweater with her hands.

"You cold?" Lush asks.

"No, it's just, well, oh dear, I think I need another hit off that joint, Lush." Lush and I laugh out loud. Brenda smiles, "Well, I am concerned, you all."

Lush lights the joint and hands it to Brenda, "Oh, the subterfuges one must employ in child rearing."

Brenda takes the joint and inhales deeply, holds it a moment and speaks in a strained voice as she continues to hold her breath, "Tell me about it. But, Charles and I believe it's teaching them it's all about moderation." She hands the joint to Lush.

"Well you've certainly got that down, Brenda, darling," I add. "Lush and I have sucked this joint down and you only had two tokes." Everyone laughs again.

"This is so much fun," Lush says, "I just love getting stoned with you two."

"Oh, me too, Lush," Brenda says, "I haven't had so much fun in ages."

"Yeah, it's really great," I say as I take the joint from Lush, inhale deeply and say in my own breath-holding tone, "Ever noticed the more you smoke a joint, the less you have to cough?"

"Well that's probably because it relaxes you so, it just calms down all those little cilia beating in your lungs. They get stoned, too!" Lush says in a loud voice.

"Is that true, Lush?" Brenda asks.

"Oh hell, I don't know, but it sounds good," she replies.

A sudden blast of wind gathers and whips the large snowflakes like white sheets hanging on a line during a gale, disturbing pigeons roosting somewhere on the roof, their faint cooing, a sine wave of sound, amplified, then washed out as it threads through the turbulence into our ears and Clark's ears, both of which, even the damaged one, perk up noticeably as he uncurls, lifts his head, turning it askew in a questioning, intelligent gesture which I adore.

"Sounds like rain crows to me, Clark," I observe. His eyes catch mine. He sighs.

"Rain crows? What are those? I've never heard of them," Brenda says.

"Oh, that's what people back home would call mourning doves. Rain crows, because it always seemed they cooed those mournful sounds in earnest before rainfall."

"Interesting," Lush states. "Maybe these are snow crows, then. You know, up this far north and all." We all laugh.

"Y'all know what sounds good to me?" I ask, smiling, shifting my eyes, arching my eyebrows.

"What, Todge?" Lush asks.

"More of Brenda's Bananas Foster."

"Oh my God, yes, Todge. That with some ice cold champagne." Brenda, perched on top of her legs, smiles her biggest smile, generating her biggest dimples.

"Please, Brenda. Oh, please, please, please," Lush begs.

"For you two, anything," she replies, "I bought plenty of bananas for snacks for the kids."

"Hey, I got an idea," I say. "It's so nice being out here. Why don't you cook it over in the outdoor kitchen?"

"Splendid!" Brenda says, clapping her hands like Emma. "I'll go over and set up. Billy's got all the utensils I need out here. You all sneak inside and get the ingredients. But be quiet, I don't want the gang finding out. I'll make a double batch and surprise them with theirs and we'll eat ours out here."

"Brilliant, girl," Lush says. "Tell us what to bring out."

"Okay, let's see," she looks up into the sky, brushes her hair behind her ears, and says, "We'll need eight bananas, two sticks of butter, the bag of brown sugar, some ground cinnamon, the bottle of banana liqueur—I put it with the after dinner drinks in the bar—a bottle of dark rum, vanilla ice cream—it's in the bottom freezer—bowls, spoons, and the champagne."

"Damn girl, you've got it together," Lush says, stands up, takes the roach from me, hits it again, grabs my hand, and says as she pulls me up, "Come on, Todge, we're on a mission."

"What kind of mission?" I ask, playfully.

"A mission of mercy, honey. 'Cause when I put that delicious Bananas Foster in my mouth, wash it down with some fine champagne, you'll be hearing me say, 'Mercy, that was good'." Laughter erupts among us as Clark finally jumps down from his warm bed to join us.

"Hey, buddy. You stay out here and keep Brenda company," I direct. He looks at me, wags his tail, turns, breaking into a trot toward his personal lawn.

"Okay, let's go, Lush," I say, pulling her away. "I gotta pee, first."

"You go pee. I'll start gathering the stuff," she replies.

"Okay, we'll be back in a minute," I say to Brenda.

We enter the kitchen quietly. I make my way out to the hall bathroom, enter, leaving the light off, walk up to one of the urinals, pull out my penis, and piss. Damn, I really had to go, and I wonder which cop is out in the living room now. I'm trying to remember if it's Officer Kelly's shift or Officer Graham's. It feels good to be stoned, temporary relief from everything. This has to be the weirdest, saddest, most confusing week of my life. What else will I find out? You think you know someone really well and it turns out, you don't really know them at all. They're only what you want them to be—people. And they continue to be what they want to be and you are what you want to be and nobody ever, I mean really ever connects and communicates in such a true and honest and perfect way that you really end up knowing who the other really is. Oh my God I'm stoned but I think I really believe what I just thought. I finish peeing and I realize my dick is getting hard. You again. Think I've been neglecting you? Well, sorry buddy, but you're just gonna have to settle for me this week. Pot always makes me so horny. I'll jack off later, when every one has turned in. I pull on my dick; it gets hard, really hard. Shit. Maybe if we smoke that other joint, I could get Brenda and Lush in my bedroom. Wow, what an orgy that would be. My dick starts throbbing as I picture Brenda, with her gorgeous slim waist and to die for tits eating out luscious Lush. I let go of my cock and bite the knuckles on my right hand. I bite them hard, really hard. Shit, I've got to get back out there. Let's see. "Ouch, shit," I say in a loud whisper as I try to bend my cock down to get back in my pants. It won't go. I'll just wear it up. Nobody will notice, especially with this jacket and sweater on. Shit. I undo my belt, unbutton my pants, pull my cock through the fly in my boxers, arranging it, pointing up to my navel. Damn, have I grown? In this dim light, it looks like it almost reaches my navel. Wishful thinking. I wonder if those penis enlargement pills I get emailed about almost every day really work? I zip up, button up, buckle up, wash my hands, shaking them dry as I quickly walk out of the bathroom back to the kitchen to find Lush standing by one of the island counters with two trays in front of her, loaded down. She is in the process of icing down a bottle of Dom she has placed in a silver cooler. "Damn, Todge. I thought I was gonna have to come retrieve you. What were you doing in there? Playing with yourself?"

I blush red from head to toe. "What? You wish, you bitch. I just had to pee a lot."

"Uhm hum. Like a race horse, I guess," she replies with a smile on her face, picking up one of the trays. "Here, take this tray, we can come back for the champagne and flutes."

"Okay," I say, my cheeks still burning, but now feeling like laughing out loud at her speculation.

We take everything to Brenda who has pulled out a large sauté pan, a knife, and a plastic spatula from the stainless steel cabinets in the outdoor kitchen. I go back in for the champagne cooler while Brenda and Lush begin preparing the dessert. When I return, Lush is peeling bananas, slicing them lengthwise with the knife, while Brenda dissolves the brown sugar in the butter in a large sauté pan on one of the gas burners.

I take the bottle of champagne from the cooler, untwist the wire guard, and peel off the foil, "Ladies, I'll pour the champagne." I start twisting the cork, but it is in tightly.

"Why don't you use the cork pull, Todge?" Lush asks.

I set the bottle down, pick up a utensil that looks like something you'd use for cracking crab claws, "Is that what this is? I wondered why you had put a crab claw cracker on the tray."

"No silly, just clamp it on the cork and twist," she replies, peeling another banana.

I follow her directions and with a twist of my wrist the cork pops right out. "Wow, this works really well. I definitely see the safety advantages."

Brenda stirs the bubbling puddle of brown sugar and melted butter while she sprinkles ground cinnamon over the mixture. Then she takes the bottle of banana liqueur and pours some into the mixture. I pour three glasses of the Dom. "Attention ladies, let's have a quick toast." They both turn around to take a glass of champagne.

"Here's to my two lovely companions and our secret, winter, dessert cookout. I'm forever grateful to you both for all your efforts this week and for holding my hand through this nightmarish week." We clink our glasses, take a sip of the golden bubbles, breathing in the wonderful buttery, cinnamon, banana aroma wafting from the stove.

"Thanks, Todge," Lush says.

"Yes, that was lovely, Philip," Brenda says. "Now, let's add those bananas." She turns around, sets her glass on a chopping block, picks up a pair of tongs, grabbing banana halves, lowering them into the boiling mixture one by one, nudging them into position with the tongs, until all sixteen halves are arranged like a pinwheel. Lush starts to laugh.

"What's so funny?" I ask.

"Oh, the three of us getting stoned, cooking Bananas Foster outside in a snow flurry in New York City," she replies.

"I think it's wonderful," Brenda says, "I'll let these cook a couple of minutes while I scoop out the ice cream."

"Here, I can do that, Brenda," Lush says and begins opening the container of vanilla ice cream. "Todge, remember that time in St. Barts when Billy got that killer pot from a bartender?"

"Oh, yes. How could I forget that?"

"What happened?" Brenda asks.

"Well," Lush says and pauses as she directs a large scoop of ice cream into a bowl. "Well, when Billy returned with the pot, which the bartender got in St. Marten, it was a half gallon Ziploc bag crammed full of the strongest smelling buds with red hairs. We had no idea what to do with so much pot. As I recall it didn't even cost much."

"No, it didn't," I reply, "And we thought we were just going to get enough for a few joints."

"Billy came up with the idea to make a batch of marijuana brownies," Lush says, scooping out more ice cream. "None of us had ever made them before, so we had no idea how much to put in the brownie mix which was a French version of a Duncan Hines box of brownie mix. Well, I asked the boys to just grind up some of the pot in a blender. They did—half the bag."

"Dear, that sounds like a lot of pot," Brenda says as she stirs the bananas.

"Well, none of us knew, so I put in what they ground up. The night we made them, Billy ate two small brownies and went to bed. The next morning Billy was sound asleep so Philip and I decided to split one brownie and lay out in the sun."

"I've never eaten marijuana," Brenda interjects, "How long does it take to get you high after you eat it?"

"Uhmm, I'd say an hour or more and it can last up to eight hours. It's usually a much longer lasting and more mellow high than inhaling it," I reply.

"Yes, that's what I remember," Lush adds. "That trip we had a charming little villa way up on the mountain at Vitez. So Philip and I go out by the pool with our bloody Marys, oil up, lay down, chatting about this and that. After a half hour or so, we realize we are both really stoned. What's

worse, the pot is the kind that makes you paranoid, self conscious, and obsessed with stupid little things."

"Oh dear, that sounds unpleasant," Brenda says, pours a healthy portion of rum into the sauté pan, swirls it over the flame, igniting the rum with the characteristic 'whoosh' sound and two feet high yellow flames.

"Bravo," I say and clap my hands.

"Yes, it was unpleasant," Lush replies. "Philip and I decided life just was not worth living anymore and we stood up on the patio wall which fell off into a deep ravine running down the mountain, held hands, contemplating jumping off."

"Oh my God, Lush," exclaims Brenda as she continues to swirl the Bananas Foster as the flames recede, "What kept you from jumping?"

"Oh, I don't think we really would have jumped, but Billy walked out onto the patio wanting to know what we were doing standing on the wall, holding hands."

"Yeah," I add, "When we told him, he just laughed his ass off and said it was obvious we'd eaten some of the brownies. They had knocked him out for over twelve hours."

"Yes," Lush says, "We were stoned the rest of the day, but it did fade into a more pleasant high, so Billy drove us to the beach."

"Lush and I fed the rest of the brownies to some of the goats that roam the hills in St. Barts. You should have heard the sounds coming from those goats that night. I think the brownies made them horny because it sounded as if they were in a rutting mode all night."

"Remind me never to eat one of your brownies," Brenda says, laughing as she dishes out the steaming bananas into the bowls of ice cream.

"Brenda, that looks heavenly," Lush says.

"Thanks. I'm going to take these inside to Charles and the kids. I'll be right back to join you two." She picks up a tray with four bowls, turns toward the kitchen with Clark right on her heels.

"We'll be back over by the fireplace, Brenda," Lush says.

"Okay, dear," Brenda says as she enters the kitchen.

"You take the champagne over, Todge. I'll take the dessert."

"Okay."

The snow flurries and breeze, increasing in intensity, create whirling spirals of snowflakes descending upon the terrace. I look up into the illuminated grey of the night sky, envisioning that we are encapsulated inside one of those plastic snow globes with little winter scenes that you shake, creating little snowfalls, while I speculate whether I've succumbed to myopia in my approach to dealing with Adrian.

"Todge, I can't believe we haven't mentioned basketball," Lush says, "Those damned Patriots knocked us out in the second round."

"Yeah, bad luck, I thought we had a chance at the championship. I managed to catch the game on ESPN in Hong Kong."

"Remember the fun we had with Billy in St. Louis last year?"

"God yes. It's hard to believe this time last year the three of us were together in St. Louis celebrating the Tar Heels win."

Lush removes the bowls from the tray, puts them on the table, sighs, "Yeah, who would have ever thought then we'd be here now to say goodbye to Billy?"

"Yeah well, life's a shit sandwich and every day you get to take another bite of it," I reply.

"My, my. Where ever did you come up with that expression?"

"Don't know. Heard it somewhere. Maybe it just sprang from my gut spontaneously," I reply.

"Actually, I like it," Lush replies, "It pretty much sums up this week."

"Hmmm, it sure does," I reply, pouring more champagne in each glass, watching the relentless bubbles rapidly swirl up inside the tall optic glass flutes, as if they were in a panic to jump out of the wide mouths of the flutes, merge with the snowflakes, making themselves more permanent, at least, until the temperature rises. A cold wet nose touches my left hand. I smile, look down at Clark, pat his head, watch his nose move toward the direction of the bowls of Bananas Foster, then turn to see Brenda approaching.

"Well, your idea to have another dessert pleased my family greatly," Brenda says to me.

"Good—a special treat for the kids, I suppose?"

"Indeed, they never get two desserts back home."

"Okay, ladies, another toast," I say, handing Brenda her glass. "To family. And you all are my family."

They both repeat, "To family." We clink glasses, take a sip, smile at each other, as the snow spirals down around us.

"It's so beautiful out here tonight," Lush says.

Lush and Brenda settle in the cushioned chairs. I sit on the hearth by Clark. We pick up our spoons and begin to eat the Bananas Foster.

"Oh my God, Brenda. This is better than the first batch," Lush says.

"I think so, too," I say.

"You both are too kind, but I think the pot probably has made our taste buds a bit more sensitive," Brenda replies.

"No, it's not the pot," Lush says, "Believe me, I'm a dessert fiend, and this is superb. The consistency is just right. The sauce is just caramelized in the perfect, softest way. How do you do that? I mean without a candy thermometer?"

"Honestly, I've made this so many times, I can tell just by the color of it and the thickness as I stir it," Brenda replies, takes another bite, savors the flavors and consistency a moment, "But this really did turn out well. Maybe the cooler temperature outside had some effect? Who knows, maybe it was the snowflakes falling in the pan?"

"That's gotta be it," I reply. "I've been observing these snowflakes all night, tasting them on my tongue, feeling them against my cheeks and on my nose, watching them, swirling, hovering, funneling down on us, protecting us. Yeah, protecting us. Let's face it; this is an unusual snow. Look out at the other buildings, it doesn't seem to be snowing much at all."

"I think that's just an illusion," Lush says. "The lights on the patio make it easy to see these snowflakes."

"Yeah, but I see hardly any snow falling in front of all those lit up buildings," I point out. "This snow is from Billy. It's his way—his spirit's way—of being here with us tonight."

"How lovely," Brenda says. We all look up into the funnel of swirling snow; even Clark raises his head, looks up, sniffs, and sneezes twice.

"I do feel his presence," Lush says. "I just keep expecting him to walk out here any second now." Clark looks at Lush, sighs, puts his head down, staring into the flames.

"Well, whether he manifests himself as flesh or snowflakes, he'll always be with me, always by my side," I say.

"Todge, how do you feel about your newly discovered half-brother?" Lush asks with a serious expression on her face, plunging her spoon into the bowl, scraping the sides, pulling out a final generous portion.

"You know, Brooker T was always part of our extended family anyway. He was someone we grew up with. Now, he's just a little closer. God knows we've all made mistakes, Mother certainly wasn't immune from them." I eat two spoonfuls in rapid succession because I notice Brenda and Lush have finished theirs.

"I wonder why your grandmother just didn't arrange an abortion for Eva?" Lush asks as she pulls out two cigarettes, lights one, hands it to Brenda, then lights one for herself.

"God, you've got a point. I wondered that today, too," I say.

"Oh dear," Brenda says.

"What, hon?" Lush looks at her.

"Well, it's just that."

"Just that you are a Catholic?" Lush replies as she sips her champagne.

"Well yes. But that's nothing to do with this. You see, well, I guess that it's all out in the open now. Charles wouldn't mind my telling you. You see, abortion was illegal in every state in the union in the 1960's. The only way to get one legally was if the unborn child was endangering the life of the mother. Charles told me that Eva told him that Fatgram had encouraged her to claim that she would commit suicide if she were forced to carry out the pregnancy—you know, having a black man's child. By saying that, the unborn child becomes a danger to the mother's health, and, especially in those days, doctors for rich women, would agree to perform the abortion."

"Dear God, another dirty family secret emerges," I say shaking my head, scraping my bowl now.

"Well," Brenda crosses her legs as she speaks, "Charles says Eva wouldn't even consider the idea. Eventually, Fatgram gave up on it too and moved on to the finishing school idea."

"I assume you know about the other child, Brenda," I say, putting down my bowl on the hearth, reaching toward the table for my own cigarettes. She nods in acknowledgement.

"For God's sake, what other child?" Lush asks looking back and forth from Brenda to me.

"Dad told me this evening, when he was grilling the steaks, that Mother was five month's pregnant when she died," I say, light my cigarette, leaning back on the hearth, taking in Lush's face.

"How very sad," she says gently, quietly, looking down at the reflections in the glass top of the wrought iron table, a thick strand of her dark hair falls over the left side of her face, her left hand automatically reaches for it, pulling it back behind her left ear. She looks up, eyes wet and shining, takes a drag from her cigarette, lips moving, forming silent, smoky words.

"What's that you're saying, dear?" Brenda asks.

"Wasted babies. The world's so full of wasted babies."

"Yes, it is," Brenda replies, reaching over to take Lush's left hand in hers.

I'm uncertain whether Lush is thinking about my unborn sibling, the children David wouldn't let her adopt, or the lives Adrian wrecked and ended.

"You're still a young woman, Lush. You can still have children if you want them," Brenda says.

"Yes, that's true, Brenda. But you can't bring back the ones that are gone."

Lush turns her head toward me, "Todge, dear. I hope you can forgive me."

"For what, darling?" I ask, smiling, trying to comfort her.

"For not telling you that I was pregnant when we broke up during our freshman year. For not telling you that I had an abortion." She weeps with a minimal display of emotion. Brenda gets up, scooting in next to her, embracing her. Clark gets up, jumps off the hearth, observes the women, yawns punctuated with a high pitch squeak, stretches, yawns again, settling at their feet. I feel a prickling, burning sensation throughout my body, particularly in my arms and legs, and I think, maybe this news has driven up my blood pressure to such a level that I'm having a stroke or a heart attack, but it passes, leaving me with a numb, cold feeling. I look at Lush and Brenda.

"Lush, I'm sorry. I hope you can forgive me for being such an immature prick back then, for putting you in such a terrible, lonely, horrible situation. I can't say how I would have reacted then had I known. But I know how I would react today. Today, I would really want that child."

She looks up at me, "So would I."

Brenda stands up. "Well, I think I'll go in now. I hope I can make it to the bathroom to brush my teeth and change into a night gown before Charles gets a whiff of this pot." She laughs, leans over and kisses Lush. "Goodnight, dear."

"Goodnight, Brenda. Thanks for your kindness."

"Yes, dear stepmother, thanks for your kindness," I add with a smile.

"Stepmother? Lord, Philip. That makes me feel ancient," she replies, eyes sparkling, dimples accenting her smile. We all laugh. Brenda walks over, gives me a peck on the cheek as she says goodnight, turns around, picks up the tray, puts the three mugs, stacks the three bowls on it, collects the spoons and napkins and heads back to the kitchen. "Enjoy this magical night darlings," she calls back over her shoulder. Clark hops up in the chair beside Lush, puts his head in her lap, melting into her caresses.

"Why didn't you tell me, Lush?" She doesn't answer, just keeps stroking Clark.

"I guess I know the answer. I was such a God-awful cad to you, how could you've told me? I sure wouldn't have told me had I been you. Do you know if it was a boy or a girl?"

"Don't know. I was only a few weeks pregnant when I got the abortion."

"Weren't you on birth control pills?"

"Yes, but they're not one hundred percent effective."

"Gee, the kid would be fifteen, now," I say trying to conjure up in my mind a male or female version of Lush and myself.

"I know," she says.

I lean over, taking her hands in mine. "I understand why you didn't tell me at the time, but why haven't you told me since then. I mean we're so close now. Don't you trust me?"

"Yes, I trust you, Todge. It's just that the closer we've become over the years, the harder it has become for me to tell you. I suppose I thought you might not forgive me for getting the abortion in the first place—for killing our child. I dunno. It's all so fucking convoluted. I mean, sometimes I feel the spirit of that child, its essence, our essence, the possibilities, the limitless opportunities, wasted, sucked out, disposed of like a malignant growth. For what? My convenience? My career? My hollow vengeance against you, Todge? At the time, I was certain, steadfast in my decision, despite my Catholic upbringing. I did it without telling anyone. I was grateful I had the right, the choice to do it. Now, I'm not so certain. If only I'd had someone like your Mother for guidance, that child would probably be alive today, whether or not you and I were close or not, whether or not you knew about its existence. Eva had the fortitude and gumption to have her baby, even facing overwhelming social stigma and the displeasure of her formidable mother. Eva did the right thing; I didn't."

"Lush, given the circumstances at the time, you did the right thing. I would have done the same thing. Don't beat yourself up—a few week old fetus is not a person yet—it's just a developing embryo, anything could happen to it."

"You mean like, of the mother's own volition, being ripped out of her uterus by means of a surgical vacuum? Is that what you mean, Todge?" she asks with vehement sarcasm, illuminating the abyss of her sadness, its sides covered with fronds of anger, growing within her soul for years, finally sensing the appropriate conditions and receptor, bursting forth upon me like some malignant pollen, spawning an allergic reaction in my soul from which no antihistamine provides relief. I breathe it in, speechless, blaming the pot for evoking these feelings and images, knowing the nascent grief I feel for this lost child will be no less painful than what I feel for its uncle.

"I'm sorry. I shouldn't talk to you like that," Lush says, her face still sad, but brightening now, like the sky in Union right after the heaviest part of an April downpour.

"Not a problem," I reply. "So, where do we go from here?"

"I think we're already on the right path, Todge. More right than ever, now."

We stand up, embrace, the strengthening breeze cutting through the radiant heat, tickling our faces with chilled air and wet snowflakes.

"Lush, let's smoke this other joint, then go in for a night cap. What do you say?"

"I say that's a plan. I'll light it." She picks up the joint and her lighter. I cup my hands around her face as she applies the flame. The flickering light bounces off the beautiful features of her face as the end

of the joint begins to glow. She takes a couple of big tokes and hands it to me. I do the same. We look at each other, holding the smoke in our lungs as long as we can, then, laughing and coughing, expel it simultaneously. This pot can pull you down if you let it, but it can also pull you up, and I'm determined to follow that path the rest of the evening.

CHAPTER 26

Something jabs into my stomach several times, sharp powerful kicks, pulling me out of a deep dream, rousing my consciousness, making me aware that Clark is also dreaming as his powerful back legs kick with rapid seizure-like thrusts into my stomach. I put my left hand against his belly and rub it gently, instantly calming his movements. The clock reads three fifteen a.m., and I have been dreaming a strange convoluted dream in which I rode a red bicycle up a large hill through a crowded mill village. At the top of the hill was a tiny green building that I recognized as an art gallery that must have been operated by Mother. The tiny dollhouse-like structure was in a lovely shade garden full of ferns, ivy, and sculpture. I focused on three tombstone-shaped pieces of granite on which Mother had painted something. As I observed the stones, I realized that she had painted faces on them: the first was Fatgram, the second Billy, and the third Uncle Adrian. A profound sense of security, calmness, and safety filled me as I gazed at the stones, the faces appeared to be living holograms etched into the stones in ethereal, glowing colors, pulsating auras, full of subatomic charged particles. I kept thinking how skilled an artist Mother was, but I could not figure out how she managed this effect of movement and luminosity in solid granite. Fatgram and Billy seemed unaware of my presence, but Adrian recognized me, I could tell, and his visage drew me in with a warm smile, making me feel all of the warm, good thoughts I used to feel about him when I was a boy. In the dream I was satisfied and contented by Adrian's smile so I confidently got back on my bicycle and rode back down the hill, through the mill village, at a speed so fast my body flew up into the air as I hung on to the handlebars, racing down the hill, slowing to a stop at the bottom of the hill by a very long sand pit, much like the runaway truck lanes on Interstate 24 on Mount Eagle near Sewanee as you head down the mountain towards Chattanooga. When I finally stopped, I looked up to see that I was on Pine Street in Spartanburg, in front of the side entrance to Converse College, the same entrance Uncle Adrian took Billy and me to and picked us up from each weekday for two weeks one summer while we attended a summer arts camp for kids. I turned around and was starting back up the hill to the art gallery when Clark's kicks awoke me.

I now feel pissed and mad at myself for dreaming something pleasant about Adrian. What the fuck was that all about? How can someone I loathe and wish to see suffer mercilessly arouse feelings of contentment and safety in me? How fucked up is that? The man rapes me as a kid, kills both my mother, her unborn child, and Billy, and I experience nirvana looking at his smiling face etched into a tombstone? I gotta pee. I roll off the bed, awaking Clark. I walk into the bathroom, turn on the light, go to the toilet and piss. I feel thirsty. I've been drinking too much this week. After tomorrow, I'll cut back. I'm going to quit the damned cigarettes, too, and I'm going to get in some Bikram classes. I finish, flush, wash my hands, look up in the mirror to see Clark standing behind me wagging his tail.

"You need to go out, boy?"

He turns and heads to the bedroom door.

"Okay, let me grab a robe."

I go into Billy's closet, turn on the light, find a plush, white, terry cloth robe, and a pair of sheep wool lined slippers, put them on, open the bedroom door and head down the hall. Clark immediately heads into the living room to where Officer Graham is sitting on a sofa reading a book.

"Couldn't sleep, Mr. Hampton?"

"No, just thirsty, and I think Clark needs to go out," I reply, squinting to try to make out the name of the book she is reading, but I can not focus enough to see the cover. Realizing my hair must be a mess, I comb through it with my right hand.

"Mrs. Richardson couldn't sleep either, she's been out in the kitchen for a while," she says, pulling the book to an upright position clearly revealing the title as *The Year Of Magical Thinking*, which surprises me a bit. I read a review of that book, and I have planned to read it. Funny, I thought I would relate to the tragic events experienced by the author, now, more than ever, I know I would.

"She's, she's been out there a while, you say?" I look in Officer Graham's eyes, observing that she is tired.

"Yes, about a half an hour."

"Well, maybe I'll go make some hot tea. Would you care for anything, Officer Graham?"

"Thank you, but I've had enough java to see me through my shift."

"Well, I'll leave you to your book. Is it any good? I read a review and thought I might get it."

"It really is. It's about how life can change in an instant, turn on a dime from one moment to the next. Joan Didion writes beautifully, expressing her emotions so well." She sighs, pulling the book close into her chest.

"You talk more like an English major than a cop," I say as I notice her looking at my calves and bedroom shoes.

"I was an English major, Brown University," she replies with a slight smile, lighting up her face, offering me an invitation for further discussion.

"My God, you from Brown and O'Daniel from Julliard! The NYPD standards and recruiting methods must have surely changed."

She laughs and says, "One might surmise that from meeting me and O'Daniel, but I can assure you we are both anomalies as far as police academy recruits go."

"I see. Was your father in the police force, too?" Clark looks up at me, panting and whimpering. "Okay, boy, just a second."

"No, he retired from the army. But he instilled the virtue of service to a higher cause in his kids, and I was in no way fulfilled as a high school English teacher, so I joined the police force."

"Wow. You must crave action, suspense, even danger?"

"No, it's more a case of using my physical and mental skills to help out others. I am planning to become a detective."

"Admirable. It must be difficult with kids and a husband."

"You know. You make things work. I'm lucky, my mom lives with us now and she watches the kids when I'm working. My husband was on the force, but he's in law school now—just one year left. He wants to become a judge someday."

"Cool. What kind of judge?"

"Well, eventually federal. He'll probably start out in the DA's office and go from there."

Clark paws at my right leg, scratching my shin with his claws. "Ouch! Somebody's nails need clipping. Well, I better let him out. Nice chatting with you, Officer Graham," I say, heading toward the kitchen, feeling her eyes watching me as I walk away.

"Thanks," she says, and I hear her opening the book in her lap.

I open the kitchen door and walk in to semi-darkness. Lush, illuminated by the glow of a laptop screen, sits erect and motionless at one of the granite counters with her back to me. She holds a lit cigarette

in her right hand, smoke curling into tight grey curls above her head, pulsating and twirling as if they were alive, and a coffee cup in her left hand. Clark, happy to discover her there, trots over, jumping up to put his front paws on her right thigh. She turns her face away from the screen toward Clark, leans her face down towards his and says, "Hello, Clarkie." He licks her face.

"Can't sleep?" I ask as I walk over to Lush.

"No, just wanted to make sure all the presentation materials for the wake are just right. And—" She pauses as she turns toward me.

"Hold that thought, Clark needs to go out. Come on, Clark." I walk over to the terrace door and open it. Clark darts past me. I stick my head out and get a rush of cold air and snowflakes in my face. I look out to see the patio covered in a couple of inches of snow. "Damn, I didn't know we were in for any accumulation, did you?"

"Yeah, two to three inches, but it's going to warm back up later today, so it will melt by the time of the wake, I hope. People will need to go out on the terrace for air and for smokes. They say we'll have a high of fifty-five.. It's thirty-five right now." She swivels her seat around toward me, takes a drag off her cigarette, exhales, takes a sip of coffee, smiles, the diffuse light from the screen backlights her body, revealing hair pulled back into a pony tail, a light green silk robe patterned with dark green leaves which look like banana leaves or palm leaves, bare feet with painted toe nails, and her long beautiful neck.

"I'm glad you're up. I was just about to come in and wake you," she says with another smile.

"Why? Wassup?"

"Mabry."

"What?"

"Mabry's up, that's wassup." She laughs this time.

"Seems he's a night owl, too. We've been instant messaging each other for the past twenty minutes. I just happened to check my emails and saw that he sent me one about thirty minutes ago."

"And, what did he say?" I leave the door cracked, walk over to Lush, take her coffee cup, which is warm, take a sip and hand it back to her.

"We have an answer from Adrian," she says, widening her eyes, nodding her head slightly.

"No shit. I can't believe it. Tell me what he said." I pull out the stool to the left of Lush, sit down, waiting for her answer.

"Well, he really didn't say anything to us, not yet anyway."

"But you just said we had an answer from Adrian," I say in a loud voice.

"Shhh," Lush says quietly, then whispers, "Keep in down, you don't want Officer Graham to hear you, do you?"

I grab her shoulders, "Just tell me, Lush."

"Okay, okay. You see, Mabry has been going through Billy's computer thoroughly. He found a couple of other email accounts that were hidden and password protected. Billy used one of those secret accounts to correspond with Adrian."

"What? I don't believe it. He would have told me." I feel shock and disgust, as if I had just felt a small sensation on the back of my neck and reached around with my thumb and forefinger, grabbed something, scab-like, brought it around up to my eyes, revealing the eight small wiggling legs of a flat, brown tick.

"I know. I'm sorry, Todge. They connected in a chat room—a chat room for pedophiles."

"Oh for God's sake, Lush. Billy wasn't a fucking pedophile. You know that."

"I know, I know, Todge. But it appears that he was doing some sort of research—probably to relive his childhood experiences in order to create and get through this last monumental artistic achievement."

"I don't understand. It's inconceivable."

"No it's not, Todge. Billy posted some very provocative photographs of himself and you as a child on that site, some of the photos Adrian himself took. Some of them had been altered with Photo Shop too,

well to create different sexual scenes, for instance, the adult Billy, having sex with himself as a child. It was just too tempting to Adrian and he revealed himself to Billy on-line."

"Fuck! Well, I'll be damned."

"Tell me about it," she puts out her cigarette, sets the coffee cup down, manipulates the touch pad, clicks a few times, pulling up a long list of emails. She points to them. "See all these emails, they go back to August of 2004, about the same time Billy began his last genre of paintings. I haven't had time to read them all, but Mabry has. In a nutshell, Adrian was mentoring Billy on each painting—just as he did your mother. Billy would email a high resolution photograph of each painting to Adrian and Adrian would critique it."

"This is too fucking weird. Goddamn you, Billy. What were you thinking? Why the fuck did you hide this from me?" Tears fall down my face. I put my head in my lap and cry. Lush strokes my back as Clark arrives, senses my distress, jumping up to stick his snout into the side of my face. I raise up to stroke his head. "It's okay, boy."

"Philip, did anything happen between you and Billy? Anything that could have put a damper on your relationship?"

"Crap, Lush. Nothing I can think of. The last big thing was that time in St. Barts, but I thought we both worked through that. I mean, the past couple of years I've been on the road constantly, but I always stayed in contact—just like I have with you, Lush."

"True, you're good about that, Todge. I just can't figure out why he kept this all a secret. I'm afraid there's a lot more to this."

"What do you mean, Lush?"

"I mean, I think we're going to find out a lot of things Billy kept hidden before we solve this thing," she says, sighs, offering a look of kindness, support and understanding to me.

"Yep, I think you are on target, Lush."

"Well, anyway, Mabry and Jonas believe Billy was stringing Adrian along, in a sense, until he could discover his whereabouts."

"What, did Mabry call Jonas and wake him in the middle of the night?"

"I guess he just walked over and woke him," she replies.

"Huh? They live together?" I ask.

"Yeah, they're partners. Julianna told me," she replies.

"Well, I'll be damned. I never would have guessed he-man Jonas and computer nerd Mabry would be gay, much less an item. Shit, good for them."

"That's right, Todge. Julianna says they are a happy couple. Hey, look at the very last email from Adrian, sent the evening Billy was drugged."

She runs her finger over the touch pad, clicks, revealing:

"Darling boy, you've achieved your greatest work to date. The painting left me breathless—the movement, the emotion, the rhythm of the colors, the detail where needed, the absence of detail where appropriate, the supreme expression of all of your technical skills. Well, I could go on, but suffice it to say that you have risen to the best of the best and without a doubt raised me to the pinnacle of my mentoring abilities. Your mother would be so proud. Well, not of the subject matter, but about everything else in the painting. And to think, it's a tribute to your dear old Uncle Adrian. You cannot imagine how pleased this has made me. I'm happy that you have finished this important collection. You deserve a long, long rest for all your efforts, including your futile attempts to locate my whereabouts. But first, go out and celebrate! A night on the town is what Uncle Adrian prescribes for you. And when the night is over, sweet dreams my most beautiful one."

"This looks like a threat to me. Surely to God, Billy could see that?" I ask looking into Lush's eyes.

"Well, it's a threat for certain, but Billy was probably feeling too good about finishing *Bloodbrothers* and the collection to worry about it. Plus, he figured he had finally found Adrian in Dubai. Jonas believes Adrian may have just instructed Benny to drug Billy, get him back to his place for sex in order to find out where Billy hid the stolen disk from Najeed, retrieve it and move on."

"I dunno. Look, Adrian killed all those other people."

"True, but he seemed to have a special place in his heart for Billy. It's incredible some of the things he said to Billy in these emails. It was almost like he was counseling his own child."

"That's all part of his con—for sex—believe me, I lived through it."

"True, but Adrian was obviously not interested in Billy as a sexual pursuit anymore, even though Billy tried to tempt him," Lush replies turning on her stool toward me.

"What do you mean by 'tempt him', Lush?"

"Well, this will be hard for you to hear, but apparently Billy has digital cameras installed in the sex chamber and he broadcast some of his sexual encounters to Adrian," she says.

"Damn, that's disgusting to me. I just can't believe he'd do that. No, yes I can. Billy had no modesty about sex. You know that, Lush." I sigh.

"Well Jonas and Mabry think he did it to try to lure Adrian in, maybe even get him to come here," Lush says waving her right hand and raising her brow.

"Well, whatever, but can't we just trace all these emails to find Adrian?"

"No, Jonas and Mabry can't trace any of them. It seems each one came from a different place, different countries, and different continents even. They all came from untraceable, highly protected accounts. Each one was coded and an algorithm was attached to decode the message."

"Amazing, but they had to have come from Adrian, I mean the mentoring and all. It had to be him."

"Or a very good imposter who knew a lot about art and your family. But Jonas thinks it is Adrian, although the sender denies being Adrian in several emails and never falls into the countless traps Billy set for him to try to force him to reveal something only the real Adrian would know."

"Well, we know he is a clever bastard. But why did Billy do this? And in secret?"

"Jonas thinks as Billy tried to draw Adrian in by revealing his works to him, that he in fact realized that he could create his best works with Adrian's help while at the same time hooking Adrian in so much that Billy could arrange a meeting. Jonas thinks Billy intended to kill Adrian."

"Oh my God. Could that be true, Lush? I mean I want to kill him. Does that mean Billy figured out about Mother? And the other women Adrian killed?"

"Jonas thinks so. He also thinks we may learn a lot more when we get into Adrian's apartment this morning."

"This morning?"

"Yep, he's already arranged for it—ten o'clock. You, Jonas, Mabry, and Julianna will go in disguised as plumbers to change a hot water heater."

"How did he do that?"

"Got to the super who let it slip that Julian complained of a dripping noise while he was there. Turns out, the hot water heater is leaking. Julian told the super to order a new one. Mabry monitored all the super's calls and found out the plumbers planned to install a new one on Monday. Pretending to be a scheduler from the plumbing company, Mabry called the super back, said they had a cancellation and would like to do the work on Friday."

"Christ, they'll know something's wrong when no new heater is installed," I say.

"Oh contraire. Brush up on your plumbing skills, darling, because you all really are going to install a new hot water heater."

"I don't know a damn thing about plumbing, and I'm sure Julianna doesn't," I reply.

"Don't worry, it is in Jonas's and Mabry's job descriptions," Lush says crossing her legs as she leans toward me.

"Well, why does he want Julianna to go and not you?"

"Because of her expertise in art. He wants her there to document things."

"I see. God, this is all unfolding so fast. But I sure feel like Jonas and Mabry are paying off."

"Indeed. They're worth every penny you've spent."

"I guess I'll be supplying Julian or Adrian with a new hot water heater."

"I guess so," Lush laughs. "Wanna night cap?"

"Love one."

"Me too."

"Lush?"

"What Todge?"

"You think I should read all these emails?"

"I think you should wait until after the wake. Maybe even a bit after that."

"Really? Why?"

"It's like you said. Too much is happening too fast this week. Give yourself some time to process your feelings before adding fuel to the fire. There's a lot of stuff in these emails that you may not like or understand, at least at this point."

"I'm so glad you're here, Lush," I say and then sigh.

"I wouldn't be anywhere else, Todge. Single malt, rocks?"

"Sweet," I reply as I light up one of her Presidentials, feeling the weight of Clark's triangular shaped head as he rests it on my right foot, looking up at me with anticipation.

CHAPTER 27

"Philip, Philip, wake up, wake up," I hear Emma's excited high voice pleading, as she shakes my left shoulder with both her small hands.

I bolt upright in bed, pop my eyes wide open, smile, and say, "Good morning, Emma darling. What's all the excitement about?"

"Today's the day. Billy's wake, you know. I'm so excited about handing out the roses and meeting all those famous people. You've got to get up to get ready, Philip." She is dressed in adorable blue and white striped overalls, a long sleeved white T-shirt, with her hair pulled into two braided pigtails poking out on each side of her head. I can't help but laugh at the sight of her.

"I've got my work clothes on, Lois and Tammy are already here, and Lois is assigning chores," she smiles and climbs up on the bed.

"Chores?" I say.

"Yes, Lois made a list of chores for all of us kids," she says as she pulls on her overall bib with both hands. She smiles, looks at me, and adds, "But I really think you ought to shave today, Philip."

"You do? Why? Am I too scruffy for you young lady?"

"Well, I don't know what scruffy is, but Mom thinks you look like a homeless person when you don't shave and with your puffy eyes and all," she states in a matter-of-fact manner, now looking down at the blue Keds she wears.

"Does she?" I ask, surprised, my feelings hurt.

"Uhm hum, she does," she says as she flings her entire body back in my lap. I instantaneously flinch forward over her in reaction to her landing her back on my morning hard-on.

She laughs as I gently push her up off my lap and onto the side of the bed, "Oh, let's see if anything good is on TV, Philip."

"Emma, dear, you just said Lois is ready for us to get to work, so we better watch TV later," I reply.

"Well, okay, but hurry up and get in the kitchen." She jumps off the bed and runs out of the room, shouting as she leaves, "Now, don't forget to shave."

I'm overcome with the thought of how easy it would be for an adult to take advantage of a child in such a situation as I just experienced. I could have easily hugged Emma, tickled her, played with her, kept her in my lap against my hard on. I can feel Uncle Adrian's breath down the back of my neck, and I break out in goose bumps down my arms and legs, my entire scalp tightens as if someone is pulling handfuls of my hair.

"Okay, Philly, on the count of three, I'll spring up and you can dive off my knees," Uncle Adrian says as I sit atop his thighs, curled up with his arms around me as he bounces up and down in the water. My teeth are chattering from the chill of the water and the thrill of having Uncle Adrian throw me up into the air to execute whatever type of dive I wish. I am so glad he's here to take me to the swimming hole. Mother says Billy is too young to go yet because he's just five years old. Uncle Adrian pulls me closer in, talking to me with his face pressed against mine, scratching me with his stubble.

"Okay, Philly, you're Uncle Adrian's brave boy. One, two, three! Up you go."

He jumps up, catapulting me into the air, and I do a sort of cartwheel into the water. I love it. I dog paddle back into his arms.

"Again, again, Uncle Adrian."

"Sure thing, Philly. We can do it as much as you like."

So I climb on again, he hugs me and begins to bounce; this time I can feel something hard against my rear.

"What's that hard thing back there, Uncle Adrian?" I say and put my hand back to feel it through his swimsuit.

He moans and says, "Oh, that's just my todger getting worked up with all this exercise and excitement."

"Your what?" I ask, pulling my hand back from it, but he pushes my hand back against it with his right hand.

"You know, your pee pee, your tinkler," he replies.

"Mother and Dad call it penis," I reply, jerk my hand away, and say, "Now launch me up, Uncle Adrian."

"Okay, Philly, but first just let me bounce a bit to get wound up enough to give you a good, high, launching."

And we did this, all that summer until I got used to his hard todger against my rump, to him holding me, to him touching me all over during the prelaunch phase, 'making certain all my parts were in order,' he'd say.

Emma must have felt my hard cock against her back and bottom. I feel nauseated as I realize Uncle Adrian was having sex with me then, rubbing his hard cock against me for sexual pleasure, probably even ejaculating in his swimsuit as he did this. A pang of guilt overcomes me as I remember that the following summer, when Billy was six, I encouraged him to partake in the launching procedure with Uncle Adrian, I helped to indoctrinate him into Adrian's carefully planned, patiently executed technique of child molestation. I can't let myself dwell on this now, there's too much to do today—Billy's day. I glance at the

clock; it's seven o'clock. Clark is nowhere around. I realize I've only been asleep for three hours. Lush and I didn't get back to bed until four in the morning. Officer Graham was sound asleep with her book in her lap as we passed through the living room so that I could say good night to Billy's ashes in the blue and white Chinese ginger jar.

"Good night, dear brother, I love you," I whispered.

"Good night, beautiful one," Lush whispered and blew a kiss to the jar.

We walked down the hall, pausing in front of Billy's room, embracing, each of us knowing how easy and good it would be to make love right now, but each of us afraid to go there. We pulled apart from our embrace, smiled at each other, said good night, turned away from a union whose lost child will haunt my dreams and deep thoughts for the rest of my life. Lush went to her bedroom, and I went to mine with Clark. I pulled off my clothes, left them on the floor in the closet, pulled on a tee shirt, and was asleep within a few minutes after getting in the bed, snuggling with Clark, releasing from my mind the thoughts of dead fetuses, brothers, and mothers.

I get out of bed, glance at Willy B's massive ebony biceps, try to picture him fucking Mother at the swimming hole, and wonder where the hell did Billy get ahold of the original Blood Brother's certificate. My primary goal in my morning routine today is to shave as close as I can. Boy, I miscalculated that; I really believed that my scruffy look would have turned Brenda on like it does so many other women. Maybe I haven't been reading her right at all. Maybe I haven't been reading anybody right. Hell, how accurately do I really even read myself? Since Mother's death I've been so careful to map out things, set goals for myself, help out Billy the best that I could without trying to be too much of a big brother. What was that all about? I mean, really. Was it just a way to deal with the loss of Mother, her love, which when it flowed, was irresistible and unimaginably fulfilling to me—it's the most intoxicating thing I've ever experienced in my life. Here I go again, Mr. Oedipus. But really, I don't think it was that. Hell, Ala Mary, Willy B, Dad, Billy, Adrian, even Fatgram were completely taken in by her. Mother had extraordinary confidence when dispersing her love—so much so that when it flowed freely, like manna from heaven, not only did she realize this, she carefully controlled it, and you could tell by the look of satisfaction on her face that she completely understood how much pleasure she delivered and that she could withdraw it with the drop of a hat. This was the power she held over all of us, as irresistible as the Sirens' calls, willing to bide our time in despair until she decided to sing again. Even Adrian, the most base and evil a human I know, wasn't immune to Mother's power. I know this to be true. He waited on her hand and foot, even when she would thrash out at him, tell him he was crazy, insane, untalented, poorly educated, unqualified to even view her works, much less criticize them, but he had a knack to draw out her best—just as he did most recently with Billy—and Mother knew this, and lavished her love upon him when she took a notion, so much so that I can remember, even as a small boy, seeing him curled up at her feet like a contented puppy at his master's feet. Odd as it may seem, I can now clearly recall Fatgram observing this once and saying, loudly, matter-of-factly, with a tinge of disgust in her low smooth flow of perfectly enunciated words, in front of everyone, "Adrian, if you were a Goddamned cat, you'd be purring." How then could he have killed Mother? She must have found out about his molestation of little boys, her own sons. She must have. My God, what a scene that must have been. I'm certain she would have confronted him, torn him to shreds. So how did he get the best of her? I just can't figure that one out. Who was with them in France that summer? Someone must have seen something, overheard something, thought something was not right between the two of them. I'll have to ask Dad. Maybe Julianna will have some clues; she's the living expert on Mother, having formulated Mother's catalogue raisonné during the 1990's.

I glance up into the shower mirror to discover I've completed shaving so I finish my shower, get out, dry off, comb my hair back, brush my teeth, put on deodorant, open the bathroom door, head to the closet, and am completely startled as I enter the closet to see Andrew standing there, staring at my naked body as I walk in. His eyes immediately fall to my penis.

"Oh, Drew, you startled me," I say, quickly moving past him to the drawer where Billy keeps boxer shorts. I grab a pair, with my back to Andrew, bend over and step into the shorts, pull them up, turning back around toward Andrew, his mass of curly auburn hair and green eyes pulling me back twenty-one years, making me feel as if I'm facing a ten year old Billy. Andrew stares at my chest and face.

"Gosh, Andrew, you're the spitting image of Billy when he was your age."

"Yeah, I know. Dad always tells me that," he says now moving his eyes around the closet. "Billy sure has more clothes than anyone, well, any man I've ever seen."

"Yeah, well you know he was a fashion model for years, and models always have a lot of clothes. It's their business."

"Humm," he says, looking back up at me, "Randy says all male models are faggots."

"I see. Good old cousin Randy's words of wisdom again. Drew, do you believe everything Randy tells you?"

"Well, he's really smart, and he's already grown up," he says, pulling at the hem of his short sleeve, green Polo shirt.

"What do you mean by 'already grown up,' Drew?" I ask as I pull out a black, cotton, mock turtleneck, thinking it will be cold outside this morning.

His stuffs his hands into the front pockets of his jeans, bending his knees slightly, drawing my attention to his left tennis shoe, an unlaced blue Nike running shoe. "Well, you know, he's already got a big hairy penis like yours and Dad's."

"Well, just because he's hit puberty doesn't mean he's grown up, Drew. And it doesn't mean he knows everything either. You better tie that left shoe before you trip over it." I search his face for a response. His eyes wander around the closet again as he bends down to tie his shoe without looking at it.

"By the way," I say as I pull the turtleneck over my head, "how do you know he's so grown up, I mean, his body and all? Do you all swim together or something?"

He hesitates, looks down, then up at me with the worried look of a child, "Well, yes, but at other times, too."

"What do you mean?" I grab a pair of some designer's blue jeans and pull them on. "Drew, what do you mean by 'other times'?"

"Oh, it's nothing," he says, turns, and starts to walk out of the closet.

"Hey, Drew, wait a minute. You know, now that we know each other as brothers, we can count on each other, can't we?"

He turns around, a worried look fading into a look of excited anticipation, "Well, yeah, that would be really cool, Philip."

"It would be cool, Drew. You see, Billy and I were close friends, more than just brothers. Well, now that he's gone, I need someone like you to rely on. We can help each other out. You know a guy needs a guy to help him out sometimes. You know. Sorta like you rely on your cousin Randy for advice and stuff." At the mention of Randy's name, Drew's face drops.

"Yeah, well, I'd rather have you than Randy. He can be such a bully sometimes."

"Oh yeah? How so, Drew?"

"Well, sometimes when I go over to his house, he makes me do things I don't want to do."

"Oh really, like what?"

"Well, I promised him I'd never tell anyone. He said if I did, he'd tell our parents that all this was my idea, that I was showing him what my gay brother did."

I'm stunned, "Drew, this is just the type of thing I was talking about. You can count on me and I can count on you. If Randy is doing something to you that doesn't seem right, I can help you out with it."

"Well, I'm afraid if he finds out that I told anyone, he'll get really mad and do something bad to me."

"Drew, I swear to you that will not happen. You can count on me. What is he doing to you?"

"Well, he practices sex on me," he says, looking up at me, his eyes framed by long dark lashes, his visage so innocent looking.

"And how does he do that, Drew?"

He sighs loudly, heaving his little stout frame up and down, searching my eyes with his for a safety zone. "He rubs his penis on me until he gets off. Sometimes he makes me bend over and he sticks it up my butt. It really hurts." He begins to cry. I fall to my knees, embrace him, pulling him into me, feeling his strong little body pulsating with grief, feeling him collapsing into me. I hold him, stoking his head with my right hand.

"It's going to be okay, Drew. You and I will take care of this together. I promise Randy will never hurt you again. Never. Nor will he bully you or do anything to hurt you or any member of our family. Trust me. I can take care of this."

"You can? How?" He pulls back, looking into my face, tear trails running down his face.

"Drew, the same thing happened to me when I was your age."

"It did?"

"Yes, it did. It was a grown man, and he did bad things to Billy and me. And we never told anyone. But we should have."

"Why didn't you tell?"

"The same reason you haven't. He tricked us into believing that if we did, something bad would happen to our parents."

"Really?"

"Yeah, really. Hey, guess what?"

"What?"

"You have to believe me, but you will not ever have to worry about this again or even think about it."

"Really?"

"That's right. I'm going to talk to your parents and we'll handle this. What Randy did to you is wrong. Sometimes when kids hit puberty, they do stupid things, but they should never do things to hurt other people. Your mother and Aunt Pam will take care of Randy. He probably needs help dealing with all the feelings that go along with maturing."

"Oh, I don't know. He'll try to get me back if you tell them."

"No he won't, Andrew. I promise. You have to believe me. I've had a lot of experience in these matters. You will be safe. And remember if anyone, anyone ever again tries to do that to you again, go straight to your mom and dad and tell them. And you know you can always tell me."

His face brightens; he smiles, throws his arms around my neck and says, "You're a great brother, Philip."

"So are you, little man. So are you."

"Philip?"

"Yes."

"Well, sometimes I get frightened when I think I'll have to grow up and get married." The worried look has returned to his face.

"That's enough to frighten anyone," I say with a chuckle.

"I just don't think I'll ever want to marry a girl. I mean I like girls like Emma and all. But I just don't want to get married." He examines my face for a response.

"Drew, you've got a long time to figure out who you are and who you will grow up to be. Don't be too worried about that now. Enjoy being a boy. Just follow your heart." I punch his chest with my right index finger. "Follow your true inside, your gut feelings and you'll be fine."

He looks relieved.

"Andrew, did Randy ever do any of this stuff to Peter?"

"No, I don't think so. They were always best friends until Randy became a teenager. Besides, Peter may act gentle and do sissy stuff like play the piano."

"Playing the piano isn't sissy, Drew," I interject.

"I know. But Randy says it is. Anyway, Peter is strong, and could beat up Randy anytime he wanted to, even now. No body messes with Peter after they see him mad."

"Interesting," I reply.

"Anyway, I was supposed to come in to tell you that breakfast is ready," Andrew says.

"Okay, buddy. I'll be right out. Now remember, your days worrying about Randy are over."

"Okay, Philip. Thanks." He smiles, turns around, and runs out of the closet.

It feels really good to me that Andrew confided in me. That had to be a hard thing for a little boy to do, but he must sense somehow that I, too, am damaged goods, that I was subjected to an unnatural sexual force as a child. I wonder what psychiatrists would say is a natural progression for children to learn about sex? Masturbation? Television? Siblings? Friends? Because of Adrian, sex was always foremost in my mind as a child, a teenager, and adult, hell, even now. Billy and I carried on like rabbits in heat until my strong desire to be with women made me dread having sex with him, even to the point of where it disgusted me. But then, I turned to masturbation, visualizing having sex with women, all kinds of women that I found in easily obtainable dirty magazines at boarding school. And then college and the first week of classes I met Lush who was so eager to go to bed with me—we did everything sexually I could imagine. She was so willing, so aggressive. How was this so, especially for a virgin? I wonder if she was sexually abused at some point in her life? She's never mentioned it. Perhaps she's pushed it back into her mind so far, se can't even recall it, much like I have done with Adrian and Billy over the years. Shit, just because I'm a product of total dysfunction doesn't mean every one else is. But still, little Andrew sensed something in me; I just know it. He knew I would understand, could help him—that's why he waited for me in the closet. Funny that phrase should come up, but I really suspect Andrew is gay. Billy used to have the greatest fear of growing up and having to marry a woman. Fatgram would always say things like, 'Now when you boys grow up and get married, I'm going to give you this pattern of sterling flatware and this set of china. I know it doesn't mean much to you now, but I can assure you your wives will appreciate it.' Billy would glaze over and confide in me later. 'Philly, do I really have to get married? I don't wanna. Fatgram and Mother will kill me though if I don't. I'll just run away when I get big—run away and never come back.' I pull on a pair of blue wool socks and slip my feet into a pair of expensive, black Italian, leather, ankle-high boots with side zippers. I find a beautiful cable knit, V-neck, cashmere sweater, softer than a down pillow, woven tightly with green, blue, and black yarns, pull it over my head, decide I don't need a belt, glance at myself in a full length mirror, feeling satisfied that I look anything but homeless. I walk down the hall, turn right down the side hall to the kitchen in order to avoid whichever officer guards over the living room and foyer this morning, and enter the kitchen where everyone is gathered around the breakfast table, eating, talking, and laughing. The warm atmosphere draws me in and everyone looks up as I enter. Clark runs over, jumps up thrusting his front paws to my waist, panting happily, awaiting a pat on his head.

"Good morning, Clarkster," I say stroking his head.

"My, don't you look handsome today," Brenda says, smiling, holding a white coffee mug in her hands.

"Why thank you, Brenda," I say, smiling, "Billy has such wonderful clothes, they'd make any man look good. My clothes are barely suited for a homeless person compared to these."

Brenda's smile fades. I immediately feel guilty for taking such a cheap shot back at her.

"Good morning, Philip. What can I make you for breakfast?" Lois asks in a voice that sounds particularly gravelly this morning, and I imagine that she must have been really partying last night.

"Oh, let's see, black coffee, wheat toast with a little cream cheese and a couple pieces of bacon. Thanks, Lois."

"Bacon's already fried. Here's some java, black, and I'll pop the toast in now." She pours coffee into a mug and hands it to me.

"Here, I'll put the toast in, Lois," Tammy says. She and Lois both are dressed in the same grey service dresses with white collars and white shoes. Tammy must assist Lois quite a bit to own her own dress, I think.

"Philip, come sit beside me," Emma says in an excited tone.

"Okay, darling."

"Son, Lush says you and Julianna have some business to attend to this morning at her gallery," Dad, who looks more rested today than I've seen him all week, says.

"Yes, a few things she wants to be completed before tonight. She would like to display a couple of his latest works at the wake. I think it is a great idea. We're going to select them this morning and go over what she plans to say about them," I reply as I squeeze in between Emma and Drew. Clark walks under the table and puts his head in my lap. I pat his head.

"We've got everything under control and lined out here," Lush says, "Ricky's crew will arrive at nine o'clock, and I have the presentation ready. It will play on all the plasma TV's in the house. Peter and I have coordinated the music so that he will play the piano for a half hour as guests arrive, then for twenty minutes before and after your tribute to Billy, which should be at eight, and then twenty minutes at nine thirty when a lot of people will be leaving. The rest of the time, Billy's favorite songs will play."

"That all sounds great, Lush. So you've got all the electronic stuff figured out?"

"I do and I must say Peter was a great help in helping me program every thing. Anything we can't handle, I'll get Mabry to work it out later today."

Peter looks up from his plate of scrambled eggs and bacon, smiles, then looks back down. "Thanks Peter," I say.

"No problem, Philip. I enjoyed helping Ms. Richardson," he says looking up at me again.

"Now Peter, I told you to call me Lush," Lush says.

"Yes mam, Lush," he says. We all laugh.

"I can't wait to see the roses," Emma says.

"They'll be here this morning, honey," Brenda says, "And you can inspect every one of them to make sure they are of the best quality." Emma claps her hands, picks up a slice of bacon, bites off a tiny piece, chews rapidly, swallows, bites off another piece, smiles up at me, then feeds the remainder of the piece of bacon to Clark, who makes a sound halfway between a grunt and a gasp as he snaps up the bacon. Lois brings over a plate with wheat toast, cream cheese, and four slices of bacon on it, sits it in front of me, and hands me a fork, a knife, and a linen napkin.

"Thanks, Lois. Perfect."

Clark looks up at me, whining, begging for bacon.

"No sir, you've had enough of Emma's bacon, you're not getting mine. Has he been fed?"

"Yes, son. I fed him at six thirty this morning, then took him out for a stroll in the snow," Dad says.

"Thanks, Dad. Did you have a police escort?"

"Yes, we did. Nice guy, Officer O'Daniel. Says he has a pit bull named Ludwig. Named him for Beethoven, he said." Dad leans back in his chair, pulling his shoulders back together, stretching his chest out.

"Well, that makes sense, you should hear him play the piano. He's a graduate of Julliard," I say, looking at Lush's face as she sips her coffee, witnessing the formation of the tiniest bit of a smile emerging on her face.

"Really," Brenda says as she looks at Peter whose attention has shifted from his food to me at the mention of Julliard.

"Yes, he played for us at Julianna's gallery yesterday. He's indeed a trained concert pianist. Isn't that right, Lush?"

"Yes, he's quite talented. You must ask him to play for you, Peter. I think you'd enjoy it," Lush says.

"Oh, I will. Philip, could I go down and ask him to come up to play?" Peter's curly blonde locks fall over his forehead, cascading over his eyebrows. I look into his blue eyes and wonder about the rage Andrew referred to. Where does that come from?

"Of course you can, as soon as you finish your breakfast," I reply.

"Oh, thanks" he replies and begins to quickly finish eating his food.

"I wonder how he got from Julliard to the police force?" Brenda asks.

"Well, something having to do with retribution, I believe," Lush replies, "You see, his father was with the NYPD and was murdered during a drug raid."

"Does everyone get murdered in New York?" Emma asks, wrinkling her delicate forehead with a worried look.

"No, darling, not everyone," Brenda replies, "Only a very few people who happen to be in the wrong place at the wrong time."

"So was Billy in the wrong place at the wrong time?"

Brenda looks at me for help answering this, so I reply, "Yes, Emma he was. He didn't realize it, or he wouldn't have gone there, but he was."

"Oh," she says, picks up a piece of white toast with grape jelly spread over it, takes a small bite, puts the toast back on her plate, looks up at me, and says, "Why'd you let him go, Philip?"

"I wasn't here in New York, Emma. I was at home in Atlanta. I didn't even know he had gone anywhere."

"Well, where did he go to get murdered, anyway?"

"At a disco," Andrew replies.

"Children," Brenda abruptly interjects, "we've got a lot to do and you all promised Lois to help, so let's get going." She stands up, collecting plates.

"But what about Officer O'Daniel?" Peter asks.

"Darling, go into the living room and ask Officer Kelly to phone Officer O'Daniel to see if he'd mind coming up to play for us. But we don't have long, we've got a lot to do, so only a song or two, Peter."

"Okay, Mom. Thanks." He gets up and heads out of the kitchen, followed by Drew, Emma, and Clark. Tammy begins cleaning off the table.

"More coffee, anyone?" Lois asks as she approaches the table with the French press.

Dad and Brenda decline, but Lush and I desire more. "Lush, since you're all done with the presentation, maybe you'd better come down to Julianna's with me. You could keep Officer O'Daniel company while I talk with Julianna."

She looks at me with a look of mistrust, but then the truth registers in her mind. "Yes, you're right. I wouldn't want him disturbing you all or trying to listen in to a private conversation about Billy's works."

"How long will you all be?" Brenda asks.

"Oh, just a couple of hours at most. We should be back by lunch," I reply.

"Good. Remember Ricky is providing lunch for us all today. I'm sure it will be wonderful," Brenda says as she gathers silverware from the table.

"Dad, I like the way you are wearing your hair now, longer, brushed back," I smile at him, wondering if I will age as well as he is aging. In my mind, his looks are frozen in his late twenties, with his dark hair, bright blue eyes, and dark complexion. Mother always said he must have Cherokee in him.

"Thanks, son. Brenda suggested it. It was hard for me to get used to it, but I like it now."

"Don't you all think it makes him look sophisticated and younger?" Brenda asks, putting the silverware in a sink.

"Very," Lush replies, "And I love that you don't try to cover up the grey, Charles."

"Thanks, Lush. I can't see myself coloring my hair," Dad replies looking a little self-conscious with all the attention.

"I agree, Lush," Brenda says, "The salt and pepper hair just enhances his good looks."

"Yes sir, Mr. Hampton, you could give George Clooney a run for his money in the looks department," Lois chimes in from the kitchen.

"Ladies, ladies, your compliments are greatly appreciated but totally blown out of proportion," Dad states looking completely embarrassed.

"Charles doesn't handle praise well," Brenda says. "Just last year he was approached by a modeling agency in St. Louis to do photo shoots and a TV commercial."

"Really, Dad? That's great."

"Oh, I didn't have time for all that. We've got a business to run."

"Charles, that's great," Lush says. "God forbid the furniture business ever hits the doldrums, but if it does, it's comforting to know you've got a potential modeling career to fall back on."

We all laugh, even Dad.

"Okay, okay. Let's get up and prepare to get this show on the road," Dad says. "Ricky's crew will be here at nine, and I will be orchestrating the rearrangement of furniture and the cleaning of the terrace for guests."

"You get the manly chores, Dad," I say.

"That's right son. We men must supply our brute strength to these lovely, but frail ladies."

Lois lets out a big laugh, "Mr. Hampton, I've been called many things in my life, but frail was never mentioned by anyone."

Everyone laughs again. "Well, while we prepare to hear Officer O'Daniel's short concert," Lush interjects, "I'm going to take a cup of coffee and a cigarette out on the terrace. Any takers?"

"Sure," I reply.

"No thanks," Brenda says, "I've got to return a few phone calls after we clear this table."

"You go ahead, Mrs. Hampton," Lois says, "Tammy and I will make quick work of all this."

"Thanks, Lois," Brenda replies, "Charles, maybe you'd better make certain the children don't overwhelm Officer O'Daniel."

"Good idea, honey."

Lush and I take our coffee and head out onto the terrace. The sky is cloudless, robin's egg blue, and calm. The climbing sun has initiated a thaw over the city and the snow on the terrace, fluffy and frozen just an hour ago is turning into a watery mush. I focus on the sound of traffic moving through the wet slush below as a flock of at least a dozen pigeons of varying colors swoosh across the terrace making a uniform direct nosedive to the streets below.

"Wow, what weird weather," Lush says as she puts her coffee mug on a brick wall, pulls out her cigarettes from a large front pocket in the belted, long black sweater she wears, and offers me one.

"Thanks, my final day," I say as I take two cigarettes from her pack.

"Final day is good, at least for smoking, anyway," she says smiling as she hands me her gold lighter. I put both cigarettes in my mouth, light them, hand her one, take a sip of my coffee, then set the mug down on the wall beside Lush's mug.

"Thanks for agreeing to go to Julianna's. It will be much easier for us to escape out her back door to meet Jonas and Mabry if you are with Officer O'Daniel."

"No problem. I'm surprised we didn't think of that earlier," she says, fishing her Chanel sunglasses out of the other pocket on her sweater.

"What a treat for O'Daniel to have you all to himself for a couple of hours in Julianna's beautiful gallery," I say in a teasing tone.

"Yes, no telling what we'll get into with all that time on our hands," she replies as she puts on the sunglasses.

"Well, as distasteful as it is to me, I think you two look good together," I offer taking a big drag off my cigarette.

"Christ Todge, just because I think he's cute and interesting doesn't mean I'll be screwing him on Julianna's sofa this morning," she says as I watch the muscles in her neck tighten.

"Well, it's as plain as day that he's smitten with you. And why shouldn't he be? You have a lot to offer any man."

She smiles, leans over, kisses my left cheek, the smell of a sweet, subtle floral perfume lingering in the air as she pulls back saying, "You're such a darling. Even after all we've been through. I really love you, Todge."

"And I love you, Lush."

We both smile, silent for a moment until Clark jumps up on the door leading from the kitchen, crying to be let out. I walk over, open the door, he runs out onto the terrace commencing a sniffing expedition as Lush and I hear the sound of a beautiful, somewhat melancholy piece of piano music emanating from inside.

"Peter succeeded with O'Daniel. Listen to that, isn't it beautiful?" I ask, wishing I could see Lush's eyes through the dark sunglasses.

She smiles, "Debussy, he's playing 'Claire de Lune'," she says, picks ups her mug, sips her coffee turning her head toward me.

"Debussy? Isn't he the composer that wrote a bunch of romantic pieces?" I ask.

"Yes, he did—some of my favorite piano pieces," she replies holding the mug close to her lips, pursing them, blowing a cooling stream of air into the steaming mug, smoke from the cigarette she still holds between the index and middle fingers of her right hand curling over and into the steam.

"Did you tell him that?" I ask, somewhat defensively.

"Tell who what?" She snaps back.

"O'Daniel, that you love Debussy!" I reply, then sigh loudly.

"I don't think I did. I suppose I could have, but no, I don't think I did. Why does it matter, Todge?"

"Well, he's obviously hot for you."

"And?"

"And I just don't think you should go throwing yourself at some young stud cop who plays the piano like Liberace," I reply already wishing I could keep my tongue at bay.

"Huh. He hardly plays like Liberace," she states, takes a drag off her cigarette, exhales, looking at me as if she wants to pout.

"Todge, don't be so protective or jealous or whatever."

I sigh loudly again and kick at the terrace with my right foot. "I know, I know. It's just, it's just a natural reaction for me. Especially now that I know about our baby and everything."

"I guess that makes me feel loved, looked after. I guess that's sweet, Todge," she says pulling off her glasses with her left hand, focusing on my eyes, "But, Todge, do you really think there's more for us than what we already have?"

"I don't know, Lush. I don't know. I mean I fucked it all up for us." I take another big drag off my cigarette, fling it into the snow; it emits a short, faint sizzle catching Clark's attention who trots over to sniff it. "Leave it, Clark," I say angrily. He immediately looks up questioning me with a surprised, hurt look on his face.

"Leave it is what we should do with this conversation, Todge."

Lush snuffs her cigarette out on the wall and sets her mug down. "We've been through it all before—all, that is, except for my abortion—and I don't see how rehashing it is going to do either of us any good. What we have is good—good for me and good for you, at least, I hope."

251

"Oh shit, I suppose. It just pisses me off thinking that O'Daniel may end up having everything with you that I could have had."

"That's a sincere, brave thing to say, Todge. You've become a very kind man."

We look into each other's eyes, searching, communicating with no words. Clark, thinking from my tone to him that he's done something wrong, walks over, nudges my right calf with his nose, looking up at me for affirmation.

I squat down, hug him, pulling his compact body into me, "You're just a little bear and a good little bear at that. I love you, Little Bear." He wags his tail wildly, licks my face as I raise it to look up at Lush with her head framed by the bright morning sunlight, her beautiful long hair gently rustling in the breeze, her white teeth showing through her gorgeous, voluptuous red lips, the picture of a magnificent angel-woman, and I become thrilled inside by the love I feel for her and for Little Bear while at the same time feeling like a little boy again, and I'm certain it is the voice of the little boy in me that says, "Lush, don't ever say 'your abortion' again, ever. That was my abortion even though it happened to your body."

The beauty of her smile fades, her visage takes on a saintly look, a look of one whose sole purpose is to dispense care and love, a look that stirs my wrecked emotions forcing tears from both my eyes as the light from the sun surrounding her face intensifies to an almost blinding level, yet I see her hands reaching for me, so I grab them, letting her pull me up into her arms, into her strength which I crave, into her control as she uses her left hand to direct my head to rest on her left shoulder as she whispers into my right ear, "Our abortion, Todge, our abortion."

CHAPTER 28

Jonas tells the building super, a plump, bald man with bushy brown eyebrows and thick, meaty, hairy hands, that the installation of the new hot water heater will take at least an hour, and to our surprise, the super replies that's okay because he has things to do and will check back in an hour or so, or to call him on his cell if we finish sooner. He hands Jonas his card and leaves us in the foyer of Adrian's apartment with the new water heater on a dolly and two large red toolboxes Jonas and Mabry brought.

"Okay, guys," Jonas says. "Let's all go into the utility closet first where we will wait for Mabry to find the surveillance controls and deactivate them. The super says there's nothing but simple motion detectors he turned off before we got here, but I'm not buying that. After we deactivate, Mabry and I will install the heater as fast as we can."

"Okay, sounds good," I say.

Mabry takes some sort of small metering device in his hands, squats down on the floor, slides his tool belt around so that the tools cover his ass, lays down on his stomach, and crawls out into the apartment on his elbows, pulling his legs behind him.

"Good luck, Mabry," Julianna calls out in a whisper. He turns his head back around, smiling as he slithers away.

"Meanwhile," Jonas says, handing Julianna and me each a pair of latex surgical gloves, "you all put on these gloves and begin searching the apartment once Mabry returns."

"Okay, Jonas. Want us to help you get this new water heater out of the box?"

"Good idea, Philip." He opens the top of the box. "Here, I'll tilt it, grab the heater and you guys just pull the box away." We do that and the heater comes out easily. Jonas sits it upright, then looks at me.

"Philip, I think we should do a sweep through Billy's unit to see if we find any bugs. After reading some of those emails from Adrian, I have a hunch Adrian was privy to more than just what went on in the secret room."

"Really, Jonas?" I ask.

"It's a good possibility," he replies.

"Well, if he has been listening, then he knows everything we're up to, even coming here today," I remark.

"I pretty much think that's the situation, but time will tell," Jonas says looking around the utility room. "Great, there's a drain in the floor here. I'm going to get started with this." He goes over to the heater, closes off the gas and water supply lines, then opens a valve on the bottom of the heater. Hot water pours out onto the floor, runs into the drain, leaving wisps of steam filling up the utility room.

"Dear, I don't think we're dressed for a sauna," Julianna remarks.

Jonas laughs, "It will dissipate quickly." He takes an adjustable wrench from one of the toolboxes and says, "I'm going to get started by unhooking the gas line." He adjusts the wrench to fit over a coupling and pulls on the wrench. "Geez, this has been on a while. Julianna, would you mind handing me that hammer with the blue handle?"

"Certainly," she says as she bends over, takes the hammer out of the tool box, hands it to Jonas, straightens back up, her eyes fixed on the wrench and coupling. Jonas taps the hammer against the handle of the wrench with quick precise strokes. The coupling begins to turn. He places the hammer on the floor, puts his hands back on the wrench turning the coupling with his own strength. The process is slow as he has to keep removing the wrench and readjusting it each time the handle reaches the floor. Finally, the coupling releases the two steel gas lines it holds.

"Okay, that looks like about a six inch nipple on the heater," Jonas says and begins rummaging through the toolbox. "Looks like we brought four, five, six, seven and eight inch nipples, so we should be okay there. I'll just leave that one on the old heater." He looks through the toolbox, pulls out some sort of red clamp device, effortlessly rises to a standing position with the clamp in his hands, and begins to examine the top of the heater.

"What's that in your hands, Jonas?" Julianna asks.

"It's a pipe cutter. I'm trying to figure out where best to cut the water supply line and the hot water output line. You see, with this type of copper piping, we have to use solder to join the fittings to the pipe. I want to minimize the number of welds Mabry has to execute to give us more time to search this place. Let's see, here and here should do just fine." He takes the cutter, turns the steel screw closing the jaws of the cutter that contains four little sharp, shiny, steel wheels. He spins the cutter around and around the pipe. After about a minute the first cut is complete.

"Wow, that was pretty fast," I observe.

"Yeah, copper is a relatively soft metal, so it cuts easily," Jonas replies as he executes the second cut even faster than the first. Right as the pipe gives way, freeing the old heater from any connections, Mabry walks in.

"All done," he smiles, taking off his ball cap and pulling his curly locks over his ears on both sides.

"Sweet, any complications?" Jonas asks.

"Negative. A lot more than just motion detectors, though. Twenty-four cameras and a microphone in every room—all remotely controlled via the Internet. I turned the mics off and the cameras will continue to transmit a shot taken an hour ago. It will take someone a while to figure out anything's wrong with the system." He radiates confidence.

"The system had to be password protected, so how did you manage that, Mabry?" I ask. "Pretty easy for me. I developed the software for this type of security system when I was in graduate school, so I know all the loopholes," he replies.

"Fascinating," Julianna remarks.

"All right, folks, let's get this show on the road," Jonas says, rubbing his hands together.

"Yes, let's get started, Philip," Julianna says, "See you two in a bit." We leave the utility closet, pass through the kitchen, and head down the hall to the living room.

"Okay, I remember the layout of the place pretty well," I reply as I scan the living room, "and from what I can see so far, it doesn't look as though it's changed much in twenty years. It even smells the same."

"You okay, Philip?" Julianna asks as she stretches a glove over the long fingers of her left hand.

"Yeah, I'm fine. It's just weird being here again after all these years," I reply, walk into the living room surveying everything. "I swear, Julianna, it's exactly as I remember, nothing's changed."

She follows me, remarking, "Exquisite taste in furniture. He certainly liked the Louis's. I don't think I've seen so many high quality French Renaissance pieces in a long time. It's easy to see where Billy got his taste for Boulle work."

"Curious, isn't it, Cindy?" I ask, turning toward her, observing how out of place she appears in the bright blue worker's jumpsuit we all wear with the company name and our phony names embroidered in red on the front pockets. It's not just the clothes that make her look so different, but it's the fact that she wears no make up at all. I've got to have a picture of this. I pull the digital camera from my pocket, aim and focus on her.

"Smile, Cindy."

"Sure, Sam. Here, get me in front of this gorgeous Louis Fourteenth armoire," she instructs, striking a game show model's pose with the armoire. I chuckle as I take the picture.

The room is large and dark, all the draperies are closed, the light from the two crystal chandeliers lights the center of the room, leaving the walls in shadows.

"It looks like some sort of religious shrine in here," Julianna remarks as her eyes adjust to the dim lighting and she takes in the artwork, panels, extracted frescoes, crucifixes, and relics. She gasps, "My God, Philip, I had no idea Adrian had such a collection of Italian Renaissance works. He's got pieces from the Proto-Renaissance through the High-Renaissance and Mannerism."

"Yeah, Mother always called it his 'Tomb of Catholicism'," I reply.

"This Madonna is definitely a Raphael," she says, then turns toward me, "I'm simply overwhelmed, Philip. This is so unexpected, and unknown in the art world. All these pieces are extremely important pieces. Why isn't it known that he had these?"

"Well, you know how secretive Adrian was, rather, is. He never entertained here, only at clubs and restaurants. Mother certainly knew about all this, she spent days in here studying pieces," I reply.

"Damn, Billy never told me that. I knew I should have picked your brains more while I was working on Eva's catalogue raisonné. I'll simply have to update it now. It's so clear to me now," she says putting her right latex covered index finger to her lips.

"What's so clear to you now?"

"The juxtaposition of characters," she replies, heading toward another fresco remnant hanging in an alcove.

"What juxtaposition?" I ask.

"What an epiphany." Julianna exclaims with a look of sheer joy on her face.

"What are you talking about, Julianna?"

"Philip, your mother was more of a genius than I ever imagined. I mean she was a major artist in her own right. But in all my years of research on her works, there was always something so familiar about the juxtaposition of many of the people she painted, especially the black field workers." She taps her forehead with her left hand. "What a dunce I am."

"I'm still not sure what you are talking about?" I reply, shrugging my shoulders.

"Your mother was heavily influenced by the position of all these, and other religious characters. I'm certain of it. What I mean is that those field hands, and white cracker dirt farmers, and garden club ladies, and you and Billy, were her angels, Madonnas, and Christ figures."

"Humm," I reply.

"Philip, remember the painting I have of Willie B lifting a bale of golden hay onto a high pile on a flat-bed truck?"

"Yeah, I remember."

"And the field workers, women with kerchiefs, men with straw hats, the agony of their labor on their faces, all handing bales up to Willie B whose expression is so serene, calm, almost holy?"

"Yeah."

"Well, think of Willie B as Christ on the cross and the field workers as the grieving disciples."

"Got it," I reply.

"Oh dear, we've got to hurry," she says, pulling a digital camera out of her jumpsuit. "Let's turn on some of these lamps, we've got to photograph everything in here. I've simply got to document this."

"Are you sure, Julianna? I mean, what's all this religious stuff have to do with Billy and Mother's murders?" I ask, frustrated.

"My hunch is an awful lot. Now, you take that side of the room. Get the furniture and relics, too. My God, that looks like a human finger bone over there in that glass dome. Let's hurry," she instructs.

"It is. Some saint's. Billy would know. He was always fascinated by it. I just thought it was gross."

As we engage in a photographing frenzy I relate to Julianna my recent discoveries about Brooker T's identity and Mother's love affair with Willie B. She listens intently as I recap what I learned from Brooker T and Dad, continuously snapping, intermittently demanding details of Mother's past I cannot supply. After about fifteen minutes, we've completed our photographic catalog of Adrian's living room. I walk over to Julianna and notice that she has tears in her eyes.

"What's the matter, Julianna?" I ask.

"I'm fine. I'm just overwhelmed by all this beautiful art and the connection Eva had to it and the influence it had on her works. I can't explain it, but it stirs me deeply."

"I think I understand," I reply, smiling at her. "Shall we move on to the other rooms?"

"Yes, let's go," she says, dabbing her eyes with a Kleenex she pulls from an ornately carved box. She stuffs the tissue into her pocket. "We can't leave a trace of anything."

As we move into Adrian's study, I turn on a couple of light switches revealing a richly paneled room with a Boulle desk, bookcases lining the walls, and built in cabinets containing slots for canvasses.

"My God, Philip, this looks like Billy's studio," Julianna exclaims.

"Yes it does, I guess I never really made that connection before," I reply. My stomach turns, and I fill up inside with dread and despair, the relentless, aching sensation permeating my bones, my soul, my essence, of understanding that I will never see Billy again, that I will never see his smile, never respond to his erratic phone calls, never feel his strong arms embracing me, never luxuriate in his presence during an evening of drink, food and conversation, never rest well in peace and contentment with the knowledge that he's there if I need him, never grow old with him. My eyes fill with tears as I watch Julianna pull out canvasses from the bins.

"Philip, we've got to photograph these, also. You realize Julian lied about vacating this apartment. These bins are completely full; nothing's been packed up and moved. He's got works from major artists in here."

Once again, as I have so many times this week, I quell my tears. I join Julianna in removing canvasses and photographing them. Most of them are unfamiliar to me, but Julianna rattles off artists' names like a confident sixth grader rattles off letters in a spelling bee, until suddenly I pull out a canvas that takes my breath away with the same ferocity as the time I fell off the jungle gym while pretending I was a gymnast in

the sixth grade, landing flat on my back on the hard dirt, gasping for breath, kids all around me screaming out to the teachers that I was dying. It is a beautiful water scene, a river flowing through a wooded area. On the near bank of the river is a sort of small fishing pier. On the far side is a blue shack. The reflections of the shack, the trees, and the sky in the water are extraordinarily beautiful. It is the same painting Mother was painting in my nightmare Monday morning. I'm frozen looking at the painting. Julianna approaches me, observing the painting.

"What? It isn't. An unknown painting by your Mother." She grabs the canvas, her eyes reading every square inch of it. "It's Eva's, alright, it couldn't be a fake, look at the signature." She flips the canvas over, "Nothing en verso. Hmmn. I wonder if our pedophile art genius has a black light around here anywhere?" She sets the painting down, moves to a built in cabinet and starts opening drawers.

"Voila," she pulls out a small light fixture, plugs it into an outlet, presses a black button, and the bulb lights up into a purplish glow. "Philip, bring that over here, I want to scan it with this light."

"Okay," I reply like a zombie. I'm dumbfounded by my visionary dream, the possibility that Mother communicated with me from the spirit world, and I pick up the painting and walk over to Julianna, knowing that she wants to check the signature with the black light and check the progression of the painting to see if Mother over painted any features or otherwise altered the original. I place the painting on an easel and Julianna waves the black light over it. Immediately, beautiful calligraphy appears in the water of the river in bright phosphorescent blue: *Happy thirteenth, darling Philip. You'd love the fishing here. Love, Mother.* Julianna's mouth is agape as she turns to look at my face.

"Mother wrote to me that summer that she was working on a special present for my thirteenth birthday. I always thought she died before she finished it," I say, tears running down my face. "I waited all summer for Mother to return with this, I've been waiting my whole life. Thank you, Mother. Thank you so much. It's beautiful." I feel thirteen again as Julianna embraces me, and I lean my head into her breast, crying as a child cries.

After a while, I look up into Julianna's face, pleading, "This has to stop at some point; I just can't cry anymore. I just can't cry anymore; there's nothing left inside me. I saw that painting in a dream about Mother and Billy the morning he died. I don't know what to think anymore. I'm just a shell."

"No you're not a shell, Philip. You're a man who's been through hell and back in a few days. But you are also answering the great questions of your life. You will emerge from this, Philip. You will emerge as a stronger man—a man with deep love and emotion for others and yourself. You will get through this; I know it."

Her words ring true to me, but in this moment I feel as if my heart is eaten up with some raging cancer that will not stop until my soul is destroyed—and I recognize that cancer as Adrian.

"Philip, I don't mean to be crass, but we must finish photographing these. We've got to move on."

"You're right," I say, sniffing, wiping my nose on the right sleeve of my jump suit.

"Oh, by the way, we're definitely taking your birthday present with us. We can put it in the box with the old hot water heater. No one will see us leave with it. After all, it is rightly yours. That evil bastard, Adrian." She goes back to removing more canvasses and we begin to photograph them. Our fast past work is punctuated by exclamations from Julianna such as 'So that's where this ended up,' 'I haven't seen this in fifteen years,' 'Certainly one of her best works,' 'This alone is worth a fortune,', and 'How did he get his hands on this one?' We continue cataloging art in the room until we finish and decide we better check in with Jonas and Mabry.

They have also worked quickly, completing the entire installation in less than thirty minutes. Julianna and I watch in silence as Mabry solders the copper fitting connecting the water supply line to the water heater. Jonas holds it in place with some type of pliers as Mabry meticulously melts the solder around the fitting with a torch, beads of perspiration shining through on his forehead where his curly bangs are parted, his glasses imperceptibly inch down his long nose as he focuses intently on the torch, his brown eyes and

the blue flame reflecting in the round lenses of his glasses. He has not shaved in a few days revealing the patchy beard of a young man, thick around his chin, upper lip and sideburns but sparse on his cheeks. I imagine he's hoping to conceal some of the eruptions of acne on his face as I notice a particularly virulent pustule under his left jawbone and I remember that during my late teens how I experienced embarrassing and painful bouts of acne from time to time which I finally got under control with a drug called Retin A. Billy sailed through his teens and early twenties without so much as a blackhead on his face. Mabry is as skilled a plumber as he is a code cracker. I wonder how someone so young acquired these skills.

"That should do it," Mabry says, pulling away the torch, shutting it off, stepping back to observe his work.

"Nice work, Mabry," Jonas says as he begins to pack away tools, "This should pass inspection with flying colors."

"Where did you learn to do that, Mabry?" Julianna asks.

"Oh, my Dad and uncle run a machine shop back home. I spent a lot of time in there growing up," he says, shyly, avoiding Julianna's eyes.

"I see," she replies, "Where's home?"

"Schenectady," he replies, glances up at Julianna, then back down to the bottom of the newly installed heater.

"Let's get this old heater in the box and on the dolly and we're done," Jonas says. "Did you all make any discoveries?"

"Only about five hundred million dollars worth of art ranging from early Italian Renaissance to recent paintings."

"Wow, the plot thickens yet again." Jonas replies. "The super told me Mr. Ainsworth comes here only once or twice a year since Mr. McWhorter's death. But get this, the only time the apartment was really used during the past year was when Mr. Ainsworth let two Asian twin boys live here while they attended school in New York. He said that they were children of a business associate of Mr. Ainsworth's and that they had just moved out this week when Mr. Ainsworth came to town."

"Moved on to their next dimension you mean, which I hope is hell. The little bastards deserve to burn for eternity," I say.

"Right," Jonas replies. "Find anything else besides art?"

"No, but we didn't have time to check all the drawers. We got through the living room and study. I thought it was important to photograph the valuable things," Julianna replies.

"Well done, Julianna," Jonas replies, "I imagine Adrian keeps all this art here as a way to store wealth here without reporting it to anyone. I wonder even if it's insured?"

"Why would he do that?" I ask.

"For a variety of reasons," Jonas replies. "He may need large sums of money from time to time in the states. He could orchestrate an arms length, all cash sale with a collector. Who knows? Maybe some of this art is actually al-Qaeda's and it's here to finance terrorist cells and destructive plots."

"Nothing would surprise me about Adrian. He brings new meaning to the word diabolical," Julianna states, lifting the red baseball cap she wears to adjust her hair.

"Okay," Jonas picks up the two tool boxes, "Mabry and I will go through drawers and cabinets in the living room and study. You all check the bedrooms and baths. I already checked the kitchen, but didn't find anything. The only food we found were several boxes of ramen noodles. Perhaps Benny and Bernie's last meal?"

"Probably so," I reply.

Jonas moves out of the utility closet. "Philip, would you help me and Mabry with this old heater? We need to tilt it on its side, then slide it into this box."

"Sure thing."

"While you all do that, I'll go get the painting and wrap it with some of this bubble wrap in here," Julianna says.

"What painting?" Jonas asks.

"We found a painting of my Mother's that she did in France the summer Adrian murdered her. Julianna shined a black light on it. Mother had written an inscription to me in invisible fluorescent paint. She said the painting was for my thirteenth birthday. I turned thirteen the summer she died."

"Heavy," Mabry says, making brief eye contact with me before looking back at the old water heater.

"Yeah," I reply.

"Okay, go get it Julianna. We need to get moving, we've got about twenty minutes left in here," Jonas says as he begins to tilt the old water heater on its side. Mabry and I pick up the bottom of the heater, put it as far as we can inside the cardboard box, then all three of us lift up the box to cause the heater to slide completely in. Mabry and I tilt the box so Jonas can get the lip of the dolly underneath the bottom. Mabry and Jonas fasten two straps around the box to secure it to the dolly.

"Here's the painting," Julianna holds it up.

"That's beautiful," Jonas says, "Look at the reflections of the trees in the water, really stunning."

"Yes, some of Eva's best works are water scenes, she always got the light right—it's flawless, possibly one of the best of all her works. Philip, this birthday present of yours would easily bring a few million at auction."

"Wow," Mabry says, "A few million?"

"Absolutely, Mabry. And that bastard Julian has hidden this from Philip all these years. We've got to bring him down."

"Julianna. If we're going to do that, we've got to hurry," Jonas says, unrolling the bubble wrap. "Okay, let's wrap the painting and put it in the box."

As they wrap the painting, I try to visualize Mother on the bank of that lovely river in France, her easel set up, painting furiously, to capture 'the essence' of the light before it faded or intensified too much. Mother was a fast painter and did most of her landscapes plein air. She did not trust photographs or Polaroids, claiming that they couldn't capture the feeling and beauty she saw with her own eyes. She was relentless and tenacious in her efforts to execute the major parts of her oil paintings in real time. One winter, we spent a week at a condominium at Sugar Mountain in North Carolina so Dad could teach Billy and me how to ski. We had a fantastic week skiing, ice skating and sledding. One day we had several inches of new snow, but by evening the sky was clear, the temperature dropped to the low teens and a full moon rose up over the landscape, illuminating a big snow covered fir tree growing in a field behind the back deck of our condominium. Mother donned a thick wool sweater, opened the sliding doors, set up her easel just inside the door, and painted for hours as the moon traveled across the night sky. Dad, Billy and I put on our down ski jackets and pants and headed out for a magical walk among our moon shadows, throwing snowballs at each other, making snow angels, howling like wolves at the bright moon, waving to Mother as she painted, exhilarating in the briskness of the frigid mountain air and the softness of the deep snow. When we became tired and cold, Dad took us inside, dressed us in warm flannel pajamas, built up the fire, and made us hot chocolate. Billy and I lay by the fireplace on a blanket, watching the flames, talking about the best ski trails, turning our heads when we felt the occasional blast of cold air rushing through the room from where Mother painted. As I fell asleep to the sound of Billy's soft rhythmic snoring, I watched Dad walk up behind Mother, put his arms around her waist, and kiss her neck as she looked up at him, smiling. This is one of the few memories from childhood I ever allow behind the secret waterfall with me.

"Philip dear, are you ready to check out the bedrooms?" Julianna peers into my eyes. "You okay?"

"What? Oh, I'm fine. Let's go." I turn away from everyone, blinking away the tears beginning to form in my eyes, "I know the way very well."

We walk down the long, wide hallway leading to the back rooms, the hardwood parquet floors covered by three long, identical oriental runners, paintings adorn the walls, several centered over diminutive, antique, gate-leg tables, demilunes, and chests.

"Philip, is everything as you remembered it—I mean the furniture, the displayed artwork?" Julianna asks as we proceed down the hall.

"Pretty much. I mean I haven't been in here in over twenty years, but it pretty much looks and feels the same," I reply and turn into the first bedroom. "Let's start in here. This was mine and Billy's room." I hit the light switch. "Well I'll be damned."

"What is it, Philip?"

"Nothing's changed in here. It's exactly as it was all those years ago."

"Goodness, what is that in the corner?" Julianna says walking across the large bedroom toward the bunk beds Uncle Adrian had custom built to resemble a tree house, complete with wooden ladders, plank sides with open holes for windows, a wooden landing with a large cushion on it halfway between the bottom and top beds, bedspreads made from a material decorated with tree limbs and leaves, and a giant live oak tree painted on the corner walls and ceiling surrounding the bed.

"It's bunk beds built like a tree house," I reply.

"How wonderful, what an exciting bedroom for little boys," Julianna says as she examines the intricate construction of the bunk-bed-tree-house.

"Yes, very exciting, very enticing, very easy for Uncle Adrian to expand his Blood Brothers ritual right into this bedroom," I reply as I recall an image of Adrian sitting naked on the landing, Billy and I sitting naked on the top bunk, our legs dangling over, our crotches face-level with Adrian.

"Oh dear, Philip, I'm sorry. I forgot it happened here, too." An expression of pity and sadness shapes the porcelain skin on her face as she reaches for my hands.

"It's okay Julianna. It's just that now that I've opened up to you all, these memories seem to flood my mind."

"That's perfectly normal, Philip. That's a good sign, that's the path to healing yourself—reliving the abuse in a safe way with people you trust, people you love and who love you."

"You sound like a shrink, Julianna," I reply with a half smile, half smirk.

"Well, I certainly hope so, I've been in therapy over twenty years," she says without hesitation.

"Wow, what for?" I blurt out without thinking.

"Well, everyone has their own demons, their own issues they can't solve alone. Mine revolve around being too tall and too bright at too young of an age—nothing nearly so horrible as what you and Billy endured. Nonetheless, it's taken me a lifetime to overcome them. I couldn't have done it without therapy."

"I'm glad you found help, Julianna. Maybe I should go see a psychiatrist after all this is over with Adrain."

"Maybe you should, but I personally think you are well on the way to healing yourself. I have to tell you I thought seeing all of Billy's paintings would have shut you down, sent you packing, or infuriated you to extremes. I apologize."

"For what?"

"For misjudging you. I just didn't think you had Billy's sensitivity, but I was dead wrong. You opened up completely in front of us Wednesday afternoon and became totally vulnerable as a man in the presence of three strong-willed women. I've only seen that happened once before and that was in group therapy. I'm glad to have been a part of that, and I greatly admire you for it."

She gives me a hug and I hug her back, pulling her into me, feeling her thin waist, long thighs, and ample breasts pushing into my body.

"Thanks, Julianna, that means a lot to me to hear you say that," I say, releasing her, releasing the sexual desire that enters my mind. She looks at me, trying to ascertain the full meaning of my embrace

and then turns around. We walk back across the room to the chest of drawers against the wall. The chest is child height—about three feet tall—with an array of small drawers, the ten on the left half of the chest were mine, and the ten on the right half of the chest were Billy's. Three black and white eight by ten photographs in wide pewter frames sit on the chest along with two large, ornate wooden chests, one ebony with swirling braids of acanthus leaves done in gold leafing, the other a harlequin pattern in ebony and gold-leaf.

"Wonderful photographs, Philip. Let me guess, Adrian took these head shots of you and Billy."

"Yes he did. I was eleven here and Billy was nine. Mother loved these shots. She also loved this one of the three of us at an amusement park in Myrtle Beach." I turn the picture toward Julianna.

"Yes, I see why, it's quite good—the composition is wonderful. My, look how happy you all were. Eva was certainly a gorgeous woman—gorgeous and talented. See how perfectly the roller coaster and double Ferris wheel fit in the background with these beautiful fluffy clouds."

"Yeah, it was a great day. Mother was in the best of moods. She and Uncle Adrian let us spend the whole day at the amusement park playing games, riding rides, eating junk food like corn dogs and cotton candy."

"Sounds delightful. What are these beautiful boxes?"

"They're our treasure chests. The harlequin one is Billy's. The other one is mine."

"Treasure chests?" Julianna asks as she rubs the fingers of her right hand over Billy's treasure chest.

"Yes. See each one has a drawer in the bottom that you can pull out." I pull out the bottom drawer of Billy's chest. It is empty. "Uncle Adrian would surprise us with clues in the bottom drawers."

"Clues?" Julianna asks.

"Yes, clues for treasure hunts in the apartment, in the building, and sometimes around the city. It was quite exciting for us on our visits here, and he did it when he visited us in Union, too. His clues were always challenging for us—always made us learn something about art or history. We could never solve them without resorting to a dictionary, encyclopedia, or bugging Mother or Fatgram for information."

"And what were the treasures?"

"Wonderful, grand things, like antique gold coins, jewels, one hundred dollar bills, savings bonds, or tickets to shows."

"Extraordinary," Julianna replies with a puzzled look on her face. "And did you keep your treasures in these chests?"

"Usually. You see, they open at the top and inside each one has a rotating lock with a combination we could each set so that no one else would know it—not even Uncle Adrian." I move toward my box and open the top. "My favorite number is four, so my combination was always 4,4,4,4." I dial in the numbers, open the chest, look inside and see a photograph on the bottom. I pick it up. "Damn, it's an old Polaroid. Who is this guy? What's that he's holding?"

"You don't know who this is?" Julianna asks, taking it from my hands. "It looks like he's holding a finial, a gilded eagle finial, that goes on the top of a piece of furniture or maybe a lamp or a flagpole or something."

"Well, I don't know who the hell he is or what his picture's doing in my treasure chest," I remark examining the slim man who has brown hair, a short beard, and gold, round, wire-rimmed glasses, framing eyes I could never trust.

"Maybe he's holding a treasure," Julianna replies.

"Well, could be, but I don't know why it's in here," I reply, take the photo from Julianna and stuff it in a pocket of my jumpsuit.

"It's so weird he left the room the same," I say, shut my chest, then, as an afterthought check the bottom drawer. "Huh! Look Julianna." I pull an ecru piece of paper rolled up and tied with a gold satin ribbon. My name is printed beautifully in blue calligraphy on the roll. Chills run up and down my spine and through my scalp, creating the sensation that someone is pulling my hair.

"Open it, Philip," Julianna quickly says.

I sniff the calligraphy. "This ink smells fresh. This is exactly how Adrian would leave us clues. This looks like his handwriting even." I untie the ribbon and unroll the paper revealing the following letter in Adrian's beautiful penmanship:

My Dearest Philly:

I've always known we'd be in touch again, and I dare say it shan't be solely through the glamorous crown prince's email. Since I am dead anyway, your threats of exposure are of no concern to me. However, you do have my disk—destroy it today. I've designated human collateral for this unwritten contract—your three little stepsiblings. If ever I have the slightest inkling that you let a copy of the disk get out, they'll be picked off or picked up, as it were, one by one. As you have gleaned by now, my reach from the grave is far and wide. Deviate at all from what I demand and they all shall perish.

You see, I'm as adept at anticipating your moves as an adult as I was figuring out what you would or wouldn't do or say when you were a child, and I knew you'd be snooping around my New York apartment. Still can't resist the treasure hunt, can you? Fine, you always were quite the Little Sherlock Holmes, and I dare say the games I orchestrated for you and Billy influenced your career path. It occurs to me that you and your three female cohorts can be of great assistance to me in locating some real treasure for which I have a client willing to pay a king's ransom.

The treasure is the Isabella Stewart Gardner Museum Art Heist items which I believe to be hidden somewhere in Kentucky. Dyanne O'Bryan's boyfriend, Ted Johnson, a skinny, worthless rogue she took up with while she was studying art at Boston University, was a security guard at Boston University who used that as a cover to supply drugs to students. He was eventually fired, committed several petty crimes becoming continually in and out of trouble with the police. Nevertheless, Dyanne was devoted to him and convinced him to move to Kentucky with her when she and her sister inherited her parents' large farm outside of Bardstown in the mid 1980's. Ted wasted no time in establishing quite a marijuana growing operation in the remote areas of the farm. In doing so, he stepped on the toes of other established growers, or traffickers from Mexico. Well, to make a long story short, his and Dyanne's young twin sons, Christopher and Noel, found Ted hanging from the rafters in one of their barns one morning. Not only was he hung, but also both his legs had been cut off with a chain saw. I for one think Ted got what he deserved. After his gruesome death, the muse grabbed Dyanne and she painted all the masterpieces for which she is known.

Naturally, I aided her and helped her out with the boys.

At any rate, Ted learned about the great value of the artwork in the Gardner Museum from his association with Dyanne, and he and one of his idiot friends managed to pull off the heist. The photo in your chest is lovely Teddie displaying a memento from the heist to entice me to pay him millions for it. But before I could get down to Kentucky to him, he met his demise in the barn. Dyanne would never admit Ted had anything to do with the heist, but I know she knew it, and I also think she knew where the artworks were hidden, but she

261

would never tell me. The night she died, I came close to getting it out of her, but failed. Her last words were a riddle, mocking me, I'm certain:

The eye of the virgin,
A fetus saved,
A piece of pie,
Marks the way.

So, take this hint of the treasure's whereabouts to your three female cohorts. Find this for me and you may just have the pleasure of seeing me in the flesh once again. Only then will I release your little stepsiblings from true harm.

Fondly,
Uncle Adrian

"That fucking bastard," I exclaim, "Threatening the kids like that. I'll kill him."

"Philip, Billy's place must be bugged. How else would he know about three females?"

"You're exactly right. We'll get Jonas and Mabry to check it out today," I reply, still staring at Adrian's perfect penmanship. "How the hell did this note with fresh ink, obviously written by Adrian, get here so fast? Is the bastard in New York?"

"It was probably delivered by our Mr. Ainsworth," Julianna says sarcastically, then asks, "What do you make of this riddle?" as she peruses the verse.

"I don't know. A lot of his clues would refer to works of art. That's how he got us to learn about certain artists when we were kids," I rub my forehead with my right hand to ease the sinus pressure I feel building.

"Well, if Dyanne was in fact mocking him, then the first two lines could refer to *The Crucifixion of the Madonna*," Julianna says, "Remember the painting, the Madonna is crucified and the baby Jesus's head is crowning through her vagina."

"Yes, I see that. What do you remember about her eyes in the painting?" I put the note down on the dresser.

"Gee, I think she is staring out with sort of a benevolent suffering expression on her face. Dyanne painted herself as the Madonna, so the eyes must be blue. We'll have to go over to MOMA and take a closer look. I'll make arrangements to get us in after hours."

"If solving this will get me in contact with the bastard in the flesh, I'm in this treasure hunt all the way," I say.

"Me, too, Philip," Julianna replies quickly with a smile, "Plus, I'd die to find the Vermeer, the Rembrandts, and the Manets Ted Johnson supposedly stole. By the way, Ted is holding a gilded bronze finial taken off of a Napoleonic banner in the museum."

"Really?"

"Yes. The thieves probably wanted the banner as a momento to their heist, but they couldn't remove it from its frame, so they probably took the finial instead," she replies.

"Assholes," I add, "Well, let's get a move on through the rest of these rooms."

"Philip, do you know the combination to Billy's chest?"

"Well, it used to be twice mine, so it was 8888. Let me try it." I open Billy's chest and dial in the numbers. It immediately clicks open. Lying in the bottom of the box is a snapshot of Julianna, myself, Mabry and Jonas emerging from the elevator toward Andrian's apartment with the new hot water heater.

"Shit, someone's in here, watching us. Let's get out of here."

We quickly leave the room and head down the hall to find Jonas and Mabry going through drawers and cabinets in the library.

"You guys, someone's been in here watching us. Look, they even photographed us coming in," I say and hand the snapshot to Jonas.

"Shouldn't we get out of here?" Julianna asks.

"Well, it's too late now." Jonas replies.

"Shit, we're toast now," I say.

"Not really," Jonas says looking up at me, "I suspect Adrian very much wanted us in here today for a very specific reason."

"And would that be this note and photographs we found in my old bedroom treasure box?" I ask, handing over the note and the photographs to Jonas who begins to read it as Mabry looks over his shoulder at the note.

"Hmmn, could very well be," Jonas replies.

"Are they still watching and listening?" Julianna asks.

"Heavens no, Mabry disarmed the system, remember," Jonas says with a big smile.

"But someone had to physically be inside here to actually have put this photograph of us in Billy's locked treasure box," I say in a perplexed tone.

Jonas looks around at Mabry and says, "Yes, but they must have exited through the service entrance in the back hall. But, I think we should finish our inspection, we've still got about ten minutes left before the Super is expecting us."

"You sure, Jonas? Are we safe in here?" I ask.

Jonas pulls up his right pants leg revealing a small revolver in a holster, then points to a leather case on Mabry's tool belt and says, "We've got you covered."

"Good," I reply while Julianna sighs loudly.

"We found a safe in here," Jonas says. "It was a tough one, but Mabry cracked the code and opened it. This is all we found in there." He picks up a leather attaché case, handing it to me.

"What is in it?" I ask.

"Open it, Philip. I think you might recognize it," Jonas says.

I open the attaché case to see many manila folders with white labels with names typed on them. I realize all the names are names of men as I flip through the folders until I find a folder with 'Philip and Billy Hampton' typed on it. I pull it out; it is empty. I spot a folder with the name Christopher and Noel O'Bryan typed on it. I pull it out, open it and am amazed to find a Blood Brothers Certificate just like the one Uncle Adrian made for us. It is dated July 14, 1994 and is signed with the bloody thumbprints of Adrian, Christopher and Noel.

"This makes me sick to my stomach. It's the bastard's track record for his accomplishments of seducing little boys," I say as I count the number of folders. "Damn, there are twelve in all."

"Do you recognize any of the names?" Jonas asks.

"Yeah," I reply, "Look, Julianna, the first one is Jonathan Zeng. And here is Andre de la Croix."

"Yes, I see," she says reaching over my arm to pull out a folder. "Oh my God. I can't believe this. Look, this one says Ricky Wallitsch."

"What? Ricky was one of Adrian's victims?" I ask.

"He's the caterer, right?" Jonas asks.

"Yes, he's catering the wake. He's at Billy's right now with his crew," I reply.

"He's our man, you all," Jonas says, "He's got to be the eyes and ears for Adrian. Adrian's seduction of him must have been so complete that he still controls him. It all makes sense now. Julianna, do you think some of the art here may be stolen?"

"I'm not certain, but my gut feeling is that several of the pieces are stolen," she replies.

"You see, Adrian probably set Ricky up in the high end catering business so he would have access to the homes of wealthy people and could find out what valuable pieces of art they had," Jonas says reaching his right hand around to scratch his back.

"Yes, that makes sense. So Ricky lied to me when he said Billy wanted him to hire Benny," I say, looking at all the folders. "Look at all these lives Adrian has ruined."

"It's almost unbelievable, we must stop him," Julianna says.

"We will," Jonas replies, "But let's run through the rest of the rooms quickly. Let's stay together this time."

"Okay, we're gonna keep these aren't we, Jonas?" I ask.

"Of course," Jonas replies, "I'll keep them and do a search on all these boys. Plus, we will need these thumbprints and DNA samples from the dried blood."

"Oh, is there anything else in this case?" I ask.

"Should there be?" Jonas asks.

"Well, I thought there might be a small black Bible in there. Adrian made us swear on the Bible during the Blood Brothers Ceremony that we'd never tell anyone."

"Yep, it's here, in the zipper pocket," Mabry says, reaches inside the case, unzips the inside pocket and pulls out the Bible. He flips it open to one of the first pages and says, "Look what's written here."

Julianna and I read the inscription silently:

Dearest Adrian,

I'm pleased to present you with your first Bible.

Study it and cherish it for its wisdom will guide you throughout your life's journey. It is of no importance that you are not my own flesh and blood for you are the brightest spot in my life and the Reverend and I would have forever been childless had chance not delivered you to us.

All my love,

Mother

"I wonder what she would say if she knew what her son had grown into?" Julianna says.

"I'm certain it would be inconceivable to her," I say as I put my hand in the case feeling for anything else. "Just think, she must have loved him a great deal. Wait, there's something else in the case. It's a flattened box of some sort." I pull out the old box to reveal that it's a box for a Swiss Army knife. "Adrian used a Swiss Army knife to cut our hands to mix the blood for the Blood Brothers Ceremony. This must be the box. I wonder where the knife is?"

"Hmmp," Jonas says, "Seems like it would be in there also."

I return the folders, the Bible, and the knife box to the attaché case and hand it to Mabry. We head off down the hall to inspect the other guest bedroom, Adrian's bedroom, and the darkroom. The guest bedroom is as I remember it: awash in neutral tones with landscape paintings on the walls, two of them are Mother's, one is a view in the height of summer down the Tyger River near Rose Hill, the secessionist Governor Gist's antebellum mansion, the other is a beautiful autumn scene of the Blue Ridge Mountains at a distance painted at one of Mother's friend's farm in Spartanburg. This room was Mother's private domain whenever she was in New York—sometimes spending weeks at a time here.

"Well, it's known that Adrian owned these two landscapes of Eva's," Julianna remarks. "Aren't they exquisite?"

"Yes, they're very beautiful," Mabry says turning toward me. "Your Mother was a great painter."

"Thanks, Mabry," I reply.

Jonas pulls open several drawers in a large chests and remarks, "There's nothing in here but women's clothes, bras, panties, lingerie, slips, blouses, sweaters."

I turn around, walk over to the chest, pick up a silk blouse, raising it to my face, inhaling deeply, Mother's scent lingers on the clothes, even after twenty years. I look up at everyone. "These are all my Mother's things. They're all hers, all of this." I fall to my knees, burying my face into a drawer full of sweaters, weeping, instantly returned to a time when I might feel the comfort of her hands, the warmth of her touch. I feel hands on my shoulders; I know they belong to Julianna.

"Philip, I'm so sorry. I can't imagine why he's kept Eva's clothes," she says softly.

"Well, for once I'm glad he did something. I've only been able to conjure up her scent in my mind. Dad and Fatgram got rid of all of her clothes. I never thought I'd get this chance again, ever."

I pick up a lavender cashmere sweater and hold it up for everyone to see. "I remember this sweater so well. Dad took Billy and me to Atlanta one December to see the Ringling Brothers and Barnum and Bailey Circus. I think I was eight or nine. The circus was awesome. The next day we went to some fancy stores in Phipps Plaza to shop for Christmas presents for Mother and Fatgram. Lavender was not Mother's favorite color, but she always said she looked so good in it, so we all decided on this sweater. She loved it. I can't believe it's here."

Everyone is quiet, just staring at me, and I realize there is not much time left. I stand up. "I'm taking this sweater, too," I say and I walk into the bathroom, turn on the light, walk over to the built in dressing table and find what I'm looking for.

"I'm taking this too," I exclaim in a loud voice. "This vanity set was Fatgram's grandmother's. Fatgram gave it to Mother a long time ago. It's sterling silver." I pick up the brush, pull out some long auburn hairs, look up at everyone, turn around, put the brush back on the silver plateau, pick it up, and walk out of the bathroom, through the bedroom, grab the lavender sweater from the drawer, and head out into the hall. Everyone follows.

"Philip, is there anything else of your Mother's you want from in here?" Jonas asks.

"No, this is enough. This door is to another studio and a dark room," I say and open the door, reach for the light switch, flicking it up.

The room is barren—not a stick of furniture, not one painting, nothing but walls, the hardwood floor, and a single light fixture in the middle of the ceiling.

"I sure didn't expect to find an empty room after everything else we've seen," Jonas exclaims.

"Me either," I reply.

The door to the dark room is open. We walk over to inspect—apart from the sinks, counters, and cabinets, it is also empty. We quickly search all the cabinets and drawers but find nothing.

"These two rooms are where Adrian kept his cameras, his photographs, and of course, did all the developing in here. I guess he took everything with him to Dubai," I say.

"Strange indeed," Julianna remarks.

"Oh well, all we have left is the crucifixion room," I say realizing I haven't uttered those words in a very long time.

"The what?" Jonas asks.

"Oh, that's mine and Billy's term for Uncle Adrian's room. Come on, you'll see what I mean." I head out of the dark room, across the empty studio, across the hall into Adrian's bedroom. I turn on the lights as everyone enters.

"Oh my God," Julianna gasps. "I've never seen so many paintings, sculptures, and carvings of The Crucifixion in my life."

"Dudes, it's a frickin' weird shrine of some sort, dying Jesuses everywhere, on the walls, hanging from the ceiling. Christ!" Mabry exclaims.

"You've got that right, Mabry," Jonas says.

Adrian's bedroom is large, the walls and ceiling are paneled in dark brown stained oak. Large, ornate oriental rugs cover the floor. The furniture is a collection of antiques, most ornately carved wooden pieces. The bed is a large mahogany canopy bed so high it has built in wooden steps on each side. The headboard is upholstered in a deep mauve raw silk, buttoned and tufted, over which hangs an antique Belgian tapestry of The Crucifixion. The bedspread and pillow covers are all silks in various shades of mauve and complementary colors. Curtains made from mauve and golden fabric are pulled back at each bedpost, but can be released to completely enclose the bed. The first time Uncle Adrian ever stuck his todger in my butt, he closed all of these curtains. He woke me up from my bed in the tree house and told me to be quiet so we wouldn't wake Billy. Everything was confusing. I couldn't wake up. Uncle Adrian made me walk around the apartment with him a couple of times and even splashed cold water on my face. Then I remember being naked on my hands and knees and feeling something cold and slippery being rubbed on my butt. Then he mounted me from behind and it felt like someone shoved a baseball bat up my butt. I screamed, I know, because he put his right hand over my mouth and told me to shut up. He told me I'd learn to like this after a while as he continued to thrust his todger into my butt. The first time was just the hardest, he said. I cried and just kept looking up at Jesus's woven face and wondered if my suffering was anything at all on the level of his. I fell back asleep quickly in his bed and the next morning he seemed annoyed that there was blood on the sheets. He told me this was just all a natural progression of the Blood Brothers' ritual—another step towards manhood but that this one was worth more than the others. That morning he gave me my first real Spanish golden doubloon. Even though my butt hurt terribly and bled every time I had a bowel movement for several days, I was ecstatic about the doubloon, so I kept my mouth shut. By the time Mother died I had collected fourteen doubloons. Billy had twenty-five. Only now does it occur to me that Adrian must have drugged us each time he wanted to have anal intercourse with one of us, because we were always so groggy afterwards. Could he have been giving us GHB back then? What a fucked up bastard. How could he do that to a kid? How could he lead the life he's leading? I look up at the tapestry of Christ on the cross and say, "If you are real, how could you let all of this happen?"

"What did you say, Philip?" Julianna asks as she takes photographs.

"Nothing, just thinking out loud," I reply.

"I suppose nothing's changed in here either," I hear Jonas say.

"It looks pretty much the same as I remember it."

Julianna continues taking photographs of all the artwork and says, "I know this display is completely morbid, outrageous, and sick, but the quality of the art is breathtaking. Gentlemen, you are looking at some of the finest renderings of the crucifixion outside of major museums and cathedrals."

"All I can say is that there must be a definite connection with these figures and Adrian's psychotic and delusional life path," Jonas smirks.

Mabry has been looking through drawers and cabinets in the bedroom and in Adrian's bathroom. "Jonas, this must be where the twins stayed. The clothes and shoes I found look like they are for a small man. Didn't find anything else except for this." He holds up a Ziploc bag with a good bit of white powder in it and four small plastic bottles with a clear liquid in them.

"The powder doesn't taste like coke," Mabry says, "I'm pretty sure it's G, and this is Liquid X."

"You think this is the stuff that killed Billy?" I say.

"Most likely," Jonas says. "Good job, Mabry. We'll dust these things for prints. Listen, we've run over a few minutes. Let's get out of here. I'll call the Super now."

266

He takes out his mobile phone and begins to dial. I grasp Mother's vanity set and her lavender sweater and feel relieved to be leaving Adrian's domain thinking that I'm glad I came here today, but I never want to be here again.

CHAPTER 29

"My, you all had a long meeting," Lush says smiling as Julianna and I walk into the lounge area of her gallery.

"Yes, long, sad, and challenging," Julianna replies. "But, I think we've ironed out everything we need to concerning what works we'll display at the wake and how we will disseminate the news about a posthumous showing of Billy's recent works."

Lush gets a look of concern on her face. "Good, but I'm sorry you had to go through that, Todge. I know it was hard."

"Thanks, Lush. It was, but it had to be done."

Officer O'Daniel observes Julianna and me, and I wonder if he suspects anything.

"Those were lovely Handel pieces you were playing, Officer O'Daniel," Julianna says. "Some of my favorite piano pieces and you play it so beautifully."

"Thank you, Miss Morgan."

"Oh please, call me Julianna."

"Yes, mam."

I can't help but smile as I think how smart Julianna was to have had Alejandraia eavesdrop on Lush and Officer O'Daniel and report back to us via cell phone as we returned from Adrian's apartment. Lush gives me an eat shit look which lets me know she's figured this out already. Oh well, it's all for a good cause Lush, darling. Everyone must make sacrifices, and I just can't wait to hear what Alejandraia tells Julianna about the conversation between you and Officer piano stud-boy. Why do I keep coiling into jealously over Lush and Officer O'Daniel? Maybe I just want to watch them fuck. I wonder if Lush would do a three-way with us? My ears start to burn.

"Excuse me, please," I say. "I need to go to the restroom before we leave."

I walk down the hall to one of Julianna's private bathrooms, go in, lock the door, turn on the fan and the water, pull down my pants and underwear, pull out my already hard cock, and beat off furiously, looking in the mirror at my face, imagining Lush naked on all fours sucking my cock as Officer O'Daniel fucks her doggy style. In less than a minute I feel hot semen rising through my groin, and I shoot off all over Julianna's granite vanity top, picturing Officer O'Daniel as he pulls out, ejaculating onto Lush's lower back, catching my eyes with his uniting us in the understanding of great sex. Panting, I look down at the mess I've made and immediately feel a pang of guilt overtaking me. "Fuck it," I mumble. "I have as much of a right to have sex as anyone else, even if it is with myself." Sometimes I feel that despite all the sex I've experienced over the years—including all the fucked up stuff with Adrian and Billy—that the best sex I've ever had is, in fact, with myself, by myself. As I wipe up my cum with toilet paper, I wonder if this is normal or not. Fuck it, I feel better. Though still erect, I force myself to pee onto the wad of cum soaked tissue in the toilet. The more I pee, the more my cock goes down, and the better I feel. I finish, flush, pull my pants up and fasten them, wash my hands, dry them, slap my cheeks a couple of times, emerging from the bathroom feeling much better about everything. I walk down the hall to find Julianna, Lush, and Officer O'Daniel chatting.

"Okay, shall we go?" I ask. "We've got a lot to do before tonight."

"Yes, let's be on our way," Lush says as she gets up out of her chair.

Officer O'Daniel stands up and I wonder what he'd say if he knew he was, for the second time in two days, a part of my spontaneous sexual fantasies.

"Julianna, dear, thank you so much for all your help and guidance," I say and take her hands in mine. "I can't tell you how much I appreciate it."

She gives both my hands a subtle shake and replies, "Oh darling, you know I'd do anything for Eva's boys."

She walks with us to the front of the gallery where we pass the sexy, radiant Alejandraia at the reception area. "Good morning," she says to everyone, smiling. We all exchange greetings.

"Julianna, dear, see you tonight," Lush says as she gives her a quick kiss on the cheek.

"Yes, Lush. We'll be there by five o'clock," Julianna replies.

"Bye, Julianna," I say.

"Goodbye, Philip," she replies.

Officer O'Daniel nods his head at Julianna as he holds the door open for Lush and me.

As soon as we get into the car, Lush's mobile phone rings. She looks at the incoming number.

"Oh shit, it's Carrie Blankenship," she exclaims.

"Who's that?" I ask.

"Just one of my friends whose two million dollar house I have for sale and wrote a contract on last week. The inspection was yesterday, and I'm sure she's calling to bitch about it. Mind if I take this call?"

"Not at all. You go ahead, business is business," I say.

"Thanks, dear. Carrie? Hi darling, how are you? Good. No, the wake is tonight and we're all working like crazy to get ready for it. Yes. He's doing fine, under the circumstances and all. Yes, Sabrina emailed me the inspection report yesterday, and I know what they're wanting repaired. What? No. Absolutely not! No honey, it will all work out. There's nothing to worry about. Everything's still negotiable, dear. What? Yes, I know, I know. Well, twenty thousand dollars is small in comparison to the one point nine they've offered, honey. Yes, I know your alimony's not that much. Oh dear, don't cry, honey, I know you have to net a million. We will work this out. Lemme tell you what I'm going to do. I think we can all split this. Well, what I mean is this. You pay five thousand or better yet we'll ask Doug to pay it for you. I think he will. Of course I'll ask him. I'll phone him right this minute. Yes, the purchaser will pay five thousand, I'll pay five thousand out of my commission, and I'll get the purchaser's agent to pay five thousand out of her commission. What? She'll do it. I know Sabrina very well. No, she's not a money hungry bitch, dear. She's tough, yes, but she's a good realtor, and she wants this deal to close as much as the rest of us. Yes, I'll call her right this minute, too. Of course it's legal, honey. It's done all the time. There, I knew we could work this out. Feel better, darling? Good. You are? You're in the tournament at the Boat Club? Well, good luck dear. I remember your wicked backhand. No, I don't think so. I just don't have the time anymore to devote to it. Well, have fun, honey. I'll call you and confirm everything and let you know when they want to close. Okay, dear. Bye."

Lush looks at me, takes a deep breath and sighs. "Hear what I have to put up with every day? Silly, simpering, bitchy, whining rich divorcees selling and buying homes. Sometimes they drive me mad. I've got to get out of this business, Todge."

"That business has made quite a lot of money for you, Lush," I say raising my eyebrows at her.

"Well, money isn't everything, as you well know. But my sanity and health are, and I feel both are eroding the longer I stay in the real estate business."

"I can't argue with that," I say looking up to see if Officer O'Daniel is watching us in the rear view mirror. I catch his eyes as he quickly looks away. "Maybe it's a good thing you're going to be off for a while. This change, even as gloomy as it is, might do you some good."

"You're right about that, dear. I'm so ready for a change on many levels," she smiles, putting her sunglasses on.

"Officer O'Daniel," I say, "Would you mind stopping up here two blocks on the right at The Sophisticated Pooch? I want to get a new collar for Clark for tonight."

"Sure," he replies, "I'll pull over and wait by the curb for you," he says.

"He has a beautiful collar now, Todge," Lush remarks, "You sure he needs another?"

"Yeah. I saw some of the collars they have on their web site, and they are truly wonderful. Why don't you come in with me and help me pick out one?"

"I'd love to," she replies.

Officer O'Daniel pulls up in front of the store. I get out, turn around and help Lush out.

"We won't be long," I say to him as I shut the door.

We enter the store. Lush pulls off her sunglasses, looks around and says, "My Lord, if this isn't swank, I don't know what is." An assortment of ornate collars, leads, and tags, many encrusted with rhinestones, are displayed in velvet-lined, lit, glass showcases. Fancy dog beds, some with fabric canopies sit in large, built-in Biedermeier style showcases, with recessed halogen lighting illuminating them. Suddenly, a large dark brown poodle wearing a green leather collar covered with rhinestone rosettes trots up to us, sits down, wagging its tail, asking to be petted. We both do.

"Why, you are an adorable princess or prince," Lush says as she strokes the dog's head. "I just love standard poodles. They're so athletic and smart." An attractive fortyish-something woman in a form fitting black dress and black stilettos walks toward us, and I think to myself as I take in her walk, her swept up coiffure, her expression of sophisticated nonchalance, that she has to be European. She smiles and says, "Good morning, I see you've met Bernard. He's such a sweet boy, that one. Bernard, viens ici." The dog immediately gets up, trots to the woman, turns around and sits down by her left side, looking up at her with an expression of adoration on his face.

"May I help you find something?" she asks.

"Yes," I reply. "I saw a beautiful brown collar on your website. It had wonderful, tooled metal rivets with cream-colored beads or buttons on them. A Weimaraner models it on your webpage."

"Oh yes, that one is beautiful, hand-made in Amsterdam. Come over here. Let me show it to you," she says, turning around and walking back to a showcase. I watch her ass and hips sway beneath the black fabric, and I imagine peeling that dress off of her to reveal tempting, lacy, black bra and panties. A faint spicy, floral scent trails her, exacerbating my lust. Lush pokes me in the side; I turn toward her shrugging my shoulders. We follow the woman who stops at a showcase, slides open a glass door and pulls out the collar, hands it to me, and says, "Beautiful, no?"

"Very nice," I say taking the collar, turning it over in my hands, feeling the rich brown leather, rubbing my fingers over the intricate tooling in the metal.

"It is exquisite," Lush remarks.

"Yes, and quite durable. It will last for years. Just clean it with a little saddle soap every so often," the woman instructs. "Do you know what size you need?"

"Yes, he wears a sixteen inch collar," I reply.

"Quarante centimeters," she replies. "Let me go see if I have that size in the back. Excuse me a moment." She heads back through a door surrounded by an elaborate wooden pediment, Bernard at her heels. I look at Lush and whisper, "Hot!"

"Yes, I can see that," she replies.

"Listen, let me fill you in on what we found at Adrian's, you just won't believe this." I proceed in an almost whisper and watch the expressions on her beautiful face change as I describe what we found: the vast amount of art, the painting mother did for me, the attaché case containing the Blood Brother certificates of Adrian's victims, including Ricky Wallitsch, the photograph of us in Billy's treasure chest

and the letter and riddle in mine. By the time I'm finished, her mouth has fallen open causing her sensuous lips to thin a bit as they stretch around her white teeth.

"Dear God, Todge. Isn't this all too much? Shouldn't we go directly to Detectives Johnson and Bell now?"

"That was my initial feeling," I reply, "but Jonas thinks we're okay. He's completed an extensive profile of Adrian. In a nutshell, Jonas thinks Adrian is the type of highly intelligent psychopath who has been so successful for so long in his malevolent deeds that he has fooled himself into believing he is so much smarter than everyone else that he can never be caught. Jonas says that, in fact, Adrian now gets the most pleasure out of taunting us, pitching us scraps, as it were, waiting to see if we take the bait and where we'll go with it."

"Well, nothing Adrian does surprises me. Can I see that note?" I hand her the note, she quickly reads it and says, "But Todge, he's threatening the kids and God only knows what Ricky may be willing to do if he is still connected to Adrian."

"That's right," I reply. "Jonas will have eight bodyguards at the wake tonight, one assigned to each child and five others dispersed throughout the party. Jonas and Mabry are coming over this afternoon to sweep the entire place for bugs. On the way back from Adrian's we were all discussing the best locations for listening devices at Billy's. Julianna mentioned that Clark was always at Billy's side, just as he has been with us this week. Jonas thinks there must be a bug in Clark's collar. Julianna told me about this place and showed me the website when we got back to her office. That's why we're here."

"Hummn," Lush says, knitting her brow and scrunching up her lips, "But what about this riddle? What do you make of it? How much is this stolen art worth?"

"Well, Julianna thinks the…"

"Well today's your lucky day," the woman says emerging through the doorway with a collar in her hand and Bernard by her side. "I have just one forty centimeter collar in that style left." She walks over, hands me the collar, and says, "Is there anything else you need for your dog?"

"Not right now," I reply, "This will do just fine. How much do I owe you?"

"That one is two hundred and fifty dollars," she replies.

An expression of surprise erupts on my face, "Wow, that's one expensive dog collar."

"Expensive, yes, but the best quality and well worth it," she replies with a smile.

"Well, I'll take it. Clark is worth it," I reply smiling back, pulling a credit card out of my wallet. The look on her face is strange, as if she doesn't trust me, so I ask, "Just out of curiosity, what's the most expensive dog collar you carry?"

She takes my credit card and replies, "Well it varies. So much of what I carry is custom made, but the ones with real jewels are always the most expensive." She points to a showcase behind her displaying a very small silver collar covered with sparkling rhinestones. "That one there, it's for a toy breed. It is woven platinum with ten carats of diamonds. It's forty-five thousand dollars." She looks at me for a response.

"Do you sell many in that price range?" I ask.

"I have the good fortune to have clients from many different countries, and yes, there is a good market for ultra-luxurious collars and leads," she replies as she walks to the cash wrap and starts poking at the screen.

"Well, it certainly is a beautiful collar," Lush says.

"Yes," the woman says, "Would you like for me to get it out for you?"

"Oh, no thank you," Lush replies.

"Would you please sign the receipt, Mr. Hampton?" The woman asks, handing it to me.

"Certainly," I sign the receipt and hand it back to her.

"Give me a moment to wrap this for you," she says.

"Of course," I reply and turn toward Lush. "I wonder if Clark would like any of these fancy dog beds?"

"Probably not. I've noticed he prefers human beds," she replies.

"You're right about that," I say. "But I think he will look fantastic tonight in this collar."

"Yes, quite handsome," Lush replies. "Look, Todge. See that red collar with the silver on it. That's Clark's collar, the one he has now."

I look closer at the collar. "It sure is, Lush. I bet Billy got it here." I turn back around toward the woman who is putting a fancy gold box with a brown bow on it into a gold and brown bag. "Would you happen to know if my brother, Billy Hampton, shopped here?"

Now she looks surprised. "Yes, when I heard you mention Clark, and I saw your last name is Hampton, I was going to ask if you are related to Billy. Billy loved this store and brought Clark in several times. Clark and Bernard got along quite well. We'd even meet at the dog run sometimes so they could play. I'm so sorry. I just can't believe Billy's gone. Such a tragedy. Such a kind, talented man. My deepest expressions of sympathy to you and your family. My name is Manon Gerard. My husband and I are planning to attend the wake this evening."

"That's wonderful," I reply. "I'm Philip Hampton and this is my good friend Sarah Richardson."

"Enchanté," Manon replies, "So good to meet you both."

"Nice to meet you, too," Lush replies.

Manon hands the bag to me. "Well, thank you for your purchase, and I'll see you both and Clark tonight."

"Yes, we'll see you this evening. Goodbye," I say.

"Goodbye," Lush says. Manon smiles. "A tout a l'heure, Bernard," Lush says to the big poodle who responds by wagging his tail and sitting down.

As we head outside to get into the car, Lush says, "Well, even in New York, it's still a small world. What a coincidence is that?" Officer O'Daniel is standing by the car with the back door open for us. He helps Lush in, then offers me a hand.

"Thanks, I'm fine," I say.

"Yes, indeed, it is a small world, Lush," I reply looking at the mysteriously beautiful Manon standing in her store as Officer O'Daniel gets in, starts the car, quickly pulling away from the curb.

Lush looks down at her watch. "It's almost noon. I'm a bit hungry. Are you, Todge?"

"Well, yes I could eat something. I'm sure everyone will be ready to eat when we return," I reply, immersed in thought, wondering about the relationship Billy had with Manon. They had to be more than friends. I mean the strange way she looked at me when I first mentioned Clark's name. He definitely would have been attracted to her for a variety of reasons. It will be interesting to meet her husband tonight. I wonder what he looks like. I wonder if he was also a friend of Billy's. I'll check the Address Book list to find out. That name, Gerard is familiar to me, but I cannot place it right now.

"I'm so glad the weather has turned," Lush remarks, putting her sunglasses back on, "It's going to be beautiful for the wake. It's warming up faster than I expected. Why, I think we'll be able to throw open all the doors to the terrace."

"I know. This evening will be perfect," I reply.

Lush makes several calls in an effort to finalize the deal for her Louisville divorcee as we head back to Billy's. My mind races as I watch the endless parade of pedestrians, and I wonder where they all came from and where are they all going. How the hell am I going to get Adrian on my turf—Billy's turf? I've got to figure out a way. Will he really come if we find the Gardner treasure? Maybe that's just an elaborate set up or trap. Fuck, who am I kidding? He's got me by the balls. I mean I have enough proof to put him away forever—murder, child abuse, grand theft, international terrorism—and he doesn't give a damn, just threatens my family and offers me a stupid riddle for a treasure hunt. The way to solve all this will become clear to me. I have to believe this to be true; otherwise I'll go crazy. All I have to do now is focus on tonight—Billy's night, everything else will fall in place. My forehead aches along the eye socket of

my skull, and I rub along the hard bone with the fingers of my right hand, but find no relief. Instinctively I press my forehead to the window in my door, absorbing the cool of the glass as I roll my head back and forth.

"Ahhh, damn that feels good," I say as I sigh. Lush is chattering away on her mobile phone, but she reaches over, pats me on the back, letting her hand linger a moment, then commencing a rhythmic tapping of her nails up and down my spine. The cold glass sucks the pain from my head, and I smile as I suppose that Officer O'Daniel's rear view mirror must offer a disagreeable view. My supposition is confirmed within seconds as he slams on brakes at a light and my head lurches forward then backwards.

CHAPTER 30

Timmy's strong hands dig into the muscles around my shoulder blades, I groan with pleasure, and I silently thank Lush for arranging massages for us today. My mind drifts over the chaos of the past three hours: each person on their own schedules rushing to get assigned tasks accomplished before tonight; the beautiful sandwich buffet set up in the kitchen by the caterer, with everyone grabbing half sandwiches, chips and brownies whenever they could; my retreat to Billy's bedroom with a plate of sandwiches and a brownie to return phone calls and emails and work on my tribute to Billy which Lush says I should do at eight o'clock promptly; Clark, nervous with anticipation, sticking by my side, begging for bits of food, sighing and whining randomly; crews from the caterer rearranging furniture, initiating set-ups for tonight; the constant arrival of flowers from friends and acquaintances of Billy; the excited outbursts of the children as they raced through their assigned duties, stopping by intermittently to inform me of their progress; the ten minute meeting between Lush, myself, Detective Johnson and Detective Bell where we ascertained that they have made virtually no progress on the case in the past twenty-four hours; and the general atmosphere of pandemonium, latent with the backbones of Lush's plan, which gives me total confidence that the evening will emerge in perfect order and everything will be as it should. I breathe slowly and deeply through the hole in the headrest on the massage table Timmy has set up in Billy's large closet and concentrate on relaxing and letting go, a futile attempt to erase the stress of the week. Timmy has put in a compact disk in the player in Billy's closet and a beautiful but haunting flute is playing.

"What is that music, Timmy," I ask.

"It's classical Indian flute," he responds in his stutter. "Do you like it?"

"Yes, it's very relaxing," I reply.

"Is this pressure okay, Philip?" He asks.

"Feels great, Timmy. I'm used to deep tissue," I reply as he continues to work around my shoulder blades and the notes of the flute bounce off my thoughts.

"Good, because you've got quite a few knots in your back," he replies, going even a bit deeper with his hands.

"I imagine your hands must be spent after giving three ninety minute massages already today," I add.

"No. They're fine. Mr. and Mrs. Hampton and Mrs. Richardson didn't want deep tissue, just Swedish," he replies, moving his hands in a kneading motion down and up both sides of my spine.

"Mmmm, they don't know what they're missing," I reply.

Timmy chuckles, "Yeah, but deep tissue takes some getting used to."

"I suppose so, but, man oh man, it's worth it," I say as my thoughts turn back to the morning. Goddamned Adrian—that crap about the Gardner Heist and treasure. It's got to be a ruse or, at least, a setup—although Julianna knew all about it and confirms it. Plus, the Polaroid of the guy holding up the eagle finial looked old and looked legitimate. Let's see what Jonas and Mabry have to say about it. Damn, I'm glad they did a sweep for surveillance devices in here this afternoon. The only thing they found was, as we suspected, Clark's collar. How the hell did someone get ahold of Clark's collar to implant that tiny microphone and transmitter? Shit, I wonder if it could have been done at Manon's store when Billy bought the collar. Maybe she's all part of this too? Maybe I'm just becoming totally paranoid. Shit. Boy, was she sexy, though? Geez, I'd love to get her naked, kiss that neck, lick her nipples, and fuck her. I picture her giving me the massage instead of Timmy.

Timmy is massaging my lower back and the pressure of his hands on my lower back pushing my groin into the soft mattress of the massage table coupled with my fantasy of having sex with Manon causes my cock to stiffen into a fully erect state which is somewhat painful as I have it pointed down towards my feet. "Christ," I think, "I better stop with this fantasy, I don't want Timmy to see me get hard." I redirect my thoughts back to Adrian. "How the hell am I going to get the bastard within my reach? Maybe he's in New York often, catching a ride on some sheikh's jumbo jet and then hanging out surreptitiously at Ricky Wallitch's."

"Hey, Timmy. Do you know Billy's catering friend, Ricky Wallitch?"

"Yes, I know Ricky," he replies.

"Very well?"

"Uhmm, well, well, not real well, but he uses me for massage sometimes."

"Really, how often?"

"Well, uhmn, maybe once every other month."

"Fuck," I think to myself, "That's a lot and people usually confide in a masseur."

"Why do you ask, Philip?"

"Oh, I was just curious. I mean with the type of clientele he has and all, I bet he has a really nice apartment," I remark trying to sound unconcerned.

"Yes he does, West side over looking Central Park, very nice," he says as he digs the knuckles of his right hand into my left rhomboid.

I take in a deep breath to offset the pain, "Oh shit, that's tight, isn't it?"

"Yes it is, but I can get it to release, just breathe deeply, and slowly, Philip," he says and I feel his breath on the back of my neck as he continues to dig in. He pins the offending knotted muscle down against a rib with the knuckles of his first two fingers and applies heavy steady pressure. The pain is intense, which causes my hard on to completely deflate as I try my best to relax into deep breaths. Finally, just as I'm breaking out in a cold sweat from the intensity of Timmy's pressure, I feel the muscle give up and release; the pain abates as a flood of sweet relief rushes through my body.

"Ahhh, damn you're good, Timmy," I say between pants.

He chuckles again, "Thanks," he replies, gingerly caressing the back of my neck with both of his hands before going deeper.

"Is Ricky gay or straight?" I ask.

"He's gay," Timmy replies.

"Does he have a partner?"

"No, he lives alone. Spends all his time working or at his place in Westport with his dogs."

"Dogs?"

"He raises some kind of English spaniel. Shows them, too. I think one of his dogs won Westminster a few years back."

"Probably English Springer Spaniels," I reply.

"Yeah, that's it," Timmy says, "He's always got one or two of them at his place here."

"Cool. Ya know he's a nice looking dude. I'm surprised he doesn't have a partner or a lover," I offer, fishing for a response.

"I'm sure he gets what he wants," Timmy replies.

"What do you mean?"

"Well, he's wealthy and can pay for sex," he replies.

"So, does he pay you for sex, Timmy?"

"Well, he has before and he always likes 'happy endings' with his massages," he replies, digging underneath my right shoulder blade.

"So you do know him pretty well, after all" I reply with a chuckle.

"Not really. Just because you have sex with someone, doesn't always mean you know them well," he says, bending over, putting a lot of muscle into my shoulder blade.

"Geez, that's intense," I remark as I let out a big breath.

"Too much?"

"No, keep on. It's just what I need," I reply and take in another deep breath.

"Ricky is pretty submissive sexually, kind of, in a weird way."

"You mean he's a bottom, Timmy?" I raise my head, turning to view Timmy's torso.

"No, I mean, I've never fucked him, but he likes me to be sort of aggressive, do most of the kissing, take charge about getting him off."

"Hmmmn, is that unusual among gay men?"

"Well, sort of. It's almost like he's a big child and doesn't know what to do sexually. And he says things like, 'Tell me what Daddy's going to do to his little boy next.'"

"Wow," I say and think how Adrian's abuse must have really fucked Ricky up sexually.

"Yeah, it kinda gives me the creeps because I have no interest in having sex with kids, but that's how Ricky acts and for five hundred dollars, it's not so bad."

"Yeah, weird," I say. "Timmy. So, how do you actually get him off?"

"His favorite way is for me to sit behind him, with my legs wrapped around him with my hard cock sort of wedged into his crack, but not inside him, and I reach around and jack him off as I kiss his neck, chew on his ear, and ask him to 'shoot a big load for Daddy.'"

"Christ," I say, "The strange things people do for sex. And does he?"

"Does he what?"

"Does he shoot a big load, Timmy?"

"Oh yes. He comes a lot. The dude's in great shape. Nice big cock and his body really turns me on. It'd really be a bummer if he wasn't."

"Wow. I wonder if he was abused or molested as a child? I mean what could make a grown man behave like that sexually?"

"Yeah, I know. I don't know anything about his childhood. Well, except that he has an uncle from England who visits him a couple of times a year."

"Uncle? Maybe he was the molester?"

"You never know. This guy is one cold fish."

"How so?"

"Well, I've given him a massage a few times and he never says a word. Ricky says his uncle doesn't talk a lot and he says he definitely is not interested in men sexually."

"That's because he's interested in little boys," I say to myself. "Well, Timmy what's this uncle of Ricky's like?"

"What do you mean?"

"What does he look like?"

"Well, he's old. Maybe sixties, I dunno. Reddish grey hair, a big beard, real white skin, blue eyes. Looks like he'd burn to a crisp in the sunlight."

"That's got to be Adrian," I think. "What's his name?"

"Ricky just calls him Uncle Adrian. He's some kind of art professor at Oxford."

"Bingo!" I scream to myself, pushing up on my arms. "Adrian could be in town this minute. That would explain his writing on the note."

"Is everything okay, Philip?"

"Oh fine, I just need to get some air," I reply as I smile at Timmy, silently thanking him for the information before settling back into the headrest.

Timmy begins working on my arms as he sits on a small stool with wheels on it. Armed with this new information about Adrian, it is easier for me to relax as Timmy works the muscles of my arms with his strong hands.

"Timmy, it fascinates me the way you make a living. I mean the different things you do, but especially the sexual services part."

"Well, I feel lucky, Philip, because I'm doing what I like. I mean I really love what I'm doing. I really get off on it!" he replies, laughing.

"I don't mean to be noisy or anything, but you know I'm a journalist. I spent a lot of time investigating the sexual trade in Thailand. I know it is alive and well here in the states but I just never have really been exposed to it."

"Well, it is alive and well," he replies.

"Do you mind talking to me more about it?"

"Not at all, Philip. Are you going to do a story on me?"

"Well, I'm not planning on it, but you never know where a conversation can lead. If I did, I'd ask your permission. I could write it so that you'd be completely anonymous," I add.

"Okay, well what do you want to know?"

"How did you get into this? Were you abused sexually as a child? Did you end up on the streets as a prostitute and work your way up to this level?"

He laughs as he works my right triceps and I feel his warm exhalation unfold around my face enveloping me with the enticing smell of sweet oats—the same smell I recall from scooping out oats from a big plastic drum to feed Picasso and Whinny, each horse nickering with anticipation as I spread the oats in their wooden feeding trays, each horse savoring the sweet oats, munching them, licking up every single small oat with their thick, strong tongues, and I wonder what his mouth would taste like if I kissed him—it feels strange, but not unfamiliar for me to be sexually attracted to a man. He is skillfully adept at employing his full lips, symmetrical features, boyish looks, and near perfect body in conjunction with soulful blue-green eyes and body gestures to exude a sexuality which, from my perspective, is neither gay nor straight, but more of a sensuous, amorphous aura—promising intensely gratifying sexual pleasure—and I realize what an asset this is in his preferred line of work.

"No, not at all. I grew up in Bridgeport—regular upper middle class suburb. My parents were really into their corporate jobs. I'm an only child, so they sort of left me to do whatever I wanted. For me that became sex. At first, with other neighborhood boys, just jacking off and stuff. But by the time I was in high school I had a steady boyfriend, and I was fucking Mrs. Doyle, a housewife down our street, almost every day. She taught me all about women."

"That's some high school life you had, Timmy," I observe and visualize the young stud fucking a sexy, forty-five year old housewife.

"Wasn't bad. After high school, I spent a year at UConn but never went back. That summer I enrolled in massage school and worked as a waiter in a fancy restaurant. That led to a few hookups with both

women and men. After a year, I signed on as the massage therapist on the yacht of a cable TV heir from Florida and traveled the world for three years on different yachts doing what I do best."

"Damn, that must have been quite an experience."

"It was. I've had sex in the most beautiful places in the world and put a lot of money away doing it."

"Timmy, have you always had that stutter?" I ask without thinking.

"Yes. Since I was a kid. No one knows why. Speech therapists didn't help."

"I'm sorry. I didn't mean to be cruel by asking; I'm just curious."

"Not a problem, Philip," he replies working down into my right forearm.

I turn my head, smile at him and notice the perspiration marks on the armpits of his white T-shirt. He has on long blue, silky, workout pants with light blue stripes running down both sides and white tennis shoes with no socks.

"Hey, you're working up quite a sweat doing this. Take off your shirt if you like," I say, situating my face back on the face rest.

"Oh, thanks, sure," he replies, lays my hand down gently, and I hear him pull off his shirt. "Better, I am getting a little sweaty," he says, picks up my right hand with both of his, entwines his fingers in mine, squeezes hard, moving my hand in slow circles. I sigh.

"Now, where were we?"

"Yachts."

"Right. What did you do after that?"

"Well I moved to the city. One of my high school friends landed a spot on a soap opera and had an apartment in the West Village. I enrolled in more massage training and got the job here as a doorman. That was four years ago. So here I am." He finishes with my right hand and rolls the stool over to the other side and begins on my left arm by rubbing oil all over it, then digs into my biceps and triceps. I turn my head toward him and glimpse a view of his chest. He must work out a lot to maintain his perfectly sculpted pecs and major washboard abs.

"Tell me more, Timmy. Tell me about some of your more interesting female clients," I say hoping to experience some of his sexual escapades vicariously.

"Let me think. Hmmn. Yes. We'll call her Madame X—a real beauty, rich, powerful, forty something woman in the entertainment industry—Broadway. She likes for me to stalk her on the streets—maybe in a café or coffee house. I pursue her to an arranged destination. Maybe a secluded warehouse or a stairwell in an abandoned building. She wears beautiful, flimsy dresses. I surprise her, pin her to a wall, drop to my knees, pull up her dress, rip off her panties, and eat her out until she comes while I play with my cock. Then I stand up, rip her dress off, just tear the shit out of it, and thrust my cock into her, pick her up, and fuck her. She comes fast, screaming sometimes."

This story is everything I hoped it would be and more. My ears are burning, my breathing is labored, and my cock is hard again.

"God damn, that is sexy, Timmy. You lucky S.O.B. and you get paid to do it. How much for that?"

"A thousand dollars," he replies, working around my elbow.

"Christ. I can't imagine," I reply. "Aren't you afraid of getting caught by someone?"

"At first I was. But she's very clever and has an aide who sets everything up. We've only been caught once and it was by a bum."

Timmy continues massaging my left arm as I drift off into a sexual fantasy, imagining myself stalking the beautiful Broadway star, following her into a dead end alley, pinning her against a brick wall, both of us anticipating, wanting and needing hot sex. I squat down, lift her dress, rip off her lacey panties, burying my face between her legs, exploring her with my tongue, breathing in her smell. With my eyes closed I find her clitoris with my tongue and begin a dance on it. She moves violently. I am relentless with my tongue and mouth, tickling her, sucking her, licking her, until she shudders and her juices cover my mouth and

cheeks. I stroke my hard cock, get up from my knees, rip her dress off with my bare hands, press my wet face into hers, lift her up with my hands under her ass and drive my cock into her warm wetness, thrusting as forcefully as I can, looking into her eyes, watching her expression change from desire, to extreme need, asking for more and more, until a painful ecstasy emerges and I shoot my load into her as she reaches another orgasm. My cock is throbbing and I feel precum on the sheet underneath me. At this point Timmy stands up, pulls the sheet off my left leg and buttocks, tucks it in between my legs and applies oil on my leg and ass. As his hands rub my upper thigh, he rubs against my hard cock, making no effort to avoid it.

"Looks as if my story has awakened something," he says rubbing my ass now with oil.

"Yeah," I say with a combination chuckle and sigh, laced with a tinge of guilt. 'Guilt,' Fatgram would say, 'is okay if it comes from within your being—it's just your soul's way of letting you know you need to change your behavior or examine all of your feelings about something; otherwise, if it is a result of some external force, doctrine or person, shuck it and throw it away, just like you do with an ear of corn. The Catholics have manipulated their flocks for centuries with guilt—for God's sake, don't let yourself fall into that trap.'

He pulls the sheet completely off of me, hops up on the table on his knees between my legs and begins to rub the backs of both my legs and my ass vigorously. It feels really good and I think to myself, what the heck, I deserve a happy ending, too, especially today. Billy would certainly approve. He continues to rub my legs and ass, occasionally rubbing the back of my hard cock. I moan and flip over to face Timmy. He looks at my erect cock, smiling.

"You're beautiful, too, Philip, just like Billy." I see a very large bulge in his pants and he slowly stands up, pulls down his pants, releasing a big, thick, erect cock, which slaps against his hard abdomen. The hair on his chest and his pubic region is dark blonde, trimmed short and neat. There are two Chinese letters tattooed in green ink right where the line of hair from his navel meets his bush.

"What do these mean?" I ask.

"They're the Chinese symbols for nurture. Which is what, I believe, I do best," he replies, pulling his cock to one side to display the tattoo. Smiling, he slowly bends back down on his knees, leans over, takes my cock in his left hand, squeezes it hard, and puts it in his mouth. He sucks it, slowly at first, intermittently licking the head or rubbing it on his face. I rise up on my elbows to watch. His own thick cock remains erect, throbbing, dripping with precum. He begins to suck with more urgency, ravenously feeding, taking my whole shaft in his throat, gently pulling and rubbing my balls with his left hand. This feels so good; his technique entices me into a state of sexual rapture. I now understand why people pay him so much money. I've never had a better blowjob. I moan, absorbing the pleasure of his mouth on my cock and the beautiful sound of the flute.

"Shit, Timmy, I'm gonna blow soon." He sucks my cock harder and more rapidly for a few seconds and then quickly pulls it out of his mouth. He pants heavily as he lowers his muscled torso over my chest, presses his warm, wet body into mine, and begins to kiss me deeply. His taste is indeed like sweet oats. He rolls his hard cock over mine and I think how I would like to fuck him now, hoping he is not wishing to fuck me.

He pulls back off my mouth and asks, "Is this okay, Philip?"

"It's fine, Timmy. It's great," I say. "Listen, sit up and face me. Pull your pants and shoes off. Cool. Put this leg over mine here and this one under here. That's right. Great. Hand me that oil." He does, and I put oil into my right hand and rub it over his cock. He groans, grabs the oil, pours some on my cock and begins rubbing it. I scoot closer into him so that our balls touch and I lift up a little, pushing and rubbing my balls into his.

"God, that feels good," I say, "My balls are really sensitive. Are yours?"

"Sorta. But my nipples really are."

I lean over, lick his right nipple, suck it, and lightly bite it. He groans and I feel his thick cock harden even more in my right hand. We sit on the table, facing each other, jacking each other off.

"Timmy, this is how Billy and I had sex when we were teenagers."

He shakes his head up and down, "I know, he told me."

I smile, lean into him, exploring the sweet taste of his mouth with my tongue. I feel a burning sensation from my prostate area, and I know the semen is rising and I'm approaching ejaculation. I peer down at Timmy's heavy balls and I see them climbing up inside him, just like Billy's always did, indicating to me that he was nearing orgasm. Just for a moment, I feel fifteen again and I'm facing Billy, as we jack each other off in our bedroom, but now, I'm not thinking to myself this really is the last time I'm going to do this with him because it's just not right, it's unnatural. I'm thinking that somehow, in this moment with Timmy, I am able to release any inhibitions I have of having sex with another man. I pull back off Timmy's mouth, thrust my cock upwards as he does the same. We shoot almost simultaneously, moaning, as hot semen sprays all over our chests—a large blob of his semen hits the left cheek of my face.

"Sorry," he says, chuckling.

"It's okay," I reply, feeling the warm liquid run down my face, not even bothering to wipe it off.

We sit looking at each other, spent, panting—the release of physical and sexual energy into the closet is palpable, the smell of sex lingers in the air like ozone after a spring thunderstorm. For the first time since Billy's death, a feeling of tranquility envelops me like a warm pink light and seals itself around me with the soothing notes of the flute, and I sense that I will find my way through tonight and the coming weeks and months. I will conquer Adrian.

"Thanks, Timmy. That was great. Well, it was more than great. I, I don't really know what to say. Just, just that I, I really needed that. You are a kind guy."

"Thank you, Philip. I needed it, too."

"Cool, we better hit the shower. Listen, you go first. I'll rest here a minute."

He lets my cock go, pulls back away from me and jumps off the massage table. He turns around and heads from the closet to the bathroom. I observe his perfectly sculpted backside, the ripples of muscles in his back, his rock hard ass, pronounced hamstrings, quads, and calves—a Michelangelo sculpture awakened from his eternal pedestal to deliver mortal pleasure. Just as he reaches the door he turns back around and says, "Philip, this one's on me."

"Thanks, see you tonight," I say, smiling, taking a towel to wipe his cum off my cheek, my mind racing back to the image of pinning the woman against the wall, and I wonder if he fucked Lush today. I'll bet money on it that he did.

CHAPTER 31

Knowing that the remainder of the day and night will pass with the speed of a vortex in a draining bathtub, I shave my face in the shower as quickly as I can. I visualize myself standing at the precipice of a misty, vertiginous ravine, ready to jump, free falling into the cool abyss with a choice of two outcomes: the instantaneous, harsh crunch of my bones against rock or the ascension of my body up through the clouds, into the warm sunlight, soaring over Shangri-La or the Garden of Eden before Adam set foot in it. I spring off the cliff in perfect swan dive formation, my body falling through the cool mist until I gather my strength into the core of my abdomen, lifting myself up and up through the darkness, until I pierce through the clouds, flying at great speed into the sunlight and over lush green hills, laced with blue rivers, confidant that I have control of my own destiny. As I complete my shower and attend to my

appearance in the bathroom mirror, I am overcome with the same optimism I experienced right after sex with Timmy—a definite feeling that everything will fall into place, and I will realize what I have to do. I emerge into the bedroom to find Clark waiting on the bed for me, wagging his tail, looking at me with the same understanding I now have. I walk into the closet to find that Timmy has packed his equipment, leaving behind an unmistakable pleasant orange scent, which I surmise must be some sort of cleaner or disinfectant. I walk over to Billy's underwear drawers, find a pair of black cotton, midrise trunks and put them on. They feel good, sort of a combination between boxers and briefs. I spot Mother's lavender sweater and her silver vanity set I put on a shelf, and I wonder what she would say if she witnessed me with Timmy. I find a pair of black nylon and wool socks, sit on the cushioned bench in the closet, and pull them on. Clark attends me, eagerly watching every move I make, yet patiently sits without jumping up on me as he would normally. I stand up and began sorting through a section of hanging white dress shirts until I spot one that is made of silk with a textured weave that resembles an intricate mosaic tiled floor. I slide my arms and torso into the silk, buttoning the shirt up to the top two buttons which I leave open. Next I sort through a hanging row of black slacks and try on a few pairs until I find a pair that fits me the best. They are flat front, snug, but not too tight, and have a thin vertical band of a satin-like material running down the outside seams similar to tuxedo pants. I look through dozens of belts hanging from a custom made belt rack and locate a black ostrich skin belt with a silver buckle I like. I put it on as I move over to the pullout shelves containing shoes. I spot a pair of semi-square toe, black, over the ankle boots, pick them up, and slip on the right one. It fits well, so I pull on the left one. All I need now is a jacket so I look through several rows of jackets until I find a black one made of a very fine wool woven into a pattern that resembles tiny honeycombs. The jacket has three buttons, a single back vent, and narrow lapels, reminding me of a riding jacket. I put it on, walk over to a full length mirror in the closet, take in my appearance, force a smile, and think that I look okay and that this outfit is appropriate for my brother's wake. Beside the mirror is a built in case containing several sliding drawers. I pull open the first drawer to see that it is full of bottles of cologne. I choose one that is labeled Tiffany For Men and spray two quick squirts in the general direction of my neck and upper body. The scent is pleasant, a little spicy, not overpowering at all. I like it. Clark, sitting by my feet watching me, sniffs, then sneezes violently several times.

"Hey boy, I'm sorry. Didn't mean to get you with the perfume." I squat down to pet him. He wags his tail then sneezes again, the wet mist from his nose sprays onto my face.

"Serves me right, Clark," I say laughing. I stand up, grab a tissue from a box on a shelf, wipe my face while looking in the mirror, throw the tissue in a waste can, then turn towards Clark.

"Well, Clark. I think we look pretty decent. Me in some of Billy's fancy clothes and you with your sharp looking new collar." Clark looks up to me, panting a little, wagging his tail.

"Okay, boy. Let's go find everyone." I walk out of the closet to get my watch, a steel, black face, Rolex Oyster Perpetual Explorer Billy gave me for my twenty-fifth birthday, which is on the nightstand by the bed. I see that it is four forty-five as I pick up the watch and put it on my left wrist. I open the bedroom door to find Lush walking past.

"Wow, Lush, you look fabulous, really stunning," I say. She is wearing a black satin blouse with a low cut neck, long sleeves and a big bow that ties in the back at the bottom of her neck, a form fitting, high waist, knee length black skirt with two short slits up each side, and, to my surprise, black suede high heels. She wears a single, short—just a bit longer than a choker—strand of black pearls and diamonds around her neck and dangling earrings each made from a short strand of three diamonds capped by a single black pearl. Her long hair is pulled back and formed into a sort of braided bun in the back with a pendant made of diamonds and black pearls fastened near the top of the bun.

"Why thanks, Todge. You look quite handsome, yourself."

"Thanks, Lush. Did you go out to get your hair done? It looks great."

She laughs. "No, no time to go out. Turns out Tammy attended cosmetology school and is a part-time hairdresser. She great with up do's. Wait until you see Brenda and Emma."

"That's great. Lush, step in here a second." She comes in the bedroom. Clark follows her in and I shut the door.

"Listen, I quizzed Timmy on Ricky Wallitsch during my massage. Turns out Ricky is one of Timmy's clients. He likes Timmy to dominate him and call him 'Daddy's boy' during sex."

A look of disgust flashes across Lush's face. "Adrian's work, I suppose."

"Exactly. And Timmy said that Ricky has an Uncle Adrian who is an art professor at Oxford who visits a couple of times a year. Timmy has massaged Adrian a few times—no sex, just massage. Said he was a real cold fish."

"Excellent, Todge. That proves our theory that Adrian works through Ricky. I can't wait to see what Jonas finds out about Ricky. He's been hot on his trail this afternoon."

"Good. Let's go see how everything looks," I say while making a mental note that Lush offers nothing about her own massage experience with Timmy.

"It's gorgeous. I was just out there and Ricky is going over everything with a fine toothcomb. I just peaked through the dining room door, he didn't see me. He may be a pervert and a pawn of Adrian's, but he can put together a party fit for a king."

"That's probably why Billy used him. I wonder how Billy met Ricky. I bet Adrian had something to do with that."

"Oh, you can be sure of that, Todge," Lush says as I open the door and follow her and Clark into the hall.

We walk down the hall and enter into the living room which I expected would be full of people doing final preparations, but we are alone. The furniture has been rearranged into several small groupings, leaving much more open space for traffic flow. The room is adorned with arrangements of white orchids of several different varieties: a large silver butler's tray contains at least a dozen different plants with their thick green leaves and tall stems capped by masses of white blooms rising out of a covering of beautiful, bright green moss; Fatgram's pair of sterling champagne coolers flank a mahogany end table and display tall orchids of the dendrobium variety with cascades of white blooms; several of Mother's blue and white Chinese pieces, placed throughout the room, contain either plants in full bloom or cut stems with blooms. The long white marble hall table has been moved to the center of the room and is set up like some sort of altar with Billy's ashes in the large blue and white Chinese jar in the middle sitting on top of a blanket made entirely of white orchids strung together. The orchid blanket is so large that its escalloped edges hang down at least a foot and a half on each side. Eight silver frames are symmetrically placed around the jar. I turn toward Lush.

"I hope you don't mind. This was my idea—the orchid altar," she says smiling and tearing up at the same time.

"It's beautiful, Lush. I don't know what to say. Billy would love it. Thank you."

We walk up to the altar. Clark sniffs the blanket of orchids as I look at each picture Lush has chosen with incredible sensitivity and insight into my brother's life.

"My God, Lush. You must have had these made. They're all eight by ten, black and white glossies."

"It's amazing what you can do with a scanner, email, and Kinko's," she replies.

There is a picture of little Billy and Bonnie Belle, Billy's head in profile as he sucks his right thumb, Bonnie Belle gazing into the lens with her ever patience countenance. Another shot shows Fatgram and Mother, both in mink coats, standing between two of the huge white columns on Fatgram's front porch. I'm half smiling, standing in front of Fatgram with my hair in a crew cut while Billy, wearing his favorite cowboy hat, is standing in front of Mother, with his face scrunched up aiming his laser gun at the photographer, Dad.

"That picture's so cute, I couldn't resist," Lush says. "Yeah, it sort of sums up Billy and me, doesn't it?"

"Indeed it does. But, in a good way, Todge."

The next photograph I see is one of Billy taken at Pawley's Island in June the summer Mother died. It was the last trip we had with Mother before she and Uncle Adrian went to France. I remember Mother looking at this photograph and gasping, "Dear Lord, Billy, I'm giving this photo to Adrian to take to New York. If this isn't the look of a model, I don't know what is." I remember being jealous at the time, but now I wish I could travel back in time to that lovely, magical evening when Billy and I were crabbing on a weather beaten wooden pier in the marsh. The sun hung very low in the sky, just over the moss draped woodlands framing the horizon at the western edge of the expansive marsh, shimmering in the brilliant yellow light. I can smell the salty breeze, almost feel its cool touch on my skin. I'm counting the number of crabs in our bucket as Billy, leaning over a wooden rail on the pier, lowers a string tied around a chicken back into the water. The muted sound of the waves rolling ashore down at the beach and crying gulls filter through the breeze. Mother is busy snapping photographs to study the light at this time of day, a time she always refers to as 'the golden hour' which she claims is the best light of the day. Suddenly Billy shouts, "Mother, Philly, I got a really big one. Look!" He is wearing only a pair of long khaki shorts and his skin is already brown from the sun. As he turns towards Mother and me, smiling, holding up the crab on the string, the breeze tossing his long, curly hair, I hear Mother's camera shutter firing.

"He was already a looker then, wasn't he? How old was he here, Todge?"

"Eleven. Just eleven, Lush." A surge of remorse, regret, and pain begins to grip my body like some god-awful desiccant sucking at my soul. I move on to the next photograph, one where Billy the child has disappeared into a young man. I know this photo well because I took it. One weekend while Billy was at St. Andrew's-Sewanee School, I caught a ride down from Asheville with a friend whose brother was attending Sewanee. Billy's roommate was away for the weekend, so I stayed with Billy. It was a mistake. I had misgivings about coming because I knew he would want to try to have sex. That Friday night as soon as it was time for bed, he started pleading with me.

"Philly, come on. Please, just one more time. Let's just SO like we used to do—just real fast. Please, please, please." Billy looked at me with a mixture of lust and love in his eyes. At fifteen, he was already taller, heavier, and hairier than I. He had more chest hair and could grow full sideburns. I couldn't yet. SO was our abbreviation for 'shoot off.' For years we never called what we did at night and in the woods 'sex', but just 'SO'. I would ask, 'Hey, Billy, you feel like SOing tonight?'

"Damn it, Billy. I told you I'm not going to do this anymore. I don't want to. I'm not gay."

"Gay, smay. What's that got to do with it? You can go screw all the girls you want. I don't give a damn."

"Yeah, right."

"Well are you, Philly?"

"Am I what?"

"Are you screwing any girls?"

"No, I'm not."

"Right. I bet you're screwing that Beverly girl. She was making eyes at you all during dinner."

"Beverly dates Ted Armstrong. I'm not interested in her."

"Well then, I bet it's that Cindy Maddox chick, then."

"No, it's not, Billy. Let's just go to bed."

"Ah come on, Philly. Just one more time. I swear it will be the last. I promise," he pleads, putting his hands around my ass. I push him back hard.

"Get off, Goddammit!" I shout.

The look of pain and hurt in his face pierces me like a shard of glass, and I immediately regret reacting so harshly.

"Why don't you love me anymore, Philly? Why?" he asks, almost in tears.

"Billy, I do love you. I love you as my brother, but I just don't want to SO with you anymore. It's not right. It's unnatural."

"But why? We've always done it. As long as I can remember, Philly," he says, still pleading.

"I know. But I'm not doing it anymore, Billy. Please stop begging."

"Well then, just let me look at you naked while I SO. I promise I won't even touch you, not even your balls." Billy would rub my sensitive balls while we were SOing and I would groan like a rutting animal. He loved this. I used to love it.

"Fuck no, Billy. No, go to bed. That's it. No more tonight. I knew that's the only reason you wanted me to come up here this weekend—just to SO. Go find some other dude to SO with. Leave me alone."

I turned my back on him, put on my pajamas, got in bed, stuck my headphones in my ears and turned up the volume on a B-52's CD. As *Love Shack* blasted into my head, I knew my brother was curled up on the other bed, whimpering.

The next day we went over to check out the campus at Sewanee. I acted as if nothing had happened the night before, but Billy was sulking and in a foul mood—so much so that he didn't even seem to notice all the girls at Sewanee ogling him. He could have laid anyone of them, and I became annoyed that he was getting more looks than I. It was one of those crisp October days that makes you wonder how the sky can be so perfectly blue, and I was determined to get some good photographs of people for a photography class I was taking. At one point, I focused on photographing a group of students sitting in a circle in the sun, books open, studying and talking. After a while I turned around to see where Billy was. He was reclined on a stone bench, twirling a small branch with yellow leaves on it between his fingers. When he noticed I was looking at him he dropped the branch and smiled. I immediately recognized a good shot, so I lifted my camera and took a photo. The following week when I developed the shot in the dark room, I was amazed. Billy was stretched out on the stone bench smiling seductively, curly brown hair and two inch long sideburns framing his perfect facial features and perfect, white teeth, advertising health and beauty. His weight was supported by his left elbow and left hip, left jawbone resting atop his left fist, right arm curled in front of his chest, left leg bent back underneath with his right leg bent like an inverted V, his right foot flat on the bench. He wore a white, button down Oxford shirt underneath an olive green cable knit wool sweater, long khakis and weejuns with no socks. His right pants leg had ridden up a bit, revealing a hairy lower leg and foot and you could clearly see wisps of chest hair in the V of his shirt and sweater. The background of the picture turned out to be the All Saint's Chapel. There was my beautiful brother, seemingly floating on a stone bench, hovering on the outside of that massive, gothic, sandstone Christian edifice with a beckoning, seductive smile on his face. My photography teacher, a woman, gave me an A plus for that black and white photo of Billy and the church and asked to keep a copy. That night, the Saturday I took that shot, I gave in to Billy's pleas. It was the last time we had sex together as teenagers, the last time before that night in St. Barts eight years ago.

I move on to the next silver frame. This is Billy's famous underwear shot—the shot that made him an instant fashion supermodel. God only knows how many pairs of tighty whities this shot sold and how many people of both sexes have lusted after him in this picture—it's just hard to imagine a more perfect looking man. I was so proud of him by this time. Somehow, after Fatgram's death and after Billy entered college, we began to grow closer again, and we both never mentioned SOing. I'm sure he was getting plenty of sex elsewhere, and he managed to separate my affection towards him from sex. God, I was so relieved. So relieved to have my brother back and not have to feel guilty about not wanting to have sex with him. He became my best friend, my confidant, my family. I was struggling at the *Atlanta Constitution* to make a name for myself—I was determined to pursue my passion for journalism, and I forced myself to live off

my salary as motivation. Everything I inherited I left in Mr. Barksdale's capable hands. Meanwhile, almost as soon as Billy moved to New York, he was discovered by a modeling agency one night at an art opening. His fame advanced rapidly, and he included me in every aspect of it and seemed to really care about my opinions. He followed my own career closely and tried in every way he could to get me connected in New York. Eventually, he introduced me to Flo, Florence MacPherson, a literary agent who specialized in pitching stories to magazines, who dared me, on the spot immediately after Billy introduced us, to write an article about the art opening we were attending. The next day at Billy's apartment I wrote the article from the perspective of an adult child of a famous artist. Flo pitched it to *The New Yorker*. They bought it. She helped me negotiate with *The Constitution*, which released me from my contract and gave me a new contract to supply articles as a Special Contributor, and my career as a free-lance journalist began. Billy and I became constants for one another and all the closeness of our shared childhood and teenage years seemed to meld into a state of mutual understanding and caring for each other—it became an unwritten fraternal code that neither one of us would ever get as close to anyone else. When Billy would enter into a down period, he'd call me for help. When I felt insecure or unloved, I'd call him for help. This was a good period. We were both on solid ground, for the most part. Goddamn Adrian McWhorter—you mother fucker. You will pay for this.

Lush holds up a photograph of Billy taken on a flats skiff at the Marquesas Keys. This is my favorite photograph of him as an adult because I know he is at his happiest here—his expression shows it: relaxed face, gentle, proud smile, intelligent eyes, and contagious serenity he could exude when the conditions were right. Stan Shultz, his fishing guide, snapped the photo of Billy who is sitting in the front of the skiff, shirtless, holding a hundred pound tarpon in his lap he has just landed after a forty-five minute fight, using a fly rod and reel and a green deceiver fly. Dad told me Stan is coming tonight.

The seventh photograph depicts Billy, barefoot in jeans and a white T-shirt spotted with paint, focused on a canvas in his studio here a couple of years ago while he was working on a series of landscapes. Unlike Mother, Billy preferred to paint landscapes in his studio. He would visit sites of interest, shoot digital photos, make quick sketches with notes, and, after a period of time he referred to as his 'digestive phase'—a period of time ranging from minutes to months during which his thoughts and observations about a particular scene would be processed and distilled into what would appear on the canvas, he would return to his studio to execute the painting. Mother's landscapes border on reality; Billy's landscapes border on ethereality.

Lush hands me the last photograph. As I take it in my hands, I look up at her to see tears running down her cheeks.

"In one of the last emails I got from Billy," she says through sobs, "Just a couple of weeks ago, he told me he had Nigel do a series of black and white shots with Clark. He was exited about the proofs and said he wanted to surprise you with one of the photographs for Christmas. I phoned Nigel yesterday and he sent over this one. He says it's the best."

I turn the frame over to see a photograph of Billy and Clark sitting on an upholstered club chair. A piece of dark, heavy brocade covers the arm of the chair toward which Billy faces. He is sitting askew in the chair with his legs stretched out and crossed, his back resting against the other arm, and Clark, with his head slightly bowed, leaning against his chest. Billy's left hand rests on his left thigh and his right arm covers the ridge of Clark's back. Clark's right paw protrudes from behind the brocade, resting on Billy's right knee. Just the top of his curled left paw is visible as it rests on the upper part of Billy's right thigh. Billy stares into the camera, mouth slightly open, no smile, but with a look of absolute contentment. Clark's damaged right ear hangs down with a sheen and texture of velvet. His eyes stare down to nothing, but his body expresses nothing but love. The background is almost completely black. Billy and Clark in the chair seem to be floating in the dark, as if the light is emanating from them. I am overwhelmed.

"This is just great, Lush." I bend down to show the picture to Clark who sniffs it, then licks the glass. "Yes, boy. You really loved your daddy, didn't you," I say as I stroke his head with my right hand. He turns to me, presses his cold nose into my chin, licking my throat a couple of times. "Good boy," I say, sniffing back the tears as I stand up, handing the photograph back to Lush.

"Thanks, Lush. This is just great. You're the best."

Smiling, she takes the photo in both her hands, and says, "And so are you, Todge."

I smile back at her. "Sounds like there's an army in the dining room. Let's take a peak," I say.

"Alright," she says, places the photo of Billy and Clark back on its place on the orchid blanket, and turns toward the dining room door.

As soon as Lush opens the dining room door, my eyes fall on Ricky Wallitsch standing by the fireplace gesticulating as he instructs his staff in the transformation of the dining room table which they have covered with white linen table cloths with swags, embroidered with acanthus leaf designs in silver thread, hanging from the sides of the table with wide strips of shiny silver fabric draped over the table and fashioned into vertical drops, gathered midway to the floor with white bows with white orchids sewn on them, then fanning out and puddling on the floor. Mirrored platforms of varying heights are arranged on the table, the flat surfaces of which are strewn with white orchid blossoms, and I realize these platforms will soon hold trays and dishes of food. The centerpiece is magnificent and consists of a circular, tiered, mirrored platform, on top of which sits a very large silver champagne cooler filled with dozens of large solid white cattelaya orchids.

"Dear God, this is magnificent," Lush exclaims, wide-eyed, looking at the table, then at me.

"Extraordinary, I reply, "Billy would love it."

"Philip. Dear Philip," Ricky says in a loud, high voice as he abruptly breaks away from his staff and heads in our direction.

"Hello, Ricky," I reply and watch as he walks with long, quick strides toward me. I take in his tall athletic build, handsome face with pointed nose and chin, black hair cropped short, extremely narrow mustache outlining the top of his lips, spilling down into a full, carefully groomed goatee, and I wonder what he looked like as a boy, and I surmise he must have been a beautiful boy, a boy with a single mother, perhaps, a mother Adrian befriended in some way, becoming an invaluable friend or a close associate who just happened to have all the time in the word for lonely little Ricky. As he approaches with his hands outstretched reaching for mine, I look into his dark brown eyes, framed with heavy, but neatly trimmed and waxed brows, and thick, long eyelashes, the kind which make all women envious, and I grab his hands, pausing as we execute a kind of awkward, four-fists, hand shake, still staring into his eyes, as he pulls into me, releasing his grip on my hands, pulling my torso into his, into a tight bear hug, overwhelming my sense of masculinity with his muscular power as he says in a softer, lower voice, tinged with femininity, "Oh God, Philip. I'm so very sorry this happened—our lovely Billy gone."

"Yes," I reply as I pull back from his arms, look again into his eyes, surprised to see tears falling.

"Yes, I've followed that on the news. Those detectives have interviewed me twice. Have they found out anything yet?" he asks, sniffling, as he pulls out a white handkerchief from his pants pocket, wipes his eyes, and blows his nose.

"Not really, nothing substantial," I reply. "You remember my friend Sarah Richardson, Ricky?"

"Of course. How are you, Lush?' he asks, giving her a hug, too.

She kisses his left cheek, "Just fine, Ricky. Nice to see you again. You all are doing wondrous things here for Billy."

"Well, nothing he wouldn't have done himself or demanded from me," he replies smiling, revealing perfect white teeth which I think must be veneers or caps.

Nothing I feel or sense from Ricky seems suspect, seems evil, evil enough to be Adrian's accomplice. My gut is usually right. Maybe Ricky is an unknowing accomplice—merely a pawn, an ignorant malefactor

in Adrian's wicked labyrinth. I look down at Clark, tail wagging, patiently standing beside Ricky, looking up at him, waiting to be acknowledged and petted. Clark would never act this way towards anyone who perpetrated murder against his master.

"Hey, Clark," Ricky says, resuming his high pitch, "How's my boy?" Ricky kneels down allowing Clark to jump up, placing his paws on Ricky's long thighs, and covering his face with licks. Ricky laughs and says, "Billy brought Clark out to my place in Westport a few times. He just loved running and playing in the woods with my dogs, didn't you Clarkster?"

"Really. I bet he did love that," I reply, glancing at Lush.

"Listen, Philip, if for any reason, there's no one to take Clark now, I want you to know I'd be happy to. He's a wonderful dog—I'm a dog person, you know. He gets along great with my spaniels. Anyway, I really mean it."

"That's really kind of you, Ricky," I reply, "But I'll be moving here now and this place wouldn't be the same without Clark."

"That's great, Philip. Glad you're moving up here, and I'm glad for Clark. That'll be less stressful on him."

"Yes, that's what I thought," but what I'm really thinking is that Fatgram said you can always trust a person who really loves dogs. Then an image of Timmy straddling Ricky, jacking him off and calling him 'Daddy's boy' appears in my mind.

"Well, listen," Ricky says, gazing out at the long dining room table, "I better get back to finishing up. Love your Dad's wife. She and I have been working together the past couple of days and all day today. I think we've got it all together."

"Yes, she's great," I reply.

"Brenda says you've got all the electronics covered, Lush. Need any help there?"

"No thanks, Ricky. I've got a young man coming to help out."

"Good. Well, everything will be on schedule just as you planned it, Lush. Brenda and I went through it carefully. It will be a wonderful evening—a fitting tribute to and celebration of Billy. I promise."

"Thanks, Ricky," I say, "I knew I could count on you."

"Well, if you all need anything, or observe something is not the way you want it, just let me know."

"Will do, Ricky," Lush replies.

He turns around, walking quickly back to a group of three women and one man who are decorating the mantel with garlands of white orchids.

"Let's go out on the terrace for a quick smoke, Todge," Lush says.

"Okay," I reply.

We walk through the dining room and out onto the terrace. Clark follows us out.

"You're going to love this," Lush says, smiling, "I think it's a bit extravagant, even by Billy's standards."

"What?" I ask and immediately spot the huge ice carving in the center of the terrace. "Oh my God, Lush. It's beautiful. Did you order this?"

"No, Todge, I didn't," she replies, pulling two cigarettes from her black clutch.

Clark trots over, sniffs the ice carving, turns to look at us, sighs, then trots off to another part of the terrace. The ice carving is a large ginger jar in the same shape as the one containing Billy's ashes; in fact, as I look at it, I realize it is a sculpture of the exact jar, with short sets of lines etched into the ice to mimic the blue lines on the vase that represent cracked ice, and beautiful rock formations, prunus, pine, and bamboo carefully carved into the ice. Surrounding the sculpture are pots of live prunus, pine, and bamboo. The prunus are covered in white blossoms. I notice all the pots are actually pots made of ice. It is a stunningly beautiful display—a great homage to my brother.

"Damn, who did this Lush? It must have cost a fortune?"

"It arrived this afternoon in a Morgan Galleries van; Brenda took the call from the bellman. It must be from Julianna. Brenda told me it took her breath away. She had the officers check it out and they said it was okay. She said she hoped you wouldn't mind putting it out here, but it was just too big to be put inside."

"Mind. I don't mind; it's beautiful. God, Mother would have loved this," I remark, taking a lit cigarette from Lush. She lights another for herself.

I take a big drag off my cigarette and walk around the sculpture, taking it all in. A slight breeze is blowing; the sun sits low in the west; the sky is pale blue, cloudless; the temperature hovers around fifty.

"It really did warm up," I remark, "I hope this doesn't melt too much."

"I think it will be fine," Lush replies, "Besides, once the sun goes does, it will cool back down quickly."

"Yeah, you're right," I reply. "It's sitting in some sort of receptacle to contain the water, anyway. Gosh, look at how intricate the carving is. Someone really skilled did this. It must have cost Julianna a fortune."

"Of course it did," Lush replies, exhaling smoke, "But you know she dearly loved Billy and would do anything for him. What a beautiful tribute."

"Indeed," I reply, sighing. "Lush, I just don't think Ricky has the capacity to do anything harmful to anyone. Do you?"

"Well, he seems pretty upset over Billy's death. But, I think it's hard to tell about those things. You know?"

"Yes, but my gut tells me he's a gentle victim. I just think if Ricky is involved, though, maybe, he doesn't really know or understand what he's doing. Adrian is that smart, you know."

"Yes, I know—as brilliant as he is evil." Lush reaches out with her left hand to stroke the ice sculpture, "Oh, I almost forgot. Look, there's a cord coming out of the ice sculpture. See. Brenda said when you plug it in, it's lit from within."

"Really?" I walk over and plug the cord into an electric receptacle in one of the brick walls. Immediately diffuse blue light shines from within the sculpture, making it even more beautiful.

"Oh my, Philip. That's gorgeous," Lush says. "Imagine what it will look like tonight."

"Yes," I reply. "I can't wait to see Julianna to thank her."

"What time is it, anyway?" I ask.

Lush glances at her watch, "It's ten after five—T minus fifty minutes and counting," she replies, smiling.

"Well, we better do a walk-through, don't you think, Lush?"

"Of course. Let's go. Oh, Mabry completed the setup on the audio visual after he and Jonas found the bug in Clark's collar. He'll also video your tribute to Billy tonight so we'll have it and so it can be broadcast on the flat screens in all the rooms. There's no way we'll get everyone in the living room when you are speaking."

"Great. I've pretty much figured out what I'll say—not too wordy, gushy, or long. Just to the point but from my heart."

"Wonderful, Todge. I know it will be a great speech."

"I hope so."

We put out our cigarettes in a stone ashtray and walk toward the kitchen door. Ricky's staff is moving about the kitchen in an orchestrated, but feverish mode. I spot Luka.

"Look, Lush, there's Luka. He must be okay."

"Yes, I see. Wow, look at the bruise on his forehead. Nasty."

"Yeah. I bet he's been through a lot of interrogation with Bell and Johnson," I reply reaching for the door handle.

"You can count on that," Lush says.

I pause. "Lush, let's not go in here. There are already too many people."

"You're right, Todge. Let's go to the studio."

We walk back on the terrace and around to the French doors of the studio. I open a door and we walk in. The room has undergone an amazing transformation—a complete antithesis to the uniformity of the living room with its masses of white orchids, for the studio has become the receptacle for the dozens of flower arrangements received today and yesterday, and Ricky has incorporated them into displays, perhaps better described as vignettes, surrounding several of Billy's most well-known paintings, some of which had to have been loaned out by their owners. How all this was done on such short notice, I haven't a clue, but I know that between Lush and Julianna, almost anything is possible. Dad is standing in front of one painting, and I see that it is the only painting in the exhibition from Billy's recent works—it is the painting of Billy swimming through Dad's legs. I turn around to look into Lush's eyes. She shakes her head back and forth, eyes widening, letting me know this is a surprise to her, and I whisper to her that Julianna is full of surprises today. She shakes her head in agreement. We walk up to Dad. I put my left hand on his right shoulder. He turns to me, and I see his blue eyes brimming with tears.

"This painting brings it back to me so clearly, son. Remember. That's the day Billy learned to swim underwater for the first time. My God, he was only four years old. Look at this. Just look at it. He was a genius even then. Look, son. Look what he remembered—all the details in perfection."

I sigh with relief, "Dad, when I saw this painting. Well, I, I didn't know how you would respond to it, the subject matter and all."

He chuckles causing a tear to spill out of his right eye, "Well, I never thought my penis would be front and center in a painting, but in this case, I'm fine with it. Do you remember that day, Philly?"

"I do, Dad. You forgot our swim trunks, so we had to skinny dip."

"Yes, I did. But what fun we had. You could already swim underwater, but Billy couldn't. That day he saw you swim between my legs. I remember the look he gave me with those sharp green eyes—a look that asked me if it was okay. Dad, was it safe? And I smiled, shook my head that it was safe, and he took a great gulp of air and followed you. I looked down at him and was just amazed that his eyes were not only open, but that he was looking up at me the whole time. Looking up at me for safety, security and confidence."

Dad begins sniffing as the tears stream down his eyes, his face reddens, framed by his thick, long, salt and pepper hair, which is combed back, layered and held in place with gel, a look both elegant and flattering. He looks into my eyes, then Lush's, clinches his right fist, gesturing with it as he begins to speak.

"And I was so confident then, that I would always be there to guide Billy and guide you, just like I did that day at the swimming hole. But I didn't. Did I, son?"

He pauses, staring into my eyes. His lips begin to quiver; he puts his fist to his forehead and begins to speak more rapidly.

"I left my beautiful boys to drown. I left them to swim alone all those years and now."

He gasps for air as the tears stream down his face.

"And, now, sweet, beautiful Billy has drowned—drowned by the evil of others, and I wasn't there to save him, as I should have been. I wasn't there to give him a hand to safety, to tell him how much I love him. I never got a last chance to tell him how truly sorry I am for that. I never got the last chance to tell him how much I love him and that I always have. How will I ever live with that, son?"

Dad looks into my eyes, searching for the answer, an answer he knows I'm incapable of giving.

"Please excuse me," he says, abruptly turns around and walks quickly out onto the terrace.

"Dad, Dad," I call out, "Wait, don't do this to yourself." He doesn't respond, but shuts the door and moves out onto the terrace. I watch him walk away, slowly, head bowed, eyes fixed on the slate floor. Suddenly Clark races past the French doors, catching up with Dad. Dad bends down, pets Clark, then embraces him.

I look up at Lush, whose eyes have filled with tears. She takes a tissue from her clutch, dabs her eyes, sniffs and says, "Damn, I'm going to ruin my mascara, Todge." She smiles at me, looks out at Dad, "That's the kind of pain no one can ease, Todge—the loneliest kind. Thank God for Clark."

I shake my head at her.

"He's a good man, Lush. I forgive him; I hope Billy would've, too. I've got to tell him about Adrian. I'll tell him in the morning before they leave."

The painting, sitting at counter level and leaning against bookshelves, is surrounded by garlands and arrangements of colorful lilies of many different types, and I'm thankful Dad approves of it, even though it's shaken him to his core.

Another painting of one of Billy's beautiful female model friends named Bitsy, perched on a rock fence on a hillside in St. Barts, hugging her knees in serious contemplation, awash in the golden light of the late afternoon sun, is surrounded by all types of tropical arrangements and palm leaves. This painting brought Billy into the limelight because of his complicated and innovative technique with the illumination of the afternoon sun on his subject, and it has subsequently become even more renowned as the model transformed herself into an Academy Award winning superstar over the past ten years. She reminds me of a twenty first century Grace Kelly because she is from a prominent Boston family and has been wooed by practically every royal and nouveau billionaire around. I don't think she ever married, though. I wonder if she will attend tonight.

Other paintings are dispersed throughout the study, some surrounded by roses, others colorful orchids, and others mixtures of flowers. Beside each painting separate food stations, each one soon to have its own chef, are set up. This must have been Julianna's idea, an ingenious way to let guests peruse the paintings as they wait for food. There is a pasta station; a beef station with a huge cutting block beside it; a seafood station, with large copper tubs containing mounds of ice where shellfish and fish will soon rest; a salad station; a vegetable station; a station with all types of cheeses; and two dessert stations. Ricky's crew has strung white lights on the Palmetto trees, the false aralias, and the ficus trees and has brought in several large palm trees, all strung with white lights, giving the room the feel of a tropical solarium.

I glance up at the fieldstone chimney of the fireplace and am surprised to see two paintings: the only painting of Mother's that Billy ever attempted—Fatgram's swimming hole. Mother executed the entire painting plein air whereas Billy did his strictly from memory. I love both; each has its own story to tell, as has so clearly become evident to me this past week. Once again, Julianna must have had these placed here because she is the owner of both of these paintings.

"Wow," Lush says, looking up at the paintings. "Both so wonderful, yet so different. Your Mother's looks so real, the light and ripples on the water, the trees. I can almost hear the stream running. And Billy's, from the same perspective as your Mom's but it looks, well it looks like a black and white photograph, Todge. It's beautiful."

"Yes, it is, Lush. Gosh, it looks almost like one of Adrian's photos. I wonder if he got ahold of one when he did this? Maybe Julianna knows." A wave of nausea runs through my gut as I reason that Billy's relationship with Adrian must have been deeper than I have thought, even deeper than the recent emails reveal.

"You okay, Todge?"

"Yeah, why?"

"Well, you look a bit 'green around the gills.'"

"Nerves, I suppose. Did you save any of those roaches?"

"I did, Todge. But you can't get stoned now," Lush gives me a disapproving look.

"No, no. Not stoned. Just a toke or two will calm my upset stomach."

"Really?" She looks surprised.

"Sure. You didn't know that?" She shakes her head. "Well, it works for a bad hangover, too."

"My, my, the medicinal properties of cannibus," she replies, taking my left arm in her right arm. "Let's go to my room and I'll get the roach. Then, we can go into your bathroom and smoke it."

"We?" I ask in a high tone.

"Absolutely. I'm gonna need help, too, to get through this night."

We both laugh and head out of the study, circumventing the kitchen by way of the back hallway. As we approach Lush's room, we hear the clickety-clack of what sounds like someone running down the limestone hallway in tap shoes.

"Philip, Lush, wait for me," Emma's excited voice rings out.

We turn around to see Emma running after us. She reaches us, out of breath, smiling. She twirls around like a petite ballerina; her white, knee length satin dress, tied in the back with a big, pastel blue bow, flares into a perfect circle completely exposing her slim legs covered in white tights and a frilly, crispy-white slip; her fragile arms, the upper parts of which are covered by puffy sleeves, held high above her head, gracefully arch into an oval; she rises up onto her toes in a pair of flats the exact color as the blue bow on her dress, her hair pulled back into a short of bun-pony tail combination held in place with a rhinestone comb and ringlets of hair hanging from her temples, executes two complete turns, stops on a dime, curtsies in perfect form and says, "Well, how do I look?"

Lush claps her hands, "Absolutely adorable, darling. You're so pretty and a dancer, too."

"Yes, I'm in my third year of ballet," she replies as she brushes the skirt of her dress back in place.

"You look beautiful, Emma," I say, smiling. "Are your brothers ready, too?"

"Yes," she replies as she begins to twist as if she were spinning a Hula Hoop on her hips, looking down at the undulating motion of her satin skirt, "Mom's making sure they look alright now." She glances up at us, smiles, pulls one of her curls with her right hand and says, "My brothers don't like to comb their hair. Mom said she's not going to have them look like shaggy dogs tonight."

"Well, I'm sure your Mother will have them looking spiffy in no time," Lush says. "Emma, dear, would you mind to go tell your Mother that Philip and I would like to meet her in the studio in a few minutes for a final run-through of things?"

"Oh, okay," she says. She smiles again, simultaneously jumps up, turns around in mid-air, lands, executes several kangaroo-like hops down the hall, then breaks into a full tap dancing gallop. We both laugh.

"Wish I had all her energy, " I reply.

"You and me both. Wonder why Brenda let her wear taps on those shoes?" Lush asks as she turns into her bedroom, a room Billy referred to as 'transitional' in its furnishings and artwork with several original Schieles hanging on the walls, walks around the large sleigh bed made of cherry with an antique finish, covered with linens, a down comforter and pillows in solid white, opens a drawer in one of the matching nightstands, picks up a silver cigarette case, opens it, pulls out half of one of the joints we smoked with Brenda last night, which seems like many days ago to me right now, shows it to me and smiles.

"We better hurry in to your bathroom to smoke this before Brenda's done with the boys."

"Right," I reply, "Let's just pop into your bath. It's got a fan doesn't it?"

"Yes, but Emma's been hanging out in here some. I don't want her to notice any funny smells," she replies.

"Well, with a fan and a spray or two of perfume, it'll be fine," I say as I walk toward the bathroom.

"Okay," Lush says following me into the bathroom, also in a transitional style, with the floor, walls, ceiling, vanity, shower, and Jacuzzi all fabricated from small, beautiful glass tiles in deep tones of aubergine, rust, and green. I love this bathroom, the warm colors, the solidity, uniformity, and steadfastness of the tiles and everything into which they are fashioned. This room and bathroom are where I stay when I visit Billy. I flip on the lights; all are indirect halogens, hidden behind rectangular troughs of tile in arrays of rectilinear designs on the ceiling, walls, and around the mirrors, connected to a panel containing several

dimmer switches, allowing for the light intensity to be controlled in zones across the bathroom. This feature is fantastic, creating mesmerizing effects of light bouncing off the glass tiles. I shut the door and adjust the dimmers for low background lighting in the bathroom, but stronger light around the vanity, so we can clearly see ourselves in the mirror. I also turn on the fans over the shower and over the toilet. Lush hands me the joint. I take it and her lighter, put the joint between my lips, flick the lighter, put the flame to the joint, inhaling deeply as I watch the tip of the joint begin to glow orange-red. I hand the joint to Lush who takes it between her ample red lips, inhales, and hands it back to me. I release the smoke from my lungs.

"Thanks, Lush. Just one more toke for me and my stomach will be fine."

I take another big hit and hold it. Lush does the same and we stand quietly, looking at each other, smiling, until we can no longer hold our breaths, and we exhale out the thick smoke.

"Whew, I can feel my eyeballs bulging already. That's good stuff."

"Yes, it is, Todge," Lush replies, turning to view herself in the mirror.

I take the joint, snuff it out on the glass tiles and then look up into the mirror at Lush.

"You're as beautiful as ever, Lush."

She smiles, chuckles, looks at my face in the mirror, and replies, "Thanks, Philip. And you are as well. Are we ready for this?"

I turn around toward her, taking her hands in mine, "I'm ready, Lush. Your presence here means so much to me. I'm not so sure I would be getting through this at all if you couldn't have come."

"That's not a possibility, Todge. Nothing would have kept me away. Over the years, you've been there for me, always. I can't begin to tell you how much that means to me. I hope you feel the same?"

"Of course I do, Lush."

"Damn, I'm sorry, Philip. There I go again, fishing for self-affirmation."

"What? No, Lush. You're not doing that."

"The hell I'm not. Didn't you know that about me, Philip? I'm always seeking approval from others—what a vicious cycle, self-disparagement, bad, weak, ugly little feelings swirling inside, making me afraid, Todge. So afraid until someone comes along—even a total fucking stranger—offers me the slightest compliment, the tiniest bit of affirmation that I'm not inferior, not bad, not ugly in a hundred different ways. Yes, only then does the ice crack, and a warm feeling of self-worth pushes through. Only then, Todge."

I feel my brow knotting up as I search her eyes, absorbing the immense depth of sadness flowing out, surprising myself that I can connect to her pain.

"Gosh, Lush. I'm so sorry. I feel like a complete idiot. In all these years I never knew that about you. Or, maybe, I just never let myself feel it. Because something so strong, well, it must have always been there. I, I just didn't see it."

A tear falls from her left eye as she sniffs.

"Well, truth is, Philip, when I first fell in love with you, that's the only period in my life when that feeling went away. It was like the highest of highs. Shit, you see the reason I fell in love with you was purely selfish, purely an antidote for sadness for one selfish bitch."

Tears are streaming down her face now.

"Dear God, Lush. That's just not true. Love makes everyone feel good about themselves. That's, that's totally normal. There's nothing wrong with that."

"Oh no, Todge. My narcissism precludes true love—I just can't feel it, I can only feel better about myself."

"Geez, that's a mouthful, Lush. Where is all this coming from?"

"I don't know, Todge. Maybe the years of group therapy are finally working." She turns around, grabs a tissue and begins dabbing at her eyes, looking into the mirror.

"Shit, maybe that's what I need—group therapy."

"Well, I think it's helping me, Todge."

"I can see that, Lush. But where is all this sadness coming from? Whatever happened to you to cause this? I mean you've always had everything."

She turns back around toward me.

"I'm so ashamed, Todge. I have always had everything—a true life of privilege. My parents, especially Mother, constantly reminded me that I was from a long line of achievers, upstanding citizens, and pillars of society. I was different from everyone else by virtue of my birth. I guess I just grew up perpetually trying to uphold this mythical standard, but never really feeling good enough or worthy enough for it—just shame and sadness."

"Lush," I say as I take both her hands again, "Listen to me. When I first met you I was attracted to a young, beautiful, smart, vibrant girl. And when we made love and would lie in each other's arms afterwards, well, what I felt and I felt that you felt it, too, wasn't just lust or physical attraction. I felt that you could look into my soul and recognize that part of me that is good, and I could do the same with you and we nurtured each other in that way. That has nothing to do with narcissism. And I was the one who blew it because I couldn't accept that intensity of pureness without a devastating fear of losing it. You were my angel, an angel I couldn't hold onto, then. I think that's why our friendship has survived all these years. That's why we're so close—we recognize and cherish that capacity to connect and love each other without conditions. My God, Lush. How many people on this earth ever have that?"

She pauses, searching my eyes, and smiles.

"Todge, thank you. I love you. You are the kindest, caring, most emotionally connected man I know."

"Thanks, Lush. As you well know, I've journeyed through hell to get here, wherever that really is."

"Billy knew this about you, Todge. Did you know that about him?"

"What do you mean, Lush?"

"Well, he was always concerned that you wouldn't find the right person—a person he would refer to as 'worthy of your love.'"

"Really, Lush?"

"Yes, really. I guess I can talk about it now."

"About what?"

"Well, Billy was in group therapy, too, for the past couple of years. He knew I was, too, so he confided in me. I just couldn't discuss this with you, Todge. I mean. I mean, that's just how it is. Respect, you know."

"Yes, yes, of course."

I look into her eyes for answers.

"Well, now that he's gone. I guess Billy wouldn't mind that I give you some idea, some comfort about his emotional state. He was really experiencing self-enlightenment, Todge. My God, you can see it in his paintings. Yet, he was so guilty about his relationship with you."

"Guilty?"

"Yes. He never told me about Adrian. But he did tell me about having sex with you. He felt he manipulated and controlled you all those years until you cut him off. In a way, he and I are a lot alike. Your having sex with him was the ultimate self-affirmation—he'd do anything to get it. Now that I know the history of the abuse by Adrian, it all makes sense to me."

"How so, Lush?"

"Well, Adrian manipulated both you and Billy as innocent children to feel good about yourselves in direct proportion to the amount of sex you had with him. He must have given you both tremendous gifts for sexual favors. I think both Billy and you transferred that to each other as teenagers and then to others as you matured."

"I see what you're saying. It feels right."

"Billy came to this understanding by becoming totally vulnerable in a group situation. You arrive at it through a series of tragedies and simple self-examination. And, it makes perfect sense to me that as sensitive as you are, whenever you got a taste of unconditional love, your greatest fear was losing it, so you bounced from lover to lover, one-night stand to one-night stand until now."

"Now, Lush?"

"Well, that's what Billy was relaying to me. You see, I didn't want to upset you, but I really believe he had a premonition that he was in danger, that there was a real chance something bad would happen to him."

Suddenly, I feel my heart beating in my throat. I squeeze Lush's hands, shaking them.

"You must tell me, Lush."

"Yes. His last email to me was Saturday, late in the evening, just as he was about to go to Splash. He wrote, well he wrote that he was feeling better about himself than he could ever remember. He said now that he was in such a good, solid emotional state, he wanted the same for you. He didn't say what, but he said that he had a lot of old baggage he wanted to resurrect with you. To clear the air, you know. He said he thought that if he could do this with you, that you might be able. Well his exact words were that 'Philly will finally be able to cast off that shame embroidered cloak of responsibility he's worn since Mother's death.'"

"Billy said that?"

"He did, Todge. He also asked me to help him think of a good time and place and way to breech all this with you. And he ended the email by saying that he was really worried what would happen to you if anything ever happened to him. He said he was ready to start over with healthy relationships in the future and that's what he really wanted for you, too."

My vision becomes blurred, I feel tears running down my face, my nose stops up, and I feel my brother's strong arms surrounding me with love.

"Thanks for telling me that, Lush. It means so much to me. So much. I can see the way through this evening now."

CHAPTER 32

Love. So much love is what I feel right now—right in the thick of Billy's wake surrounded by people who adored my brother. The two tokes of pot and a glass of good champagne have lulled the usual frenetic rhythms of my brain where my thoughts are conceived, born, and put to death with such rapidity like shooting stars in a meteor shower that it's often hard for me to focus on what people are saying to me; in other words, I am not usually a good listener with much capacity of truly understanding what someone is relating to me without forceful, conscious effort. In this current, magic, trance-like state—a state I often imagined Billy entered during his creative bursts, Mother, too. Of the dozens and dozens of people who've arrived and I've met this evening, I can remember something about virtually everyone of them— it's as if I am a sponge absorbing all these events so that I can squeeze them out later in a bucket to give to my brother as a tribute. I realize, even as it all transpires, I will write about this at some point in time, in some fashion. Peter is playing the piano for the second time, an indication that I must give my tribute to Billy soon. My father, Brenda, and Emma are tireless greeters at the elevator, with smiling Emma, demure one moment, loquacious the next, proudly giving each arriving woman a beautiful Tropicana rose

in its own sterling silver bud vase with the phrase 'In Memory of Billy Hampton, April 1, 1975-April 6, 2006' engraved down the neck. Gentlemen receive a silver ballpoint pin with the same engraving. Dad and Brenda are elegant and gracious together, skilled at getting the people in rather quickly. Drew looks splendid in a black wool blazer with a white shirt, a black and grey striped tie, and grey wool pants, curly auburn hair in disarray despite Brenda's attempts, brushed behind his left ear, but covering his right ear, so much like Billy's, Clark calmly at his left side in the newly purchased collar, both unabashedly working the crowd, Drew showing off Clark, talking to complete strangers, many of whom are famous, Clark patiently licking hands, sniffing legs and feet. Peter is in all black—even his shirt and necktie, which I suspect is his preference. He sits at the piano playing for the crowd as if it were a nightly occurrence for him. Mabry has brought in two people with digital cameras, one focusing on Peter as his body sways, his long blonde curly locks tussling about his face, his image broadcast on all the flat screens in the house. My agent, Florence shows off her slim, voluptuous body, clad in a shimmering black satin dress, with a row of shiny black buttons, sewn on a richly embroidered trim running up the entire front of the dress, working the crowd accompanied by a handsome young man from Kansas who she says has just completed the most fantastic novel. In a few swift seconds of conversation, she displays to me a range of emotion from utter sadness over Billy's death to abundant joy about the two new assignments, both of which will involve extensive travel, she has obtained for me during her London trip. As the reticent young author listens, she tells me to take as much time as I need to come to some resolution about Billy's death because she can get the deadlines for the two articles pushed back, if necessary, and that her preeminent concern is my emotional well being. She hugs me, kisses me on the cheek, and grabs the young man by the hand, leading him over to a well-known movie producer and his wife. God love her, the metonym 'has balls' certainly applies to this woman, yet she is a mélange of femininity, finesse, fierceness, and fortitude guided by a keen intellect and an honest desire to help others, not merely use them, as she climbs ever higher in the publishing world. It wouldn't surprise me at all to find her owning or at least running one of the media conglomerates in a few years. Thank you, dear brother, for introducing us.

Lush, with her intense beauty and striking figure, looks every bit as resplendent as Florence, and is a real 'head turner' in this New York City 'A' crowd. I watch her absorbing the looks, the attention, and I'm happy for her. She needs and deserves this after years of living with the emotionally abusive dolt, David. I think she hasn't quite got all that mess about her narcissism figured out; for instance, despite all the attention she's receiving, she is careful to check in with me every few minutes to see how I'm doing, and if everything is going to my satisfaction. There's nothing narcissistic about that. I love Lush. What would I do without her?

Even though it's a wake, the mood is light, warm, perhaps even a tinge of levity is emerging—Billy would be the first to appreciate and probably instigate this. The crowds have spilled into all the rooms, even into the bedrooms and guest suite. Ricky's staff is everywhere, working quickly and quietly to service the guests. He seems to be everywhere at once, giving subtle, forceful direction to his staff, relentless in his orchestration of this affair, gesticulating with many sharp, erratic, hand signals, the meanings are only understood by his staff. I couldn't be more pleased with him, yet I find myself fantasizing, pushing him into Billy's sex room, chaining him up on the scaffold, stripping his shirt off, beating him with a leather whip or perhaps choking him with the silk noose until he reveals the extent of his knowledge about Billy's murder and Adrian. I force myself to release this negative image and move on from the living room into the dining room. The long dining table is now full of all types of food, food that is as beautiful to behold as it is to taste. Many things are unrecognizable to me, small, individual works of art which guests curiously observe, carefully pick up, sometimes sniff, then pop into their mouths, closing their eyes, smiling, as the tastes tantalize their tongues. There is one silver tray full of confections that are almost indistinguishable from white phaleonopsis blossoms. I haven't the slightest desire to eat anything at this point because I know it will distort my magic state. I notice a flash and turn to see a photographer taking pictures. Security

personnel at the security screening process in the lobby informed all guests that all photographs and videos made by the family are for family use only. Absolutely no copies will be distributed to the media or anyone else, for that matter. They also asked everyone to refrain from taking photographs with cell phones. All the bodyguards have been instructed to stop anyone they see doing this. I do not want Billy's wake to become fodder for the tabloids—God only knows what they've published already. I look outside to see groups of people on the terrace, the red glows of cigarettes moving about like fireflies on a June night. The ice carving of the ginger jar is plugged in and a pale bluish light floods the terrace. I must find Julianna to thank her for this. I wonder if she has arrived yet. Janet Ostro, looking like a different woman, dressed in a pants suit of black silk brocade with designs of five-clawed dragons chasing flaming pearls woven into the fabric, her short hair, appearing longer, probably coiffed with a hair piece or extensions, a large hair clip in the form of a Chinese dragon, sparkling with rhinestones, maybe diamonds, fastened on the right side of her head, make-up carefully applied by a skilled artist, arrived about half an hour ago. I told her how beautiful she looked. She smiled self-consciously and said it was all Julianna's design. She told me Julianna had some last minute business to attend to at the gallery, but would be along before my tribute to Billy. Brooker T, dressed in a black suit, white shirt and black tie, arrived at the same time as Janet. I introduced Brooker T as my brother to Janet. She didn't seem a bit surprised. They seemed to hit it off, and I watched Brooker T accompany Janet into the crowd. Stan Shultz, Billy's fishing guide from Key West, arrives arm in arm, with a tall, young, lithe, woman named Sabre, with thick, brown hair, hanging down past her ass, wearing a sleeveless, tight, short, black dress, revealing long brown arms completely covered in delicate, curvilinear, henna tattoos. Stan's countenance is striking: thick hair, sun-bleached into a bright white-blonde, half way covers his brown ears and surrounds a furrowed lined, deeply tanned forehead, grey-white eyebrows arch over his dark brown eyes which frame a slightly bulbous nose with more of a red hue than brown, and a grey white mustache and goatee setting off thin lips and a strong jaw. The roughness of his hands are apparent as I shake his right hand, and I can't help but think how out of place he looks in a black, pinstripe suit. As he and Sabre offer their condolences, I focus in on her New England accent and wonder if she was one of those Key West vacationers who went down for a week or two, was intoxicated by the unhurried, unfettered, unadorned lifestyle, fell in with a fisherman like Stan and stayed on. I shift my attention to telling Stan about Billy's wish to have him take me to the Marquesas to spread some of his ashes. Stan and Sabre exchange a look that tells me how much they are touched by Billy's request and so happy to do it. As I am discussing with Stan the timing of the ceremony, Drew engages Sabre in a conversation about Clark. I hear Sabre say she knows Clark, had met him when Billy brought him down to Key West last April. I had forgotten about that. Maybe I should take him with me to Union, Key West, and St. Barts. I think I must. I thank Stan and Sabre for coming and they walk off into the crowd with Drew.

I continue my walk through the crowd. People stop me to express their condolences about Billy, comment on how shocking the murders of Billy and Elliott are, and thank me for such an extraordinary, wonderful affair. My closest friends from Atlanta, Buck and Turley Madison, who both started at *The Constitution* with me, come up to me and we embrace in a sort of group hug. The three of us banded together from the onset and became friends dealing with our new careers and the bar scene in Atlanta. Buck and I competed for Turley's affection in an unspoken manner, but I believe Turley sensed that beyond sex, I probably wouldn't have much to offer in a relationship at that time. Buck and Turley eventually fell in love and got married. They never excluded me or pushed me aside as their relationship deepened, and I was best man at their wedding. Besides Lush and Florence, they are the only friends of mine I invited. I really don't have that many friends in Atlanta, in part because I travel so much, but, in truth, because I always considered my real home here in New York with Billy—I relied on forming relationships with his friends much more than seeking out my own friends in Atlanta. In the past ten years I've live in Atlanta, Billy has only been there a couple of times—once for a modeling job and once for an art exhibition. Buck and Turley live in my neighborhood and have been so generous over the years inviting me over to dinner,

sending over home cooked meals, including me in family events and outings with their three young children. I love them both; they make me feel grounded in Atlanta. I'm always welcome in their home, in their family, anytime—no strings attached, no questions asked. Periodically, I do become annoyed with them when they try to fix me up with some unmarried or divorced woman Turley is certain will turn out to be my perfect life mate. I also adore their three dogs, Cosmos, a frisky Australian Cattle Dog, and Gus and Ruby, two cute French Bulldogs. We chat a minute and they instinctively release me to continue on my circulation among the crowd. I avoid the kitchen and continue down the hall into the studio. The room is packed with people viewing the art and waiting in little groups at the food stations. Detectives Johnson and Bell stand over by the French doors surveying the crowd. Detective Johnson is dressed in his usual dark pen-stripe suit. Detective Bell looks stunning in a short, black, sleeveless dress, with a wide, lacey, black ruffle collar made out of some diaphanous material covering her cleavage, which I suspect will be occasionally revealed with the movement of her body. They notice me watching them; Detective Johnson nods his head, and I move toward them, thinking that even an unpleasant confrontation with Detective Bell is worth a glimpse of her cleavage, but notice that a group of people are standing around discussing Billy's painting of my nude father from an underwater perspective. It is Timmy, Manon, and a handsome man with a closely cropped beard dressed in a dark grey suit, probably Armani. Timmy introduces him as Manon's husband, Sebastian. It's easy to see that Timmy is familiar with this couple, and I quickly surmise that Billy must have had sex with both Manon and Sebastian, maybe even participated in an orgy with Timmy involved—how hot would that have been, I think. As Sebastian speaks to me, his blue eyes seem to reach inside mine, startling me at first, then evolving into what feels like a violation of my personal space—uncovering information I don't freely expose, focusing on my emotional weaknesses, ascertaining things I probably don't even know about myself, overwhelming me with the urge to turn around and run away. I can't figure this out—few people, besides Billy and Fatgram have ever had this effect on me before. I have this uncanny feeling that Sebastian is some sort of wizard, sorcerer, or savant. I forcefully tear my gaze from his, look down at my feet, look back up and him, and ask him what he does for a living. He replies that he is a psychiatrist. My body tingles; I can't believe I didn't make the connection in Manon's store. Sebastian is Billy's psychotherapist, Dr. Gerard. Why the hell didn't Manon tell me this? No wonder I feel as if he knows my deepest, darkest secrets—he probably does. I'm jolted out of my magic state, and I pull Sebastian aside and put my lips close to his right ear.

"Dr. Gerard, have the detectives questioned you yet about Billy's death?"

"Yes, they have," he replies with only a trace of a French accent.

"Well, do you know anything about who might have killed Billy?"

He clears his throat loudly, hesitates, then says, "Mr. Hampton, you probably already know I can not and will not discuss my patients' confidential information, of any type."

"But...."

"Please wait, Mr. Hampton. You see, I have told the police that, to the best of my knowledge, I have no information that would be useful in identifying who might have killed Billy. I told them that if they have a suspect or could identify a potential suspect, then my opinion might change."

"Indeed, Dr. Gerard," I reply, leaning, over putting my lips almost against his right ear, whispering, "I know very well who killed Billy. It was Adrian McWhorter."

I pull back to look at his face which is contorted, drawn—a look of nervous surprise. His lips open to speak; nothing comes out. I lean in again.

"I'd appreciate it if you wouldn't say anything to anyone. I haven't even told the police yet, but I have proof. I'm sure of it. I just have to get the bastard back in the states so he can be arrested and tried. Once he's over here, I'll deliver him to the police."

"Mr. Hampton. What you're planning is beyond the law. It's not right, and it could be dangerous if, in fact, Adrian is the killer."

"It's worth the risk for me. You see, the bastard killed my Mother, too, and others, several others. Not only is he a notorious pedophile, he's also a serial killer, and I intend to stop him, if it's the last thing I ever do."

"Mr. Hampton, please don't act rashly. You must trust the authorities."

"Trust? Trust, Dr. Gerard? I have assembled a skilled team to get this job done, and I trust that we will do it. Please, Sebastian, don't betray me, don't betray my brother. And if there is anything you know, anything you really know that might help me, I trust that you will tell me."

My body language is forceful, on the verge of becoming overbearing, and I sense that I am becoming offensive to Sebastian. I take a step back and fold my arms.

"Mr. Hampton, your brother described you very well. I can tell you, he really knew you," he says, narrowing his eyes.

"Yes, I'm sure he did. And you know how much we loved each other. So you know I'm dead serious about this." We both stand there looking at each other.

"I tell you what, Dr. Gerard, I'll become your patient, too. Now that my brother's gone, there should be no real conflict, right?"

"Well, that's not completely true, Mr. Hampton."

"But, it's not completely untrue either. I could really use your help, dealing with Billy's death, dealing with the sexual abuse in my past, trying to figure out where I go from here."

"I don't know, Mr. Hampton," he replies and I see that even though Manon and Timmy are engaged in conversation, Manon appears nervous as she periodically glances at us.

"Please, Sebastian, give it a try—just one meeting, to begin with. I can be there Monday."

He reaches into the inside pocket of his suit jacket, pulls out a card, hands it to me as he says, "I'm completely booked, but come by my office at noon and we'll talk."

"Thank you, Sebastian, I'll be there." I glance across the room to see Detective Bell watching me; I quickly turn toward Timmy and Manon.

"So, how do you all know each other?"

"Well, Billy and Timmy first came to my store, hmm, maybe a year ago." She glances at Sebastian and then looks back at me. "Clark and Bernard got along so well Billy and sometimes Timmy would meet me at the dog park so the dogs could play. We all got to know each other. Sebastian and I began using Timmy as our masseur. He really is marvelous. Have you tried him?"

"Oh, yes, I have. He's quite good," I reply, quickly smiling at Timmy.

"Yes, it's, how do you say? A tiny, no, a small world, Philip. It wasn't until a couple of months ago that Sebastian and I realized than my dog-walking friend, Billy, was Sebastian's patient."

"Really," I reply, "You didn't know Billy was a famous model and painter?"

"No, I knew he was an artist, but that was all. I've lived in New York only three years—just since Sebastian and I married," she replies raising her Tropicana rose to her nose, turning her head away from me, revealing a beautiful profile. The long sleeved black dress she wears has ruches starting at a V-neckline and running down the front in double panels cascading over her curves and accentuating her tiny waist. The back is cutout and ties at the top, similar to Lush's blouse. I can't help myself, my eyes follow her curves longing to see and know her body.

Some one taps my back; I turn around to see Detective Bell standing there with a half-smile, looking directly into my eyes.

"Good evening, Mr. Hampton. Could I have a quick word with you?"

"Certainly," I reply and turn back to Manon, Sebastian, and Timmy, "Would you all please excuse me?"

"Of course," Manon says.

Detective Bell and I walk over to some of the storage bins where there is no crowd.

"Are there any new developments, Detective Bell?"

She chuckles, "How odd, Mr. Hampton, that's exactly what I planned to ask you."

"Here we go again," I reply, shaking my head, looking out over the crowd.

"Yes, here we go again. Or maybe you'd like to tell me why you all decided to change out the hot water heater in Adrian McWhorter's apartment this morning?"

"Ha," I laugh, "I should have known you tailed us."

"We do our job thoroughly, Mr. Hampton," she replies. I notice she holds onto a rather large black satin evening purse.

"Do you have a gun in that purse, Detective Bell?"

"Of course I do, Mr. Hampton. But, back to my question. What were you looking for in Adrian McWhorter's apartment?"

"Well, anything of my Mother's and brother's. You see, Julianna and I thought that Adrian might have kept some of their works that he had no right to keep—you know, before he died."

"I see," she replies, "Before he died…."

"Yes, you see Julianna can not place the whereabouts of a couple of known works by Mother and by Billy and she thinks Adrian had them."

"Well, why didn't you ask Julian Ainsworth about them?"

"We did, but we just didn't believe him when he denied knowing anything about them."

"Did you find anything, Mr. Hampton?"

"We found one painting, one done by Mother. A river scene done in France the summer she died."

"I see. Did you take it?"

"I did. You see it was a gift from Mother to me—for my thirteenth birthday."

"How do you know that?"

"Mother wrote me a birthday message in the river water, a message in fluorescent paint that shows up only under a black light."

"How interesting," she replies. "Did you find anything else?"

"No, nothing really, but the place is crammed full of important art."

"Really?"

"Yes. I'm not sure why Mr. Ainsworth leaves it all there. It's got to be worth a fortune, Julianna says."

"That's a good question," she replies.

"So you all had surveillance on Adrian's building while we were in there?"

"Yes."

"Did you notice anything else?"

"Like what, Mr. Hampton?"

"Like anyone else entering or leaving while we were there."

"Why, do you think you were being followed by someone else?"

"Come on detective, cut the BS. Just give me a straight answer," I say glancing into her eyes, then down into the lacey cleavage.

"That's so interesting, Mr. Hampton. You expect 'straight answers' from us, yet you tell us none of the findings you and your expensive private investigators glean."

"Just forget it," I say, looking at my watch. "Listen, I have a eulogy to give in about five minutes. I need to go."

"Yes," she says and grabs my left arm as I start to walk away. "Mr. Hampton, we really do care about your safety and the safety of those around you. I don't know what you have found out and what trail or trails you are following in connection with your brother's death, but I suspect you are in over your head. If you would just trust us, we could help you immensely."

"Thank you, Detective Bell. That gives me great comfort," I reply in a tone of disdain.

"I really mean it, Mr. Hampton. I did check on Adrian McWhorter as you asked me to. I found three complaints of pedophilia files against him, two in the 1980's and one in the early1990's. There was also an on-going investigation into his involvement in an international ring of child pornographers at the time of his death."

"Really. I see. Thank you for checking on that, Detective Bell."

"Well?" she asks.

"Well, what?"

"Isn't there anything you want to tell me, now that I've told you what we found out about Adrian?" She crosses her arms, holding the clutch in her right hand.

"No, there isn't, Detective Bell," I reply turning away.

"Mr. Hampton," she quickly says, "The charge filed in the early 90's was by a Sally Wallitch. She was Adrian's personal secretary and your caterer's mother. We photographed Ricky pulling out of the garage of Adrian's building about twenty minutes after you all entered the building."

"Very interesting," I reply. "Have you questioned him about it?"

"Yes, right before he came over here. Seems he was employed by Mr. McWhorter until he died and then by Mr. Ainsworth to take care of the New York apartment. We confirmed this with the building's superintendent. Ricky said he was there today to make sure everything was alright when the super called him to tell him about the water heater."

"I see," I reply.

"So, I suppose Ricky didn't reveal himself to you all in the apartment?"

"No, he didn't," I reply. "We thought we heard someone leaving through the back door. That's why I asked you if you all saw anyone leaving."

"Well, he must know it was you and Miss Morgan in there today," she replies, her eyes rolling over the crowd.

"I suppose he does, but he hasn't said anything to me today. I don't care if he does, I'll just tell him the truth."

"The truth, Mr. Hampton?" she asks locking her eyes on mine.

"Yes, detective, the truth. Now if you'll excuse me, I must go."

I quickly walk away, through the studio and into the back hallway, my mind racing now over the new information about Ricky. If he's that involved, he could kill me or any of my family in an instant here tonight. I've got to find Jonas before the eulogy. Two teenage girls, dressed in black outfits, one in a short skirt and blouse, the other in a short black dress, both with makeup on, stop me in the hallway.

"Like, you're Mr. Hampton's brother, right?" The taller blonde girl says as she twirls the strand of pearls around her neck.

"Yes, I am," I reply.

"Like, I told you he was, totally, Hilary," the brunette says to her friend.

"Well, like, we're so sorry about his death," Hilary says.

"Yeah, totally," her friend joins in, "He was like so totally cool, being a famous model and all and a fab artist."

"Yeah, he was friends with our parents," Hilary says.

"He was. Like Hilary still has an underwear poster of Billy hanging in her bedroom," the brunette says.

"Ewwww, Daphne, you midge. How totally crude to bring that up now," Hilary says.

I smile. "Thanks, girls. Are you two sisters?"

"Well, like half sisters. We have the same father. He's like an art critic for the Times," Hilary says.

"I see. Well, thank you girls for coming, and thank your parents," I reply. They look at each other and giggle. "There's plenty of good food out there, great desserts. Be sure and have some." They giggle again.

"Nice to meet you, ladies," I say and walk on down the hall. On a whim I head into Lush's bedroom and, to my amazement, she is standing in there talking with Officer O'Daniel. They both look up at me, abruptly ceasing their conversation.

"Oh, Todge, I was just coming to find you. Five minutes until you go on, darling," Lush says, her face reddening as she speaks.

"Yes, I know. But first, I need a word with you, Lush. Alone. Could you excuse us, Officer O'Daniel?"

"Of course, Mr. Hampton," he says, glancing up at Lush as he walks out of the room.

"Well, I see this relationship continues to develop," I say in a whisper.

"Stop it, Todge. We were just talking. No big deal," she replies, her face now completely red.

"Yes, well. Well, anyway, Detective Bell told me she had us trailed today—saw us do the whole water heater thing at Adrian's."

"Dear God," Lush says, her mouth wide open.

"Right, but anyway, she told me they observed Ricky Wallitch leaving the building about twenty minutes after we went in."

"Shit," she says.

"I know. Where's Jonas? We need to talk to him before I make the speech."

To my amazement, Lush picks up a small beeper-looking device from the bedside table and presses a button. In a second I hear Jonas's voice, "Lush, you need something?"

She presses a button and speaks, "Yes, come back to my bedroom. Hurry please."

"On the way," he replies.

"Damn, why didn't I get one of those?"

"Because you are being shadowed," she replies. "Look outside the door."

I stick my head outside the door to see a tall, muscular man with short brown hair, in a dark suit standing there. I saw him once this evening and just thought he was one of the guests.

"Gee, I had no idea he was watching me all night."

"Good, then he's doing his job well," she says, "There's an officer assigned to each member of your family."

"That's good, especially after what Detective Bell just told me," I reply.

"What did she say?" Lush asks, opening a compact to look at her face in the mirror.

"Everything okay, Lush?" Jonas, dressed in a charcoal suit with blue windowpane patterns and a white shirt with a necktie with blue and black diagonal stripes, jacket unbuttoned, asks as he walks into the room.

"Fine, Jonas. Philip has some news from Detective Bell."

"Yes, she told me she had us followed today into Adrian's apartment. She said they observed Ricky Wallitsch leaving the building about twenty minutes after we arrived."

"Interesting," Jonas says, rubbing his chin with his right hand.

"There's more. She also told me that Adrian had three charges of child molestation filed against him during the eighties and nineties, the last one was filed by Ricky's mother, Sally, who was Adrian's secretary. I've already told Lush that while Timmy was giving me a massage today I asked him if he knew Ricky. He said he did, that he was a client. Sexually, Ricky likes to play the role of the little boy and make Timmy play the domineering daddy. He also said he has massaged Ricky's Uncle Adrian, an art professor from Oxford who visits a couple of times a year."

"Yes, it all fits together," Jonas says, leaning into us and speaking quietly. "Sallie Wallitsch committed suicide in 1998, supposedly. Adrian became Ricky's legal guardian. Ricky was seventeen at the time. Adrian did indeed, as we suspected, mastermind the catering business as an avenue to get into major collectors homes, to establish a secret catalog of sorts for whatever reason, legitimate art dealing or theft, probably both. His attorney was the original incorporator and the original address was Adrian's apartment for Ricky's business."

"He plans everything, doesn't he?" Lush asks with a look of disgust on her face.

"Yes he does," Jonas replies, "He engages in detailed and long range planning. He pretty much blows the mold of the typical serial killer because he forms very close relationships with his victims for gain—both sexual—their children—and monetary—their art. No telling how he took out Sallie Wallitsch, but we'll find out."

"Well it's obvious Ricky is Adrian's mole," I reply. "Aren't we all in danger with him here? What if the food is poisoned?" I ask.

"Unlikely," Jonas replies, "He and his crew went through NYPD screening and our screening to get inside—we found nothing. He runs a stellar business, no question about that. Even Julianna uses him. I called her and discussed him with her this afternoon. She said he's never let her down and that he and Billy were also good friends. From what I've learned about him this afternoon, he is well liked on many levels: business, social, the dog show circuit. I just don't think he would knowingly kill or contribute to the killing of a close friend. I think Ricky is carefully manipulated by Adrian, more or less for informational purposes, but I think Adrian uses others, like the twins, to carry out his dirty deeds."

"Can you really be so sure, Jonas?" Lush asks.

"Nothing is certain, Lush, but I think I'm right about Ricky," he replies in a confidant tone making me instinctively trust him. He turns toward me, "Adrian wants something from you, Philip. I have not yet worked it out completely, but you are the key. Perhaps the key to finding the Gardner heist? It seems as though that's what he really wants—now anyway. He's got you by the balls with the al-Qaeda disk. He must have controlled Billy in the same way. So why did he really kill him—Elliott, too? We're missing the most important, fundamental piece of this puzzle. It has to be something Billy knew, something he probably shared with Elliott, and, now, Adrian must have reason to believe you know it, too, Philip."

"Oh, crap," I say, placing my right hand on my forehead and rubbing it in. "What the hell could it be? I've racked my brain for the past few days trying to come up with everything I know about Billy, about Adrian, about Mother. I just don't know."

"It's okay, Philip. Calm down," Jonas says, patting my right shoulder with his right hand. "I didn't mean to put you on the spot. Sometimes things take time to reveal themselves to us, particularly things we hold in closely."

"You sound like a shrink, man," I reply, smiling and sighing at the same time.

"I have my masters in psychology," he replies, smiling.

"I should have known. Billy's psychotherapist, Dr. Gerard, has agreed to meet with me on Monday—sort of as a new patient. Maybe that will help."

"Yes, I think that's a great idea," Jonas says. "Maybe you can get some information from him about what Billy was thinking during the last few weeks of his life—what really was bothering him. The only other thing that comes to mind is was Billy in some way a threat to Adrian—a major threat, more than the pedophilia, more than the al-Qaeda connection. What could it be?"

"Maybe he was just planning to kill the bastard like you conjectured yesterday, Jonas," Lush interjects. "Maybe he had figured out about Eva's murder and the others. Maybe he was planning to do what we all would take great pleasure in doing. Maybe that is why he really went to Dubai in such secrecy. Maybe that's why he learned Jiu-Jitsu." Lush crosses her arms; her eyes burn cold.

"Well, Lush, if Philip can corroborate that hypothesis with Dr. Gerard, I'd say it is a solid motive," Jonas replies, "Yes, a solid motive."

"Todge, you ready for the eulogy?" Lush looks at me, her thick lips spreading into a smile.

"I'm ready, Lush. Let's go."

We all leave the room, walking down the hall into the living room. People are still arriving and we look into the foyer to see Dad, Emma, and Brenda greeting three women and several men. I immediately recognize Julianna, the ravishing Alejandraia, and another woman, although she looks

familiar, an attractive brunette; I'm not certain who she is. Julianna bends down to hug Emma, who has just presented her with the Tropicana rose. I focus on a tall, handsome, young Arab man surrounded by four large bodyguards in dark suits. I immediately recognize the young man from Billy's painting—it's Najeed.

"Julianna is just full of surprises today," Lush says, looking at Jonas and me. "Let's go meet her guests." We walk over to the foyer. Julianna turns, sees us, and a huge smile erupts on her face.

"Hello, everyone. I'm so sorry I'm late. I had some business to attend to as well as meeting some last minute guests. Lush, dear, you look radiant," she says as she leans forward to give Lush a peck on each cheek. She does the same to me as she says, "And don't you look dashing, Philip?" She pauses in front of Jonas, looks up and down his body, kisses him once on the end of the nose, smiles, turns toward Lush and me, and says, "Well, didn't I tell you he was worth the money?"

We all laugh. I appreciate the warmth, humor, and elegance Julianna brings with her grand entrance, complete with an entourage of royalty. Her dress is stunning, a perfect contrast of an intricately ruffled, white silk halter blouse with a long, hip-hugging, black velvet skirt, fanning out, flowing at the bottom, just touching the floor. She wears a diamond choker with an immense, marquis-cut diamond in front, dangling diamond earrings, and diamond bracelets on each wrist, the contrasting colors of her outfit punctuated by the sparkling diamonds completely captivate Emma who can't take her eyes off of Julianna.

"Please allow me to introduce my guests." She turns toward Najeed and says, His Royal Highness, Crowned Prince Najeed bib Khalid bin Faysal bin Abd al-Aziz of Umm AlQuwain and Miss Isabella de la Croix of Sante Fe, St. Barts, and Paris. You all remember Alejandraia."

The prince smiles, revealing perfect white teeth, and bows slightly. Julianna immediately switches to the familiar address and says, "Najeed, Isabella, this is our host, Billy's brother, Mr. Philip Hampton, his friend, Sarah Richardson, and the gentleman I told you about who is helping us with our investigation, Jonas Grey."

"How do you do, Crowned Prince Najeed," I say, wondering if one shakes a sheikh's hand as he immediately offers me his right hand. We shake; he has a firm grip, and he shakes my hand for longer than usual as he looks into my eyes, his smile dissolving into a serious expression, then clasping his left hand over my right hand.

"It's a pleasure and an honor to meet you, Mr. Hampton. Please accept my deepest sympathies. The world has lost a genius, and I have lost a true friend. I will do whatever it takes to help you gain justice for this horrible crime."

"Thank you, your Highness. I can't tell you how much that means to me," I reply, somewhat stunned by his warmth and directness.

"Please call me Najeed," he replies, releasing my hands.

"Of course, so long as you call me Philip," I reply with a grin.

"It's done, then, Philip. I know you have many guests to attend to and Julianna tells me we're just in time for your eulogy to Billy. I would like a word with you before I leave, though."

"Of course. Perhaps after the eulogy," I reply, totally mesmerized by his royal persona.

"Good. So, if you don't mind, I'm going to have a look around. Billy described his home to me, and I can't wait to see it."

"By all means, Najeed. Please, have a look around and make yourself at home," I reply.

"Thank you, Philip," he replies and turns toward Lush and Jonas. "Miss Richardson, Mr. Grey, a pleasure to meet you both," he says as he shakes their hands before moving off, the four big bodyguards flank him in front and behind, moving in unison, almost as if appendages of the prince. He moves off, then stops, turns around, smiles, and says, "Alejandraia, won't you walk with me? I'm sure you can fill me in on the details of Billy's art collection."

"Certainly," says Alejandraia, dressed in a black cocktail dress with a fluffy black shawl, woven of loosely knitted cashmere yarn with bright silver threads running through it, draped over her lovely shoulders and arms, says. She turns toward us, "Would you all please excuse me?"

"Certainly," Julianna says, "Run along, dear. Keep Najeed company."

Julianna turns toward us, "Everyone, I took the liberty of phoning Isabella yesterday, Najeed, too, for that matter. I've done business with his family for years. Anyway I explained to both of them what was going on. Well, as you can see, they both came immediately. I hope you all approve."

"Of course, Julianna," I say as I reach for the hand of Miss de la Croix. "Welcome, Miss de la Croix. I'm so pleased to meet you," I say shaking her hand.

"It's a pleasure as well, Mr. Hampton. Please, call me Isabella," she says.

"Isabella, I'm Sarah Richardson," Lush says, shaking her hand, "But, please call me Lush."

"Oh yes, Lush," Isabella replies. I'm captivated by her French accent and the lovely way her mouth moves as she speaks. She is as pretty as I remember her from the magazine article in which I first saw her the last time I was in St. Barts with Billy. As Jonas introduces himself to her I let my eyes explore this goddess: she's rather petite and slim, wearing a black V-neck dress, revealing a touch of cleavage, and a black jacket with a silk shawl lapel. Her thick, straight, brown hair, brushed back behind her small, delicate ears, lobes holding diamond studs, hangs down her back, flashing with a healthy luster as her body moves. Her skin is a beautiful olive brown with its own fresh aura; I imagine it must feel like silk. Her large brown eyes and high forehead project intelligence. Another group of people arrive in the foyer, so I turn around inviting Julianna and Isabella into the living room.

"Philip, it's five after eight," Lush says.

"Yes, I know, " I say with a big sigh.

"Are you ready for this?" she asks, taking my left arm in her right arm.

"I am," I reply.

I walk up to the table with Billy's ashes in the porcelain jar. Mabry, dressed entirely in black—tight fitting jacket with narrow lapels, thin silk tie, and straight leg pants, looking more like a punk rocker than a detective—walks up to me with a cordless microphone in his outstretched right hand.

"Thanks, Mabry," I say, noticing a beautiful, wide, silver and gold band covering his hairy right wrist, and I wonder if that was a gift from Jonas. Peter observes me, immediately transitioning the piece he is playing to a gentle ending. As I think what a gifted kid he is, my half-brother, a warm feeling of belonging to a family arises at the base of my spine moving deep into my gut, surprising me, grounding me, giving me courage and comfort as I pause a moment, looking out over the crowd around me, watching the wave of silence spreading out radially from me. I glance up at a large flat screen monitor that has been temporarily installed at the other end of the living room and notice my face in the center of the screen. I look around to see two men focusing cameras on me. I clear my throat.

"Thank you, everyone. Thank you all for coming this evening," I pause, look down at the floor, my heart thumping in my throat, butterflies awakening in my stomach.

"Thank you all for coming to help me celebrate the life of my brother, Billy Hampton. It is a great honor to him that so many of his friends are here this evening. Billy was an extraordinary man, and I'm certain that he touched each of you in some meaningful way, and that each of you, as individuals, shared something unique and good with him. Billy was and is full of love, a love that, when focused on you, whether you had just met him or had known him for years, made you feel as if you were the center of the universe." I chuckle, smile, then look directly into one of the cameras. "You all know exactly what I'm talking about." I pause as murmurs flow through the crowd like a gentle breeze. "You know that when Billy locked his eyes onto yours, it was difficult to refuse him anything. I can assure you he was born with this gift, cultivating it throughout his life—his short life." I pause as a surge of emotion erupts through my throat, my eyes welling up with tears. "I love my brother Billy more than anything. He is the one constant

in my life. His birth is my first memory. We have journeyed through the years, for the most part, deeply connected, though vast distances and lengths of time sometimes separated us physically. Together, as children and through our teenage years, we experienced the loss of the loved ones closest to us—tragedies which fortified our bond as brothers." I feel tears streaming down my face, but I have found my voice and I proceed, my emotions propelling my speech. "I want to share a story with you which epitomizes the depth of my brother's compassion. We were standing beside the grave of our Mother, her coffin had just been lowered, the minister threw a clump of soil onto her coffin, that terrible thud ringing in my ears as he said a final prayer, my right hand squeezing Billy's left hand, my knees weak and wobbly in the overbearing August heat that day, the day after which I had just turned thirteen, Billy was eleven, and as we turned to walk away, Billy whispered into my right ear, 'It's gonna be okay, Philly. You've still got me. We've still got each other.'" I pause again, and I hear audible weeping in the room. I look over at Lush, who is standing with Dad, Brenda, and Emma. Tears are running down all their faces, except Emma, who, with an expression of urgent concern, keeps looking up at her mother. "Everyone should be so lucky to have a brother like Billy, and in my mind, Billy's greatest achievement was being a truly great brother as well as a loving person." I pause to clear my throat. "It is certainly not an overstatement to say that Billy was and is a genius. I'll admit that sometimes I felt a bit shortchanged in that he got the best parts of our mother and father—the great looks, the artistic ability, the loving nature. Yet along with those fantastic gifts that afforded him great peaks in his life and career, he was plagued with the deepest valleys of self-doubt, despair, and loss of direction. He would call me up, sometimes in the middle of the night, and say, 'Oh, Philly, I've got the mean blues again something fierce.' We'd talk it over and somehow he always found the strength to persevere, to overcome those blues, to move on to his usual greatness. His work as a fashion model and as an artist have left enduring images—whether simple, complex, mesmerizing, thought provoking, erotic, harsh, beautiful, thrilling, or frightening—that all reveal the truth that is Billy, his truth. It saddens me beyond words to know that the source of these great images has been snuffed out in the prime of life. Yes, tricked into drinking a poison which destroyed his brain, the cradle of his genius, then, executed in his hospital bed by a merciless perpetrator who injected the same poison into his body." People gasp throughout the room. "I think it is important that the truth be known. Billy was all about the truth, and as you all will see in his upcoming exhibition, he was in the process of solidifying his own truth. And to the murderer I'll say, you made one part of my obligation to my brother easy for me: you removed him from a vegetative state. You see, Billy made it very clear to me, that should he ever have the misfortune to arrive at such a state, I was to do everything in my power to let him go, even if, as he told me on more than one occasion, it meant holding a pillow over his face. So, murderer, thank you for that, because, I don't think I could have ever done that. Now, you hear this. I will find you and deliver the retribution you must know has been waiting patiently for you, lurking on the margins of your life, all these years." I look out among all the faces to see looks of confusion, but I feel like I've made the point I want to make to Adrian.

"So now I ask all of you dear people to join me in a toast to my brother," I say and reach for a glass of champagne served to me by Luka, smiling at me with a large, shiny black, blue, yellow and green bruise over his right eye. I take the glass from his right hand, covered in a short white glove, smile back, and say, "Luka, please take a glass and join the toast."

"Really? Thank you, sir." He steps back, places his silver tray down on Billy's altar, picks up a glass, smiling at me. I look around to see that all the waitresses and waiters have done a fine job getting champagne to everyone.

I raise my glass with my right hand, holding the microphone in my left hand, and say, "On behalf of Billy, I thank each of you for coming tonight. It is Billy's deepest desire that you enjoy this party, eat well, drink well, socialize, celebrate his life, your lives, and experience all the love and positive energy in this house. Dear Billy, right now I am the luckiest man alive to have you as my brother. I want to thank you

for everything you've done for me," I pause, crying audibly. "You have been and, I know, always will be there for me. It breaks my heart to know I will never see your smiling face in person again, never hear your actual voice, never feel your comforting touch. It breaks my heart that you will never know your brothers Andrew and Peter and your sweet sister Emma. It breaks my heart to know that you will never know that Brooker T is also our brother. But a broken heart is not something you'd want me to have, not for long anyway. I promise to be true to your mission and help guide your great legacy of art so that as many people as possible can experience it, enjoy it, know you from it. I promise to take care of Clark and give him the loving, secure environment you've surrounded him with. I promise to keep you in my heart, always. Dear brother, I know someday, in some shape form or fashion we will walk together again, holding hands. Until then, Billy, I will miss you so much, so, so much. I love you, Billy. Here's to you, my lovely brother." I raise my glass, clink it with Lush's, Dad's, Brenda's, and Luka's. Then I turn the glass up and drink the whole thing in one long gulp. Instinctively, I wipe my mouth on the left sleeve of my jacket, smile through my tears, turn around toward the Kangxi jar, reach up, kiss it, and say, "Goodbye, dear brother."

Suddenly, people, smiling and crying, sad and happy, surround me. They are all telling me what a wonderful, touching speech I made, how much Billy meant to them, how lucky Billy was to have me as a brother, what a horrible thing his murder was, and a million other comments and questions. A hand reaches in to take the microphone from me. Mostly, I just stand there giving and receiving hugs. It feels really good. I look up at the flat screen as pictures and videos of Billy play and the voice of Chet Baker singing *Time After Time* fills the room. Lush hit the nail on the head with that song, one of Mother's favorites, probably Billy's favorite, and I feel the urge to drop to the floor and cry but I find myself moving into the dining room, Julianna guiding me by my left arm and Lush guiding me by my right.

"Todge, dear, we're going to get you out on the terrace for a breather," Lush says, "You look like you could use it."

"Thanks, ladies. That would be nice. Maybe even a smoke," I reply.

We manage to navigate through the dining room without stopping, Julianna and Lush sweetly returning people's comments as I attempt to nod and smile. We enter the terrace, the night air, cool, yet warmer than I expected, smacks my face, travels down my body, shocking me with a cold sensation as it meets my perspiration-soaked shirt, sending waves of chills up and down my body.

"Philip, your teeth are chattering. Are you cold?" Julianna asks.

"A bit. I mean I'm soaked through. I guess, as Fatgram would say, I was sweating like a whore in church on Sunday while I was speaking."

"Well, let's go back inside," Lush says.

"No, no. I'm fine. It actually feels good. I just want a smoke and maybe a stiff shot of bourbon."

"Waiter!" Lush waves her hand at a young man walking with a tray of empty champagne glasses. "Bring this man a shot of Four Roses, no ice. There's a bottle in the bar. Please hurry."

"Of course, Madame," the tall young man with thick, wavy blonde hair and blue eyes says. He looks at me, straight in my eyes, boldly, but just for an instant, and in that look, I read the invitation that, just as he was for my brother, he's available for me, if I so desire, and I sense that he thinks I do desire him, and I wonder which category of aspiring artist he is as I think that tonight what I really desire is to entwine my limbs with those of the magnificent and mysterious Isabella. "Anything for you ladies?" he asks.

"Sparkling water for me, please," Julianna replies.

"Oh hell, I'll have a shot of the Four Roses, too," Lush says as she pulls out two cigarettes from her clutch, handing me one.

"Certainly," the young man says, turns, moving quickly towards the dining room.

"Let me light them for you," Julianna says, taking Lush's gold lighter from Lush's hand.

"Thanks, Julianna," Lush says, puts her cigarette between her lips, leaning forward as Julianna holds up the small flame to the tip of the cigarette. Lush inhales deeply, takes the cigarette between her right

index and middle fingers, withdraws it gracefully from her mouth, parts her red lips, exposing her front white teeth as she exhales a stream of smoke.

"Your smoking is so eloquent, Lush," Julianna says.

Lush laughs, "Well, God knows I've had enough practice at it."

Julianna smiles, turns the flame toward my cigarette. I inhale, pull it from my lips, turn my head, dramatically exhaling. Both women laugh.

"Making mockery of my smoking, darling?" Lush asks.

"As if I could ever be a challenge to your beautiful style of smoking," I reply as I feel the nicotine calming me, elevating my spirits.

We all turn to look at the ice carving, with the faint blue light emanating from it.

"My, what an exquisite ice carving. Who did this for you?" Julianna says as she hands Lush the lighter.

"What? You should know. Brenda said it came from you. Why it was delivered by one of your trucks," Lush replies with a concerned look on her face.

"It's not from me, Lush. I wish it were; it's so beautiful," Julianna replies.

"Brenda said it came in a truck with your gallery name on it. And the delivery man said it was from you." I reply

"How extremely odd. I don't have any trucks. I use a service to deliver all my art. I'd never advertise like that. We'd be sitting ducks for any thief. My insurance company would never allow it."

"Well, who the hell is this from?" Lush asks. "And why did they want it to appear to be from you?"

"So that they could get it inside here, without questions," I reply.

"Dear God. It could be a bomb, Todge. A bomb from Adrian." Lush states, shock in her eyes.

"It had to go through the police inspection, and I know they had bomb sniffing dogs down there, Lush. Surely they would have detected it."

"How can we be sure of that?" She asks, then pulls out the pager from her purse, presses a button on it and says, "Jonas. Get out here on the terrace. We're by the ice sculpture. Hurry."

"It truly is exquisite," Julianna says. "There are only a couple of people in town capable of doing such fine ice carving. I'm sure I can find out who did it."

"Whoever sent it had to know that Billy's ashes were to be put in the Kangxi jar. The ice carving is almost an exact replica," I say, and then take a drag off my cigarette.

"And someone went to all the trouble to get the plants, even blooming prunus," Lush says.

As we stand observing the ice jar, the blue light begins to rotate, slowly at first, then more rapidly. The light attracts people on the terrace and a crowd begins to gather around it.

"Todge, I don't feel good about this. I think we should clear everyone off the terrace." She leans into me and asks in a whisper, "What if it is a bomb?"

Suddenly, with a loud piercing, cracking sound, the sculpture shatters into hundreds of pieces, collapsing in a large mound on the terrace, turning over the plants surrounding it. Everyone is startled and moves back. A shot of burning adrenaline races through my body and I grab Julianna and Lush, pulling them back behind me. We all stand still a minute, breathing heavily.

"What the hell was that?" Lush exclaims out loud.

"Dear, it just shattered into a million pieces," Julianna says.

"God, what happened?" Jonas asks as he and Mabry run up to us.

"Well, we don't know. The blue light started spinning and then the whole thing just shattered as if it were a vase dropped on the floor," Julianna says.

"Jonas, Julianna says she didn't order this or have anything to do with it. Someone used her name to get it in here. She doesn't even have any trucks with her gallery name on it," Lush says.

"Damn!" Jonas says.

"Look, you guys. There's a gold box sitting on top of the blue light," I say.

We all walk up to the mound of ice. Mabry walks up into the pile of ice, observing the light, the box, and the pile of ice. He bends over, pulling at something.

"Ingenious design. This thing was made to shatter on command. The ice was frozen with dozens of these tiny wires. See? And right here is a transmitting device. Someone must have activated this with a remote switch."

He walks over to us with a handful of tiny metal wires. "The wires were a heat source or maybe a shock wave source from the box with the blue light." He turns back around, climbs up the pile of ice, picks up the gold box, returns, looks at me and asks, "Any idea what's in this?"

"Not a clue, Mabry," I reply.

"I know what's in it," I hear a man's voice say and we turn around to see Najeed standing there surrounded by his four bodyguards, Alejandraia is no longer with him.

"Did you send the ice sculpture, Najeed?" Julianna asks.

"No I did not, but I have a good idea who did," he replies as he takes a drag off of a cigarette.

"Who is it, Najeed?" I ask.

"Adrian, of course," he replies, coolly, smiling. "And in that gold box, I imagine you'll find an old, red, Swiss Army knife."

"What?" I ask, taking the box from Mabry. I open it. Sure enough there is a red, Swiss Army knife. My mouth falls open. "This is the knife Adrian used to cut our hands when we became blood brothers."

Najeed motions us to come closer around him, forcing his bodyguards to move back. He leans in and whispers, "Billy planned to kill Adrian. He wanted to do it himself, with his own bare hands, but he could never get close to him, not even with my help. Adrian is too sheltered, too protected, and much too powerful. So, after Billy told me the story of how Adrian had sexually molested him and you and many other boys and how he had murdered the mothers but made them all appear as suicides or accidents…."

"So Billy had figured out that Adrian killed our mother?" I interject.

"Yes, he had. He and Ricky Wallitsch, who had been friends for a long time, ended up having an affair a couple of years ago which didn't last long but led them to figure out Adrian's heinous methods and that he had actually murdered both their mothers. I agreed to help Billy find an assassin to do the job. The signal for the assassin to implement the job was that this knife would be in a certain locker, at a certain time, in the men's locker at the Riddles Bay Golf Club in Bermuda." He pauses.

"Damn, that explains everything," Lush says. "Elliott would have been the one delivering this, so that's why Bernie was sent there to kill him, to stop delivery of the knife to Riddles Bay. So this is a message from Adrian. A message that he's a step ahead of us."

"Yes, unfortunately that's right," Najeed says, lowering his voice even more as more people stream outside to see the crumbled ice sculpture. "Billy instructed the assassin to strangle Adrian with a pink and black silk necktie and to plunge this knife into his heart. He was willing to pay two million dollars for this. The assassin uses Bermuda as a base, so it was convenient to have Elliott deliver the knife. Billy and Ricky never dreamed any harm would come to Elliott."

"Wait," I interject, "Ricky was in on this, too?"

"He was, or, rather, he is," Najeed says, "I would imagine he's fearing greatly for his own life at this point and probably acting as if he knows nothing. Adrian has to know it was either the Boonmee twins or Ricky who betrayed him. I suppose you know what happened to Bennie and Bernie?"

"Yes, I do," I reply, "But how did you know? The police haven't release any details yet."

He smiles, "Philip, I have my own Mr. Grey, in fact, several. After Billy and I became close, I became fascinated with Adrian, myself. I met him once a few years ago on a visit with my father to Julian Ainsworth's compound in Dubai to view a Vermeer Charles was brokering for sale and trying to bid up among wealthy Arabs. He was introduced to us as Claude Blackmore, the first cousin of Mr. Ainsworth. I found it quite odd that this British man was dressed in a Disdashah and a Gutrah." He pauses a moment,

looks up at the crowd forming around the pile of ice, then says, "Can we meet tomorrow, Philip? I have more to tell you, and I see now is not a good time."

"Of course," I reply. "What's a good time for you, Najeed?"

"Well, I'm sure you have a lot to do in the morning after this large gathering. Perhaps we could meet for dinner?"

"What a good idea," Julianna says. "Please, let me host dinner at my house. We can have our privacy for conversation and Najeed can see my art collection."

"How very considerate of you, Julianna," Najeed says.

"Thanks, Julianna, that would be fine," I say.

"Good," Julianna says, smiling. "Let's say seven thirty, okay?"

"Sounds good," Lush says.

"Very well," Najeed says. "Philip, it's been a pleasure meeting you. I'm so sorry for the circumstances, but I believe I can help with Adrian. Thank you for your hospitality." He bows and holds out his right hand.

"Thank you for coming all this way and for your willingness to help, Najeed. I look forward to talking to you tomorrow," I say as I shake his hand.

"Goodnight everyone," Najeed says, turns toward the dining room, his four body guards surrounding him completely as they move off in unison.

"What a nice fellow," I say to Julianna.

"Very nice, and he told me he has a good deal of information about Adrian," she replies.

"Mabry," Jonas says with a wrinkled brow, "Take the box and knife and put them in one of our cases before the police get out here. We don't want them asking questions. I'll meet you by the service elevator in a few minutes. We need a word with Mr. Wallitsch."

"Right," he replies as I hand him the knife. He takes it, puts it in his coat pocket and walks back inside, holding the gold box. The blonde waiter returns with our drinks and several glasses of champagne on his tray.

"Madame, a shot of Four Roses for you and also you, sir," he says as he hands Lush and me our drinks.

"Sparkling water for you, Madame," he says to Julianna.

"I've changed my mind," she replies as she takes a glass of champagne.

"Yes, I'll have one too," Jonas says as he takes a glass, and I observe the waiter issuing the same invitation with his eyes to Jonas as he did to me and I discern, at least I think I do, that Jonas likes the look of this kid as his eyes follow the waiter who turns and walks away. It's still hard for me to picture Jonas with Mabry. Well, as Fatgram always said, 'You can't judge a book by its cover.'

"Here's a toast to Najeed and learning more about Adrian tomorrow night," Lush says, holding up her glass.

"Indeed," I say as we all clink glasses and I put my glass to my lips, pulling the warm, smooth, sweet, woody liquid into my throat in one gulp, shutting my eyes as it burns a trail down my esophagus into my stomach.

"Ah," I say, opening my mouth, gasping for a breath, "Just what the doctor ordered."

"Whew, Todge," Lush says, "This should stop your teeth from chattering."

Janet, Isabella, and Brooker T walk up to us.

"What happened to the ice sculpture?" Janet asks.

"It seems it was rigged to crumble at the press of a button," Lush replies.

"Whatever for?" Isabella asks.

"A message, perhaps warning, from our aspiring nemesis," I reply.

"Au contraire, Todge, we're his nemesis," Lush interjects.

"Yes, darling, you're right about that," I reply.

Brooker T has a confused look on his face. I do not want him to feel that way or be uncomfortable at all.

"Brooker T, how do you think this wake is going?" I ask.

"Just fine, Philip. Billy would have been real proud of your speech," he replies, shifting his weight from one foot to the other, hands in his pant pockets.

"Thanks," I reply.

"Everythang sho is nice in here. Lots of fine, nice people, too. Some fancy people, but fine and nice," he adds, pauses, shifts his weight again and says, "I sho wish daddy could've seen all this."

"Me, too, Brooker T," I say, "We're making a DVD of it all. I'll send you one and maybe Newt can watch it."

"Thanks, Philip. That would be nice. Daddy'll like that."

"Brooker T," I say, "Dad, Brenda and their kids are leaving tomorrow. Why don't you move over here and stay a few more days?"

"Oh, Lord, thank you, but I gotta get back to the farm, to Daddy. Got a lot of work to do now that spring is here. But that's real kind of you, Philip."

"Well, when I come down there to spread some of Billy's ashes, maybe I can stay a few days to visit," I say.

"Yes, I hope you will, Philip," Brooker T says, "It'll be nice to have you back a while. Ain't much changed."

"Well, let's plan it then. It'll be sometime this summer. Maybe around the peach harvest?"

"Yes sir," Brooker T says, smiling. "We'll put you to work. This man knows how to pick some peaches. How many bushels you think you've picked in your life, Philip?"

"Oh God, I can't begin to count, Brooker T, but I know, thanks to Fatgram, that's how Billy and I learned about working and earning a wage," I reply.

I look into Brooker T's yellow-green eyes, and I remember working beside him, loading bushels of peaches from the field onto a flatbed, little Billy always close by, working, or attempting to work, in starts and fits, picking peaches a while, then, distracted by a grub hole in the red earth, trying to entice it to lock its pinchers on a straw, so he can pull it out and exclaim about how gross it is, and I can hear his voice as he looks up at me and Brooker T as we load peaches.

"Philly, how many bushels do I need to pick to get enough money for a Battle-Armor He Man?" Billy is picking his nose with his sticky left hand and fishing for a grub with a piece of hay with his right hand.

"Billy, stop picking your nose." I say to him, wiping the sweat out of my eyes with a rag. "About a hundred or so, I reckon," being good at math, I'm able to answer quickly.

"Naw, you gotta be lying, turdface," he smirks up at me. He's almost nine and gotten hardly any growth yet, still short with plenty of baby fat on him.

"Don't you be getting smart with me, son." He hates it when I call him son, but I'm almost eleven, already a head taller than Ala Mary. "He Man costs about ten bucks. There's ten dimes in one dollar, so there's ten times ten or one hundred dimes in ten dollars."

"Damn nation and I'll be a son of a bitch," he looks at me, lets go of the straw, picks up a perfectly good ripe peach and hurls it into the orchard, causing one of the workers to duck down to keep from getting hit upside the head.

"Shut your mouth," I say to him. "Mother wouldn't want you cussing like that." He sighs real loud, getting red around the gills and poking out his bottom lip like he does when he's fixing to get into one of his temper tantrums. Well, all I can say is, on a good day, I can pick fifty bushels. Poor little Billy hasn't broken fifteen yet, but he can flat out milk Magnolia, Fatgram's cow. Fatgram likes fresh milk with the cream in it.

"Little brother, you take my milkings the rest of the week, and I'll split the cost of the He Man with you. We'll ask Fatgram to drive us to the Kmart in Spartanburg this Saturday and get it."

Billy smiles real big up at me, sticks a finger in his nose and says, "Aw, gee, Philly, that's just great."

"Well, Philip. Thank you for your hospitality," Brooker T says, focusing me back to the present. "I'm gonna head back to the hotel. Gotta be at the airport by seven in the morning."

I lean forward, put my arms around him, and he does the same to me.

"Thanks so much for coming, Brooker T. Thanks for caring, brother," I say.

We release each other and step apart. He smiles, looks down, looks up and says, "It was nice to meet all you folks."

"So nice of you to come, Brooker T, and to finally meet you," Lush says.

"Well, thank you, Miss Richardson. Good to meet you too," he replies.

"Oh, Brooker T, I really enjoyed meeting you and spending time with you tonight," Janet says, smiling at him.

"Me too, Miss Ostro. Good to meet you," Brooker T says, shaking both of her hands. "And I mean it, you're always welcome down in Union. Some pretty scenes to paint there."

"Yes, indeed," Julianna says, "Eva showed the world that."

"Brooker T," Isabella puts her right hand on his right shoulder, "Thanks for sharing your passion about the forests and the wild animals with me. It was fascinating. You're a lucky man to be so connected with nature. I hope you and Landrum will come to Sante Fe some time. You'll both love the high desert and its wildness." Her brown eyes gleam, and I focus on her elegant lips as she speaks.

"Thank you so much Miss de la Croix," Brooker T says, beaming, "We just may take you up on that sometime."

"I'm counting on it," she says as she reaches up to kiss each of his cheeks.

"I'll escort Brooker T to the door," Janet says. "We'll find Charles and Brenda and the kids on the way out so you can tell them goodbye," she says putting her left arm around his right arm and turning toward the dining room doors.

"Bye, Brooker T," I say.

"Good night, y'all," he says and walks away with Janet.

"Fascinating man," Isabella says, looking up at me, "And he's your half-brother, Philip, I understand?"

"Yes, he is. Something I didn't know until yesterday," I reply, feeling a buzz from the bourbon, thinking how I'd love to take Isabella back into Billy's bedroom.

"Life's full of surprises, Mr. Hampton. I hope that was a pleasant one for you," she says, ever so slightly raising her chin, its lovely skin inviting my hands to touch it, stroke it, feel its softness, its warmth.

"Very pleasant, Miss de la Croix and an honor," I reply.

"Please, call me Isabella," she says.

"Of course, Isabella. Please call me Philip," I reply.

She nods her head as Lush interjects, "Todge, we aught to eat something, don't you think?"

"Yes, Lush, we should. I'm a little hungry. Let's go into the study. I'm craving raw oysters and shrimp."

"Sure, sounds good," she replies. "Are you all hungry, too?" She asks Julianna, Isabella, and Jonas.

"Nothing for me, thanks," Jonas replies, "I need to go meet Mabry. If you all will excuse me, Philip, ladies," he says and walks back into the dining room.

"There are some people I want Isabella to meet, Philip," Julianna says, smiling. "We'll see you both before we leave."

"Okay," I reply, "Go forth and mingle and have fun."

Isabella smiles at me and she and Julianna head into the dining room. I notice two men from Ricky's company are sweeping the ice fragments into dustpans and dumping them into a large black garbage can. Lush and I walk around toward the studio and are stopped by numerous people who compliment me on my eulogy and offer anecdotes about Billy. After about ten minutes we finally make it to the seafood station where Dominique Montaigne, wearing tight black leather pants and a black leather jacket, its back festooned with silver rivets in the shape of a human skull, has the attention of several people. An assortment of stainless steel bracelets adorn his wrists, jingling as he gesticulates, his eyes animated, moving from face to face.

"Yes, neither one of us was about to lose our bet, so having stripped off all our clothes, we walked down to this pristine lake, fed by melting snow and stuck our toes in. Christ, I'd never felt anything so cold in my life. So I turned to Alysse and asked, 'Lady are we going to do this?' and with that she ran as fast as she could into the lake and dove in. Well, I wasn't going to let this gentrified white lady show me up, so I held my breath, ran after her and dove in. Mother Mary can I tell you I thought I was going to die from shock right then and there—much, much too cold for a poor black boy from the tropics. The funny thing was that after the first instant, it didn't feel cold to me anymore, but hot, like my skin was burning, like a million hot needles sticking all over my body. Alysse and I could barely catch our breaths, but we both managed to scream and laugh at the same time. She says, 'okay Dominique let's go under one more time to make certain it really counts,' so we did and then both high tailed it back to shore as fast as we could. I'm telling you, I've always been proud about my man thing here, but it was swiveled up smaller than a little boy's. Alysse was pointing at me and laughing and I said, 'That's all right girl, look at your titties, you could etch glass with those nipples.' She felt her nipples and said that I was right about that so maybe we should warm each other up. Well, naturally I was all for that, so we sat down on a grassy area by the lake and began to warm each other up. We knew we couldn't take too long, because we were over eleven thousand feet up, and Alysse with her snow-white skin and no sunscreen on anything but her face and arms would burn to a crisp. Well, we finished warming each other up and walked back to where we took off our clothes and what do you think we found? Not a damn thing, not even our shoes. They had vanished into thin air and we were a good three mile hike back down to the lodge."

With that one woman gasps, a man laughs, and another woman asks, "Whatever did you do, Dominique?"

"What did we do?" He turns to a young woman with long dark hair, blue eyes, and pale skin who is dressed in a tailored and stylish black pants suit and says, "Tell them what we did, Alysse."

She smiles, moves her Chanel clutch from her right hand to her left hand, pulls her hair back behind her right ear and says, "We hobbled, barefoot, naked as newborns, down the side of that Goddamned mountain, slapping at biting mosquitos and flies, all the way back to the lodge. We arrived, hand in hand, limping, me beet red with sunburn, hell, even Dominique burned, and walked straight up onto the front porch of the lodge where everyone was gathered for afternoon cocktails to watch hummingbirds at the feeders. You should have seen the look on the faces of those people. Dominique walks over to the proprietor, an older crusty man who is trying not to laugh and says, 'What sort of animal steals people's clothes?' The man bursts out laughing and says, 'That'd be a teenage mountain biker, son.' Well, so much for our Colorado vacation last summer," she says and laughs.

I can tell at once I like Alysse. Her elocution supports Dominique's description of her social class—I'm guessing Boston Brahmin. Lush is laughing at the story when Dominique turns around toward us.

"Philip, Lush, what a grand party this is. Your brother would love it." He opens his arms wide, breathes in deeply, smiling, and says, "I feel his presence here; he is definitely with us now."

"Thank you Dominique, that's kind of you to say," I say, turning toward Alysse. "Welcome, I'm Philip Hampton and this is my friend Sarah Richardson."

Alysse smiles, extending her right hand to me, then immediately to Lush, "I'm Alysse Lowell. It's so nice to meet you both, but I'm so saddened by Billy's death. What a terrible crime."

"Did you know Billy, Miss Lowell?" I ask.

"Oh yes, but please call me Alysse. My sister, Bitsy modeled with him quite a bit and Billy introduced me to Dominique."

"Oh, you're Bitsy's sister. I wondered if she'd be here tonight. Did you see the painting of her Julianna put up tonight? It's right over there."

"Yes. I opened up Bitsy's place so Julianna's people could get the painting. Bitsy sends her love and condolences. She's on location in Argentina filming and couldn't get here because of the schedule. You know how it goes—always over budget and under the gun to finish."

"Well, I'm pleased to meet you, Alysse."

"Thank you, Philip. This is a wonderful affair, and I'm glad to be a part of it."

"Philip, I was just getting ready to look for you. Thanks for your kind note, and I was happy to help, but I don't think this thing worked," Dominique says as he pulls out a thin black plastic case the size of a credit card with two round gray buttons on it, both marked 'On'. I'm shocked as I take what I think must be some sort of transmitter in my hand, turn it over and over and stare at it.

"Yes, I pushed the 'On' button exactly ten minutes after you finished the eulogy, just as you instructed in the letter, but nothing happened. So I pushed the other 'On' button. I kept looking up at the TV screens, but the special tribute to Billy never started. You know, pictures of Billy just kept flashing up, no special tribute at all. I pushed both buttons several times, but nothing happened."

Stunned, I'm not sure how to handle this, so I say, "Dominique, thank you so much for trying. I'm sorry to put you through this. You just never know with electronics."

"Yes, that's right," Lush says. "Sometimes these systems are sensitive. I'm sure we checked the battery in this thing," she says and takes it from my hands.

"Well, I'm sorry it didn't work. Maybe you have another and can get it to play now? I understand that you wanted the spontaneity of someone from the crowd doing it, but I still think it would be a good time now."

"You're exactly right, Dominique," I reply. "Would you all excuse us, please? Let's go see if we can get this to work, Lush."

I grab Lush's left hand pulling her across the study into the back bathroom beside Billy's sex chamber, and I shut the door.

"Call Jonas on your walkie talkie, Lush."

She pulls the small device from her purse, presses a button and says, "Jonas, it's Lush. Please hurry to the back bathroom behind the study—the one beside Billy's secret room."

Immediately we hear, "Roger, on the way."

I sigh, "Lush, is this getting out of hand?"

"Maybe, I don't know, Todge."

"You think this thing controlled the ice sculpture?"

"That's my guess," she replies with a nervous expression on her face. "I don't think anything else happened. Do you?"

"No, like what?"

"Like, well, I don't know. I just have this bad feeling."

"Me too. It's almost as if Adrian were here, here in the flesh doing all this stuff."

"Yeah, Todge, I know what you mean," she replies as we hear a knock on the door. I open it and Jonas and Mabry enter.

"What's the matter?" Jonas asks.

I show him the device and explain what happened with Dominique. Mabry takes the device and begins to examine it. He looks up at us, "You all didn't push either of these buttons did you?"

311

"No, I didn't," I reply, "Did you, Lush?"

"No. Well, I don't remember pushing them, why?"

"Well, look here. This little clear plastic bulb is an infrared transmitter. This is what the receiver in the ice sculpture responded to. So when Dominique pushed it ten minutes after the eulogy, it activated the destruction sequence in the ice sculpture."

"Okay, I see that," Lush says, "But why are there two 'On' buttons, Mabry?"

"My guess is to confuse the operator," he replies and turns the unit over. "See this array of gold wires on the back?"

"Yeah, they're so thin, you barely notice them," I say.

"Thin, but powerful," Mabry says, scratching his forehead with his left hand. "It's some sort of antenna, I believe. It transmitted a signal to something else, something that had to get through to a protected area, like thicker walls." Everyone immediately looks toward the secret sex room.

"Shit," Jonas exclaims, "no one has seen Ricky Wallitsch for the past twenty minutes. We've been searching for him everywhere." He quickly moves over to the shelves, pushing hard on the molding. The unit swings open and we notice the light is on in the hallway. Jonas turns around and looks at everyone, then he opens the door to the chamber. Ricky Wallitsch is lying on the floor face down.

"Oh my God," Lush says, "Is he dead?"

Jonas squats down, carefully turns Ricky over, puts his left hand on Ricky's chest, and picks his right wrist up. "He's breathing," Jonas says, "He has a pulse. Thank God. He's not dead—just unconscious. Look at this nasty gash on his left temple."

Lush and I both sigh at the same time.

"Who hit him in the head, I wonder?" I ask.

"No one," Mabry says. "Jonas, check his left hand."

"Christ, look at this burn," Jonas says. "There is a small entrance wound on the index finger, but look at the charred wound coming out of the bottom of his palm."

"Just what I thought," Mabry says, "Electrocution."

"What?" Lush says. "But how?"

"Look at this satellite phone here," Mabry says, pointing to a device on a wooden stool under the scaffold. "See the metal receiver, see the push buttons are even metal."

The satellite phone is contained in a metal box about the size of a car battery. It looks as if it would be the type of phone used in combat or on an archeological expedition to Outer Mongolia. The receiver, attached to the phone by a black, curled, phone cord, lies on the floor. I bend over toward it.

"Don't touch it," Mabry says with alarm and shoots his right arm out, pushing me back away from the phone. "It's probably still activated. In fact, it's really an electrocution device. Pick up the receiver with one hand, dial with the other and the instant you touch the first number a current of probably around 100 milliamperes runs from your finger through your heart, stopping it or causing it to go into irreversible fibrillation, and through to the other hand holding the receiver. Very clever, no? Only, in this case I suspect Ricky picked up the receiver with his left hand and while holding it in his left hand, used his left hand to dial the number. You can tell this by the entrance and exit wounds made by the current in Ricky's left hand. The designer did not anticipate this method of operating the phone. He received the shock that went in and out of his left hand, but didn't travel through his body affecting his heart, but did cause him to lurch back, hitting his head on the wooden scaffold. Ah ha, look right here—see there's blood and even a bit of hair. Is the back of his left hand bruised, Jonas?"

Jonas looks at Ricky's left hand and says, "Very badly."

With an extremely satisfied look on his face Mabry replies, "That bruise saved his life because the electrical shock would have made his hand clench tightly to the receiver, but when he fell back and hit his head, he also hit his left hand on this part of the scaffold here—see the blood here—and the force knocked

the receiver out of his hand. Then he fell forward unconscious. I believe this thing was activated when Dominique pushed the other 'On' button. Adrian must have instructed Ricky to come in here to call him or call somebody overseas."

"Nice work, Mabry," Jonas says. "Let's call an ambulance, fast. He seems to be stable, but he could be in shock and we need to get these wounds and burns treated."

I am dumbfounded by Mabry's observation and deductive reasoning skills.

"Jonas," Lush says, "He's okay right now? I mean he doesn't need CPR or anything?"

"No, he's just had a bad shock, followed by a concussion, most probably. He's a lucky man, though."

"What are we going to do about the detectives and the other four hundred people out there?" Lush asks.

"Christ," I say, "I forgot all about the detectives. How can we cover this up? Should we even try?"

Everyone looks at one another for what seems like a minute.

"Ricky's well-being is the most important thing," I reply. "I'm sure this is Adrian's doing. I'm going to get the detectives in here. Ricky will need police protection. Everyone okay with that?"

"I agree," Jonas says, "But let's get Ricky out into the bathroom and Mabry, disarm that thing, please. We don't want any cops to get electrocuted tonight."

Mabry pulls a small leather case of tools from his inside coat pocket and smiles at Jonas in such a way that causes me to suddenly understand why they are indeed right for one another.

"Lush, darling," I look at her as I widen my eyes, "What have we gotten ourselves into?" I sigh before she answers. "Would you mind going to round up Dad, Brenda, and Julianna and filling them in?"

"Not at all, Todge," she replies. "I'll keep them away from here. I'll also make certain the party keeps moving along on its natural course."

"Okay, I'll be right back," I say and walk out.

CHAPTER 33

I've been asleep for a while. I can't even remember going to bed, but now I lie awake, the luminous numerals of the alarm clock bathe my face in an eerie pale green light, as images of the events of the day pop up on my mental screen culminating with the come to Jesus about Adrian with Detective Johnson and Detective Bell after they arranged to get Ricky to the hospital virtually unnoticed through the service elevator and finally, the overwhelming state of exhaustion I experienced as the wake wound down around midnight. I hope Ricky will be okay. I wonder how much he can reveal about all of this. Now, the detectives will have first crack at him when he regains consciousness. But I'm glad I brought them in. Who knows what Adrian has up his sleeve? He must have figured out Ricky had turned against him. I just feel deep inside that I will get my chance at Adrian. I really believe I will. I try my best to force all these thoughts away by retreating behind my waterfall, curling into a fetal position, concentrating on the sound of the water, hoping desperately to pacify my brain. I find no physical comfort either as I begin to toss and turn, searching for a restful position—belly down, my lower back protests with an ache; left side, my left arm goes to sleep; right side, my right shoulder throbs; back down, I feel open, vulnerable, unprotected. Each time I turn I glance at the clock, counting the passing minutes—one forty five, one forty six, one forty seven…. Clark emits a long groan, stands up, sighs loudly, walks to the foot of the bed as far away as he can get from me, rapidly digs into the covers with his front paws as if he's ferreting out some rodent from

the ground, pauses, looks up at me, sighs again, spins around in a tight circle four full rotations, plops down hard, grunts, licks his muzzle, curls into a tight ball and closes his eyes.

"Sorry to disturb you, boy. I know you're tired out after all the people and commotion here tonight." I say out loud as I roll out of bed, heading toward the bathroom. I turn on the light, walk to the toilet, pull my penis through the right leg of my boxers and begin to pee. As I pee I can't decide if I should beat off or take one of Billy's sleeping pills or do both. The thought of masturbating causes my penis to start lengthening while I pee. Christ, what I need is rest, not sex, so I focus on emptying my bladder rather than stroking my cock. I finish, flush the toilet, go to the medicine cabinet, search the labels for Ambien, locate it, open the bottle, take out one of the small blue pills, put it in my mouth, turn on the water faucet, rub my hands in the cold water, cup my left hand under the faucet, suck up a bit of water from my hand, swallow, turn the faucet off, dry my hands on a towel, look at my disheveled hair in the mirror, turn around, flick off the light and head back to bed, noticing that Clark has paid no attention to me and is sound asleep. I get back into bed, turn the clock face away from mine, grab a pillow, stuff it between my knees, settling on my right side as I await the pill's effects. Thoughts flood my mind again and Brooker T's face appears. What a gentle man. I wonder how I grew up around him and never fully realized his sensitivity, his kindness, his compassionate nature. It is probably because, in the seventies and eighties, Union was still a place where prejudice against blacks, although largely unspoken among the 'nicer' families, reigned. God knows my parents taught us that everyone was equal, but everyday living in a small southern town demonstrated to us otherwise. Black people were generally poor inhabitants of the projects, random trailers, or small houses on the wrong side of town. I recall a few who, through education or hard work, had risen up into the realms of retail management, banking, and business ownership, and there even was a black, female general practitioner, but most had minimum wage type jobs in fast food joints and restaurants or worked as maids, gardeners, farm hands, and handymen for white people. I remember on some of my first visits to New York as a child being amazed to see black men walking on the streets in business suits, carrying nice brief cases, hearing them speak with no discernible accent, and mingling freely with white people. Mother would catch Billy and me gawking at such sights and say with a look of disgust on her face, "Really, boys, must you be so provincial? You both act as if you have no sophistication whatsoever. I told Mother and your father it was a mistake to raise you in Union. If I had gotten my way, we'd be living in Provence or Tuscany this very moment, although I can't imagine how a furniture salesmen like your father would be gainfully employed in Europe." Sometimes Mother was such a snob, yes, a snobby bitch—as if she were too good for Union. But at the same time, I know she loved it, you can tell from her paintings of the people and landscapes of South Carolina, and I can remember in the springtime, sometimes she'd bend over in her flower garden or jump off her horse beside a freshly plowed field at the farm, scoop up the soil in her hands, bring it to her nose, breathe in deeply and exclaim, "Oh, boys, there's nothing like the smell of earth, especially our rich red soil here in Union County." She may have been a snob but never in the sense of an elitist or racist, but only in the sense that she believed Europe and the big east coast cities of America had so much more to offer than Union. Fatgram, on the other hand, had enigmatic views about blacks. Strictly reared and taught by her father that she was the crème de la crème, Fatgram outwardly portrayed an elitist demeanor, especially in society, yet inside her heart, I know she cared greatly for Ala Mary and her family and many other black families in Union. She knew them all and whenever news reached her that someone was in need as a result of sickness, a death in the family, a runaway husband, a new baby, or just plain hard times, she would load her station wagon with clothes, groceries, or casseroles she and Ala Mary prepared, and they would deliver the goods. Fatgram and Ala Mary always beat any organized charitable effort by the ladies of the various white churches by at least a day, sometimes several. Often Billy and I would accompany them on these 'missions of forced mercy' as Mother always referred to them. Once Billy asked Fatgram why she never gave anything to poor white people. She snapped back that "White trash have every opportunity to succeed, they're just shiftless;

whereas, black people, because of our system, don't stand much of a chance of success at all. Take that redneck Darrell Coots, with whom your mother is so enamored. Hmmp, she says he's the perfect male specimen for a model. Some model. Remember when he dropped out of high school, Ala Mary, and I felt sorry for him and engaged him to be a night watchman at the big mill after we closed it? And all he did every night was get drunk on cheap beer and then passed out that night in the parking lot while the mill burned to the ground. And dear Mother's collection of spinning wheels stored in there. Why Daddy would roll over in his grave if he knew I let that happen." Ala Mary nodded her head in agreement—despite the disparities in income, education, and race between them, those two women were like two peas in a pod when it came to views about their society. I was amazed to discover after her death when I was going through boxes of old bank statements before throwing them out to find dozens of checks Fatgram wrote over the years, some for thousands of dollars, to charities and educational institutions benefiting African Americans. As for Darrell being white trash, I agree with Fatgram's views on that topic, but he must have had a model penis, one Mother certainly liked. God, how did I get on this tangent? As I yawn, my thoughts drift back to gentle Brooker T and my feelings about him. That took guts to do what he did, even if Dad instigated it. I bet he and Landrum have a good relationship. Landrum is another person Fatgram would categorize as white trash. Perhaps his success on the farm would change her thinking? I bet Brooker T is totally devoted to him—just like he was to mine and Billy's safety, just like he was to Hedda and Max. God, I'll never forget when someone left a coffee can of anti-freeze in one of the barns and Hedda drank some of it. Everyone, even the vet thought she would die, but Brooker T stayed by her side for days, giving her water with a turkey baster every few minutes throughout the day and night, stroking her, gradually coaxing her back from the brink of death. A sharp feeling of guilt overcomes me as I think that if I had stayed with Billy like Brooker T did with Hedda, Benny could not have gotten in to kill him. Dear God, Brooker T treats his dogs better than I treat my own brother. Why did I leave his side? It was all so overwhelming. I remember I had to pee, and then I just had to get out of that hospital. I remember Brooker T lying beside Hedda in that hot horse stall all day and all night. It had to be July or August. Ala Mary would take him breakfast, lunch, and dinner, and we would take him jugs of iced tea and cold water, but he barely touched his food or drink, just sat there stroking Hedda's head with Max patiently snoozing beside them, flies buzzing everywhere in the relentless heat. And I couldn't even last in an air-conditioned hospital room with my brother for a day. Fatgram, telling Mother that it was time we started learning about death, made Billy and me dig the graves for the five barn cats that also drank the anti-freeze. We tried to get help from Uncle Adrian, who was visiting, but having just been bitten by Hedda when he tried to pet her, was nursing the wound on his right hand, so he refused. He said all cats were nasty and carried disease and that Hedda was a wild dog and should've been put down anyway; some forgetful farm hand had done the world a favor. No one would admit to the mistake, but Fatgram overtly accused Uncle Adrian of perpetrating the poisoning because of the recent bite and because no one in their right mind under her employment would be using anti-freeze in the dog days of summer. Mother said to Fatgram that that was a vile and wicked accusation directed toward her guest. Uncle Adrian said he wouldn't know what a jar of anti-freeze looked like if it dropped from the sky onto his head. Fatgram called him an idiot and said everyone knows anti-freeze doesn't come in jars. Now that I think about it, I am certain Adrian poisoned Hedda. He wasn't thrilled when, after several days, Hedda got to her feet one morning, ate an entire bowl of kibble and acted as if nothing had ever happened. She went on to produce three litters of puppies and lived to the ripe old age of fourteen. One thing I remember for certain, she would never go near Adrian again once she recovered. Billy, Oh sweet Billy, Bennie did the same thing to you. No, Goddamit, it was Adrian who did the same thing to you. I've got to talk to Brooker T to see what he remembers about this— to see if he thinks Adrian poisoned Hedda. Oh, Billy, I'm so sorry, I'm so sorry I didn't stay with you when you needed me. Tears roll out of my eyes onto the sheets and I feel the sleepy, tugging sensation of the drug mixed with the booze I've had tonight—such a powerful effect now that I find I can't even lift my

head or move my hands to wipe the tears away. I drift into sleep mourning the death of my brother, knowing I probably could have prevented it.

Icy, cold air rushes over my face, stinging the inside of my nose as I inhale, creating frigid, audible eddies in both of my ears that mix with the rhythmic beat of pounding hooves. We are galloping in pursuit of something, following the lead of a pack of hounds. I realize it is not a pack of hounds but a pack of elegant Weimaraners, all wearing jewel encrusted leather collars, like the ones in Manon's store. Hedda and Max are out in front, leading the pack. My horse is big, at least seventeen hands, and coal black. I feel the fire in this horse through my reins; I know he is a stallion. My riding boots, jodhpurs, shirt, jacket, gloves, and ascot are all black. I'm not wearing a helmet, but a top hat that somehow stays on my head. My jacket has long tails I feel flapping behind me. My saddle, reins, and bridle are all black leather. I notice a black leather quiver full of arrows attached to the saddle behind my right leg, and I realize that a bow is resting on my right shoulder with its string under my right armpit. What is it we're hunting I wonder? I look over to my right to see Billy, Mother, and Fatgram, all dressed in white formal riding clothes and boots, galloping on magnificent white stallions. Even their saddlery is white. Fatgram has on a white top hat, but Billy and Mother are hatless and their long auburn hair flies back in the cold air, and they are both laughing and Fatgram is smiling.

"We're going to catch the God Damn thing and Philly's going to shoot it," Billy yells out to Mother and Fatgram.

"Shoot what?" I holler to Billy who ignores me as he shifts his weight more forward, moving his steed ahead of the others.

The sky is grey and heavy with clouds and a light snow begins to fall. Up ahead on a hill I see a herd of deer dash out of the woods, running and leaping in a diagonal across a field, their white tails in full alert, warning of incipient danger. Hedda and Max, who delight in pursuing deer whenever they can, don't even seem to notice the deer as they lead the pack toward the point in the woods where the deer emerged. I look around to see if I recognize the field we are in, but I don't at all. The landscape, the vegetation doesn't look like Union county. The dogs leap over a stone wall and we follow. My big stallion, with his long strides, clears the wall with ease and I notice the wall is actually a stone fence, constructed of thousands of stones. It appears to be very old. There are no fences like this in Union County. We enter the woods, a growth of deciduous trees with huge circumferences and heights, forcing us to slow down to a steady trot. There are no ancient forests like this left in Union County. As I began to post, I catch a glimpse of something white, ahead, in the distance, darting through the trees. Barking madly, the dogs increase their pace, moving way ahead of the horses. "They're gaining on him, boys," Mother yells, laughing, showing her beautiful teeth.

"Yes they are, dear," Fatgram screams out, then turns her face toward mine, smiling, nodding at me and suddenly everything turns into slow motion, even the cadence of the horse beneath me.

"You must kill it, Philip," Fatgram commands me.

"Kill what, Fatgram?" I scream back at her.

"You'll know what to do, darling. Just do it," she replies, tapping her horse's rear with a white riding crop to catch up with Billy. Mother pulls her horse up behind Fatgram's and I follow them, confused, lost, still wondering what we are pursuing. The dogs are out of view now, but I can hear them barking, and after a while, we enter a clearing in the woods. Ahead, I see a stone springhouse, ancient, its walls and slate roof covered in moss and lichen. A stone fence surrounds the springhouse and the small pond beside which it sits. We increase our pace to a canter and jump over the fence. I hear gurgling sounds from a brook flowing from the pond and through the clearing. I look down and notice a heavy frost on the ground around the brook; a chill runs down my spine; my ear lobes and fingertips feel numb and frozen. The dogs, there must be twenty or thirty of them, are circling the spring house, barking wildly, trying to jump up on the roof, some are even trying to climb up the stone walls, but keep falling back. We pull our horses up to the

agitated pack and begin scanning the roof. Suddenly, a large white wolf, twice the size of the Weimaraners, appears on the crest of the roof. It pulls back its lips in an evil snarl revealing long white fangs as it glares down at the dogs with its light blue eyes, then, it turns its head toward me, looking right into my eyes. My heart races with fear, I hesitate a moment before I look down at the quiver tied to the saddle and quickly pull out an arrow. The slow motion of events slows even more as I focus on the arrow—its beauty, a work of art in itself, amazes me; this footed arrow was fashioned by an expert fletcher. The fixed blade broadhead arrow head is shining, highly polished sterling silver with razor sharp edges skillfully hammered out and designed to cause massive bleeding in the target; the shaft, gleaming and lacquered, is exquisite with a short spine constructed of heavy, dark, ebony to which is attached a longer rod of some pale coniferous wood, much lighter in weight. The fletching consists of two black feathers, perhaps from a crow or raven, and a solid white cock feather, all carefully cut into the shape of a half shield. I wonder if there is such a thing as an albino raven or crow. The nock is tortoiseshell. I drop my reins, confidant my horse won't move, remove the highly polished black, recurve bow, carefully put the nock of the arrow on the string as I rest the arrow on the shelf, pull the string tight with my right hand, line the wolf up in the sight. Just as it leaps from the roof over the dogs, aiming its canines for my throat, I release the arrow and watch it fly right into its chest. It screams like a wounded puppy, falls to the ground, and is immediately covered by the pack of Weimaraners. I hear the others clapping and shouting praises to me. I jump off my horse, screaming at the dogs to get away because I want to see the animal before they devour it. I move into the pack and am astonished that they are not ripping it to shreds at all, but are gently and playfully licking it, their tails wagging with joy. But it is no longer a wolf. I push the dogs aside to find a small boy, dressed in grey wool knickers, argyle wool socks, black leather half boots, a grey wool jacket with a blue shirt and a grey newsboy cap. The boy is curled into a fetal position; the arrow penetrates the center of a blood soaked bull's eye on his blue shirt. I kneel down, pulling off his cap to look at his face. He has straight red-brown hair, pale skin with freckles and the wolf's light blue eyes, now staring into nothingness. Overwhelmed with grief, sorrow, and guilt, I close his eyelids with my left hand. My eyes fill with tears, blurring my vision. I look up to find that Billy, Mother, Fatgram, and the pack of Weimaraners have all vanished. I fall to the ground beside the boy, pull my knees up to my chest and weep. I ask myself how I could have done this. It's like a bad dream from which I need to wake up. Then, slowly, I realize that it is a bad dream and I can wake up whenever I desire. I force my eyes open, turn over, reach for the clock, turn it around to see the time—it's 6:14 a.m., and I feel so relieved to be out of the nightmare.

I decide to get up because my T-shirt is soaked and I don't want to risk lapsing back into that dream. I roll out of bed, go into the closet, take off the wet shirt, put on a pair of jeans I brought with me, a long sleeve, green Izod pullover of Billy's, and slide my feet into a pair of black slip on sandals I find. I grab a baseball cap that has 'Key West' embroidered on the front and put it on to cover up my bed hair. I walk back into the bedroom to find Clark yawning and stretching on the bed. I sit down to pet him. He immediately walks over to me, plops down beside me and rolls on his back offering me his belly. I begin rubbing it; he groans with pleasure. "You're just a love sponge," I say as I bend over to kiss his muzzle. He lets out an explosive sneeze that wets my face. "Christ, you got me good, boy," I say as I stand up, wipe my face with the sleeve of my shirt and head into the bathroom. While I'm peeing I try to decide how I feel physically. Okay, I think. I'm glad I purposely drank a lot of water yesterday; that certainly helped. I think I will go to yoga today after Dad and Brenda leave. That will help my focus. It will help me get back on track. I flush, wash my hands, and then brush my teeth and begin to wonder what all Najeed will reveal tonight at dinner. Shit, I promised the detectives I would meet with them today to tell them everything I know about Adrian. Well, I just don't think I'll tell them about Najeed or about the Gardner treasure. We'll see. I spit out the foam, rinse my mouth by taking water in my left hand. I look at my face in the mirror as I dry my hands on a towel. I tell myself, "Today will be a good day. Today I will make progress toward getting Adrian." I smile, walk out of the bathroom, motioning for Clark to follow me. We go out into the

hall and walk down and turn into the kitchen where I see Brenda and Dad sitting on bar stools drinking coffee and talking.

"Good morning, Philip," Brenda says, smiling, holding a coffee mug in her hands.

"Good morning. You guys are up early," I reply, noticing that Brenda looks great, even at this early hour. She is dressed in a beige V-neck, cable knit sweater over a white button down collar oxford cloth shirt with khakis and burgundy weejuns. She wears a necklace with alternating beads of gold rice and small white pearls and her hair is pulled back into a simple pony tail, revealing her lovely face on which she has already applied a hint of make-up, eye shadow and lipstick. Dad is dressed in a blue button down collar oxford cloth shirt and has on a pair of jeans and loafers with no socks. A blue blazer is folded on the bar stool beside him.

"Morning son," he says as I approach them. He stands up and embraces me. "I was so proud of you last night, son. You delivered a wonderful, heart-felt tribute to Billy. It touched me deeply."

"Thanks, Dad," I say as I hug him tightly. "I'm so glad you all were here."

"We wouldn't have missed it for anything," he replies, releasing me. He doesn't look rested and his eyes have dark circles under them.

"You all look like you're ready to leave right now," I say as I walk over and give Brenda a hug. She remains seated as she hugs me. "Your father and I have found out things move more smoothly if we ready ourselves before the kids when we're traveling."

"That sound like a good plan to me," I say as I release my embrace on her and take in her wonderful smell and think what a damn lucky man Dad is to have her.

"Our flight leaves at eleven forty-five so we plan to leave here by eight thirty," Brenda says. "We'll wake the kids at seven. We had them pack last night before they went to bed."

"Wow, I can't believe it's time for you all to leave so soon," I say.

"Son, Brenda needs to get the kids back to get ready for school Monday, but I can stay longer if you like. I mean, if you need me, I'd be happy to stay," Dad says with an awkward expression on his face.

"Oh, thanks Dad. No, I'm sure you need to get back, too. For business and everything. I'll be okay. Lush is here. I mean, I'd love to have you stay—as long as you like. I mean, if you wanted to, but really I'm fine," I reply having trouble getting the words out to express what I'm feeling. We both look at each other and smile.

"Want some coffee, Philip?" Brenda asks.

"Sure, thanks. Just black."

Clark is standing by the door to the terrace. I walk over, open the door, let him out, feel that it is not too cold, so I leave the door ajar just a bit so he can let himself back in.

"What time did you all get to bed?" I ask. They both look at each other, smiling.

"Well, son, Brenda and I never made it to bed," he replies looking into his mug of coffee.

"What? Why? Did something else happen?"

"No son, not at all. We knew you were preoccupied with the detectives after you all found Ricky. And Ricky really didn't have a second in command here, so your Mother and I assisted Luka and the rest of Ricky's crew in cleaning up and getting the place back together."

"You mean you all worked all night?"

"We did and we had a blast," Brenda replies, handing me a steaming mug of coffee. "We had Luka and six of his co-workers, Lois and Tammy, and Officer O'Daniel and Lush. We finished about an hour ago."

"My God. How did I sleep through all of that?"

"Son, you were dead tired. After the last guests left around midnight, you took a B and B and sat down on the floor by the fireplace in the study. I walked past and found you asleep on the floor. Lush and I helped you to bed. Don't you remember?"

"Really? No, well maybe. But then I woke up and couldn't sleep, so I took a sleeping pill. No wonder I slept through the cleanup. Damn, I'm sorry you all had to do that. I could've helped."

"Philip, it wasn't a problem and there was no way your father and I were going to leave town today with this entire place in disarray," Brenda says in an authoritative tone.

"Wow, you guys are the best. But I thought Ricky's crew were scheduled to come back today to clean up and straighten up."

"They were," Brenda says, "But after they learned of Ricky's accident they decided it was best to just stay and get it done. Luka said it wouldn't take all of them, so six of them stayed and the other ten went home. Lush worked relentlessly, all night. Philip, she is a wonderful woman. I'm so glad I got to know her this week."

"She certainly is, Brenda—she's my rock."

"Son, what are your plans for the day?"

"Well, I have to meet with the detectives for a while. Then, I definitely plan to go to yoga—no more smoking starting now."

"That's great, Philip," Brenda says, "I need to pattern myself more after you."

"Gee, Brenda, you're in great shape. You must work out," I reply.

"Thanks. I do Pilates three times a week and your Dad and I take two or three long walks every week."

"It shows," I reply. "What about you, Dad?"

"Unfortunately, besides the walks, nothing," he replies, sighs, looks down then back up. "But, I really would like to take up something—something that's not hard on the joints. I pretty well beat myself up running all those years."

"Gosh, I'd nearly forgotten about your running," I reply. Memories flood back of Mother taking Billy and me to watch Dad finish in different road races. He competed in ten k's, half mini's, and full marathons and he was good, usually in the top ten or fifteen in his age group. He ran track in college at Chapel Hill. I can't believe I haven't remembered that in such a long time.

"Yeah, well, I gave it up after your Mother died, but it had already taken its toll on my knees. Maybe I should try this yoga you do, son?"

"Dad, it would be great for you. It's called Bikram yoga or a similar one is Barkan yoga—I recommend either one. I know you can stand the heat. I remember you training for races in the middle of summer in Union. You'd come home, bare-chested, soaked running shorts, white salt trails on your arms and sides and all you wanted to do was find a cool patch of hard floor or concrete and lay down and take a nap."

He laughs, "Yes, I did. The hard surfaces always felt so good on my back after a long run. I can't believe I fell asleep that way."

"Well, I'm certain there are these type yoga studios in St. Louis. Look them up when you get back and give it a shot. Just remember to be well hydrated before you do class. I mean drink a lot of water the day before you do it and on the day you do it."

"Okay, I can do that. I'm going to give it a try. Want to do it with me, hon?" Dad asks Brenda as he taps both hands on the back of the bar stool.

"Oh dear, Charles. You know I'm not a heat person unless I'm on the beach with a nice breeze," Brenda replies. "But I think you really ought to do it. At least give it a try," she says as if she asking a question, then a look of concern shapes her face. It's so obvious to me that she really loves and cares for my Dad. I'm so happy for him.

"Dad, Brenda," I say, sensing this is a good time to tell them, "I have two things I want to talk to you about. Well, first, it's about Drew."

"Drew?" Brenda asks. "What is it, Philip?"

"Brenda, how close are you with your sister?"

"Sister? I don't have a sister, Philip," she replies with a confused look on her face.

"Well, who is Pam?" I ask.

"Pam is my brother Harry's wife. I just have one brother, Harry. Why?"

"I see. So cousin Randy is their child?"

"Yes, he is, why?"

"Does Randy have any siblings?"

"He does, an older brother, Harrison who's in his early twenties. Why do you want to know about them, Philip?"

"Because Randy has been sexually abusing Drew," I say flatly.

"Oh my God. Is that true, Philip?" Brenda asks, clasping her cheeks with both hands.

"Son, are you certain?" Dad asks.

"I'm certain. Drew came into Billy's closet when I walked in there after showering yesterday. I was naked and sort of embarrassed so I quickly dressed while Drew started talking again about Billy being gay. He was referring again to his cousin Randy and how he was knowledgeable and all grown up. I asked him what he meant by 'all grown up' and he replied that he has a 'big hairy penis like mine and Dad's.' So I asked him how he knew that and he told me that he had seen it when Randy practiced sex on him."

Brenda bows her head, shaking it. Dad reaches over to touch her shoulder.

"I'm sorry to be the bearer of this news, but I think you guys need to deal with this as soon as you get home. I promised Andrew that I would take care of it and that he never would have to worry about it again. He told me Randy only does it to him, including anal intercourse, when they are alone. He threatens Drew and tells him that if he ever tells anyone, he'll tell everyone that it's really Drew's idea, because Drew is really just like his faggot half-brother, Billy."

"Dear God," Brenda says, "How often did it happen?"

"Well, Brenda, how often were they left alone?" I ask.

The color drains from her face and she begins to cry. Dad embraces her. "Honey, it's all right. We can deal with this. We will deal with this."

"God, I'm so stupid. I just blindly trusted Randy. He was always an aggressive child, but so very, very bright, I thought his influence would be good around our boys. And they are cousins."

"Well, in my opinion, Drew is fine. He's a hell of a strong personality himself as I'm sure you all are well aware of. He confided in me for a reason. I told him that Billy and I had been abused in the same way as he had but by a much older man. That seemed to help him a lot. I really think he'll get through this okay, provided you all deal with Randy's parents directly."

"You better believe we'll deal with them directly. I could just kill Harry. I've always told him he gave his kids too much free reign," she says wringing her hands. "Oh dear God, it was true, then," she explains.

"What was true, honey?" Dad asks.

"Well, when Harrison was about fifteen, he was accused of molesting a younger boy in his neighborhood. Pam and Harry told me it was just a misunderstanding and that it was pubescent boys just exploring their sexuality. Damn, Harrison has been nothing but trouble for them—in and out of different boarding schools and now colleges. He probably abused Randy for all we know."

"That's a real possibility, I think," I reply. "At any rate, I think you should confront Harry and Pam, let them know this is not just a case of pubescent boys playing around, and recommend that they get help for Randy. If in fact his older brother sexually abused him, he's going to need help with it. And, even if he wasn't, he still needs help because of what he's done to Drew."

"Philip, I suppose you're right," Brenda says with a sigh, dabbing her eyes with a napkin.

"Brenda, I know I'm right. I speak from experience. You need to be strong but firm with your brother and sister-in-law and insist on this. And I think you should do it without bringing Drew in for questioning or anything. That's my advice and I only give it because I love you all, and I don't want to see any of you hurt or suffer."

"Son, thank you. You are right," Dad says with a sad look on his face, his hands on Brenda's shoulders, and out of the corner of my left eye, I think I see his right hand trembling, and it nearly breaks my heart. I walk over and embrace them both.

"Well, what about Drew? Do you think he'll need treatment as a result of this?" Brenda asks.

"I'm certainly no expert on children, but my impression is that he is strong and together and as long as you guys love and support him, he's going to be just fine," I say.

"Well, we do love and support him, Philip," Brenda says. "Do you think we don't do it enough?"

"No, I didn't mean that, but what I really mean is that I think Andrew is gay and will discover this in himself in the coming years."

"Really, Philip?" Dad asks. Brenda begins to audibly weep.

"Well, I do think that. Having grown up with a brother who is gay. I just see so many similarities between Drew and Billy."

"Excuse me, Philip," Brenda says. "I'm not crying because he's gay. That's not a problem at all with me. I'm crying because I've always suspected it and have been too much of a coward to admit it to myself or to Charles."

"That's nothing to be ashamed about, Brenda," I say. "You love your children and want the best for them. Being different from others is a challenge you wouldn't wish on anyone. Even as open sexually as Billy was, there were times when he'd get really blue and depressed about it—about being different, being gay."

"It's so funny," Dad says, "Maybe I'm an insensitive dolt, but I never saw Billy as being gay, and I don't see Andrew as being gay. They're both my sons, and I love them just the way they are. Your Mother always suspected Billy was gay and told me. I never saw it. It never, ever mattered to me. And it doesn't with Drew. I'll support him as the person he is until my dying day."

"That's really a nice thing to say, Dad."

"Well, thanks for telling us, Philip. You really have been a savior to my family and me in so many ways this week. You have become a man I truly admire, would aspire to be like, and am so proud to call my son." Tears seep from his eyes as he says this and I feel a huge smile burst forth across my face even though I'm crying, and I'm back to the same fantastic feeling I remember when I was ten years old and was fishing alone with Dad and I hooked a nine pound large mouth bass and brought it in as Dad watched, then clapped his hands, jumped up and down with delight, and picked me up while I was still holding the fish, twirled me around, kissed my neck and told me how proud he was of his little man.

"Gee, thanks Dad," I say smiling at him and Brenda, "It feels so incredibly good. I mean Billy and I have really had only each other all these years. And now it feels like I have my family back."

"Yes, I know, Philip," Dad says, smiling, "I feel the same."

"And so do I, Philip," Brenda says, smiling through her tears, "You're stuck with us now and how lucky we all are, especially the children, who'll grow up knowing and loving you as the wonderful man you are."

"Thanks, Brenda. You are indeed as kind as you are beautiful—inside and out. Dad has to be one of the luckiest men alive to have you in his life everyday."

"Well, what about me? Don't I count for anything in this family?" Lush says, startling us all as she sweeps into the kitchen dressed in a light green silk kimono covered with curvilinear designs in iridescent shades of lavender, pink, and white, her luxuriant hair held back with a scarf made of the same material, a Presidential in her right hand, her gold lighter in her left hand, her face, free of make-up revealing near flawless skin, drawn into a look of exhaustive dismay, punctuated by a slight furrow in her forehead, her full lips puckered into a near pout.

"Oh darling," Brenda quickly says as she dabs her eyes with a napkin, "You count for everything and you are indeed a part of this family."

"Absolutely, Lush," I reply, "You're my angel, my rock. I was just telling Dad and Brenda that."

"Really, Todge?" Her face relaxes as she begins to smile.

"Yes, yes, of course," I reply.

"Well thank you. Thank you all. I don't know why I felt so left out as I was walking in here hearing you all expressing your familial bonds so wonderfully." She sighs, lights her cigarette, exhales a stream of smoke, looks toward the floor as she says, "Sometimes I can be such a selfish, rude bitch."

"Dear, you are not that way at all," Brenda says, gets up off her stool, walks over to Lush, lifts her chin with her right hand, looks into her eyes and says, "You are one of the most kind, compassionate, caring, selfless, and genuine women I've ever met, and I am proud to call you my sister."

Lush throws her arms around Brenda, holding the cigarette well away from Brenda's back. "Oh Brenda, that's one of the sweetest things anyone has ever said to me. Thank you so much." She releases Brenda, steps back, takes another drag off her cigarette and says, "You'll all have to excuse me. It's been such an emotional week for us all, and after that wonderful wake last night, and now the fact that you all are leaving today, and somehow we must all go back to some sort of normalcy. Well, I guess, I guess I just felt lost and alone."

"Aren't you staying on here a bit, Lush?" Dad asks in a soft tone.

"Oh yes, Charles. I mean as long as Todge wants me here."

"Want. I expect you here, Lush. You know that. I'll never get to the bottom of the Adrian thing without you. I need you to help me get back on track, and I want to help you get back on track, you know—post-David and all."

"And you know I will," she says, taking another drag off her cigarette. "I think when I heard you all talking about family, I realized how much I miss Mom and Dad and how I've desperately but unsuccessfully tried to build a family with David all these years."

"Here, dear. You need some caffeine," Brenda says as she hands Lush a steaming mug of black coffee, takes the Presidential from Lush's right hand, takes a big drag from it, smiles at Lush as she exhales the smoke, hands the cigarette back to Lush, and picks up her own mug to take a sip.

Lush looks at Brenda, then Dad, then me and emits a sort of combination sigh, smile, and chuckle, snuffs out her cigarette in an ashtray on the counter, before she says, "You know, despite the horror and tragedy of Billy's death and Elliott's death, I've felt in many ways more alive and connected to all of you this week than I have with anyone in years. I guess I just panicked this morning when I woke up, heard you all talking in here, and longed so much to be in here and be a part of it, of you all. So I threw this on and as I walked in here as fast as I could, I thought this wonderful nirvana of connections might end today when Charles and Brenda and the children leave. And, what if Todge doesn't really want or need me here? And, shouldn't I just really go back to Louisville and deal with David? And, so you see, it just overwhelmed me."

I walk up to Lush, look into her eyes and say, "Lush, I do want and need you here. I want you here as long as you want to be here. You are a part of my family, our family, this family here. And you always will be. Aren't we all planning Christmas in Aspen this year?"

"Absolutely we are," Brenda says.

"Yes, a white Christmas with all of you, something so wonderful to look forward to," Lush says, smiling.

Clark nudges the door open wider with his nose, trots over, stops, and looks up at us, his mouth open, panting, rapidly wagging his tail. "And you're welcome in Aspen, too, Clark," Dad says.

"Really?" I ask.

"Absolutely, son. He gets along well with other dogs. He and Henry will have a blast playing in the snow with the kids."

"Cool," I reply. "You all don't mind shipping Henry on a commercial flight?"

"We'll only do it in the cool months," Dad replies. "In the summer, we usually drive if we take him with us to the beach."

"Well, we'll cross that bridge when we come to it, Clarkster," I say as I squat down, sitting on my heels, stroking Clark's face with both of my hands. He licks my face twice, rapidly. I laugh. "I bet you want some breakfast, boy."

"Here, son. Let me get it," Dad says. "I really will miss Clark. He's just the best. I love his spirit. He and I have sort of bonded this week. In a lot of ways, he's helping me cope with Billy's death."

"I know what you mean, Dad. It's like he can read your mind or your emotions or something like that," I say as I push up to a standing position.

"Yeah," Dad says and continues to speak as he gets Clark's food. "I've found myself talking to him on our walks—even telling him how I feel or, at least, how I think I feel. Hell, I've even asked him questions. I suppose passersby wrote me off as a crazy man."

"Charles, that's so nice—it's touching," Brenda says, her worried expression easing into the beginnings of a smile.

"Someone once told me that stray dogs you take in or dogs you rescue from the pound are really angels sent to help you," Lush says, her eyes appearing unfocused but fixed on a nothingness only visible to her through the panes of glass in the French doors.

"I love that, Lush," Brenda says, "What a kind and wonderful thought."

Lush does not respond for a second and then with a look of anger picks up her cigarettes from the counter, pulls one out, quickly lights it, inhales deeply, and as the blue smoke spews from her nose and mouth, she looks down at her nails, inspecting them, sighs, and says, "And I allowed my angel to be sent away." A single tear falls from her left eye onto the counter.

"No you didn't, Lush," I reply. "David made you get rid of Clark. He wouldn't let you keep him."

As she looks up at me, I can see that she is reining in her emotions. She swallows, smiles, replying, "But I'm a grown woman, Todge. I gave in to him when I absolutely didn't have to. It was my choice." She picks up her mug of coffee with her left hand, takes a small sip, turning her eyes to mine. "I'm so glad Billy got Clark. They were perfect for each other. I just regret that I gave David the satisfaction of depriving me of a heavenly being he recommended a long time ago when I first met him."

Lush's reply sends an icy shock wave through my heart that quickly melts into jealousy as I realize that she did indeed love David, and I barely hear Brenda saying in a soft voice, "Oh, dear, Lush. I'm so sorry you've suffered so much in this marriage. What torture you must have endured. You deserve so much better."

"Thank you, Brenda. I appreciate your compassion and caring. In a thousand different ways, the horrors of this week have transformed me, even inspired me to follow what has been deep inside me all along. I know what I have to do," Lush sighs, "I will do it and I will be fine. I can't thank you all enough for your emotional support."

As Dad walks back to the counter, I hear the clinging of Clark's tags on the metal bowl, and I feel a surge of emotional energy emanating from my hip joints, wrapping through my guts, surging up through my heart and throat and I force myself to breathe deeply and slowly as I pull out a barstool and sit down, focusing my eyes on the black granite, knowing that I must tell them about Adrian.

"Philip, dear," Brenda says, gently touching my left shoulder with her right hand, "Are you alright?"

"Yes, yes," I reply, "Just a little dizzy, or maybe drowsy. I'm sure it's just an after effect of the Ambien. Listen, Dad, Brenda, we found out yesterday that Adrian McWhorter is very much alive and well."

"What?" Brenda says, "Is this really true, Philip?"

Dad walks over towards with his hands turned out.

"How could this be, son? He burned to death."

"No, Dad, he didn't. Lush figured it out earlier this week. Adrian faked his death by killing a migrant worker, pulling the guy's teeth out, then putting a set of Adrian's dentures in the worker's mouth. So the dental records make it appear that Adrian was killed."

"But why would he do that, Philip?" Brenda asks.

"We don't know exactly," I reply, "But Adrian is living in Dubai now, is an operative in al-Queda, and is still up to his insidious crimes. Dad, he had Billy and Elliott Fields killed."

Dad shakes his head, "That son of a bitch, that Goddamned son of a bitch."

Lush looks at me with a questioning look, and I nod to her affirmatively. She says, "Brenda, Charles. There's something else you need to know. Philip and I have been focusing on Adrian all week with Julianna and a private investigator we hired. We're certain that Adrian murdered Eva as well as several other women artists, including Dyanne O'Bryan, whose sons he was sexually abusing."

Dad's face turns red, he gasps, puts both hands on the counter, looks up toward the ceiling, and in a high-pitched voice says, "Oh God, Ina! Dear God, I should have listened to you."

"Dad, what did Fatgram tell you? Did she know anything?" I ask, hoping that Dad doesn't start hyperventilating again.

"She never approved of or trusted Adrian. Once, at a cocktail party at her house, while Adrian was babbling on about some painter to a small crowd, including Eva, he held transfixed, Ina walked over to me, smirked at me, and said, 'Charles, if you were any kind of real man at all, you'd kick that little queer's ass, tar and feather him, and send him packing back to New York and threaten to castrate him if he ever sets foot near Eva or the boys again.'"

"Damn, Dad," I reply, "Do you think Fatgram knew what Adrian was doing to Billy and me?"

"No, she would have said something," he replies, sighing, "I just think she had a really strong, bad feeling in her gut about him—that bastard."

"Dad, Billy has corresponded with him for the past two years. He even let Adrian mentor him on his recent works."

"But, why, son? That makes no sense."

"Yes, it does, Dad. It makes perfect sense. Billy was trying to ensnare Adrian, find out where he was, and kill him."

"Yes," Lush interjects, "Billy had discovered Adrian had killed Eva and the others. You see, Adrian killed Ricky Wallitsch's mother, too. Billy and Ricky were working together. Ricky didn't electrocute himself with a blow dryer last night. He was using a satellite phone supplied by Adrian to report the progress of the wake. Adrian meant to kill Ricky. You see, Adrian discovered Billy and Ricky were planning to kill him. At least that is what we are thinking at this point. We hope Ricky recovers from the coma he's in, so that we can ask him."

"This is almost all unbelievable," Dad says.

"It gets worse, Dad," I say as I look at him.

"Yesterday morning, Julianna and I, along with two private investigators broke into Adrian's apartment to see if we could find anything. Adrian left me a note demanding that I return an al-Qaeda operational compact disc that Najeed purchased from a maid in Adrian's compound and sent to Billy. He said if I exposed him to anyone, that he would attack Emma, Drew, and Peter."

"What!" Brenda says. "My God, what are we going to do?"

"We will arrange, through our detective, Jonas Grey, to get good people to shadow the kids until we catch Adrian," I reply.

"Do the police know about all of this, son?"

I hesitate a moment. "Yes, well almost everthing. Things have been happening so fast, it's been a challenge to report everything."

Lush widens her eyes as she looks at me.

"So how do you think you're going to catch Adrian?" Dad asks.

"There's something he wants badly," I reply.

"What is it?" Dad asks.

"A half a billion dollars worth of priceless artworks stolen in 1990 from the Isabella Stewart Gardner art museum in Boston," I reply.

"What's that got to do with you, son?"

"Adrian believes that Dyanne O'Bryan's husband pulled off the heist and hid the stolen works, which include a Vermeer and a couple of Rembrandts, on their farm in Kentucky. Adrian thinks that I will be able to successfully convince Dyanne's son, Christopher, who is now a monk living in Southern Indiana, to reveal where the works are hidden. If I can deliver the works, Adrian has agreed to personally inspect them and pick them up."

"This all is too much to comprehend," Brenda says.

"Why would anyone trust Adrian at all, son?" Dad asks.

"You're right, Dad," I reply. "But, if those stolen artworks are hidden in Kentucky, I have to at least give it a shot. Otherwise, we may never catch Adrian."

"I don't know, son," Dad replies, "Hadn't you better just let the police handle this?"

"They are, Dad, but if Lush and I, with the help of Jonas and his associate Mabry, help apprehend Adrian, I'm going to do it. I owe it to Billy and to Mother, and now, to all the others who he has killed or wrecked their lives."

"Be careful, guys," Brenda says.

"We will, Brenda," I say. "Gosh, I feel weak all of the sudden."

"You need to get something in your stomach, Todge," Lush says. "How 'bout I make fried egg sandwiches for everyone?"

"Oh, that sounds good, Lush," Brenda says.

"Yes, that would be great," I add in, as I force out a smile.

"Good," Lush replies. "Brenda, I'll make them for the children, too. Will they eat them?"

"Oh, yes, Lush. They'll love them. Emma and I will split one, though."

"Great," Lush replies, moving into the kitchen. "Six fried egg sandwiches coming up!"

Emma, dressed in an ankle length, lacey, white, night gown, runs into the room, rubbing her eyes with her small fists, stops at her mother's stool, stretches out her thin arms to her mother without saying a word.

"Good morning, my sleepy angel," Brenda says, bending forward, pulling the child up in her lap, pulling her into her bosom, wrapping her arms around her, unconsciously rocking her, planting little kisses on her head. Speechless, Emma closes her eyes, drifting to sleep, absorbing her mother's love.

"She's like you, Philly," Dad says, smiling at his wife and child, "It always takes her a while to wake up."

"Was I like that? Really, Dad?" I ask.

"Just like that," he replies.

"Yes, I can vouch for that, Todge," Lush says from the kitchen as she places two large frying pans on the gas burners. "I learned quickly, a long time ago, to give you your space in the morning."

I feel my mood brightening as I recall sitting in Dad's lap before breakfast in the morning. I can even smell the newsprint as he turns the pages of the paper he's reading as I lay against his chest, drifting in and out of sleep, waiting for Ala Mary to finish fixing our breakfast. Billy, always quick to jump out of bed and get going, is playing with toy cars underneath the kitchen table, generating various sound effects through his lips. And then I feel an anxious feeling in my stomach as I anticipate Mother's mood this morning. God, how many days did I begin in the arms of my Dad, wondering which Mother would descend the stairs that day, ushering in a day of wonder, love, and learning, or a stormy day full of fear and despair. Maybe this is why I have recurring dreams of enduring and surviving devastating tornados, their giant

325

funnels sucking me in, exploding structures around me, tossing cars, cattle, and trees about like match sticks, clutching my hands over my head, crunched into a fetal position, my heart thumping madly in my throat as I'm violently hurled through the air, wanting to be set down on wet ground, awaiting the moment when I can look up, thankful that I have survived another storm.

Clark, having finished his breakfast, trots around the bar, sniffs Emma's bare feet, before licking them. She stirs, groans, opens her eyes, looks down at Clark, giggles, looks up at her mother and says, "Mommy, that tickles."

"I know it does, darling," Brenda says, "Clark's just telling you good morning."

"Good morning, Clark," Emma says, wriggles from her mother's lap, plops down on the floor beside Clark, embracing and kissing his head. Clark looks up toward me, mouth open, pink tongue out, barely panting, smiling. He closes his mouth, puts his nose into Emma's right ear, sniffing heavily.

"That tickles, Clark!" Emma shouts.

He pulls back, then licks her right on the lips.

"Haaah! Now he's kissing me, Mommy," Emma shrieks.

"Yes, he is darling. He loves you," Brenda says.

"I love him, too, Mommy," Emma says.

"I know you do, sweetheart. Go put on your slippers. Darling, wake up your brothers, then take Clark out on the terrace," Brenda says.

"Okay," Emma smiles, then starts to run out of the kitchen.

"Emma dear, wait a moment," Brenda says. "Won't you tell everyone else good morning?"

Emma pirouettes twice while she says without looking at anyone "Good morning everyone, good morning Daddy, good morning Lush, good morning Philip, good morning Officer O'Daniel in the front hall," then dashes out of the kitchen, down the hall, Clark trailing her.

We all laugh and Lush says, "Oh my, is Brent still here?"

"Brent?" I ask. "I see we're on a first name basis now."

"Oh hush, Todge. He was a real trooper last night, helping us with the clean up."

"He certainly was," Brenda replies, "And such a well mannered, nice, young man."

I look at Dad and ask, "Well, I suppose you're a member of his fan club too?" Dad gets a worried look on his face, so I break out laughing. "Just kidding, just kidding, just giving Luscious a hard time."

"Todge, I'm in the middle of cooking. Why don't you take him a cup of coffee?" She pours coffee into a white mug and hands it to me.

"How do you know he likes it black?" I ask.

"Just take him the damn coffee!" Lush demands.

I smile, "Yes, yes, dear, I'll take him the coffee."

I pick up the coffee mug, head through the dining room, living room, and into the foyer where I observe O'Daniel in a sound sleep, gently snoring, stretched out on his back, feet hanging off one end of one of a pair mauve silk, upholstered settees. His face is covered in dark stubble, yet he looks so young. His uniform shirt is partially unbuttoned, exposing a white V-neck t-shirt that reveals the top of his hairy chest. I know Lush likes men with hairy chests, and I reckon that her hand must have slipped through that shirt at some point last night or this morning for a sensual rub. Why is it that I don't like this guy? He's nice. He's talented. He's dedicated to his job. He's not in a line of work just for money. He's, he's, oh my God, he's the spitting image of Darrell Coots. That's it. They could be brothers. No wonder I don't like this guy. God, how I hated Darrell, especially after Billy and I witnessed him fucking Mother—I wanted to kill him, I wanted him dead. I was so afraid Mother would divorce Dad, marry Darrell, and we'd end up with a redneck for a stepfather. Fatgram said he got his just rewards when he was smashed in his old Chevy pickup by a train out on Carem Road, but it was such a shame that that young, cute Bennet girl, not even out of high school, happened to be in the truck with him. I felt so guilty, certain my evil wishes

caused the terrible accident to happen, and I prayed for forgiveness to God every night for over a year. I finally couldn't hold it in anymore so one day, distraught and crying, I revealed it all to Fatgram. She hugged me and told me that it wasn't my fault at all, that Darrell and Carrie Bennet were both drunk, out joy riding, and did a stupid thing which cost them their lives. She looked me straight in the eyes and said, "Now Philip, people don't have any control or power over such things, it doesn't matter what you wish, only God controls such things." Well, that eased my guilt, but it started me thinking about what kind of God would let something so terrible as being smashed to smitherings by a train happen to anyone. I was around eleven at the time, and I have progressively pulled away from any organized religious views or beliefs since. Even though I talk to God and pray to God, especially this past week, I do not envision the image of a man, but only of swirling galaxies and the vastness of the universe. O'Daniel opens his eyes, sitting up abruptly. He must have sensed me watching him.

"Here you go, hot coffee," I say handing him the mug.

"Oh thanks, Mr. Hampton. I guess I fell asleep. Sorry," he replies as he takes the mug.

"No need to apologize. I hear you worked all night with the others getting this place back in order," I say as I watch him take a sip of coffee and begin buttoning his shirt with his right hand.

"I was glad to help," he replies looking down at his watch, "Wow, that bacon smells good."

"Yeah, Lush is making bacon and egg sandwiches. Why don't I have her make you one?"

"Oh, no thanks, Mr. Hampton. It's almost seven o'clock. Officer Graham will be here soon to relieve me."

"You sure?"

"Yes, but thanks a lot, Mr. Hampton."

I pause just as I'm about to tell him to just call me Philip. "Well, listen, thanks again for your help last night, Officer O'Daniel."

"Oh, glad to do it, sir," he replies. "Is it alright if I use the restroom down the hall?"

"Of course," I reply as I turn to walk back into the living room. "Help yourself," I say as I make a mental note to ask Dad, when the time is right, how much he knew about Mother's affair with Darrell.

The next hour and a half goes by almost in a flash as Dad, Brenda, Peter, Andrew, Emma, Lush, Clark and I come together one last time during this strangest of weeks. Lush's fried egg sandwiches are a hit with the kids who are all abuzz with stories about the wake, about the famous people they met, about what the best food was—all three children voted for the desserts—about who was the best dressed, about all the beautiful flowers, about how cool it was to meet kids who lived in New York, and about how good each one did in their assigned tasks. Dad, Brenda, Lush and I chime in every now and then, but this table talk is clearly orchestrated by the children and we adults delight in this. It is so much fun that I am mildly shocked when Brenda looks down at her thin, diamond encrusted watch and announces that it is time to gather their luggage for the airport. I realize my bond with this family, my family has materialized and grown strong this week, and just as Lush felt earlier this morning, I do not now want this to end.

"Oh dear, Brenda" I say, "Don't you think you could call the school and ask for another week of spring break?"

"Yeah, mom," Andrew says.

"Cool," Peter adds.

"Oh, please Momma," Emma begs, "Let's stay another week."

"Now kids, we've got to get back to our routines. We'll come back to visit Philip soon. I promise," Dad says.

"When, Daddy?" Emma asks as she focuses her big blue eyes on her father, her face a study in seriousness.

"Well, maybe during summer break if it's alright with Philip," he replies, smiling at me as he raises his eyebrows.

"Of course you all can come this summer. And who knows maybe Clark and Lush and I will come to St. Louis to see you all before then," I reply as I look at my half-siblings.

"That would be so cool, Philly," Andrew says.

"Yeah, it would," Peter adds.

"Oh, please come to visit Philip. Please come, too, Lush," Emma says.

"I'd love to come Emma," Lush says.

Chills run up and down my spine and a warm, gushing feeling of love pours through and out of my body, and I feel so very happy in this moment—so very happy and so grateful, even in the midst of Billy's death these positive feelings flow, and I wish he was here to feel it, too. I sit back and watch the children continue to talk about our upcoming visits and all the things they want to show us in St. Louis, and all the things they want to do in New York. Suddenly, I get the sensation that Billy has put both his hands on my shoulders and is leaning down to whisper something into my left ear, the way he always did when we were out for dinner, at a party, or some other social gathering. He would be returning from the bathroom, the bar, or wherever, approach me from behind, I'd feel his hands clasp my shoulders, feel his weight on my shoulders, and realize that he was about to share something meant only for my ears, some observation, thought or feeling that only true brothers could know and understand and share, in secret. It was always one of my favorite feelings. I smile as I feel his breath in my left ear, and I know that he is here and that he does feel all of this.

CHAPTER 34

Detectives Johnson and Bell watch me as I take a seat on the other side of a small, rectangular conference table in the small room where they have taken me. I feel as if I'm a criminal about to be interrogated, and I suddenly wish that Lush had decided to come with me instead of remaining at Billy's to work on some of her real estate deals.

I sigh, "Do you guys work every day?"

Detective Johnson looks at me, emotionless, as he takes a seat across from me, "We do, Mr. Hampton, when we're working a case like this."

"Yes, I suppose," I reply, placing both my hands on the table.

"Mr. Hampton," Detective Bell begins, still standing, but placing her hands on the table, leaning in towards me, "What can you or, rather, what are you willing to tell us about Adrian McWhorter today?" Her brown eyes focus in on my eyes, and I notice what appears to be some sort of copper and silver pendant dangling from a copper chain around her slender neck. She wears a white blouse with a tailored khaki jacket and matching slacks. Suddenly I realize the pendant is the Ohm symbol, and I wonder if she is a yogis as well as a detective.

I take a deep breath in and exhale, "Adrian McWhorter is alive and well; lives in Dubai with Charles Ainsworth; is a major player in al-Qaeda who supplies the terrorist organization with sophisticated encryption software revolving around pedophile-based pornographic websites and web transmissions; is a major dealer of fine art to wealthy Arabs; comes to New York at least twice a year; orchestrated the death of my brother and Elliott Fields through the Boonmee twins; murdered my Mother in France because she

found out that he was sexually abusing Billy and me; sexually abused Ricky Wallitch and murdered his mother; sexually abused Christopher O'Bryan and his twin brother Noel, murdered their mother, Dyanne O'Bryan; sexually abused Andre de la Croix and murdered his mother, Janine de la Croix; sexually abused Jonathan Zeng and murdered his mother, Hi Lu Zeng, and probably sexually abused many other boys and murdered their mothers as well."

Detective Johnson's eyes have widened, he clears his throat and asks, "And do you have proof or evidence which supports your accusations, Mr. Hampton?"

"We have in our possession a disk obtained from the home of Mr. Ainsworth which proves the al-Qaeda connection. However, Adrian has threatened to kill my younger step siblings if a word of this gets out."

"I see," Detective Johnson says, "But we'd rather pursue the accusations of pedophilia and murders. It will be easier to extradite him on those."

"You'll never extradite Adrian, I can guarantee it. He'll be camped in some unchartered cave in Afghanistan or Pakistan, probably bunking in with Osama bin Laden," I reply with a smirk.

"What makes you so sure, Mr. Hampton?" Detective Bell asks.

"I'll tell you what makes me so sure, Detective Bell. I know the bastard, inside and out! I know what it feels like to be drugged by him and have his body pressed against mine and have his ugly purple cock pushed up inside me! I know what it's like to succumb to his charm and his schemes! But most of all, I know what he has taken from me, and I know him well enough to get even with him!" I realize I am half standing, shaking my finger at Detective Bell, and I see the glistening flecks of spit that have landed on the table from my mouth.

"Take it easy, take it easy, Mr. Hampton," Detective Johnson says. "We know you've been through utter hell this week. We're trying to help, that's all. But you've got to work with us, not against us."

I sit back, wipe my lips off with the back of my right hand, take a deep breath, and sigh. "Yes, I know, I know. That's why I'm here. That's what I'm trying to do."

"Good," Detective Bell says sharply, "Then you'll turn over all the evidence you and your minions pilfered from Adrian's co-op yesterday?"

"Jesus," I say, just about at flash point, again, and bang my right fist down on the conference table, "Do you sit up at night, Detective Bell rehearsing how you can best address me so as to elicit the most anger from me?"

"Afraid not, Mr. Hampton," she replies nonchalantly, "but I do sit up sometimes focusing on how I can help solve the murders of Billy Hampton and Elliott Fields."

"Touché," I reply as I roll my right hand toward her and bow my head.

"Mr. Hampton," Detective Johnson addresses me in an authoritative tone, "We really need everything you all took out."

"The only thing which would help you is an attaché case full of files detailing Adrian's victims. Each complete with its own Blood Brother's Certificate."

"Certificate?" Detective Johnson asks.

"Yes, that was part of his ritual. He showered us with gifts and attention and amazing treasure hunts all leading up to this sacred ritual men and boys do. Right, some ritual—that is if you classify pedophilia as a ritual," I say and pause looking down at the table.

"Please, go on, Mr. Hampton," Detective Johnson says.

"Well, you see, Adrian made such an elaborate game of the whole thing—that is, his wooing or courtship of boys leading up to the first act and subsequent acts of sex. I can't believe I'm saying this, but it was thrilling, exciting, a big adventure for a boy of nine, ten, or eleven. On the day Adrian first had sex with us, we had to swear on the Bible—his little black Bible which is also in that attaché case—promise to never tell a soul at the risk of death, and then cut our hands with a Swiss army pocket knife, rub the blood

on the certificate and sign our names over it. He even photographed that first day at our grandmother's swimming hole in South Carolina. He is an accomplished photographer and sold his black and white photographs of naked young boys and of himself engaging in sexual acts for a lot of money using the pseudonym Nairda—Adrian spelled backwards. The artist Dominique Montaigne, himself a victim of a wealthy pedophile, gave me some of the original pictures Adrian took and developed of Billy and me on the day we were inducted into the Blood Brothers' Circle. I suppose the rich pedophile with whom Dominique lived as a child purchased them, at great expense, from Adrian. After Adrian initiated us, he pretty much had us by giving us incredible gifts, such as real gold doubloons, whenever we would have sex with him. Now I know that when we'd visit him in New York, he'd actually drug us, probably with GHB, to make it easier for him to rape us."

There is calmness in the room, and I think I can discern a trace of sadness in the eyes of Detective Bell and a look of disgust in Detective Johnson's face.

"Adrian McWhorter is the smartest person I have ever known," I offer. "I suspect his I.Q. is off the charts. My mother was a very bright and gifted individual and strongly independent. Yet, she fell completely for Adrian's charm and knowledge. I really believe he was a genuine mentor to her, but, as it turned out, a lethal one."

"Do you know anything else about Adrian?" Detective Bell asks as she fingers her Ohm pendant with her left hand.

"Well, Lush and I suspect that Billy and Ricky had put two and two together to figure out that Adrian had killed our mothers. I think they were actually going after Adrian."

"Going after him?" Detective Johnson asks.

"Yes, going after him to kill him." I state flatly and then add, "Just like I would love to do."

They both look at me as if to stare me down, remaining speechless.

"Well, haven't you already interviewed Ricky, Detective Bell? I'm sure you know everything I know by now."

"Do we, Mr. Hampton? Do we know everything you know?" She asks observing my every breath.

"Indeed you do. I'm sure Ricky filled you in, no?"

"Unfortunately not, Mr. Hampton," she replies, glances at Detective Johnson, then back at me. "The blow he sustained to his head when he was electrocuted was strong enough to bruise his brain resulting in a hematoma. The build up of pressure has caused him to go into a coma. He is being operated on as we speak."

"Dear God, not another death," I say scrunching my entire face.

"The doctors think he will survive if they can stop the bleeding, but he may not awaken for days or even weeks," Detective Johnson states.

"So you see, Mr. Hampton," Detective Bell says looking straight into my eyes, "We need you to tell us everything," she slaps her right hand down on the desk, "Everything you know."

"I've told you everything, Detective Bell," I reply holding her gaze to keep my eyes from shifting.

"Oh really, Mr. Hampton? Then why do I sense that you haven't?" She asks with a crescendo in her voice.

"Probably because you haven't trusted me from the first moment you laid eyes on me, Detective Bell," I reply.

She smirks. "Mr. Hampton, just because you and Mrs. Richardson had success in your investigative journalistic techniques in graduate school, does not mean you are qualified to solve this case and enact justice."

I smile, "Detective Bell, I can assure you that I'm relying on karma to take care of Adrian, but what I really want to know is what you all intend to do about him?"

"We intend to keep twenty four hour surveillance around you, Miss Richardson, Ricky Wallitsch, and your family headed back to St. Louis," she replies.

"Okay, that's fine, but what's that got to do with catching Adrian?"

"We're not certain," she replies, leaning back in her chair, running her slender right hand up and down a gold Cross pen which she taps on the table, "But we think he will most definitely try again to kill Ricky. And I have a hunch there's something he wants from you."

"Oh you do? And what would that be, Detective Bell?"

"Like I said, it's just a hunch, nothing definite at all. Perhaps you'll find it prudent to reveal it to us at some point," she says, smiling.

"Well, I'm sure I will, Detective Bell. Whenever it reveals itself to me."

"Can we have the attaché case and its contents, Mr. Hampton?" Detective Johnson asks.

"Yes, yes. I'll call Jonas and tell him to have it delivered to you. I'm sure he's done with it now anyway. But the other things, I intend to keep. They are personal, they're my Mother's—some of her clothing, hairbrushes, a painting she painted for me—and have nothing to do with this investigation."

"Are you certain?" he asks.

I pause to reflect. "Well we did find drugs. Probably the GHB Bennie used on Billy. You can have what's left of that. I'm certain Jonas had it tested. I mean, it's okay with me for you to interview Jonas and Mabry. I'll tell them to do it. I'll even pay them to do it."

"How kind of you, Mr. Hampton, to save us from the effort of getting a search warrant," Detective Bell says flatly.

"Well, I guess you'll be searching Adrian's place?" I ask.

"Oh yes," replies Detective Bell.

"Tell me, Mr. Hampton," Detective Johnson leans toward me. "What do you make of the self destructing ice sculpture? Wasn't it a sort of copy of the urn your brother's ashes are in?"

"Good observation, Detective, but sloppy work by your staff. They let the sculpture in because it was delivered in a truck from Morgan Galleries. Julianna has no trucks with her name on it. Adrian knows this. I believe he's testing you, even taunting you—now he's laughing, I'm certain."

"I apologize for our oversight, but we did determine there were no explosive devices in it, and one of our officers did call Morgan Galleries and a woman there confirmed that it was from Julianna," he replies.

I try to contain my shock and amazement and ask, "Oh really, and who was this woman?"

"Miss Morgan's assistant, Alejandraia Espinoza," Detective Bell says.

"Impossible," I reply, "Julianna didn't send that sculpture, Adrian did."

"Yes, we suspect that. We interviewed Alejandraia this morning. She said Miss Morgan never told her about the sculpture, but that a representative from the company that carved it phoned and asked for a fax number to fax over the invoice on the rush job Miss Morgan had ordered for the wake."

"Ah, I see now," I reply, "Adrian and his minions at work once again."

"And so it seems," Detective Bell says, "We now know from the ice sculptor that Ricky Wallitsch ordered the sculpture saying it was for Morgan Galleries."

"I see, he didn't want to blow his cover with Adrian," I reply, "But somehow Adrian caught onto him—no telling how."

Detective Johnson clears his throat. "We'll find that out eventually. Is there anything else you want to share with us, Mr. Hampton?"

"No, Detective Johnson. I've conveyed everything I can to you."

"Can convey or want to convey, Mr. Hampton?" Detective Bell asks.

"May I leave now?" I ask.

"Of course," Detective Johnson replies.

I walk out into the hallway where Officer Grissom, a, pudgy, middle aged man, with closely cropped grey hair along the sides of his head, crowned by a large shiny bald spot, who is assigned to me today, waits.

"Thank you for your time and help, Mr. Hampton," Detective Johnson says.

"You're most welcome," I reply. "Now I'm going to hot yoga to try to regain my sanity." I turn toward Officer Grissom, "You're welcome to join in Officer Grissom, it's just ninety minutes of fairly intense yoga in 105 degree heat and fifty percent humidity."

His eyes widen as he lifts his brow creating furrows in his forehead and looks toward Detective Johnson. I laugh looking back at Detective Bell, who is smiling and fingering her Ohm charm with her right hand. My ears begin to burn. I abruptly turn and walk down the hall.

So far so good I tell myself as I move into Eagle pose, the final pose in the warm up series of Bikram. My lungs feel a bit compromised from the week of smoking, but I'm generally okay as I wrap my right arm under my left elbow, intertwining my forearms and palms, thumbs facing my face. I lean forward, wrapping my right leg over my left leg, around my left calf, with my toes pointing to the floor. I sit back and down, bending my knees, noticing that my legs feel really strong as sweat pours off my face and oozes from almost every area of my skin. I breathe deeply and try to focus on my third eye and sure enough, in a second, a distinctive yellow-white glow lights up around my body, a glow I have come to know as my aura. Thank God it's still here after all that has happened this week. I'm so focused on myself that I don't even hear the instructor when she says release.

"Philip, you can release now," she says.

"Philip, release the pose, please. It's important we all stay together."

Then I realize she's talking to me. I instantly release the pose and stand erect mouthing, "I'm sorry," to her general direction.

"Begin left side, eagle," she ejects from her mouth, as if she were a platoon sergeant going through a morning drill. "Inhale, arms overhead, left arm under right arm at the elbows, wrap your arms and palms, thumbs facing inward. Good. Now, left leg way up high, as high as you can go over right leg—the higher you go the easier it is to wrap around. Good. Around the calf, toes visible in the mirror and pointing straight down. Nice. Shoulders back, sit back more, pull your hands down, fingers below your chin, now chest up and out, sit down, more down, more down, more down! Breathe! Hold It! Good! Now release! Arms overhead and down by your side. Good! Take a break, dry off your hands and grab a sip of water, not too much, just a sip. This is the only water break we'll take together. From now on take the water, when you need it, between poses. Moving into the one legged balancing series, we'll begin with standing head to knee pose, dandayama janurshirshasana…." She continues to bark orders as I attempt my least favorite pose, and I began to lose my focus and concentration. I don't particularly like this teacher, she's way too thin and her boobs are way too big for her skinny frame. What is it with all these women who get boobs made totally out of proportion with their bodies? It just doesn't look right to me, and I've never liked big breasts anyway. I much prefer proportional, perky breasts, than pendulous ones or ones that broadcast 'Here I am, now come and get me!' But who am I to criticize? I suppose if men could have penis enlargements the way women have breast enhancements, three quarters of all men would be strutting around with huge packages bulging out the front of their pants. I silently groan as I focus on my left knee, locked like a lamp post, as I try to kick out my right leg parallel to the floor, holding underneath the ball of my right foot with both hands interlocked. I feel a painful sensation in one of my right hamstring muscles near where it attaches in the butt area, but I manage to kick out all the way. I try to pull back on my right foot to flex it in toward my body, but I just can't do it, nor can I pull my shoulders back, stand up straighter, bringing weight more forward in my left foot, while opening up my chest at the same time. The women surrounding me execute the pose seemingly effortlessly. They are all flexing their feet way back and are curling in bringing their elbows around their calves and their foreheads to their knees. My left leg begins to wobble furiously and I fall out of the pose, panting as if I just completed a hundred yards sprint when, miraculously, she says, 'release'. She, the instructor, whose name is Griffin, which I hope is some sort of

family name, as it is such an odd name for a female, or perhaps she changed her name because she felt some sort of kinship or camaraderie with the mythical beast with the body of a lion and the head and wings of an eagle; although, as I watch her prance about the room, she seems as if she may become airborne at any second, and she keeps reminding us that 'the tighter you are, the lighter you are' and I focus on her micro shorts and surmise that she must have such a tight pussy that she could practically fly out the friggin' window at any moment, is really getting on my nerves, so much so that I can't focus on my third eye, I can't calm my breathing, and I am trying like hell to kick out my left leg at this point, but it will only go halfway, and oh shit, the griffin with the tits of a strip tease dancer is heading my way."Philip, your right knee is not locked and is wobbling way too much for you to try to kick out. Just stand up straight and hold you left thigh up at a ninety-degree angle to the floor. That way you'll take the pressure off your lower back and still get many of the benefits of the pose."

I shake my head yes and follow her instructions, and immediately, I can breathe better and I feel better as the struggling stops. Damn, she's right. Why do I have bad feelings about Griffin? I mean, she's just doing her job, and she really acts as if she cares about it and cares about her students. I just don't like her demeanor, but I quickly realize that it's really my problem and not hers. I begin to focus on my breath, trying to slow it down, trying to focus only on my right kneecap in the mirror as I try as hard as I can to draw it up into my right thigh for stability. As usual, the ratio of women to men in this class is four to one—today there must be forty women and about ten men. As I try to keep my mind and focus on my right knee cap, I notice that a slim dude up in the front, two rows ahead of me has kicked his left leg straight out and has curled his head all the way to his knee. He has a really interesting tattoo on his right shoulder on his back—it's some kind of plant or vegetation, not the omnipresent cannabis tattoo, but something else, I just can't make it out from here. We are now going into the standing bow pose, which is one of my favorites because my legs and abs are strong enough that I can get my belly parallel to the ground. I just wish I could get my lifted leg higher, but I've never been able to go much higher than seeing my toes just barely pop up over the top of my head in the front mirror. As I begin the pose and quickly reach forward and bend at the hips until my belly is parallel to the ground, Griffin notices me again and shouts out, "Nice reach Philip, belly perfect, now all you need to do is kick. Go ahead, Kick! Kick! Kick! Kick like your trying to kick a field goal from the forty-yard line. Kick! Kick! There you go!" And with those words I fall forward out of the pose and come close to knocking down the woman in front of me. Several women around me fall out of their poses like dominos at the same time. The redhead to my left shoots me a dirty look. Christ, calm down, honey, this is yoga, not competition hot stretching. "Good, Philip," the griffin says, "Falling forward means you are doing the pose right. You just need to kick harder and soften your back a little more and you can hold this pose forever!"

Between pants, I try to smile at her, but I'm really feeling a bit nauseated, and I think that if I kick any harder, I'll cause myself to projectile vomit all over the people in front of me, which, thank God, has only happened to me once in my life, that I can recall, and that was when I was doing a travel article about Acapulco for a magazine, and I was spending a couple of days going to the city's finest restaurants with a well known local food critic. One evening as I was descending in the elevator of my hotel to meet the critic in the lobby, I suddenly became very sick to my stomach and without warning, it felt as if someone had slammed their fist into my gut and vomit literally spewed out of my mouth with geyser-like force covering the other people in the elevator who, because it was the middle of the summer, were all members of a large Mexican family on their summer vacation. I just remember hearing shrieks from the women and children and cursing in Spanish from the men and when the elevator door finally opened at the lobby, all the vomit-drenched people ran screaming out. The smell was so foul I can't even describe it, and I was wondering if I had shit in my pants, too. At that point, I didn't know if I was going to faint, burst into tears, or just shrivel up into a ball and fade away, but the food critic, whose name was Emmanuel Garcia, took great pity on me, escorted me back up to my room, held on to me as I vomited again and again over the

toilet until nothing came out but bile. Then he ordered ginger ale from room service, filled the bathtub with warm water, took off my soiled clothing, bathed me, dried me off, got me in bed, called a doctor in to see me, and stayed with me until I fell asleep. Emmanuel, who had raised six children, taught me a thing or two about compassion for others that night, and although I've never been back to Acapulco since that trip, I remained friends with Emmanuel and met him twice when he came to New York before he died from lung cancer last year. Emmanuel was a two pack a day smoker. Suddenly, I regret all the cigarettes I've smoked this past week. I continue through the rest of the standing poses reasonably well, but my mind is roaming, and I'm not focusing on my third eye, my breathing, or anything else but this running faucet of thoughts that is flowing at full force and I am powerless to shut it off. By the time we get to the floor poses, I am literally exhausted, and during the two-minute floor savasana pose, I fall asleep.

"Change, CHANGE! Philip, change into wind removing pose, pavanamuktasana!" I hear a loud, harsh, screeching voice over me and I realize it's the griffin and that I'm waking up. I grab my right knee and pull it up as high as I can to my chest. "Damn it, Hampton," I yell at myself under my breath, "Get your shit together! Wake up! Focus on your yoga!"

I try my best to focus and my breathing has slowed somewhat from the soporific effect of savasana, so I am able to begin to shut down the thought train. I focus on the sound of my breath and visualize it as the sound of ocean waves breaking on the beach and receding back to sea—this works for me and before I know it we are through the cobra series and the only stray thoughts I've had are of Billy and me playing on the beach at Pawley's Island as kids. I get through fixed firm and half-tortoise just fine, thinking that I'm in the homestretch and feeling good about myself and glad that I came to yoga today. Sweat pours off my body and my towels and mat are soaking as I rise to my knees to begin the major back bend pose, the camel. Camel is not my favorite but today I try to push it a little further, pushing my hips out a little more towards the mirror and looking back to the back wall a little more and then as Griffin says release, and I am pushing my torso up out of the back bend, an emotional surge envelops me, and I realize that the sweat running down my face is not sweat at all, but tears—a whole lot of them. I flip over on my back, shut my eyes tightly, trying to hide my convulsive whimpers, but I can't, and I know I'm about to break down into another full fledged bout of crying. At once I grab a towel, jump up, quickly walking to the door, looking at the floor as I cover my face with the towel. I run into the men's room, run into a shower stall, pull the curtain shut, turn on the water to luke warm, fall to my knees, wailing and crying under my breath, until I curl up into a fetal position on my right side underneath the stream of water and before I know it, I'm safe behind my waterfall.

"Hey, you alright in there?"

"Hey, sir. Are you okay?"

I hear a soft male voice calling out to me, and I think if this guy sings, he must be a tenor. My convulsive crying has ceased, and I realize I don't know how long I've been in the shower curled up like this, but I look at my fingers and they are shriveled up and the water is no longer warm. I stand up and shut the water off.

"Hey, thanks, I'm okay, man. Just a little sick, that's all," I reply.

"You sure?"

"Yeah, man, thanks."

"Okay. Sure you don't need anything?"

"Yeah, thanks. Well, maybe a dry towel."

A slender, muscular arm shoots through the curtain handing me a dry white towel.

"Thanks, man."

"No problem."

I slip off my wet yoga trunks and dry my body, starting with my hair and progressing to my feet. I feel drained and my face feels swollen. I wrap the towel around my waist, comb my fingers through my hair,

pick up my wet trunks, and head out to my locker. The guy with the tattoo is sitting on the bench a few lockers down pulling on a pair of brightly colored striped socks, and I recognize from his arms that it was he who handed me the towel. My eyes are focused on the floor, but I see him turn to look at me. Although I can tell from his face that he is older than I am, his body looks like that of a young man. His brown eyes and almost feminine facial features project a warm, friendly feeling.

I try to smile, but I don't think it works, "Hey, thanks for the towel."

"No problem. I noticed that you left class during camel and you've been in that shower for quite a while so I thought I'd better check on you," he says turning toward me. He has on briefs with blue, orange and white stripes on them, and I immediately think this guy's got to be gay.

"Was I in there that long?"

"You don't know? Probably twenty minutes. Did you pass out?"

"Well, I'm not sure, maybe."

"Hey, you better sit down. Oh, I brought in your mat, towels, and water bottle. They're right here," he says as he stands up. I see his legs are slim and hairy, but covered in sinewy muscles, his belly is flat with well-defined abs, and his chest, which is hairless, is built like a swimmer's. He is shorter than I am by a couple of inches.

"Oh, thanks a lot," I reply bending over to retrieve my stuff. "I'm much better now," I reply, hesitate, and then feel compelled to explain my behavior to this gentle stranger, "You see. It's just that. Well, I've had a horrible week. My brother was murdered a week ago, and we just had the wake last night, and something about that camel just caused me to crack. I don't know what it is, man."

His facial expression drops into a look of sadness; he looks up at me and says, "Gee, I'm sorry to hear that. I can't imagine how terrible that must be."

"Thanks," I say and sit down in front of my locker, unfasten the key pinned to my yoga shorts, and open the locker.

"Camel and any of the hip opening poses can really draw out emotions. You're really offering your heart in camel and are really vulnerable," he says, pauses, looks down, then looks up at me, "Hey, I don't mean to be nosey, but was Billy Hampton your brother?"

I turn to look at the guy and reply, "Yes he was—I mean, he is. Do you know him?"

He shakes his head quickly side to side, "No. Well, I met him once when I went with a friend to one of his openings, but I didn't know him. You look a lot like him, so I figured you must be his brother when you told me about the murder." I realize this guy is from the south from his accent and word choices, so I turn around and offer him my right hand.

"It's nice to meet you. I'm Philip Hampton."

He bends over, shaking my hand, and replies, "Good to meet you Philip, I'm H.R. Ferguson."

"H. R., what's that short for?" I ask.

"Harper Reed," he says quickly.

"Harper," I reply, "Well that's a family name if I've ever heard it, and I know you must be from the south."

"Yeah, you've got me pegged, Philip. Harper Reed Ferguson the fourth from Montgomery, Alabama," he replies in a pronounced southern drawl in his soft, warm voice.

He pulls a pair of faded Levi's from his locker and steps into them. I can't help but look at his body and wonder what I would have to do to get such definition, such appearance of strength and health. "Well, Mr. Ferguson," I reply in my own southern drawl, "We probably have some things in common seeing as how I'm from Union, South Carolina."

H.R. laughs out loud with an infectious, likable laugh, like an eleven-year-old boy full of life and enthusiasm who has just heard a semi-dirty joke from his best buddy, as he rolls a Speed Stick under his arms, pops the top back on the deodorant, throws it in his black backpack, reaches inside his locker, pulls

out a white T-shirt, slips it over his head in one motion, and smiling with a big smile showing two rows of straight, yellow-white teeth replies, "I'm sure you're right about that, brother." I am drawn into him, his boyish demeanor, his innate friendliness and compassion; even his hair is cut short like a boy's in the summer, and I notice he has a cowlick sticking out of the left crown of his head. I am aware that his eyes are on me as I stand up, drop my towel, reach into the locker for my boxers, step into then, and pull them up. I grab my hairbrush out of my gym bag and begin brushing back my hair as I turn around to face him and ask, "Are you visiting or do you live in New York, H.R.?"

"Awe, I live here. Have for the past twenty years," he replies as he zips up his pack. "Came here when I was fresh out of Auburn, determined to make it on Broadway. Been here ever since."

"Jesus," I reply, "I'd never guess you were forty."

"Forty two this summer," he says, smiling, and I observe that his chin and upper lip are covered in fine stubble, as I watch his well defined biceps and triceps move.

"Well, did you make it on Broadway?" I ask.

"Hell, no," he replies, "A few minor roles and lots of chorus gigs, but not enough to really make a decent living." He's sitting back down, bent over lacing up what appear to be some type of bowling shoes.

"Well, if you don't mind my asking, what do you do now?" I reach inside my bag for my own Speed Stick, and start to apply it.

"I teach yoga here and at two other studios, I'm a waiter at The Metropolitan Club, and I'm an aspiring writer," he quickly replies.

"My, you've got a lot going on," I say.

"Well, Mr. Hampton, I'm sure you know what it takes to live in this city, unless you're wealthy or have a high paying job, you work several jobs," he replies in a voice without any trace of his southern accent.

I laugh. "Is that how you speak at The Metropolitan Club? No southern drawl?"

"That all depends on who the client is. I learned a long time ago, you have to bend like a willow to adapt to any situation," he says, turning his head toward me, smiles, winks at me with his right eye and continues putting on his shoes.

"I imagine that's a good skill to have in this town," I reply reaching in the locker for my pants.

"So, Mr. Hampton," he says.

"Please, just call me Philip," I interject.

"So, Philip, what do you do for a living?"

"I am a free lance journalist."

"Cool. That sounds like an interesting career. You travel much?" he asks, sits up facing me and straddles the bench with a graceful arching motion of his right leg.

"I do travel, quite a bit. What kind of writing do you do, H.R.?"

"Oh, well, I've been working on my first novel for about twenty years, now," he laughs a bit. "But, seriously, I've taken a bunch of creative writing courses, and in the past four years, it is finally coming together."

"Do you hope to publish it?"

"Right now, all I'm worried about is finishing it. I figure I'll worry about publishing it once it's done, once it's complete, I mean, exactly the way I want it to be," he says with lessening confidence.

"I've done a lot of Bikram yoga around the country and around the world, and I don't think I've ever seen a man do the poses as well as you, especially the standing bow—your leg was straight up, a perfect split."

He face lightens and he smiles again, "Well, thanks. I kind of had a head start with all my years of dancing."

"Yeah, I imagine that helps. Hey, listen. What's that tattoo on your back? It looked really cool, but I couldn't quite make out what it was."

In another unified motion he pulls off the T-Shirt, lifts both legs high, pivots one hundred and eighty degrees on his ass, exposing his bare back to me. I study the tattoo.

"Well I'll be damned I say. It's the three friends of winter and beautifully done."

I hear him gasp as he turns his head around toward me, "You're shitting me! You're the first person I ever met who knew what this is."

"Oh, I know alright. You see, my mother was an avid collector of blue and white Chinese porcelain and took great pains to educate my brother and me about the different motifs on her pieces. Why do you have it tattooed on your back?"

Harper sighs, flips back around facing me, scoots to the end of the bench, with a sad, worried look on his face, and begins, "Well when I was in my early thirties and coming to grips with the fact that I was not ever going to make it on Broadway or Hollywood, I was having a pretty rough time. I started partying too much, drinking too much, doing some drugs, and just not taking care of myself or of relationships that were important to me. All this was precipitated by a bad knee injury I sustained in a show I was in. After my knee surgery, a friend recommended Bikram to me. I started doing it and after a few months, it changed my life. I went to teacher training and then later got into Barkan and went to that teacher training. During this whole time I became more spiritual, gave up my partying ways and generally got my life back on track. In some of my readings about eastern religions and philosophies I came across the three friends of winter, and I was always drawn to these images and Chinese paintings of them because they can all endure cold weather and flourish under adverse conditions. Hell, the plum even blooms during the winter. I could really relate to that coming from the south, and I hate the cold weather and the long gray winters here in New York. So the three friends became my secret personal symbol, and when I completed the Barkan training in Ft. Lauderdale eight years ago, I found a great tattoo artist down there, took him a picture of the three friends from a fourteenth century Chinese scroll painting and voila, here it is on my back now, and I truly love it."

"Wow, H.R., that's admirable of you. It's one of the best reasons I've ever heard for having a tattoo. I remember from my Mother that the three friends also together symbolize longevity, perseverance, and integrity—the virtues of the ideal scholar-gentleman. They also represent the three main religions of China: Buddhism, Daoism and Confucianism."

"Yes, I've read that about them, too," he says and pulls his shirt back over his head.

Officer Grissom walks into the locker room, sees me, pauses, executes a combination wave and points with his right hand toward me and says, "Oh, excuse me, Mr. Hampton, just checking to see if everything's okay in here. I'll be out here in the lobby, just let me know when you're ready to go."

I sigh loudly, "Yes, yes, thank you Officer Grissom. I'll be out in just a minute."

I roll my eyes while H.R. studies my face, anticipating an explanation.

"You see, because my brother was murdered, the police are covering our immediate family members until the murder is solved," I offer.

H.R. blushes pink in his face and replies with an embarrassed expression, "Gosh, that doesn't sound too good. You're not in any danger are you?"

"Danger? I'm not sure, after this week, I even know what danger is anymore, H.R. But what I do know is that I've got a pretty long journey ahead of me to get myself back together. I sure hope yoga can do for me what it has obviously done for you."

I look up at him and he walks over and puts his left hand on my bare left shoulder, gently squeezes it, and says, "It will, brother. Just keep doing it." He releases his grip and smiles at me.

"Will you be in New York long, Philip?"

"Oh yes, I'm moving here permanently," I reply.

"Great. I hope you'll come take some of my classes. Griffin is a great teacher, but I offer more of a spiritual flow yoga with a lot of hip openers and back bends." He laughs, "Those'll really flush you out emotionally."

"Thanks. I will come to your class."

"Great. You can pick up a schedule at the desk. I'm gonna be late for work—gotta a big luncheon at the club today. Take care, man." He pulls his backpack on, turns and walks out.

"Yeah, you too. See you around," I say watching him walk out, leaving me helpless to quell the viscous feeling of loneliness and despair oozing out of my hip joints, into my gut and up my esophagus where it congeals, forcing an abrupt, deep, painful, suffocating swallow reflex as my throat clenches around what feels to me like a cold, hard-boiled, rotten egg.

"It's the absolute truth, Todge," Lush looks at me with an expression of sorrow on her face, takes a long drag from her cigarette, turns her head toward the right, blowing out the smoke from her lungs, letting the breeze catch the smoke, directing it away from me. "You really don't mind if I smoke in front of you?"

"No, not at all. I'm fine," I reply, looking at her as I reach down to stroke Clark's head as I feel him push his body weight against my right leg. The day has warmed up pleasantly, even though the sky is filled with a grey haze, and I can feel the warmth of the mid-day sun. We are sitting on the terrace, sipping pinot noir, after having just finished a wonderful lunch Lush put together from leftovers from Billy's wake.

"You see," she continues, "I liked David a lot, and the sex with him was very good, but I never loved him, not even a tiny bit. I knew he would be successful, especially with our family's drug stores, and I felt so pressured to get married to please Momma. But I never loved him."

I try to let the truth of her admission sink in. I've always assumed that she must have loved him, at least, in the beginning, and that, like so many other marriages, they just grew apart, or sunk into some vapid routine neither could bear. She watches me, seeking my reaction. Lush intuits body language like a dog.

"I see you're surprised, Todge," she states, takes a sip of her wine, then another long drag.

"Well, I did believe you must have loved him in the beginning. And, I'll have to admit, the way he used to dote over you, I believed he cared an awful lot about you," I reply as Clark nudges me to continue petting him.

"David loved me, Todge. He loved me completely. And I did not love him, and I watched this crush him over the years as he realized this. And he accepted this completely as I stood by, doing nothing, watching his heart break, piece by piece. Yes, I've never told you this, but there was a period during our marriage, after about five years, when he would get down on his knees and beg me to love him. He would tell me he was going to find some way to make me love him. He even pleaded with me to go to counseling with him. But I wouldn't budge. I was nice to him. I had sex with him. But, in my heart, I did not love him, and, despite my best efforts, I could not bring myself to admit this to him, truthfully; I'd just tell him I loved him in a different way than he loved me. What a cold-hearted bitch I was, Todge. And instead of leaving me, he let his hurt and pain poison his soul, harden him into the disgusting man he is today, into the man who treats me so badly. But how can I blame him? If I will not or can not give him my love, then all he has to hang on to is torment—both his and mine, a constant reminder that he loves me, but I do not reciprocate."

She looks at me with clarity in her eyes, and I know she is telling me this truth, her truth, for the first time—the first time she's ever spoken this out loud.

"You've never revealed this even to your therapy group, have you, Lush?"

"Never, Todge. Never had the courage until this week. It has always been that dirty little secret—not so little, I suppose—that I kept conveniently tucked away inside myself."

"There's no reason to be so hard on yourself, Lush. Lots of people enter marriages not in love. You know that," I reply, taking my wine glass in my left hand, bringing it to my lips, taking a small sip of this wonderful Willamette Valley pinot noir, that has the perfect combination of fruit and spice for my taste, as I continue to rub Clark's wide forehead.

"Of course I know that," she flashes at me in a tone of condescension. "You know that's not what I'm talking about," she states with challenge in her voice.

"You're right, Lush," I reply. "It's, it's, well, the truth is that it scares me to hear you talk about this."

Through some internal metamorphic process her confrontational demeanor is now serene, calm, even compassionate. "Awe, Philip. That's what I love so much about you as a man. You are unafraid to show your vulnerability."

I emit a nervous giggle, gather my courage, swallow, look up at her and ask, "So, you probably know why it scares me then?"

She smiles as she puts out her cigarette in an ashtray. "I can think of two reasons: one, you are afraid that I couldn't love David because I really loved you, and two, you're at the point where you're recognizing some little truth within yourself that you've never brought out into the open."

Instantly relieved, I sigh. "Damn, Lush. You are good. You hit the nail on the head twice in a row. I mean, in some strange way, I have felt guilty about your declining relationship with David. I felt like I inundated you with the force of my love so quickly and violently when we first met and once you fully succumbed to it, I yanked it away. You know, we've discussed this—I've always felt guilty about this. But even more so, I've always suspected it had somehow interfered with your relationship with David."

"I suppose there's a touch of that in there, Todge. I did fall deeply in love with you, and by the time I met David, I had resigned myself that I would probably never love anyone the way I loved you—it was so pure, so innocent, so sexual, and I felt sometimes as if we were the same person."

My anxiety starts to rise with this statement, so I close my eyes while I reply, "I felt that way too, Lush, but it overwhelmed me, swallowed me, and I felt that if you left me, for any reason, I wouldn't be able to exist, so I purposefully forced you away by hurting you. I've told you this before. I feel so bad about that, and now knowing that we had a child, I feel even worse."

"That's not what this is about, Todge. I have no desire to make you feel bad about this or about the abortion. I'm just giving you my truth because I trust you now not to hurt me," she says leaning toward me.

"I will never purposefully hurt you again, Sarah," I reply taking her hands in mind. Clark does not like the transfer of my attention and he immediately jumps up placing his front paws in my lap, sticking his muzzle up to my face. Lush and I both laugh.

"Now there's a creature that's not afraid to ask for love," Lush says, pulling her hands from mine so she can stroke Clark's head. Then she looks up at me. "Todge, I learned so much about myself this week. It's appalling that it took such horrifying events—my God the death of Billy and Elliott—to elicit such self-recognition, but that's what happened. I suppose some good comes out of even the worst events."

"It's not appalling, Lush," I reply, "It's life, plain and simple. You can look at it as if you are just a helpless victim, or, you can tell yourself, I'm going to get through each day without judgment against myself or anyone else and do the best that I can."

"I can tell you've been to yoga today," she replies, smiling, "And that's a great philosophy by which to live, Todge, but how do you reconcile that with Adrian?"

"Hell, I don't. There's not a perfect solution, Lush. I've gotten to the point where I live my life each day as if I am embarking on a multitude of different journeys—each one to a different place, but all from the same origin, my central truth. As long as I don't stray too far from that truth, I feel okay. When I stray too far, things don't feel right and, generally, things don't go right."

"Wow," she replies as she runs her nails up and down Clark's spine causing him to stretch his neck and head toward her face, "And what is that central truth?"

"A black hole."

"A black hole, Todge? Whatever do you mean?"

"Well, it's like this. I kind of envision myself and my life like a mini-galaxy—take the Milky Way, for example. In the center is a large black hole that somehow drives the motion of billions of stars around it, spiraling them out into the heavens."

"Okay, I can picture that. But how does that model fit you, your central truth?" She asks as she sits up to pick up her wine glass.

"Well, the black hole is my gut feeling—that unknown yet all-knowing force deep within my innards that I know powers everything in my body. How can I put this? My food goes there and is digested and it powers my body, but moreover there's some spiritual or celestial force connection in there also. I follow the feeling in my gut and things generally come out right for me or at least somewhat right. I feel like my gut feeling is that unknown black hole and everything else, my bones, my skin, my muscles, my blood, my thoughts, my emotions, my soul, my spirit spiral around that. When I listen to it, I'm grounded and in sync with nature. When I defy it, I'm out of equilibrium. This applies to everything from when I need to masturbate to how much food should I eat to how to best construct a sentence to get a point across or to describe a glorious scene in nature."

"That's a great model, Todge. I think it's serving you well," she replies, putting her wine glass down and picking up her pack of cigarettes.

I sigh, "As far as Adrian goes, I feel hate towards him, yet I remember so many incredibly wonderful times with him. I just feel so awfully used and betrayed by him. One minute I want to kill him, get my retribution, and the next minute my gut feeling tells me I must somehow find it within myself to forgive him. But at any rate, my deepest gut feeling tells me, I will never rest until I can meet with him, face to face and let him know what my truth is."

"Do you really think he gives a good Goddamn what your truth is, Todge?" She asks as she lights another cigarette.

"I know he doesn't care—he couldn't care. But it's not about him. It's about me, Lush. It's about what I need to do so that I can go on living each day and my many little journeys without judging myself too much." Clark jumps up into my lap. I hug him, feeling his warmth, lean my face into his back, taking in his dog smell, so pleasant to me.

"Todge?"

"Yes, Lush."

"I hope you don't think all this soul bearing is just a manipulation on my part to try and win you back in some way?"

"Win me back, Lush? But, you've already got me. I love you."

"Yes, I know that, Todge. And I feel so blessed that you do. And I love you. But I'm talking about, winning you back as my partner or husband—I'm not trying to do that at all."

"Damn, and I was planning on popping the question at any moment!"

We both break out into laughter. Clark smiles, panting, and appears to be laughing with us. I push him down off my lap.

"Go get your bone, boy. I know there's one out here," I instruct. He looks up at me, cocks his head sideways, then turns around trotting off, wagging his tail.

"Seriously, Lush. I don't feel that or think that. I don't want it either. I feel so close to you and so connected with you. That's what I want to keep pursuing—that kind of a relationship."

"And I, too," she replies.

"Although, I have to admit, I get a little jealous when I see the spark between you and O'Daniel. But believe me, I'm really happy you can have that spark with him."

"Thanks, Todge. That's sweet of you. I really like Brent. But you know, I'm not looking for anything right now. I just need to come clean with David, so he and I can go our separate ways."

"How and when do you plan to do that?" I ask.

"Soon," she replies. "As soon as we figure out our game plan here, I'll fly home for a day or two, meet with him, then come right back."

"I'm glad you know what you have to do now, Lush. Do you think David will be surprised?"

"No," she replies looking down at the terrace, "I think he'll be relieved, as will I, so relieved."

I smile and ask "Did you have sex with Timmy?"

"What? No, Todge, I didn't. Did you?"

"Actually, I did."

"Was it good?"

"It was."

"Exploring your gay side, Todge?"

"I don't think so. It just sorta happened during the massage. It felt good. My gut feeling let it happen. It felt good, that's all."

"Well, there you have it, Todge. All is good. We're good." She smiles takes a drag, picks up her wine glass, heading toward the kitchen, "I gotta pee. I'll be right back." I smile at her as I grab hold of the rawhide bone Clark has just plunked down in my lap, and wonder if she intends to dig any deeper after my own unexposed truth when she returns.

CHAPTER 35

As Officer O'Daniel drives Lush and me to the Upper East Side to Julianna's for dinner, I sense by the brightness of the sky that the sun has not yet set and that the days are getting noticeably longer—the lengthening days in the spring have always renewed my general feeling of well being, allowing me to approach everything with more energy and more confidence. This is the time of the year I relish, a time that always thrilled me as a boy when the sweet scents of honeysuckle and wild roses filled the air, and the woods were ablaze with the purple hues of the redbuds and the vivid whites of the dogwoods. I feel warmth and love as I glance over at Lush who is intently focusing on a piece of scrap paper she has pulled out of her Chanel clutch, which is the same chocolate color as the long silk evening dress she wears. Her shoulders are wrapped in a beautiful loosely woven, cream color, cashmere shawl with bands and ribbons of long fringe of varying lengths, knotted with thousands of tiny seed pearls, woven into it. We spent most of the afternoon napping, Clark going back and forth between my bedroom and hers, cuddling up beside me for a while, then getting up to check on Lush, resting with her for a while. My sleep was fitful, punctuated with sporadic short dreams, vignettes from my childhood, images of Mother, Billy, Ala Mary, Dad, Fatgram, Adrian and others, the details of which have evaporated from my mind, leaving me only with general feelings of frustration and dissatisfaction because I am aware that I was some type of outsider in the dreams, merely observing the others who were not even aware of my presence as I tried in vain to interact with them, just as if I were some sort of phantom. I do not want my happy mood to change, so I force the dream images out of my mind while I try to read Lush's list. As long as I have known her, Lush has had the habit of tearing off strips of paper from envelopes, brown bags, blank areas of magazine pages, paper napkins, cereal boxes, almost anything that would provide her with a small writing area

where she diligently formulates lists of things she wants to do. If she had saved the hundreds of lists she has made during her life and compiled them into a volume of lists and if you could decipher her illegible handwriting, you could pretty much determine everything about her. Her lists have always aroused my curiosity because they usually contain a combination of everything she plans or needs for an upcoming period of time from half a day to a week and might include items as varied as appointments, major life goals, ingredients for a casserole, phone numbers, deal-breaking discoveries from home inspections, medications to refill, and names of people to invite to a dinner party. This disarray is somehow assimilated in her mind to produce perhaps the most goal oriented, organized person I know. Lush is the type of person you can always rely upon when you need to get something done—she probably scratched out ten different lists in orchestrating Billy's wake—a complete success by any account.

"What's on your list?" I ask as we head down Fifth Avenue.

She looks up at me, focusing her eyes on my face. I can tell she has been in deep concentration. "Well," she whispers as she leans toward me, "Mainly questions I intend to ask Najeed and Isabella tonight, plus a few things I need to get from the drugstore tomorrow. Oh, and the name of a boutique Manon recommends."

I laugh, "I wish I had your organizational skills—simple yet incredibly effective."

She smiles and asks, "Remember my mentioning my great grandpa Kendrick?"

"Yeah, the one who taught you never to put off until tomorrow, blah, blah, blah," I reply sarcastically.

Her mouth falls open and she pokes me in the left side with her right index finger, "Don't make fun of my great grandpa!"

I laugh and scoot over toward the door as her finger jabs at me again. I notice Officer O'Daniel watching us in his rear view mirror.

"Okay, okay. Stop. I'm just jealous, that's all. So, I suppose he started you on list making, too?"

She smiles, "Yes he did. When I first started having homework in school, I complained to him that there was just too much to do every day, and that I'd be up all night trying to get things done, he just chuckled and said, 'Sarah, just make a list every night before you go to bed of what you want to do tomorrow. Sleep on it and the next morning pick the five most important things you want to do. Do them first and then tackle the others as you have time.'"

"Sounds like great advice," I say.

"Yes, I practiced it my entire life, but I still do it the old fashioned way with a pen. You'd think by now I would have transferred the process to my Blackberry."

"Why haven't you, Lush?"

"Don't know. Well, perhaps it's the connection I feel by writing it out in my own handwriting. It just seems that it really matters when I do that." She sighs, looks back down at her list, picks up her clutch, pops it open, pulls out a compact while she stuffs the list into the purse.

"Well, it works, so I wouldn't change anything," I reply. "It is absolutely amazing how, excluding Adrian's intrusion, how flawless Billy's wake transpired and it was all because of your planning and execution, Lush. I will never be able to thank you enough for all your help."

"You know I'm glad to do it, Philip. It was a challenge, but we all pulled together and did it. Brenda was a big help, you know." Lush has opened her compact and is reapplying lipstick as she speaks.

"Yes she was," I reply. "She's a good person, down to the bone."

"I totally agree," Lush replies. "Her idea to send all those flowers to nursing homes was superb."

"Yes, a great idea—so generous, so caring for others, much more so than Mother ever was," I quickly reply.

Lush turns her head toward me with a questioning look on her face.

"I guess I have some pent up anger with Mother," I reply thinking that I just blurted out something really shitty and not altogether accurate.

"Well, don't get me wrong—Mother was a very caring person. It's just that. Well, it's just that. Fuck. I'm not going to defend her. I always felt like she cared more for her art—her career—than she did for Billy and me and Dad. There you have it." I sigh, look up at the rear view mirror and see a look of compassion on O'Daniel's face.

Lush is quiet for a few seconds, then she closes her compact, stretches her lips out together, looks at me, and says, "Todge, that sounded like a spontaneous gut feeling. Don't judge yourself. Just go with it. It's how you feel and that's okay."

"Yeah. I loved my Mother. It's just that. Well, I guess I'm just still mad that she died so young. I'm pissed about all the time she spent locked up in her studio painting; time she could have spent with Billy and me. And, then, when she wasn't painting, it seemed like she was always having cocktail parties or running around with her best friend Aunt CC."

"Well, I didn't know your Mother, but I knew Billy really well, and I saw a lot of that in him. Didn't you, Todge? I think that's part of the make up of a lot of artists—that seemingly selfish introspection and preoccupation with themselves and what they are creating."

"Yes. I know, but he was so much more approachable than Mother. I suppose because he and I were so close, so connected. He was always glad to see me, to be with me, whereas Mother seemed to be at her happiest when she was leaving us for a trip to set up an exhibition somewhere or to go to Europe or wherever to paint. When she would return home, she always looked so happy, so refreshed. Sometimes I felt as if all of us in Union, especially her family, somehow sucked the life blood out of her, forcing her to escape for however long she could, to rejuvenate, to revitalize."Lush pats my left thigh with her right hand, "Dear, Philip, I think you took on a lot of the burden of your family's emotional dynamics. I could see that from going through all the old, family photos while I was putting together the video presentation for the wake."

"How's that?"

"Well, you looked worried, anxious, somehow unsettled in a lot of the photos—kind of like you had the weight of the world on your shoulders, whereas Billy usually looked carefree, happy, sometimes defiant."

I squeeze my eyes together, tilting my head down toward my lap; as some of the fear I felt as a child creeps back into my guts, I begin to fell shaky and sweaty. I take a few deep breaths to try to calm down; a single tear falls from my left eye.

"Philip, are you okay?" Lush asks as she cups her hands around my left hand.

"Yeah," I reply as I sigh deeply. "You're right, Lush. I spent the younger part of my boyhood worried that my folks would split, and I tried to shelter Billy from those worries. Then after Mother died and Dad left, well, you can imagine what kind of fear resulted from that."

"I'm sorry, Todge. I didn't mean to be cruel," Lush replies as she tightens her hands around mine.

"You're not cruel, Lush. You saw what I really felt. You know, as weird as this sounds, some of the most comforting and calm times I remember were when Adrian was around—even with the Bloodbrothers stuff and all. Even with all that, he had a way of making us feel really wanted, really accepted, really confident that everything would be alright." I feel tears running down my face now and I look up at Lush and ask, "How could that be? How could that be? It makes no sense, no sense at all. It's all so fucked up, Lush."

She pulls my head down into her lap, stroking my hair and head, enveloping me with her warm torso. I cry silently, embarrassed that O'Daniel is witnessing this, but at the same time, not really caring. We drive along this way for a while as I take in the warmth and compassion Lush exudes, the particular soul soothing comfort only a woman can give, an innate part of her womanness, a familiar feeling, doled out sparingly from Mother and Fatgram, profusely from Ala Mary—a feeling I have never trusted completely, the sting of having it withdrawn haunts me. O'Daniel maneuvers the car

through traffic, the city noises fill my right ear, mixing with the pulse of my heartbeat vibrating in my left ear, like some syncopated rhythm of humanity, so I push my left ear harder into Lush's thigh, searching for the sound of my waterfall, but what comes through is the sound of Mother and Aunt CC in a fit of drunken laughter—their favorite summer drink was gin on the rocks with a splash of Indian Tonic and a generous squeeze of fresh lime, a drink I know well because I made so many of them for them—lounging on the large rattan sofa on our screened in back porch, chain smoking, reminiscing, both wearing shorts and midriffs, an ensemble Fatgram despised, telling them both on many occasions when she got word that they were drinking, usually from a surreptitious phone call from me, that they looked like complete white trash and could at least put on something more suitable, especially in front of young boys like Billy and me.

"Oh dear, Mother. Not the white trash lecture again," Mother says returning Fatgram's look of disapproval with her own, somewhat unsteady, look of disapproval. "Must you be so....so...."

"So Goddamn condescending!" Aunt CC shouts, then laughs furiously, her loud rolling laugh at present infectious, but soon to border on obnoxious after another gin or two. Mother joins in the laughter. Billy is sitting on the floor, rolling around a large, yellow, toy dump trunk, in which sits Geisel, the worn out old Teddy Bear he's had since he was a toddler, ignoring everyone. I'm lying down in a very large chair with overstuffed cushions covered in a tropical pattern of palm trees, with my legs barely reaching onto the large ottoman pushed up against the chair. Bonnie Bell is nestled up beside me with her eyes closed, her tail thumping a few beats every time Mother laughs. The evening July air is thick, lightning bugs have begun their nightly luminous display, orchestrated to a vast chorus of tree frogs and cicadas. I pretend to ignore Mother and Aunt CC and even Fatgram, but what I'm really doing is carefully monitoring Mother and Aunt CC for their stage of drunkenness. Each drink I've made for them, I've made progressively stronger, with lesser amounts of Indian Tonic each time. My aim is to get them both so drunk that they pass out before Dad gets home, thus reducing the chance that there will be a nasty fight between my parents. Mother, although never known for keeping thoughts and opinions to herself, becomes excessively outspoken when inebriated, especially toward Dad, picking on his weaknesses and shortcomings, verbally magnifying them for those around to see, prodding and pressing him until he finally explodes, and a nasty fight ensues. She used to do that to Billy and me, to a lesser extent, until last Christmas. We were all lounging in Fatgram's main living room around the fireplace after a large, early afternoon Christmas dinner. Billy and I were playing with our toys, while all the adults were drinking, talking, and smoking. Mother had been hitting Ala Mary's eggnog all morning and had started drinking champagne during dinner. I could tell she wouldn't last too much longer, and I was praying that she would just go up to her old bedroom and pass out. Instead, she started in on Billy and me about how we really didn't appreciate the nice things we got for Christmas, which included a painting for each of us from her, a lot of new winter clothes, and several art books for children. She said that all we cared about were the cheap toys, made in China, with their garish battery powered bells and whistles meant to attract the mindless masses. After a few minutes of this, Billy looked up toward her and in his gruff, deep voice said, "Shut your ugly face, bitch!" Mother was speechless; I about crapped in my pants, and I saw a wide smile develop on Fatgram's face. Since Christmas, Mother's been on her guard and nicer to us when she's drinking. Maybe Dad should employ this strategy, but anyway, most of the time, if Mother and Aunt CC are out cold, or close enough, he'll just carry Mother up to her bed and tuck her in. Then he'll come back down and get Aunt CC and carry her up to the guest bedroom. Aunt CC is not really our aunt, she's mother's best friend from childhood. Aunt CC's family is the richest family in Union County; we're number two, Fatgram says, because, not only did Aunt CC's grandfather have cotton mills as large as ours, but he had the foresight to buy up practically all of downtown Union plus all the land where the surrounding suburbs and shopping centers were built. Fatgram is very close to the Atwell family. She and Aunt CC's mother, Big Carol, are

best friends. Fatgram says Aunt CC is a very bad influence on Mother because Aunt CC is an alcoholic—has been since she was not much older than I am—and will probably kill herself by drinking so much.

"You two just don't know when to stop," Fatgram replies, "You're both on the road to feeling like hell tomorrow."

"Oh, quit your bitchin and sit right down here and have a drink with us, Ina," Aunt CC replies, swinging her long legs off the sofa, then patting the space between her and Mother with her right hand, balancing a long, lit cigarette, between her index and middle fingers. Aunt CC is a tall, beautiful woman with blonde hair and aquamarine eyes—a former Miss South Carolina and first runner up to Miss America. She used to be on several different regional television commercials when she wasn't drinking so much.

"Not tonight, CC," Fatgram replies with a sour look on her face, "I'm on the way to your mother's soiree in honor of your future sister-in-law. I surely thought you'd be attending. And so did your mother; she just phoned me to ask if I knew where you were. Naturally, I didn't know you were down here. I just popped in to see if Eva had changed her mind about going with me."

"No, Mother," Mother replies, staring out into the back yard, expressionless, "I've not changed my mind. I intend to sit here with CC and continue our little visit."

"Could! I mean, good!" CC says with a snicker, swinging her legs back up on the sofa, "I knew I could count on you Eva to keep me company over going to honor that snooty, skinny bitch, Mary Louise, from Charleston. Heaven knows what Bobby sees in her."

"Darling," Mother says to CC as she kicks CC's left foot with her own right foot, then pushes all of her toes into Aunt CC's, their twenty perfectly painted red toe nails blending together. "It's not what he sees in her. I believe it's more of a case of what she sees in him—a man with a whole lot of money whom she can easily pussy-whip."

"You are so Goddamned right, sister," CC replies, "Bobby's gotta be the most easily pussy whipped man in the entire state of South Carolina!"

"Except for your father, darling!" Mother replies and both women break into hysterical laughing.

Billy starts to laugh, too and shouts, "Geisel is pussy whipped, too, Mother!"

This sends CC and Mother into a deeper state of laughter, causing Aunt CC to make a snorting noise like a hog. It always bothers me that Mother and Aunt CC are always touching each other, pecking kisses and hugging, stroking each other's hair.

Fatgran shrugs her shoulders, "You two are incorrigible. Speaking such trash in front of these children, here. Neither of you girls was raised in such a manner. Now that's a fact."

"Don't lecture us, Mother. We're just trying to have some fun," Mother replies turning up her empty glass to get a piece of ice which she begins crunching loudly between her molars.

I become tense because I suspect Fatgram and Mother and even Aunt CC are getting ready to get into it, but I notice Fatgram glancing down at her slender, small watch, encrusted with tiny diamonds and attached to a band also covered in diamonds.

"Well, I'm late already," she replies, "I don't have the time or energy to lecture you girls, anyway. It falls on deaf ears. Eva, you ought to be out in your studio getting ready for your Sante Fe show and CC, well, I don't know what the hell you should be doing, but you surely shouldn't be drinking again. When I think of all the money your poor mother has spent sending you to rehab clinics, and nice ones, too. Well, I guess you'll quit when you're good and ready."

"That ikzaxtly right, Ina, when I'm damn good and ready to," she replies, the slurring of speech a good indication to me that my plan is working.

"Philly dear," Mother calls out to me, "Be a good boy and go fix Auntie CC and Mother one last drinky poo."

I hate it when Mother talks baby talk to me because I'm ten years old and it humiliates me. Of course, she only does it when she's pulling a long one, as Dad refers to her drinking binges. I get up and walk over

to take their glasses, knowing they both like their drinks to be made in their used glasses. Mother calls them 'seasoned' glasses which make all the subsequent drinks taste better. I take their glasses and turn to go into the kitchen, not making too much noise so I can continue to hear the conversation.

"Eva, it's Friday, Charles should be back in town this evening. What time do you expect him?" Fatgram asks.

"I don't really know, Mother. And furthermore, I don't really care."

I was afraid that response was coming, and even though I anticipated it, it still sends a feeling of despair through my gut, and I decide that I will do almost all gin in the glasses this round with just the thinnest layer of Indian Tonic on top and a big squeeze of lime, careful not to stir, so their first taste or two won't taste too strong, and after that, they won't even notice. I'm confidant this round will knock them out so that Dad won't even have to talk to them—he'll just pick them up like potato sacks and haul them up to bed. I wish Uncle Adrian would hurry up and get down here. These kinds of situations never happen when he's around—he arranges everything so perfectly.

The car hits a bump, I open my eyes, push myself up out of Lush's lap, comb my fingers through my hair, straighten the sleeves of one of Billy's navy blazers I'm wearing, look over at Lush, who smiles at me as she hands me a wad of tissue. I'm thinking about how Aunt CC seemed to be the most distraught person at Mother's funeral, barely able to walk to the gravesite, Big Carol on one side of her and her brother Bobby on the other, practically carrying her the entire way. She sobbed and whimpered like a little girl during the graveside service and, even though I was still in shock and consumed with my own guilt and fear, the look of grief and hopelessness on her pretty face frightened me. Aunt CC bought our house from Dad after we moved in with Fatgram, and, except for the nicest pieces of furniture and Mother's porcelain and art collection which were taken to Fatgram's, left everything, especially Mother's studio, the way it was. Years in and out of rehab never worked for Aunt CC. Towards the end, out of desperation, Big Carol, hired a full-time housekeeper/caretaker from the north, Gertrude, whom Fatgram and Big Carol referred to as Gert the Nazi, to constantly monitor CC, making it extremely difficult for her to get a drink. Aunt CC eluded her on several occasions, got rip-roaring drunk, returned home, always threatening to kill Gert. One morning, after such an episode, Gert simply left town, never to be heard from again. I'll never forget the buzz in town when CC, having escaped from Gert, pulled her red convertible Mercedes up to the gas pumps of the Swifty Mart to buy gas and cigarettes, got out of the car stark naked, pumped her gas and walked into the store with an empty Scope bottle in her hand demanding more Scope and a pack of Marlboro 100's. Big Carol walked into Mother's studio one morning a couple of years after Mother died to find CC dead on the sofa, having choked to death on her own vomit. What was her pain, I wonder, and I wonder if it had to do with how Aunt CC must have loved Mother? I wonder if they were ever lovers? They must, at least at some time, have been sexually involved with one another. I wish I could discuss this with Billy. It makes sense, CC never married, never even had a boyfriend that I remember. I wipe my eyes, blow my nose, ball up the tissue while stuffing it in an inside pocket of the blazer. Lush opens her compact again and begins touching up her lipstick and makeup. We remain silent as O'Daniel pulls the car over. I look out the window, count five stories of an imposing Renaissance Revival townhouse with an ornately carved whitish-gray limestone façade, becoming luminous as darkness falls, capped with a verdegris copper Mansard roof. I've never been to Julianna's house, but as I open the car door and step out onto the curb, I'm overcome with a deep feeling that I will find answers within the opulence housed within these walls.

"My, what a lovely townhouse," Lush says as she slides over to get out on my side. I turn around to offer her my hand but find O'Daniel already offering his. I smile, stepping back, turning toward the house, waiting for the sound of the car door shutting. I turn back around, offer Lush my left arm, which she takes, and we walk up to the front door which opens as soon as we arrive.

"Good evening, Mrs. Richardson, Mr. Hampton," an elderly, grey headed butler, formally dressed, greets us. "Won't you please come in?"

"Thank you," I reply. "This gentleman behind us is Officer O'Daniel, from the New York City Police Department."

"Good evening, Officer O'Daniel. Miss Morgan is expecting you, too," the butler says with a semi-bow of his torso.

We enter into an interior entrance porch way with a tall barrel vaulted ceiling, ornately paneled in mahogany, from which hangs a large crystal chandelier, illuminating the limestone walls and stairway leading up to the breath-taking main entrance—a massive pair of paneled mahogany doors hang beneath a limestone transom richly carved with acanthus leaves over which sits a magnificent Louis Comfort Tiffany semi-circular leaded Favrile-glass fanlight of a spring landscape with blooming dogwoods and blue iris in the foreground and mountains and the sunrise in the background. A man in a dark suit stands beside the left door, holding his hands behind his back, looking forward motionless. I recognize him to be one of Najeed's bodyguards. We all stare at the entrance for a moment.

"Exquisite," Lush remarks.

"Absolutely," I reply, "Billy raved about this Tiffany window. There are others inside."

The limestone stairs are covered in a dense black carpet uniformly dotted with small gold fleur de lis designs with thick braids of black and gold braided fringe defining its edges. I notice the stair rails are the same mahogany as the doors and ceiling, but the porch is so wide we walk up the center without using the rails. The butler, with the deeply wrinkled face of a lifelong smoker, pulls a magnetic fob from a pocket in his waistcoat, waves it over a sensor on the doors, initiating a clicking sound; he pushes open the right door by its large, pewter colored, hammered metal, handle motioning for us to enter into a larger entrance hall, itself another ante-foyer, constructed in the Romanesque style of columns supporting archways, which contain alcoves displaying works of art, except for the main entrance archway which opens to the left, with a intricate ribbed vaulted ceiling covered in painted stucco depicting celestial scenes overlooking the highly polished white marble floor, the center of which contains a starburst medallion constructed of black, brown, grey, red, and yellow marbles with the four cardinal directions in bold cursive, capital letters, fashioned from black marble, inlayed at the four longest points of the starburst. Small pin-like halogen lights are embedded in the ceiling like dozens of little stars, and the artwork in each alcove is lit from recessed lighting in the archways. I recognize a Van Gogh, a couple of Old Masters, Billy's *Self Portrait in Reverse*, one of his most famous and critically acclaimed paintings which depicts him looking into a mirror at himself, and a few other paintings I do not recognize, which appear to be contemporary in nature. Two of the alcoves contain sculpture: one appears to be an antique Greek or Roman male torso, and the other is a life-size bronze of ballerina in the midst of a pirouette on toe.

"Oh, my, how beautiful is this room?" Lush asks as we all turn our heads, taking in the architecture and artworks.

"It's wonderful," I reply, "It's like a museum."

"Yes, beautiful," O'Daniel says.

"Welcome, welcome," Julianna says, sweeping through the entrance archway in a long, black velvet evening gown with very short sleeves, a deeply cut V-neck, and a skirt which tapers from just above the ankle in the front to a short train in the back, her hands, wrists, neck and ears sparkling with diamonds.

She approaches me and we kiss lightly on the lips. "My God, you look beautiful tonight, Julianna," I say.

"Thank you, Philip dear," she replies as she turns toward Lush.

"Lush, you look so lovely this evening," Julianna says taking both of Lush's hands in hers. Lush is stunning, ravishing, as she takes off the shawl, hands it to the butler, and I see that her chocolate color evening gown has a low cut, tight bodice, richly embroidered, held up by two thin spaghetti straps,

accentuating her lovely breasts, smooth back and shoulders, beautiful long neck, and buttery soft skin. The dress hugs her waist and thighs, complementing her womanly curves, before it flares out from just above the knees to the floor. She wears her wedding ring and engagement diamond on her left hand, a large canary diamond, which I've never seen before, on her right ring finger and matching canary diamond studs in her ears. She wears her luxuriant brown hair parted in the middle, brushed back, with thick long curls cascading down her shoulders.

"Thank you, Julianna," Lush says, smiling as they embrace. "You look like a princess."

Julianna chuckles, "Well, since I'm entertaining a prince tonight, I thought I might as well dress like a princess, even if I'm not one!" Her eyes widen as she smiles. We all laugh.

"Well, I think you are a princess, Julianna. My God, you live in a palace—this place is magnificent and we haven't even seen the main rooms yet," I say as I open my arms and hands toward the ceiling, turn my body in a small circle, trying to take it all in.

"It's amazing what a family can accumulate when they've lived in the same house for over a hundred years," Julianna replies.

I walk over to Billy's self-portrait. "Do you always have this painting in such a grand location, Julianna?" I ask.

"Oh my, yes, Philip. It's every bit as good, if not better, than this Vermeer beside it."

"My," Lush replies, "That's an impressive comparison."

"I truly believe that in a hundred years, Billy will be recognized as one of the greatest painters of the early twenty-first century," Julianna replies, "And it is such a tragedy, well—" She sighs shaking her head side to side. "Well," she claps her hands together once, "Let's go in for cocktails. Officer O'Daniel, nice to see you this evening."

"Thank you. Good to see you Miss Morgan," he replies.

"Maybe you'd like Darcy to give you a tour of the place so you can get your bearings—you know, all the entrances and exits, secret stairways and tunnels," she laughs.

"That would be fine, Miss Morgan," he replies.

"Good, then, Darcy please attend to Officer O'Daniel, and I'll take care of Miss Richardson and Mr. Hampton."

"Yes, indeed Madame," the old butler says and moves through the entrance archway motioning with his right hand for Officer O'Daniel to follow, holding Lush's pearl encrusted shawl over his left arm.

"You should have seen the sweep Najeed's body guards did when they arrived," Julianna says. "They even took a bomb sniffing dog through. Turns out, the dog is part of Najeed's entourage!"

"My, my," Lush says turning toward me, "This is going to be a most interesting evening."

Julianna leads us through the archway into an imposing elliptical entrance hall with a highly polished white marble floor, the perimeter a border of a Greek key pattern in black marble, and another larger starburst pattern of various colors of marble in the center of the floor. A magnificent sweeping staircase constructed of limestone with stairs capped in white marble with intricately carved balusters painted white and a richly polished, mahogany balustrade rises from the hall along the east side of the room. The ceiling is a complex array of octagons with borders of leaves, fruit and flowers. I can not determine if it is carved wood or plaster because it is painted a beige color with the borders in gold leaf. A grand crystal chandelier hangs in the center of the hall directly above the center of the marble starburst. I stare at it and wonder how one would ever clean it. The curved walls of the room are covered in a very pale yellow material, I believe it must be silk. I count four elaborate doorways leading from the entrance hall, each one an elaborate construction of columns, pedestals, and ornate pediments. I realize by the carvings on the pediments that each doorway represents one of the four seasons. There are, of course, paintings, on the elliptical walls, and on the walls up the staircase. It feels as if we're inside a giant Faberge egg, and I'm so overcome with the beauty and complexity of the architecture, I can hardly focus on the paintings and as we walk closer to

the staircase heading for the Spring entranceway, I notice that the staircase winds up the entire five story structure with the top of the stairwell covered with a glass dome. What a great way to add natural light to such a large house. We enter through the Spring entrance into a large salon filled with ornate furniture, which I think is in the French Regency style—similar to Billy's ormolu encrusted desk in his studio. The upholstery, carpets, and drapes all feature shades of green, white, and gold in designs of spring flowers, vines, and leaves. Janet, Jonas, Mabry, Isabella, a man with Asian features and light skin whom I don't know but who looks somewhat familiar, and Najeed, accompanied by two of his body guards, are all standing around an easel looking at a painting.

"Darlings," Julianna says to Lush and me, "I have a couple of surprises for you!"

As we approach everyone, they turn from the painting to greet us. I immediately see that the painting is Dyanne O'Bryan's, *The Crucifixion of the Madonna*.

"My God," I say, "Is that the original painting?"

Julianna smiles, "Yes, dear, it is. You see, it has been part of an exhibition in Europe and has just arrived back in the states. MOMA won't redisplay it for another two weeks. I made a phone call and 'voila', here it is. I wanted to get the other two, but they were doing some minor restorative work on them, so I have copies we'll bring in later."

"Wonderful, Julianna," Lush says. "I saw the painting at an exhibit in Louisville in the nineties when Dyanne first painted it and the other similar ones. You wouldn't believe the stir they caused."

"Oh, yes I would, dear," Julianna replies, "They still are very controversial almost everywhere to this day."

"Well, I can't wait to get a close look. I know we can solve Adrian's riddle. I just know we can," Lush says.

A young waitress dressed in a short grey dress covered with a sexy, frilly white, bibbed apron approaches us and asks with a British accent, "Madame, Sir, may I bring you a beverage?"

"Champagne, please," Lush replies.

"Vodka martini, up, with a twist, please," I reply.

"Thank you," she says, smiling, turns around and walks out of the room, carrying a round silver tray. My eyes follow her graceful strides. She looks like a friggin' Barbie Doll, blonde hair pinned up under a little lacey ornamental headband, blue eyes, firm, young breasts, pushed up in the bodice of her corseted mini dress, long, slim legs in dark hose with seams along the backs, and black patent leather high heels. Damn, I'd just love to corner her in one of Julianna's bathrooms, sit her up on a counter, kiss her lips while I gently pull open her legs, work her stockings and panties off, pull down my pants and undershorts, grab her by the hips, still kissing her, fucking her until she moans in ecstasy. I wonder why the hell Julianna has her servants dressed this way: the formal butler, now the French maid. My God, what a show.

Najeed, looking every bit a crown prince dressed in a dark, pin stripe, six on two double-breasted jacket with peak lapels and matching trousers; white, French cuffed dress shirt with large, square, gold cufflinks in a basket weave design; a crimson silk tie with black, grey and white diagonal stripes and a crimson silk pocket square with white dots; and shiny, black leather lace ups with square toes, all probably custom made in Italy, steps forward, "Philip, Lush, so good to see you again. I must say the wake you held for Billy was quite wonderful, unforgettable."

I bow toward Najeed, "Thank you, Najeed, it is so kind of you to say that, and I am so honored that you came so far to help us celebrate my brother's life."

"Your brother was a special man, a force unlike any I've ever met, and it was my honor and duty to pay him my respects, Philip," he replies.

"You are most kind," I reply, sticking out my right hand. As we shakes hands, I notice the watch on his left hand, exquisite, gold, with all the gears and mechanisms visible through the crystal, and I think it probably cost a quarter of a million dollars. He then embraces me, and I embrace him back.

"Good to see you again, Lush. You look so beautiful tonight," Najeed says as he releases me and faces Lush.

"Thank you, Najeed. It's certainly a pleasure to see you this evening." Lush replies smiling and pushing her hair back behind her right ear with her right hand.

"Yes we are real friends, here. We all have much in common," he says, smiling, waving his right hand toward everyone, splaying out his slender, dark, hairy fingers.

"Good evening, everyone," I say. "It's so nice to see you all in this magnificent setting."

"Hello, Philip, Lush," Jonas says, "Mabry and I have been very busy today. We have a lot of news tonight."

"Wonderful, Jonas," I reply, noticing that both he and Mabry are dressed in suits and ties, and I realize that I'm the most under dressed person here tonight, wearing only a blue blazer, grey wool slacks, and rather casual cordovan loafers with a matching belt. Thank God I put on this white dress shirt with French cuffs at the last minute. But I chose not to wear a tie and the top two buttons of my shirt are open. Oh well, I tell myself that it really doesn't bother me.

Lush and I shake Jonas's hand and then Mabry's, who seems a little shy and out of place in these opulent surroundings. We then turn to greet Janet, who looks wonderful in an oriental inspired, long, black silk jacket, with designs of lotuses, chrysanthemums, and peonies embroidered in it. She wears long black silk pants, and black pumps. She reaches out both of her hands taking my right hand in her right hand and Lush's right hand in her left hand, "It's so good to see you both this evening. I can't tell you how lovely Billy's wake was. It was truly an event filled with love."

"Thank you, Janet," I reply, "I'm so glad you were part of it."

"Thank you, Philip," she replies, gently shaking Lush's hands and mine before releasing them.

"You look lovely, tonight, Janet," Lush says.

"Oh, thank you Lush," she says with a short laugh, "Julianna has become my new wardrobe consultant." She raises both her shoulders, giggles, and says, "I must say I love her tastes."

"Nothing's too good for my next star in the art world!" Julianna says. "I'm going to treat you all to a few examples of Janet's exquisite talent tonight after dinner."

"How wonderful," Lush says, "I can't wait to see."

"Yes, that's exciting," I add.

"Yes, we're all anticipating the exhibition," Isabella says, walking over to us, looking so beautiful, in a sumptuous, floor length, richly ruched gown of an iridescent slate color, with a fitted bodice, and spaghetti straps.

"Good evening, Miss De la Croix," I say, "It's so good to see you again." I can't stop my eyes from looking up and down the curves of her body. All that I really want to say to her is that she is simply ravishing.

"Lovely to see you and Miss Richardson," she replies, smiling. "After my conversations with Julianna last night and today, I think we have a lot to talk about."

"Yes, indeed," I reply, "Unfortunately not a pleasant topic, but necessary to both of us having peace of mind, I think."

"Yes," she says in a drawn out tone, and I see sadness in her lovely brown eyes.

"Tonight's dinner conversation may help give us all some peace of mind," Lush says.

"Amen," I say and turn toward the man with Asian features, offer my right hand, and say, "I'm Philip Hampton, and this is my friend, Sarah Richardson."

He smiles, shakes my hand with his right hand and in perfect enunciation with a hint of a British accent says, "Please to meet you, Philip Hampton, Miss Richardson. I'm Jonathan Zeng."

My mouth falls open; I steal a quick glance at Lush, who also looks completely surprised. "So very nice to meet you Jonathan," I reply as Lush nods her head in agreement, smiling.

"I'm so sorry about your brother's death. What a tragedy," he says. He is dressed in a beautifully tailored dark grey, wool, business suit with matching vest, a French blue shirt with French cuffs and cuff links, made of round bars of onyx mounted on gold.

"Thank you," I reply. "It seems that all of us here are all linked by tragedies—tragedies precipitated by Adrian McWhorter."

Jonathan smirks at my remark, raises his champagne flute to his lips taking a sip of the pink nectar; everyone else falls silent. He clears his throat, looks me directly in the eyes and says, "That's rather an unpleasant accusation aimed toward my father, Mr. Hampton."

"Dear God," I reply, "I knew you looked familiar when I saw you. I can tell you are Adrian's son."

"Yes, I am, Mr. Hampton," he replies, smiling now, "the son of Adrian McWhorter and Hi Lu Zeng."

"But how?" Lush asks in a sharp, acrid tone, glaring at him, her shoulders visibly tense. "Everyone knows Adrian is a pedophile and not at all into women."

Jonathan laughs sheepishly as his gaze drops to the floor in response to Lush's display of anger, and it appears he is almost bowing to Lush as he says in a much softer tone, "I didn't mean to upset you, Mrs. Richardson. It was unkind of me not to be completely forthright quickly under such circumstances. Although Adrian is my biological father, he is nothing more to me than that. I hate him and have for years. I always sensed he was the real demise of my mother, and now, after talking to Jonas yesterday, I know the truth."

"The truth, Jonathan?" I ask.

"Yes, I'm convinced Adrian killed my mother, just the same as he did yours and Miss de la Croix's. It would have been so easy for him with my mother's drug habits," he says, still looking down.

Lush, letting her anger melt into sympathy, reaches and gently touches Jonathan's right shoulder with her right hand, "But I still don't understand him sleeping with your mother, Jonathan."

"You see, Miss Richardson," he says.

"Please, call me, Lush," she says, her hand resting on his shoulder.

"My mother was very close to her sister, my Aunt Bao Yu, who had escaped from China and married a wealthy banker in Hong Kong around the time mother was becoming famous in New York. Mother and Auntie wrote many letters to one another, telling each other about every aspect of their lives. After I was grown, Auntie gave me all of mother's letters. Mother, it seems, was desperately in love with Adrian—this British God in the art world who could change her life. I suspect strongly that Adrian realized that the only way he could get what he wanted out of my mother was to sleep with her, and so he did, until he found that he could easily replace himself with drugs. It's all in the letters, everything. I suppose mother thought she was the one with all the goods, but it was really Adrian. By the time I was entering grammar school, she had already produced her best and most famous works, and Adrian had her hopelessly hooked on heroin. Well, she wasn't around much for me, but guess who was? That's right. Lovely, Uncle Adrian, who could make everything just right for a lonely, lost, little boy. Thank God for Auntie Bao Yu who had the financial ability to gain custody of me when I was twelve. I never told her the horrible things Adrian did to me. I never told anyone, until now."

As Jonathan looks up toward me, a single tear runs from his left eye, "I guess you and I are brothers, Philip, Blood Brothers."

Lush sighs, turning away from him with a look of sorrow on her face, as I walk over and embrace him. "I'm glad to be your brother, Jonathan, blood or no blood."

"Thank you, Philip. Thank you," he says.

Isabella is staring at us. I can tell she wants to say something, but she remains silent.

"Here comes Celeste with more drinks," Julianna says in an upbeat voice. The waitress hands champagne to Lush and Julianna and gives me my martini.

"I propose a toast," Julianna says, raising her sparkling, intricately carved, crystal champagne flute. "To an evening of discovery—not the discovery of the evil that is Adrian McWhorter, no, for that has

revealed itself and will continue to reveal itself this evening and in time as we seek and implement justice against him, and we will be successful in getting that justice, but the discovery of the strength and love that bonds all of us in this room as we begin to heal the wounds he has inflicted and the discovery of the unique paths each of us will take as we regain control of our lives!"

"To discovery!" I shout, holding up my glass and everyone else joins in.

"To discovery!" We clink each other's glasses, smiling at each other.

"Alright," Julianna says, "I've mapped out a general plan for the evening because we all have so much to discuss and because Najeed, Isabella, and Jonathan are here in New York for only a short time. The first thing we'll do, while we're having drinks and hors d'oeuvres, is examine and discuss Dyanne O'Bryan's paintings and her riddle. Jonas and I have filled everyone in on that story. After that we'll go in to dinner where we can have a general discussion of how all this fits together. Each person will have a chance to add or reveal anything to the others. After that, we'll wander up to the palm court for dessert and after dinner drinks. On the way up, we'll look at art and chat. There'll be plenty of opportunity during this time for you to discuss things privately with one another, if you like. Finally, we'll reassemble back down in the winter salon where I will introduce you to the wonderful paintings by Janet Ostro." She pauses a moment, smiling, "I hope this schedule is okay with everyone?"

"It's perfect, Julianna," Lush replies, "Just what we need to maximize our effectiveness in communicating with each other tonight. After all, this is not your run of the mill dinner party!"

Lush's remark elicits several chuckles from the group.

"Well, let's get started, shall we?" Julianna asks. "I'll give you an overview of Dyanne's paintings. I'm hoping something I say will spark a connection that will help us solve the riddle. Please stop me and ask questions as we proceed, this is a group effort."

"Splendid, Julianna," Lush says with the reaction of a schoolgirl who just learned she made the cheerleading squad.

Julianna takes a sip of champagne, sits her flute down on a small, round, ornate, marble top table and clasps her hands, "Well, let's begin. Everyone please gather around Dyanne's painting and observe while I talk. Celeste, please ask Henri to bring in the copies of *The Rape of the Rosary* and *The Hanging of St. John Houghton.*"

"Yes, Madame," she replies, turns around and walks out of the room. My eyes are again drawn to her legs.

Julianna clears her throat and continues, "I think it is important to view them as well as we proceed since they are tied in so closely to *The Crucifixation of the Madonna.* Dyanne O'Bryan was truly a genius, albeit a tormented one. She is probably the most gifted figure and portrait painter of the late twentieth century, and certainly one of the most controversial artists ever to reach international fame and success. Her darkness, as is the case with many of us, resulted from unpleasant and abusive behaviors wrought upon her during childhood. Most of what we know about her is documented in the copious amount of letters she wrote to the novelist, Cara Bridgefield, who was Dyanne's roommate and lover at Centre College in Kentucky. Dyanne was devastated when Cara left to pursue her Masters in Creative Writing at The University of Iowa and Dyanne returned to the family farm in Bardstown for a while before entering the Sisters of Charity of Nazareth in Bardstown. Interestingly enough, Cara is currently working on a biography of Dyanne that she intends to call: *Portrait of a Tortured Genius: The Life of Dyanne O'Bryan.*" She pauses, looking at everyone, then continues, "Catholocism's roots in Bardstown are deep and old with the diocese of Bardstown being established by Pope Pius VII in 1808, which was one of four carved out of the original archdiocese of Baltimore. The other three were New York, Philadelphia, and Boston—not bad company for a small Kentucky settlement. The Bardstown diocese was created to cover the expanding territories to the west. Dyanne's great, great, great grandfather immigrated to Bardstown from Ireland in the 1820's and by the Civil War had become a successful Kentucky planter with over a thousand

acres and dozens of slaves. The family remained in Bardstown through the generations, maintaining its farming operations and retaining most of the land. Today, the farm and its operations are owned by a trust established by Dyanne's father. Dyanne's older sister, and only sibling, Joan, and Joan's husband control the trust. Dyanne's son, Christopher, who, of course, took the vow of poverty when he entered the Benedictine Abbey at St. Meinrad in southern Indiana, owned half of the trust but gave it all to Joan. Joan, like her sister, became disenchanted with Catholocism, holds Christopher's share separately in case he ever leaves the order. Upon his death, it will go to whatever charity he specifies. Interestingly enough, Joan controls another trust that owns Dyanne's unsold works and collects any residuals from copyrights. This, too, would be turned over to Christopher should he ever leave the order. Joan has one son who I believe helps his parents run the farm operations. I apologize for all the information, but I think the more we know and explore, the better the chance we have of solving the riddle Dyanne supposedly gave Adrian the night she died. Anyway, Dyanne was educated in Catholic schools in Bardstown from a young girl through high school. In her letters to Cara, she talks about physical, mental, and even spiritual abuse from some of the nuns, but the biggest offender was the priest she refers to as Father X, with whom Dyanne had a sexual relationship from the time she was fourteen until she left for Centre College. It is clear that the priest forced himself upon the young Dyanne at first, but as she grew older, she began to accept the sexual meetings, as he convinced her what they were doing was in the name of the Holy Father. No one knows why Dyanne never revealed the identity of Father X. Cara believes it is an older cousin who was a priest in Bardstown. At Centre, Dyanne fell in love with Cara. When Cara left for Iowa City and made it clear to Dyanne that both of their lives had to go on, that they were too young and unformed to stick together, Dyanne entered into the Sisters of Charity of Nazareth. Her two years there were a complete disaster and some of the unhappiest in her life. Joan finally convinced her to pursue her painting and enroll in Boston University where her talent blossomed and she met and fell in love with a campus security guard named Ted Johnson. They had the twins while still in Boston. After she received her MFA, Ted, Dyanne and the twins moved to her parents' farm in Bardstown. Dyanne painted; Ted grew marijuana. I think from this point on, you all are familiar with Ted's gruesome death and Dyanne's demise with Adrian. It is no wonder that the vast majority of her works portray the dark side of human nature and of herself. The only positive portraits she ever did were of Ted and of her boys, and a few landscapes of the farm. She was such a complex woman, living a life full of diametric opposites: amorous, often intensely erotic based relationships with both women and men; hating the Catholic Church, exposing it in her paintings and letters to Cara on the one hand, but, on the other hand, loving the Church by sending her children to the same Catholic school she attended and giving thousands of dollars to the Church over time. There you have it, a brief history of Dyanne O'Bryan."

"Good heavens," Janet says, holding her champagne flute with her left hand and placing her right palm on her bosom, "Such horrible turmoil she experienced throughout her life; it's really so sad. What happened to the other son? The twin?"

"Noel," Julianna replies, "He committed suicide when he was fifteen—hanged himself in the same barn where he and Christopher found their father hanging years earlier."

"It's all so sad, but, on the other hand, possibly, and I think probably, the driving force which molded her genius," Isabella says and adds, "It's not at all an uncommon type of situation among great artists, take Von Gogh, for instance, or my mother, Jonathan's mother, or Philip's mother."

Janet shakes her head in agreement and focuses her attention on the painting. A tall, slim, boney young man with closely cropped brown hair, high cheekbones with sunken cheeks, shifting, bright, blue-grey eyes, and dressed in a formal waiter's attire with a bowtie and tails, enters carrying two folding wooden easels and two large leather portfolios.

"Ah, Henri, montez s'il vous plaît les chevalets de chaque côté de cette peinture," Julianna says in perfect French.

"Oui, Madame, MOMA a juste livré ceux-ci pour vous. Ils sont les peintures originales, " he replies in a bass voice.

"Magnifique!" Julianna replies, clasping her hands together. "Henri said MOMA has just delivered the other two paintings. Now we have all three originals to examine."

Henri quickly sets the easels up on either side of *The Crucifixion of the Madonna*, opens the portfolios, removes the canvases and sets them on the easels. He executes these tasks with a look of disapproval, turns around and leaves the room.

Julianna takes a step back, looking at all three paintings and says, "I think it would be useful if we go over the paintings in chronologic order. Let me read Dyanne's riddle first.

The eye of the virgin,

A fetus saved,

A piece of pie,

Marks the way."

Julianna pauses and I watch everyone's expressions as we all ponder the riddle.

"Well, we have the virgin in two of the paintings, I say we look at her eyes," Lush states with enthusiasm.

"Precisely my thought," Julianna replies as she picks up a small leather case sitting beside her champagne flute. "This jeweler's loupe magnifies 30 times. Mabry, would you do the honors?"

"Sure, Julianna," he approaches her, takes the loupe, pulls off his glasses, and asks, "Shall I start with this first one?"

"Yes," Julianna replies, "Start with *The Rape of the Rosary,* it was painted first."

I observe the paintings as Mabry approaches *The Rape of the Rosary*. I've seen these paintings before on a visit to MOMA with Billy, and I am overcome with the same eerie feelings now as they evoked in me then, which I think arise out of the conflicting and dual messages evident in them. The paintings look old, like something you'd see in a cathedral built four centuries ago, with the light focusing on the central characters and the margins of the paintings darker, yet the appearance of the characters appear very modern. In *The Rape of the Rosary* the priest is forcing himself on Dyanne, his black cassock, completely unbuttoned in the front, is pulled back and thrown over his left buttocks and back, exposing his muscular, hairy ass and legs, the type of physique you would expect on an athlete, not a priest, his balls hanging down as he thrusts his erect penis, which is not visible, into Dyanne. A pair of yellow boxer shorts with little brown and white designs on them is down around his ankles partially covering his black leather shoes and black socks. A large gold cross on a gold chain is slung over his left shoulder and lies on the back of his cassock. Sweat glistens on his muscular torso exposed on his right side. The back of his head is visible as he hunches over Dyanne, whose face is turned slightly to the left, her red-blonde hair in disarray around her shoulders, her blue eyes wide open in a dissociative, expressionless state, her entire body appears limp, unmoving, receiving the priest without struggle, her left hand open, a beautiful, delicate set of gold and lapis lazuli rosary beads with a golden crucifix on the end dangles across her slender fingers. A simple white blouse, white bra, and white panties lay crumpled on the floor, her Tartan scooter, in shades of green, red, white, and black, is pushed up, inside out, fanning over her chest covering her right breast, her left breast and its rosy pink nipple, rises erect and firm from the cloth. The priest's hands clamp onto her knees holding open her slim legs which straddle his thighs, white knee socks cover her calves, one black Mary Jane shoe is on her left foot, the other shoe, turned upside down is on the floor. The rape is set in the priest's office and on top of his desk where the priest has pushed aside a brass desk lamp, a telephone, and a large, leather bound Bible, which is open with a red silk ribbon marking the page. Dark paneled, built-in bookcases, full of leather-bound books, religious bric-a-brac, and a round antique mantel clock, black with Rococo gilding around the pie crust dial pan, reading three o'clock, flank the desk. From the light entering through the leaded glass window behind the desk, it must be three o'clock in the afternoon. I feel myself

becoming aroused as I look at the painting when suddenly a feeling of guilt shoots through me as I picture myself doing this to Julianna's young maid, Celeste. But there is one difference, this is obviously a rape, I could never rape anyone, it's just not in me. If Celeste were to reject me, that would be that. And then an image of me fucking Adrian in the ass enters my mind, which annoys and confuses me because I have no sexual desire toward Adrian whatsoever, but the image persists and I visualize him on his hands and knees, bent over, his hands handcuffed to a steam radiator like the ones in his apartment, and I'm choking him with a silk tie with my right hand and grabbing his long red beard with my left hand, as I force my cock into his ass, fucking him so hard, that the sensitive tissues in his ass and rectum tear and bleed, and I relish the feel of the hot blood on my cock as I continue to force myself in him.

"Incredible detail," Mabry says as he leans over the painting with the jeweler's loupe and the troublesome image of Adrian rapidly recedes from my mind. "Really astounding, Julianna. These little brown and white designs on his boxers are hounds and foxes. How on earth did she paint such small detail?"

"She was known for that, Mabry—that's why her paintings are so realistic. But what about her eyes? Look at her eyes," Julianna implores.

"Yes, yes. Just shades of blue, grey, white. Oh, my God, this is unbelievable!" Mabry shouts.

"What is it, Mabry?" Lush asks.

My heart begins to race; I feel it thumping in my chest.

"She's even painted the curvature of the eyeball and in the left side of each iris is the reflection of the priest's face!" Mabry says turning around facing us.

"How detailed is it, Mabry?" Julianna asks.

"I think, with additional magnification, detailed enough to recognize this person."

"I'll be damned," Lush says.

"Unbelievable!" Janet says.

"Mabry, let me see that loupe, please," Jonas says as he moves closer to the picture.

"Julianna, why hasn't anyone ever noticed this before, or have they?" I ask.

"No one has, to my knowledge, Philip," she replies. It's not usual to go over a painting with magnification, especially one created within the last ten years. Generally speaking, paintings are creations for the human eye alone. Although I will say, this type of thing is not unprecedented in religious art. For instance, the famous Virgin of Guadalupe image which supposedly miraculously appeared on the tilma of Juan Diego in the fifteen hundreds has multiple images of faces in her right eye."

"What's a tilma?" I ask.

"Darling," Julianna replies, "It's a sort of cloak or robe Juan Diego was wearing with his encounter with the Virgin Mary in the mid-fifteen hundreds in Mexico when she sent blooming roses in mid-winter via Juan Diego to the Spanish Bishop, Fray Juan de Zumarraga, as a sign of her existence and to entice him to build a shrine to her—this was the so-called Miracle of the Roses. In fact, Juan Diego was canonized by Pope John Paul II in 2002."

"Interesting," I reply, "How do you know so damned much, Julianna?"

She smiles, chuckles, "That comes with the territory when you're pursuing a doctorate in Art History."

Jonas is carefully examining Dyanne's eyes in *The Rape of the Rosary*. He quickly moves over to *The Crucifixion of The Madonna* and starts to examine her eyes with the loupe. "Nothing here, just layers of color." He turns around toward us, "What I think is that *The Rape of the Rosary* depicts O'Bryan's memory of being raped the first time by this priest, hence, she would have been a virgin, which corresponds to the first line of the riddle, 'The Eye of the Virgin'. I'm betting that the image she painted in the eyes is the actual priest who raped her. Mabry get your camera and photograph her eyes. We'll blow the images up large enough to identify the man. That's where our search for the treasure begins, I'd say."

"Yes, that makes sense," Julianna says, "Jonas, take the loupe to the Bible. See what passage is there and if you can read anything."

Jonas does and immediately says, "Incredible. It's Chapter 4 of the Gospel of Mark and verses thirty-five through forty-one are actually underlined in red."

"Can you read them, Jonas?" Lush asks.

"Yes, it's incredibly small though. How the hell did she paint this? With a big magnifying glass? Here it goes:

> *And that same day, when the evening had come, He said unto them, "Let us pass over unto the other side."*
>
> *And when they had sent away the multitude, they took Him even as He was in the boat; and there were also with Him other little boats.*
>
> *And there arose a great storm of wind, and the waves beat into the boat, so that it was now full.*
>
> *But He was in the hind part of the boat, asleep on a pillow; and they awoke Him and said unto Him, "Master, carest thou not that we perish?"*
>
> *And He arose, and rebuked the wind and said unto the sea, "Peace, be still." And the wind ceased, and there was a great calm.*
>
> *And He said unto them, "Why are you so fearful? How is it that ye have no faith?"*
>
> *And they feared exceedingly and said one to another, "What manner of man is this, that even the wind and the sea obey him?"*

"Whatever can that mean?" Lush asks, "It's the passage where Jesus calms the Sea of Galilee, I believe."

"Lush, you're exactly right," Julianna states. "*The Storm on the Sea of Galilee* is a Rembrandt painting—one of the one's stolen in the Gardner heist."

"Oh my," Janet says.

"Well, this certainly connects Dyanne O'Bryan to the Gardner heist," Jonas says.

"I think you're entirely right, Jonas," Lush says. "Was her hatred of the church so great that somehow she had to possess this painting? I believe we're on to something here. It just doesn't make sense that a deadbeat security guard could have masterminded the Gardner heist. Let's move on to the next line, 'A fetus saved.' She walks up to *The Crucifixion of The Madonna*, takes the loupe from Jonas and begins to examine the crowning fetus in the painting. This is by far the most famous painting of the three and it depicts Dyanne as The Virgin Mary, nailed to a cross, large spikes are driven through both wrists and one through both heels which are stacked, red blood oozes from the wounds. Blood drips down her forehead from cuts made by the crown of thorns on her head. Her blue eyes gaze out to the viewer, and it seems to me they are seeking answers, that she is in fact asking, 'Why is this happening to me?' She is naked with a large, distended, pregnant belly, navel popped out, and an infant's wet, blooding head pushing through her vagina. Water and blood run down her legs and her red-blonde pubic hair is wet and matted. Two other crucifixions are painted in the background, one is Cara Bridgefield, the other is Ted Johnson, and both

victims are naked. The setting is a hilly area that Julianna tells us is somewhere on the O'Bryan family farm in Bardstown. A stone fence runs behind the crosses, late afternoon sun illuminates the figures.

"Ah ha!" Lush says in a loud voice, "It's just as I thought!"

"What is it, Lush?" Julianna asks.

"Does anyone have a pen and paper?" Lush asks.

"I do," Jonas says and pulls a small black leather notebook from his coat pocket.

"Write this down, please," Lush says as she steadies the loupe in her hand over the crowning head of the baby. "These letters are written around the circumference of the baby's head: P U E R I N P R A G N A T U S D I E S M E R C U R I I X X I I I J U N I U S M C M L X X V I I, that's it."

"Oh my," Julianna says, "It's Latin."

"Exactly," Lush replies, "It's a date. And if my Latin is right it says, 'Boy born on June 23, 1977. I believe this painting is about an illegitimate child Dyanne had by the priest when she was a girl."

"Mon Dieux," Isabella says, "Is this possible?"

"Quite possible," Julianna replies. "Dyanne would have been fourteen years old at the time."

"Yes," Lush says, "I grew up Catholic in Louisville, I went to an all girls Catholic school through the eighth grade. Believe me, this type of thing was not at all uncommon. A young girl gets pregnant, the family will not consider an abortion because of the religious beliefs, young girl gets sent away for a year to a 'boarding school' (Lush makes quotation marks with her two hands as she says this), young girl has baby, nice white babies are in big demand for adoption, young girl returns to school as if nothing happened."

"But why wouldn't anyone have known about this?" I ask. "I mean, Dyanne O'Bryan is a very famous artist and has been studied a great deal. Why wouldn't Adrian have known about this?"

"Some secrets go to the grave, Todge," Lush says, looking at me.

"Well, I suppose so, but you think she would have told someone like Cara. Well, Joan, her sister must know," I add.

"I suspect she knows, but has never revealed it," Jonas says. "I think a trip to Kentucky is imminent."

"Absolutely," Lush replies, "And you are all welcome to stay at my house!"

"Thanks, Lush," Jonas says.

"This is incredible," Najeed says, "We've already gotten through the two lines of the riddle, 'The Eye of the Virgin, A fetus saved', so somehow the priest who raped Dyanne and fathered her child is involved with the whereabouts of the stolen Gardner treasures?"

"Yes," Isabella says, "That leaves only one line, 'A piece of pie' because that 'Marks the way'. But what can that mean?"

"It could be anything," Lush says, "We found the first answer in the first painting and the second clue in the second painting, let's focus on the third painting now."

We all turn to examine *The Hanging of St. John Houghton*. Celeste arrives carrying a tray of tiny blinis with caviar and crème fraiche and radish finger sandwiches. They are delicious. This painting, the last one painted, is by far the most complicated and intricate of the three, and perhaps, the most disturbing as it depicts in graphic detail the hanging of the English priest who defied Henry VIII's denunciation of the Catholic Church. Here again, Dyanne's own face is the face of the saint as he is being hanged nude. His eyes bulge as he gasps for breath, and a large blue vein is evident on his forehead as well as on his large erect penis that ejaculates as brown fecal matter runs down both his legs. He hangs from a grey-green noose that almost appears to be intertwined serpents rather than fibers of a rope. The scaffold, a massive structure of weathered, rough-hewn timbers, has a crossbeam wide enough to hang a half dozen people at once. This graphic image is painted in a large central circular region in the painting. Six smaller perfectly circular inserts show him being dragged, fastened to a hurdle, to the hanging site by a horse; being taken down from the scaffold while still alive; being castrated and eviscerated while still conscious; watching his entrails and genitalia being burned; having his heart cut out, head cut off, and body quartered; and

finally, his head, heart, and four body quarters being paraded around on spikes for public viewing. Because the figures are so life-like and the horrific details of the torture are painted with such precision, it is hard for me to look at the painting for very long. The scaffold is erected in a forest clearing circled by immense trees, a small, ancient looking stone building is in the background, it is surrounded by a stone fence, and a brook flows past the building. I notice Jonathan has turned completely away from the painting. He has not spoken in a while. I walk over to him.

"Are you okay, Jonathan?" I ask in a half whisper while Lush goes over the painting with the loupe.

"Yes, thanks, Philip. Just a little jet lag and that painting, well, it's not the kind of painting I like. It gives off bad energy."

"I understand, completely. The painting is a bit much to take in. It's hard to believe that that was the punishment for treason against the crown for many centuries in England," I reply.

"Right," Jonathan says with a wince, "Those British, take Adrian for example, can be a rather brutal lot, don't you think?"

"Well, I hate to generalize, but I see your point, Jonathan," I reply, then noticing that he really appears green around the gills so I ask, "Perhaps you should sit down?"

"Yes, maybe so," he replies and walks over to an ornate armchair behind the three easels and sits down. Celeste walks over to him and asks if he needs anything. He orders a ginger ale on ice with a lime.

"Damn it! I am not finding anything but incredibly detailed painting," Lush says, "Here, Jonas, take the loupe. See if you can do any better."

Mabry's eyes are fixed on the painting like cat eyes fixed on a chipmunk. As Jonas bends over with the loupe in his hand, Mabry says, "She was brilliant. I believe I have the answer for the third part of the riddle."

"What is it, Mabry?" Julianna asks.

"Well, 'A piece of pie' may really be 'A piece of pi' where pie is spelled pi, representing the Greek letter pi. It is probably the most well known mathematical constant—you know, the circumference of a circle divided by its diameter. There are six small circles and one big circle in this painting; 'A piece of pi—p i' could be any one of them or a portion of them. Yes, the clues are in the circles and I see it now. Jonas, let me have the pad and pen."

Jonas turns around, hands Mabry the pad and pen, smiling, and says to everyone, "I can tell he's on the trail of cracking a sequence."

Mabry takes the pen and pad and quickly starts sketching a series of circles. As he sketches he looks up at the painting and back down at the pad several times.

"Whatever is he onto?" Lush asks.

"We'll see in a very short period, I suspect," Jonas says in the tone of a proud parent.

A smile erupts across Mabry's face and he turns the pad around to all of us to reveal the following.

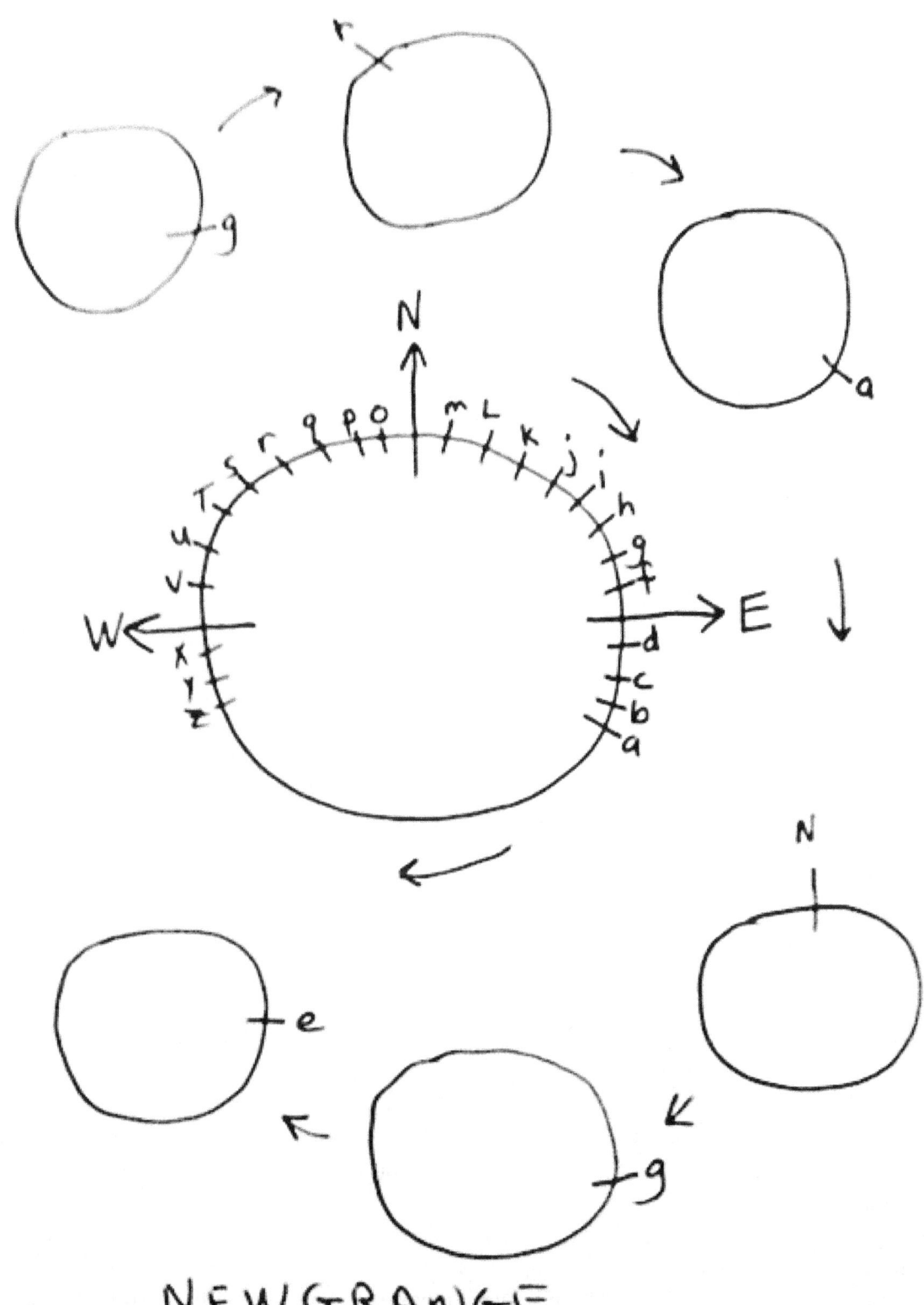

NEWGRANGE

"The answer was right in front of Adrian's eyes and he couldn't see it," Mabry says. "That really surprises me considering he must know quite a bit about sequencing."

"Right, Mabry," Lush says with an urgent tone, "Tell us what it means!"

"Alright. The central directional inlays in Julianna's entrance halls gave me the answer. See the big circle here. It represents the central figure in the painting. If you look at the painting, Dyanne has painted in faint directional arrows here for north, at the top over St. John's head, east, on the right side of the crossbeam, and west, on the left side of the cross beam. Notice she has left out an arrow for south, which would have come out of his feet. Now look at each of the six smaller circular inserts. See how each one has an individual directional arrow pointing out, and see if we start in the left hand top corner of the painting and go in a clock-wise direction how the first and fifth circle have the same directional arrow. See that, yes? Now see how the fourth and sixth circles have directional arrows corresponding to arrows on the big circle? Yes? Here's how you solve it. There are eight letters in the alphabet between E for east on the big circle here and N for north. So we have eight equal marks representing the letters f, g, h, i, j, k, l, and m which takes us up to N for north. From N for north to W for west guess what? We have eight letters also. In the same manner we have o, p, q, r, s, t, u, and v until we get to W for west. Now I just write in a, b, c, and d using the same approximate spacing before the E for east and x, y, and z after the W for west and we have the complete alphabet. Identify the letters corresponding with the positional arrows in each of the smaller circles and start reading the puzzle at N for north on the big circle and move around it clockwise, then around the series of smaller circles in a clock-wise manner and we have: N E W G R A N G E. New Grange! Does that mean anything to anyone?"

"Oh my God!" Julianna shouts. "That's the name of the O'Bryan's farm in Kentucky."

"Well, there you have it, the treasure must be there," Mabry says, smiling while he makes a slight bow.

Everyone claps enthusiastically. "You are the brilliant one, Mabry," Lush says, runs up to him, embraces him, and plants a huge kiss on his right cheek.

"Thanks, Lush," Mabry replies with a giggle as his face turns bright red.

"Okay everyone," Lush says, clasping her hands together, "I think I can bring this baby home, so to speak. What I think the riddle is telling us is that Dyanne got the priest who raped her to help her conceal the treasure somewhere on the family farm. She forced him to be her accomplice, otherwise she could have destroyed him by revealing his sexual abuse of her and the fact that she bore his child."

"Yes, that would make perfect sense, Lush," Janet replies.

"Yes, I agree, Lush," Jonas says, "Very good thinking!"

Lush beams, and I smile back at her, "Thanks, Lush. Thanks, Mabry. Thank you all."

"This has been quite an extraordinary cocktail hour," Najeed says.

Jonathan, looking somewhat revitalized, has rejoined the group, and he points to the priest's ass and remarks, "I guess one could say his cock ended up telling after all!"

Laughter erupts.

"Oh dear, Jonathan," Julianna says, "That's a good one. I misjudged you entirely dear. I halfway thought you were going to be the stick in the mud of this group."

We all laugh even louder.

"Well, we've got a lot to discuss during dinner," Julianna says. "Ladies, gentlemen there are several restrooms down here. Why don't we freshen up and then reconvene in the main dining room behind the staircase? Come along with me ladies. I have a sumptuous ladies lounge off of the Autumn Salon."

The ladies depart while the guys remain standing around the paintings.

"Geez, pretty incredible what just happened." I remark.

"Yes indeed," Jonas replies. "The energy is flowing tonight."

A big smile surfaces on Najeed's princely face, "And the night is very young, gentlemen."

"Quite young," I reply. "Excuse me, gentlemen. I need to pee." I turn to walk away when something in *The Hanging of St. John Houghton* catches my eye: it's the old stone building. I approach the painting to examine it closer. I break out in a cold sweat—this is the same springhouse in my hunt dream from last night, the same place where I killed the white wolf, which turned into the little boy, a little boy that I now know was Adrian. I turn away from the painting and head for the bathroom near the back of the salon.

CHAPTER 36

I walk into the bathroom and am surprised to see two full-length urinals, side by side. I suppose these come in handy when Julianna entertains a large number of guests. The doors to two smaller rooms, each containing a toilet, are partially open, and I imagine there have been parties here where men and women are using this bathroom at the same time. The décor is a continuation of the Spring Salon with a Chinese flair; a mural depicting springtime in a large Chinese garden with lakes, rivers, pavilions, pagodas and temples is painted over the walls. Groups of people, dressed in beautiful, brightly colored robes stroll in the gardens while groups of children play games, climb blossoming trees, chase dogs, and pick peonies. Servants are working the gardens. Mother would have loved this mural; I'm certain she must have been in this room on several occasions. I walk over to one of the urinals to pee. Each urinal has a mirror with gilded wooden frames, carved with blooming lotuses, peonies, and chrysanthemums, hung over it at face level. I look into the mirror as I pee and wonder how, within the space of a week, have I had dreams so strongly connected to paintings: first, the river painting Mother did for my thirteenth birthday and now the springhouse in *The Hanging of St. John Houghton*. I've never considered myself psychic, but I've experienced enough déjà vus and strong, gut-level, intuitive feelings in my life to realize that communication beyond our tangible senses must exist. This week has been the most stressful in my life, or at least, it feels that way now. Mother's death was like having the wind knocked out of me for a long period of time—I could hardly feel anything, I was just a body going through the motions of everyday life. This week I have really been connected to my feelings. Perhaps that's why I'm having these dreams, which are in fact messages from the other side. The other side of what I don't exactly know, but somehow I've always equated spirits with energy and something about yoga helps to connect all this. That guy at yoga today, Harper, was really interesting. I must go to his class tomorrow. My hunch is, and I'm so glad I'm listening to myself right now, that even though I'm a little buzzed from that martini, because this is a real gut feeling, a message to me that I need to connect with Harper because he has something to teach me. This realization inundates me with a feeling of hope and almost joyful anticipation that somehow lessens my worry over these bizarre dreams. I shake my penis and put it back in my pants, zip up, flush the urinal, walk over to one of the sinks in the vanity, made of some beautiful green marble or granite, wash my hands, dry them with a thick cotton hand towel I remove from a basket full of them, straighten my hair in the mirror, and turn to walk out. As I open the door, Najeed enters, followed by his two bodyguards.

"See you in the dining room," I say.

"Oh yes, I expect the dinner to be as interesting as the cocktail hour," he replies as he heads to one of the urinals.

I turn to walk away, and I think it must be rather odd to have to go to the bathroom with bodyguards. I suspect Najeed must be used to it. I pass back through the Spring Salon, take one more look at Dyanne's three paintings, turn around, and walk out into the elliptical entrance hall, pass under the staircase and into the

dining room where Jonas, Mabry, and Jonathan sit in a group of upholstered chairs arranged around a coffee table in front of a large fireplace with a large white, wooden mantel held up by fluted Doric columns. Mabry is pecking away on a laptop. A round dining table, beautifully decorated with a very tall, cut crystal, pedestal bowl, full of dozens of feathery, pink and white parrot tulips, spilling out over the sides of the scalloped bowl, and several cut crystal votives containing burning candles of the same pink shade as the tulips, sits in the center of the large rectangular room on top of a large, round, silk oriental rug woven in various shades of green, red, white, and yellow. The table is covered with a floor length white tablecloth and is surrounded by nine dining chairs, fully upholstered in a beautiful plaid, raw silk of the colors in the rug. Sterling flatware and chargers reflect the light from the votives and I notice place cards, done in pink ink in calligraphy, resting in crystal holders. I find it interesting that Julianna wants to control the seating arrangement tonight. I realize that this circular table was probably brought in for tonight's intimate dinner, and I'm certain that a large, banquet table and chairs must be in storage somewhere, probably in the basement. I walk over to the men sitting by the fireplace in which real logs make crackling, popping, and hissing sounds as they burn.

"Jonas, were you surprised that we've most likely already solved Dyanne's riddle?" I ask.

"Not at all, Philip," he replies shaking the ice in his crystal glass, holding about an inch of pale golden liquid I guess must be scotch, "Given the number of very bright people here tonight, it does not surprise me a bit." He sips his drink.

"Well, that is true," I reply as I walk in front of the fireplace letting my rear and the back of my legs absorb its warmth, "But it somehow bothers me that Adrian wasn't able to solve it. Doesn't that seem odd to you guys?"

"I remember how much Adrian loved riddles and treasure hunts," Jonathan states.

"Oh yes," I reply, "Every time he visited us in Union or we visited him in New York, he had a new adventure, revolving around a riddle or treasure hunt, he had carefully planned."

"Well," Jonas says, "We do not know that Adrian has not solved the riddle. Perhaps he has? Perhaps he's sent his minions on clandestine treasure hunts to the O'Bryan farm on numerous occasions, only to come up empty handed. A thousand acre farm is a lot of ground to cover and the treasure could be anywhere. Mabry was just telling us that Bardstown is in a karst region and there would likely be numerous caves and sinkholes on the O'Bryan farm. A cave, with its even temperatures, might be a great place to stash treasure."

"Yes, I see your point," I reply, "But why did Adrian give us the riddle?"

"Because I believe he realizes that you have a better chance at finding the treasure than he has," Jonas replies.

"Precisely the point that has been running through my mind, Jonas," Lush says as she and all the ladies enter the dining room. "I've been thinking, we know the priest in the painting must know where that treasure is, but Christopher and/or Joan might know something about it too. Possibly even Cara may know something."

"Okay," Mabry says, looking up from his laptop, "The priest in the painting will not be much help to us."

"How do you know that, Mabry?" Julianna asks.

"Because he's dead," he replies and turns his laptop around to show us an obituary from *The Courier-Journal*, the newspaper in Louisville. The caption reads: Father Joseph Patrick O'Callaghan, OSB Presumed Dead. A photograph of a middle aged man with dark hair and a friendly face accompanies the article.

Mabry continues, "I photographed the right eye of the virgin in the painting, enlarged it greatly, and produced this image." He turns the laptop around, runs his fingers over the touch pad, clicks the mouse bar a few times, and up pops the face of the priest, undeniably a younger version of the same man pictured in the obituary, in the throws of an orgasm, gasping for air, eyes wide open.

"How did you know he was dead?" Lush asks.

"Well, I figured that if Adrian knew who this guy was, he might well be dead. Once I had this image to work with, I just did a search for priests' obituaries in The Louisville, Kentucky Roman Catholic archdiocese. It seems our alleged rapist was a nature lover and avid outdoorsman as well as a priest. While on a mission trip to South America in 2001 he went scuba diving in the Galapagos Islands where he vanished and is presumed dead. He was fifty-four years old, so he would have been thirty years old in 1977. The obituary says that he served as Associate Pastor of Saint Joseph Proto-Cathedral in Bardstown from 1976 until 1981."

"No question, that's our man," Lush says, "Or rather, that was our man."

Najeed and his two bodyguards enter the room.

"Najeed, Mabry located the rapist priest," I state, "He went missing off of the coast of the Galapagos Islands on a scuba-diving trip in 2001."

"Not surprising. Adrian's work, no doubt," he says.

"So this means Adrian has in fact solved the riddle?" Janet asks.

"Probably so, Janet," Jonas replies. "My hunch is that he believes Philip has a better chance than anyone else of locating the exact location of the treasure on the O'Bryan farm."

"Well I have no earthy idea why he believes that," I reply, "I can't imagine what advantage I have over anyone else seeking the treasure."

"Philip," Jonas stands up as he addresses me, "I think Dyanne's son, Christopher, must know something about the treasure, and I think Adrian believes that you might be able to connect with him and draw out the information."

"Jonas," I reply, "I just am not following you. Why would anyone think I might have a break-through with Dyanne's son? I don't get it."

"Look at it this way," Jonas continues, "You both are from rural backgrounds with famous artist mothers. You both had brothers with whom you were very close, you both lost your mothers and your brothers, and you both suffered sexual abuse by Adrian. I'd say you have a lot in common. Someone as bright as Adrian is acutely aware of this."

I try to take this in and reply, "Well, I see your points, Jonas, and forgive me for being obtuse, but it just doesn't come together for me."

"I think I can be of assistance here," Najeed says, separating himself from the bodyguards as he walks in front of the fireplace, stops, turns around, facing everyone. "Adrian did reveal his knowledge of the Gardner heist to Billy and probably Ricky, too. He convinced Billy that Dyanne O'Bryan's son, Christopher, whom Adrian refers to as the 'little monk,' knows the whereabouts of the stolen art. Adrian wanted Billy to go visit Christopher, gain his confidence, seduce him, and find out where the artworks were hidden by his mother. Adrian told Billy that 'the little monk' was as gay as anyone he'd ever seen and that someone with Billy's great looks and reputation for sexual prowess should have no problem getting to him. In fact, Adrian offered to meet with Billy if he could deliver the artworks, which I suspect he has done with you, Philip. Billy was planning to go visit Christopher when he accompanied me to the Keeneland two-year old in training sales this week. When all this talk came up, I suggested to Billy that there were better ways to deal with Adrian."

I am stunned at Najeed's matter-of-fact delivery of being involved in Adrian's planned assassination. "Najeed," I ask, "Why on earth would someone with all the power, status, and privilege you have risk getting involved with an assassination attempt of someone whom you barely knew."

Najeed flashes a smile, "Philip, you are mistaken. I was and am completely in love with your brother. I'm sure if Mabry spends a little more time with Billy's hard drive, he'll bust the latest encryption code I used in corresponding with Billy. I actually thought that when Julianna phoned me Thursday that this had occurred."

"The only email we found from you was the one you sent two weeks ago where you're inviting Billy to Keeneland and you refer to having something to celebrate. Adrian's assassination, correct?"

"Yes, that's right, Lush. I'm not sure how that one got through the encryption, but apparently it did, probably negligence on my part." Najeed releases a heavy sigh and continues, "You see, I don't believe in violence at all, but I knew Billy would not stop until he got at Adrian with his bare hands. Billy would have been killed in any such attempt. I wouldn't risk that. In my world, arranging an assassination is not a complicated matter, so I offered my assistance to Billy and he accepted. When we realized the enormity of crimes and murders Adrian had perpetrated and continues to cause through his connection with al-Qaeda, it was an easy decision for us. I think all Ricky wanted was to be released from the almost life-long grip Adrian has had on him."

Darcy and Henri enter the room.

"Excuse me, Najeed," Julianna quickly interrupts, "Please, everyone let's all be seated. We'll continue this discussion at dinner."

We walk over to the table to find our seats. Darcy and Henri seat the ladies, then the men sit down and the servers unfold our napkins, putting them in our laps. Julianna sits facing the doorway in order to see the servants entering and leaving through the east doorway, I conjecture. Najeed sits to her right and I sit to her left. Isabella sits to my left, Jonas to Isabella's left, Lush to Jonas's left, Mabry to Lush's left, Janet to Mabry's left, and Jonathan to Janet's left. I look down at the place setting and know we are in for a wonderful meal—there are four forks to the left of my plate and three knives to the right.

"Julianna," Lush says, "This table is gorgeous."

"Thank you, Lush," Julianna replies, "Mother loved china almost as much as she loved art. When she died, we had eighteen full settings of different china in this house. I managed to whittle it down to six."

Celeste and the middle age Asian woman, Jiao, who served us at Julianna's gallery, enter the room pushing a large silver serving cart on which sits a silver wine cooler containing two bottles of wine. Jiao opens the doors of the cart, reaches in, and takes out two small plates, steps aside to let Celeste and Darcy each get two plates. Henri waits for them, then reaches in and takes three plates. Celeste and Darcy serve the women first, after which Jiao and Henri serve the men. The waitresses and waiters step back from the table.

Darcy clears his throat and says in his eloquent British accent as Henri and Celeste pour white wine into our glasses, "Ladies and gentlemen: Sautéed Alaskan halibut with steamed and poached artichoke heart, poached quail eggs, grilled asparagus, micro greens, and Hollandaise sauce made with lime infused butter accompanied by a wonderful Sancerre. Bon appetit."

"Thank you, Darcy," Julianna says. Jiao and Henri roll the cart out of the room. Henri and Darcy follow.

"Julianna," I say, "May I propose a toast."

"Oh yes, Philip," she replies.

I smile, stand up, raise my glass, and begin:

I raise my glass to the Lord above,
An invocation of thanks and love.
Bless this wine
Bless this sumptuous fare
Bless this time
We so gratefully share.
As the seasons come and go,
As we travel near and far,
Keep us safe from Satan's show,

Let us conquer every foe.
And before I say 'Amen'
May God always be our friend,
Grant us truth and love and mercy,
Oh Lord, we are all so thirsty!

"Amen and cheers!" I offer. We clink our glasses and take a sip of wine. I sit down.

"What a divine toast, Philip!" Julianna says, smiling at me, "Where ever did you find that one? Wait! Let me guess. Fatgram?"

"You got it!" I laugh.

"Who is Fatgram?" Isabella asks.

"She's my indomitable grandmother," I reply, "She always said this toast was something she picked up from her band days. You see, in the nineteen twenties she traveled throughout the south as the only female member of a twenty piece band. She was full of clever toasts and pithy sayings."

"How interesting," Janet says, "What did she play?"

"Oh, she was the pianist," I reply.

"From the stories I've heard about her from Philip, she was quite the 'ball of fire,'" Lush says.

"Indeed she was," Julianna says. "I had the pleasure of meeting Ina on several occasions. I've entertained her here with Eva. Ina was a force to be reckoned with. You certainly never had to second guess her," Julianna laughs. "She and your mother were like oil and vinegar, Philip."

"Oh, yes," I reply, "Couldn't live with each other, couldn't live without each other. You shake them up enough; it was a thing of beauty, like a delectable dressing."

Everyone laughs. I smile, but sadness fills my core because I miss Fatgram so much.

Julianna picks up a fork and knife, everyone else does the same, and we begin to eat. The servings are not too large, for which I am thankful, because I'm certain there are several more courses to follow. I cut a piece of the halibut, put it in my mouth, biting into its warm, sweet, rich, buttery texture tasting a slight hint of lime in the Hollandaise sauce. I take a sip of the Sancerre and think what a wonderful pairing this wine and fish are.

"Julianna," Lush says, "The halibut and artichoke are divine. Who is your cook?"

"Her name is Kathy Thomas. She trained in the states and in Paris. I use her whenever she's available for my dinners. There are five or six of us in this neighborhood who keep her pretty busy. I haven't had a full time cook since father died three years ago."

"It's delicious," Janet says, "After growing up Catholic, I've never been a fan of fish, but this is so light, so fresh, almost sweet tasting, and the sauce is divine."

"Thank you," Julianna replies. "Kathy's a genius in the kitchen. I'll introduce you all in a bit."

"Good," Lush says, "Maybe she'll share the recipe for this wonderful Hollandaise sauce."

"Oh, I'm sure she will, Lush," Julianna replies. "She's not one of those secretive chefs." She smiles then turns toward Najeed. "Najeed, please continue with your story. And please forgive me for interrupting you earlier. I just didn't want any of the waiters to hear what you were saying. You never know who may be listening."

He smiles at her, "I understand. You see, the dessert also has ears of its own, and when Billy and I talked about our plan concerning Adrian, unbeknownst to us, someone was listening."

Najeed notices me diverting my glance toward his two bodyguards.

"No, no. It had to have been someone working for my father. It's impossible it could have been my people," he quickly states.

"Your father?" Julianna asks.

"Yes, that's what I believe. It's the dirty side of our oil production," he says, picks up his fork, cuts into the halibut, spears it, and puts the piece in his mouth, chewing slowly as an expression of satisfaction blooms across the brown skin of his face.

"What do you mean by that, Najeed?" Lush asks.

He swallows and replies, "Just look at history, Lush. Every few years we have a major terrorist attack somewhere around the globe. After that, crude oil prices skyrocket, sometimes for months or even years before they go back down. Think of the hundreds of billions of dollars in revenue this creates for oil producing countries."

"Astonishing," Jonas says. "So you're saying your father supports terrorism, for example, the kind that someone like Adrian McWhorter is involved in?"

"Yes, Mr. Grey, sadly enough, that's exactly what I'm saying," Najeed says looking down at all of us with his large brown eyes.

"And you, the future king of your country, seem so outspoken about this horrendous secret," Lush remarks.

"Ah yes, I'm a pacifist at heart, Lush, but not stupid. As you can see, I try to protect myself well," he says and waves his left hand toward the two bodyguards who sit near the fireplace, scanning the surroundings. "I'm sure you've figured out by now that I'm a rather unconventional Arab. My father is not a bad man; I love him, dearly. But he is blindly protecting the single resource our country has—oil. Someday, it will run out. He feels it is his duty to use the tremendous flow of income from it to build an infrastructure in our country and educate our people so that in the future they may sustain themselves when the oil is gone. He's rather an astonishing individual. When he was born in 1952, oil had not yet been discovered in our country, now we are the eighth largest producer in the world and father has built a fantastic metropolis in under twenty years."

"And an extraordinary art collection, too," Julianna remarks as she lifts the crystal wine glass to her lips. Najeed smiles at her.

"Does your father know your feelings about terrorism?" Lush asks.

"Oh yes. He knows I'll never support terrorism of any type," Najeed replies scratching his brow with the thumb of his right hand.

"Fascinating," I remark.

"Complicated," Najeed says, smiling. "My father is relentlessly building our country, I suppose, so that by the time I take over, we'll be less dependent on the oil. But his attempt to shield me from involvement in this business is futile. My uncles and cousins will simply continue to support the terrorism. I have no power to stop them."

"Najeed, it seems to me you are in real danger of being assassinated if your beliefs are so well known," Lush says.

"Only twice, so far, that I know about. But I am not worried. I have four younger brothers who share my views. They'd have to kill us all."

Lush smiles, "Is your mother a Buddhist?"

A large smile erupts across Najeed's face, "Close, Hindu. You are most perceptive, Lush."

"Thank you, Najeed," she replies, holding her wine glass with both hands.

Najeed's big brown eyes focus with intensity as he looks at Lush. "My mother is a Saudi Princess. She attended boarding school in Switzerland and befriended an Indian princess whose grandfather was the last Maharaja of Mysore. The princess introduced my mother to the Hindu beliefs and traditions and Mother embraced them completely and has practiced them her entire adult life, much to the chagrin of her parents and my father's siblings. She and the princess, who lives in a beautiful palace in Mysore, are best friends to this day."

"So her children are all Hindu?" Lush asks.

"Strictly speaking no, we're Islam and brought up that way by my father's family, but we were heavily influenced by our mother's beliefs," he replies.

"Doesn't that cause conflict between your parents, Najeed?" Julianna asks.

"Not to my knowledge. My father has always been totally in love with my mother. She's been his only wife and will always be."

"Najeed, thank you for sharing all this with us," I say.

"You're most welcome," he replies, looks down, smiles, looks back up at me and says, "Forgive me, Philip, but I see the same look in your eyes I saw in Billy's, and I know your heart is set on killing Adrian yourself."

I am stunned, start to reply, then say nothing because I know he's pegged me.

"You're very perceptive for such a young man, Najeed," Lush interjects.

"Young in body, Lush, not in spirit and soul," he replies, smiling at her. Then he turns toward me. "But I can tell you right now, Philip, you'll never get near Adrian unless he desires it."

"Why do you say that?" I ask.

"Because he is extremely powerful among the terrorist groups, practically a legend. The boys he supplies from his training camps have been some of the most effective assassins, suicide bombers, and perpetrators of evil-doing in the past decade."

"Decade?" I ask. "But he was living here until he staged his fake death in the late nineties," I reply.

"Yes, that's true, but he had already established a school in Amsterdam and a training camp outside of Kabul during the nineties," he replies.

"My God," Lush says. "But why? What does he get out of it?"

"Millions of dollars to buy art and a continual fresh supply of young boys," Najeed says. "Disgusting, isn't it?"

"Absolutely," Lush replies.

"Let me show you how far his reach is," Najeed continues. "It was Billy's desire that the assassin present Adrian with a gift immediately before killing Adrian. That gift was to be the red Swiss Army knife Adrian used in his ritualistic Blood Brothers ceremony with his victims. Billy and Ricky broke into Adrian's safe, just as you all did. Billy kept the Swiss Army knife and your Blood Brothers certificate. As you probably have realized by now, those two things inspired his last painting, Blood Brothers."

"You've seen the painting, Najeed?" Julianna asks.

"Oh yes, he emailed me a picture the night of his murder. I find it extraordinary," he replies.

"But weren't you jealous of Elliott Fields?" Lush asks.

Najeed looks at her and smiles, "You forget, Lush. I come from a land where it is customary for men, especially wealthy men, to have many wives. So, as a gay man, it is not a far stretch for me to have many lovers. So, no, I wasn't jealous of Elliott. I still loved Billy deeply. I hoped we could somehow find a way to be together someday. You must know, I never thought or believed Billy felt that way. I know he cared for me a great deal—we fed off of each other's energy, but I know in my gut he never desired to spend his life with me." As he finishes speaking, his eyes drop, his smile fades, and I begin to feel sorry for him as I feel his sadness.

"Oh, Najeed," Lush says, "I can see how much you cared for Billy—how beautiful."

"Yes, yes, I cared a great deal. I cared so much that I risked a great deal to protect him from Adrian. But as you can see, I failed him greatly."

"No you haven't failed him, Najeed. Or you wouldn't be here right now helping us," Jonas says. "Tell us more about the Swiss Army knife. Obviously Adrian was sending a message by delivering it in the ice sculpture."

"Yes, indeed—a message carefully planned and delivered to hurt those closest to Billy and to broadcast Adrian's proven ability to persevere and triumph," Najeed says. "You see, the assassin with whom we made arrangements for Adrian's demise maintains a residence in Bermuda. Delivery of the Swiss Army knife to a certain massage therapist at the Willow Stream Spa at the Fairmont Southampton in Bermuda was to initiate the assassination. The assassin guaranteed Adrian's death within seventy-two hours of this

delivery. Billy had wired one hundred thousand dollars to an offshore account just to initiate the pick-up. The assassin was to receive an additional one million nine hundred thousand dollars upon proving Adrian's death."

"So how does one prove the death of someone as elusive as Adrian?" I ask.

"By delivering a part of the body which would cause a mortal wound," Najeed remarks in a matter of fact manner.

I feel a sinking sensation in my gut. I'm afraid to ask, but I do anyway, "And what part of Adrian did Billy want, Najeed?"

"His gonads, intact."

"Dear God," Julianna says.

"No wonder the price tag was two million dollars," Jonas remarks.

"Yes, but there's more," Najeed continues, "I do not want to go into details during dinner, but Billy wanted Adrian to be alive and cognizant while this was being done to him. He wanted Adrian strangled first, and then, well, let's just say, something similar to Dyanne O'Bryan's *The Hanging of St. John Houghton* would have happened to Adrian."

"Dear God," Julianna says again, "I am going to ring for a shot of calvados for us all. Right now I feel as if I need more than my palate cleansed."

I am shocked at the horror of Najeed's story. Could my brother have been capable of orchestrating such horrific acts on another person, even Adrian? Was Adrian more abusive to Billy than he was to me? Am I blocking out something—not remembering something? Yes, those pictures of Adrian with the boys in his training camps were pretty horrible, but would Billy stoop to Adrian's level? It's not that Adrian doesn't deserve such a fate, but at the hands of my brother? Is this Najeed for real? Perhaps he's really an ally of Adrian's? I just don't know. I look at Lush, who looks back at me, and I can see her mind is churning. Oh how I wish we could speak right now without words. Henri enters.

"Henri," Julianna says. "I know chef is planning to serve one of her delightful lemon sorbets now, but might you let her know we'd all like a bit of calvados first?"

"Oui, madam," he says in his flat baritone and walks out.

"Najeed, did Elliott Fields know about any of this?" Lush asks.

"No, not to my knowledge. But Billy had arranged for Elliott to have a massage at the Willow Stream Spa while Elliott was staying at the Fairmont for his Bermuda shoot. He asked Elliott to deliver a package to the masseur who Billy described as an old friend from the past. Billy nor I ever intended any harm to Elliott."

"No, I know you didn't," Lush says. "Now it is all coming together. Benny must have been instructed by Adrian to use GHB to get the whereabouts of the Swiss Army knife from Billy. But Benny put too much GHB in Billy's drink—he probably was unaware of how much alcohol Billy had consumed already. I bet Benny had planned to take Billy back home, maybe have sex with him, get the information from him that way."

"That makes sense," Jonas says. "Killing Billy before he had revealed where the knife was wouldn't have helped Adrian. That's why Benny came back as a waiter on Monday, knocked out the other waiter, and opened Billy's safe. He didn't find the knife because Elliott Fields had it. We know from the police department that Elliott Fields' apartment had been ransacked that night too. That explains why Bernie was sent to Bermuda—to get the knife from Elliott before it was delivered to the masseur, thus stopping Adrian's assassination."

"But why did Benny go to the hospital Monday morning to kill Billy?" I ask. "Surely he would have known Billy was in a vegetative state when he saw him lying there?"

"Maybe he didn't know it until he got there?" Jonas says.

"If that's the truth, then why did he go ahead and administer more GHB to him?" I ask.

"Instructions from Adrian, I would say, Philip," Jonas replies.

"Yes, I suppose you're right," I reply, but something in my gut tells me that's not the whole story, but I cannot put my finger on it.

"Yes, that makes sense," Lush says. "But Najeed, when did you and Billy discuss the details of the assass, uh uh the plot?" She looks at the door as Celeste and Darcy enter with a cart and move toward the table to remove plates.

"Well, when he came to visit me in January," he replies.

"What? He visited you in January?" I ask in amazement.

"Yes, for a week. I showed him my country in more detail than his first visit. We had a splendid time. We camped in the desert, rode horses and camels, hunted with my falcons, spent hours looking at my father's art collection, toured our thoroughbred stables, had a discotheque party in our palace, did yoga with my mother and the Princess of Mysore, and made the plans we have been discussing tonight." Najeed's face fills with calmness as he relates this story.

"January. I was in China working. Billy told me he was going to Key West for a week to fish. That's when he went to visit you. I suppose even Lois didn't know. How did he get there?"

Najeed smiles, "I came and got him in my plane. We stopped in London for a day going over to stay at my father's townhouse. I couldn't come back with him because of engagements with my father. He flew back via India to escort the princess home, then Hong Kong and New York—almost an entire day of flying for him."

Celeste and Darcy have quickly removed the plates and reset the silver, and are leaving as Henri comes in carrying a silver tray filled with crystal shot glasses of calvados and carefully sits a shot glass down in front of each person. I notice the white gloves Henri wears as he places my glass on the table. He quickly leaves the room when he finishes placing all the glasses.

"Everyone, feel free to shoot this or sip it, whatever is your pleasure," Julianna says as she raises her glass of calvados. "Myself, I need the fortification of a quick shot as I suspect this evening will be a challenge for us all."

"I'll second that!" Lush says.

"Moi, aussi!" Isabella says.

"Oh dear, me as well!" Janet chimes in.

Julianna pauses, looks at all the men around the table, "And gentlemen, are you all with the ladies?"

"Absolutely!" Najeed says.

We toast and everyone turns up their shot glasses and I feel a warm, sweet, apple taste running down my throat and into my stomach.

"Very well," Julianna says, "That's more like it. Please continue Najeed."

"I'm afraid I'm at the end of my story, Julianna," he replies wrinkling his forehead.

"But you must have an idea of how your father found out," she states.

He lets out a heavy sigh, setting his shot glass back on the table, his lips bending into a frown. "It could have been anyone, even the assassin, vying for more money. Hardly anyone can compete with my father when it comes to sheer buying power. He does in fact have as much wealth as anyone on this planet."

"Have you confronted him about Billy's death, Najeed?" I ask. "I mean if you loved Billy as much as you say you do, aren't you pissed at your father for participating in this?" I ask as I feel the heat rising underneath my collar.

Najeed's eyes narrow at me and he lifts his chin a bit, and I feel as if I am about to receive a blast of arrogance the likes of which I've never experienced, but to my complete surprise, his face softens, almost childlike, his shoulders slump, he looks at me, his eyes watery, and he says in a soft, pleading voice, "I'm so sorry, Philip. I'm so very sorry. I had no idea it would end this way. I should have kept out of it. I just wanted to make it right for Billy. I wanted to be his hero. I, I just wanted to make him love me."

I feel like someone has just driven a dagger through my heart. Najeed is speaking to me the exact way Billy did when I wouldn't have sex with him all those years ago at Sewanee, and it becomes obvious to me that, for whatever convoluted reason, probably a result of Adrian's sexual abuse and manipulation of Billy and me at such a young age, that my having sex with Billy was more than just two horny teenagers beating off together, but it was his way of attaching to me emotionally and feeling loved by me, something I know deep in my heart I forced on him after Mother's death. This realization is almost more than I can bear, my heart skips a beat, then another, then starts beating furiously, my throat tightens, and I think to myself that I am having a heart attack right here in the middle of dinner. I feel breathless, and my vision begins to fade as I feel a million tiny needles piercing my brain, pulling my face and torso down toward the table.

"Breathe, Todge, breathe, for God's sake," I hear Lush's urgent words. I feel her hair in my face; the floral scent of her shampoo or conditioner fills my nostrils. I open my eyes to observe her worried face peering into mine as she fans my face furiously with her napkin. "Thank God, you're awake," she says. "Are you okay, Todge?"

I try to focus on her pretty face and a flood of recollection hits me. "Yes, yes," I reply, "Just give me a moment." I sit up in my chair and breathe in and out, slowly. An image of Harper in his beautiful yoga asanas runs through my mind, and I decide that I will go to his class tomorrow. I notice Janet is on my other side and her left hand is on my left shoulder.

"Philip, I thought you were going to hyperventilate and pass out," she says.

"No, it's just that when Najeed was speaking. Well, it was. It just. Najeed, forgive me for doubting your care and concern for Billy. I know this is a terrible thing for you, too," I say.

He looks over at me and I observe that he has regained his composure as he says, "I know I can not understand half of what you are going through, Philip. You are every bit the man and brother Billy described to me. It's an honor to be with you tonight."

With those words, I feel tears pooling in my eyes, "Thank you, Najeed," I reply, "Please excuse me, everyone. I'm going to the restroom."

Lush helps me up and the two of us walk out of the room.

"I gotta pee," I whisper to her as I try to hold back the tears.

"So do I," Lush says.

"Come with me into the ladies lounge, you're not going to believe it." She holds my right arm as we proceed through the hallway, into Autumn Salon and into the lounge.

"Oh, my, this is tremendous," I say as I observe the walls of the large bathroom, covered with beautiful tropical jungle scenes with waterfalls, rivers, and lagoons, exotic flowering plants, huge hardwood, trees, vines, palms, colorful parrots, macaws, toucans, and beautiful butterflies. "It's got to be Zuber."

"Yes," Lush replies, "Julianna told me it is an original design made in the 1830's."

"Wow, it's got to be worth a fortune. How exquisite. You know it is made entirely by hand with small wood blocks," I add, "Billy explained it all to me. Fatgram had a screen covered with panels of Zuber in sort of a chinoiserie design. I don't know what happened to it."

"Glad this is a two staller," I say.

"Me too," she says.

We each go into a toilet room, but neither shuts the door. I start to pee and I hear her peeing.

"God, I had to pee like a race horse," she says.

"Me too," I reply.

"Are you really okay, Todge?"

"Yeah. It's just that my emotional circuits keep getting overloaded and zap, I'm down."

"You don't have high blood pressure do you, Todge?" she asks.

"No, I don't think so. Why?"

"Well, I just wondered. You've passed out twice this week, and I know you've been under incredible stress and all. Or maybe it's low blood pressure that makes you pass out easily. I can't remember."

"I think the truth is that I'm reconnecting with some powerful and unpleasant memories, Lush. It's like a circuit overload and my mind just goes blank."

"You mean, like you dissociate?"

"Well, yeah, but worse. I black out. But, you know what. I'm getting a handle on this. I'm not going to let it get the best of me."

"Maybe you should go see a doctor, Todge?"

"I'm going to see Dr. Gerard tomorrow."

"Yeah, but I mean for yourself, Todge."

"I'm gonna be okay, Lush. Right now, I feel as if I've turned the corner. I have a lot of guilt over Billy's death and I know I'll continue to have it, but I also know it's not all mine and I know Billy would never have laid that on me."

"I'm glad to hear you say that," she says and I hear her straining to get the last bit of pee out as I shake my cock.

"As cruel as it seems sometimes, Lush. Life does go on and so must we."

"No, it's not cruel, Todge. It's the way of the universe."

We both exit the toilet rooms at the same time. I'm zipping my zipper and Lush is adjusting her skirt. We walk over to the sinks and begin to wash our hands.

"I believe the elegant crown prince was truly enamored with Billy," I say.

"Quite, but understandably so. After all, you know as well as I that Billy could have anyone he wanted," she says.

"True. And when did he have you?" I ask.

Without missing a beat she replies, "Oh, that first time we all went to St. Barts, the night before you arrived."

"Oh, okay, that makes sense," I reply as I grab a towel to dry my hands. Lush does the same, throws the towel in a basket, turns back around to the mirror to arrange her hair.

"Was it good?" I ask.

"Yes, as good as drug induced sex can be," she replies.

"Really? That good?"

"As if you don't know for yourself," she smirks as she touches up her lipstick.

"You ready to go back?" I ask.

"Ready, Todge," she puts her lipstick back into her clutch, smiles, grabs my left hand with her right and we walk back into the dining room.

All the others are sitting at the table talking.

"Are you alright, Philip?" Julianna asks.

"Fine, much better, thank you," I reply. I look at Najeed, nod, and smile, and ask, "Najeed, how do you know so much about Adrian?"

"I have my own personal Jonas Grey based in England. I don't have a Mabry, but from what I see, I surely need one." Mabry and Jonas both smile.

"Sorry, your highness," Jonas says, "But we're a package deal."

Najeed laughs, "That's exactly what I thought, Jonas. And please, you must call me Najeed. Everyone here, please do the same. We are all brothers and sisters here. We are all royalty. My grandfather was a glorified camel driver, I'm no one's highness."

"Would you mind telling us what you found out about Adrian, Najeed?" Jonas lengthens his spine to a more erect position as he speaks.

"Not at all," he replies, takes a sip of water, looks up toward the ceiling, sighs, "I'm not sure where to start—it is such a dark, convoluted story. Well, to begin with, Charles Ainsworth is not who you think

he is. Julianna told me what he told you all—all of it lies. He is in fact Charles McWhorter, who was an Anglican Rector in the little town of Eckton. It was Charles and his wife, Edith, who took in Adrian after Adrian's parents, peasant farmers, were killed in a barn fire, trying to save livestock. Adrian was just three years old and his sister was five. A wealthy merchant from Liverpool adopted the sister, but Adrian was shuffled from home to home until the Rector and his wife took him in. By all accounts, life was difficult for little Adrian because Charles was a stern taskmaster and a perfectionist. Apparently life was difficult for Edith, too, and Adrian discovered her hanging from a rafter in the attic of the parsonage when he was ten. The day of her funeral, Charles lost his right eye. Medical records from the local hospital show that his eye was stabbed with a pencil. My investigator found and interviewed the McWhorter's housekeeper who found Charles screaming in pain in his study with a lead pencil sticking in his right eye. She said he was screaming at Adrian, calling him a little bastard for doing it. She said things were never right in that household and that no love ever existed there. She said Charles abused Adrian and Edith, emotionally and physically. In fact, most of the townsfolk suspected that Edith didn't hang herself, but that Charles murdered her. He had a strong alibi, however, for he was visiting another Rector in a parish some fifty miles away on the day of her death. At any rate, as soon as he was out of the hospital from the loss of his eye, he and Adrian simply vanished, never to be heard from again."

"Dear me, what horror," Lush says, staring down at her plate, "It seems to be so true…."

"What's so true, Lush?" I ask.

"Well, that abuse can persist for generations."

"Christ, I hope you're not feeling sorry for Adrian, now," I reply feeling the anger rise in my chest.

"No, Todge. Not for him, not now anyway. But, certainly I feel sorry for that little three year old who lost his parents, was torn from his sister and put into the lap of evil. I just can't help it; I feel sorry for that little boy."

No one says anything for a few moments as the silence builds. The image of the little boy in my dream, the little Adrian with the arrow through his heart, flashes in my mind, and my anger begins to dissipate.

"No, you're right, Lush. I have to believe that even Adrian must have started his life in innocence," I reply, letting out a big sigh.

"That's so kind of you, Philip," Isabella, who has been noticeably quiet all evening, says. I look over at her, and I notice a tear fall from her left eye.

"Thank you, Isabella," I reply sitting back in my chair. "Are you alright?"

"Yes, thank you. These past two days have been difficult—learning about all these horrible things, piecing it together with my own life, wondering if I will attain any sort of resolution at all." I am totally mesmerized by her emotion and her lovely French accent, yet I'm yearning to get out of her the details of what she knows or recalls about Adrian.

"So, do you think Adrian abused your brother and even killed your mother?" I ask in a compassionate tone.

"Yes, I do. It all makes perfect sense. It explains why Jean Paul was so troubled his whole life until he took his own life. It explains why the airbag on mammon's side of the car did not deploy. It explains why Adrian never sued the automobile company." She pauses a moment, looking into the side of her crystal wine glass as she slowly turns it in her hands. "It's so strange. Adrian would always scold Jean Paul whenever he was mean to me, even though I was the older child by two years. He'd say, 'Jean Paul, vous devez être plus agréables à votre soeur. Elle est la seule que vous avez.'" She looks up from her glass, "Oh, excuse me, Adrian would say, 'Jean Paul, you must be nicer to your sister. She's the only one you've got.' Adrian never laid a hand on me except to comfort me. He was always there for me until his supposed death. Perhaps he saw me as the sister he lost all those years ago?"

"Oh, Isabella," Janet says as she gets up from her chair, walks over to Isabella, leans over the back of her chair, puts both her hands on Isabella's shoulders, leaning her face against the top of Isabella's head. "I'm so sorry you have to go through this. I can't imagine how terrible this must be for you."

Isabella takes Janet's hands in her own and says, "Thank you, Janet. I really appreciate your concern. I will get through this. I will be okay."

There is something so familiar in what Isabella is describing and suddenly I'm back in South Carolina again, back in the oppressive heat, back into one of our secret kudzu caves where Billy and I could hide from the world. I am sitting inside one of those great mounds of kudzu, redolent with the sweet, heavy scent of its purple flowers, one July day, hugging my knees, crying my heart out after Mother and Dad had a particularly bad argument the night before during one of Mother's cocktail parties. Mother ended up yanking Billy and me out of bed, loading us in her car, and driving up the street to Fatgram's house crying in a rage, telling us that she was going to divorce Dad this time for certain and that we would be moving to New York. I was so distraught the next morning, fearing that Mother would carry through with her threat and move us to New York that very day that I ran away and hid in the kudzu. Uncle Adrian was visiting for a while, and before too long, he and Billy discovered my hiding place. Billy was more interested in looking for the purple-black racer snakes that inhabited the expanses of kudzu than worrying about our imminent move to New York.

"You're nothing but a cry baby, Philly. Cut it out, let's go catch some snakes."

"Shut up, leave me alone, Billy. I don't want to go to New York and leave Dad."

"Here, here, Philip," Uncle Adrian says, crawling into the darkness of the thick vines. "Christ, I don't see how you all can stand this stuff. Ala Mary says it will make you swell up like a toad if it touches your skin."

"Awe, that's just an ole wise tale," Billy says.

"I think you must mean an 'old wives' tale' Billy," Uncle Adrian says as he sits down beside me. "Anyway, I suppose you're right. We've been in here before, and I've never gotten swollen limbs, itchy yes, swollen no."

"Whatever," Billy says, smirking at Adrian, "Let's look for snakes."

"In a minute, William," Uncle Adrian says, as he takes me in his arms, pulling me into his lap. My sobs explode into his chest.

"Awe, here he goes again," Billy says. "Fatgram would say you're a big sissy for bawling so much, Philly."

"Billy," Uncle Adrian says in an urgent tone, "You've got to be nicer to your brother. He's the only one you've got."

I know Billy is jutting out his lower lip, I hear it in his voice as his says, "I'll be out here hunting snakes whenever anyone cares to join me." I hear him crawl out of the cave.

Uncle Adrian pulls me in closer, gently rocking me. "Listen here, young man. Your parents just had an argument, that's all. Sometimes adults do that, especially high-strung artist types like your mother. She's not going to leave Union—not for long anyway, I dare say. This place is in her blood. She loves you boys and she loves Charles. It'll all be resolved by this evening. You'll see. Don't worry, Philly. You know Uncle Adrian is here for you. I won't let anything bad happen to you or to Billy."

His words do comfort me, and I do feel safe now even as his hands begin to rub between my thighs.

"Do you ever have mixed emotions about Adrian, Philip?" I hear someone asking me, but I'm not certain if it's Jonas, Jonathan, or Mabry.

"What?" I reply.

"Well, maybe I should put it another way," Jonathan says. "Did Adrian ever really show you love?"

"Love?" I ask in disbelief. "Love?" I ask with indignation. "And why are we having this conversation?"

"Well, to be frank, I observed you fading away when Isabella was describing a more compassionate side of Adrian. I am curious as to whether you ever experienced anything similar with him?"

I feel opposing forces churning within my gut. I feel nauseated. I feel anger. I feel love. I feel horny. What the hell is going on? My face is turning red; I am starting to sweat. I feel drops of perspiration dripping from my armpits. Breathe, I tell myself. Breathe, I'll be damned if I'm going to let myself pass out again in front of all these people. I begin to take slower, deeper breaths. I take my glass of water, almost emptying it in a few gulps. I am conscience that everyone is focused on me, awaiting my answer.

"Yes, Jonathan," I reply and it feels as if I have to pull the words out of my throat with a large pair of pliers, "As best as I can tell it, and tell it truthfully, I have experienced compassion and even love from Adrian. If what he directed toward me was in fact only a grand seduction to dupe a little boy into doing nasty things, then so be it. But to me, at the time, I loved him, I felt safe with him, despite the sexual abuse, and I guess this is the first time I've ever really admitted this to myself much less saying it out loud in front of all of you. You see up until now, I've always cloaked these feelings in a deep shame, a shame that still persists like a deep, dark, pool of water, but now, just maybe, just maybe, I am beginning to believe my head is above water."

I look around the table to see many watery eyes. Jonathan looks at me, puts his hands together below his chin as if he were praying, bows his head toward me and says, "Thank you for the truth, Philip. And so it is with me, but you are the braver man to admit it first."

"Jonathan," I reply, "I think we are all brave to be here helping each other."

"Yes, indeed, Philip. Well put," Julianna says. "I think it's time for the next course."

Darcy enters the room and addresses Julianna, "Madame, do you still want the sorbet?"

"Yes, please, Darcy," she replies.

He nods, turns around and walks out.

My eyes fall on the crystal bowl full of exquisite pink and white parrot tulips in the center of the table, and although I'm conscious of the conversation at the table, I am drawn inward, home again, as I recall how much Mother loved crystal bowls and vases full of flowers, so much so, that she always included fresh flowers in the household budget, even in the dead of winter, even in Union, South Carolina. How much that cost, I do not know, but whenever Mother wanted or needed something beyond the range of Dad's income, she'd simply asked Fatgram who rarely denied her daughter anything. I notice a tiny dark ant scurrying up and down the petals of a bloom bowing its head toward me.

"What do you think, Todge?" Lush asks me.

I avert my gaze from the ant toward Lush, "I'm sorry, Lush. What do I think about what?"

"We were discussing why Adrian has stayed with Charles all these years," she replies.

"Gee. Who can say? Another terribly sick and dysfunctional relationship, I suppose."

"Yes. Perhaps a love-slash-hate relationship carried to the extreme?" she directs her question to everyone at the table.

Jonas begins to say something but pauses as Celeste and Henri enter carrying silver trays with sorbet in small silver compotes. They place the sorbet and a small sterling spoon in front of each person, leaving the room as quickly as they entered.

Jonas clears his throat and says, "Adrian is an anomaly as far as pedophiles and serial killers go because he is so highly functional among people and particularly brilliant. I believe he has an extremely high intelligence level, probably at or near genius level. At his core, he is a psychopath with essentially no self worth, fashioned by years of abuse by Charles. I think the turning point must have been when, at ten years of age, he stabbed Charles in the right eye. You see, I believe he put out his eye for a specific reason."

"Whatever could that be?" Julianna asks.

"I'm not certain, but I have an idea," Jonas replies. "Najeed, did your investigator give you any more details of Charles' life?"

Najeed tastes his sorbet, swallows, looks at Jonas, sniffs loudly, and replies, "Yes he did. The housekeeper told him that Charles himself was the son of a rector from a nearby town. Charles had

dreamed of becoming an artist, but his father would not permit this, and forced him to study to be a clergyman. She said Charles had volume after volume of books on fine art and would spend hours in his study looking at pictures. The only outings the family ever took were to art museums in London. He particularly liked religious paintings, especially those of the crucifixion of Jesus. She said the only really pleasant times in the house were when Charles would let Adrian look through his volumes of art books while he taught Adrian about the artists and their techniques."

"Yes, that fits in perfectly," Jonas replies, "I proffer that Adrian blinded Charles's right eye on purpose as retaliation against Charles for causing the death of Edith, whether or not he did it himself or drove her to suicide. By putting out his eye, Adrian deprived Charles of the full enjoyment of observing art and the little ten-year-old genius got the upper hand of his guardian and abuser. From that point on Charles always lived with the threat of Adrian poking out his other eye. I can only imagine how those two lived with one another in Amsterdam as Adrian matured. Has your man researched that period, Najeed?"

"No. No he hasn't. But I can get him on it immediately."

"It might be helpful," Jonas replies.

"Yes, indeed. I'll do it immediately," Najeed says, "Oh, but I do think Adrian was trying to blind Charles completely the first time. The housekeeper also reported that Charles had a stab wound from the pencil on his left temple."

"Yes, that supports my theory," Jonas replies.

"If you asked me, I'd say it is all rather disgusting," Jonathan says as he places his silver spoon on the table, grazing the side of the silver compote generating a bright metallic sound. We all look at him; he appears nauseated.

"What's so disgusting?" Julianna asks.

"That I'm a blood relative to those two," he replies, then wipes his mouth with his napkin.

"But you're only related to Adrian," Lush says. "I mean he's your father, but Adrian and Charles aren't even related. Charles is just the father through adoption." Lush sits back, erect in her chair, placing her hands in her lap.

"I'm not so certain of that," Jonathan replies. "Adrian always talked to me about his uncle in England and how he'd taught him all about the great artists. That had to be Charles. I think perhaps Charles was the brother of one of Adrian's biological parents, which would make him my great uncle."

"Now that you mention it, Jonathan," I say, "I do recall Adrian telling us about how he was taught to appreciate art as a small boy by a very smart and special uncle. Yet I do not recall him ever mentioning the name of this uncle."

"Najeed?" Jonas asks, "Did your man allude to any of this?"

"No he didn't, but I suppose I'll shall direct him toward it now."

"Yes, a good idea. You might also see if he can find Adrian's older sister. She may well have more memory than Adrian of the parents and their blood relations."

"Well, I may be taking all this the wrong way," Isabella suddenly says earnestly as bright red flushes across her cheeks, "And I know I'm just getting involved in all of this, but why are we wasting time focusing so intently on the past of Adrian and Charles? Doesn't it make more sense to learn more about them in their present state if we're to capture them?"

Everyone but Lush seems confused by Isabella's questions. A big smile develops across Lush's beautiful jaw exposing her perfect teeth, and I wonder how they remain so white after years of smoking, she leans towards Isabella, "Darling, you and I think a lot alike. Capturing Adrian is the goal!"

Isabella smiles at Lush, "Thank you, Lush."

"I see your point too, Isabella," Jonas says, "Yet accurate information from people who were close to the perpetrators in the past may help to reveal important internal motivators."

"I can see that, Jonas," she replies, "But haven't we already confirmed that Adrian is motivated by greed, lust, power, and evil doing?"

"Yes, we have," Jonas replies, "But we don't know exactly why Charles and Adrian have been a pair all these years. Jonathan's hypothesis that they are in fact blood related might help to explain that."

"Yes, that's true, but how will that help us apprehend them?" she asks.

"I don't know the answer to that yet, but it could prove to be a valuable piece of information."

"Yes, I know you're right," Isabella replies, "But I just keep thinking about what he did to Andre and Billy and my mother and all the others, and what little consideration he has for life, and great talent, and how he has so recklessly snuffed out so much, that I just don't give a damn about his past, I just want him brought to justice." Her eyes scan the faces of everyone at the table as she picks up a silver water goblet.

"Well spoken, Isabella," Lush says, "I've been wondering myself how we're actually going to catch the bastard. I don't think the police will be of much help, and I think Adrian's Gardner Treasure challenge is merely some sort of manipulative ruse. Why on earth would he put himself in a vulnerable position, even for those treasures? It just doesn't make sense to me."

"Maybe he wants to tell his story," Janet interjects.

"Tell his story?" Lush asks, directing her attention to Janet.

"Well, I don't know," Janet replies, dabbing her forehead, which has begun to perspire, with a handkerchief she has pulled from a pocket, "But maybe, just maybe, he senses that his game is about over and he wants to make himself known to someone who he knows, someone who might understand him. I see this quite a bit working in the ICU. People on the verge of death will often forcefully, willfully delay death until they are able to convey something, something vitally important to them, something they want understood or carried forth."

"Interesting, Janet," Lush replies. "As heartless as the man is, I'll have to say some of the correspondence between Billy and him, some of those emails where he mentored Billy over the past two years, might support what you're saying."

"You really think so, Lush?" I ask. "I still haven't read any of those emails on your advice to wait a while."

"I do, Todge," she replies. "Jonas, Mabry, you guys have read them all, what do you think?"

"Even the most ferocious dog seeks comfort from someone it trusts," Jonas replies, "It is possible, Philip." He looks into my eyes and asks, "Does Adrian trust you, Philip? Does he trust you at a deep level?"

I feel shock, then anger, then embarrassment, yet woven throughout all of these feelings is a thin thread of truth, truth which whispers into my ear that Uncle Adrian is always there for me, and I'm always there for him and the memories flood into my mind, the true knowledge that I always held that, even though Billy was clearly his favorite, I never, ever disappointed him the way Billy sometimes did, throwing off his affections for the pursuit of something more immediate, more exciting, like the pursuit of a snake or an invitation to the roller skating rink from a friend, instead of treasure hunting with me and Adrian. Yet he abandoned me too, just like Mother and Dad. Why? Did Fatgram have something to do with that? Did Dad?

I open my mouth to respond, nothing comes out. The inside of my nose below the bridge begins to burn and I know that tears are not far behind. I clear my throat, forcing myself to speak, "I know that when I was a boy, when Adrian was so involved in our lives…. I know that he trusted me on a deep level then. Does that sort of thing last?"

Isabella turns toward me, "I think it does, Philip. I think he trusts you in a strange way. How do you say it in English? Level playing field?"

"I don't follow, Isabella," I reply, sighing, trying to hold back more tears.

"I think the ten year old Adrian trusts the ten year old Philip," she enunciates slowly with tender emotion. "I certainly trusted Adrian when I was ten. I feel certain he trusted me, too."

I feel my eyes draining tears, but I'm not crying. "Yes, I understand now. I think you're right, Isabella." I take my napkin, dry off my wet face, sigh again loudly, look around the table, smile, and declare, "Well, I'm compelled on many levels to carry this thing through, but I'm going to need the support of everyone at this table to achieve the sort of éclat necessary to capture Adrian." Everyone erupts into phrases of support bordering on adulation. I laugh as tears stream down my face, grab Isabella's and Julianna's hands in mine and, almost instantaneously, everyone around the table joins hands sending good and powerful energy through my body the likes of which I have never known. This is what it feels like to be truly blessed.

The rest of the dinner seems to pass quickly; I feel as if I'm having an out of body experience even though I eat the delicious food, drink the outstanding wines, and participate in conversation, which shifts from Adrian to topics as varied as the malevolent military regime in Burma, the record prices for fine art spurred on by the almost worldwide economic boom, global warming, the exponential pace of technology, and Elizabeth II's upcoming eightieth birthday. Julianna remarks she has met the Queen once. Najeed smiles and after prodding from Lush reveals he has met the Queen on numerous occasions. The meat course is delectable: a stew Julianna refers to as Kathy's Triple B Stew, explaining it contains beef, boar, and buck. It reminds me of Beef Bourgunon, but this stew has morels, carrots, pearl onions, and parsnips in it. She serves a full-bodied Burgundy with the stew and as we eat, several different conversations occur. Isabella is curious about Billy's recent works and Julianna and I describe them to her. Julianna and I invite her to come for a viewing tomorrow before her return to Sante Fe. Najeed and Jonathan are discussing the rise of China and Lush, Jonas, and Janet listen to Mabry talk about encryption technology. We finish the meat course and a small salad is served which consists of a bed of baby arugula tossed in a dressing of reduced duck stock, a bit of balsamic vinegar, olive oil, Dijon mustard, and garlic. Thinly carved strips of duck breast and pretty, ribbony swirls of radishes top the salad. A red Zinfandel is served. Isabella remarks that it is often difficult to pair a wine with a salad because of the acidic tastes of most vinegars, but Chef Kathy has done an outstanding job with the peppery arugula, the choice of only a small amount of balsamic blended with duck stock and olive oil and the red Zinfandel. We all agree and the conversations dwindle as we eat the salad. Julianna suggests that we eat dessert in the Palm Court on the fifth floor, the only area in the house in which she permits smoking. Lush looks at me, raises her eyebrows, and smiles. I would truly love a cigarette now, but I am determined not to succumb. Everyone gets up from the table, some head to the elevator, some to the grand staircase, and I head to the men's room beside the Winter Gallery.

I enter the restroom and am immediately drawn into the warm finishes: raised paneled wooden walls of a deep brown color; dual full length black urinals encased like fireplaces with ornately carved wooden mantels supported by pairs of fluted, Ionic columns; a travertine floor, which looks as if it was taken from a thousand year old monastery in Europe, Persian runners in front of the urinals and the vanity; dual sinks, built into a paneled and carved wooden cabinet with wide fluted molding framing the front and sides; a large mirror, the width of both sinks, in a wide, gilt wooden frame, carved with scenes of pointers on point in the field, hangs above the sinks; two brass sconces cast into the shape of pheasants eating bunches of berries, the berries themselves consisting of clear and frosted glass beads surrounding small halogen lights, are anchored directly in the glass of the mirror above each sink; the ceiling, paneled with the same type of raised panels as the walls and outlined with wide, intricate crown molding, dotted with small halogen spot lights, four of which direct light toward four different Flemish tapestries hanging on the walls, all of hunting scenes and, on closer inspection, each one depicts one of the four seasons; two tall doors at the far end of the room, each with twelve raised panels, conceal the commodes, I suspect; placed in between the two sinks on the vanity is a large basket woven of some type of thick vine, filled with plush, white hand towels, and sitting in front of the vanity is an oval silver serving tray with raised sides, embossed with hunting scenes, holding bars of soap, mouthwash, small paper cups, a glass cylinder full of plastic combs

soaking in a sterile, blue solution, a small silver cup containing toothpicks, a bottle of men's hair spray, a bottle of men's hair gel, and a box of Kleenex under a silver cover. I walk up to one of the urinals, unzip my pants, and begin to pee. The door opens; I look back and up to see Mabry enter.

"Wow, this looks more like a library than a john," he says as he walks over to the other urinal and unzips his pants.

"Yes," I reply, "It certainly is a cozy, manly restroom."

"Awe," Mabry sighs as he lets out a strong stream of urine, which hits the urinal so loudly that I automatically look over to observe that his flaccid penis is quite large as it ejects a thick yellow stream of urine. I notice that he is looking at my penis at the same time out of the corner of his left eye, so I quickly avert my gaze back down to my own penis. I feel self-conscious about my smaller penis and my smaller stream of urine so I strain a bit to increase the flow of urine but in doing so I accidently let out a loud fart.

"Oh, excuse me," I say and look up at Mabry who starts laughing, then he squints his eyes, strains, and suddenly lets out a very loud and long fart.

"Boy, that was a good one," he says. "Must be all this fancy food. It sure is good dude, but I'm not use to it, especially with all the different wines," he replies, giggling like a child.

I realize Mabry must be a bit tipsy, and I find it so interesting that someone I categorized just a couple of days ago, with little thought on my part, as a computer nerd, albeit a brilliant, gay one, who happens to be the partner of a savvy, tough, handsome, commando, private investigator of the highest sort, could have so many facets in his personality, so I smile, visualizing a Ken Doll with a G.I. Joe Commando, and I finish peeing. I shake my cock, zip up, flush the urinal, and walk over to one of the sinks.

"So Mabry, what do you think the odds are that we catch Adrian?"

"Uhmmmm, well uhmm, I really think you're going to have to set a trap for him like he is doing for you. But only, your trap has to be more intelligently formulated and most importantly more enticing to him than his is to you," he replies in a matter of fact manner.

"Interesting," I say as I turn on the faucet and look up at my reflection in the mirror. "Why do you think we must entice him with a trap?"

I look into the mirror to watch Mabry as he turns his entire body slightly to the left toward me before turning his head further to the left to respond to me. His penis is visible again and I observe that if he turns anymore his stream of piss will escape the urinal and hit the wooden columns. He notices where my eyes fall and turns his body back toward the urinal. He is more intoxicated than I thought.

"Uhmmmm, because his profile, a least a narrow part of it, resembles mine, to some extent, anyway. People who like to encode generally like to decipher, too," he replies as I observe him shaking his cock with his left hand.

"Yes, that makes sense," I reply. "Does Jonas agree with this analysis of yours?"

"I haven't said anything to him about it. It just now occurred to me when you asked me if I thought we'd catch Adrian." He turns and walks to the other sink, turns on the water, takes a bar of soap, sniffs it, then rubs it vigorously in his hands underneath the stream of water.

"Well, do you think Jonas will agree with you when you tell him?"

"Oh, no, I don't intend to tell him. Jonas is the leader and the strategist. I can assure you he is not a trap setter but a stalk-and-ambush kind of guy. That's his training and that's definitely his style—to catch his prey by surprise."

"Interesting," I reply. "And what's his bag rate?"

"Pretty darn good. Let's just say we don't advertise, most of our clientele use us more than once and we work for the….well we work for several very high level organizations. We've recovered priceless art works for Julianna before. If you weren't her friend, it's unlikely we'd be working for you now."

"Well, I'm a fortunate man then, and I'm very happy you guys are on my team," I say as I dry my hands and throw the towel in a basket on the floor.

"I'll see you up in the Palm Court, Mabry," I say as I walk out.

"Okay dude," he replies, looking down at his hands as he continues to thoroughly wash them.

I walk back out into the elliptical hallway looking around to see if anyone else is around as I head toward the staircase to climb the five stories hoping to burn some calories after the lavish dinner. I hear Julianna's voice coming from above describing some technique an artist used in a painting. I observe the three paintings hanging on the walls of the initial curved flight but I cannot focus on them, as I am preoccupied with Mabry's advice on entrapping Adrian. What enticement or inducement could I devise that Adrian would find irresistible? This is something I must work on for it is my only chance to get Adrian alone. Even though Lush could probably help me figure this out, I will not include her in these plans, for she would never allow me to go through with them, whatever they may be. As I make my ascent I try to focus on what I remember about Adrian, what it was he liked about me, I mean really, really liked about me. I know he abused me first before Billy. I know he explored my body first after we had the Blood Brother's ceremony. What was it that really turned him on? I feel butterflies in my stomach and my cock suddenly begins to harden.

"Philly, your Mother's taking Billy to the doctor, he has thrown up again, he has a fever, and we can't determine what is the matter," Uncle Adrian says as he enters my bedroom. "Ala Mary's up at your grandmother's helping with some canning, so it's just the two of us. What do you want to do today?"

"I don't know," I reply.

"Well, it's still raining, so we'll have to stay inside or we could go see a movie."

"Do you have more gold coins, Uncle Adrian?" I ask, looking up from the thick album of colorful stamps collected by my grandfather, Fatgram's husband, when he was a boy.

"Oh yes, I have some delightful ones this trip. So you want to have a treasure hunt without Billy?"

"Well, he's sick and probably couldn't do it anyway," I reply.

"I see," he smiles, "Well, it will have to be an indoor treasure hunt. I haven't had my shower yet and you're still in your pajamas. Let's hit the shower together, and I'll give you the first clue."

"Okay," I reply excitedly already expecting to have to get naked with Uncle Adrian in order to get a clue.

"Come on then," he says, "We don't have that much time until Billy and your mother return."

I follow him down the hall to the guest bathroom, we enter, he closes the door and turns the lock.

"You get undressed, Philly while I turn on the water."

"Okay," I reply strip off my pajama top and bottoms and walk over to the toilet and start to pee. I hear Uncle Adrian turning on the shower and as I pee a thrilling sensation rolls through my belly as I imagine finding the gold coin. When I finish peeing I turn around and Uncle Adrian is standing behind me naked. His todger is hard and throbbing. He bends down to his knees, pulls me closer to him with his left hand on my butt, then takes his right hand and repeatedly runs it up and down the front of my chest to my own todger as if he were rubbing a dog's belly. He traces the contour of my nipples with his index fingers and makes small circles around my navel. He slowly spins me around, rubbing my butt and my legs.

"You're growing up, my pretty, pretty boy," he says to me. "Right now you are perfect, perfect, perfect, just on the precipice of puberty, just beginning to grow down around your todger and under your arms—sheer Heaven; you'll never ever be like this again—the most beautiful creature God ever made," he sighs deeply then takes my todger in his mouth as he strokes his own. My todger gets hard, really hard, so much so that it hurts, but then I feel a strange burning sensation in my groin area which culminates in a good, pleasant sensation in the head of my todger.

Uncle Adrian pulls his face back and smiles, "I think by the time I come back in July, you'll have matured even more. Here, rub my todger the way I showed you," he says as he sits on the edge of the

bathtub, the shower turned on full force behind him. I straddle his left leg and take his todger with my right hand. He pours a little baby oil on it and I begin to rub the long slippery todger as he grabs my still hard todger with his right hand and fastens his eyes on it.

"Oh, God it feels so good, Philly. Oh, yes, yes, yes."

I keep the pace up, thinking that this is such a weird way to get to do a treasure hunt, but it's worth it, and at least, he's not trying to stick his big cucumber in my butt today. I close my eyes and imagine that I'm climbing behind my waterfall where a pile of gold doubloons awaits me. Suddenly I feel his todger convulsing and it shoots out thick, white, warm, gooey stuff all over my chest. Uncle Adrian moans like a heifer dropping a calf, and I'm relieved this is over, for now anyway, and I get to pursue my treasure. Uncle Adrian is always true to his word about the treasure. If we keep our bargain by never telling anyone what we do with him to get the treasure, we always get more.

"Aw yes, good show, Philly. Let's jump in and wash off now."

We both get into the shower and Uncle Adrian takes a bar of soap, works up a good lather in his hands, and begins washing my body all over.

"Let's see, Philly, the word for you today is fenestration," he says as he kneels to scrub my butt and legs with a washcloth.

"Fenestration?" I ask. "That's a funny word."

"It's a good word," he replies. "Look it up and present me with a written sentence using it correctly. Then we'll start the hunt for the treasure."

"Okay, okay," I reply. "Let's hurry."

He stands up. "Shut your eyes. Let me wash your hair quickly." He directs me under the shower, turns me around to rinse me off, then squeezes shampoo onto my head and massages it in to a mass of lather while I keep my eyes tightly closed saying the word fenestration over and over in my head. He stops lathering and lets the shower rinse my hair and turns me around one more time.

"Perfect, Philly, you're as clean as can be. Hop out, dry off, and go get dressed. Then look up fenestration and write your sentence. I'll be along in just a bit."

I climb out, grab a towel, and begin to dry off, the excitement of the treasure hunt building with in me to such an extent, I can barely breathe.

I blink my eyes rapidly because the painting I'm looking at seems to be in black and white. The color returns instantaneously, and I realize that I'm looking at a painting of me Billy did a few years back when he came to Atlanta to stay for a couple of weeks to get away from New York. I didn't even recognize myself. I'm standing behind the sofa in my den—a cozy room with a large, beige, overstuffed sofa with big goose down pillows, two comfortable, brown, leather chairs with matching ottomans, a glass coffee table, built in bookcases, a couple of antique chests of drawers and a large Persian rug from Union, a Tiffany lamp Billy gave me, all arranged in front of a big bay window which looks out into my back yard, a shady enclave of tall deciduous trees in my urban neighborhood. I remember when he was sketching and painting in the den, and I couldn't figure out why the hell he was painting that room. That evening we stayed in and I had grilled strip steaks and cooked baked potatoes, his favorite dinner. He had been painting all day while I worked around the house, glad to be home from the road for a chunk of time. I walked into the den with a glass of red wine in my hand to tell him dinner was ready. I had decided to grow a beard, and I was wearing worn out blue jeans and a beat up blue and white stripe, button down oxford cloth shirt. I had not even showered all day. My neighbors had given me a good joint, so I had a couple of tokes while I was cooking. Billy looked up at me and shouted for me to stand there and just talk to him while I finished my glass of wine. I told him the steaks had finished resting and would be perfect now, so we really should eat, but he wouldn't let me move. So, I finished my wine while he talked to me. We ate dinner and the next day, the painting was gone and he didn't work on it anymore. I had never seen

the finished painting, but a year later, Lush sent me a picture of it in an art magazine article announcing that Billy had won a prestigious prize for it. I think it was $10,000. I'm going to miss my low-keyed life in Atlanta, but I know now that phase of my life is over, and I most certainly know I will build my trap for Adrian. Yes, indeed Uncle Adrian, I learned the word fenestration well that day, and I'll have another sentence for you soon. And suddenly I experience a sick realization: it was Uncle Adrian's vocabulary challenges and puzzles that first got me interested in writing, the passion I pursued and fashioned into my career. It's so strange, though, in the week since Billy's death, I haven't written one word.

"I'm headed up, man," Mabry says as he races up the stairs past me.

"I'm right behind you, bro," I reply, forcing a smile as I try to keep up with Mabry, thinking about how wonderful I'll feel when I figure out how I'm going to trick Adrian into meeting with me.

We both arrive on the fifth floor, breathless, and walk into the stunningly beautiful palm court, an elaborate, spacious, Victorian style, botanical conservatory fabricated atop the townhouse, containing a lush array of palms, philodendrons, orchids, hibiscus, bougainvillea, and other tropical flora. I immediately hear the sound of a waterfall, so soothing and grounding to me, and I noticed that a slender pool winds through the court. We cross over a small bridge with stone balusters and rails and I look down and observe several large orange, black, and white koi swimming. To the right of the bridge is a small limestone gazebo in the shape of a rotunda and to the left the path leads past an aviary containing a flock of vividly colorful finches.

"Wow, those little birds are beautiful," Mabry says as we pause to admire them.

"Yes, they are called Gouldian finches. They are native to Australia," I remark, feeling pleased that I'm able to teach Mabry something.

"Really? Are you a bird lover?"

"Well, I like most animals and birds, but I've done enough nature articles to have been exposed to a lot. I met up with these little guys in their native Australia in the Northern Territory a few years ago when I was working on an article. Sadly, they are extremely endangered in their native habitat. Yet, they are widely kept and bred in captivity here and in Europe."

"Cool, they're really cool. They don't look real, especially these," he says pointing to the colorful males.

That was a great assignment—thank you, Florence—to deliver an overview for *National Geographic* of a place most people know so little about. I spent nearly two months there traveling over the vast region touring the national parks, camping with Aborigines, learning about their rich and long heritage, visiting the cities from tiny Yulara in the south, to view the famous Ulura, to the largest city Darwin in the north, to Katherine, a city at the hub of the cattle raising area in the north which harbors the largest remaining wild flock of Gouldian finches, and yes, where I first made love to Katherine, the photographer from Sydney for *National Geographic* who joined me on the journey. Neither of us fell in love, but sexually, our chemistry was so intense, it catapulted us into a region of extraordinary vulnerability, each to the other, so much so, that after a night of intense love making, it was hard to look each other in the eye the next day, and we both yearned to escape from one another, which worked out well because she was one of two photographers on that trip, and she was on a dual assignment, so we would join together for hours of heated sex, fucking deeply, slowly, intensely, her damp, wavy brown hair, falling over my shoulders as she sat on my cock, and I, bending forward to lick her nipples and breasts, thrusting my cock up into her the entire time, sweat pouring down my body, each of us sending unspoken, yet audible signals to one another as to our nearness to orgasm, and when we achieved simultaneous orgasm as we did so many times together, we truly felt as if we were one and couldn't risk being torn apart, yet as I squirted my semen into her, her pelvic floor contracting around my throbbing cock, punctuated by the echo of her rhythmic, dual syllabic moans and her sweet salty taste, we both knew we could never sustain this level of intimacy beyond the realm of intense sex, and as we lay together, sometimes for a minute, sometimes more, intertwined after orgasm,

my erect cock still deep within her, we knew once we physically separated, the intimacy would recede like a tidal wave leaving the destruction behind, in our case, tortured souls. And after a period of several days or a week, we would meet up after work for cocktails, our eyes searching one another's, wondering if we could merge into ecstasy again, and so it went, for several weeks, and since that time, neither one of us has contacted the other. My cock is almost hard, and I realized I have both hands in my pocket guiding it down my right leg to conceal it. I clear my throat, looking at Mabry out of the corner of my left eye.

"Yes, I had no idea Julianna was a bird keeper," I abruptly say.

"Well, I'm not really," she says, walking toward us down the path. "They were father's passion. Mr. Darcy knows everything about them, too, so we keep them going. They really are a splendid part of the palm court."

"This court is spectacular, Julianna," I say.

"Thank you, Philip. It certainly helps one get through the New York winters," she replies, smiling, then she makes an inviting gesture with her hands, "You all come join us over here. We're getting reading to have dessert."

"Great," Mabry replies, rubbing his hands together as if he were cold, "Dessert is my favorite part of the meal."

"Do you like chocolate, Mabry?" Julianna asks.

"Oh, yes," he replies.

"Splendid," Julianna says, hooking her left arm around Mabry's right arm, "Kathy has prepared her lovely chocolate soufflé."

"Great," he says and they begin walking down the path. I smile and follow them. The path opens up into a central courtyard or patio area under the pinnacle of the conservatory with white, wrought iron chairs and lounges with thick cushions, covered in a pale yellow fabric with interlaced designs of white and gold rope crisscrossing through the fabric, trimmed with elaborate white, gold and yellow bullion fringe and large yellow and gold tassels. Two square white wrought iron tables with glass tops have been placed together. Our companions sit around the table in the cushioned chairs. Henri and Mr. Darcy stand around a serving cart, covered with a white tablecloth, upon which sits a very large, oval, sterling silver vessel with stag heads on either end, containing four bottles of champagne and ice. Tall crystal champagne flutes in the shape of a trumpet vase sit on an oval silver tray with the same stag head handles as the vessel. Celeste and Jiao pull open the lid on another serving cart and I see several individual chocolate soufflés, each with puffy light brown tops rising four or five inches above the white ramekins in which they were baked.

"I found them enjoying the finches," Julianna says as we approach the table. I look around for Najeed's bodyguards, but I don't see them. They could be observing, unseen from many places in this room. I hear the waterfall, but I don't see it either. Lush is sitting at the far end of the table so I walk over to her and take a seat next to her. She smiles at me, and I hear the pop of a champagne bottle as Henri opens one. He hands it to Mr. Darcy who begins pouring it into the flutes. Mabry takes a seat beside Jonas at the other end of the table and Julianna sits in the middle between Najeed and Isabella. Jiao and Celeste begin placing the soufflés, along with small silver cups containing whipped cream, sprinkled with something sparkling and orange, in front of each guest. There are yellow linen napkins and a sterling dessert fork and two sizes of sterling spoons at our places.

"We've have several good toasts this evening, and I would like to propose another," Najeed says, picking up his champagne flute in his right hand. "To our elegant hostess," he says, delivering his mesmerizing smile directly to Julianna, who absorbs it with an intense look of pleasure and satisfaction, much the same as will be on most of the faces around this table once we begin eating the chocolate soufflé. "To new friends," he says, still smiling, his head turning around the table as he looks into each person's eyes, "And to an old enemy we shall most certainly vanquish! Cheers!"

"I'll drink to that!" Lush says.

"Yes, indeed!" Jonathan shouts.

We all clink our flutes, take a sip of an almost perfect pale, golden champagne, with myriads of bubbles, forming and rising from the slender, delicate crystal flute bottoms, as if each glass contained an aeration stone powered by a pump, racing through the neck of the flutes, escaping into the air with minute pops and splashes I feel as I lean my nose close to the mouth of my flute to smell this nectar which upon sipping imparts on my palette a crisp, rich flavor of nuts, toffee, and honey. I watch Julianna take the larger spoon, scoop up a large blob of whipped cream, and plunged it into the middle of her soufflé. I, as well as everyone else, do the same. Then we begin to eat the soufflé and moans of satisfaction and phrases such as 'Oh my God', 'This is incredible', and 'I've never had such a great soufflé' fill the air, but I'm too focused on eating spoonfuls of mine, alternating with sips of this fine champagne to notice who says what. The soufflé is indeed outstanding: it is not too sweet, not too chocolaty; it is just the right warmness, and it is so fluffy that it dissolves on your tongue. Billy would have loved this. I truly hope he had at least one of these here before he....before he...before he died. It is so hard for me to say that he is dead. Even though he was murdered, he is dead. I sigh, take a sip of champagne, take a large spoonful of the soufflé, put it in my mouth, close my eyes, and say to myself, "this bite's for you my brother."

Night has fallen with a slight breeze; I hear dead leaves rustle; and even though it is unseasonably warm, the smell of autumn inundates everything. We are standing on the front porch of Mrs. Mobley's house, ears of Indian corn, their dry husks peeled back displaying shiny rows of red, white, black, and yellow kernels, hang on the door. To the right of the door someone has arranged a few bales of straw, upon which sit several large jack-o-lanterns aglow with fiery mouths, noses and eyes. Billy reaches out to stick his finger in the mouth of the one closest to him.

"No son, don't do that," Dad says, "You'll burn your finger and might catch your costume on fire."

Billy pulls his finger back and says, pouting, "Dad, I wanted to be a Battlestar Galactica Cyclon Centurion."

"I know you did son, but Mother didn't have time to make that costume. You guys look great as ghosts."

"But I don't wanna be a ghost," he whines.

"But you are a great looking, scary ghost, Billy. So is Philly," Dad says, looking down at me, and I dread what I know he is going to say. "Go ahead and ring Mrs. Mobley's bell, Philly. You can reach it."

I freeze. Even in a costume, I feel shy, and I hate all the attention these women give, and all the things you have to say and do just to get a piece of candy. I'd rather walk up to the store and buy a Baby Ruth bar than get dressed up in a costume and parade around town.

"Go ahead, Philly, ring the bell," Dad repeats in a more encouraging tone. I look at him through the two holes Mother has cut in this sheet. I wish she had cut a nose hole, too, because I'm getting hot and it's hard for me to breath in this thing. At least she cut holes for our arms, but she made us wear long sleeve white shirts, which adds to the discomfort. I sigh, reach up and push the doorbell. I hear the sound of Mrs. Mobley's toy poodle, Bubbles, yapping. The door opens and Mrs. Mobley's formidable figure appears. Bubbles, a tiny muff of black, curly hair, barking furiously, rushes at my feet, growling, flashing two rows of sharp white teeth, then retreats, then rushes again.

"Bubsy, these scary ghosts won't hurt you," she says in baby talk as she leans her bulk down to pick the dog up.

"Shhhhhh. Calm down. Momma won't let these scary ghosts hurt baby girl."

The dog shuts up, then whines, then growls again.

"Well, what have we here!" Mrs. Mobley exclaims through lips painted bright red, her grey hair in tight curls, like springs, all over her large head. She wears a calico smock dress with a pattern of tiny black

cats with arched backs, witches flying on brooms, and bats flying in front of a full, yellow moon. A pair of black, cat-eyes glasses hangs on a silver chain over her large bosom. I look down at her feet stuffed into black mules; her ankles and shins seem massive to me.

Billy pushes in front of me, holding up his plastic jack-o-lantern toward Mrs. Mobley and shouts, "Trick or treat!"

I hold up my jack-o-lantern and say, with much less enthusiasm than Billy, "Trick or treat, Mrs. Mobley."

She laughs and bends toward us holding Bubbles, who is growling, now revealing her considerable set of fangs for such a small dog, in her right arm.

Billy points to Bubbles, "That dog bit Brooker T."

Mrs. Mobley gasps, "Oh, sweet Bubsy wouldn't hurt a flea, Billy. She just doesn't like colored people, except, of course, my maid Beulah."

I'm thinking that silly excuse for a dog doesn't like anyone but Mrs. Mobley. Every time we ride our bikes past here she runs out and tries to bite our ankles. Hedda and Max would make minced meat out of her.

A convertible, full of teenagers rolls by slowly, Blondie's *Heart of Glass* blaring on the radio, and I hear female and male voices singing, 'Once I had love and it was a gas, soon turned out to be a pain in the ass' and they all shout the word 'ass' as loud as they can looking up at us, then laughing loudly.

Mrs. Mobley snarls, "Who was that in that car, Charles? Did I see Betty Jean Hays's girl in there? Riding around acting like white trash? I'm going to call Betty Jean up this minute and let her know what her daughter's up to."

"Trick or treat!" Billy shouts again, holding up his jack-o-lantern. "Got any chocolate?"

"Chocolate? Why no son, that'll rot your teeth out. I never give out candy. I've got these delicious red apples from North Carolina." She turns around, grabs a large red apple from a tray and puts one in Billy's jack-o-lantern, turns back around, grabs another apple and puts it in mine. Her husband used to be the best dentist in town before he disappeared, all of the sudden.

"Thank you, Mrs. Mobley," I say as I peer down at the giant and heavy apple, which takes up way too much room in my jack-o-lantern, room where candy should be.

"You're welcome, Philip," she replies.

Billy says nothing, but just keeps peering down into his jack-o-lantern.

"Billy, aren't you going to thank Mrs. Mobley?" Dad asks.

But I know he is not, because he's fixing to throw a fit. As soon as I think it, I hear a high-pitched wail that develops into a full-fledged cry, "But I don't wanna apple, Dad. I wanna chocolate candy bar!" He drops his jack-o-lantern on the porch, it rolls toward the steps, then bounces down the steps, throwing out pieces of candy, but not the big, red apple. Bubbles bolts from Mrs. Mobley's arms, letting out a trill of sharp yaps, chasing the rolling jack-o-lantern. Billy is heaving now and slowly turning a circle. His costume is off kilter and his eyeholes are on the side of his head. He falls to the porch in a screaming rage, kicking, trying to get out of the costume, gasping for air, and screaming, "I want chocolate."

"Bubbles, you git yourself back here right now," Mrs. Mobley shouts, hands curled into fists on her large hips, elbows pointing outward. The little dog obeys, scurrying back to his mistress who sighs, bends over, picks it up, kisses it on the head, and says, "Mummie doesn't want little girl to get run over chasing that nasty little boy's jack-o-lantern."

"Help your brother, son," Dad barks at me then turns to Mrs. Mobley, "Mrs. Mobley, I'm so sorry. Billy's just getting tired. I should have stopped. I should've taken them home fifteen minutes ago."

Billy is flailing around on the porch, so I set my jack-o-lantern down, squat down, grab him, and pull the sheet back around so he can see out of the holes. His sobbing begins to subside. I lean over and say to him, "Don't worry Billy, you can have my chocolate. I'll trade you for your Mary Janes and Sweet Tarts."

His sniffs loudly, and I can tell he needs to blow his nose, "Really, Philly?"

"Sure, now get up and let's go get your candy." I help him up and we walk down the stairs to get the spilled candy. As we are picking up the candy out of the front yard I hear Mrs. Mobley talking to Dad in a scolding voice.

"Charles, Ina always gave Eva anything she wanted, spoiled the girl rotten. Now I can see the same thing happening to your boys. It's a crying shame. You need to take a stronger stand in raising these children. You hear?"

Dad mumbles something to her but I whisper to Billy, "Fatgram's right about her, she's nothing but a sour old bitch. No wonder her husband ran off on her."

Billy says, "Yeah, but you're the best brother in the world, Philly."

I look up to see Henri filling my champagne glass and I look down to see I've consumed my entire soufflé. I look over at Lush who is leaning back smoking a cigarette, talking to Janet, who is also smoking.

"You were in some sort of chocolate consuming reverie, Todge."

I chuckle, "Yes, I was."

"Good memories?"

"Good and bad." I reply.

"Is that why you have tears in your eyes?" she asks.

"I do?" I reply, rubbing my face with my right hand, feeling the wetness on my face. I take my napkin and wipe my mouth, then my face.

"Geez, Lush. It's so weird; I keep having all these flashbacks. Things I never could've possibly remembered. Yet, I do. Vivid memories from way back. When I was a little boy. Six years old and younger."

"Philip," she says, putting her left hand on my right leg, "That's totally understandable, considering everything you've been through this week."

"You think?"

"Yes, I think," she replies, smiling beautifully, then takes a drag off her cigarette.

I look at her. I sigh. "You know, Adrian is setting us up with this treasure hunt. He has no intention of meeting me, ever."

"Of course, why would he? I can't figure out why he hasn't abducted Christopher and tortured the young man until he reveals the whereabouts of the Gardner heist."

"I was thinking the same thing, Lush."

"There's more to this, Todge. Even though the Gardner art is worth a fortune, is that what Adrian is really after?"

"I don't know, Lush, but something just doesn't fit," I reply.

She stares into my eyes, sighs, looks down, then back up at me, "You're planning something on your own. Aren't you, Todge?"

"You know me too well," I reply.

"What are you two talking about so secretively over there?" Julianna asks, looking at Lush and me.

"Just comparing notes," I reply.

"Hummn, scheming, I should think," she replies, "But aren't we better off joining forces?"

I look at her, smile, wondering if I am that fucking transparent, and reply, "You are absolutely right, Julianna. We are better off joining all of these fine minds. So, I'll put it to the floor. What are we going to do? Jonas?"

He looks me straight in my eyes, "Philip, what is it exactly that you want?"

"I want my brother's life back. And, Jonas, if you can't deliver that, then I want the life of the man who took Billy's life."

Dead silence. I immediately feel like shit for saying that; for being such a prick to Jonas. I stand up and slam my napkin down. "Where the hell is this waterfall I hear? I just wanna go crawl into a hole behind it." I begin to walk away from the table toward the sound of the water. I walk around a grouping of palm trees and follow the path along the koi pond until I arrive at the north end of the conservatory where I see the waterfall, a beautiful tall structure made of some sort of limestone or creek stone stacked high, surrounded by lush tropical plantings. A powerful pump must create the waterfall because it rushes down the stones with great force and volume. I kneel down beside the waterfall, feeling the spray thrown from it, wrap my arms around my knees, close my eyes, and cry. I cry for Billy. I want him back so badly. I wish this waterfall had a cave behind it, a cool, safe cave, in which I could curl up and sleep for eternity, knowing that I'm guarded by the creatures of the forest. I feel a hand on my back, and I expect it to be Lush or maybe Julianna. I turn my face up over my left shoulder and observe Jonas kneeling beside me, looking down at me with kindness in his blue-grey eyes.

"I'm so sorry for being such a prick back there," I say, sniffing and wiping my eyes.

He pulls out a clean white handkerchief from the inside pocket of his jacket and instead of handing it to me, he begins to gently dry my face with it, all the while looking at me with kindness, compassion, even love. I'm so surprised by this that my mood begins to change quickly. How could this macho private investigator, ex-cop, special agent be so gentle, so kind? He hands me the handkerchief, then wraps his arms around me, hugs me, pulls my face against his, and I feel the stubble of his beard.

"Philip," he whispers in his deep voice into my left ear, sending an avalanche of chills down my spine, "I know you are hurting deeply. I know what it is like to lose someone so close, someone you love so deeply." My gut feeling is that he speaks the truth and that this man is suffering as much as I am. "The details are unimportant, but, six years ago, while I was still with the NYPD, my partner—someone I loved more than I can put into words—died in my arms. His lifeblood poured out, literally squirted out all over me with each beat of his heart. I couldn't even begin to stop it, and I knew each beat of his heart was one beat closer to the last, and as I held him, and I told him I loved him, he smiled, he was too weak to speak, and I stared into his beautiful hazel eyes. I locked my eyes onto his; he locked his onto mine, and I watched the life recede from his body, from his eyes. He just faded away, the light in his beautiful eyes dimming to nothingness, and I could feel the life, his very soul emptying out."

He releases me from his grip, and I look up to see tears streaming down his face. I hand him back his handkerchief. He smiles, wipes his face and says, "Philip, let me catch Adrian. I am your man. I can do it. Don't risk your life; I know this business; I know his kind; I can bring him to you."

"Do you really know his kind, Jonas?" I ask. His eyes searching mine, looking for hidden meaning, his voice silent. "I know his kind, Jonas," I tell him. "You see, I am one of Adrian's kind."

His eyes open wide. "I don't understand, Philip."

"I've done my share of hurting people, Jonas, people I love very much."

He stares into my eyes, all his mental and physiological sensory receptors activated in full force. I stand up hoping his gut feeling about me will prevail.

"I think we all have, to some extent, Philip," he replies as he stands up, turns, and walks away.

We have all assembled in the Winter Salon, which is, in fact a library, the walls and ceilings fabricated in rectilinear raised panels of oak, stained a rich chestnut color; leather bound volumes fill bookcases built in all four walls between the paneled sections; the floor, an intricate diagonal parallelogram herringbone parquetry with threes shades of stain—light, medium, and dark—is covered with very large oriental rugs, which look like the big Heriz rugs Fatgram had in her house that auctioned for thousands of dollars when Billy and I liquidated her estate and sold the house ten years ago; large antique wooden library tables are dispersed throughout the room on which sit various ornate reading lamps, some Tiffany, I suspect; a huge old globe is positioned between two tall windows, adorned with silk brocade draperies with a pattern of

floral designs in white, gold and green on a red background, held back by ornate bronze holdbacks in the shape of acanthus leaves, the cornices are covered in the same fabric; antique tapestries with various scenes of medieval life hang from the exposed paneled sections; there are several groupings of upholstered furniture, some in leather, some in fabric, and side tables dispersed throughout the room; and a large fireplace, containing burning logs, with an ornate mantel carved out of black and grey marble is located at the far end of the room and a large painting of a woman in a silver, evening gown, her slim waist is accentuated by a long sash tied around her waist and by the full, floor length skirt and train, the bodice is low cut, exposing a voluptuous cleavage, the sleeves are short but full and puffy, her hair is pulled and pinned up, she wears a strand of diamonds around her neck and holds a large feather fan, she stands in front of a tapestry. Five easels, each covered with a white cloth are arranged in front of the fireplace. We all approach the fireplace.

"What a marvelous painting, Juliana," Lush says walking up to observe the portrait over the fireplace. Darcy and Henri arrive with silver trays containing the after dinner drinks for those who requested them. Henri gives me a disapproving look as he hands me my B&B in a carved crystal sniffer. I just smile at him as I take it.

"Thank you Lush," Julianna says as Darcy hands her a glass of champagne, "That is my great great grandmother, Elise. The painting is a Sargent done in 1900 at the Biltmore Estate in North Carolina. Elise was a close friend to Edith Stuyvesant Dresser, who married George Washington Vanderbilt."

"How wonderful it is," Isabella says with a look of sadness, "And how wonderful that you have such a long, rich family history that such a masterpiece still remains in your home today."

"Why thank you, Isabella. Mother's family goes back to the roots of New York. Now father's, on the other hand," she continues with a laugh, "Well, we've never gotten any further than one generation back in the steel mills around Akron. But it doesn't matter one bit. I loved my father more than I can say, and he was certainly one of the hardest working people I've ever known." She looks down at Isabella who now looks as if she is about to cry and asks, "Darling are you alright?"

"Oui," she replies, sighing, then smiling. "I'm just thinking that the only time in my life I really had a family was when mother and Andre and I were virtually living on the streets of Paris. Father had run away, God knows where, and we never knew from one day to the next where we would be sleeping that night or how we were going to get our next meal. But mother was always positive and almost made a game of it for Andre and me. We were poor, but happy, and we were a family."

"Isabella," I say, "But didn't you ever feel that Adrian was part of your family?"

She focuses her large brown eyes on me, "Yes, Philip, I did. But after all I know now, I can't consider him family, can I? Mon Dieux. Et vous? Can you?"

"No, I can not." I reply and take a sip of the warm, sweet, thick B&B.

"Well," Julianna says, "I certainly consider you all my family here. We are a group of people who care about each other and have some similar interests. One being Mr. McWhorter, but I think we've spent time enough on him this evening. I'd like to end the evening on a very positive note. I've learned over the years that good things do in fact come out of bad or unpleasant experiences. Sometimes they are not readily apparent, sometimes they are. One thing I'm certain of is that an angel has descended among us—the same angel that cared for Billy Hampton in his last hours on earth and tenderly held his hand as he took his last breath. This angel is Janet Ostro, and I would like to reintroduce her to you all tonight as not only an angel in her vocation as a nurse, but as an angel who captures the very essence of what it is to be human in the wonderful oil paintings she has created. Behold these five paintings. They speak for themselves."

Julianna nods her head and Darcy and Henri quickly remove all the white cloths covering the easels, revealing five portraits of people, all painted on canvases of the same size which appear to me to be about two feet wide by three feet tall. My eyes quickly scan the five portraits until they settle on the middle one which is of a thin, old woman sitting in a Lazy-Boy type reclining chair, peeling a potato with a knife.

Something seems so disturbing or out of whack with this painting. What is it? Yes! I see it. The woman is dressed as if she came out of the nineteenth century, but she is in repose in an upholstered recliner in a late twentieth century den. Her long sleeve dress is black with buttons running all down the front. She wears a white, crocheted shawl around her shoulders. Her grey hair is pulled back into a bun. Her grey eyes peer down at the potato she holds in her bony, arthritic fingers. I know she must have peeled thousands of potatoes in her day because half of the potato is peeled and one long continuous ribbon of skin hangs down, curling at the end, underneath the potato. A basket of unpeeled potatoes sits on the floor to the left of her feet, a bowl of peeled potatoes sits to the right of her feet, and a newspaper onto which the long curls of peelings have fallen lies in front of her feet. She sits by a window, through which you see three little girls in bathing suits, one whirling a hoola hoop around her waist, playing around a water sprinkler. Her face and her eyes tell the rest of the story. I know this woman must have immigrated to America in the 1930's or 40's. She must have come from Eastern Europe, maybe Poland. Janet told us her heritage is Polish. Perhaps she lived through World War II in Europe? Her face is so aged, sagging and wrinkled, but her eyes, though tired, do not look old. She must be thinking about her youth, her home country, her own parents, the man or men she loved, the children she had, the children she lost, the world she knew which has vanished. I want to reach out, touch her cheek, and tell her I admire her for all she has been through and that the love in her heart keeps all those memories alive. I cannot believe how alive this old woman seems to be here in this moment. I sigh deeply, literally pulling myself away from this painting to the next one beside it. Holy smokes! What a contrast. This is a painting of a real babe—a genuine motorcycle chick in cut off jeans, white sandals, and a halter-top. She is not a tattooed chick, but a feminine babe with darkly tanned skinned, red lipstick, red toe nails and fingernails, and an incredible set of large tits, nipples evident through the white fabric, with a life of their own, wanting to burst out of the white halter top. Her blonde hair is pulled back and braided into one long, thick strand; she holds a lit cigarette in her left hand; she gazes out looking at someone with a mischievous smile on her face. Her eyes are bright and blue and inviting; she is sultry. The look on her face says it all—she knows how to have fun and she doesn't give a shit what other people say about her. Her right arm is around the waist of a well-built dude, his muscular, hairy arms sticking out of his tight, white T-shirt, revealing a skull and cross bones tattooed in black on the bulging bicep of his left arm. They sit on a beautiful blue and chrome Harley Davidson, his feet still on the ground, just preparing to start their ride. He wears long, faded Levi's, dusty black cowboy boots, and a thick black leather band on his left wrist. His aviator sunglasses reflect the gauges of the motorcycle as his face, framed by mutton chop side burns and a goatee, tilts down; a cigarette with a long ash hangs from his lips; his wavy brown hair almost reaches his shoulders. I am instantly jealous because I know he gets to fuck this babe. Who are these people? Are they related to Janet? I wonder as I look at the next painting to the right of this one which is a young woman holding a chubby, diaper clad infant, an image that immediately brings to mind a Mary Cassatt painting, except that this painting is not impressionistic, but realistic, and the setting is modern. I see that she has a pleasant round face with arching eyebrows and a button nose as she smiles adoringly at the baby, her baby, I presume, sitting in her lap, facing her, her left hand, a gold wedding band and a small diamond engagement ring on the ring finger, supports the back of the child who reaches up both of its chubby arms, fat fingers and thumbs curled into its palms, its round face broadcasting an exuberant, toothless smile, and big brown eyes open wide with excitement, toward a plastic rattle the woman dangles at the child in her right hand. She wears a sleeveless, boat neck, shift made of white and red polka dot fabric with a braided red and white tie around her waist; long brown hair curls around her shoulders, framing the healthy, clear skin of her face and neck. Her arms are not muscular, but youthful and toned. They sit in a white wicker chair on the front porch of a house. A green, potted fern, a small folded towel and a baby bottle sit on a round table next to them. Mother would have loved this painting.

We all make way silently for one another as we peruse the paintings. I walk over to the first painting on the left where Lush stands and begin to examine it. This painting is also of a woman holding a child,

but it tells a much different story than the other one. A grim-face, big-boned woman, clad in a stretched out T-shirt with holes in the tail and tight fitting, black, stretch pants, stands in the front doorway of what literally appears to be a shack, holding a large, sleeping baby, its right leg dangling, its left leg, head, and torso, curled into the woman's large bosom. Her brown hair is stringy, greasy, hanging down in curving strands to her shoulders. Tightly drawn lips, furrowed brow, and sad brown eyes project her state of despair. A naked light bulb hangs from the ceiling behind her throwing light on five small grimy faced children who peer out from behind the women. I remember Janet saying she had volunteered in Appalachia; this scene has to be taken from there. This painting transfixes Lush. She pulls close into me.

"Todge, when I was in high school, our church youth group spent a week one summer helping out the poor in Eastern Kentucky. This painting captures everything I witnessed about those poor people. It's amazing. Janet is truly gifted."

"I agree," I whisper to her, "I'm so glad Julianna found her."

She shakes her head in agreement and we both turn toward the next painting, a self-portrait of Janet with her two dogs Harry and Sally. I love this painting; the expression on her face exudes the care and compassion I've experienced from her. She is not smiling, but the corners of her lips are slightly turned up as if she were about to smile. Her blue eyes portray confidence, contentment, and peace. She is seated in a large, overstuffed chair, covered in a blue and brown houndstooth pattern fabric, with one dog sitting in her lap and the other on her right side. The dog in her lap, ears alert, eyes confidant, pointed snout facing the viewer, has a shaggy, tri-colored coat of rust, black, and white. The other smaller dog, mainly having a black and tan coat, lies beside Janet, its head resting on its front paws, its ears also alert. Janet wears a white blouse and black pants. Her right hand rests on the smaller dog and her left hand holds the chest of the dog in her lap. A tray table containing books, magazines, and a basket with several skeins of yarn and a pair of knitting needles sits to the right of the chair. I wonder if she painted this from a photograph of if she composed it from her mind? She doesn't hide her obesity, but the painting is not about a fat woman at all, but about a woman who loves her life and her situation in life. The dogs seem to be saying to me, "You can look at this treasure, this tower of kindness, love, and compassion, but if you get to close, we'll bite you!" This is my favorite painting of the bunch because I have experienced the truth of it first hand.

"Well, everyone," Julianna says, "I can tell you've all been engrossed in these paintings. What do you think?"

We all turn around to face Julianna. Janet, a worried expression on her face, stands beside her. In unison we all begin clapping our hands, and I watch an enormous smile unfold across Janet's face.

CHAPTER 37

The elevator door opens into Billy's foyer where Clark sits, wagging his tail. He jumps up to greet us as we enter the hallway.

"Hey, pretty boy," Lush says as she bends over to stroke his head.

"Do you think he hears the elevator?" I ask. "But how does he know it's going to stop here and that we are on it?"

"The little boy is psychic," Lush replies as she continues petting him.

"Must be," I reply. "The only time I've seen him come out here is when someone actually is coming here."

"Well, the doorman always rings up to announce a visitor," Lush says. "Maybe he relates that call to people getting off the elevator."

"Yeah, but, no one rang up to announce us, and here he is," I reply.

"Duh, stupid of me. You're right, Todge. Somehow he senses this."

I look at my watch as I lean over to pet Clark, "Damn, it's eleven thirty!"

"You tired, Todge?"

"No, not really, Lush. But tonight's dinner seemed to last forever," I reply. "Not that it wasn't outstanding and the information we gleaned astonishing, it just seemed like we were there for hours and hours."

"I know what you mean, Todge. Wanna night cap here or are you ready to turn in?"

"You know what, Lush. I'd like a sidecar. Want one?"

"Sure."

"I'll make them. It's not too cold. Let's have them on the terrace. You can smoke and Clark can pee."

"It's a deal," Lush says, "I'll meet you out there in five. I'm going to get out of this dress and into something comfortable."

"Okay, see you shortly," I reply.

Lush walks into the living room and turns down the hallway to her room. Clark follows her. I hear her say hello to Officer Graham who is sitting on a sofa in the living room reading a book. I walk into the living room, which has been returned to normal, except for several additional pots of white orchards dispersed throughout, and I walk over to the large hall table on which the blue and white ginger jar containing Billy's ashes sits.

I say to myself, "Dear brother. I will get to the bottom of this for you. You must have known more about all this than I know and it cost you your life. Guide me, Billy. Help me catch Adrian. Help me, please."

My eyes drift over the jar taking in the exquisite detail of the bamboo branches, the pine branches and gnarled trunks, the delicacy of the prunus blossoms, the three of which form the 'Three Friends of Winter Motif', and I smile and think how similar this is to H.R.'s tattoo on his back. No wonder I feel so connected with him.

"Hello, Mr. Hampton?" Officer Graham asks.

I look over at her, "Oh, good evening Officer Graham."

"Did you have a nice evening at Miss Morgan's?"

"Yes, it was very nice. Quiet around here, I suppose?"

"Yes, very. Clark kept me company all evening," she replies, and I notice a Styrofoam cup of coffee on the end table next to her.

"It's a shame you don't just make some coffee here. You're more than welcome, Officer Graham," I say, scratching my head with my right hand.

"Thank you, Mr. Hampton. I really appreciate your generosity, but I prefer to remain as unnoticed here as possible. I am here to protect you all, not to mess up your kitchen," she says, smiling.

"Yes, I understand, but if you need anything at all, make yourself at home," I reply, turn around, touch the jar with my right hand, and I turn to walk to the bar to make our sidecars. I take out the Cointreau and the Courvoissier and find a lemon and an orange in the bar refrigerator. I ice two martini glasses, fill them with water and get out the shaker and a jigger. I begin to make the drinks without even thinking about it. My mind wanders over the events of the past week, but it keeps returning to Adrian. Is the Gardner heist really enough to bring him out, bring him to me? Julianna says the value of all the works stolen probably exceeds half a billion dollars—in fact, she says it's the largest single property theft in recorded history. I suppose that would be big enough, even on the scale of the immense wealth of the Middle East, to get Adrian's interest. He probably really does already have the works placed as he said in his letter. No way

390

in hell, even if I did find the stolen art, would I give it to Adrian. It would go straight back to the Gardner Museum. So, I go to Kentucky, go to that Abbey where Christopher is, reveal Adrian's evil doings. Then what? Can I possibly hope to gain Christopher's trust, someone who has committed his life to the Catholic Church? Can I possibly convince him to take me to his family farm in Bardstown and just give me the Gardner treasure? Oh shit, that's ridiculous. But I have to try. Somehow. I have to talk to him. I have to try. I have to go to Kentucky this week. How am I going to maneuver through all this with Jonas and Lush and Juliana? I promised to come clean with Jonas tomorrow, and I will. He has to know what I did to Billy and how deeply I am connected to Adrian in such an evil way. I look down to observe that I've already poured the liquor and lemon juice in the shaker, so I put ice into it, put on the top and begin to shake vigorously. Lush likes her drinks shaken hard enough to cause little ice crystals to float on top of the liquid. The phone rings, I put the shaker down and answer it."Yes, hello."

"Philip, it's Timmy downstairs. Mr. Grey and Mr. Whittaker are down here. They say it's urgent that they see you."

"Oh, yes, well please send them up right now, Timmy."

"Who was that?" Lush asks as she walks into the bar area wearing jeans, a pair of fleece lined bedroom slippers and a white turtleneck underneath an unbuttoned, navy and white cardigan. Clark is by her side and he stands there looking up at me, wagging his tail.

"Timmy. Jonas and Mabry are on the way up now. Something urgent."

"Oh crap," Lush replies, "What could it be?"

"Don't know," I say as I pick up the shaker and begin to shake it vigorously again. Lush pours the ice and water out of the glasses.

"Want me to sugar the rims?" She asks as I continue to shake.

"Not for me. I think the drink is sweet enough, already."

"Me, too," she replies.

I pour the drinks into the glasses and Lush garnishes them with an orange twist. Clark's ears perk up, he turns, and trots through the living room to the foyer.

"There he goes, intuition working again," I say with a smile.

"Amen," Lush says. "Cheers, Todge."

"Cheers, Lush." We tap glasses and taste our drinks.

"Let's go greet them," I say.

Before we get through the living room, Jonas and Mabry are in the foyer.

"Hello, Clark," Mabry says.

"Where's Officer Graham?" I ask Lush.

"She was going to the bathroom when I walked through to the bar," Lush replies.

"Big news," Jonas says as he walks into the living room.

I put my right index finger to my lips and make a 'shhhh' sound.

"Oh, okay," Jonas replies in a hushed voice, "Ricky Wallitsch died this evening. The surgery to relieve the pressure from the subdural hematoma formed in his head when he fell was not successful."

"Oh how awful," Lush says. "Yet another needless death at the hands of Adrian."

"Speak of the devil," Jonas says. "Mabry received an email from him directed to you, Philip. It was short. It said: 'My Dearest Philip. Now that my little Billy and little Ricky are gone and can't help me with my treasure, you're the only one left. You have seven days from today to retrieve it. Please contact me when you have it. Uncle Adrian.'"

"Shit! So Billy and Ricky were looking for the treasure for him!" I shout in a whisper. "What's he going to do if I don't deliver?"

"I'm afraid we know that, Todge," Lush says. "He's already threatened the children."

"Yes. But why the urgency?" I ask. "Something's going on we don't know about."

"It could be anything, Philip," Jonas says.

"Yes, but why all of the sudden, that art heist took place in 1990. Why does he have to have it within seven days?" I ask.

"Well, maybe Adrian's gotten himself into a major pickle, and that treasure is his only way out," Lush says and takes a sip of her sidecar. "Hmmm, this is good, Todge. Jonas, Mabry. Would you fellows like something to drink?"

"I'll have a scotch on the rocks with a twist, Lush. Thanks." Jonas replies.

"Nothing for me, Lush. Thanks." Mabry says.

"We were going to sit out on the terrace with our drinks," I say. "I hope it's not too cool."

"It's forty-eight degrees," Mabry replies, "Not too cold."

"Okay, let's go by the bar for Jonas's scotch," I reply.

I taste my sidecar again. It is a good drink. It tastes like a margarita made with brandy. We walk into the bar and I take out a bottle of 18-year-old Glenlivet.

"This okay, Jonas?" I ask.

"Perfect, but I'll have that neat," he replies.

I take out a crystal bar glass and pour in a healthy shot of the scotch and hand it to Jonas.

"Thanks, Philip." He holds up his glass. "Well, cheers. Here's to Louisville, I suppose?"

We clink our glasses and take a sip.

"Well, logistics-wise, it's a good week to go," Lush says, "Everyone can stay at my house. I've got plenty of room and my husband will be in Florida fishing."

Jonas looks at me, "What do you think, Philip?"

"Well, I have nothing against going to Kentucky, but something just doesn't seem right."

"Let's go outside," Lush says. We follow her out onto the terrace to one of the wrought iron tables. We all sit down. Clark sees that we are settled, turns his muzzle up into the breeze, sniffs deeply, and then trots over toward his grass patch. Lush smiles as she observes Clark, takes her cigarettes from a pocket in the cardigan and lights up.

"What if Adrian is just trying to get us out of New York?" I ask. "I mean we are not certain that Benny was after the Swiss Army knife here. What if there's something else he's after?"

"Well, that's possible, Philip," Jonas replies, "But my gut tells me he really thinks you can find the stolen artworks through Christopher O'Bryan," he replies, looks over at Lush, raises his eyebrows, then takes a sip of his scotch.

"Do you really think that, Jonas?" I ask, noticing that I can see my breath, and I see Officer Graham peering through the kitchen windows at us.

"I really do, Philip. Half a billion dollars of art is even a huge amount in Adrian's circles," he replies.

"Yes, I guess you're right," I say, pulling my blazer around me as a breeze is picking up and the air feels cold to me, "I was wondering about that just a minute ago. It is a lot, even for Adrian."

"It's scary to think how far his reach is," Lush says. "I mean, how many people in this city could know that Ricky died just a few hours ago? Yet Adrian already knows."

"Yes, he has a strong network here in New York," Jonas says, "We're trying hard to penetrate it, but it's taking some time. What I'm finding out is sketchy. But, I have a CIA buddy who owes me big time. He thinks he may have something for me by tomorrow."

"That's good news," I reply.

"Yes, keep your fingers crossed," Jonas replies. "Listen, Philip. Julianna told me Cara Bridgefield lives in Chicago. I think I should fly there tomorrow and try to meet with her."

"Sure, sounds like a good idea. No telling what she really knows about Dyanne and the Gardner heist," I reply.

"I'm certain a meeting will be beneficial. Then I could meet you all in Louisville on Tuesday," Jonas replies. "Mabry can hold down the fort here."

I look over at Mabry who is being especially quiet, so I ask, "Are you okay, Mabry?"

"Oh, I'm fine. Just a little tired. I think I drank too much at Julianna's."

I see Jonas look at Mabry with concern. "He's been fighting a cold for a couple of days. He needs rest. I better get him home."

"Yes, you better," I say, standing up. "Look, let's go with your plans Jonas. I'll try to get in touch with Christopher tomorrow to see if he'll meet with me. Maybe we can get to his aunt Joan also through him. Julianna says they are very close."

"Okay, sounds good," Jonas says. "We've done a thorough review of the Gardner heist, and I have a friend who worked on the case. He told me today that all the evidence leads to a Mafia connected heist, but two men dressed in police uniforms did it in an extremely amateurish way. Ted Johnson and Dyanne O'Bryan are not suspects at all. Although, I cannot explain the Polaroid of Ted holding up that eagle finial. It could have been a fake I suppose. Maybe he was trying to swindle Adrian out of some money." He pauses to take a sip of his drink. "Meanwhile, the police are going to be buzzing after Ricky's death because it is now a murder. I'm sure they'll want to see you tomorrow, Philip."

"Yes, I'm sure you're right, Jonas," I reply.

"Okay, we'll talk tomorrow," Jonas says, turns up his glass, emptying it. "Thanks for the drink. Mabry, let's go buddy."

"Alright, I'm ready," Mabry says, standing up. "See you all, soon."

Clark hears the wrought iron chairs moving and trots back over.

Lush stands up, too. "Gentlemen, I have a good feeling about the Bluegrass. Something will turn up, and I intend to show you a good time."

"Can't wait, Lush," Jonas says and turns to walk back inside. Lush, Clark and I escort Mabry and Jonas to the elevator. Officer Graham is sitting in the foyer writing in a little notebook. Mabry and Jonas exchange greetings with her. She gives me a look of suspicion.

"Goodnight, Jonas. Goodnight Mabry," Lush says.

"Night," Mabry replies.

"Goodnight, Lush," Jonas replies.

I wave to them as the elevator door closes, and I turn around to Officer Graham, "Well, I guess you know Ricky is dead?"

"Yes, I do. He died at 8:43 pm this evening," she replies. "I suppose that's the reason for the late visit from Mr. Grey?"

"Yes, indeed," I reply. "Goodnight, Officer Graham."

"Goodnight, Mr. Hampton, Mrs. Richardson," she replies.

"Goodnight," Lush says.

We turn and walk down the hall to the kitchen, followed by Clark.

"I can't believe that bastard has given me an ultimatum, Lush."

"Really," Lush says yawning, "Who the hell does he think he is? With all the police involvement and our hiring Jonas, I'd say he's walking on thin ice. I don't care how connected he is to al-Qaeda."

I pull my cell phone from my coat pocket and see that I have two messages, one from Florence and one from Dad. "Wonder what Dad wants?" I ask as I dial my voice mail and hear Dad's voice.

"Hi Son. Sorry to bother you. Gosh, it was good spending time with you. Brenda, the kids, well, we all really loved being there with you. Listen, Emma left her little pink backpack there. She says she hid it in the closet in the guest suite. She said there's a secret compartment in the main clothes closet. Brenda and I aren't sure what she's talking about, but we didn't have the pack when we got home, so Emma probably

did leave it there. Please see if you can locate it. I'd really appreciate it if you could UPS it to us. Thanks, Son. Love you."

"Oh my God, Lush. Listen to this message." I press "1" to replay the message and hand it to Lush. After a moment, her mouth falls open and she snaps the phone shut.

"Crap, Todge, let's get in there now," she says and begins to run toward the studio.

"Wait up!" I yell. Clark runs ahead of me as I start after Lush. By the time I get there, she has all the lights on in the guest suite and is opening the closet door. It is a large walk-in closet with built in drawers, compartments for shoes, lots of shelving, and six different rods for hanging clothes. We begin looking around, opening drawers, pushing on shelves, and feeling the walls.

"Well, nothing's in these drawers and it doesn't appear they come out too easily," Lush says.

I notice that there are two one-foot sections of raised paneling separating two of the hanging sections. "These two areas are wide enough to have something between them," I say. I press against the lower panel on one of the sections and it immediately springs open revealing a tall narrow storage space. "Look over here, Lush!"

Sitting on the floor of the small closet is Emma's pink backpack.

"Well, I'll be damned," Lush says. "Anything else in there, Todge?"

"No, it's empty."

"Wonder if this one does the same thing?" Lush asks as she pushes against the panels. Sure enough the panel is actually a door with hidden hinges and it pops right open. We look inside to find several large canvasses and a portfolio.

"What are these?" Lush asks.

"Don't know, but let's take a look. Here let's pull out the biggest one first." I grab the edge of a canvass that must be a little over five feet tall. I carefully pull it out to reveal a beautiful oil painting of a sailboat on a stormy sea. Lush looks at the painting as I turn it around illuminating it.

"Dear God, Todge, this couldn't be, could it?"

"Couldn't be what, Lush?"

"One of the stolen paintings from the Gardner museum. Julianna was talking about Rembrandt's *The Storm on the Sea of Galilee* tonight. This looks just like it, I think."

"Do you think Billy already found the Gardner heist, Lush?" I ask still wondering what the hell I'm looking at.

"Does the canvas look old, Todge?"

I flip it around. "Look, it's definitely got some age on it, Lush, but I really have no idea."

"We need Julianna over here, Todge. Put that one over here and see what else is in there."

I lean the large painting against a shelf and take out the next canvas, which is almost as large as the first one. I rotate the front of the canvas to the light.

Lush gasps, "Oh my God, Todge, that has to be a Rembrandt. Look at it."

It does indeed look like a Rembrandt and is a scene depicting a standing gentleman in black with a wide, round lacey collar lying flat against his shoulders and upper torso and a seated lady in a black dress with a round white erect collar that looks like some kind of medical neck brace. She sits on a chair with a brilliant red cushion and another chair in the foreground of the painting has the same red cushion.

"It does indeed look like a Rembrandt," I say. I lean this painting against another shelf and retrieve another canvas. This one depicts a seated lady in profile playing a piano or a harpsichord. A gentleman, whose back is to the viewer, sits beside her. Another lady is standing, facing the viewer, and holding what must be music. The floor is black and white marble squares, and a couple of paintings hang on the wall above the harpsichord.

"Hmmm, I don't know whether that's Dutch or maybe Spanish," Lush says.

"Yeah, me either," I reply.

"Todge, see what else is in there, I'm going to get my computer and Google the Gardner heist," Lush says and quickly leaves the room.

Clark, who has been sniffing the paintings profusely, trots after her. I pull out two more paintings. One is oil on board roughly a foot and a half tall by two feet wide and is a beautiful landscape painting with an obelisk in the distance. The last painting is even smaller and is oil on canvas of a man in a black suit and tall black top hat writing in a journal with a glass of wine beside him. I pull out the portfolio and open it to find five charcoal and watercolor drawings on paper: two are equestrian scenes, one of a city somewhere, and two showing musicians and perhaps a couple dancing. Something shiny catches my eye in the portfolio and I lean over and pull out a small, clear plastic sleeve, which contains what appears to be an etching of an unshaven man with long curly hair cascading from underneath a cap. The etching is only a couple of inches tall and wide.

Lush walks back in the room, accompanied by Clark, who has a rawhide bone in his mouth, with her laptop open in her hands. She surveys the artwork.

"Dear God in Heaven, Todge. It is the Gardner heist. We're looking at half a billion dollars worth of art on the floor here. Take a look at this article." She turns the screen around toward me and I read about these eleven works of art, one Vermeer, three Rembrandts, five by Degas, a Manet, and one by Govaert Flinck.

"Billy must have gone to visit Christopher or Joan," I say, "Somehow he managed to discover these. The only pieces missing are the finial and the Yu. There's nothing else in the closet."

"Well, now we can land Adrian," Lush says.

"Yes," I reply looking at Clark, who has settled on the floor by Vermeer's *The Concert*, vigorously gnawing his bone. "Do you think it's too late to call Julianna?"

"Well, it's one a.m., probably so. Let's call her first thing in the morning," Lush replies, and then yawns. "What an exciting find. Thanks to little Emma. Did you get her pack?"

"No. I'll get it. Bless her heart," I reply. "Now I can go to sleep and dream about dealing with Adrian." I walk over and pick up the pack.

"Damn! What's she got in here? It's so heavy for a little girl."

"Open it, Todge," Lush demands.

I unzip it and to our amazement, I pull out a large bronze Yu vessel and the eagle finial.

"Well, I'll be damned," Lush says. "Maybe Emma found the Gardner heist. I think she should get the five million dollar reward. Yes, indeed Todge, you'll definitely dream about dealing with Adrian now," Lush says with a devious smile erupting across her face. "I suppose we should call Julianna and Jonas first thing in the morning."

"Yes, let's do that. Maybe I'll try to get ahold of Christopher O'Bryan, too. What's the name of his abbey?"

"It's called Saint Meinrad's; it's about an hour west of Louisville in the hills of Southern Indiana," Lush replies. "It's lovely. I've been there a couple of times."

"Well, do you think if I just call a general number there and ask for Christopher O'Bryan, they'll let me talk to him?" I ask.

"Well, I don't see why not, Todge," Lush replies, looking at the Vermeer, "It really is a lovely painting."

"Yes, it is," I reply.

"I have a good friend in Louisville, Joe Stutts, who's a Catholic priest," Lush says, now looking at *The Storm on the Sea of Galilee*. "Why don't I call him in the morning and ask him what would be the best way to contact Christopher?"

"Good idea, Lush. I'd appreciate that. I don't want to scare Christopher off or anything. I really want to talk to him, even if we don't go to Louisville now that we have the Gardner treasure here."

"I guess I'm going to turn in, Todge," Lush says, yawning.

"Yeah, me too. It's been a long day."

We walk out of the closet, shut the lights and close the door.

"Gosh, Lush, there are hundreds of millions of dollars worth of art in this house right now," I say in a whisper.

"I know. Good thing we've got Officer Graham out there to protect it!" She smiles as we turn down the hallway to the bedrooms. She pauses by her door, leans forward, stretches her body up and gives me a peck on the left cheek. "Goodnight, Todge."

"Good night, Lush. Hey, you really looked beautiful, ravishing tonight in that dress."

She smiles up at me. "Thank you, sweet heart. Sweet dreams."

"Sweet dreams to you, too, Lush," I reply and walk toward my room with Patsy Cline's version of *Sweet Dreams* playing in my head. Mother loved that song so much. She played it often and sang it often. Suddenly, I really want to hear that song, so I run into Billy's room and into his closet to find my duffel bag. I root around in it until I find my iPod. Clark is right beside me, curious to see what I'm after. He sticks his head in the bag and sniffs while I connect my earphones into the iPod and scroll to find Patsy Cline's *Sweet Dreams*. I click on the song and all at once I am gripped by the slide of the violins from high notes to low notes, the dramatic prelude to Cline's angelic voice singing the words, 'Sweet Dreams'. I walk over to the bed and fall onto my belly, looking up at Mother's birthday gift to me I've put on an easel in the room next to the chaise longue. The orchestral opening fades into a twangy honky tonk beat, and I become a twelve-year-old boy again full of fear and worry about my Mother. Who is she singing about? It couldn't be Dad; he loves her. When Patsy yells out, 'You don't love me, It's plain' it sounds like Mother screaming at Dad. How many times did I hear that? 'You don't love me, Charles. You don't.' But he did, Mother. He does Mother. Why couldn't you realize that? Why couldn't you see that we all loved you? But it wasn't enough for you. It was never enough. She wears Dad's wedding ring. Who is this other man? Is Mother planning to divorce Dad? Is she planning to run off with some other man? And now I, the thirty-two year old man, emerge, and I wonder if Mother was singing about Willie B? Perhaps even Aunt CC? My eyes trace the incredible way Mother painted the light on the Marne River, with the reflection of the tall trees in the river, the little blue, dilapidated fishing shack on the far side of the river, the rotting fishing pier in the foreground, and in invisible paint in the river, her birthday wish to me, "*Happy thirteenth, darling Philip. You'd love the fishing here. Love, Mother.*" Tears are streaming down my face as I think about my beautiful Mother—she actually resembled Patsy Cline with dark hair, high forehead and red lips, but Mother was more beautiful, I think—standing in front of her canvas, painting this picture all those years ago. Was she with some man she loved more than Dad? Was Adrian there when she painted this? Was he there planning her murder at that moment?

> *Why can't I forget the past?*
> *Start loving someone new,*
> *Instead of having sweet dreams about you.*

The song ends and I'm facedown on the bed weeping. Clark is lying down beside me. I get up and head to the bathroom knowing it's going to be another Ambien night.

I'm kneeling in front of an immense white marble throne and some giant king, or perhaps God himself, sits upon the throne, I cannot tell because a blinding light, like the sun, but whiter, maybe a white star, hovering over the figure bears down upon me; I feel the heat, and I fear to look up, knowing I'll be instantly blinded, so I focus on the feet, but I cannot even see the feet because they are covered in a billowing robe of shiny white silk, rustling in the swift breeze created from the heat of the star. I am

petrified. I feel so young, not even old enough to speak. I do not know why I am here. I wish that I could escape to my waterfall, but waterfalls vaporize in the intensity of this light.

"Philip, what is it that you want from me? What do you desire?" The reverberating baritone of a true giant resounds.

I cannot speak. I have no words. Why I am here? Then my mind races forward many years. Why the hell am I here, I wonder? I rise up on my knees, opening my torso toward the giant, keeping my face and eyes down, and I open my mouth to say 'I', but my voice quivers; my body shivers, and I withdraw down like a beaten mongrel.

"You are here because you willed yourself here, Philip," the giant booms then laughs like thunder, and I see flashes of lightning in my peripheral vision. "You have a question you want answered. Do not be afraid. Ask me the question, Philip. I know what you want to ask, but you must ask it in order for me to answer you." When the giant speaks, wind rushes over me, I feel the warmth of his breath, and I smell a smell that is familiar. I realize it is the smell of ozone after a spring thunderstorm.

I rise up again, my hands in a prayer position at the level of my heart and pulled in tight against my chest. "Why didn't Mother love me?" I ask in a tiny child's voice. I realize that I'm probably not really speaking at all, but only thinking.

The giant takes a deep breath in, I feel the air rushing up toward his face, and then he sighs, expelling a gale. "Philip, your Mother always loved you and still does. Her love shone on you like a revolving beacon shines light on the sea, the light is constant but it is not always on one particular spot."

My body is gripped with the strong recognition of a deep, intuitive truth. "That's true," I say. "She did love me, but was constantly withdrawing her love and then offering it up again. I, I never knew when it might come my way," I reply in my adult voice.

"Philip, my son," the booming voice is full of compassion. "You give your love in the same way as did your Mother. She was unable to understand that her love should shine forth in all directions like the sun's light. And you do not realize this. You must learn how to do this or you will never be at ease with yourself."

I feel a choking sensation as he speaks these words, and I am shocked to realize he is exactly right. I am my Mother. I do disperse my love in Mother's random, indiscriminate manner, even to Billy and Lush. It's always been too painful for me to direct my love to anyone for too long a period—better for me to direct it elsewhere before someone's love for me vanishes. "But how do I do this?" I ask, and I realize the giant has withdrawn an immense distant from me and I look up to see a white star in the night sky. The star is one of millions and millions I see in the night sky and I am on a mountaintop bald in the Pisgah National Forest, a place Dad would take Billy and me hiking and camping. At night we would look out at the immensity of the universe and Dad would point out the constellations. But Dad and Billy are not here; I'm alone; I'm squatting down, hugging my knees. A cold wind is blowing; I'm chilled; I'm frightened. I look around at the path I am on, and I realize I have no idea where I am, how I got here, or how I can find my way home. And when I think of home I don't want to go back to New York, I don't want to go back to Atlanta, I want to go home to Union before Dad and Mother started fighting, before Uncle Adrian came into our lives, back to the time when Fatgram and Ala Mary and Billy and Brooker T were constants. And I know if I can just get back there Mother will love me now. She will love me unconditionally and constantly. I know she will; I will make her. A large bird swoops by and below me, startling me. It alights on a large boulder below me, and I see that the bird is a great-horned owl. It is facing away from me, peering out over the night mountains, then it pivots its head toward me, and I see that it is holding a tiny mouse in its beak. The little mouse is squirming and squealing sharp, high pitched chirping sounds, and I pick up a stick so that I can hit the owl and knock the little mouse out of its beak. As I stand up and begin walking toward the great owl, it transforms into a giant size, and its eyes are the eyes of Uncle Adrian and in its beak Billy is writhing in pain and screaming out to me, screaming my name, "Philly, Philly, help me! Help me, Philly! Save me! Save me, please!" My anger explodes. I run as fast as I can, and I dive into the owl with my hands around it throat,

and I expose my teeth, my canines now long and razor sharp, like a crazed wild animal. I bite through the feathers and into the great bird's throat, and I rip into its flesh with my teeth, biting down hard, and I feel bones crutching and the warm blood releases into my mouth, and I yank my face back and feel the flesh and blood vessels hanging from my mouth. I spit it out and turn my face up to the sky where there is now a full yellow moon and I begin howling like a wolf, and the owl, Billy, and I fall off of the mountain and into the darkness of a deep valley, and we fall and fall and fall, and I lose sight of Billy and the owl and I begin to float without falling and I realize I can fly, so I fly upward. I am naked with an erection so hard it hurts. I fly up and over the mountain. On the other side I descend into a sunny desert terrain where I see a lone adobe edifice. I circle down and around the edifice. Something draws me to the house, and I see that the windows are openings with no glass, so I fly into one window into a bedroom and before me on a bed covered in white silk sheets lies Isabella, completely naked with her arms and legs open, wooing me. I descend upon her and begin to sniff her entire body, like a dog sniffing another dog. Her pubic hair is golden and smooth like silk and I bury my face in it, finding her clitoris with my tongue and I begin to pleasure her. She moans in pleasure, clamping her hands around my hair. The more she moans, the harder my cock gets. I feel a hand reaching from behind me, grabbing my cock, stroking it, and I feel a tongue rimming my asshole. I begin to moan. It feels so good. My moans blend with Isabella's, and I realize I'm in some sort of orgy. I wonder who is eating my ass and stroking my cock when I feel stubble rubbing on my ass and I realize it has to be a man. Isabella pulls me up toward her face and guides my cock into her vagina. I am overwhelmed with pure sexual pleasure and I can barely believe I am fucking her. As I get into my rhythm, she pushes her pelvis up to meet my thrusts and I look into her beautiful face. I feel a body leaning over me, and suddenly I feel a sharp pain as a penis is thrust into my ass. This man begins to fuck me as I continue to fuck Isabella. It now feels good, and I look over my left shoulder to see it's Uncle Adrian and then I wake up, my heart pounding, my breathing heavy and my head dizzy from the Ambien. My cock is hard, dripping pre-cum. I look around to see Clark stretched out beside me, his legs quivering in his own dream, his lips slightly parted, revealing his formidable canines, and I notice his lipstick-red penis is half way extended, and I think about my dream, and I wonder if somehow our dreams crossed over and merged in some weird way. And, in an instant, I become clairvoyant, peering into the soul of the little boy Adrian and all I see is fear; and I know all he feels is fear. I fast forward to Adrian's current psyche to find the fear completely hidden from himself, hidden by a master of manipulation, who even must control death to keep the fear from emerging.

CHAPTER 38

"My God, what marvelous work. Simply exquisite," Julianna says as she peruses the eleven masterpieces from the Gardner museum Lush and I have set up on easels and tables in the guest suite to keep them as far away as we can from the officers on duty. She holds a mug of coffee in her left hand and her right hand touches her chin as she turns around to us and says, "For the life of me, I never knew Billy was such an accomplished copier."

"Copier?" I ask.

"Oh yes. These are all forgeries. But excellent ones."

"You mean Billy did these?" Lush asks.

"Well, I certainly suspect he did. Or perhaps he hired someone else to do it, but these are really outstanding copies," Julianna replies.

"I suppose he was going to try to fool Adrian with these," I say now feeling empty handed and crestfallen.

"Well, he might have fooled him from a photograph of these, but once Adrian saw them in person, he'd know they were forgeries," Julianna replies.

"That's it!" I shout.

"What, Todge?" Lush asks.

"That has to be why Adrian would expose himself. He would have to see the Gardner art pieces in person in order to determine if they were real or not," I reply.

"Yes, I would agree, Philip. It's unlikely there's anyone Adrian would trust authenticating such valuable pieces. I doubt I would. These are really, really good, but just look at the back of the canvasses, there are no inventory control numbers; the real paintings would have them from the museum. Also, even though these are older canvasses, the thread counts are not the same as sixteenth and seventeenth century thread counts." Julianna states.

"Wow, I never realized all that," I reply, "So the Gardner Museum and the thief would be the only ones to know those control numbers?"

Julianna gives me a strange look, "Well, of course, Philip. Sometimes the police will 'leak out' phony control numbers to differentiate the phonies from the real perpetrators."

"Fascinating," I reply.

"But what about this finial and this bronze vessel, Julianna?" Lush asks holding them up for Julianna to see.

"Hmmm, let me see those," she says as she sets her coffee mug down on an end table. She takes the bronze vessel in her hand and turns it around and around. "Well, I'm no expert on Chinese bronzes, but I'd say this is a fake and the finial, too. It wouldn't be hard to replicate those."

"Really?" Lush asks.

"Oh yes. Billy could have sent photos to China and had these made easily," Julianna says, sets the vessel on the table and picks her mug up.

"I wondered where everyone was at. Morning!" Lois says, smiling, as she enters the guest suite dressed in her usual grey maid's uniform.

"Hi, Lois," I reply, "How are you?"

"Just great," she replies in her deep, gruff voice. "You all are getting an early start. I was going to change all the bed linens today. Figured I'd start in here."

"Okay, we'll be out of your way in a few minutes, Lois," I reply.

"Aw, take your time. Anybody need any coffee or anything?"

"No thanks," Lush says.

"I'm fine, thank you," Julianna replies.

"Oh, I see you all are looking at them copies Billy made. I really like that one with them people in the fancy collars," she says. "Look at that woman. Bet that's uncomfortable," she says pointing to the Rembrandt. Our eyes are riveted on Lois's expressive face.

"You saw Billy paint these, Lois?" Julianna asks.

"Lord, yes. He did these this winter. I'd forgotten about them. I know he stashed them in the closet in there. I told him he didn't need any more art schooling," she says, hands on both hips, with a red and white striped kitchen towel in her right hand.

"Art schooling, Lois?" I ask.

"Why, yes. Him and that Claus fellow spent all hours of the night working on these. Billy said it was high time he learned to paint like the greats and Claus was the best teacher in the world. Hell, I like Billy's paintings way better than these. And those ones on the paper, well, I can't say much about them at all," she says screwing up her face with a look of disgust.

"Lois," Julianna approaches her. "Lois, do you remember much about Claus?"

"Huh! Dude could put down scotch like iced tea. He always drank a whole fifth himself every time he'd come over. Kind of a gruff, grizzly old bear. Chain-smoked and wouldn't eat nothing but cheese toast—had to be white bread. Funny last name, Van Fielder, Van Flipper, Van…."

"Vangilder?" Julianna asks.

"That's it. You know him, Miss Morgan?"

"Yes, I do. Not well, but I know him. He's probably the most well known art forger alive today. He has been convicted of fraud on numerous occasions and has spent time in prison."

"Damn!" Lois replies, "Oh, excuse me, but damn, I wonder why Billy was hanging around him for?"

"Because Claus is an incredible art instructor, one of the best. I heard that when he was released from prison the last time, part of his parole included giving art lessons to children in some of the poorer inner-city schools," Julianna states.

"Fascinating," Lush remarks. "Just how good is he?"

"He's beyond good. He can fool many art experts. He's fooled me on a few occasions," Julianna says.

"But how did you know all these were fakes before Lois got here?" I ask.

Julianna lets out a big laugh, "Because, darling, I spent hours and hours and hours studying artwork at the Gardner Museum. I did my Master's thesis on Vermeer. I know *The Concert* like the back of my hand." She walks over to the Vermeer and strokes the painting as if she were stroking a kitten. "This is as fine a copy as I've ever seen, but it is not the real thing."

"Lois, do you know anything about this eagle finial and this bronze vessel?" I ask.

"Well, I know they arrived by UPS from China, cause Billy had me open the package when it arrived a couple of weeks ago. He seemed excited to get them. I haven't laid eyes on them since."

"Shit," I let out with a big sigh, "It looks as if we're off to Kentucky tomorrow, then."

"Yes it does," Lush says.

"Well, my old man's out of town on a job," Lois says. "I can stay here with Clark if you want me to? Billy told me he was probably going to be out of town this week anyway, so I had already planned to stay here."

"Yes, I expect he was planning to go to Kentucky with Najeed," I reply. "Let's put all these fakes back in the secret storage area."

"Okay," Lush says, "Julianna, are you available to fly down to Louisville if we should discover the Gardner heist? I mean, we'd need to have it authenticated and would need someone to oversee the handling."

"Certainly, Lush. You find it. I'll even charter a plane to get there."

"Good," Lush replies as she picks up the fake Vermeer, "I know our chances are slim to nothing, but I have a good feeling about this, about Christopher. I think Todge is going to have good luck with him."

"So you want me to plan on staying over tomorrow, Philip?" Lois asks.

"Yes, please. How long could you stay?"

"I could stay 'till Saturday. Rocky gets home Saturday night."

"Great," I reply. "We should be back by Saturday, no matter what."

"Well, I've got to run," Julianna says, "I'll see you both this afternoon. I'll bring Isabella by about two o'clock. Is that okay?"

"That's fine, Julianna. Thanks so much for coming. Sorry for the dry run," I say as I pick up the big fake Rembrandt and shove it back into the hidden space.

"No problem. It's always a treat to see Claus's work."

"You're certain it's not good enough to fool Adrian?" I ask.

"Yes. It would be almost impossible to fool Adrian, I'm afraid," Julianna says, "It's hard to fathom the incredible pool of knowledge he possesses of the techniques and characteristics of world class artists

from the Renaissance to today. That's what made him such a great mentor; that's what made him pull the best out of his artists, rather his victims, I suppose we should call them now."

I look up at Julianna and a vision of Uncle Adrian looking over my shoulder, helping me with a book report, pointing out words to delete, showing me how to construct sentences to better express my thoughts, how to produce something elegant in a form as mundane as a book report. Yes, he was a great mentor, even to me. Dear God, how can such extremes of good and evil reside in the same body?

"Won't you stay for a bite of breakfast, Julianna?" Lush asks, and I snap out of the past, back into the present process of putting back the forgeries.

"Thank you, Lush, but I've got to meet a client for breakfast."

"Julianna," I say, "Lush and I had such a wonderful evening at your house last night, thank you so much."

"You are so welcome," she replies, "Wasn't it fascinating how we accomplished so much by putting our heads together?"

"Yes it was," Lush replies. "Mabry is one sharp cookie."

"Oh yes, extremely bright," Julianna replies. "Jonas tells me his I.Q. is one of the highest ever measured in the Schenectady public school system."

"I don't doubt it," I reply, as I think about Mabry's advice to me to set a trap for Adrian, a trap I've been formulating in my head since last night, a trap which I thought I had perfected, but now, with no Gardner treasure, I'm back to zero.

"You all may not remember this, but it made the national news. When Mabry was twelve years old he successfully hacked into one of the FBI's main computers," Julianna says.

"Oh my God," Lush says, "I do remember that."

"Wow," I say, "Yep, I remember that, too. I forget what happened. Were any charges pressed?"

"No," she replies and takes a sip of coffee. "Mabry did it on a dare from some older friends. Jonas says the government spent time with him, though, to 'reprogram' his mindset. He's been on contract with the FBI ever since. They paid his way through M.I.T."

"Amazing," Lush says. "He seems like a nice guy to me, a little nerdy, but very nice. How did he and Jonas meet?"

"At a party on Fire Island five years ago. It was love at first sight, and they've been together since then."

"Good for them," I say, "To be such a macho guy, Jonas is a very compassionate man."

"Yes he is, and I, for one, would trust him with my life," Julianna says.

"Todge, I'll see Julianna out and then come help you put these back," Lush says.

"Awe, I can help him, Lush," Lois says.

"Thanks, Lois," Lush says.

"Good bye, Julianna," I say.

"See you later, darling," Julianna says. She, Lush, and Clark walk out.

"Lois, did Billy ever say anything to you about stolen artworks?" I ask as she helps me slide the larger canvasses back.

"Stolen artworks? Naw. Not that I recall," she says.

"Did you know that all of these copies are of artwork that was stolen from a museum in Boston in 1990?"

"Really? No, I didn't. Billy just said he was 'perfecting his technique' by copying famous works."

"Can you think of anything else Billy said about these, Lois?"

"Well, no. Well, he did say the real ones were worth a king's ransom, but that these were worth a lot more than that to him."

I smile, yes I suppose they are worth more than a king's ransom, I think to myself. "Thanks, Lois," I say as I put the drawings in the portfolio and slide it into the storage area. I pick up Emma's pink backpack and head to Billy's bedroom to call Mabry.

I walk into the bedroom and quietly shut the door, head back into the closet where my cell phone is charging. I know I entered both Jonas's and Mabry's cell phones into my contacts. Mabry's last name starts with a W I know. I scroll through the W's until I find Mabry Whittaker. I select it and place the call. The phone rings five times. I think to myself, shit, I'm going to get his voice mail. But then he answers,

"Hello, Philip, wassup?"

"Hi Mabry. Are you feeling better today?"

"Feel much better, just needed some rest."

"Good, glad to hear that. Is Jonas there?"

"No, he left on an early flight to Chicago to see Cara Bridgefield."

"Yes, good," I reply. "Listen, Mabry. I have a favor to ask you.""Sure thing, dude. What is it?"

"I don't want to talk about it over the phone. Is there anyway we could meet alone somewhere today?" He does not reply.

"It has to do with the trap thing we discussed last night at Julianna's. You see, I have an idea and I need some advice."

"You don't want Jonas to know?" he asks.

"I'd prefer he didn't. I think if anyone knows besides you and me, the plan will not work."

"Okay, where do you want to meet?"

"Have you ever done yoga, Mabry?"

"Yoga? No, I haven't."

"Well, I'm planning to go to a hot vinyasa class in Chelsea this afternoon. You could go and sign up and we could meet in the locker room before class. You don't have to take the class if you don't want to, but I highly recommend it."

"Yoga, hot yoga? I dunno dude," he replies.

"It's about the only thing I could come up with where no one would know, especially the detectives," I reply.

"Well, okay, Philip. I'll meet you. I could use some exercise. What time?"

"Class starts at one thirty, but get there twenty minutes early. I'll meet you in the locker room."

"Okay. What's the address?"

"I'll text it to you. Listen, Mabry. I'll pay for this. Just add it on my tab."

"No prob. Later dude." He hangs up before I can say goodbye.

"Yes!" I say out loud to myself. A surge of fresh energy and excited anticipation races through my body. I smile. "The hunt is on, Fatgram!" I pick up the little spiral bound notebook I use to keep notes in for work, and I find the address of the yoga studio and text it to Mabry. He fires back a text that says, "Got it. C u." I slip my cell phone in my pants pocket, leave the closet, walk through the bedroom, and out in the hall to find Lush. I avoid the living room and head to the kitchen. My hunch is that Lush is outside smoking. I'm right. I see her through the French doors, so I go out on the terrace.

"What a shame about the forgeries," she says holding her right elbow in her upturned right hand at mid-chest level with a newly lit cigarette held between the index and middle fingers of her right hand.

"Yes, I know. I thought we had him," I reply trying to hold back my enthusiasm from Lush. I just can't risk letting anyone but me get close to Adrian.

"I talked to my priest friend, Joe, just a minute ago. He doesn't know Christopher O'Bryan, but he gave me the general phone number of St. Meinrad's."

"Thanks, I'll put a call in and see if they will let me talk to Christopher or at least get a message to him that I urgently need to see him tomorrow."

"Good, Todge," Lush says. "But how are we going to get around the police? They'll certainly not want us traipsing off to Kentucky. Will they?"

"No. Not at all, but it's a free country. Besides, we're not under any kind of legal orders are we?"

"No, but they'll fight us. I don't think they'll pay to send along a police escort. Do you?"

"No, Lush, they won't. But I've been thinking. There's no use taking too much risk. I think we should charter a jet. Billy was a Net Jet member. His card would be in his desk in the studio."

"That's probably not a bad idea, Todge. An expensive idea, but not a bad one."

"Well, you know I'm not one for extravagance, but the sooner we can get there, the better," I reply.

"I agree. I'll find his card and give them a call."

"Thanks. Are there any little airports in Louisville?"

"Yes. There's Bowman Field near the Highlands. Small jets land there. That's a good idea. We'll be less noticed there."

"Great, Lush. You arrange that. Can you rent a car there?"

"No. I can get my yardman's son to pick us up in my car. No need to rent one."

"Perfect. I'm going to go get a bowl of cereal, then return some calls. I have to be at Dr. Gerard's at noon."

"Okay. I've got plenty to do, too."

"Lush. I really want to do yoga again today. It starts at one thirty. Would you mind helping Julianna show Billy's work to Isabella?"

"Not at all. Happy to do it."

"Good. I should be back by four. I imagine they'll still be here then."

"Yes. There's a lot to see."

Clark trots up, demanding attention.

"Hey, little bear," I say. "Have you been out on morning patrols?"

He wags his tail as I pat his head.

"Speaking of patrols, we have a new officer in the house this morning," Lush says.

"Really, who?"

"He's a really big young man, Officer Dennison. He looks more like a linebacker than a policeman— not very friendly—very serious—has a 'don't fuck with me' look on his face."

I snicker. "Well would you?"

"Would I what, Todge?"

"Would you fuck him?"

"You're incorrigible. Sex always on your mind!"

"Me?"

"Yes, you," she says, puts her cigarette in an ashtray, grabs my right arm, and says, "Come on, let's get breakfast."

Sebastian Gerard's office is like a piece of white bread, you can tell nothing at all about it, except that it is a piece of white bread. I wonder if there is some interior designer who specializes in decorating shrinks' offices in such banal finishes as to minimize the chance that patients might glean something about the real person behind the medical doctor who tries to pry open their brains, their souls, their very selves, wide open like spilling a glass jar of old coins onto a table so that you can pick each one up turning it over and over in your fingers for careful observation, hoping to find the rare one, the special one, the one that explains the purpose for the collection.

"Please take a seat, Mr. Hampton," Sebastian says as I walk into his office. He is sitting behind some nondescript desk reading a computer monitor.

"Thank you," I reply, eyeing the two beige, wingback upholstered chairs and a large beige sofa surrounding a rectangular wooden coffee table. I choose one of the chairs. Sebastian, dressed in a dark grey suit with a black shirt and a black tie, walks over and sits in the other chair, and smiles, looking into my eyes.

I sigh, "So, Dr. Gerard, I guess you know my dirty secret?"

"Why don't you tell me about it, Mr. Hampton?"

"But you do know don't you? I mean I could tell you knew by the way you looked at me, looked right through me, at Billy's wake."

He clears his throat, crosses his left leg over his right leg, causing his pant leg to rise up revealing socks with a black and white checker board pattern, and repeats, "Why don't you tell me about it, Mr. Hampton?"

With my gaze down on the socks, I become annoyed and reply, "I don't like you calling me Mr. Hampton. Just Philip. Okay?"

"Very well, Philip. Tell me about it."

"God dammit! God dammit! God dammit!" I shout and slap both arms of the chair with the palms of my hands. "I don't know why I did it. I really don't. I was so mad, so mad with everyone." I sigh, my cheeks are flaming, and I feel a prickly sensation all over my scalp. "You see, Mother died, then Dad left, and Uncle Adrian just disappeared. Three of the people I, we, Billy and I, loved more than anything just vanished. I, I was so confused. Ala Mary was wounded, but her kind, loving self wouldn't tell us the complete truth, even if she did know, because she wanted to protect us. I know now she must have gone to her grave bearing the truth. What a burden for her. And Fatgram, well, she took over and was so good to us, but she was such a strong, rigid, force. She was a great force, so much so that there was no way to ever defy her. And she was not emotional like Mother. Fatgram loved us, I know, but it was a cold love, especially to two boys who lost both parents. Fatgram really loved Mother the best, yes her own daughter—that's the only time she ever let her guard down, really let it down, was when she was caring for my Mother. I recall watching Fatgram's face, time after time, the way she simply lit up like a Christmas tree whenever Mother walked into the room. Sure, Fatgram could turn on a dime and become mad as hell with Mother, in an instant, but her deep, deep love of Mother was unquestioned, by everyone. Dad was jealous of it. The truth is, even Billy and I were jealous of it. Uncle Adrian, on the other hand, saw it as a great opportunity to divide and conquer. And that's just what the bastard did." Tears are running down my face and my nose is becoming snotty. Dr. Gerard pushes a box of Kleenex, sitting near him on the coffee table, toward me. "So I suppose, really, I was just a ball of anger, a big ball of anger who felt unloved and Billy simply withdrew into himself and what was left was just a shell, a shell of a little boy. And he was still a little boy, and I wasn't. I was the oldest, and I knew better. God dammit, I knew so much better, but I did it anyway. That little boy had always relied on me, and I was, I was a good brother. I was the best big brother I knew how to be. And I would pray every night, every single night for as long as I can remember. I'd pray to God to guide me to be a better brother. I promised Mother and Dad I'd take care of him, and I did. I did until they left me, left us. And Billy, in his shell, would not respond to me, no matter what I did, no matter what I said, no matter what I gave him or brought for him. No matter how much I prayed to God to help. God wasn't listening. And that's when I realized there wasn't a God. There wasn't anyone. There's just each one of us, alone within ourselves, trying to make some sense out of life, of living. And I just couldn't take it. So I beat Billy. In rages, I would beat him. And then I started fucking him, having sex with him—just the same way Uncle Adrian did to us. If he resisted sex, I would beat him. I would beat my dear little brother, slap him hard in the face, hit him in the head or the back with a broom handle, and I would choke him. Yes I was a great choker, a superb choker, the very best. I would get him hard, suck his

cock, and when he was close to cumming, I would choke him until he almost passed out—sometimes he would and his cock would get so hard and he would shoot an unbelievable amount of cum."

"Oh God, this feels good, Billy," I say as he rapidly stokes my cock with his right hand, and I stroke his cock with my right hand. We sit facing each other, my left leg stretched out under his right leg and his left leg stretched out under my right leg.

"Yeah, it does, Philly," he replies, leans over and squeezes a large blob of spit through his lips, letting it drop onto the head of my cock.

"Oh, yeah," I groan, "Stroke it, Billy." I reach over and stick my tongue in his mouth. He pulls back. "Come on, man," I say.

"Your braces cut my tongue," he replies, wincing, his full lips pouting, his long, curly hair falling over his eyes, beads of sweat trickling through the thick peach fuzz sprouting down the center of his chest.

"Okay, okay," I say, leaning over to spit on his cock, which decreases the friction of my hand, and I feel the head of his cock throb even harder in the slime.

A cacophony of freakish sound reverberates through our room. Startled, we both stop stroking and listen.

"Goddamn starlings," Billy says, "They're nesting in the attic again."

"Christ, that scared me," I say, resuming my stroking. "Fatgram shouldn't be home from bridge club for at least another hour, though. The coast should be clear." Billy gazes into my eyes, squeezes my cock, and slowly begins to stroke it again.

"Hey, Billy, I'm sorry for slapping you," I say. "It's just. Well, it's just when you ignore me. I mean I ask you a friggin' question and you won't even answer me?"

His says nothing but his eyes shift to my cock as he squeezes it harder.

"Yeah, that feels so good, little brother," I say.

"Little? Huh? My todger's bigger than yours," his voice has deepened dramatically and lost its childish tone in the past few months, sometimes startling me.

"Rub it in, why don't you? I know yours is longer and fatter than mine. But so what? It's not like mine's tiny. Yours is just bigger, that's all."

Even though Fatgram had the house air-conditioned a few years back, our bedroom on the second floor never gets cool, and it's a hot afternoon in late May. I'm covered in sweat, but I don't care, the heat and the musky smell of sex and my brother are intoxicating, a high unlike anything I've ever known, and I plan to take it higher and higher and higher.

"Hey, you anywhere close to coming, Billy?" I ask. He shrugs his shoulders, and I see his balls are still hanging heavy so I know the answer. I feel guilty for slapping him when I asked him if he wanted to SO and he wouldn't answer me. But I know what he likes—I mean really, really likes, so I'll do it, even though I think it's nasty and disgusting. I stop stroking him and push him back with force on the bed with my two hands. He makes a grunting sound. I take my hands, push his legs back and up exposing his ass that is getting really hairy, especially around the rim, spread his cheeks apart with my hands, and in one quick motion, nose dive into his butt hole, thrusting my tongue into his anus, tasting the bitterness of fecal remnants at first, but ignoring it as Billy lets out a massive groan.

"Oh my God, Philly. Lick me, yeah. Lick my asshole," he moans.

I pull my tongue out and lick around the rim of his ass, picking up a couple of small balls of toilet paper.

"Shit," I shout in disgust, spitting on the dark green matelassé bedspread, rubbing my tongue on it, shedding the toilet paper balls, leaving a wet streak. "This is what you taste like down there little brother with the big todger," I say as I lean over his torso, thrusting my tongue deep into his mouth, pressing my body into his. We kiss deeply for almost a minute, rolling over and over on each other. When we release,

we are panting. I roll off the bed, get on my knees, and pull Billy by the legs so that his ass is at my face level. I push his legs back and resume tickling the rim of his ass with my tongue. He begins to emit a low groan that evolves into a kind of ethereal feline growl that turns me on and makes me feel ecstatically wonderful in this bodily knowledge and experience of turning my brother on so much. My cock throbs and drips with precum and I rub the precum all over the head as I continue to rim him. Billy continues to growl, his hairy ass and legs writhing in pleasure. He takes the silk tie I formed into a noose, loops it over his neck, placing the end of it in my left hand.

"Here we go. Ready?" I ask. He says nothing but continues to moan and growl. I push his ass up higher, stand up and start to rub the head of my cock around the rim as I begin to tightened the noose with my left hand and stroke his hard cock with my right hand. It's hard work, but highly satisfying for both of us. I keep rubbing my cock on his ass, tightening the noose, and stroking him fast and furiously. I see his balls begin to climb upward, I pull the noose as tight as I can, and I feel his cock go rock solid hard, his face takes on a bluish hue, and all at once his body begins a violent convulsion as his cocks spews forth an unbelievable amount of cum covering his chest, his face, the bedspread beyond his head, and spraying on the hardwood floor clear off the far side of the bed. Immediately my cock explodes, I drop the noose, grab my cock, aiming it towards his chest, watching my own cum merge with his, covering his chest, hitting him in the face. Exhausted I fall on his chest, wedge my arms under his back, roll onto my back, with him on top of me, and I take my hands and gently pull the noose loose around his neck. He exhales and goes limp. I lie there in the sticky heat, engulfed by the heavy smells of sex and ass, waiting for Billy to take another breath, once again briefly and absurdly defiant and triumphant over the dark pain of nothingness, even as I face it, desperately rushing headlong into it, without any real hope of stopping it for good. Fatgram always says the true definition of insanity is repeating the same behavior over and over again while expecting a different result—it's finally becoming clear to me exactly what she means.

"And I, I carried this on and on until, after a while, Billy got used to it. He seemed to be climbing out of his shell and he became more and more interested in the sex. I suppose that's when I really begin to realize that he was indeed gay. And, as strange as it may seem, the more interested he got in it, the less interested I became, and the more guilty I felt about using sex to get closer to him. It's like I had created a sex monster, awakened some deep insatiable craving within him. The more responsive he became to me, the less abusive I was toward him. Until finally, the pendulum had swung the other way and Billy started getting angry when I didn't want to have sex and even began hitting me. By the time I was fifteen and he was nearly fourteen, he was bigger and stronger than I was. My sexuality had definitely shifted toward women. I had much rather masturbate alone looking at a *Playboy* than have sex with Billy. It was all so fucking confusing. I was so happy when I was able to convince Fatgram to send us to separate boarding schools. Who knew, she was so smart, maybe she had figured out what was really going on in that big white mansion of hers. The rest doesn't matter much, Dr. Gerard. You see, I had become the abuser; I had become Uncle Adrian. And I have been such a coward my whole life, that I've been running away from this truth, running away until last night. Until, I simply couldn't run anymore. And that is, my only real regret with Billy, the fact that I never came clean with him about this, never really asked him to forgive me for it. My God, he knew I loved him, but I never had the guts to apologize for all the times I abused him." My face is soaked with tears and my nose is running, I feel snot on my lips. I grab a big wad of Kleenex, blow my nose hard, and grab another wad to wipe my face. I hold a wad of Kleenex in each fist as I look up at Dr. Gerard. His face is expressionless. He blinks his eyes twice.

"Philip, you have been on a long journey of self discovery, a process of self-healing, that has been occurring for a long time, long before your brother's death. Billy's death has been a catalyst to bring this healing process to closure for you. You may not realize it now, especially as you are still in shock and burdened with great grief, but you are healing from the horrible, horrible abuse you suffered as a child.

Billy told me essentially everything you've told me. He never blamed you for what you did to him; he blamed himself for remaining locked within himself for so long. He told me he loved the sex with you, always, even when it involved physical abuse. He knew you were not gay, and he always feared losing the close physical contact with you. I know you are feeling a great amount of guilt and shame about this. Don't be too hard on yourself. Adrian warped your sense and Billy's sense of how to be close and intimate in a healthy way. I'm not here to judge you; you have to be your own judge. Billy certainly didn't judge you, Philip. He loved you."

My heart feels like it's breaking as I hear these words. I fold over my knees, "Oh, God. How could I have ever treated him so badly? I don't deserve to live. I should have been the one murdered." I cry for a while, feeling so alone, so cold, soulless, and I wonder if Adrian ever feels this way, for it would take a truly soulless person do to the things that he has done. Dr. Gerard and I are both silent for a long while. I slowly regain my composure and ask him, "Why did you looked so surprised when I told you Adrian was the killer?"

"Because Billy never mentioned anything at all that would lead me to suspect Adrian. He described Adrian as a genius, quirky, pedophile who was now in the process of helping Billy create his greatest works. I cautioned Billy to stay away from Adrian, and when he wouldn't, I suggested that he confront Adrian about the abuse and let him know how much he had suffered during the abuse and all his life since then."

"Did Billy do that?"

"He told me he did and that he was planning to visit Adrian in person at his home in Amsterdam."

"Billy was not coming completely clean with you, Dr. Gerard. You see, Adrian doesn't live in Amsterdam. He lives in Dubai. We have concrete proof that he not only killed Billy, but he killed my mother, as well as at least seven other women artists whom he represented and whose sons he sexually abused."

"Is this really true, Philip?"

"Yes, it's true. And it is true that Billy was planning to kill Adrian. He even hired an assassin to do the job. When Adrian found out about this, well, that's when, that's when he arranged for Billy's murder."

"I see."

"Are you surprised Billy wasn't truthful to you?"

"No, I'm not. Billy was making good progress at becoming truthful with himself. But he wasn't all the way there yet. If you can't be truthful with yourself, then how can you be truthful with anyone else?"

"I get your point, Dr. Gerard. I really get your point." He remains emotionless, peering into my eyes.

"Well, I suppose I could sit here and tell you the whole story, Dr. Gerard, but I get the feeling you don't even want to know it. Am I correct?"

For the first time, I feel a great amount of love pouring out of this man's heart as he smiles at me and replies, "Philip, it's is not a question of wanting to know the whole story. Have you told me as much as you need for me to know?"

"Yes, I think I have."

"Then, I do in fact know enough already."

"Dr. Gerard, I thank you for your time. I think you must have really helped a great many people in your career, and I think you'll help many more."

"I love my work. And, I love people. You will get through your grief, Philip. In my opinion, you do not need my help. I am glad we spent this time together."

"Me too. Thank you so much," I say as I pull out my checkbook.

"No, no," he says, "There is no charge today."

"Well, that's kind of you. Thank you. Thanks for doing this during your lunch hour."

"Glad to do it, Philip."

I turn around and walk out of his office into the waiting area. A middle aged women with stringy brown hair and a distraught look on her thin, ashen face stares at the floor, not acknowledging my presence. I walk over to the receptionist area, but no one is there. I turn around, look at the woman once again, observing with surprise that she is dressed extremely well, probably a Chanel suit, and several rings with a lot of diamonds glistening on her tightly clenched fingers. I walk out into the hallway wondering how life got her to this point and see Officer O'Daniel waiting for me.

"Ready to go, Mr. Hampton?" he asks with a smile.

"Yes, thanks. Listen, please just call me Philip."

"Yes sir. Yes, Philip. I will."

"I've decided to go to yoga. Can you take me to a yoga studio in Chelsea?"

"Certainly."

We walk to the elevator and I take out my cell phone to dial Lush.

"Hello, Todge?"

"Hi, Lush."

"How did it go with Dr. Gerard?"

"It went very well."

"Good. Is Brent with you?"

"Who?"

"Officer O'Daniel—Brent."

"Yes. Yes, he is. Listen, everything okay there?"

"Yes, I've made the arrangements for tomorrow. We need to be at the airport by eight thirty. That'll get us into Louisville by eleven. We can grab lunch at my house and you can be at St. Meinrad's by two. Did you make contact with Christopher?"

"No, but I explained to a receptionist there that I would be there at two tomorrow and had an urgent, family matter to discuss with Christopher. She said she would get the message to him and someone would get back in touch with me."

"Good," she says, "I've heard nothing from Jonas or Mabry. You heard anything?"

"No. Well, I'll see you after yoga. Bye."

"Bye, Todge."

I close my phone, put it in my blazer pocket, and look over at Officer O'Daniel. "Well, Brent. Is it okay if I call you Brent?"

He shifts his weight from foot to foot nervously, "Well, yes, I guess so, Philip."

"Listen Brent. I can tell Lush is attracted to you and that you are attracted to her. God knows you're setting yourself up for a complicated situation. Anyway, I have to tell you, she is the most important person in my life now, and I love her deeply."

"Yes, I can see that, Philip." He looks me directly in my eyes.

"Well, you see, I have no claim on Lush, and I don't expect that she and I will ever be anything but the closest of friends. We had our chance at being lovers a long time ago, and I basically blew it. I mean, I don't want her as a lover, but she's the closest person in the world to me, and I couldn't bear to see her hurt."

"Yes, I understand," he replies.

"I hope you do, Brent. She is one hell of a woman—smart, beautiful, kind, compassionate, loving. She's everything a man could hope for. I just want to make certain you know that."

"Yes sir, I know that," he replies.

"Good," I say as the elevator door opens in the garage. We walk to the car and Brent opens the back door for me. I get in. He looks down at me.

"You really think I have a chance with her?"

I look up at him, "Yeah, I do. Half a chance anyway."

He smiles, carefully shuts the door. I watch him walk behind the car and I observe him jump up, rubbing his hands in joy and excitement. Damn, what a great feeling he must be feeling right now. Lucky bastard.

Brent takes a seat in the hallway leading to the yoga studio. I enter the studio, sign in, pay for my class and proceed to the men's locker room where I find Mabry sitting on the bench in front of the second row of lockers looking at the screen of his laptop. Two other men are in the room changing.

"Hi Mabry," I say.

He looks up at me, "What's going on man?"

"Thanks for meeting me here," I reply. I notice he has a rather large, green backpack with him.

"Are you planning to do the class?" I ask.

"Might as well, since I'm here. I went on-line to check it out. Seems like a good way to get some exercise," he replies.

"Well, I can attest to that. I've been doing it for almost five years. It's really helped me out. I hope you like it." The two other guys in the room are standing by the sinks talking. One guys is washing his hands. I hear the water stop, and I hear him pulling out paper towels. They walk out of the locker room.

"Listen, I have to talk fast before anyone else comes in, Mabry."

"Okay," he says as he shuts his laptop and leans over to stuff it back into the backpack.

"I know you can hack your way into probably most any computer on this planet. Julianna told me about what you did when you were twelve. I remember it from the news, too."

A big smile erupts across his face, "Yeah man, but I gave that sort of hacking up a long time ago."

"I'm sure you did, but haven't you had to do it in your investigative work?"

"Yep, I have." He replies, pushing on the nose bridge of his glasses that are slowly sliding down his nose.

"Good, because this is investigative hacking. It will help me set the trap for Adrian—just like you suggested. Last night Lush and I found what we thought was the Gardner heist in a hidden closet in Billy's guest suite."

Mabry's eyes widen. "Really, dude?"

"Yes, it was all there, including the finial and bronze Yu. But this morning Julianna came by and confirmed that they were all fakes, very good fakes, but fakes nonetheless." I realize my voice is getting loud, so I begin to whisper. "Anyway, Lois, the housekeeper came in and said that she had seen Billy paint the works this winter under the guidance of a man Julianna knows to be one of the best art forgers alive."

"Claus Vangilder?" Mabry asks.

"Yes. How did you know? Have you spoken with Julianna this morning?"

"No. Jonas and I had a case that involved Vangilder. He really is an expert forger."

"Well, here's the deal. Julianna says the fakes are really good, but not good enough to fool Adrian if he inspects them himself. She says the real paintings would have special inventory control numbers on the back of the canvass and that the museum would have photographs of these as well as close-ups of the paintings and close-ups of the backs of the canvases to reveal their thread counts."

"Oh, yes that's true, we've worked with these things before," Mabry says, his interest clearly peaked.

"All that has to be stored digitally at the Gardner Museum, doesn't it?"

"Definitely and also at the insurance company," Mabry replies.

"If you can get them for me, we can send them to Adrian and along with photographs of the pieces in Billy's surroundings, he'll be fooled into thinking we found the real McCoy during our trip to Bardstown this week. That's a trap he won't be able to resist." Just as I finish, two more men walk into the locker room.

Mabry looks up at me. "Done! Give me a couple of days. Jonas will probably ask me to do this anyway when he finds out about the fakes."

"Well, hell, go ahead and tell him. I don't want to ask you to do anything unethical with your partner. But, please, ask him not to tell anyone else. I just don't want to endanger Lush, Julianna, or Janet anymore than they already are."

"Great!" Mabry says. I reach my right hand out to give him a high five. He smiles and slaps his right hand against mine.

"Listen," Mabry says as he bends over, reaching into his backpack, "I've found evidence that someone is trying to track my calls over the past week. I can safely communicate with Jonas through encryption on the Internet, but you and he may not be able to communicate, depending on where you both are the next couple of days." He pulls out a pad and a pen and scribbles something down, tears out a sheet, and hands it to me. "Here's the number of a payphone I randomly use in town. Call me from a payphone Wednesday at noon. Remember, it has to be from another payphone. I'll have your answer by then."

"I'll do it. We better get dressed," I say, "Class starts in five minutes."

"Okay," Mabry says. He pulls off his glasses and slips off the grey turtleneck he is wearing, revealing his slim hairy torso. I'm shocked to see that both of his nipples are pierced with silver loops. A giant multi-colored tattoo of some kind of bird covers most of his back and shoulders.

"Wow, that's some tattoo. What is it?" I ask.

"It's my version of a Thunderbird. Cryptozoology is one of my hobbies," he replies looking at me with an expression that tells me he is cognizant that I was surprised to see the nipple rings and the tattoo.

"Oh. Isn't that looking for mythical creatures?" I ask as I unbutton the blue Oxford cloth shirt I'm wearing.

"Well, it's more like the search for animals whose existence has not been proven," he replies as he wads up his shirt, stuffs it in his bag and pulls out a black T-shirt and a long pair of cotton warm-up pants.

I slip off my shirt and T-shirt, hang them in a locker and unbuckle my belt. Mabry has slipped off his jeans and I notice he has on a pair of boxers with a plaid pattern on them. His long slim legs are very hairy and I notice the Greek letter pi is tattooed in blue above his right ankle. He leaves the boxers on and slides into the warm up pants.

"Mabry, didn't you bring any shorts?" I ask as I slip off my loafers and unzip my khakis. "You are going to burn up in those warm-up pants."

"No, this is all I brought."

"You really need shorts. You'll sweat right through your boxers and those thick pants. Look, I have an extra pair with me. They are mediums, but they'll probably fit you." I unzip my bag and pull out a pair of black running shorts and hand them to Mabry.

"Okay, thanks," he says. He takes the shorts, stands up and pulls off the warm up pants and boxers in one motion, revealing his large penis, more formidable in full view than the glance I got in Julianna's bathroom last night. Damn, I wonder what Jonas does with that. I would expect Mabry to be the bottom, but who knows. You never know when it comes to sex. People always surprise you. He slips the shorts on and looks up at me. "Should I wear a T-shirt or not?"

"You can, but you are going sweat right through it. I wouldn't wear one if I were you."

I grab my other pair of shorts and slip off my khakis and boxers, again feeling a little self-conscience about the size of my penis compared to Mabry's. I feel Mabry's eyes on me, so I meet his gaze head on. I get the impression that he likes what he sees, so I smile and say, "I think you will really like this yoga. Just remember to keep breathing and if you get too tired or hot, just lie down on your mat."

"Okay, Philip," he replies then turns his attention to stuffing his backpack in a locker. I put my shorts on, get my things together, put them in the locker, close it, grab my mat, towels, and water, and ask Mabry, "You ready to do this, dude?"

He smiles, stands up, and I see that, even though he is slim, he has good muscular definition, and I suspect he's probably pretty strong, pound per pound, and he replies, "Ready, dude!"

We walk out of the bathroom and into the yoga room. H.R. walks up to us.

"Hi, Philip. Good to see you again."

I transfer everything into my left hand and arm and stick out my right hand to shake H.R.'s hand. "Good to see you H.R. I brought a friend along. This is Mabry Whittaker. He's new to yoga."

"Nice to meet you, Mabry."

Mabry sets his mat, towels, and water on the floor, stands up, sticks out his right hand to H.R. and says, "Good to meet you, too. Whew, it's hot in here. Hope I don't keel over."

H.R. laughs, "You'll do fine Mabry." H.R. bends down, picks up all Mabry's stuff and says, "Here, I'm going to put you back here in the third row so you can watch the people in front of you. Don't worry, I'll be giving careful instruction."

"Enjoy," I say to Mabry.

He shoots me a worried look and says, "Thanks."

H.R. unrolls Mabry's mat and towels and stands in front of him demonstrating the beginning Pranayama breathing technique. I walk up to the second row and place my mat behind and to the right of H.R.'s mat.

H.R. walks up to his mat, faces the front and instructs us to begin. We, probably thirty women and ten men, begin pranayama breathing by inhaling through our noses as we lift our elbows toward the sky with our hands interlaced beneath our chins, then exhaling through wide open mouths as we push our chins up to the ceiling, bringing our elbows together. Indian music plays softly in the background. My eyes keep returning to the tattoo on H.R.'s right shoulder and I think about how much better looking his tattoo is than Mabry's.

"Final two breaths," H.R. instructs.

A trickle of sweat runs down between my pectorals. My neck and upper shoulders feel tight and I try to direct my breath to that area to ease the discomfort.

"Come back to Tadasana, reset your foundation by engaging all the leg muscles, keep those toes spread wide apart, scoop the tail bone slightly, and bring your hands in prayer to heart center," H.R. says in a loud, but soothing voice. "Close your eyes, focus on your third eye, and set your intention for today's class. It can be whatever you want. You can dedicate the class to someone; you can promise yourself to get through the class without judgment against yourself; you can strive to have your best class ever; whatever you like, but it is important to set your intention."

My intention is to see if I can fully accept what I did to Billy, own it, forgive myself for it, and somehow manage to get on with my life. Geez, how the hell is that going to happen? I know I'm the only one who can make it happen. Okay, that's my intention. I wonder what Mabry's intention is.

"Slowly open your eyes. Surya Namaskar: Sun Salutaion. Inhale, hands over head, interlace the fingers, flip the palms to the ceiling, stretch up tall, while rooting your tailbone down. Breathe, in and out, through the nose," H.R. says. "Inhale, lift the chest. Exhale, swan dive forward with a flat back, bending your knees as much as you need to in order to get your hands on the floor by your feet. Relax, let everything hang loose in our first forward fold of the day, Uttanasana."

We progress through the sun salutation and into the moon salutation. I glance at Mabry in the mirror several times and am happy that he seems to be keeping up. I really like H.R.'s soothing voice and flowing rhythm, his selection of peaceful, Indian-style music, and his constant direction on when to inhale and when to exhale. By the time we get to the warrior series, I'm feeling strong and good about myself. I look at my sweat-covered body in the mirror and know, deep down inside, this yoga is good for me in so many ways. H.R. does most of the poses, but occasionally he jumps up and walks over to adjust someone. He adjusts Mabry several times, always offering him encouragement. I notice H.R. constantly scans the room watching everyone, even as he does the poses, giving almost constant verbal instructions. When does he

ever have a chance to breathe I wonder? I guess he's done it so much that it's second nature. We move from Warrior One and Warrior Two into Revolving Triangle.

"Philip," H.R. says as I feel his hands on my hips from behind, "Draw your right hip back a bit to the back wall."

I allow my right hip to follow his gentle pull.

"Nice adjustment, Philip. Perfect Paravritta Trikonasana."

Yeah. I remember when I could barely do this pose. Now I'm nailing it.

"Release forward into Downward Dog, with optional Chattaragna Flow," H.R. says as he falls forward on his own mat to start the triceps push-up flow. I notice that Mabry's thick, curly hair is soaked, his face framed with wet ringlets of hair. Today I am focusing on my intention, despite the fact that there are at least ten women in here I'd bang in a heartbeat. With each push up, each asana, each breath in and out, I'm focusing on my body, my breath, and my brother Billy. Every asana I push to my maximum ability and I dedicate each one to Billy, each inhale I recognize and try to accept my abuse of him, each exhale I try to forgive myself—just a little bit each time. I focus in this manner for several minutes, almost unaware of what my body is doing. The last ten minutes of the vinyasa is the hardest with One-legged Downward Dogs, Half-Wheels, Side Planks, and Triagnua Push-ups. My heart rate is racing, sweat and a noticeable alcohol smell are pouring out of my pores, puddles of sweat have formed on the floor beside my mat, but I am keeping up with H.R. as I alternatively push myself as hard as I can as retribution for hitting Billy and forcing him to have sex with me, then breathing out and forgiving myself for doing it. By the time the vinyasa is over and we are sinking into the Gentle Warrior position, I'm spent, on the verge of passing out, and very emotional.

"From Gentle Warrior, turn around, lie on your back, feet toward the back wall, heels together, toes fanned out, arms below the heart, open your under arms a bit, palms toward the ceiling, chin down, eyes closed, focus on your third eye," H.R. instructs. "Now slow the breath down, breathing in and out through the nose only. Relax the shoulders, relax the hips, and breathe."

I follow his instructions, but my heart feels as if it is about to pound right through my chest wall.

"Visualize your breath as a white ball of energy, starting at the base of your spine," H.R. says in a softer voice. "As you breathe in, this white ball of energy travels up your spine and out the crown of your head, melding with the energy of the universe. As you exhale, you draw this ball of energy through the crown of your head, back down your spine, radiating it out into every cell of your body delivering fresh energy, life force, prana. Visualize this white ball of energy as you breathe in and as you exhale. Slow the breath down, relax." I try to visualize the white ball of energy, and to my surprise, I can see and feel it clearly in my mind's eye. Is this the third eye, I wonder? This visualization technique almost immediately slows my heart rate, and I begin to get my wind back. I visualize my white ball of energy leaving my head and merging with Billy's energy in the universe. Immediately, I'm filled with a warm presence, a presence I know well, Billy. He is here with me now—I feel him in every cell of my body, and sense a feeling of calmness, no, not quite that, but, more of a feeling of 'everything is alright'. Now it hits me—it is a feeling of forgiveness. Billy has indeed forgiven me. I know that to be true. Now, I must try to forgive myself.

"Wiggle your fingers, wiggle your toes to bring awareness back into your body," H.R. calls out. "Slowly open your eyes. Inhale, bend your knees and walk your feet in about forty-five degrees, feet hip width apart on the floor. Good, slowly let your knees falls toward the floor as you turn the soles of your feet to touch. Just breathe and let your hips open. Do not force them. Put your mind and your breath into your hips, the largest joints in the body, and let them open."

I do as he says, but my hips are really tight. I shut my eyes, trying to send my breath to my hips, trying to open them ever so slightly more.

"Today is Monday—Hip opener day," H.R. says. "Apart from a few asanas in the Cobra series, all we will do is hip openers on the floor today. Be mindful of your breath as we open our hips, the largest joints in our bodies and the seat of many of our emotions."

We progress into wind releasing pose, gentle side twist, then flip over on our bellies for a quick Cobra series. After that, it is all hip openers, several of which are new to me. We do something called Janupadasana One and Two, Ninety-ninety, and Gomuktasansa (Cow-faced pose). H.R. hands out blocks and I take one, because my hips are so tight, one side is usually up off the floor. My left hip seems tighter than the right. H.R. tells us the left hip is associated with emotional issues related to your mother and the right hip your father. Great, I think, no wonder my hips are so tight. I keep my breath moving in and out smoothly all during the hip openers, and even though, it is painful to me, I begin to feel a bit of release. Our last pose is Pigeon and as we go into Pigeon on the left side from Downward Dog, a beautiful rendition of *Amazing Grace* comes on and H.R. points out it is sung in Cherokee. I stretch into Pigeon with my left leg turned inward toward the center of the mat and my right leg stretched out behind me. By using a block on the flat side to help support my left hip, I'm able to get down on my elbows and then stretch my arms forward, lying my forehead on the map, stretching my arms out, palms down into sleeping pigeon.

"Close your eyes and breathe," H.R. gently instructs to the class. "Put your mind and your breath into your left hip. Ask it to open a little bit more with each exhale."

I do this. We stay on this pose a long time. After a couple of minutes of breathing into the pose and listening to this haunting version of *Amazing Grace*, I realize the sweat pouring off my face is tears. I feel Mother's presence envelop me; I can even smell Chanel Number 5. I cry as I tell her how much I love her and how angry I am that she left Billy and me. I cry and cry and cry. It is so obvious to me that I directed my anger with Mother for dying toward Billy. It is so painfully obvious now. God, how stupid, weak, ignorant, frail, and vain was I to do that? What a sick soul I had then. I know you have forgiven me Billy. Can I ever forgive myself?

"Wiggle your fingers, wiggle your toes, and gently push back into Downward Dog," H.R. says. I do this and grab a towel to wipe my face and blow my nose. I hear muffled sobs throughout the room. "Now on the exhale take the right knee, behind the right wrist, and carefully flow into Pigeon."

I do as he says and to my amazement, my right hip has opened much more than the left—I don't even need a block or rolled towel under it because it is resting on the floor. I smile thinking of my sweet Dad and stretch out into full, sleeping pigeon, closing my eyes. My sobs over Mother and Billy are calming and I feel so much love as I breathe into this hip. A vision of Dad, Billy, and me walking through the woods in the early springtime, myriads of small woodland flowers in bloom in hues of white, yellow and purple; the hardwood trees sending out their blossoms in shades of gold, yellow, and red; a freshness in the air that is so short lived, especially in the south; and the perfect time for hunting salamanders in the brooks and streams. Dad carries an orange backpack filled with sandwiches, apples, potato chips and drinks for lunch and a couple of jars for salamanders we hope to catch to use for bait for bass fishing tomorrow. We get to spend an entire weekend with Dad. Billy and I are so excited. Dad smiles as he walks between us; I look up at his stubbly face as he takes my right hand in his left and then takes Billy's left hand in his right.

"Hang on tight boys. Let's take a short cut up the side of this hill," Dad says as he leans forward toward the steep incline and pulls us up along with him. This is the greatest. This is the good life. The forest birds sing in unison a glorious hymn of life as they build their nests and feed on the plethora of springtime insects.

I have the urge to open my eyes and look up to H.R.'s mat, so I do, and I witness him in full Pigeon. My God, what a beautiful sight: his back, a canvas of well-defined muscles, arches back into a graceful curve, his heart lifts to the sky, his arms, laced with sinuous muscles, reach over his head allowing his hands to hold his right foot, the sole of which touches the crown of his head, and the contracted hamstring muscles of his right leg ripple in the glistening sweat and waves of furry brown hair covering his legs. His eyes are open. He sees me watching him. He smiles at me, and from somewhere deep with me, a huge grin blossoms across my face and I feel love and I feel the spirit of the universe coursing through my body

with each beat of my heart and I feel a part of everything and that everything is a part of me and I begin to forgive myself for hurting my brother.

'Slowly release Pigeon. Inhale and exhaling through the nose push back into final Downward Dog," H.R. instructs calmly. "Compare this Downward Dog to the first Downward Dog at the beginning of class, and gauge the state of your body. We've worked every muscle, joint, tendon, and organ in the body. We've stretched out the fascia, the connective tissue. Every cell has been flushed clean and filled with fresh prana. Breathe in and out through the nose."

I do feel refreshed and revitalized. My body is warm and my muscles feel limber and stretched. My upper back and neck feel relaxed. I look back at Mabry who has made it through to this final downward dog.

"Now drop gently to your knees," H.R. continues, "Cross your shins and sit back in Indian style. Bring your hands into prayer at heart center. Remember the intention you set at the beginning of class."

I am amazed that I have really focused on my beginning intention, felt forgiveness from Billy, and have a feeling that I will be able to forgive myself. There is something about this flow, the breathing, and the unique combination of it all that awakens something deep within me. Maybe there is something to all this chakra business. I need to learn more about this.

"Turn over on your back for final Savasana," H.R. says quietly as the music fades and the sound of gentle ocean waves breaking on shore fills the room. "Close your eyes, focus on your third eye. Heels together, toes apart. Hands below the heart, palms open and up. Open the underarms. Relax completely. Let your hips relax. Let your shoulders relax. Slow the breath down. Breathe in and out through the nose."

H.R. is silent for a while and I focus on slowing my breath down. My heart is thumping, but I try to ignore it as I breathe in and out through my nose and try to mentally focus on my third eye.

"Refocus on the white ball of energy we visualized earlier," H.R. says. "Breathe in as the white ball of energy travels up your spine and through the crown of your head, melding with the energy of the universe. Exhale as you pull this fresh energy back through your head, down the spine, flowing into every cell in your body. Slow the breath down, relax."

The sound of the ocean waves is so calming. I feel almost as if I am on a beach somewhere. I fall into a deeper state of relaxation as I focus on my breath and the white ball of energy rising up and down my spine.

"Now, as your breath slows and the chatter of the mind calms, take a moment or two between breaths to experience the breathless state," H.R. says, almost in a whisper.

I follow his instructions and have no fear or problem remaining in a breathless state for several seconds between breathing in and breathing out.

"Imagine a summer sky," H.R. continues, "with a bright blue sky dotted with white puffy clouds floating by. Let the clouds represent each breath, and the blue sky between the clouds represents the breathless state. Focus on this state and relax."

I do this and a flood of warmth and calmness enters my body. I feel as if I'm floating.

After a while, H.R. says, "Now send out a white beam of light from your third eye. Send it out to every person in this room. As you send it out, you are also receiving it from each person in the room. Breathe. This light unites us all in our practice today and in our meditative state we begin to find the answers to the questions we seek as we connect to the universe. And so it is. Shanti, shanti, shanti. Thank you for coming today. Stay here in savasana as long as you long. Namaste."

Apart from the sound of the ocean waves, there is no other sound in the room and we all lie still in savasana. After a while, I hear H.R. get up and tip toe out of the room. The lights go off and ceiling fans come on, sending out waves of warm air over my sweat-covered body. I lie here in a calm state, motionless except for my breath. I feel warm, secure, connected, content, and safe. I feel at home.

"Philip, Philip," I hear H.R.'s warm baritone whisper to me, and I feel the touch of his hand on my left shoulder. I open my eyes and chills run down my chest and my legs. I'm cold and I wish I had a warm blanket to cover my body.

"You must've fallen asleep, Philip," H.R. says, smiling down at me. I smile back, astonished as I discern from the sunlight streaming through the front windows, reflecting up onto his face, that his dark brown eyes are actually beautiful, multi-hued marbles—a kaleidoscope of brown, black, green, amber, and even deep blue shades.

"Sorry," I reply. "How long have I been here?" I ask as I roll over on my left side, pushing my body up into a sitting position, goose bumps erupting over my body in waves.

He chuckles, "About thirty minutes, but there's not another class until four pm, so I left you alone," he says as he stands up, then bends over, draping a large, warm towel over my shoulders.

"Mmmn, thanks," I moan with satisfaction.

"I thought you might be chilly in here. I just pulled this out of the dryer. You sweat as much as I do. Once you start cooling off, you can get chilled pretty fast."

"Yes, I'm chilled to the bone," I reply, shivering even as I pull the warmth of the towel around my body.

"Your body guard out there, Officer O'Daniel, seemed pretty concerned about you lying here for so long, after everyone left and all. I told him to just let you alone, that you probably need this time of meditation and rest. Oh, your friend Mabry did really well. He said he would be coming back. He left the shorts you lent him in a plastic bag on the bench in the locker room. He said to tell you good bye."

"Thanks, H.R. You're right. I did need it. And thanks for a great class. One of my best yoga classes ever," I say as I look up at him observing that he has changed into a pair of black running shorts and wears a tight fitting, brightly colored tie-dyed T-shirt. I roll onto my knees and push my torso up with my hands, standing on my knees, then pull the still warm towel tightly around my shoulders. His muscular, hairy quadriceps are right in front of my face, and I wonder if I keep up with this yoga if my muscles will pop out like his. H.R. looks into my eyes. He must really be a turn on to women and gay men; I suspect he is gay.

"Are you gay, H.R.?" I look up at him as the question just pops out of my mouth.

His face shows a look of surprise, then he smiles and replies, "Yes, I am. Why do you ask, Philip?"

"I don't know," I reply, "I guess I just wanted to know, that's all."

"You are not gay. Are you, Philip?"

"No, I'm not. But I have nothing against gays at all," I reply.

"Yeah, I could tell you are not gay," he replies.

"How?" I ask.

"Oh, the way you look at the women in the class," he replies.

"Geez. Am I that obvious? Do I ogle that much?"

He laughs. "No, no, Philip. At least, no more than any normal straight man. It's just that I picked up on it immediately when I saw you in class yesterday."

"Oh, okay," I reply, "At least, I guess it's okay. I hope I didn't make any of the women feel uncomfortable?"

"Oh no, Philip. I didn't mean that at all. Crap, you could have half the women in here. I mean. I observed how they looked at you, too."

"Really?" I ask.

"Oh yes. I mean, what's not to like? You're a friendly, handsome, well-built dude," he replies.

"Gee, thanks, H.R. You are, too," I reply. "Plus, you are a great yoga teacher, and I can tell you must be really well balanced. I mean, you must have it all together about yourself and your life. Otherwise, you couldn't teach the way you do, and share with others the way you do, and give so much of yourself, the way you do."

"Gosh, thanks, brother. That is so kind," H.R. says, approaches me, reaches out his hands, pulls me up, takes me in his strong arms, pulls me into his chest and hugs me. I wrap my arms around his waist, hugging him back. The towel falls of my shoulders, he releases me, bends over, picks up the towel, and hands it back to me with a smile on his face.

I smile back and say, "You know, I'm going to be living in New York now. I'd love to get together with you sometime maybe for a drink or something. Do you drink?"

"Sure, I'd love it. I drink, but not like I used to," he replies with a big smile.

"Great. Let's exchange phone numbers when I get out of the shower," I say.

"Sure," he replies as we begin to walk out of the yoga room into the lobby. A slim young woman wearing what appears to be a bikini is behind the front desk, and Officer O'Daniel has come inside and is sitting in a chair reading a newspaper. He looks up as we enter the lobby.

"Listen, Philip. I've got to go to another studio now for a private instruction, but I'll leave my card with Jana at the front desk for you," he replies.

"Okay, cool," I reply. "You teach private yoga lessons?"

"Yeah, I do."

"Hmmn. How much do they cost?"

"A hundred and fifty dollars an hour," he replies.

"Maybe I should do that sometime?"

"Sure. It's a good way to improve your technique," he replies.

"Great. Listen, H.R., thanks for everything. I'll give you a call. It may be a couple of weeks, though."

"Cool. Take care, Philip," he says sticking out his right hand. We shake hands.

"Great. Thanks again for a great class. I'll see you, H.R."

"Good," he says, turns around, walks past Officer O'Daniel heading into a back hallway.

"Brent," I say as I walk over to Officer O'Daniel, "Sorry, seems I fell asleep in there."

"Yes, I know. Mr. Ferguson told me. He said to leave you alone, though. Miss Richardson phoned me. She was a little concerned when we didn't return by three thirty."

"I'm sorry. Listen, let me grab a quick shower. I'll be right out."

"Take your time," he replies. "Oh, Detectives Bell and Johnson want to know if they can meet you at your house when you return."

I sigh, "Sure, Brent. What the hell? Tell them I'm happy to meet them there," I say as I turn around, observe that Jana has been watching us, and walk toward the men's locker room.

"Detective Bell, Detective Johnson, how are you both today?" I ask as I walk into the same sitting room we've used all last week on the first floor of Billy's building.

"Fine, thank you, Mr. Hampton," Detective Johnson says, getting up from one of the armchairs. Detective Bell remains seated in another armchair typing something on her Blackberry. She looks lovely today, in a tailored suit made of a chocolate brown fabric with Tiffany blue pinstripes, a silk blouse to match the pinstripes, and brown pumps. She wears the same Ohm necklace she had on yesterday, and gold loops in her ears. She finishes typing, looks up at me with an annoyed look on her face, and stands up.

"Hello, Mr. Hampton. I know you've heard about Ricky Wallitsch. Now we have five murders involved in this case."

"Five?" I ask.

"Yes, even though they're criminals, don't forget about the Boonmee twins," she replies, raising her left eyebrow producing a look of strong intelligence which I find incredibly attractive.

"Awe, yes, Adrian's little murder machines," I reply. "Have you figured out yet why he disposed of them, Detective?"

Her brown eyes darken, I see a faint flush in her cheeks, she purses her lips with a smacking sound and replies, "No, we do not know the motive for their murders."

"I do," I reply. "It's simple. Their usefulness to Adrian had expired; therefore, he deleted them. I'm surprised you all haven't picked up on this pattern of Adrian's."

"I'm unimpressed with your unsubstantiated speculations, Mr. Hampton," Detective Bell blurts out in a loud voice. "We're here to ask you more questions, if you don't mind."

"Just trying to help out, Detective Bell," I reply, "But, by all means, proceed with your questions."

"Thank you," she replies looking over at Detective Johnson who is wearing a blue pinstripe suit, white shirt, and a silk tie with a dark yellow and white herringbone pattern. He has a dark yellow handkerchief folded and inserted in the breast pocket of his jacket so that four small peaks protrude form the pocket. He looks elegant today.

"Mr. Hampton, we've interview Jonathan Zeng and Isabella de la Croix this morning," Detective Johnson says. "Based on their testimonies and your testimony we have ample evidence to extradite Adrian McWhorter from Dubai on grounds of sexual abuse of minors. We've also interviewed Dominick Montaigne this morning and feel certain, with the help of agents in the Netherlands, we can add trafficking in child pornography charges soon."

"You'll never find him," I state flatly.

"How can you be so sure?" Detective Bell asks.

"Because he doesn't want to be found," I reply.

"Don't be so sure, Mr. Hampton," Detective Johnson replies, crossing his arms. "The Crown Prince would not meet with us, but we did speak with him over the telephone, and he gave us the exact address of Adrian's compound in Dubai. We've begun paperwork for the extradition already. That's why we are here, to get as much detail as possible about Adrian's sexual abuse of you and your brother."

"Oh dear God," I reply, "I could write a friggin' book about it! There's so much, so many occurrences. It would take a very long time."

"Time is not what we have, Mr. Hampton," Detective Bell says. "That is, if you want to insure the safety of your niece and nephews."

I squint my eyes at her and feel my mouth and nose convulse into a snarl. "If he so much as lays a hand on them, I'll tear his heart out with my bare hands."

"Perhaps it would be a better idea to direct all your emotions into recalling specific acts of sexual abuse on specific dates against you and your brother," she replies.

"Why don't we all sit down?" Detective Johnson directs.

I sigh and walk over to a sofa, sit down, fold my arms, and try to begin digging deep within myself to reveal the Blood Brothers story to the detectives. They return to their wing back chairs to sit and Detective Johnson pulls out a digital recording device from his brief case and sets it on the coffee table in front of me.

"I know this will be unpleasant, Mr. Hampton," Detective Johnson says in a low, kind, gentle tone, and I think he must be a really good father, that is, if he has children. "Let's start at the beginning, the very beginning. Tell us what you remember and try to include specific dates and places when you can."

"Oh, I can, Detectives. You will be amazed at what I can tell you," I say, looking down at the floor, feeling my eyes well up with tears. "Let's go back to the summer of 1982. Remember that summer? Boy, I do. I was nine years old, going on ten, and Billy was seven. The very first time Uncle Adrian sexually abused Billy and me was Sunday, the fourth of July, 1982 around noon at a swimming hole in the Fair Forest Creek very near to where it dumped into the Tyger River which ran through a large farm in Union County, South Carolina, owned by my grandmother, Fatgram…."

The elevator door opens and Clark awaits me, tail wagging, mouth open, smiling, panting. He takes one look at me; his ears perk up forward, but quickly fold back. He stands, tail tucked between his legs,

walks over to me, his entire body in a submissive posture. I sit down on the floor Indian style and offer my right hand to his nose, letting him sniff it. I embrace him, pull him into my lap, fold around him, place my face on the top of his head, and cry. I stay in this position until I hear footsteps in the foyer and I look up to see Lush, Isabella, Julianna, Janet, and Officer O'Daniel all looking down at me.

"Oh, Todge," Lush says squatting down to embrace me. "I'm so sorry you had to go through that—my God, almost two hours. Brent filled us in on what was going on." Julianna, Janet, and Isabella surround me, bending down to touch me, then squatting to hold me too.

"I guess this is what they call a group hug," I say with a snicker through my tears. "You all are the best. I can't thank you enough for your compassion and kindness."

Clark becomes uneasy as the nucleus of the group and begins to struggle to get out. He stands up and pushes through the women.

"I better get up, too. My knees are killing me," I say.

The ladies peel back, Lush grabs my left shoulder, Julianna takes my right shoulder, and they help me stand. Brent stands in the foyer nervously observing the scene.

"Thanks. Thank you all," I say. "I'm okay. I'm fine. Just emotionally spent. I could use a drink, and I'm starving."

"We've got you covered," Lush says. "Come sit in the living room. I'll fix you a drink. What would you like?"

"Something strong and cold. How about an Old Fashioned, no soda?"

"You got it, Todge. Food will be here shortly. I ordered from an Italian restaurant that delivers; Timmy suggested it. There are hors d'oeuvres out here. I invited the ladies to dinner. I hope that's okay. I'll be right back."

"That sounds wonderful, Lush. You're the best."

We walk into the living room to the central sitting area where I see on a coffee table a large wooden cutting board with several different types of cheese; a platter with water crackers and melba toast; a tureen of mixed olives; and a tray containing red and green grapes, strawberries, and chunks of pineapple. The ladies have been enjoying cocktails and appetizers while they waited for me to finish with the detectives. I cut a piece of blue cheese, put it on a cracker and shove the whole thing in my mouth—it tastes wonderful, so I make another and eat it.

"Sorry to be such a pig, but I'm ravenous," I say as soon as I swallow the second cheese and cracker. "I haven't had anything to at all day but a bowl of cereal at breakfast."

"Poor dear," Julianna says, "I know this has been a long day for you, but now you can relax and enjoy a wonderful dinner with four beautiful ladies."

"Yes, I am a lucky man, indeed," I reply as I sit down on one of the sofas. Clark immediately jumps up beside me, sits down, resting his head in my lap. "And don't forget the best doggie in the world, too," I say as I stroke his head. His lets out a big sigh.

"He really loves you, Philip," Janet says. "I believe he was waiting for your return all afternoon."

"Yes, I think he was," Isabella says. "He seemed nervous or anxious until just now."

"Is that so?" I ask.

"Oh yes," Julianna says, "He was pacing in the studio as we went through Billy's paintings. Lush would let him outside, he'd go out, look around, then come right back in."

"Wow. Maybe since he just lost Billy, he's worried the same thing will happen to me?"

"That might be the case," Lush says as she enters the room holding my Old Fashioned. "He kept coming up to me, looking up at me, as if he wanted to ask me a question. Kind of strange," she says, handing me my drink. I take a sip.

"Oh, two things I cherish from Kentucky, Lush and good bourbon," I say with a smile.

"Sometimes you are so irresistibly charming, Todge," Lush replies smiling back at me.

I smile, take another sip of the Old Fashioned and ask, "Any news from Jonas?"

Lush immediately draws her right index finger up to her lips and purses them. She points with her left index finger toward the foyer where I have forgotten Officer O'Daniel is sitting. I shake my head in acknowledgement.

"No news from anyone," Julianna quickly interjects, but we've had a successful afternoon going through Billy's works. Do you feel like hearing about what I think we should do, Philip?"

"Of course, Julianna, tell me," I reply.

"Well, I think we should have a posthumous showing of his new works in the fall. It will be the buzz of the season. We can do teaser advertising throughout the summer, and by fall, I predict it will be one of the biggest openings of the season."

"I think that is a great plan. I'm in," I reply.

"Good," Julianna replies, takes a sip of her champagne and continues, "Isabella has agreed, provided it meets with your approval, to represent Billy on the west coast, through her gallery in Sante Fe."

"It meets with my approval. Thank you, Isabella for agreeing to do this."

"You're most welcome," she replies from where she is sitting, legs crossed, in a winged back chair. She is lovely this evening dressed in a black pants suit with a raspberry colored blouse and a white silk scarf with shades of pink and green in it. "I'm certain I have clients who will embrace with enthusiasm your brother's recent works."

"Wonderful," I reply, trying not to stare at her.

"We have other good news, Philip," Julianna says, her voice becoming higher in pitch. "Later in the fall, I'm having an opening for Janet and Isabella will also be representing her on the west coast."

"Fantastic," I say, looking over toward Janet who is sitting in an armchair adjacent to the sofa where I sit. Janet, also dressed in a black pants suit, but with a black blouse, smiles, shrugs her shoulders, and clasps her hands together.

"I just can't believe this is happening to me. It's like I'm dreaming and I do not want to wake up."

"Darling, you deserve this," Lush says to her. "Great talent deserves to be broadcast. Your time is coming."

"Yes it is," I reply. "You are so fortunate to have Julianna take you under her wing, Janet. Some artists, some very good artists struggle a life time without ever having someone like Julianna understand their work and present it to the rest of the world."

"Oh, yes. That is so true, Philip," Janet replies. "Why, just last week, I was focused entirely on my art classes. I never even had any thought of having my art shown to the world and now, well now, I, I,..." Her eyes fill up with tears. "It's just so wonderful and you all have been so kind to me, especially during such a tragic period for all of you."

Lush walks over behind Janet's chair, puts her hands on Janet's shoulders, and says, "Darling, it's you who has been so kind to us and to Billy. We'll never be able to thank you enough for that."

"That is so true, Janet," I say. "You've been our angel through all of this, and I'm forever grateful to you."

"Thank you," she says to me in a whisper. "Thank you."

The telephone rings.

"I'll get it," Lush says, walks over to a phone on one of the end tables and picks it up.

"Hello? Yes. The service elevator? Okay, thanks, Timmy." Lush turns toward everyone. "Dinner has arrived. It is being delivered on the service elevator. I set the table earlier, so we can eat whenever you all are ready."

"Well, just let me wash up and I'll be ready," I say.

"Go ahead, Todge. We'll get everything set out in the dining room. I ordered everything in large portions so we can just pass things around family style or do a buffet."

"You all are family to me. Let's do it family style," I reply as I gently shake Clark awake and lift his head from my lap and stand up. He's reluctant to leave his comfortable position, but he hops on the floor, yawns, stretching his mouth wide open emitting a high pitch, then stretches by doing a downward dog stretch.

"You're a sleepy boy. Time to wake up," I say to him as I stand up.

"Time for his dinner. I'll feed him while you freshen up, Todge," Lush says.

"Great," I reply, pick up my drink, turn toward everyone, "Excuse me, ladies, I'll join you all in the dining room in five minutes."

"Take your time, Philip." Julianna says.

"Come on Clark," Lush says, "Time for dinner."

His ears perk up and he trots after her as she walks toward the kitchen.

I head down the hall toward Billy's bedroom. Well, I guess it's my bedroom now, but I suppose I'll always call it Billy's bedroom. I really do think I'll live here permanently. Even though I love living in Atlanta, the short winters, the long summers, the slower pace of life in the south, I am ready for a change, a new direction. I think one of my biggest fears has been that I've been living my life as if I am just a shell of a person—always on the run, always traveling from one assignment to the next, never really settling down, not even in Atlanta, never really committing fully to anything or anyone except the next story. I walk through the bedroom, glance at my birthday painting from Mother, glance up at her painting of Willie B, and glance up at a self-portrait Billy painted of himself at eighteen years old. He was completely untrained, but I can't think that anyone could have better captured the essence that he was at that age—beautiful and defiant. His eyes broadcast the message, 'I know I'm beautiful and I know you want me. You can have me, if I so desire, but you better be careful, because I'm not afraid of anyone, and I'm on a journey deep within the darkness of my soul. You may be elated, satisfied, comforted, loved; or you may be shocked, frightened, horrified, mortified; but, you'll probably experience all of these feelings together in some combination because I live my life like a gyroscope, spinning rapidly around myself, yet free to go wherever I choose.' Yes, that's my brother, and I see parts of him in me, but I know the part of me that has to go on without him now, has to be that part of me that is uniquely me—the feeling in that shell, that void, that coldness, the deep dark space really just an extension of my own Mother's turmoil. I splash water on my face and look at my face in the mirror, beads of water running down my face, the drops splattering into dark spots on my blue Oxford cloth shirt, and I ask myself, "Who is this man I see? Who are you Philip Hampton? What is your reason for being? What do you need to do to be more than a shell? Why does it matter you are still living and Billy is not?" And deep within my eyes, and deeper within my heart, I know I do not know the answer to any of these, yet. But what I do know and I feel with a great welling of energy arising from deep within my gut is that I am now on the right path, the way that will reveal the answers to these questions, a journey which I can only describe as spiritual. Yes, the word spiritual feels right, not in any religious sense, but in a natural, worldly, universal sense. At this moment I feel as if I am a part of everything and everyone in this building, in this city, on this planet, in this solar system, in this galaxy, in this universe. I look into my eyes and I see visions of giant spinning galaxies, exploding stars and forming stars. And in all this cosmic display of evolution, the one feeling I feel is love, just pure love like a bright light, not toward me or anyone in particular, just pure distilled love, and I know, deep down inside myself, that if I can feed myself and others around me with this feeling of love and light, that cold darkness in space within myself, that innermost fear that sucks in everything, like a giant stellar black hole, is really nothing unknown at all. That's who you are Philip Hampton, that's who you really are. I dry my face off and say, "Mother, I love you and I forgive you. Fatgram, I know you must have arrived at a similar pool of knowledge as I have. Thank you for helping to direct me here." I walk out of the bathroom and into the closet to get a fresh shirt, and I know that I'll be doing a lot of yoga here in my new hometown.

"Todge, you sit here at the head of the table," Lush says. "You're the man of the house."

"Thank you, Lush," I reply. "Tonight I don't feel like a man as you would most likely define a man. I feel like a blessed citizen of the universe. Just a happy part of it all."

"What a beautiful feeling, Philip," Isabella says.

"Yes it is," Julianna says.

Lush sits to my right and Janet sits to her right. Julianna sits to my left and Isabella sits to her left.

"I don't normally pray," I state, "But tonight I would like to offer a prayer. Ladies, please indulge me. Let's all join hands. Let's stand up so Isabella and Janet can reach across the table and complete the circle."

Everyone stands up and we join hands.

"Dear God, God of the universe, God that is a compilation of every single minute particle in this universe and all the universes, I am but one small speck of light in the enormity of it all, one small speck of light who shines my light with all the love instilled in me, the love which comes from being a part of you. And in my blessing of light I thank you and I thank these four other beautiful specks of light whose hands are joined with mine tonight, and I pray that your light and love shine within each of us and that we, in turn, share this light and love with you and all those within our presence. Amen."

"Oh, Todge, that was beautiful," Lush says. We're all still holding hands.

"It was lovely," Janet says.

"Yes," Isabella says.

"So spiritual," Julianna says.

I squeeze Julianna's hand and Lush's hand, look around at each person and let go. We all sit back down.

"Thank you all. It's funny. I've always been taught and told that there was a God, but I never really knew God or even felt that there really was a God—especially this week. But somehow last night, looking at those paintings of Dyanne O'Bryan's, a woman so tortured physically, mentally, and spiritually by her own religion, so much so that it is likely she may have orchestrated the Gardner heist, I came to the realization that those paintings, those beautiful yet horrific paintings were merely a plea, a cry for that which she did not find, could never find in her own religion—that light, that love to which and about which I just prayed."

No one says a word for what seems like minutes, and I think they must be all thinking I am a complete fool or have gone off my rocker.

"Philip," Julianna says, peering deeply into my eyes, "That was one of the most insightful things I've ever heard in my life. You have a God given gift with words, with expressing what artists strive to do in their works. You, my friend, are an artist."

"Oh, thank you, Julianna," I reply with a rush of relief going through my body, "What a kind thing to say."

"Kind, but true," she replies. "Philip, it would be a great honor to me and Billy, if you would write the catalog for his opening this fall."

"Really?" I ask.

"Absolutely," Julianna replies.

"I, I, don't know what to say." I reply.

"For God's sake, say yes, Todge," Lush says, smiling.

"Well, okay. Yes, I accept," I reply.

"Wonderful. Then it's done!" Julianna says. "Let's pour some wine and toast to this."

"I opened two wines from the Piedmont region, one red, one white," Lush says. "Who wants what?"

"Piedmont? I'm guessing that's Italy, not South Carolina," I say to Lush.

"You're guessing right, darling. I've never heard of any wineries in South Carolina. But, I suppose there are some now. It seems almost every little town has a winery these days."

I laugh. "Just teasing you, honey."

We pour the wine and Lush stands up and says, "Here's to the older brother, Philip, a man unafraid to share his wisdom and his kindness with others, a man who is truly committed to the ones he loves, a man I am so honored to call my best friend."

We toast, take a sip of wine and everyone focuses their attention on me, and for the hundredth time this past week, my eyes fill with tears, but this time it's not from grieving, it's from feeling loved, so I raise my glass up again, tears rolling out of both eyes, and I say, "Here's to you Lush, my darling one, the woman I betrayed but who transcended that gut wrenching hurt to accept and embrace me and lift my spirit, and direct me to a higher way of living; and here's to you, Julianna, a woman who possesses both great knowledge and great capacity to love; and here's to you Janet, a woman who possesses great compassion and an immense talent with the canvass; and here's to you Isabella, a woman whose kindness and inner strength is commensurate with her great beauty; and finally, to Clark, whose capacity for unconditional love is only exceeded by his immense intelligence concerning human nature."

"I'll toast to that, Todge," Lush says, holding her glass of white wine high up into the air. The other ladies all stand up in a synchronized fashion and suddenly, I feel left out for being the only man around the table.

CHAPTER 39

The sleek, small, white jet lifts into the air, rapidly ascending through the chilly mist. Lush is seated across the aisle looking out of the window and Clark sits beside me, my arms around him. He glances up into my eyes every few seconds for reassurance. Then finally satisfied that this strange vehicle meets my approval, he sighs, relaxes, and leans his head onto my chest. I stroke his head.

"You're a good boy, Clark," I say to him. "It's okay. You're safe with me up here."

Lush smiles at me, "Is he okay?"

"He's fine. He's relaxing. He'll be an old pro at flying by the time we get to Louisville," I reply.

"Good," Lush says, "I'm so glad you brought him. I think he would have been really sad if you had left him so soon after Billy's death."

"Yeah. It just occurred to me last night that even with Lois staying there, he might be worried that we were never coming back."

"I wonder if dogs have a sense of the future?" Lush asks.

"I have no idea, Lush, but I do know they have the ability to read a person's emotions."

"Oh, yes," Lush says, "I know that is true, certainly in Clark's case. Sometimes I think it must be a combination of visual and olfactory senses. I imagine our bodies release different odors under different emotional states."

"Fascinating," I reply as I stroke Clark's head.

"How did you ever manage to convince the detectives to let us come to Louisville alone?" Lush asks.

"It was not easy," I reply, "But when I told them Jonas would meet us at the airport and be our bodyguard during our stay, they began to back down. Perhaps you were hoping they would have sent Officer O'Daniel?"

Lush rolls her eyes and grimaces, "Really, Todge."

"I'm just kidding; I'm sorry. I shouldn't have said that. I'll have you know I'm beginning to like Brent. He is a very good guy."

"Thanks, Todge. He is nice. However, my focus is dealing with David, then focusing on myself to see where I'm going with the next phase of my life."

"That's important, Lush. God knows you owe it to yourself and, as much as I hate to say it, to David."

"Yes. Yes indeed," she replies stretching her long fingers out, observing her nails. "I'm going to my salon this afternoon while you go up to St. Meinrad—manicure, pedicure, facial, hair cut, the works."

"That sounds restful. You should schedule a massage as well, darling," I reply.

"Maybe I will, but, my regular masseuse is not nearly as good as Timmy," she replies.

"Timmy is great; he knows what he's doing," I reply. Apart from Adrian and Billy, Timmy is the only other man I've ever had sex with. It was pleasurable enough, but it is just not what I crave deep within. Women, on the other hand, draw me in completely. I want to caress their breasts, touch their soft skin and lips, lick their nipples, and lower myself onto them. The sight of curved hips in a skirt drives me wild. Christ, why do I think about sex so fucking much? It's always on my mind, even in the most grievous of times such as now. I feel compelled to go back to the bathroom and jerk off, but we are still climbing and I tell myself to put the brakes on the sexual urge. Crap, I feel like a total pervert—sex, sex, sex, that's all I ever think about. Get it together and focus Hampton.

"I've been thinking about what Jonas said on the telephone last night," Lush says. "Cara describes Dyanne as brilliant, unstable, highly emotional, and highly sexual with both men and women and she used her intelligence to manipulate people."

"Well, I suppose the rapist priest taught her well," I reply still annoyed at myself that I want to beat off.

"Todge, that's a bit severe," she replies reaching in her purse for sunglasses as the plane clears the cloud layer, shooting up into the blue sky. She puts her glasses on and turns her head toward me. "However, I get what you are saying. He must have been a master of manipulation to get her to do what he wanted for such a long time and to make Dyanne lie to her parents and say the father of the baby was a high school boy.""Yes, that's quite a lie to keep up, but look at my family, we've had a few zingers like that over the years," I reply.

"A lot of people have," Lush replies, "But, what I'm wondering is even though Cara thinks the whole Gardner thing is mere speculation, she describes Dyanne's and Ted's relationship to Jonas as almost entirely controlled by Dyanne. Couldn't Dyanne have masterminded the heist and convinced Ted to do it?"

"It seems plausible to me," I reply.

"The mysterious death of the priest and the gruesome death of Ted Johnson just smell of Adrian to me. The more I think about it, the more I feel certain of it," she says leaning back in her seat and turning her head toward the window.

"Adrian likes nooses and Ted was found hanged," I reply.

"Jonas did say Cara confirmed that Adrian was 'courting Dyanne' prior to Ted's murder," Lush says, still looking out the window.

"That means he probably visited her in Bardstown," I reply.

Lush sighs, reaches in her bag and pulls out a brown envelope. "Todge, I think you better look at these now. I looked at them again last night." She hands me the envelope. Clark sniffs it as I take it. I hesitate a moment, then open the envelope and pull out the glossy eight by ten black and white photographs. The

first one is obviously Jonathan Zeng. He is standing nude in front of a full-length white porcelain urinal. His body is in profile, but he is looking boldly at the photographer. His uncircumcised penis is half erect as he holds it for display with his left hand. A faint ring of dark hair rings the base of his penis. The next picture is more disturbing. It shows Jonathan bent over on his knees, spreading his ass cheeks open for a full view of his asshole. He peers out over his left shoulder at the camera, smiling. The next three pictures are of Jonathan and a nude, erect Adrian. Adrian's face is not in any of the photos. Then I come to the photographs of Billy and me that first day of our Blood Brother's initiation at Fatgram's swimming hole. To my surprise, I am not shocked or angry, just sad, very sad. There are ten of these photos that range from Billy peeing in the creek, to Billy and me sitting on Uncle Adrian's legs—all naked—to Billy sucking my cock, to Uncle Adrian sucking Billy's cock, to Billy and me smiling, leaning on Uncle Adrian's chest which is damp with sweat and white cum. That is pretty much how I remember it. The next picture does shock me because I have no recollection of this at all—it is a photograph of me bent over naked holding onto the wooden arms of one of Adrian's antique chairs in his New York apartment while Adrian fucks me—his erect penis almost fully inserted into my ass. My mouth falls open and I gasp. Lush gets up, walks behind my seat and puts her hands on my shoulders.

"I'm so sorry, Philip. I know this is awful for you."

"Lush, I must have been drugged. I just don't remember this happening at all. Maybe I dreamed it; but I don't remember it."

I move to the next picture—Uncle Adrian's right arm under Billy's knees, his left arm under Billy's lower back, pulling him up as he sucks on Billy's hard cock, surprisingly large for such a young boy, Billy's left arm draped around Adrian's neck, his right arm falling straight down toward the floor, revealing his new growth of underarm hair, Billy's head is slung back, his eyes closed, his wavy hair in disarray. This picture really bothers me. It looks almost like a perverted version of the Pieta—something Dyanne O'Bryan would have dreamt up. The next three photographs are all nude portraits of Billy. He must have been eleven; it had to be our final visit to New York the spring before Mother died because I remember Billy began maturing fast that summer, getting hair under his arms, on his pubic region and on his legs. Each photograph zooms in on one of these areas. Billy is not aroused in any of them but does peer into the camera so seductively—a preview for his future modeling career. The final ten photographs are all of two prepubescent twins, who I know must be Christopher and Noel, probably during their Blood Brother's initiation ceremony because the photos are so similar to mine and Billy's. The final photograph is of a boy, just entering puberty; he is standing on a rocky area on a beach. He wears a pair of low cut, white, tight swimmer's briefs, he has pulled out his erect cock from the front of his briefs and is holding it, as he smiles, defiantly at the camera. He already has a small bush in his pubic region and a faint line of hair running up to his navel. He is muscular for such a young guy. He has thick, shaggy hair, hanging halfway down to his shoulders. I see Isabella in his face.

"That has to be Andre de la Croix," Lush states.

"Yes, I think it is," I reply.

"He's as beautiful as Isabella," Lush says.

"Yes," I reply, "But what a sad life he must have led to end up hanging himself in prison."

"Chalk another destroyed human up to Adrian," Lush says with a sigh.

"His time of reckoning is coming," I say as I stuff the photographs back into the envelope.

"I don't suppose he'll reckon with anything, Todge. Even if you string him up and execute him with slow slicing. I imagine he'd relish each cut," she says, vehemently.

I turn around, looking up at her, "My, how do you know about Chinese Imperial torture?"

"Oh, picked it up from a guide when I went up the Yangzi River with Momma," she replies. "A fitting demise for Adrian, I should think—one slice for every life he's ruined." She walks back over to her seat, sits down, pulls off her sunglasses, and looks over at me. "Can I smoke in here?"

"No, darling, this is a non-smoking plane," I reply.

"Well, I suppose I can make it to Louisville," she replies.

I push the call button and the captain immediately responds, "Mr. Hampton, may I help you?"

"Yes, about how much longer will it be before we land in Louisville?" I ask.

"It should be about an hour and fifteen minutes, sir."

"Thanks," I reply.

"Everything alright, sir?"

"Yes, fine, thank you," I reply as I look over at Lush.

"Well, I'm going to get some coffee," Lush says as she gets out of her seat again. "Want some, Todge?"

"Sure," I reply. She walks back to a bar area on the plane to pour the coffee. Clark jumps up and follows her. We have leveled off now and I look out my window at the earth below. Through breaks in the clouds I can see mountain ridges, giant spines running parallel to one another along the earth. Everything looks so small and I cannot make out highways, just scattered cities, so I surmise we must be flying at a higher altitude than commercial flights.

"Lord, they have all sorts of wonderful Danish, muffins, fresh fruit, and yogurt back here, Todge," Lush says. "You care for anything besides coffee?"

"Hmmn, I'd love a cheese Danish if there's one," I reply.

"You're in luck," she replies, "Coming right up. Why don't you come back here and sit, Todge? There's a table back here."

"Okay," I reply. I get up and walk to the back of the plane. "Wow, this is nice," I say as I sit down at the table. Lush serves coffee and Danish.

"Nice china on this plane," Lush says. "Did Billy always fly this way?"

"No, just when he needed to get somewhere quickly or when he didn't feel like being exposed to paparazzi," I reply taking a sip of the hot coffee. Clark pushes my right knee with his nose. "I suppose you want a bit of Danish?" I ask, looking down at him. He peers up at me, panting. I take my fork, cut off a small piece of cheese Danish, pick it up with my right hand, noticing that it is warm to the touch, and feed it to him. He takes the Danish, swallows it, and begins gently licking my fingers. "Good, huh?"

Lush sits down across from me. She has chosen a blueberry muffin. She takes her knife and splits open the muffin. It is smoking hot. "I think I nuked this one a little too long," she says, puts down the knife, picks up her coffee, takes a sip, and smiles at me. I wipe off my fingers with a linen napkin.

"If we find the Gardner heist, how do you plan to trap Adrian?" Lush asks.

"Well, according to Julianna, he'll definitely want to inspect it himself, so he'll have to come to us. I think it would almost be impossible to get the works out of the country, and I would never do that anyway. Adrian will never get those works if we find them. They'll go right back to the Gardner Museum." I take a sip of my coffee to find the taste rich and strong, the way I like it. "Mmmn, really good coffee."

"Yes, it is," Lush replies. "Do you plan to set this up in New York?"

"We'll have to get Jonas's input, but that seems logical since it seems Adrian gets to New York relatively easily." She shakes her head in agreement. I feel guilty so I try to change the subject.

"Is it easy to get to St. Meinrad's from your house?"

"Very easy. I'm about a mile from I-71. You hop on that, it merges directly into I-64 downtown and you drive west on I-64 all the way to the exit to St. Meinrad. It'll take an hour at most."

"Good," I reply, then hesitate a moment. "I'm really anxious to meet Christopher. I'm hoping I can get him to go to Bardstown with me. I think that will be our best chance to find the treasure."

"Yes, I think that will be crucial," Lush replies. "If he has trouble remembering being abused by Adrian, those photos should come in handy."

"Yes, I thought that, too—as cruel as it is, it would most likely do the trick."

Lush takes a sip of her coffee and looks at me, "I'm just afraid Christopher's decision to become a monk is merely an escape from everything hurtful in his life. I mean, I don't know him at all, but having some idea of what he's been through, it is a logical explanation."

"I think you are right, Lush. I expect this is going to be a real challenge. I think you and Jonas should go ahead and contact Dyanne's sister, Joan, to see if she would meet with you later today or tomorrow."

"Sure. She's got to be a plethora of knowledge," Lush replies. "I've been thinking about her. I know she is ten years older than Dyanne. I think Julianna said her son helps run the farm."

"Why is that important?" I ask and take a bite of the cheese Danish. Yum. It is definitely from a nice bakery.

"Well, take Brooker T for example," Lush replies. "Often illegitimate children are kept close within a family, especially if the family is established and affluent. Perhaps Father O'Callaghan and Dyanne's child was given to Joan to raise as her own."

"Wow, good thinking, Lush. I'll ask Christopher if he has any cousins and what ages they are."

"Since Joan now controls all of Dyanne's estate, she had to be close to Dyanne—had to be. I expect she knows much more than Cara knows about all of this," Lush says her eyes drifting down to her coffee cup.

"Well, I'll leave Joan to you and Jonas, and I'll tackle Christopher," I state.

We continue to make our plans for Bardstown, eat our breakfast, and chat. Clark has curled up on the floor under the table and is sound asleep when the captain announces that we will be landing in fifteen minutes, so it's time to fasten our seat belts. We clear the table and return to our seats. I tell Clark to get up in the seat with me. He does, and I hold him as we begin our descent.

"These small jets ascend and descend much more rapidly than commercial airliners," Lush says.

"Yeah, it kinda feels like we're nose-diving on a roller coaster," I reply. I look out the window to discover a cloudless sky and green farmland and forest beneath us. In the distance I see a large river snaking around the landscape. "Guess that's the Ohio River, Lush?"

"Yes, it's a big river," she replies. "Someday you'll have to go boating with me up the river. Just a few miles north of Louisville, it's pristine. You just wouldn't believe it, Todge."

"I didn't know you were into boating," I say.

"Yes, daddy always had houseboats and cabin cruisers. I'm a good captain. David and I kept Daddy's fifty foot motor yacht." She gets a sad look on her face. "Out on the boat, well, it is about the only time we get along anymore."

"When do you plan to talk to David?"

"I don't know. I may just stay here and talk to him when he gets home Saturday night, then fly back up to New York on Sunday. That is, if you don't need me."

"That sounds like a good idea to me," I reply, relieved to know that if Mabry delivers, that's just one less person I have to worry about getting between Adrian and me. I look out and see roads, neighborhoods, shopping malls, and strip centers. The captain announces, "Final approach, Mr. Hampton."

"Here we go, Clark, buddy," I say rubbing his head. "We'll be on the ground soon." I look out as the plane drops over rooftops, then a golf course, and then I see runway underneath us. The pilot lands the plane smoothly and engages the reverse thrusters causing us to jerk a bit. Clark stiffens his legs, pants anxiously, but the plane slows quickly and we begin a slow taxi to the terminal. I look out the window to see rows and rows of small airplane hangers and a few larger, curved roof hangers in the distance. We pull up to a large hanger at the far end of the runway, the plane stops, and the pilot cuts the engines. A big blue Mercedes, driven by a young Latino man, pulls up beside the plane. Jonas sits beside him in the front seat.

"Now this is service," I say to Lush.

"Yes, these small airports are the best. And to think this was once the main airport for Louisville," Lush says.

The young, blonde, co-pilot opens the door from the cockpit and begins to open the door of the plane. Clarks sniffs the air as the door opens. I take his leather lead and latch it to his collar. The co-pilot turns toward us and says, "Just a moment as the staircase opens up." Lush puts her sunglasses back on and picks up her purse. I pick up the envelope with the photographs and take hold of Clark's lead. He immediately heads toward the door, pulling hard on the lead.

"Whoa, boy," I say.

The co-pilot bends down to pet Clark and says, "Did you have a nice flight, boy?" Clarks jumps on his thighs and licks him in the face.

"Well, I take that to mean you did," he says, laughing.

"Thank you," I say to the co-pilot and head down the stairs with Clark. I hear Lush thanking the co-pilot as she descends behind me. As soon as we hit the ground, Clark sniffs the base of the stairs, lifts his right leg and begins peeing all over the staircase.

"He's certainly getting his money's worth," Lush says, already holding a cigarette and a lighter in her hands as she steps on the ground. The Latino man and Jonas walk up to us.

"Good flight?" Jonas asks, smiling.

"Excellent. What a way to fly," I reply, shaking his right hand.

Lush lights her cigarette and takes a big draw. "Jonas, darling, good to see you. I see you've hooked up with Javier. Javier, darling, thanks for picking us up."

"No, problem Miss Richardson," the young man says with a heavy Mexican accent. He smiles, revealing a gold cap on one of his top molars.

"This is Mr. Philip Hampton, Javier," Lush says.

"Hello, sir," Javier says.

"Hello, Javier," I say as I shake his hand.

"Was your flight from Chicago okay, Jonas?" Lush asks.

"Just fine, Lush. Got in at nine o'clock, Javier was there to greet me, and we drove straight here."

"You all don't mind if we stand out here a moment while I smoke?" Lush asks.

"Not at all," Jonas says.

"Oh, this weather is perfect. Spring is the best time of year in Kentucky," Lush says.

Spring is much further along here than in New York, leaves are popping out on the trees, and I see redbud trees in full bloom in the distance. "Is that brick-deco-looking building the terminal, Lush?" I ask.

"Well, it was, originally, Todge." Lush says. "Now it is a bunch of offices and a very fine French restaurant called *Le Relais*. It's quite charming inside, the food is excellent and the owner, Anthony, is a doll. In fact, I thought we might dine there tonight or tomorrow night if it fits into our schedule."

"That sounds nice," I reply.

"I've got some news," Jonas says.

"Good," Lush replies. "Javier, would you please help the co-pilot with our luggage?"

"Yes mam," he replies and walks to the other side of the plane where the co-pilot is unloading our luggage.

"Mabry has been really busy busting into al-Qaeda communication sites. Adrian's disc gave him insight into their encryption methods. He's found out some amazing things. Most importantly, someone high up in the organization is arriving in the United States through Canada sometime this week. We think it must be Adrian. He could already be here."

"Crap," I say. "Why wouldn't he just come on some sheikh's jumbo jet like he always does?"

"Because our friends at the NYPD have filed for extradition. These sheikhs won't be helping him anymore," Jonas says.

"No, but his resources and network are still enormous," Lush says between drags.

"Why do you think he's here?" I ask.

"To make good on his threat to you. Saturday is the deadline. I think we have to believe him," Jonas says squinting at me as the morning sun shines in his face.

Javier and the co-pilot load our bags into the trunk and close it. Lush drops her cigarette, crushes it with the toe of her shoe, looks up, and says, "Time to get going, fellows." Jonas, Clark and I get into the back seat. Lush sits up front. Javier starts the car, navigates through a chain-link gate, turns right down a small lane, and makes another right down a two-lane road. My mobile phone rings. I look at it and see it's Dad's number. I flip it open.

"Hello, Dad?"

"Philip. Something horrible has hap-happened," his voice cracks and he weeps.

"Dad, what is it?"

"Drew has apparently been abducted from school this morning."

"What, are you certain?"

"Yes, yes. He went into the bathroom after homeroom. The guard waited outside. When Drew didn't come out in a reasonable amount of time, the guard went in. A ground floor window was open. Drew was nowhere to be seen."

"Oh, my God, Dad. It's Adrian. Jonas just told us there's evidence that he's in the country."

"Son, I don't know what to do. The St. Louis police are already in contact with Detectives Johnson and Bell."

"That son-of-a-bitch," I shout.

"What is it, Todge?" Lush shouts.

I pull the phone away from my face, "Drew was kidnapped at school this morning."

"Oh no," Lush says. Jonas sighs. Clark pushes his nose against my chest and Javier glares at me in the rear view mirror.

"Listen, Dad. You and Brenda do everything the police tell you to do. I'm in Louisville with Lush and Jonas. We just got here. We're here to look for the Gardner heist. That's what Adrian is really after."

"Do you think you'll really find it, son?" Dad asks.

"Dad, you have to trust me. The police do not even know about this. Adrian has threatened to harm my family if I tell them."

"But we have to tell them now," Dad says.

"No, we don't Dad!" I shout. "Listen, Dad. I didn't mean to shout, but I know Adrian better than anyone. Let me deal with him. I promise you he will not hurt Andrew. I promise. Please trust me."

"I trust you, son. I trust you."

"Listen, tell Brenda what I told you, but don't tell anyone else. Tell her I promise I will get Drew back to you all safe and sound."

"But, son,"

"Tell her, Dad! I will do this. I promise. I promise."

"I'll tell her, son. Son, please be careful. I love you."

"I love you too, Dad. Call me if anything turns up."

"I will."

"Okay, I'll be in touch soon. Bye."

"Goodbye, son."

I slap the phone shut. "Oh shit, God damn, what am I going to do?" I shout and slap my head with my right palm. Clark lowers his head, laying his head on my lap. I rest my left hand on his back.

"Philip, calm down," Jonas says. "We can deal with this, we can deal with Adrian. He's on our turf now; we have the advantage."

"How is that, Jonas?" I ask. "We've never had it before."

"We were dealing with unknowns, Philip. Now we are dealing with him."

I think to myself, "Come on Mabry; don't let me down." Jonas gives me a knowing look, and I realize he must be thinking about the identification numbers too.

"Yes, we have collected a lot of information about Adrian," I say. "So how do you see this playing out, Jonas. My major concern at this point is Andrew's safety."

"Andrew is like the ultimate catch to Adrian," Jonas replies.

"What do you mean by 'ultimate catch'?" Lush asks.

"Well, he's beautiful and he's on the brink of pubescence—combinations Adrian has specifically sought out over the years. Adrian would probably really rather have Andrew than the Gardner treasure."

"Really?" I ask.

"Yes, really," Jonas replies. "Adrian follows the typical pattern of a pedophile in wooing and courting his prey. I think whatever time he spends with Andrew, Adrian will be doing just that, wooing and courting him."

"That thought disgusts me to my core," I reply.

"Yes, disgust you it may, but isn't it better that he's courting Drew than torturing him?"

"I see your point, Jonas," I reply.

"But he's holding Drew for ransom, Jonas," Lush replies.

"True, but Adrian could have chosen anyone, Lush—anyone close to Philip. He could have chosen Emma, Peter, you Lush, or Clark here. Look who he chose. Someone very much like Billy."

"Did Adrian ever torture or hurt you or Billy?" Jonas asks me.

"Well, no, not that I remember. But it must have been torture when he, well when he sodomized me. I have a picture of it right here."

"Do you remember that happening, Philip?" Jonas asks.

"No, I don't."

"But you remember other sexual acts he performed on you?"

"Oh yes, clearly."

"Then, he most likely drugged you, so you wouldn't resist, and so you wouldn't feel the pain."

I sit back and sigh. "Yes, yes, that feels right, Jonas."

"So I think it's safe to say, Andrew will probably be treated very well until we rescue him," Jonas says.

"And how, pray God, do you plan to do that?" Lush asks.

"By giving the bastard exactly what he wants," Jonas replies.

"And what if we don't find the treasure here?" she asks.

"Oh, we will. We will find exactly what Adrian is looking for," Jonas replies shifting his eyes and shaking his head toward Javier. Lush and I both realize Jonas doesn't think this conversation should go any further with Javier in the car. I've noticed we've passed through some pretty nice neighborhoods, and through some large park, and a reservoir that has to do with the water company. Javier turns the car left, up a short, steep hill.

"We're almost home, fellows," Lush says. "This is my street."

"Very nice street," I say.

"Yes, beautiful homes," Jonas says.

Javier turns the car into a large circular drive way and Lush's house comes into view. It is magnificent: a gorgeous, French country style house made of stucco and limestone with a green slate roof. The house is large, with numerous separate sections—some protruding and some recessed, all with tall narrow windows framed with shutters. A large three story round turret separates the main house from a smaller section that angles toward the drive. Large, perfectly sculpted boxwoods accent the front of the house, in front of which are beds full of white azaleas and white tulips, all in full bloom.

"Wow, you certainly grew up privleged, Lush," I say in a high-pitched, mocking tone.

Lush turns her head around, rolls her eyes at me, and says, "That's the proverbial pot calling the kettle black!"

"Touché!" I reply, "But this is really, really beautiful, Lush. And so big. Just the two of you live here?"

"Just us and our housekeeper, Gladys," she replies as Javier navigates the big Mercedes around the back on an offshoot of the front circular drive, through an electric gate, and onto an area paved with cobblestones. The back of the house is even more massive than the front.

I let out a long whistle, "Damn, Lush, this is amazing house," I say. "How much land is with it?"

"Oh, it's just over four acres, Todge. My grandparents built the house in the mid twenties. Momma doubled the size of it in the seventies. She did a pretty good job—it only took her four architects and two contractors to get it the way she envisioned."

"I remember meeting your parents at Chapel Hill," I state. "Boy, was I scared half to death? Your mother looked into my eyes, and I felt as if she could read from my brain all the sexual stuff I'd been doing with her daughter. It was really intimidating for me."

"Yes, not surprising," Lush replies. "Momma, I think, had many of Fatgram's traits—she'd tell it like it is come hell or high water, and she didn't give a damn what anyone said. Only, I think my Momma felt even more entitled than Fatgram."

"Really, Lush?" I ask. "Why do you say that?"

"She just did. Her family had been close to the top of Louisville society since the late eighteen hundreds. That sort of thing meant a lot to Mother."

Javier pulls the car up in front of four garage doors and parks. Clark's ears are erect and he begins a nervous, high-pitched whine.

"I think he remembers this place," I say.

"Oh, I'm sure he does," Lush replies, "He liked it here."

I open my door to get out and Clark jumps over my lap to the outside and runs to the back lawn and into a wooded area. I get out quickly and begin running after him.

"Clark, Clark, come back, boy, come here!" I shout.

"Todge, don't worry," Lush says, "The whole back is fenced in with an aluminum fence. He can't get out."

I stop, "Whew! Good. I couldn't bear losing him, too. That's great. He'll have the time of his life in all this open space."

The back yard is beautiful with areas of manicured lawn curving into beds of azaleas in full bloom, rhododendron heavy with large buds, trees, and shrubs. I see a terraced area with a swimming pool, a loggia, and a pool house. Stone walkways start from the formal flower and boxwood gardens close to the house and wind through the back areas.

"Javier," I say, "I can see how this must keep you really busy."

"Yes sir," he replies, smiling, "Very busy, me and my father."

"Yes, Javier and his father do great work. They take care of several houses in this neighborhood," Lush says.

"It is beautiful, Lush," Jonas says.

"Thank you, Jonas, I hope you'll be comfortable here," Lush replies.

Javier opens the trunk and begins taking the luggage out.

"Javier, please put the luggage in the front hall," Lush says.

"Yes, mam," he replies.

"Come on in fellows," Lush says, "We've got work to do."

As we enter a back entrance hall, Clark comes sprinting through the back yard and enters the back door without hesitation. His tongue hangs out of his mouth as he rapidly pants. He looks up at us with the happiest expression on his face.

"You remember all of this? Don't you, boy?" Lush asks. He wags his tail and trots down the hall making a right turn.

"I suppose he knows where he's going?" I ask.

"I'm sure he's headed to the kitchen to see Gladys," Lush says.

The back entrance hall is long, dark and rather narrow, and I see that it runs directly into the round turret. The floor is random width oak, stained dark brown. Two identical, long, red and beige oriental runners are centered in the hallway. Dark oak wainscoting runs about four feet up the walls that appear to be stucco above that. Groupings of antique benches, chairs and tables are placed on either side of the rugs and in between various doorways. Wall sconces and torcheres light the hallway. There are several large oil paintings in richly carved gilt frames, all of rural scenes with livestock, mainly cows, hanging in the hallway.

"Momma loved her cow paintings," Lush says, as she makes a right turn just before we arrive at the entrance hall in the turret. We turn into another shorter hallway that opens up into a spacious and beautiful kitchen with travertine floors; and a high, flat ceiling with large, exposed, wooden beams. On the outside wall between two sets of windows, an immense hammered copper hood rises up over two large stoves containing several burners, a griddle, a grill and four ovens. On the right side of the hood a large metal rack is suspended from the ceiling and contains an assortment of copper cooking utensils. A long rectangular island covered in red-brown granite with two sinks, one large and one small, and lined with bar stools on the side closest to us, divides the kitchen. The cabinetry is a chestnut color with a thin strip of a darker wood outlining each raised panel. To the right I notice a large built-in refrigerator and two wall-mounted ovens. Cabinets surround the ovens and refrigerator and the top row of cabinets have glass doors and recessed lighting. To our left, the kitchen opens up into a very large den on the far side of which is a large fireplace. I see several French doors that open onto the back patio.

"Welcome home, Sarah," a slim, middle aged woman with short brown hair, wire rimmed glasses, dressed in white shorts, a white shell top, and white sneakers says as she emerges from a doorway in the right corner of the kitchen which I presume leads to a pantry. Clark trots behind the woman with a strip of rawhide in his mouth.

"Hi, Gladys, so good to see you," Lush says, walks over, embraces the woman. "Gladys, these are my friends Philip Hampton and Jonas Grey."

"Nice to meet you, Gladys," I say.

"Hello," Jonas says.

"Good to see you both," Gladys replies as she approaches us. "I remembered we had some of these treats left in the pantry, so I got one for Clark. He looks really good."

"Yes, my brother took good care of him," I reply.

"So sorry to hear about your brother, Mr. Hampton," Gladys says.

"Thanks, Gladys," I reply.

"Gladys," Lush says as she walks over to the island and places her purse on the granite top, "I'm going to put Philip in the blue guest room and Jonas in the green one."

"Sure," Gladys replies, "Everything is ready, fresh linen on the beds. I thought you all might be hungry, so I made a little brunch."

"How wonderful, Gladys," Lush says, pulling out her cigarettes from her purse. "That should work out great. I know Philip is anxious to get on the road to St. Meinrad." She takes out a cigarette and lights it. Gladys looks at her as if she is about to say, 'Please don't smoke inside,' but she says nothing.

"I'd like to visit the restroom and make a couple of calls first, if that's alright," Jonas says.

"Absolutely," Lush replies.

"Gladys, will you show these gentlemen to their rooms?" Lush asks.

"Sure thing, follow me guys," she says and heads out toward the turret.

431

"Javier put the luggage in the front hall," Lush says. "Holler out back for him if you need him to help carry it up."

"Thanks, we can manage, Lush," I reply, "We don't have that much."

"Okay. See you all back down here in fifteen minutes?" Lush asks.

"Sounds good," Jonas says.

Jonas, Clark, and I follow Gladys into the round front hallway. The floor is large, rectangular blocks of limestone. A wide spiraling staircase with an ornate metal newel post, balusters of dark hammered metal, and a sleek metal handrail in a deep bronze color sweeps up around half the circumference of the turret to a landing on the second floor. A large metal lantern hangs by three chains and a center pipe from the ceiling. I see flames flickering in the lantern and realize it is gas. Four round, evenly spaced, stained glass windows are located near the top of the turret and I notice each window has a letter in it depicting which direction it faces, reminding me of Dyanne's painting, *The Hanging of St. John Houghton*. The front door is tall, constructed of darkly stained wood cut into a semi-circle at the top, and is hung underneath an archway made of blocks of limestone. Two tall narrow, leaded glass windows flank the doorway, and metal sconces that match the hanging lantern are mounted between each window and the doorway. I see gas flames dancing in each sconce.

"Do these lights burn all the time, Gladys?" I ask.

"Yes, they do," she replies, "It's too difficult to light them every day."

Clark sniffs the three pieces of luggage sitting by the stairway and trots up the stairway and disappears, his clinking toenails suddenly muffled. I suppose he's walking on a runner or carpet.

"He really knows his way around," I comment, "I thought David made him stay in a crate?"

Gladys laughs, "Each morning as soon as David left for work, Sarah would release him and he had the run of the place all day. He's a great dog. I miss him."

"How long have you worked here, Gladys?" Jonas asks.

"Lord, almost thirty-four years. Miss Lottie, Sarah's mother, hired me right after she and Mr. Gordon got back from their honeymoon and took over this house. Sarah came along about nine months after that."

"That's a long time," Jonas replies.

"Yes it is; I was just twenty-five years old. Been a great life for me—I'm a part of their family and they're a part of mine," she replies.

"You married, Gladys?" I ask as I grab my duffle bag.

"I was; twice—that's enough. Got married at eighteen to my high school sweet heart, Danny. He was killed in Vietnam in 1968. We had our boy, Randy, in 1967. The Richardsons have been so good to us—put Randy through Centre College and hired him in the drug stores. He's an executive at Wal-Mart now; lives in Bentonville."

"That's great," I say, "So you remarried?"

"Yep," she says as she carries Lush's bag up the stairs. "Married Sam Bennet in 1981. We were pretty happy, peaceful life. He was a truck driver—his rig slid off an icy overpass in Cincinnati in the big snow, January 1994. He was a great truck driver; I think he must have fallen asleep. He was pulling a long haul from Boston, trying to get home to see our grandson who was born that day. Good and bad, always happen together," she sighs and continues up the stairs. Jonas and I follow.

At the top of the stairs I see that there are two hallways; one running down the longer side of the house and the other running down the shorter side which angles off toward the driveway. Gladys leads us down the longer hallway, which is wide and well lit from a high Palladian window at the far end and two large, crystal chandeliers hanging from plaster medallions in the ceiling. I see Clark looking out the Palladian window, his tail wagging.

"That window looks out at a big oak tree that's full of squirrels. He use to sit there for hours watching them," Gladys says.

The hallway is very formal and is indeed covered with a long wide runner with a pattern of repeating Greek keys in dark brown on a beige background with a border of solid brown. The doorway to each room is encased in wide, fluted columns supporting swan neck pediments. The wood is richly carved and painted with white, high gloss paint. It looks as if we are in a very fine hotel.

"This is beautiful," I remark.

"Yes it is," Jonas replies.

"Miss Lottie hired an architect from New York to do all this back when Sarah was still in grade school. She had the front turret, new kitchen and right wing of the house added on first. Then we moved everyone over to that side while they renovated this side that used to be the entire house. Lord it took almost two years."

"Wow," I say, "They did a great job. And Lush grew up in this big house all alone?"

"Alone?" Gladys asks, "Hardly, it was always full of cousins and friends—always something going on here."

"You live here, Gladys?" I ask.

"I do now," she replies. "I moved in to take care of Miss Lottie when her cancer spread, and I just never went back home—Randy was gone, Sam was gone. I still have my house over near Hikes Lane, but I just rent it out now."

"Do the Richardsons entertain much?" I ask.

"Seems like less and less nowadays, but they used to all the time," she replies. She stops in front of the second door on the right. "This is the green room, Mr. Grey. It has its own bath. Let me know if you need anything."

"Thanks, Gladys," he replies as he walks into the room. "I'll be down in a quarter hour."

"Okay," I reply. I poke my head in—the room is green and lovely and looks like something from the pages of *Architectural Digest*.

Gladys crosses the hall and opens a door. "Here's the blue room, Mr. Hampton. Let me know if you need anything."

"Thanks so much, Gladys, I will," I reply. Before I walk in, I turn to Clark, "Hey, boy! Come on down here with me." He turns his head toward me, wagging his tail, then turns back to the window for an instant, then turns back around and begins running to me. "Good boy!" I say. He runs past Gladys and me into the room and jumps right up onto the canopy bed and stretches out facing us. We both laugh. I walk in, turn around, close the door, and turn back around to survey my room, which is not really blue, but blue and white. It is beautiful: the walls are covered in pale blue silk with designs of scrolls and vines woven in white; fluted molding, painted white, runs in vertical drops from wide crown molding down to the floor, framing pieces of furniture and paintings; the bed is an exotic wooden canopy bed, with the same silk fabric on the walls covering a tent-like wooden frame mounted on the top of the four round posters. Eight panels of the same fabric hang like curtains from the rails mounted on the posters, each panel is tied back to a poster, but it is evident that if you release the tie-backs, you can completely conceal the bed with the panels; two tall narrow, leaded glass windows face out over the front yard, each window has a cornice covered in solid blue silk fabric with silk drapes of the same fabric hanging to the floor in a puddling fashion; the drapes are pulled back with ornate, white metal pull backs, white sheers hang between the curtains; the thick white carpet through which run light-blue triangular designs is wall-to-wall; an overstuffed chair and ottoman, in a blue and white houndstooth pattern, sit by the window on the right; a fluffy white cashmere throw is folded over the arm of the chair; a large bombé chest, made of a light-colored burled wood, with a grey-veined, white marble-top serves a dresser; a large, rectangular mirror in a white, metal frame, with cut-out designs of pagodas in a Chinese garden, rests against the wall; a pair of lamps, made from blue and white Chinese porcelain vases with designs of ladies and banana trees Mother used to call 'long ladies' flank the dresser top; a tall armoire, painted in chinoiserie on a sky-blue

background, probably eighteenth-century Italian, sits between two of the vertical pieces of fluted molding; a mahogany writing table with pretty turned and fluted legs, brass castors and white porcelain wheels, and twin drawers is against the wall near the door; a Gainsborough style, fixed desk chair in blue leather sits in front of the desk; a vintage, blue, slag glass, bronze colored, table lamp, with wonderful filigree designs in the shade sits on the writing table; and a large, eight-arm, white porcelain chandelier with blue shades hangs from a white plaster medallion in the center of the ceiling. I put my duffle on the bed and sit down next to Clark.

"How you doing, boy? You glad to be back in your home town?"

He rolls over on his back, tail wagging, wanting his belly rubbed. I oblige him and observe how his red-orange fur turns to gold and white and thins out on his belly. I can see his skin is mottled and freckled, and I see he has at least eight little nipples, like small buttons running up on either side of his chest. He groans in pleasure, sticks his tongue out, swallows, and then sneezes violently three times in a row, spraying me with mist.

"Christ, boy. You got me good," I say as I get up to head into the bathroom. It is small and cozy, with a white marble floor; a corner shower with two sides tiled in the same white marble as the floor, and two solid glass sides, one of which is a door; a white toilet, with an elongated bowl, situated between the shower and the outside wall; and a built in, marble top vanity containing a single round white porcelain sink. A small window, under which is mounted a metal towel rack, separates the vanity and the toilet. Built in glass corner shelves are to my left in front of the shower. All the fixtures are polished nickel, and all the towels are blue. A Roman shade in a dark blue, raw silk, is pulled half way up over the window. I walk over to the toilet, unzip my pants, and pull out my cock to pee. I notice the color of my urine is dark yellow, so I make a mental note to drink more water. I'm probably a bit dehydrated from two days in a row of hot yoga. I wonder what Christopher will be like, and I wonder if he will help me. My heart sinks when I think about little Andrew missing. God, everything is happening so fast. I just have to focus, stay calm, and get through this. Treasure or not, this trip is necessary, if only to fool Adrian. I feel hungry. I need to grab a bite before I leave. I finishing peeing, flush, and walk to the sink to wash my hands. I look into the mirror at my face. All I see is worry and grief. That is not good. I've got to take control. I've got to get through this and make things happen the way I need them to happen. The outcome will be that I get Andrew to safety, and I get Adrian's neck in my bare hands. I hold my soapy hands up to the mirror and observe.

"By God, these are the hands that will choke that bastard to death," I say. The grief and worry have vanished from my face. Now I only see hate and anger, but deep inside I feel fear. I quickly rinse my hands, dry them off on a blue hand towel, and walk back into the bedroom.

"Come on Clark, let's go downstairs. I can unpack later today." He jumps off the bed and follows me back downstairs.

"Darling, Gladys has made a wonderful brunch for us," Lush says, looking up as she thumbs through a pile of mail on the center island. "She made her wonderful strata, which is full of eggs, sausage, Gruyere, spinach, and Italian bread."

"Mmmn, is that what I smell?" I ask as I walk up to Lush, pull out a stool and take a seat.

"Yes, it is," Lush replies. "She also made her butter kuchen. Oh my God, it's to die for. And we have fresh fruit, fresh squeezed OJ, coffee, and I'll even make you a bloody Mary if you like."

"Sounds great, but I'll hold off on the Bloody Mary. I want to be on full mental throttle when I meet with Christopher," I reply.

"I don't blame you, Todge," Lush says. "Every minute counts now that Adrian has Andrew."

"I know," I sigh.

"Todge," Lush says, her dark eyes fixed on mine, "It's going to turn out alright. I sense that it will. I mean, I have a gut feeling that it will."

"Thanks, Lush. That means a lot to me."

Gladys enters through a French door from the den, "It's so nice outside, I set up places on the terrace. Why don't y'all go on outside, and I'll serve you?"

"Sounds perfect, Gladys," Lush says. "We'll go ahead and eat, Gladys. Jonas may be a while. Philip needs to get on the road. He has a meeting at St. Meinrad this afternoon."

"Certainly. Philip, what would you like to drink?" Gladys asks.

"Coffee and orange juice would be great, Gladys," I reply.

"Good. It's already on the table; help yourself. I'll be out in a minute," she says and walks over to one of the ovens, puts on mitts, and opens the door. The smell of the strata intensifies, and I feel my mouth watering. I get up and follow Lush out back. Clark trots along beside Lush and bursts out the door as soon as she opens it, disappearing somewhere in the back yard. We walk onto the terrace.

"This is a great backyard, Lush. The big trees are great."

"Yes, it's an old neighborhood. Momma was a gardening fanatic and took good care of these trees. We used to have a lot more, but we lost a bunch in the tornado in 1974. Momma was devastated. I'll have to show you the photos."

"Geez. Was the house damaged?" I ask.

"Yes, quite a bit. In fact, that's what caused Momma to enlarge the house—rebuilding after the storm. She was pregnant with me at the time. Daddy was downtown at the office and called Momma to tell her that a tornado was headed her way and to get to the basement. She got all three dogs and two cats down there and rode out the storm. When she emerged from the basement, all the walls of the house were standing, but the roof was torn off completely."

"Wow, that's incredible. Must have been frightening for her."

"She said it sounded like a freight train rolling through the house. They were able to save most everything inside. Daddy told a funny story about a man who called him a week or so after the storm. It seems the man was working in his back yard in Cincinnati and saw something sticking out of a bush. He picked it up and saw that it was a dividend check from AT&T made out to Daddy."

"Christ, how far is Cincinnati from here?" I ask.

"Oh, about a hundred miles north," Lush replies.

"So that check was sucked out of your house and carried all that way?" I ask.

"It seems it was. Daddy said he had received it the day before and had it on his desk here to take to the bank."

"Amazing. I didn't realize Kentucky was in tornado country." I say.

"We certainly have our fair share of them," Lush says. "Especially this time of year. The seventy-four tornado was in April."

We walk over to a round table with a large beige umbrella in the center. Gladys has set three place settings. There's an insulated coffee pot, a pitcher of orange juice, and a pitcher of tomato juice on the table. We sit down. Lush pours us each a glass of orange juice. The gardens along the back of the house are full of tulips and hyacinths, but unlike all the white in the front, these are mounds of pinks, reds, and yellows. Pear trees, pruned and anchored to the house, climb upward between the windows and doors in espalier fashion, their arms resembling giant candelabra. White, red, orange, pink, and lavender azaleas are in full bloom in different plantings throughout the back yard; white and pink dogwoods are beginning to bloom.

"Spring is a little early this year," Lush remarks. "I just hope we don't have a late hard freeze. That would kill everything. Seems like every few years that happens."

"I hate that," I reply. "Sometimes that even happens in Atlanta."

"Remember how pretty spring was at Chapel Hill?" Lush asks.

"I do. Yes, indeed. To be nineteen again in the spring," I say.

"Where does the time go, Todge?"

"I don't know, Lush, but it sure as hell goes," I reply and take a sip of juice. "On second thought, I'll have a Bloody Mary, Lush."

"Good, I'll join you," she replies with a smile. "Let me make it; Gladys has everything here."

I notice Clark trotting back toward us; he is carrying something in his mouth. As he gets closer, I can see it is something furry and brown.

"Oh dear, looks like Clark made a kill," I say.

"Probably a rabbit or a mole," Lush says as she pours pepper infused vodka into two tall glasses.

"Come here boy; let me see what you've got," I say.

Clark trots right up to me, displaying a small brown rabbit.

"Clark, give that to me," I command. He immediately releases the bunny into my hands. It's a baby, and it's alive. It is shaking. I look it over. "Damn, Lush. I think it's okay; he didn't appear to bite into it. Clark, you sit right here." I walk over to the nearest area of trees and sit the bunny on the ground. It immediately runs for cover.

"That's one lucky bunny," I say. "I sure as heck wouldn't want Clark's jaws around my neck."

"Well, Clark is as gentle as he is fierce," Lush replies. "Isn't astounding how he reacted around Benny? Too bad he didn't chomp into his ankle."

"Yes," I reply. "You know, I'm so glad we brought him. I think I'll take him with me to St. Meinrad. He might help break the ice with Christopher." Clark wags his tail and stretches out on his left side on the patio, soaking in the sun.

"Oh Todge, that's a good idea," Lush replies.

"Yes, I wanna see how he reacts to Christopher," I say.

"You like yours spicy?" Lush asks.

"Today, yes. I need a zing and a zap."

"You got it," she replies and puts a healthy dab of horseradish into each glass and stirs them vigorously with a bar spoon.

She sticks a celery stick into each glass and hands me one. "Here's to getting Christopher to open up," she states.

"I'll drink to that!" I reply, clinking my glass with Lush's.

I take a sip, "Yum and wow. It certainly has a bite. I love it."

"Good, Todge," Lush replies setting her drink down and picking up her cigarettes.

"Sooner than later, you're going to have to give those up, Lush," I say.

She pulls out a cigarette, clicks her lighter, inhales deeply, lets out a long stream of smoke, smiles, and says, "I know, Todge. Thanks for caring. Let me get my life in order the next few weeks. Then, I promise I'll stop."

"You really promise me you'll stop, Lush?"

"I do, Philip," she replies.

"Good," I reply and take another sip of my drink.

"Where do you think Adrian took Andrew?" Lush asks.

"They could be anywhere, but my hunch is New York. I mean if he really thinks we'll bring back the Gardner heist, New York would be the logical place."

"Yes," Lush says and takes another long draw off her cigarette and begins to talk as smoke spews out of her mouth. "I have a hunch that Adrian must know every square inch of the O'Bryan's farm."

"Yes, I know what you mean. But why would he have killed Ted, the priest and Dyanne without first getting from them the whereabouts of the treasure?" I ask.

"Good question. We don't know for certain that he killed Ted and the priest. Perhaps Dyanne found out about his abuse of the boys and that's why he killed her." Lush states.

"God only knows," I reply.

Gladys opens one of the French doors in the back and rolls out a serving cart.

"What a lovely, day. Blue sky and highs in the mid-seventies," she says.

"Beautiful weather," I state. "Kentucky is so green and lush, Lush." I say with a giggle.

"Yes it is," Lush replies. "Momma always said the reason the Kentucky Derby is held the first Saturday in May is because there's no place more beautiful than Kentucky in the spring."

"She sure did," Gladys replies. "I don't think anybody loved the Derby more than Miss Lottie. My Gosh, the parties we use to have," she says as she opens the serving cart revealing the strata, the butter kuchen and a large bowl of fruit.

"Oh, that looks delicious," I say.

"May I serve you, Philip?" Gladys asks.

"Oh, yes, please." I reply.

Gladys gets a white plate from the bottom of the cart and slices into the strata with a silver pie server. "Yes, Miss Lottie was a card. She loved to throw parties, especially at Derby. And her parties were always the best—top notch."

Lush is smiling, "Yes, Momma would start planning her Derby parties in the dead of winter right after New Years. She so loved the parties and the horses."

"And the cows, too," I remark. "Was she raised on a farm?"

"No, here in town, but her family has always had a big farm north of here in Oldham County. They raised cows, tobacco, and thoroughbreds," Lush says.

"Really. Interesting. Did they ever get a horse in the Derby?" I ask.

Lush glances at Gladys and they exchange a look of pain. "The year Momma died, one of her horses, Bird Charmer, ran in the Derby," Lush says.

"How did he do?" I ask.

"Fourth, just missed showing by a hair. What a race. Mother was so sick, but we got her to the track—she looked so pretty that day. From the time he was a colt, for some reason, little songbirds would always hang around him—in the fields, on his stall door, even at the tracks. That's how he got his name. We've got photographs of him looking out his stall door with little birds lined up on it. He was a gorgeous bay horse. Mother absolutely loved him."

Gladys hands me a plate of food and begins to serve Lush's plate.

"Thanks, Gladys," I say. "So he must have been pretty good to make it to the Derby."

"He was—the best we've ever produced. He certainly had a shot at it. He had a bad start that day, but by the time they turned into the final stretch he was in the lead by half a length. You should have seen Momma light up. I prayed and prayed to let Birdy win, but he couldn't hold the pace and three other horses pulled past him on the final stretch. Mother took it well, but I could see she was devastated. Six weeks later she died."

"Gosh, what a story. I'm sorry, Lush."

"Thanks, Todge. I just miss her so. And it's been ten years. She still had so much life in her; she was only fifty-six. Cancer is such a horrible death—it just ate her away to skin and bones and she looked like she was ninety years old. Just horrible." Lush's eyes have teared up, so she takes her napkin and dabs at them.

"I'm sorry," I say again.

Gladys smiles, "Here, Sarah. Eat some of this, sweet heart." She sets a plate in front of Lush and then pats her shoulders lovingly. Lush reaches up with her right hand and strokes Gladys's right hand. "Thank you, Gladys."

Jonas emerges through the back, "What terrific weather! I'm really liking Kentucky." Clark lifts his head to observe Jonas, groans, and lays his head back down, sighs, then closes his eyes.

"Spring is the best time of year here, Mr. Grey," Gladys says. "Please sit here and let me fix you a plate."

Jonas walks over, looks at the food, and says, "Wow, that looks wonderful."

"Jonas, care for a Bloody Mary?" Lush asks.

"No thank you. Just some coffee."

I pick up the coffee thermos and pour a cup for Jonas. Gladys prepares a plate for him and sets it in front of him.

"Just black, Jonas?" I ask.

"Yes sir, thanks."

"Everyone okay?" Gladys asks.

"We're fine, Gladys," Lush says. "Thank you so much."

"Good. I'll leave the cart here in case y'all want more," she says, turns around, and walks back inside.

We all begin to eat. I take a bite of the strata—it is divine, a wonderful combination of eggs, cheddar cheese, sausage, and bread.

"Oh, this is so good, Lush," I say.

"Yes, it is," Jonas adds.

"Gladys can cook anything," Lush replies. "She's the best. I'm so lucky to have her in my life. She's like a second mother to me."

"Well, I have a lot of news," Jonas says.

"Mabry has all the artwork inventory information you asked him to retrieve from the Gardner Museum," he says, his look revealing a bit of disapproval which I know results from my going around him directly to Mabry. "I think, whether or not we find the real McCoy's, we can certainly entice Adrian to present himself to inspect the works."

"That's good news," I reply, "But I still hope we can find the real deal."

"Yes, well, anything's possible, but the chances are slim," Jonas says. "I've been going over topographic and geologic maps of the O'Bryan farm. If it is hidden on the farm, it could be anywhere. There's over three thousand acres of karst terrain on that farm; part of it is even a virgin hardwood forest that has never been cut—ever."

"Wow," I reply. Lush stops chewing and looks up.

"Oh, dear," she says. "Let's pray Christopher knows something."

"Yes, let's hope he does," Jonas says. "Cara told me Joan and her husband, Carl are currently on a river boat traveling up the Yangtze River, so they are not going to be of much help."

"Shit," I state and take a bite of the butter kuchen. It melts in my mouth into a sweet, chewy slush of goodness.

"However, she says Joan's son, Geoff really runs the farm now. I put a call into him, but he hasn't gotten back to me. I figure we just go, disguised as spelunkers. I also called Jonathan Zeng to see if he could get in touch with Joan in China."

"That's great," I reply. "I'm hoping I can get Christopher to take me there tomorrow."

"Good," Jonas replies. "He's probably our only hope of locating the heist at this point."

"Jonas, may I go with you to Bardstown?" Lush asks.

"Certainly," he replies, "I was hoping you would. I'm going to need some assistance. Listen, I think Adrian may be in the area."

"You mean here in Louisville?" I ask.

"Yes, that's what I mean," he replies.

"But why, Jonas?" Lush asks.

He takes a sip of coffee. "Well, think about it. If he thinks we are close to finding that treasure, he's not going to waste any time getting his hands on it. He has Andrew as his hostage. I think he'll want to make the trade at the source, that is, on the farm."

"Hmm, I dunno," I say.

"Well, there's more," Jonas says. "Najeed's jumbo jet landed in Lexington this morning."

"That's not surprising," Lush replies, "We knew he was headed to the spring sales in Keeneland this week."

"True," Jonas says, "But it's obvious someone in Najeed's camp works for his father. How else would Billy's plan to assassinate Adrian have been foiled?"

"That's a good point," I reply. "Even Najeed hinted at that when he said 'the desert has ears.'"

"Lush, can you shoot?" Jonas asks.

"A gun?" she asks, her eyes widening.

"Yes, a gun," he replies.

"Well, yes, I suppose. I've shot rifles before. You know skeet shooting," she says.

"You're not afraid of guns?" he asks.

"No, I'm not," she replies.

"Good. I had several of my favorites delivered on your flight this morning. We'll stop by a firing range on the way to Bardstown, and I'll acquaint you with some of them," Jonas says, then cuts a large piece of strata and puts it in his mouth and begins to chew.

"But, whatever for, Jonas?" Lush asks.

He smiles, continuing to chew for a while, hold up his right index finger, swallows a couple of times, takes a sip of coffee, and says, "Because I do not think we will be the only people in those woods today."

"Really?" I ask.

"Yes, I think we may have Adrian's people there as well as Najeed's father's people," Jonas replies.

"Why would Najeed's father's people be there?" Lush asks.

"He's one of the richest men in the world. Jonas checked out his art collection. He collects Old Masters. These are the types of paintings he desires. And, he doesn't own a Vermeer. Not yet anyway. Despite Najeed's description of him, he's known to be rather a ruthless despot. It wouldn't surprise me if he circumvented Adrian."

"Crap," I reply. "Do we even have a chance at this, Jonas?"

"We have every chance," Jonas states, sitting up straight in his chair. "We are in the position of power and they all know it. We've checked out Christopher O'Bryan, too. You are going to encounter an amazingly strong, and dedicated young man—a man who has dedicated his life to the Church and who has excelled every step of the way there. Philip, I do believe you are the only person who has a chance of getting through to him. Adrian knows this. Najeed knows this, so his father knows it, too."

"Amazing work, Jonas. You are really good," I reply.

"Thanks, Philip. I'm just an observer—an observer of human nature. All the answers are out there. All you have to do is watch people, and they'll give you the answers whether or not they ever open their mouths."

"Fascinating," Lush says. "Well, let's eat up and get moving. My trigger finger is antsy!"

I look up at Lush and then over at Jonas and I feel butterflies in my stomach.

CHAPTER 40

The drive to St. Meinrad along Interstate 64 is beautiful, the rolling hills are covered with trees awash in the yellow, green, gold hues of early spring, interspersed with the vivid lavender of redbuds. Clark

rides shotgun, sitting up straight with ears erect and forward, peering out the windshield and side window, observing everything, intensely interested in the surroundings, eyes locking onto images, nose constantly twitching, discerning the many complex odors, undetected by me, entering the car's ventilation system. Lush's big blue Mercedes smoothly glides over the roadway on cruise control as we listen to a relaxing, new age, spa station on the satellite radio. Every few minutes Clark gives me a reassuring stare, then directs his attention to the road and the landscape. Lush and Jonas took her Land Rover, which seems a suitable vehicle for their mission to Bardstown. I'm really worried about Lush and the potential danger she and Jonas face, but she had absolutely no qualms about hurling herself headlong into the fray. I suspect Jonas really needs assistance or he wouldn't put her at such risk. What the hell is Adrian planning to do? God, I will kill him if he touches Andrew. How could he resist Drew, though? He looks so much like Billy, Adrian's favorite. I've always thought Billy's features were so much like Mother's, but, after spending time with Dad again last week after so many years, I now realize Billy received mainly his skin and hair color from Mother, not the bone structure—the perfectly symmetrical features come from Dad, and he has passed these down to Billy and me, as well as Peter, Andrew, and Emma. Adrian has probably devised exciting treasure hunts in order to entice Drew and lavish gifts on him. I have to break through to Christopher. I must. I'm afraid that Adrian will somehow see through the hacked data from the Gardner Museum. Hell, with his command of technology and his vast network, he's probably already done that himself. I feel my heart begin to race, and a feeling of anxiety descends upon me, my chest heaves, as I emit a long sigh. Clark immediately turns his attention toward me. He pushes his nose into my right shoulder twice and then, without hesitation, climbs into my lap, curls into a little ball, rests his head on my left thigh, sighs, runs his pink tongue over his muzzle, then closes his eyes. I'm so shocked by this that the thick fog of anxiety burns off and is replaced by a bright, warm, feeling of sunny love, and I feel so blessed to have this humble creature in my lap. I steer the sedan with my right hand, stroking Clark's head with my left hand. He opens his eyes, sighs, crescendos into a loud groan, and closes his eyes, falling asleep, and for the duration of the journey on the highway, he remains content in my lap, and my brain enters into a state of activity over which I am helpless to control, with multiple layers and levels of thought entering and leaving, some as fleeting as an evaporating cloud, some as dark and foreboding as a tornadic thunderstorm, while others are as beautiful as the blue summer sky. The net result of this thought process is that I am barely conscious of driving, so that I am startled when the female voice on the car's navigation system announces that I should take the next exit in one-quarter mile. I see the sign for Exit 72 Bristow/ Birdseye. Clark, disturbed by the sound of the voice, moves back into the passenger seat, manages to execute a downward dog stretch, and then resumes his patrol of the surroundings. I put on the blinker and pull into the deceleration lane, causing Clark to emit an urgent, pleading whine, so I crack his window just enough for him to stick his head out. He puts his front paws on the arm of the door, pokes his head out, his nostrils flaring in rapid motion as he takes in the full brunt force of the complex smells in the country air. I slow to a stop and make a left turn. We pass through a rural area along a river bottom and then in the distance I see the twin spires of St. Meinrad's cathedral soaring up to the skies, sitting on a hill overlooking a small town—it is lovely and reminds me of so many small towns in Europe. We follow the navigation system's verbal instruction up to the abbey and to the guesthouse. I pull into a parking space and turn the car off. Clark begins to whine.

"Here you go, boy. Let me put your leash on," I say in a loving tone as I clasp the lead to his collar. He sits down in the front seat, wags his tail, gives me a quick lick on my right cheek, opening his mouth into a smile, panting.

I flip down my sun visor, slide open the mirror, checking out my face to see how I look—a little tired, I think, but otherwise okay.

"Let's go, Clark," I say as I open the door and get out. Clark jumps out after me and immediately sniffs the pavement. I close the car door, push the lock button on the key, and guide Clark over to the

grass, which has the deep luxurious new deep green growth of spring. Clark walks over to a small pear tree in bloom, lifts his right leg, letting out a stream of yellow urine, holding this position for a good half a minute.

"Damn, you really had to go, boy," I say, "I bet you have to poop, too." He looks up at me with an alert countenance, finishes peeing, moves off from the tree sniffing the grass, pulling rather hard on the lead. I submit to his force and follow along behind him as he explores the grassy area surrounding the parking lot. Clark starts to eat individual blades of the grass. I let him. I've seen dogs do this my whole life; I suppose they need the chlorophyll or the vitamins or the minerals in the grass. He grazes for a couple of minutes, then suddenly stops, sniffs the ground with a snorting noise, squats on his hind legs, whirls around in a circle for three turns, grunts, then moans as he emits a long, well formed brown turd. I reach into my pocket, pull out a doggie bag, and scoop up the turd.

"Damn Clark. That's some smelly shit. What did you eat?" He looks up at me with a look of complete satisfaction as I tie the bag. I look down at my watch.

"It's two o'clock on the nose, boy. Let's go into the visitor's center and find Christopher."

As we walk toward the entrance I observe a slim man emerge through the glass door dressed in a solid white monastic habit. I swallow. I find this hooded outfit intimidating, and I dread my task with this man. He looks around, sees Clark and me, smiles, waves his right hand at us, proceeding towards us. Clark, immediately energized, begins to wag his tail, pulling on the lead, trying to get to the man. I notice the man's reddish-brown hair and beard are closely cropped to the same length and his skin is very pale. I rein Clark in close to my left side as the man approaches. He is a couple of inches shorter than I.

"Hello, you are Mr. Hampton, I presume," he states in a soft voice, the words spoken with a precise, gentle dialect, bordering on the feminine, sounding almost affected to me, or even what Fatgram would call 'piss-elegant.' I suppress the urge to judge him on his voice and enunciation. He wears round, gold rimmed glasses with thick lenses, sheltering pale blue eyes, weak, but broadcasting immense intelligence and some peculiar type of remote compassion. He smiles.

"Yes, Philip Hampton. You're Christopher Johnson?"

"I am, but I go by Brother Paul now," he replies as he drops to his knees, offering out his hands to Clark, who displays his like of the stranger by vigorously wagging his tail. Clark stiffs his hands, puts his paws on Brother Paul's thighs, stretching his head up to lick Brother Paul's face.

"This is Clark, my dog," I say, pulling Clark down off of Brother Paul, amazed that Brother Paul would approach a strange pit-bull in such a confidant and loving manner. This makes me feel instantly more at ease with the young man, even though now I'm confronted with his new religious name, and I wonder how he came about taking the name Paul.

"He's fine. I'm an animal lover; I grew up on a farm," Brother Paul says, leaning his torso forward, giving Clark a big hug. "He's a beautiful dog." Brother Paul stands up, offering me his right hand. I transfer the bag of poop and the lead to my left hand, taking his hand with my right hand. We shake. Brother Paul's grip is neither firm nor weak, but his hand is warm and as he looks into my eyes and says, "I'm pleased to know you, Mr. Hampton, welcome to St. Meinrad," with that calm, serene voice, now seeming more educated than affected to me, and I sense that I am in the presence of a very holy person, and I begin to get a feeling that this interview may go well after all.

"I am so pleased to meet you," I say, releasing his hand. "Please just call me Philip, though."

"Certainly," he replies. "Let me have that," he says, taking the bag of poop out of my hand and placing it in a trash can a few steps to his left.

"Thank you," I say.

He turns around from the trash can, faces me, claps his hands together as he lifts up both his heels, bending his knees in a little quasi-squat-jump, energizing his demeanor, and asks, "How can I be of

441

assistance to you today, Philip? You said on the phone that I could help you with some family matters that related to my mother?"

"Yes, indeed," I reply, looking around. "Is there somewhere we can go to talk in private?"

He smiles. "Of course. It's a lovely afternoon. Let's walk through the gardens and along the lake. I'm sure Clark would enjoy that. It's very private."

"Wonderful," I reply.

"Good," he says, "The path starts right up here," he directs.

We move off toward the path, Clark walks between us, nose to the ground.

"Brother Paul. Do you know anything about me or my family?" I ask.

"No, I'm sorry, Philip. I don't believe I know anything about your family. I can tell you are a pleasant person, and that you have some burden, a burden with which you believe I can help."

"You are very perceptive, Brother Paul," I reply. "I have a grave burden, and I believe you are the only person on this earth who can help me."

He pauses, looks into my eyes, searching, and he says, "I see. Well, by all means, please begin, Philip."

I sigh; a gentle breeze brushes my face. Suddenly, I hear birds singing, and the clear, loud mating call of a male cardinal fills the air, rising above the chirps of the other birds. I swallow, and begin. "My mother was Eva Hampton, a well known artist, not as famous as your mother, but nonetheless well established and widely collected. She and your mother, Dyanne, shared a mentor, Adrian McWhorter."

"Yes, of course—Eva Hampton. Now I know the connection, Philip," he says, his face jovial, his eyes focused on me, the mention of Adrian having no visible effect on him.

"Well, it's a long complicated story, Brother Paul," I continue, "And I hardly know the best way to get it all out to you." I pause, still examining his face for answers. He looks so young, even with his beard, yet he acts so wise, almost omnipotent.

"Might I suggest you start with the bad and work your way up to the good," Brother Paul says.

I sigh, "There is no good Brother Paul—it's all bad, terribly bad, base, evil," I reply.

"Nonsense," Brother Paul snaps back at me, his facial expression instantly revealing a slight look of frustrated annoyance, and I feel like a little boy who has said a cuss word out loud in grammar school and is about to receive a smack on the back of his hand with a wooden ruler from the teacher. "There is some good to be found in all evil, Philip—you only have to look deep within your heart to find it."

Now, this person I perceived to be almost a saint, seems to be melting into a brain-washed idiot, and my good feelings toward him begin to fade, and deep inside I begin to sense that possibly I have made a big mistake by coming here, and that I'll never get through to him at all with all those layers of Catholic dogma that must be ingrained into his mind—his very soul. But as quickly as these feelings manifest themselves in me, they begin to subside as Brother Paul grabs both my hands, holding them in his, looks into my eyes and says, "We all have different types of faith, Philip. No matter how horrible your story is, the fact that you have come a great distance on short notice to seek my help means that you care about someone a great deal. That in itself is all the goodness I need to hear you out."

"Thank you, Brother Paul," I reply with a sigh, withdrawing my hands. "Could we just go sit somewhere for a bit? Somewhere private?"

"Of course. I know the perfect place. It's just down this pathway a few hundred feet," he replies, pointing down the hill with his right hand.

"Good," I reply, giving a slight yank on Clark's lead to divert his attention from the base of a tree he's sniffing. We head down the sloping, curving path, that enters into an arboretum with a copper plaque on a metal stake driven in the ground in front of each tree and bush. Each plaque lists both the Latin and common name of each plant and gives the date planted or the estimated age of the larger trees.

"This is quite beautiful. Someone spent a lot of time on this, " I remark.

"Yes, it is," Brother Paul replies, "This represents the life work of Brother Frederick, who designed this garden and spent his life installing and maintaining it. He passed away in the 1960's but his legacy is enjoyed daily by the brothers and seminarians here, as well as our guests. Now, several of the monks here maintain it."

We come to a turn in the path where it widens enough to accommodate a granite bench. Brother Paul motions for me to sit down.

"Thank you," I say as I sit down. Clark jumps up beside me, and I pull him in close with my left arm, stroking his head with my right hand. He pants, turns his head toward my face, displaying a look of happiness. Brother Paul smiles as he sits down beside Clark. I feel a sensation of butterflies in my stomach, just like the first time I jumped off the high dive at the Union Country Club swimming pool when I was ten years old.

"Brother Paul," I say, pausing, looking into his eyes, "Adrian McWhorter is alive."

Brother Paul's head twitches for an instant, and I see a look of confusion arise on his face, and I decide just to get it all out.

"He murdered your mother, my mother, and at least four other women artists over the years, as well as many other people. Brother Paul, last week he murdered my younger brother, Billy, in New York." I speak slowly, my attention fixed on Brother Paul's face. His pale blue eyes shift back and forth rapidly before locking on mine, "But why? How?" he asks.

"Well, in a nutshell," I continue, "And this information is a compilation of profiling from experts at the New York City Police Department and from an expert private investigator, Jonas Grey, I've hired, Adrian is a sociopathic pedophile and a serial killer with the intellect of a genius."

"Oh my," Brother Paul says, looking down at his hands now clasped together, knuckles whitening. "So, that wasn't Uncle Adrian they found with mother after the fire? But the dental records?"

"No," I reply, annoyed that he calls Adrian uncle, too, as I rub Clark's ears with both my hands, "We think it was probably a migrant worker who was working on your family's farm at the time. Adrian had a full set of dentures. We believe Adrian killed the worker, pulled the worker's teeth out and stuck his own dentures in the worker's mouth before he set fire to your mother's cottage."

"I see," he says, still looking down at his hands, now slowly turning them as if he were rubbing lotion into them. "And how did he kill my mother?"

"We're almost certain he would have drugged her before he let her burn to death," I reply in a soft voice.

I keep looking down at his hands to avoid seeing the pain in his eyes. I notice drops of water on his hands. I look up at his face. His head is bowed, tears streaming down, hitting the inside of his glasses and dropping onto his hands. I sense that his basic emotions have taken over, dissolving his religious demeanor, and I wonder if this news is powerful enough to shake the beliefs and vows he has embraced in order to settle into a life of monasticism, and I begin to feel sorry for him, so I reach over with my right hand, clasping it on top of both his hands, "Brother Paul, I'm so sorry. I know what you are going through. Adrian murdered my mother too in the summer of 1986 when I was twelve years old and my brother was ten."

"But why? Why didn't he just let us die too?" Brother Paul asks. "He's the one who carried Noel and me out of the burning house that night. I was so afraid. I knew my mother was still in there, and Uncle Adrian promised us that he'd go in and bring her out, he promised. I watched him go back in, and I waited and watched. Noel and I just sat there holding each other, trembling. We saw the flames pouring out of the windows, but no one came out. The flames just got higher and higher, and we couldn't even get near the house it was so hot, and then the roof collapsed and we never saw Uncle Adrian or Mother again."

"I'm so sorry, Brother Paul, such a horrible thing for you and your brother to have witnessed," I whisper. Clark gets up, nudging his muzzle into Brother Paul's face. Brother Paul hugs him. Clark turns

around toward me and sits down against Brother Paul who continues to embrace him with his right arm. Brother Paul reaches into a pocket on the left side of his robe and pulls out a white handkerchief. As he does, a chain of blue and gold beads with a golden cross on the end falls onto the granite bench.

"Those are the same rosary beads in *The Rape of The Rosary*," I say almost with a gasp, "They must have been your Mother's."

He puts the handkerchief down on the bench and picks the beads up, "Yes, they were my great-grandmother's and were given to my Mother at her confirmation when she was seven years old. I carry them with me every day. Somehow, they were unharmed in the fire." He stuffs the rosary beads back into his pocket, picks up the handkerchief, removes his right hand from Clark, takes his glasses off, wipes his eyes, blows his nose rather loudly, then folds the handkerchief and stuffs it back into the pocket, puts his glasses back on, and looks at me with a look of confidence that tells me he is rapidly integrating this horrible information I have delivered into his particular set of morals and beliefs. I sigh.

"I know Uncle Adrian profited greatly from dealing in my Mother's works," he says, draping his arms around Clark. "I suppose he did the same with your mother and the other women artists, and I imagine the value of the paintings increased after the artists' deaths. Hence, his motive, I presume?"

"That's part of the picture, we believe," I reply, wondering why my news did not shatter the foundation of this young man's beliefs, "However, we think his primary motive was to associate himself with female artists who were not in a marriage or a strong relationship with a man and who had male children—hence an almost effortless supply of victims to feed his pedophilic urges. We think he murdered the women when they became aware he was sexually abusing their sons, rather than strictly counting on profiting from escalated values. Sometimes artists' works do not increase in value upon their deaths."

Brother Paul looks down at the stone pathway, and I think I know the images swirling in his mind, so I push on with a gentle but emphatic tone, "You must remember what he did to you and Noel? I have your original Blood Brother's Certificate, Brother Paul."

His chest expands as he draws in a big breath, exhaling in a loud sigh. In an owl-like maneuver, Clark turns his head up toward Brother Paul's face. Brother Paul's pale blue eyes begin to fill up with tears again. He looks directly into my eyes. "You must understand, Philip, that I have the deepest faith in God and that my path to God was marked by immense personal tragedies, and that now I am settled in my family of brothers here, a very loving and kind family, and we all share in a lifelong conversion to Christ. You know about Adrian and my mother, so I assume you know about the murder of my father and Noel's suicide when he was fifteen. You see, Noel couldn't ever accept or get over Dad's death, Mother's death, or the sexual abuse from Uncle Adrian. These things tormented him, drove him mad, until he couldn't bear to live with himself any longer. Somehow, someway, God came into my heart, and despite the horrible suffering I endured as a child, I knew—somehow, I always knew—the remainder of my life would be one of love and light. I knew that my destiny in life would be to spend every day in the pursuit of becoming closer to Christ and God."

My feelings are divided between immense admiration for the faith of this young man and total resentment for his naïveté and gross oversimplification of the horrific acts Adrian directed upon him and his family. I blurt out in an angry tone, "So, you're telling me you forgive Adrian for murdering your mother?"

"I'm telling you that I will forgive him," he replies. "I will need to pray and think this through, but, yes, I will forgive him."

"I see," I reply, knowing my tone reveals my dissatisfaction with his response, "Well, let me ask you something, Brother Paul. Do you think Adrian should be brought to justice for his crimes?"

"Only the Lord can be the judge of any one of us, Philip," he replies.

I flash, feeling the heat rising out of my shirt collar, "That's bullshit! Adrian must be accountable according to the laws of our society. How can you condone anyone going around perpetrating heinous

crimes against innocent children and their mothers and simply dismiss it by saying 'Only the Lord can judge them'?"

He swallows hard. "Please, I do not mean to upset you, Philip. I do think Adrian has to be accountable to our laws and legal system. He must suffer whatever earthly consequences accrue to him as a result of his actions. But these things pale in comparison to divine judgment."

"I'm sorry, Brother Paul," I reply looking at the ground, aware that my mouth has filled with a vile taste, so I turn my head back around to the left over toward a bush behind the bench and I spit, "Pardon me," I clear my throat and swallow, wishing that I had a drink of water or maybe something stronger like bourbon, "But I do not share your faith, and yesterday Adrian kidnapped my ten year old half brother and has threatened to kill him if I do not deliver something he wants. Brother Paul, you are the only person who can help me get Adrian what he wants!"

His eyes shift back and forth again several times, the smooth skin on his brow wrinkles, and he replies, "I don't understand, Philip. How can I help you?"

"Did Adrian ever play 'treasure hunt' with you and your brother?" I ask.

"Yes, often. He orchestrated rather elaborate treasure hunts on our farm with rather extravagant prizes, too," he replies.

"Yes, especially when you let him sodomize you. I bet he gave you all real gold Spanish doubloons." I reply, trying to see if I can elicit something I can identify as a more normal emotional response from him.

His eyes narrow at this comment, and I observe he is unconsciously holding his breath. After a moment he says, "Please tell me how I can help you, Philip?"

I suppress my anger and continue, "It has to do with treasure, Brother Paul. You see, Adrian believes that artworks worth upwards of half a billion dollars are hidden on your family's farm somewhere."

I continue to scan his face carefully; his eyes shift to the left for a split second.

"So you are aware of what I am referring to?" I quickly ask.

He looks down at Clark and says, "I do remember Adrian telling us that a great treasure was hidden on our farm somewhere, but that we could never tell anyone about it. He made us swear in blood—it's part of our Blood Brother's agreement."

Damn, I should have read all those agreements through, I think to myself and ask, "Did he say anything specific about the treasure?"

"He said my mother knew where it was, and that we should try our best to get her to reveal where the treasure was hidden."

"And did you ever hear her talk about it?" I ask.

"No, not really," he replies, sitting up, straightening his spine. " I do remember Dad, before he was murdered, telling us that if we ever saw any strangers on our land to let him know immediately because we had to protect our valuable property, but I always thought he was talking about livestock or machinery."

"Do you have any idea what this treasure is?" I ask abruptly.

"No, not at all," he replies, sighing.

"It is the artwork stolen from the Isabella Stewart Gardner Museum in 1990—the largest art heist in history, reported to be worth up to half a billion dollars," I state. "It consists of one Vermeer, three Rembrandts, five Degas, a Manet, and one by Govaert Flinck as well as an ornate finial and a Chinese bronze piece."

"And why would anyone think it was hidden at Newgrange?" he asks.

"I think your mother and father hid it there," I reply.

"I don't understand," Brother Paul says.

"Brother Paul, your mother's three paintings *The Crucifixion of the Madonna*, *The Rape of the Rosary*, and *The Hanging of St. John Houghton* have an extensive and intricate hidden message. Last week in New York a group of us cracked it." I pause. .

"What kind of message?"

"Brother Paul, it's not the most pleasant message," I reply.

He nods his head from left to right and sighs, "Please, tell me."

"Okay. In *The Rape of the Rosary*, your mother painted the reflection of the rapist's face in her eyes: it is a priest named Joseph Patrick O'Callaghan."

Brother Paul appears shocked at this revelation and he says, almost in a whisper, "Father O'Callaghan was my mother's first cousin."

"There's more," I say, "In *The Crucifixion of the Madonna*, your mother left a message inscribed in incredibly small Latin letters on the baby's head: Boy born on June 23, 1977."

Brother Paul quickly says, "Oh, well, my first cousin, Geoffrey—that's his birth date." Simultaneously, we both make the mental connection, I can see it in his eyes and he can see it in mine; his face flushes red. "You think Geoff is my half-brother? You think Aunt Joan raised him as her own?"

"Yes, I think so, Brother Paul," I reply watching him carefully, trying to see if his faith can withstand the onslaught of depravity connected with his family I am revealing.

He sighs again and says in a childlike tone, "I don't see what Geoff and Father O'Callaghan have to do with the Gardner treasure."

"Adrian left me a letter saying that on the night your mother died, after he had drugged her, in defiance to him, she recited a riddle to him about the treasure. It goes like this:

> The eye of the virgin,
> A fetus saved,
> A piece of pie,
> Marks the way.

I pause to let the words sink into Brother Paul's mind, and then I resume in a calm, soft voice, "You see the eyes of the virgin revealed your mother's rapist, the Latin inscription on the baby's head indicates that it is the birth date of your cousin, but we now know that it is really your half brother, hence, 'A fetus saved'." I pause again. Brother Paul is now holding Clark tightly, looking down at the ground.

"And finally, one of the private investigators we hired is a brilliant young code cracker. He realized the clue 'A piece of pie' really refers to the mathematical pi taken from a circle. From observing the circular panels in *The Hanging of St. John Houghton* he realized that your mother had encoded letters that spell Newgrange."

"But I still do not see how the riddle or the solving of it has anything to do with the Gardner heist or it being hidden at Newgrange," he says looking up at me.

I reach inside my jacket pocket, pullout the Polaroid of his dad, and hand it to him. A look of affection is evident on his face as he examines the photo.

"How was your relationship with your father, Brother Paul?"

"I loved dad very much. He loved my brother and me a great deal. You see, he grew up in the city—Boston. When he moved to Newgrange, he fell in love with the farm and rural life. It changed everything for him and he spent so much time with Noel and me—showing us everything about the farm and farming he had learned. Sometimes it was almost like having a kid for a father. He was so enthusiastic about everything. And mother, she, well, I suppose you know what a troubled and tortured person she was. And she was moody. She suffered from manic depression and bounced from extreme highs to extreme lows. She focused much more on her work and basically let dad raise us until he died. Then, well, then Uncle Adrian came along."

As I sit here, listening to Brother Paul talk, I understand that he and I are much more similar than I could have ever believed, and my eyes fill with tears.

"Why are you crying, Philip?" he asks.

"Just because your story is so similar to mine, and because I can tell how much you loved your dad."

"Yes, I loved dad more than anything. Noel did too. The day we found Dad hanging in the barn, well, only God's love gets me through those nightmares," he replies.

"I'm glad your faith in God can do that, Brother Paul," I reply, "I've pretty much had to do it on my own. But anyway, listen, this is so hard for me to say. Did you know your Dad grew marijuana on your farm and that he had been arrested in Boston several times for selling drugs and petty larceny?"

"I've heard rumors over the years that his murder was drug related, but I have no knowledge of any criminal record from Boston," he replies.

I point to the Polaroid. "This photo was sent to Adrian from your dad. It shows your father holding the eagle finial that was stolen the night of the Gardner Heist. Your dad sent it to Adrian as proof that he had the stolen art and he demanded millions for the stolen works from Adrian."

"I see," Brother Paul remarks catatonically.

"Adrian probably would have paid a king's ransom for the works," I continue, "but before he could get to Kentucky, your father was murdered. So you see, after the murder, Adrian became your mother's mentor and confidant, and well, well, you know the rest of the story. And now Adrian is holding my little half brother hostage. He gave me this Polaroid with the instructions to get to you and to find the treasure."

"So you think my father was such a brilliant criminal that he orchestrated the largest art heist in history?" Brother Paul asks abruptly.

"I think your father probably loved your mother a great deal and that he would have done anything to please her," I reply. "I don't know how much you know about your mother's love-hate relationship with the Catholic church, Brother Paul, but it was grandiose. For God's sake, a priest raped her repeatedly from the time she was fourteen until she was seventeen. She was forced to have his baby as a teenager and give it up to her sister. I can't imagine how much anger, hate, and disgust that generated in her, when her entire life as a child she was taught that the Catholic church was the way, yet those teaching her were the biggest sinners? How does one resolve that, Brother Paul? Just tell me how faith in God can get a fourteen year old girl through brutal rapings from a priest who was a family member?" I stop, out of breath, almost panting, and I realize my voice is too loud.

"Each person's path to God is an individual thing," he replies.

"I'm not talking about each person, Brother Paul. I'm talking about your mother," and I point my right index finger at his chest as I say this. Clark jumps down off the bench, turns around looking at each of us. "It's okay, boy," I say in a calm tone, looking down at him.

We sit in silence for what seems like a minute. "Look, Brother Paul, I'm not here to debate religion or theology. I just want to save my little brother and bring that bastard, Adrian, to justice. Will you help me or not?"

"Do you really believe my parents stole that artwork?" he asks.

"I know your mother spent many hours in the Gardner Museum studying those masterpieces. In particular Rembrandt's *The Storm on the Sea of Galilee* is a painting she studied. In fact, the Bible she painted in *The Rape of the Rosary* is opened to Chapter 4 of the Gospel of Mark and verses thirty-five through forty-one are underlined in red in her painting." I pause again. "I don't know, Brother Paul. It seems to me your mother was questioning God in this painting. If Jesus could calm the storm on the Sea of Galilee, why couldn't he calm the horrible storm in her life—the continual rapings by her older cousin, the priest?"

"Yes, but how does that prove she stole the paintings?" he asks.

"It doesn't. But we think your dad probably knew how much your mother was drawn to that painting. The security at the Gardner Museum was really lackluster at that time period, and we think your dad, an ex-security guard, and a buddy of his, probably got high on something one night and pulled it off to get that Rembrandt painting for your mother. There's really no rhyme or reason for the other paintings they

took. Perhaps your dad had been to the museum with your mom and she pointed out the Vermeer and the Manets, but a knowledgeable art thief could have taken a lot more in the time the heist took place."

"Philip," he says with a big sigh, "I'll go with you to Newgrange. I have no idea where to look, the farm is over three thousand acres, there are several caves there, it could be anywhere."

I feel a wave of relief run through my body, "Thank you so much, Brother Paul."

"It's already getting late, so we'll have to spend the night there. I need to get permission from the Abbot. Give me a half an hour or so, and I'll meet you back at the Guest Center. There are refreshments there and a bathroom if you need it. You can take Clark inside with you."

We stand up.

"Thank you, Brother Paul. I'm sorry I had to deliver all this bad news so quickly."

He smiles, "You did what you needed to do, Philip. I'm going down this way. I'll see you back up at the Guest Center in thirty minutes." He nods his head at me, touches Clark's head with his right hand, turns around and walks down the path. I look up at the soaring twin spires of the arch abbey church and say to myself, "Please God, let this man who carries your light, show me the way." Clark lifts his leg, pees on the granite bench, and we head back up the hill.

CHAPTER 41

Brother Paul, who has changed from his monk's habit into khakis, brown loafers, a white oxford shirt, and a colorful crew neck sweater, with alternating horizontal bands of maroon, navy, and yellow, drives ahead of me in a minivan owned by the monastery. He will not drive above the speed limit, which irritates me greatly. Clark began the trip in his sentinel position in the front passenger seat, but now, after about half an hour, he has curled up in the seat and gone to sleep. I keep trying to call Dad, Lush, and Jonas, but I have had no reception on my cell phone. I find myself biting my nails, sighing constantly, and continuously shifting in my seat as I keep imagining what could be happening to Andrew. I force myself to take a few slow, deep breaths. I see a sign that indicates Louisville is twenty miles away. I sigh again. My cell phone rings. I pick it up and flip it open.

"Hello."

"Todge?" I hear Lush's voice say my name, and I sigh with relief.

"Yes, Lush," I reply. "I'm following Christopher, well, he's called Brother Paul now. We're about twenty minutes west of Louisville."

"Great!" Lush says. "Your talk must have gone well?"

"It went okay, I guess. How's it going in Bardstown?" I ask.

"Well, we've done a lot. Thank God for Jonathan Zeng. Jonathan somehow managed to get in touch with Joan while she was on a riverboat on the Yangtze. He explained the situation in broad terms to her, and she agreed to contact her son, Geoff, who pretty much runs the farm now. Geoff has been very helpful and has given us complete access to the farm this afternoon. Todge, you're going to love this place, it's beautiful!"

"Lush, Geoff is Dyanne's son by the priest. Brother Paul confirmed that his first cousin's birthdate was the same as inscribed on the head of the infant in *The Crucifixion of the Madonna*."

"But of course!" Lush shouts. "It makes perfect sense the older sister would have taken the baby as her own. Listen, Todge, there are three caves on the farm, but none of them are really that large. We've been in them all—it's unlikely anything is hidden in them."

"Bother Paul doesn't really know anything about the whereabouts of the treasure as far as I can tell. He did mention the caves…." I hear a beeping sound on the line, and I look at the phone and see that Dad is calling me. "Listen, Lush, I'll call you right back. Dad is calling in."

"Okay, bye," she says.

I push a button to accept Dad's call, "Dad?"

"Hi, son. Just checking in to see if you all have found out anything yet."

"No, not really. Lush and Jonas are at the O'Bryan farm now. They've searched three caves for the treasure and have found nothing. I'm following Christopher O'Bryan to Bardstown right now. We'll get there in about an hour. Have you all heard anything?"

"The St. Louis police have been in touch with Detectives Johnson and Bell in New York," he says, and I can tell from his voice that he is on the verge of tears, "Some sheikh's jumbo jet landed in Toronto yesterday. They are guessing that Adrian was on that plane. But, who knows."

"Dad, I promise you we'll find Adrian and get Andrew back to you safe and sound," I say with total conviction in my voice.

"Son, I just don't know what we're going to do if anything happens to Drew. First Eva, then Billy, now Drew—how can this be? How can one man be so evil?" His voice cracks, and I know the tears are falling now.

"Dad, how are Brenda and Peter and Emma?"

"Peter isn't saying much. Emma won't leave Brenda's side. And Brenda, well, she's not doing well at all. I forced her to take a Valium."

"Anything else from Johnson and Bell, Dad?"

"Nothing that I know of son."

"Just hang in there, Dad. Give us another day. We'll get Drew back, I promise."

"I know you are doing all you can, son. Do you think I should drive over to help you all?"

"Dad, I'll call you if we need you when I get to Bardstown. I think Brenda and the kids need you the most right now."

"Yes, I suppose so. Philly, if I could just get my hands on Adrian, I'd choke him dead. I never did trust him, those cold, light blue, un-human eyes. I never could see what Eva saw in him—never could."

"Dad, we will get him. You have my solemn promise. We will get him."

"You're right son. We have no other choice." My phone beeps again, and I pull it away from my ear to see that it is an unknown number.

"Listen, Dad, somebody's calling me. I'm not sure who it is, but I better answer it. I'll call you soon."

"Okay, son."

"Love you, Dad."

"Love you too, son," he says and hangs up. I push the accept button on my phone.

"Hello," I say.

"Philip?"

"Yes. Drew! Drew is that you?"

"Yes. It's me, Philip." My heart begins to race, and I feel as if I might start to hyperventilate.

"Drew, where are you? Are you okay?"

"I'm fine. I'm with Uncle Adrian," he replies. His voice sounds fine. He doesn't sound nervous or stressed at all.

"Drew, where area you?" I ask again.

"We're on this cool little jet, and Uncle Adrian says we're flying seven miles up in the sky, way above all the commercial planes."

"Oh. Where are you going, Drew?" I ask.

"You know—on the treasure hunt," he replies, laughing.

"What treasure hunt?" I ask.

"You know—the one you convinced mom and dad to let me go on with Uncle Adrian. He's so cool. How come you didn't tell us you and Billy had an Uncle?"

"Uncle?" I ask.

"Yeah, your Mom's older brother."

"Oh, yeah, well, gee, I guess I don't know. Just forgot. Where is Uncle Adrian taking you?"

"You know, on the treasure hunt!" he says, loudly, almost with exasperation.

"Yes, yes, but where will the plane land?"

"Well, that's a secret. Uncle Adrian says everything is a top secret to keep spies and bad people off our trail. They'll swoop in and try to steal the treasure from us."

"Yes, yes, I see. So you're okay being away from home and all?"

"Oh, yes. This is so cool. Uncle Adrian is the coolest. He's got all kinds of cool stuff for the treasure hunt—real machine guns, cool machetes, cool electronics and computers and stuff."

"I see," I say, "Well I'm glad you're having fun, Andrew. Is Uncle Adrian with you now?"

"Yes, he's sitting right beside me," he replies.

"Can I talk to him, Drew?"

"Here you go," Drew says.

"My dear, Philip. How are you?" The same, precise, upper class, British accent I remember so well fills my right ear.

"You so much as lay one little finger on Andrew, I'll rip your throat out, you sick bastard," I say gritting my teeth. Clark uncurls, looking up at me.

"So good to hear your voice too, Philly—it's been too long, hasn't it, dear one?"

"Go to hell!" I shout.

"Well, we're not going there—not just yet," he replies, coolly. "Look, Andrew. see here on the screen. That green dot is the car your Uncle Philip is in. Looks as though he's about ten kilometers west of Louisville, Kentucky."

"What's a kilometer, Uncle Adrian?" I hear Drew ask.

"It's a unit of measure, like the mile, Andrew. In fact there are approximately one and one-half kilometers in every mile," Adrian replies.

"So you're tracing Lush's Mercedes. What of it? You know I'm going to Bardstown. It's what you demanded, isn't it?" I ask, extremely pissed that he has used his charm to lure Drew in already.

"Indeed, but one must keep track of things. Organization is the key to success, Philip, my boy," Adrian says, sarcastically.

"Whatever," I reply, "Why did you have Andrew call me?"

"We just wanted to check on your progress. You see, in order for Drew and me to find the treasure we are seeking, we must have your piece of the puzzle first. N'est-ce pas?"

"I'm doing the best I can. I'm following Christopher to Bardstown right now," I snap back.

"Well, you better hurry, and don't be surprised if you come upon some rather unsavory characters on your journey. You see, my client, who desires those paintings more than you can imagine has double crossed me and is trying to get the goods on his own so he won't have to pay me. I've eliminated as many of his thugs as I can, but even I can't compete against this man's vast resources."

"Christ, are you telling me I'm walking into a trap?"

"I'm telling you in order to win this and preserve what's so dear to you, you're going to have to convince the little monk to reveal what we need to know. I'm confident you can do it, Philly—you always managed to get what you wanted, didn't you?"

"Alright, I'll do it. But you have to tell me where you are taking Andrew."

"Never you mind that. I'll email you a number to call when you've found your part of the treasure. Until then, goodbye, Philip." He hangs up the phone.

"Shit! Goddammit!" I scream, shut my phone, and smack the steering wheel with my left hand. Clark sits up, pushing his nose into my face.

"Christ, I don't know what I'm going to do, boy. I just don't know," I am frightened. I feel like a child; I feel myself tremble; I gasp for a breath, my eyes filling up with tears. I start to cry. Clark watches me intently.

Through my tears I look out to see that we are at the top of some vast promontory with the Ohio River valley stretching out in front of us, and in the distance I see the tall buildings of downtown Louisville as the car begins its descent toward the river. I open my telephone and speed dial Lush's number.

"Todge? What did your Dad say?" She asks. "Todge are you crying? What's the matter? Oh, darling. Tell me. What is it?"

I am sniffling and drooling. I feel so sad and so scared. "Lush, Adrian just called me," I sniff as snot begins to run out of my nose. I grab a paper napkin out of the side door and blow my nose loudly.

"Philip, are you okay. What did Adrian say?"

"Is Jonas with you?"

"Yes."

"Good. Put me on your speaker phone so he can hear this, too."

"Jonas, Adrian had Andrew call me. Andrew is fine. He thinks Adrian is my

Mother's brother. He's even calling him Uncle Adrian." My sobbing slows as I continue to talk to Lush and Jonas.

"How disgusting," Lush says.

"They are on a private jet going somewhere. I couldn't get them to tell me where they are going. Adrian has convinced Andrew that they are going on some sort of important treasure hunt, and that I talked Dad and Brenda into letting Andrew go with Adrian.""Oh, my God!" Lush says.

"Adrian has some sort of tracking device on this car. He's probably tracking the Range Rover, too. He knew that I was ten kilometers west of Louisville a few minutes ago. Shit, he's probably listening to our conversation right now," I say.

"That bastard!" Lush says.

"Listen, Lush. You and Jonas, we all are in great danger. Adrian told me that the client he wants to sell the Gardner treasure to is double crossing him and is trying to recover the treasure himself, and he has employed some real nasty types to do it. They might be in Bardstown right now."

"Holy shit, Todge!" Lush says. "We've not run into anyone."

"Well, Adrian says he knows Christopher—Brother Paul—knows where the treasure is. He said I must squeeze it out of him and find it before these other people do."

"Shit!" Lush says. "Well, hurry up and get here, Todge and we'll deal with it."

"I don't know what to do."

"We'll figure it out, Todge. We have no choice," Lush says.

"Philip," Jonas says, "Try to calm down. We can handle this. Mabry and Julianna are in the air right now on the way to Bardstown. As soon as we talked to Geoffrey, I realized we were going to need more help. Mabry is bringing a ground-penetrating radar. I had a sneaking suspicion we might have company, so I asked him to bring plenty of firepower. If we find the heist, its authenticity has to be quickly confirmed, so I asked Julianna to come too."

"That's great, Jonas," I say, feeling somewhat relieved. "But I really don't think Brother Paul knows where the treasure is hidden. I mean, he really seems sincere. Well, he's a monk—I just don't think he would lie to me."

"Philip, sometimes people push bad things out of their minds, even monks. Don't worry, if I have to, I can hypnotize him to see if he can remember," Jonas says in a matter-of-fact tone.

"Really? You can do that, Jonas?" I ask.

"Yes," Jonas replies, "Sometimes it works like a charm, other times it doesn't. But I know the techniques of instant hypnosis extremely well."

"Amazing, Jonas," I say.

"You guys should be here in about an hour," Jonas says, "Do you know what part of the farm you are coming to?"

"Yes, the main house," I reply.

"Great," Jonas says, "Julianna and Mabry will be here by then. We'll all meet there and initiate our plan."

"Thank God. Thank you, Jonas," I say.

"It's just what I do, Philip," Jonas replies.

"Do you think I should call Dad and let him know I talked to Andrew?" I ask.

"Philip, I would advise you not to use your phone anymore," Jonas says. "It may be how Adrian is tracking you. Did he call you when you were talking to someone?"

"Why, yes. I was talking to Dad."

"I thought so," Jonas replies. "After we hang up, do not use it, unless it's an emergency."

"Okay," I reply.

"Philip, get here as quickly as you can," Lush says.

"I'm trying, but Brother Paul drives like an old lady," I reply. I hear Lush and Jonas laugh.

"Nothing wrong with slow and steady," Jonas says. "Philip, keep your cool. This will all work out. Let me direct this. I do my best work in situations like this. I thrive on it."

"I trust you, completely Jonas," I reply.

"Good, thanks," he says. "Let's get off these phones now."

"Bye, Todge," Lush says.

"Good bye, y'all," I say and close my phone. I put the phone on the center console, begin stroking Clark between his ears with my right hand, sigh, and steady the car as we cross over the Ohio River on a double decker bridge.

As we drive around the west side of Louisville on an inner-beltway, I feel as if I have had three double espressos, or as Fatgran would say, 'I could climb the walls'. My underarms are sweating and occasionally a part of my shirt that has grown cold with wetness touches a part of my upper arm, so I reach up and pull the shirt away, a small but definite attempt to ameliorate my almost unbearable situation. And I think to myself, "Why me, God? What the hell did I ever do to anyone to deserve this? How could I be pressed any harder? What is it? Do you want my life for Andrew's? Then, by God, take it, you bastard! You know I'd give it—no questions asked. That little guy has a whole life ahead of him. Take me. Spare him. What kind of God are you anyway. I know what kind. The same kind that let that priest rape Dyanne, that let Mother torment Dad, that let Adrian abuse all those little boys, use, deceive, profit from, and murder their mothers, murder my brother, and get off 'scot-free' without so much as one iota of remorse or, God forbid, retribution from anyone. I know you God. You are not there. You do not exist, that is, you only exist in the minds of those that have nothing else to believe in but you. How I pity those people. All they really need to do is look at themselves in the mirror and say, 'I am who I see. I like what I see. I control my destiny. I am stardust. I am light. Therefore, I am God.'"

My mind plows deeper into this fertile soil of my soul, and as we pass the airport and merge onto Interstate 65 South, a vision flashes before my eyes: I will persevere; I will triumph over Adrian, but it will be a bloody affair. I see blood. I smell blood. I taste blood. I am ready. My fear has evaporated. Henceforth,

I must and will focus on the finish. I toggle the channel switch on the steering wheel until I find a 1990's station. Ace of Base's *The Sign* begins to play and I go back to my early twenties, when I was graduating from college, after my break up with Lush, before graduate school, back to the time when life was so fresh. The music thrills me and when I hear the line, 'No one's gonna drag you up to get into the light where you belong…' the meaning of it all becomes crystal clear to me now. My life will only unfold as I will it. I, you, we, everyone deserves to be in that light, that starlight from where we all hail, but the only way to really get there is to understand and know that we must take ourselves there, no matter how selfish that may seem, in the end, when it all comes down to each person's final breath on this planet, if we don't feel that starlight shining brightly on our face, then we have no one to blame but our own selves. My God, this is what Fatgram tried to tell Billy and me so many times. Billy listened; I didn't, but I see now. Thank you Fatgram; I love you and miss you so much. Thank you Ace of Base for singing this song of light to me—I won't ever let it go again.

The rest of the drive I spend flipping the satellite radio stations back and forth from the nineties station to a current hits station, and I focus on the cascade of pop music, trying to remember if I associate any event in my life with the songs. My mobile phone rings twice: one call is from Florence and the other call is from a friend in Atlanta, but I do not answer, determined not to assist in Adrian's surveillance of me. We've exited from the interstate and have been driving through beautiful forest covered hills for the past ten minutes, and now we are approaching the outskirts of Bardstown. We pass gas stations, strip centers, residential developments, and make a right turn into town. As we pass through the downtown area, I am astonished at its beauty. Most of the brick buildings look really old, well maintained and charming. It seems to be a vibrant, functioning downtown, with banks, cafes, retail shops, churches, and an old fashion drug store. We arrive at a traffic circle in the center of which sits the county court house, an imposing brick, Victorian-style structure, enter the circle and take the first right driving past an old tavern and many other old brick buildings. A little way down the street we pass a large red brick church with a big, white portico with six huge columns on its front and a towering white steeple with a large clock in it. I see a sign designating this as the Basilica of St. Joseph Proto-Cathedral, and I scan the surrounding buildings and wonder in which one did Dyanne O'Bryan endure the rapings. I also know this site must be the seat of Brother Paul's deep faith in the Catholic church, and I am overwhelmed with a strong sense of dichotomy this church represents to the O'Bryan family: a torture chamber for Dyanne, yet a place of intense safety, peace and love for her son. Brother Paul makes a left hand turn and we head out of town and back into a rural area. He told me his family's farm is located about ten miles south of Bardstown in the knob region of the county. Soon I notice what appears to be an array of small mountains in the distance, rising up a few hundred feet, all covered in forests, some grouped together, and some standing alone resembling small volcanoes in the vast flat fields. I've never seen a landscape quite like this, and it is beautiful. At intervals the two-lane road rises up on top of large knobs and the views, where there are breaks in the forests, usually where farmhouses are located, of the surrounding countryside are gorgeous. Redbuds and dogwoods bloom in profusion, the green understory plants turn their leaves toward the sun, soaking in as much as they can before the tall trees leaf out fully. On the top of one particularly tall knob, I can see back to the west, and I am surprised to see an ominous line of dark grey clouds far in the distance. I did not think it was suppose to rain here today. We proceed down this knob, and after traveling a couple of miles through the flood plain area of a small river, we head up another broad knob. Near the top, I notice an old stone fence on the right side of the road. It looks as if it was erected a couple of centuries ago, and I realize that it probably was. Brother Paul slows down the van and puts on the right turning indicator and makes a right turn into a driveway framed by two, tall red brick columns, supporting large, black, wrought iron gates that are open. The columns are capped with weathered limestone and a bronze plaque mounted on the column to my right reads 'Newgrange'.

"Clark, we finally made it," I say. He sits erect in his seat and makes a whining noise. I push the button and roll down his window just enough to let him stick his nose out and take in the smells.

We proceed down an asphalt paved driveway through a wooded area which soon opens up into an extensive lawn area with groups of big trees spaced throughout. In front of us, up a hill, surrounded by large hardwoods, stands an imposing, federal-style, red brick, mansion. The main house is three stories tall with a pitched slate roof. Four tall, brick chimneys rise up from the roof. The front windows, two on either side of the front door with identical windows stacked above these on the second floor, are each crowned with limestone lintels and framed with black shutters. A round portico with four large white columns covers the front entrance, a limestone archway with a paneled wooden door. The center of the second story, above the portico, is a large Palladian style window over which is built in the roof line on the third floor an ornate, triangular shaped, wooden cornice, with a carved wooden, elliptical medallion in its center. Two identical two-story additions flank each side of the main house. I wonder if these structures, recessed to the front line of the main house and containing two dormer windows each, are hallways or loggias possibly with French doors in the back. Each one terminates into a large room or rooms, built perpendicular to but in line with the front of the main house. The roofs of these rooms are pitched, triangular structures with pediments similar to the center triangular cornice in the main house. Each addition has a single large widow with black shutters facing outward. A circular drive leading to the front door surrounds a garden of old boxwoods of different types, trimmed into conical and circular shapes. The center of the garden is a perfect circle of green grass. Several vehicles are parked in the front. I recognize Lush's black Range Rover. I park the Mercedes, turn it off, and open my door. Clark bolts out over my lap before I can get out of the car and runs over to Brother Paul who is closing the front door of the minivan.

"Clark! Come back here," I yell.

"He's okay," Brother Paul says, bending down to pet Clark's head. I can hear dogs barking inside the house.

"Is he okay around other dogs?" Brother Paul asks.

"Oh yes," I reply, "He is well socialized. He goes to dog parks in New York quite a bit. He loves to play with most dogs."

"Good," Brother Paul says, "He can play out here with Sophie and Ben, my cousin's dogs."

At that moment the front dog opens, a beautiful Weimaraner bitch and a male, black and rust colored, beagle/hound mix rush out of the house barking. Lush and a tall, young man with dark hair follow. The dogs, their tails lifted, immediately surround Clark. Clark lifts his tail, and the three dogs start a little dance of butt sniffing.

"Sophie, Ben, be nice! Go on and play," The man shouts. The two dogs look up at him, then dash out down the driveway. Clark runs after them.

"Don't worry, they won't go far," the man says approaching me. He sticks out his right hand. "Hi, I'm Geoff Mulvaney."

"Pleased to meet you, Geoff. I'm Philip Hampton," I say as he firmly shakes my hand.

"So glad you're here, Todge," Lush says, smiling, pats me on the shoulder as she approaches Brother Paul.

"Hello, I'm Sarah Richardson," she says to Brother Paul.

Brother Paul shakes her hand and replies, "I'm Brother Paul. Nice to meet you Miss Richardson."

"Geoff," I say, "It is so kind of you to receive and help all of us on such short notice. I don't know how I can thank you enough."

"It's not a problem. My folks wanted to help out after they talked with Mr. Zeng, so I'm glad to do it," he says with a pronounced drawl in his speech, then walks over to Brother Paul and embraces him. "Good to see you, Chris."

"Thanks, Geoff. Good to see you, too," Brother Paul says.

The dogs are playing chase and come barreling toward us, mouths open, tongues wagging.

"Watch out, everyone!" Geoff says as they run in between us, not slowing a bit, and disappear behind the house.

"Looks like they're having a ball," Lush says.

"Yes, they are," Geoff replies, "Let's go on in." He waves his right hand toward the front door and we all begin to walk up onto the porch. Geoff is about an inch taller than I and has muscular hairy forearms. He is wearing Levi's, brown leather work boots, and a short sleeve green polo shirt unbuttoned, exposing dark chest hair.

"Look at this view, Todge," Lush remarks.

I turn back around and gaze out over the circular garden.

"Wow. How beautiful," I say. The south-facing mansion sits near the top of a knob, and the view from the front is of a river valley and its flood plain. Great patches of land along the meandering river, which is flowing to the south and west, are under cultivation. Another long ridge of knobs rises up along the river to the south. I see only a few farmhouses and silos in the distance. Most of the knobs and several large tracts along the river are covered in forests.

"Yeah it is," Geoff says. "Most of what you see down to the river and along the river to that hairpin turn to the west is part of Newgrange. Our great, great, great, great Grandpappy, Patrick O'Bryan settled here in 1815. He built the main part of the house here in 1840. Today we have just over three thousand acres."

"Wow," I reply, "That's a lot of land to care for."

Geoff laughs, "Well, it sure is. Brother Paul and I can tell you about that."

Brother Paul smiles at his cousin, and, despite the difference in size, I can see they are closely related. I conjecture that Geoff gets his size and muscular build from Father O'Callaghan, the rapist. We turn back around and walk through the front door. A very wide hallway runs down the center of the house with a wide, curving staircase, sweeping up to the second floor situated at the far end of the hallway. A large opening behind the stairway leads into what I think must be a kitchen. Four wide entrances, two on each side of the hallway directly opposite one another, with doors open, lead into large rooms.

"Everyone's down here in the big den," Geoff says.

The house is not an interior designer's showcase, but it is beautiful, with furniture and oriental rugs that have most likely been in the family for generations. I can immediately tell from the clutter of jackets, gloves, hats, stacks of papers, magazines, and various other items strewn about, that this house is lived in, and moreover, that it is the center of a large working farm operation. The floors are old, wide plank oak, stained dark, and worn in places—I bet they are original. The hallway walls have darkly stained, oak raised panel wainscoting, up to a height of about three feet with plaster, painted a light shade of yellow, above that to the ceiling. The doorways and the top of the hallway walls are framed in a wide, oak crown molding, stained dark to match the wainscoting. Two lovely matching metal, seven arm chandeliers, with each curved arm terminating in a metal tulip petal candle holder, painted black with small gold leaf designs, in the center of which is an off-white, electric candle, hang in the hallway. The chandeliers must be on a dimmer because the lights are just barely lit. A tall grandfather clock, which looks old to me, stands against the wall in between the two doorways to my right, begins to chime. I glance down at my watch to see that it is five o'clock. Damn, we need to hurry; we only have, at best, about three hours of light left. Two matching drop leaf tables with turned legs and beaded bands on the molded panel sides facing out into the hallway sit facing one another on opposite sides of the hallway. Above each hang beautiful, large landscape paintings in ornate, thick, wooden frames, painted gold. I am almost certain these are by Dyanne O'Bryan. I catch an odor, which is a mix of sweet pipe tobacco, earth, burning wood, and something like beef stew—I really like this house; I really like its ambiance. We turned into the second doorway to our right into a large room that appears to be a combination, den, library, and farm office. Jonas, Mabry,

Julianna, and a very pregnant young woman with long brown hair are all looking at a large topographic map spread out on a large, wooden desk. They all turn around and look up as we enter.

"Here they are," Lush announces and says, "This lovely young woman is Lindsay Mulvaney, Geoff's wife."

"I'm Philip Hampton. Pleased to meet you, Lindsay," I say as I extend my right hand to hers. She is dressed in black riding boots, black tights, and some sort of brown and beige striped combination sweater, shawl, and wrap that is draped over her extended belly, on which her left hand is resting. She has large green eyes and a beautiful face. She smiles. Her teeth are as white as puppy teeth.

"Very nice to meet you, too, Philip," she says as she gently shakes my hand.

"When's the baby due?" I ask.

"May first," she replies, "But I'm hoping he comes a little sooner."

Geoff walks up behind her, drapes his arms around her, pats her belly with both his hands, and says, "Linds really misses her horses, and she's tired of carrying this big ole boy around."

Brother Paul smiles as he walks over to Lindsay, embraces her, kisses her left cheek, and says, "Lindsay, you look lovely."

"You're too sweet, Chris," she replies.

"Is this your first child?" I ask.

Geoff and Lindsay both shake their heads up and down and Lindsay says, "Yes."

"Well one thing's for certain," Julianna says, "He's going to be a beautiful boy."

"Oh, thanks, Julianna," Lindsay says, smiling.

"Brother Paul," I say, "These are my friends from New York who've come down to help in the search. This is Julianna Morgan, Jonas Grey, and Mabry Whittaker."

"Very pleased to meet you all," Brother Paul says, his face taking on a more serious appearance. "The news of the kidnapping of Philip's young half-brother and the general suspicion that my mother and father may have hidden stolen paintings on this farm worth a fortune is indeed shocking. I'm sure it was stressful news to your parents, Geoff, as well as to you and Lindsay." He pauses a moment, his eyes wondering over each person, almost if he is in the middle of a sermon, desiring to let some poignant words sink into the minds of the congregation. "Nonetheless, I feel, deep down inside that I, and my family, must endeavor to help you out as best as we can. Accordingly, I've spent the better part of the drive down here coaxing my mind to slip back into my childhood years to see if I can recall anything at all about this. I am sorry to report that I have turned up nothing from within myself. As you all know, on a farm this size in this terrain, there are an infinite number of places where something could be hidden. None the less, I do know my father spent a lot of time fixing up the old gristmill, and I recall our house had quite a large cellar beneath it, but I believe much of the rubble from when the house burned was simply bulldozed into the cellar. I would recommend focusing on either of these two sites."

"Outstanding, Brother Paul," Jonas says, walking over from the map, "That's just the sort of information we need. We've explored the three caves today, and I just do not think we should focus on these at this point. Geoff, would you mind showing Mabry the location of the gristmill and the burned house on the topo?"

"Sure," Geoff says. "They are close together, about a quarter mile from here, up on Shepherd's knob in the big woods."

"Big woods?" Jonas asks.

"Yes, when Patrick O'Bryan came here, most all of these knobs were covered in virgin forest. He was determined not to ruin his land by cutting the ancient woods down, like the English did to his beloved Ireland. Because of that, we have over five hundred acres of virgin forest on this farm, one of the largest tracts left in Kentucky."

"How wonderful," Julianna says. "What a divine legacy."

456

"Brother Paul," Jonas says, "I'd be most grateful if I could talk to you just for a few minutes, in private, about what you remember from your childhood. It could really help our investigation."

"Oh, absolutely, Mr. Grey," he replies. "Lindsay, may we use the front parlor?"

"Of course," she replies. "I think I hear Sophie barking out back, I'm going to check on the dogs."

"Okay, hon," Geoff says, smiling at his wife. I observe them and their apparent happiness, and I look over at Lush, and I see her watching them. I think to myself that they could be Lush and me. What if I had shown more interest in our farm and Fatgram had left it to me, and Lush and I had married and ended up there? I could have had a life like this.

I walk over to the topo map where Geoff runs his finger from where we are to the area of the big woods and the gristmill and burned house.

"Here we are," he says, "And right here, at this elevation is the gristmill, and over here is Aunt Dyanne's house. It was actually Patrick O'Bryan's original house, but when he acquired this part of the farm in later years, this knob had such an incredible view, he built this house here."

"That is a pretty steep area," Mabry says. "And it's covered in thick woods?"

"Yes," Geoff says. "There never was a paved road to the house, and once it burned, no one went there, so in the past five years, it has become overgrown and is impassable. We'll either have to take ATV's or ride horses to get there."

"Would my Land Rover get through?" Lush asks.

"Mmmm, it's possible," Geoff replies, reaches over to a shelf by the desk, picks up a pipe, and a metal tin, and to my surprise opens the tin and pulls out a wad of tobacco and begins to stuff it in the pipe. "But I wouldn't want to take that nice vehicle up Shepherd's knob. Y'all mind if I smoke?"

"Not at all," Lush says. "May I join you with a cigarette?"

"Sure, Miss Richardson," he replies.

"Just call me, Lush, Geoff," she replies, "All my friends do—it's a nickname Philip pinned on my in college and it's stuck."

"So you two met in college?" Geoff asks as he pokes the tobacco evenly into the pipe.

"Yes, University of North Carolina," she replies.

"Oh yes, know it well. Well, in basketball anyway. What teams they've had," he says.

"I know," Lush says as she lights up a cigarette, "Coming from the land of the Cardinals and Wildcats and graduating from UNC, well, most March's I'm a traitor to my friends here."

Everyone laughs, except Mabry, who is still examining the map and Julianna is looking over the many silver trophies in the room. The room is large and comfortable with floor to ceiling bookcases on the south wall on either side of the doorway. The cases are crammed full of books, silver trophies, boxes, stacks of agricultural magazines, framed photographs, and dozens of other items. There are two large wooden executive type desks in the room, each in front of a bookcase. On either side of a large doorway in the west side of the room are rows of wooden file cabinets and a large wooden map cabinet, with several wide narrow drawers. The tops of the cabinets are cluttered with silver trophies, some of which have cows and horses on them, engraved silver goblets, and photographs. A large fieldstone fireplace sits between two windows on the north side of the room. Three impressive, fourteen point, mounted buck heads hang in a triangular pattern on the chimney. On the left side of the large mantel is a growling wildcat, on the other end stands a beautiful red fox. There are also several mounted ducks and a large turkey, all preserved by some taxidermist, hanging on the walls of this den in their final resting place. I imagine all these animals lived and lost their lives on this land. In front of the fireplace, there is a long, brown leather sofa and two large, brown leather armchairs surrounding a rectangular coffee table completely filled with stacks of books and magazines. I see red coals in the fireplace. On either side of a doorway leading from the front room on the eastern wall are several gun cases, all completely full. The primary lighting in the room is another large, metal chandelier. This one resembles a large wedding cake with three layers, each with

electric candles sticking up, from the largest layer on the bottom to the smallest one on the top. It is also painted black with gold designs of leafy vines on it. The desks both have three candle brass lamps with black shades on them, and there are four tall brass floor lamps situated around the sofa and chairs. The floor is the same, old wide plank oak as the hallway. The floor rugs in this room are all large, handmade, hooked rugs that appear to be old.

"Well, I graduated from UK with a degree in agricultural management," Geoff says, then sticks his pipe in his mouth, pulls out a lighter, lights it, applying the flame to the tobacco as he sucks the pipe. The smell of the burning tobacco fills the room.

"Brace yourselves, everyone!" Lindsay yells out from down the hall, "Here comes the pack."

Sophie and Ben, followed by Clark, come rushing into the room, happy mouths open, panting, water dripping from their muzzles, trotting around greeting everyone.

"Hey, Clark, buddy," I say as he jumps his front paws up on my thighs. I pat his head. "Did you have fun?" His tail wags rapidly. Sophie trots over to me and without hesitation jumps right up to me, knocking Clark off of me, her front paws landing right below my shoulders, her face almost in mine, and she licks me right in the mouth.

"Sophie, get down," Geoff says as everyone laughs.

"Oh, it's okay," I reply. "I love dogs." I grab her back, pulling her further into me. She turns sideways and lays her head against my chest in a gesture I can only describe as loving. Clark stands below looking up with a happy face, not at all jealous over Sophie's abrupt intercession. "What a great dog!" I say.

"She's my pretty girl," Lindsay says. "She and I will be giving birth about the same time!"

"Really?" Lush asks. "She's pregnant?"

"Yes. Very pregnant." Lindsay replies. Sophie jumps down, trots over to the fireplace, yawns, and stretches out in the warmth of the coals.

"She doesn't look really pregnant, except her nipples are sort of big," Lush says.

"I know," Lindsay replies, "Lucky bitch. Dogs only have a gestation period of sixty-three days. Lord, I wish it were that way with humans."

We all laugh.

"Is Ben the father?" Julianna asks.

"Oh no. He probably thinks he is. He's neutered. He's a rescue dog we got last year when our old Weim, Max, passed away. Sophie was devastated. We had to get her another companion right away. A friend of mine knew about this coon hound/beagle mix they were getting ready to euthanize down in Bowling Green. I plopped Miss Sophie in the car. We drove down there to meet him. It was love at first sight, and they've been inseparable ever since."

Lindsay is resting both of her hands on her stomach as she smiles down at Ben. "Isn't that right Benny boy?" Ben wags his tail, and as he smiles up at Lindsay, I notice he has what appears to be thick black eyeliner around his eyes, the rest of his face is an orange brown, the same color as his eyes.

"Gosh, his eyes are beautiful—like Cleopatra eyes," I say.

"Yes," Lindsay says, "That's just a narrow line of black fur. He's a handsome boy."

"Who is the father of Sophie's pups, Lindsay?" Lush asks.

"Oh, a champion from Rhode Island. You see, I show Weimaraners. After Sophie finished, I decided to breed her. Everyone says I'm crazy doing it with our own child coming, but, what the heck, I'll probably be up most nights anyway."

"You are going to be one busy woman," Lush says, blowing her smoke away from Lindsay's direction.

"Well, I'd rather be busy than not," she replies, then looks over at her husband, "Honey, would you mind putting some logs on. Sophie wants her fire."

Geoff nods, walks over to the fireplace, puts his pipe on the mantel, bends over, stacks some kindling on the coals, pokes it with a poker until it ignites, then stacks several logs on top. We all watch as the flames begin to engulf the logs. Within a couple of minutes, the fire is roaring.

"I just love this room," Julianna says. "It speaks volumes about your family and it is such a pleasant place, a place where you can tell people live their lives."

"Thanks, Julianna," Geoff says as he sets the poker against the fireplace and picks his pipe up off the mantel. "It's been this way as long as I can remember. I think it was pretty much the same when Mom and Aunt Dyanne grew up here."

It is indeed pleasant, I think, so how the hell did such horrible turmoil occur in Dyanne's life? There's more than meets the eyes here. I wonder what Dyanne's parents were like? I wonder why Mabry is so quiet? I look over at him. He now has a laptop out and he is typing in something.

Brother Paul and Jonas walk back into the room, both with calm expressions on their faces.

"Well, we had a pleasant chat," Jonas says, clasps his hands together, interlacing his fingers. "Brother Paul and I really both feel we should focus on the gristmill."

"Sounds good," Mabry says. "We should hurry, your weather scanner will pick this up any second," he adds as he points to something that looks like a radio sitting on one of the shelves. "A line of powerful thunderstorms is expected to hit the Louisville area in about an hour. They'll be here twenty to thirty minutes after that. Conditions are favorable for fueling these storms. They could easily become tornadic."

"Oh dear," Lush says, extinguishing her cigarette in an ashtray on the desk opposite from where Mabry sits.

"What's your plan, Jonas?" I ask.

"You, Brother Paul, Geoff, Mabry and I will take three ATV's to the gristmill. Not being chauvinistic, but ladies I don't want any of you out in these approaching storms." He walks over to the other desk on which three large black plastic cases sit. He opens one of the cases revealing two large pistols. He flips open another cases which contains what I think is an assault rifle. "We've got plenty of fire power here, in case we have any uninvited guests."

"Wow, what do we have here?" Geoff asks.

"Mabry bought two AK-74M's with grenade launchers and four Glock 18's," Jonas replies as he picks up one of the Glocks and hands it to Geoff.

"Pretty, look it has a flashlight attached to it," Geoff says as he observes the black handgun.

"You and Philip take a Glock," Jonas says, "Mabry and I will take the 74M's, plus we have our own pistols already." He turns around toward Lindsay. "Something tells me you know your way around guns."

She smiles, "You've got good intuition, Mr. Grey."

Geoff laughs, "Linds can break a longneck on a fence post at two hundred yards with an iron-sight Ruger twenty-two."

"Impressive," Jonas says, "I'll leave you a Glock."

"I'll take one, too," Lush says, "I'm not as good as Lindsay, but I can hold a gun steady, and I shoot straight."

"Great," Jonas says. "Julianna, would you like a weapon?"

"Oh dear, I've only fired a gun a couple of times in my life. Do you have anything smaller?"

"Don't worry," Lindsay says. She retrieves a brown leather purse from one of the bookshelves, fishes around in it with her right hand, and pulls out a small pistol with an ivory handle. The pistol is some type of engraved metal. She hands it to Julianna.

Julianna takes it, "Oh, my, look at the engraved vines. This is handmade."

"Yes," Lindsay replies, "it was a gift from my father. It's a replica of a Baby Browning made by PSA. Here's the safety. Release it when you want to fire it. Just aim, Julianna, pretend it's a sponge and squeeze it."

"Hmmm, I see," Julianna says.

"It may not kill your attacker, but it will certainly stop him in his tracks," Lindsay says.

"I do hope none of these firearms will necessary," Brother Paul remarks, and I realize he is not armed. I wouldn't think a monk would be, but I imagine, growing up here, he's very familiar with firearms.

Geoff sticks his pipe in his mouth, claps his hands, and says, "Good plan, we're armed; come on boys. The ATV's are out back in the barn. I've got rain gear for everyone there, too."

Lush, Julianna, and Lindsay are grouped together, and they all have worried looks on their faces.

"We are going to find that treasure," I say to them. "We are going to bring it back, Julianna is going to verify its authenticity, and we're going to get my little brother back to safety."

"We will," Lush says, and I see her eyes are tearing up.

We all start to walk down the hallway to the back and the dogs immediately follow.

"Hon, why don't y'all stay in the den for a while and keep the dogs there. I don't want them following us," Geoff says.

"Okay," Lindsay says, "Y'all be careful. When you get back, I'll have supper ready. I'm cooking a big pot of beef stew."

God that sounds good even though I feel butterflies in my stomach as my adrenaline builds, and I try to sense deep within my gut if any real danger awaits us. I send out a silent prayer to Brooker T, seeking his guidance and wisdom of the forest and all its mysteries.

Jonas directs me into his ATV, Mabry and Brother Paul are in front of us in another two-seater, and Geoff leads the way in a one seater pulling a utility trailer. The sun is out, but I see high, thin clouds moving in. From the barn area we travel down a dirt road that circumvents a large pasture in which I see dozens of black and brown cattle grazing. The road veers to the left into the woods and down a rather steep hill.

"How did it go with Brother Paul?" I ask Jonas.

"Perfect. He relaxed easily and didn't even realize that I hypnotized him," he replies, turns his face toward me, smiling.

"And?" I ask.

"Pay dirt!" Jonas replies. "The Gardner heist is definitely hidden in the gristmill, and we will find it unless someone has beat us to it."

"What did he say?" I ask, my heartbeat elevating.

"I was able to get him back into being a little boy on the farm. God, was he close to his brother, Noel. I imagine Noel's death was more devastating that his mother's or father's. Anyway, he recalled how much fun he and Noel had playing in and around the gristmill the first summer they moved here in 1991. They were seven or eight years old. His mother was usually painting all day and left the kids with Ted. Ted spent most of his time working on the gristmill. When I asked Brother Paul what sort of work his dad did on the gristmill, Brother Paul replied, 'a lot of digging.'"

"Yes!" I say, "Digging to hide the artworks."

"Correct," Jonas says, "And he went on to say that his dad and his friends would smoke funny smelling cigarettes, marijuana, I presume, and dig all day long. I asked him why his dad was digging so much and he replied, 'to make a secret shortcut to China where treasures were hidden.'"

"I guess that's what Ted told the kids, then," I reply.

"Yes. It makes sense," Jonas replies. "I asked him if he could show me where the secret passageway was in the gristmill, he replies that it was under the big stone. So, I bet Ted moved the grist stone over his dugout chamber."

"Right," I reply. "Crap, those things can weigh tons, how are we going to move it?"

"No problem," Jonas replies, "Mabry brought down ten pounds of C-4."

"Plastic explosives?" I ask.

"You bet," Jonas replies, "We anticipated we might be blasting through rock."

"Great," I reply, "Let's just hope we find it intact. Ted's cronies could have stolen it years ago. Maybe they were the ones who murdered him?"

"That thought passed through my mind, too," Jonas says.

The road has faded into more of a trail as we make our way down to a shallow, wide stream that the ATV's cross easily. We proceed up another hill and stop while Geoff hops off his ATV to open a steel gate. I see long rows of fence posts strung with barbed wire, and I guess we are entering another grazing area for cattle. We proceed through mainly pastureland with some trees and as we near the crest of the hill I notice a old stone fence on the right outside of the barbed wire fence. This all looks so familiar to me and as I look into the distance up the hill, I can see that this pasture is surrounded by really big trees. We stop again near the top and Geoff opens another steel gate. We proceed into an extraordinarily beautiful woodland.

"Wow," I say, "Look at the size of these trees."

"Yes," Jonas replies, "This is where the old growth forest begins. Geoff told us earlier that there are oak, beech, chestnut, maple, hickory, black cherry, black walnut, and yellow poplar in here, some of which are hundreds of years old."

The air cools in the hardwood forest, the sunlight flickers through in patches, I gaze up at one giant tree after another, and I marvel at the dedication and consistency of a family who preserved this for almost two centuries. Suddenly, the hair on the back of my neck stands up when I realize this is the same forest in my dream where Mother, Fatgram, Billy and I were riding with a pack of Weimaraners. How is it that my dreams are becoming so prophetic? We proceed slowly through the woods for several minutes until we enter a clearing in the forest. Here it is, just as it was in my dream and in Dyanne's painting: a stone springhouse with a slate roof, built at the foot of a small pond. Three large, old weeping willows covered in chartreuse leaves, surround the pond, and as we approach I see a rusted, metal, water wheel jutting out of the far side of the building. We drive through a collapsed area in the stone fence and proceed up to the building. The wooden aqueduct that diverts water from the pond to the water wheel is rotten and has collapsed. The stone dam which forms the pond appears to be holding well and a stream of water flows through a small spillway over the dam and down past the building. The walls of the rectangular building are taller than in my dream with four small glass pane windows high up on each of the long sides. The foundation of the building is also high, I suppose because it is constructed so close to the stream and pond. We all get off the ATV's and form a group. Jonas and Mabry turn their heads, listening, scanning the area with their eyes, memorizing the lay of the land.

"Alright, guys," Jonas says, "Brother Paul, Mabry, and Philip will go inside with me. Geoff, you stay outside and keep watch. I'll come out and get you when we find something."

"Got it," Geoff says, "But shouldn't I have one of the AK's while standing guard?"

"You ever fired one?" Jonas asks.

"Oh yes," Geoff answers, smiling.

"Okay, take one, and keep a Glock, too," Jonas replies.

"Shhhh!" Mabry says. We all look at him, listening. Then we hear it, the rumble of distant thunder. "The storm is approaching," Mabry says, "Let's get going."

I reach down and feel the Glock in the holster strapped around my waist, and I look up at the tall trees behind the gristmill and I see the wind beginning to move in them.

"Here's the key to the door, Jonas," Geoff says as he hands it to Jonas. Jonas takes the key, grabs two black cases and instructs Brother Paul and myself to each take two cases. Mabry picks up two stainless steel cases. We cross over a small wooded bridge built over the stream and walk down a sloping area to the wooden door located about ten feet beside the water wheel. Geoff walks up on the bridge to begin his surveillance. Jonas puts his cases down, sticks the key in the dead bolt, wiggles it, it turns, and he pulls open the door. He picks up his cases and proceeds through the door, we follow. I imagined an old, dusty,

wooden mill, with big metal gears, big grinding stones, and wooden trays for handling grain strewn about. It is not at all like that. To our right, there is a large circular, metal gear attached to a big wooden shaft penetrating through the stone wall connecting the water wheel to the gear. Apart from that, the other traces of the mill have vanished, and the interior of the structure is finished out to resemble a hunting lodge. In fact, that is exactly what Ted transformed this into: a hunting lodge. The old wooden floor has been sanded, stained, and shellacked. There are two large old, worn upholstered sofas in the center of the room and three old leather arm chairs, all surrounding a big, square, iron, wood burning stove, with a cooking surface on top with several cast iron pots and pans stacked on it, and a round metal exhaust stack going from the back of the stove straight up to the roof. I look up to see the exposed wooden rafters and wooden cross beams, all seated directly on the stone walls. There are two large black ceiling fans hanging from cross beams and an assortment of stuffed animal busts mounted on the walls. I see several bucks, an elk, a black bear, a cougar, a red fox, a large coyote, a wild boar, a bobcat, and a bison. I look back toward the rear of the large room, and I see a wooden stairway that leads to a loft that has four twin beds lined up on the wall. The wooden rail in the loft area has three beautiful old quilts folded and hanging on it. To the right side of the room underneath the loft is a kitchen area with a refrigerator, a large utility type stainless steel sink with a water faucet. Shelving above the sink contains dishes, utensils and cutlery stacked in ceramic crockery, stacks of kitchen towels, and spices. Underneath the loft to the left is an enclosed closet that I assume must be a bathroom. Brother Paul flips a switch, and to my surprise, the room lights up from track lighting installed high up on the four walls. He flips another switch and the ceiling fans begin to turn.

"This place is way cool," Mabry says. "A hunter's retreat."

"Yes," Brother Paul replies, "My father converted the mill into a hunting lodge. He had electricity run over here, drilled a well for water, and installed a septic system for the bathroom."

"Nice," Jonas says. "What happened to the millstones?"

"I don't know," Brother Paul replies. "I don't remember ever seeing them"

"Judging from the size of the foundation, there has to be a basement in here," Jonas remarks.

"Oh, yes, there is," Brother Paul remarks. He points down to the old, half bald, oriental rug on which we all stand. We move off of the rug and Jonas grabs an end and pulls it toward himself revealing a large rectangular cut in the wooden floor with recessed handles on the either end of the short side of the rectangle. Brother Paul goes to one handle, and I go to the other.

"Let's lift on the count of three. Jonas, Mabry, if you men would grab a side when we lift. I remember this is really heavy. Here we go: one, two, three...."

I squat down, grab the metal handle and pull up, trying to use my legs rather than my back. The door lifts, but it is extremely heavy.

"Okay guys, grab it," Brother Paul says as we pull the door up three or four inches. Jonas and Mabry each take a long side of the door in their hands instantly making the weight manageable. "Let's walk it over this way and set it down. Careful, Mabry. Walk back toward Philip. Good."

We manage to place the heavy trap door on the floor. I see wooden stairs leading up from the basement. Mabry opens up one of the cases and retrieves two long black flashlights. He hands one to Jonas.

"Okay, let's go down," Jonas says. He turns on his flashlight and starts down the stairs. "Be careful guys." I follow Jonas. Brother Paul follows me. Mabry turns on his flashlight and follows us, shining the light on the stairs for the rest of us. The basement is large, running the full length of the building. I'm surprised at how deep it is; I judge the dirt floor must be ten feet beneath the floor above. Jonas and Mabry shine their lights around illuminating the beams and joists of the mill. It is amazing how close the joists are spaced—less than a foot and each board is about two inches wide and at least a foot in depth; this floor was built to support very heavy loads. Mabry and Jonas shine the light around the basement, revealing only a dry, dirt floor and the stone walls of the foundation.

"Damn, I don't see anything down here," I remark.

"Let's look at bit more," Jonas says. "Mabry, go get a lantern."

Mabry hurries up the stairs. Jonas continues to shine his light along the length of the walls illuminating the densely stacked and mortared stones of the foundation. Towards the rear of the basement he pauses the light for a long while.

"See anything?" I ask.

"Maybe," he replies. "The stone pattern looks a little different in the center of the back wall."

I strain my eyes to see something, anything, but it all looks the same to me. I hear Mabry coming down the stairs. The room becomes awash in light as Mabry descends into the basement with some sort of very bright lantern. I turn around to look at him.

"Don't look at the lantern everyone! It's far too bright," Mabry says. He sets the lantern on the dirt floor in the middle of the room. We all proceed to the back wall.

"Yes, these stones in this area, have definitely been removed, restacked and re-mortared," Jonas says as he makes a sweeping motion around a central area on the back wall. He pushes on the mortar with his fingers. "Okay, we'll blast right in here. Mabry, lets get the pick axes and the explosives. Everyone, let's go upstairs. Mabry and I can set this up in a few minutes. Then we'll all have to get out of the building when we detonate the C-4."

I feel relief as we climb back up the stairs.

"Philip, Brother Paul," Jonas says, "You guys just have a seat up here. We'll be done in ten minutes. If you want, go out and tell Geoff what we're doing."

"Sure thing," I reply. I head out the door. Brother Paul follows me. We walk up to the bridge where Geoff is standing, talking on his cell phone. I notice the wind has really picked up, and I hear the branches and leaves of the trees rustling.

As I approach Geoff, he says 'Goodbye' to someone, turns toward me and says, "That was Lindsay," he says. "Bardstown is under a severe thunderstorm warning and a tornado watch. A huge line of thunderstorms storms running from Owensboro to Louisville and producing straight-line winds in excess of seventy miles an hour is headed our way. They seem to be intensifying and will reach Bardstown in fifteen minutes. That means they'll hit us about the same time since we're southwest of Bardstown."

Just as he finishes speaking, a clap of thunder resounds and rolls lasting for several seconds. Right after that, another clap folds over it. I look up to see swift moving grey clouds headed eastward. The sun is gone, and it appears that dusk is falling. I look at my watch. It is almost six o'clock. We should have had another hour and a half of good light.

"You better come inside, Geoff," I state. "Seen anyone or anything out here?"

He shakes his head from side to side, "Naw, not a thing."

Brother Paul wrings his hands, looking up at the sky with a nervous expression on his face. Lightning flickers to the west. As we head back into the gristmill, another clap of thunder rolls over us, this one, even louder than the others. I close the door behind us.

"Mabry and Jonas are downstairs setting up explosives to blow part of the back basement wall out," I state. "Jonas detected an irregularity in the stonework and believes it has been removed at some point and the stones re-laid."

"Interesting," Geoff says. "As far as I know, Uncle Ted removed all the mill stuff that was down there. It's been empty ever since. Can you remember anything about the basement, Chris?"

"No, not really," Brother Paul replies, "I just remember Dad always told us to keep out of there because it was dark and dangerous and there might be poisonous spiders and scorpions down there."

I look at Geoff and he looks back at me, and I know we are thinking the same thing.

"Does anyone ever use this as a hunting lodge anymore?" I ask.

"No," Geoff replies. "There's plenty of game to hunt closer to the big house, so there's really no reason to come out here and 'rough it' so to speak. It was different when Aunt Dyanne and Uncle Ted lived nearby. Their house was pretty small, so it made sense to finish this into a lodge for hunting guests."

"I see," I reply. "But when was it last used as a grist mill?"

"Oh, the family operated it on a part time basis well into the sixties, grinding corn, wheat, and even sorghum for our family and for friends," Brother Paul says. "It was pretty much abandoned during the early seventies. It wasn't until we moved back to Kentucky in the early nineties that Dad decided to refurbish it. He and some of his friends did all of this themselves. He was really proud of it and spent a lot of time here."

"What happened to the grist stones and the other mill parts?" I ask.

"Well, a lot of it is stored in one of the barns up near the house," Geoff says.

"The grist stones, too?" I ask.

"Not the big ones. There are a couple of small ones up there, but there were two really big stones in here originally. I remember seeing them when I was a little boy. I don't know what Uncle Ted did with them. Do you know, Chris?"

Brother Paul looks down toward the ground, squints his eyes, takes his right index finger, pushes up his glasses which have slid part way down his nose, sighs, looks up at both of us and says, "It seems like I remember a lot of men here one day with a tractor or a back hoe and big heavy chains. But I can't recall what they were doing. It could have been moving the grist stones, but I just don't know."

I hear Jonas and Mabry coming up the stairs and another loud clap of thunder echoes much closer to us.

"Guys, we're ready," Jonas says. "To be on the safe side, let's go outside back to the bridge."

He opens the door and the wind rushes in. We all walk outside. The trees are whirling back and forth. We look up to see dark, black, boiling clouds rushing eastward.

"Christ, the skies are getting reading to open," Jonas yells, "Hurry up everyone. Leave the door open to equalize the pressure from the blast." Jonas runs up on the bridge. We all follow and turn toward the building. Lightning flashes in the sky, the loud thunder descending upon us.

"Do it now, Mabry," Jonas yells.

Mabry pushes some type of transmitter in his right hand, and all at once we hear what sounds like thunder coming from the gristmill, and a cloud of dust blasts out of the open door.

"No use going back in for a few minutes," Jonas says, "You won't be able to breathe from all the dust."

"But we're going to get pummeled out here by the storm, we've got to take shelter somewhere," I reply.

Geoff flips open his cell phone, pushing it up against his right ear. "What, you're kidding. Oh my God, honey. You all get to the basement, and we'll do the same. Go now. I'll call you soon." He slaps the phone shut. "Tornado on the ground in Hodgenville. That's five miles southwest of here. It's headed northeast. We've got to get inside the mill. Come on."

As we make our way back to the building the wind is so strong, it's hard to walk, and I feel something stinging on my face. I look up to see golf ball sized hail falling down. By the seconds it takes us to get inside, the hail is falling so hard, you can hear the slate shingles breaking. Inside the dust is thick in the air and the light coming from the track lights is hazy, but we can breathe. Mabry passes out white nose masks, and we all put them on. Windowpanes on the west wall begin to break, lightning flashes, and the thunder is deafening. And then we hear a low, deep base rumbling.

"What is that noise?" I yell.

"Tornado!" Mabry shouts back.

"Everybody in the basement!" Jonas directs.

As we head down the stairs, I hear a cracking sound; the lights flicker and die. Jonas and Mabry both turn on their flashlights, but the light barely penetrates the thick fog of dust in the basement. I'm in the front, but I cannot see the stairs.

"Sit down, Philip. Everyone grab hands and scoot down the stairs until we hit the floor."

The dust stings and is blinding. "Shut your eyes," Jonas shouts, "This dust could blind you."

I shut my eyes, sit down on a stair, grab it with my left hand, reach up to grab Brother Paul's hand, and I slowly scoot down stair to stair until I feel dirt and rubble with my left hand. I scoot over to make room for the others. We instinctively form a huddle with our arms around each other's waists, and our heads leaning in the center, touching. The noise is deafening. It sounds as if a freight train is running over the building, I feel air rushing around my face, and suddenly I feel like I'm being sucked upward and we all huddle together tighter, and I feel my feet leaving the ground, and I feel the huddle splintering apart in the air, and I think to myself this is it, this is how I am going to die, and right at that moment I am abruptly slammed into the ground and I feel the left side of my face hit something hard and sharp. I know I've been injured. The noise recedes quickly and I'm lying face down in the dry dirt basement floor on what feels like a bed of rocks. I open my eyes slowly, but everything is blurred; I can't see a thing.

"Everybody, everybody," Jonas shouts, "Keep your eyes shut. Keep your eyes shut. The dust from the blast can blind you. I have a canteen of water. Let me wash my eyes out, then I'll move around to each person. Is everyone here and alright?"

"I'm fine, Jonas," Mabry says.

"Me, too," Geoff says.

"I'm okay," I reply, "But I think my face is cut pretty badly."

"Okay, Philip, we'll get to you," Jonas says.

"Brother Paul. Brother Paul, are you okay?" Jonas asks. There is no reply.

"Shit," Jonas says, and I hear water dripping.

"Got a canteen, too," Mabry says.

"Shit," Jonas says again. "Here's my flashlight. Mabry you look okay," Jonas says.

"You do, too, Jonas," Mabry replies. "There's Brother Paul lying by the stairs."

"I'll check on him," Jonas says, "You go wash out Geoff's and Philip's eyes."

"Geoff, here, tilt your head up this way," Mabry says. "Good, keep your eyes shut. Good. Now blink a little bit. Let the water wash over your eyeballs. Good. Can you see?"

"Yes, thanks, Mabry," Geoff replies, "I can see fine."

I'm sitting up Indian style. I feel warm blood running down my left check, down my neck, soaking my shirt.

"Oh, shit that's a nasty cut," Mabry says. "It needs suturing. Tilt your head up, Philip. Let me pour some water over your eyes for a second or two, then start to open them and let the water flow over your eyeballs." I feel the cool water hitting my eyes, then I start to open them. It stings my eyes, but it stings the cut on my face much worse. Mabry stops pouring the water. I open my eyes. I can see. He is shining the flashlight on me. He takes a cloth from his pants pocket and instructs me to hold it tightly on the wound on my cheek. I do so and look over to see Geoff and Jonas helping Brother Paul, who is propped up, unconscious, against Geoff's chest. Jonas is pouring water onto Brother Paul's face. After a few seconds of this, Brother Paul groans, begins to open his eyes and Jonas pours more water onto his eyes. Brother Paul's hands fly up, knocking the canteen out of Jonas's hands.

"It's okay, Chris, it's okay," Geoff says, "Relax. Just relax. You've had a nasty bump on your head. You were unconscious, probably a concussion."

Brother Paul groans again, then says, "Where are we, Geoffrey?"

"We're in the basement of the gristmill, Chris," Geoff says in a gentle voice. "Remember, we had to come down here because of the tornado. We're here helping Philip and Jonas and Mabry find the Gardner paintings."

"Oh, yes, I remember," Brother Paul says, squinting his eyes open. "The tornado was sucking us out of the basement and then everything went dark."

"That's exactly right, Brother Paul," Jonas says as he picks up his canteen. "It appears that you were more airborne than the rest of us, and you hit the top of your head on one of the floor joists. You've got a nasty bump there. I know your arms and hands are fine. Can you move your legs okay?"

Brother Paul shakes his legs and nods affirmatively.

"Good," Jonas says.

"Jonas," Mabry says, "Take a look at this cut on Philip's face."

Jonas walks over, shines the flashlight into my face, bends over, and gently pulls my hand away from my left cheek. "Geez," he says, scrunching up his face. He takes the cloth from my hand, dabs the wound, then looks at it again. "Keep your head above your heart and keep applying pressure with this cloth, Philip. That should stop the bleeding within a few minutes. It then needs to be washed out and sutured, but it will heal just fine. Might leave a little scar, but it will be a manly one."

"Gee thanks, doc," I reply.

"Guys, guys!" Mabry shouts. "Look, look at the back wall."

The tornado has sucked all of the blast dust out of the basement, the air is clear now. Mabry's flashlight illuminates the collapsed foundation revealing a large round hole. Piles of rock and large hunks of what were two large grist stones lie on the ground.

"Just as you thought, Mabry," Jonas says, "he used the grist stones to cover the hole he dug. Brilliant placement of the plastics. Superb work, kiddo!"

Mabry beams with delight. I slowly get to my feet. Geoff is helping Brother Paul up. We all walk carefully through the rubble toward the hole. Mabry and Jonas shine their flashlights inside the round hole which I judge to be about six feet in diameter and running back about twelve feet. Stacks of small white bags cover the floor of the hole. Jonas picks up one of the bags.

"Drugs?" Geoff asks.

"No, desiccant," Mabry replies and he quickly leans over and begins throwing out the small bags into the basement as rapidly as he can. "Voila!" he shouts. "Look, Jonas, here it is."

"What is it?" I ask.

"A big cedar box," Mabry replies. "Shine the light for me, Jonas," Mabry instructs as he climbs up into the hole and starts throwing out more of the small bags. He works his way back into the hole, leaning on the right side of the dugout space. After a while he emerges, smiling, holding something in his hands.

"It's the bronze Yu vase from the Gardner. No need to incase it in a cedar box," Mabry says. "There are two large, flat, rectangular cedar boxes in there."

"That's where we'll find the paintings," Jonas says. "But first, let's go up, survey the damage, and call the ladies."

We carefully walk back to the stairway and as soon as we start to ascend them, I sense that something is terribly wrong. As we climb the stairs we enter into a realm of total destruction. The roof of the gristmill is completely gone as is almost everything in the room: there is no furniture, the wooden burning stove is gone, all of the mounted animals, the refrigerator, the quilts, the twin beds, as well as our guns, and all the cases. The rain has stopped, and I see blue sky through a break in the clouds. We look over to where we parked the ATV's and they are all gone, too. The little bridge is gone, and all around us the old growth trees are splintered and broken, uprooted, and snapped in half like matchsticks. It looks as if a big bomb exploded overhead. I feel a sick feeling in my stomach as I look at the expressions on Geoff and Brother Paul's faces.

Geoff's mouth hangs open. "Oh my God, Linds!" He pulls his cell phone from his pants pocket, flips it open, pushes a button, and puts it up to his right ear. We all wait.

"Linds. Lindsay, baby, are you okay?" He asks, "Oh, thank God," he says, hanging his head, crying. "Thank you, God." He sniffs loudly. "We're all okay, honey." He pauses, pulls the phone away from his ear and cries, then puts it back to his ear. "I'm okay, baby. I'm just so thankful you are okay. The tornado hit the millhouse and we were all in the basement. You did. You watched it through binoculars! Oh, you silly, girl, you cudda killed yourself. They did! You crazy women." He pulls the phone away from his ear again and turns toward us, tears streaming down his face. "The girls saw the funnel cloud coming and judged that it wasn't going to hit the house. They watched it skip from knob to knob, hitting the tops and skipping the valleys and they watched it as it hit us here on Shepherd's knob." He puts the phone back to his ear. "Listen, we're stranded here, and Philip's face is cut pretty badly. I think you can reach us the back way. Bring the Jeep and have Lush follow in her Rover. She gets her wish after all. Hurry, we need to get Philip some medical attention. It's a laceration on his cheek. Yeah, I figure you could. What? Oh, yeah. We found it. Hurry, honey. Bring your guns, too. Love you."

Geoff is smiling now as he turns back around toward us. Help is on the way, and he looks as if he is the happiest man alive.

"A couple of little stings, like a bee sting, that's all, Philip, honey. Now, just keep real still. That's nice. Good."

I try not to think about anything as Lindsay talks to me as if I were a little boy as she injects something to numb my left cheek before she sutures it. It was quite a surprise to learn that she is a practicing emergency room doctor on maternity leave. I never would have guessed that in a million years. I'm sitting on a stool by the sink in the large kitchen, and I've changed into one of Geoff's polo shirts that is too large for me. Lindsay has washed my laceration with warm soapy water. She wears latex gloves. I really want to be in the den where Lush, Julianna, and the men are opening the two cedar boxes.

"Now just relax, Philip, honey," Lindsay says. "Why don't you take another big sip of that bourbon before I start?"

"Sounds good," I say as I reach over to the counter and pick up the crystal glass with an inch and a half of Four Roses Small Batch in it. I put the glass to my lips, take a deep sniff of the beautiful, silky, tea-colored, honey aroma liquid, and then I take a big sip, hold it in my mouth a second, then let it slide down my throat. "Awe," I say as I open my mouth, exhaling, releasing the warmth and the burn rising in my esophagus.

"Good, that'll help," Lindsay says. Clark is sitting down by my right side watching everything carefully. "Clark is such a sweet dog. I can see how much he cares about you."

"Yes, I just couldn't leave him in New York after all that's happened," I reply.

"Philip," Lindsay says looking down at me, "Lush and Julianna told me everything. I just want you to know my heart goes out to you. I can't even begin to imagine such loss. Geoff and I will do everything we can to help."

"Thanks, Lindsay. You both are so kind. You both have done so much, already. I'll never be able to thank you, enough."

"Well, you don't need to thank us. I consider us family now, bound by common threads through the art world and by this crazy tornado."

"Thanks, Lindsay, I feel the same." I really do, but I feel bad that she doesn't know the true identity of the love of her life. I promised Brother Paul that I wouldn't reveal that. He wants to meet with Joan and her husband when they return from China next week and let them know he knows the truth, and that he thinks it's time for Geoff and Lindsay to know. I truly respect his wish.

She has threaded the curved needle and is holding it up in her right hand. "Just close you eyes; keep them shut until I'm done. You'll barely feel a thing." She leans over and her belly pushes into my left side. "Oh, I'm sorry. I hope that doesn't bother you, but there's no where else to put my big belly."

My eyes are shut. I smile, "It's fine."

"Good, now relax your face, no smiling. Here we go."

I feel pressure on my cheek, but no pain. I feel the thread as she pulls it through my skin. It's a weird feeling, but it isn't painful, and I imagine I'm simply flossing my teeth. I keep my eyes closed, trying to relax. I smell her breath as she exhales, a sweet, warm, wet smell, and I feel her warm belly pushing against me. I try to focus on the wonderful smell of the big pot of beef stew on the stove, and I am conscious of Clark's shallow panting. I start to wonder how many stitches this will take when I feel it, something I have never felt in my entire life—a baby kicking inside the mother. This is amazing; it's almost like a little fist punching from inside her stomach.

"Sorry, Philip. Please hold still; I can't stop now. That little bugger is at it again. I swear sometimes he kicks me so hard, it hurts."

I freeze, and I don't reply for fear of messing up her needle work on my face, and while I wouldn't mind a manly scar, as Jonas described it, I don't want it to be too big or too jagged. The baby kicks again, and I begin to feel truly bonded to this incredible woman who is not only a doctor, but an expert markswoman, a respected dog handler, an accomplished rider, and soon to be a great mother. I start to wonder what she is like in bed with Geoff, and then I abruptly cut that thought off. Today, maybe for the first time ever, and I really mean ever, I just do not want to go there. I wonder why this is. Why now, Hampton? What's so special about this moment unlike all the other moments in my life when I freely thought about sex with anyone and everyone. Well, you know what it is. I think I'm finally growing up. Finally! Finally, I can admire and respect someone, especially a woman, without having to judge her on any sexual basis at all. For God's sake, it's obvious that this woman is leaps and bounds above me in maturity. She is clearly living her life to the fullest, and this is so obvious after barely spending thirty minutes with her. I mean, Julianna and Lush are two of the strongest and most successful women I know. Yet, it was so clear when they arrived to rescue us storm-ravaged men, that Lindsay was the undisputed leader. And not only was she the leader, she had already gained respect and unconditional love from both Lush and Julianna. It was a sight to behold. I guarantee these three women will be in contact the rest of their lives. I just know it. I think because of this and maybe because, deep down inside, I know that there is a whole lot more to each of us than just our sexual beings, that I am able to put the thought of Lindsay and Geoff having sex, or me and Lindsay having sex, or me and Lindsay and Geoff having sex, completely, well almost completely, out of my mind, and I feel another piece of the damage Adrian forced upon my body, mind, and spirit, draining away.

"There we go, dear," Lindsay says. "All done. We could put a bandage on it, but unless you just want to cover it for cosmetic reasons, I'd leave it exposed."

I open my eyes, and smile up at her. "That's fine. I'll leave it like it is." I stand up. "Thanks so much, Lindsay. And thank you, too little man," I say to her belly."

She giggles out loud. I pick up my drink. "Come on," I say, "Let's go see the treasure."

She peels off her gloves, throws them in a trashcan under the sink, turns around, and walks with me down the hall into the den. We enter the room to find everyone standing around the two large desks. There are also four card tables set up in the room. Paintings are spread out everywhere.

"Well, what's the verdict, Julianna?" I ask. Lush smiles her beautiful smile at me.

"The verdict, my dear, Philip, is that you are gazing upon some of the finest paintings the world has ever seen. These are definitely the real things. This is indeed the Gardner heist and it is, oh, so beautiful."

I clasp my hands together, "Splendid! Now we'll get my little brother back," I shout. I really want to say, "Now I'll have my chance at Adrian."

"Todge," Lush says, "Julianna says the paintings have been well preserved. Whoever did this, and we presume it was Dyanne and Ted, knew what they were doing."

Everyone walks around examining and admiring the artwork. A big fire is burning in the fireplace and all three dogs are lying in front of it as well as a big white cat with a black tail and one black ear. I hadn't noticed the cat earlier today, and I'm surprised Clark is tolerating it so well. I remember Billy telling me that Clark did not like cats, and would growl at them whenever he came upon one.

Lush walks over to examine my face and says, "Lindsay did a good job. Let's see, I count seven stitches. It probably won't leave much of a scar."

"I hope not," I reply. "I am so thankful we found the stolen artwork, that is, everything but that eagle finial."

"Yes, it's hard to believe it's really here," Lush replies. "I imagine Ted kept that finial as a token of his successful heist."

"Probably so," I reply, "After all, that was his lure in the Polaroid to tempt Adrian."

"Right," Lush says.

Geoff has been on his cell phone for some time in one of the other rooms. He walks back in. "Listen, I've talked to several different neighbors. There are trees down across the road in several places. You guys are gonna have to stay here tonight. It'll be tomorrow at the earliest before the roads are cleared."

"We've got plenty of room for everyone," Lindsay says. "I'll show you the bedrooms and bathrooms and y'all can freshen up before dinner. I've got two bedrooms with two twin beds and one with a double bed. Y'all can decide who goes where." We follow her into the hall and up the big staircase to the second floor and down another hall to our left. Lindsay points out the rooms. Julianna and Lush take a room with twin beds, as do Jonas and Mabry. I get the room with the double bed. I sit down on the bed and pull out my cell phone to call Dad. "Why don't we all meet back in the den in fifteen minutes for drinks and we'll eat after that?" Lindsay shouts as she walks back down the hall.

I hear Lush holler back, "Lindsay, hon, I'll be down in a minute or two to help you."

"Thanks, Lush."

My cell phone rings and it shows that the caller identification is unavailable. I flip it open. "Yes?"

"So I see you survived the tempest," Adrian says rather sarcastically.

"Indeed, I did," I reply, clinching my teeth.

"And did you retrieve the paintings?" he asks.

"Yes. Yes we did."

"Splendid! Has Julianna examined them?" he asks in a somewhat urgent tone.

"Yes, she has. She says they are in very good condition and that they are the real paintings," I reply trying not to reveal any emotions in my voice.

"Perfect! Then my instructions for you, my dear Philip are quite simple. Even an idiot could follow them. Have the paintings at Billy's place tomorrow at 4 pm. I will bring the child to you and exchange him for the paintings. And, Philip, you will truly be an utter fool to let the police know about this, or let your fancy private investigator, Mr. Grey, interfere whatsoever." He abruptly hangs up the phone.

A feeling of immense anticipation overwhelms me, and I rise up off the bed, walk over to a dresser with a mirror and look at my face. I'm surprised to see the cut is in the shape of the number seven. I look into my eyes, smile at myself, and imagine what I will feel when I have my hands around his neck.

Jonas, Mabry, Lush, Julianna, and I are sitting in front of the fireplace in the den having drinks. Geoff and Lindsay are setting up a buffet in the kitchen, and Brother Paul has not come down yet. Jonas and I got down here before everyone else, discussed Adrian's latest call to me, and then called Dad and Brenda and got them to agree not to reveal any of our plans for tomorrow to any of the police in St. Louis or New York.

469

"So are we really going to let that bastard get away with the Gardner heist and not pay for any of the crimes he's committed?" Lush asks, a bourbon on the rocks in her left hand, a cigarette in her right hand.

"I'm willing to go in SWAT Team style to retrieve the artwork from Adrian once he has turned Andrew over to Philip," Jonas says.

"We could even disguise ourselves as the thugs who are double crossing Adrian on behalf of his client," Mabry says.

"Yes, that is a good idea," Jonas replies. "But it is really up to Philip," Jonas says.

I cannot believe how incredibly lucky I am. Adrian is putting himself right where I want him, and I don't have to worry about anyone else, my team, the police, or his team interfering. There's no way in hell he will leave with that artwork because I intend to kill him. If he shows up with anyone else with him for protection, I'll still kill him. They may get me, but, by God, I'll get him first. I've never been more determined or committed to anything in my life.

"I just can't risk Andrew's life," I reply. "I want to play it just as Adrian has requested. I cannot take any more loss in my family. I just can't do it. Adrian can have the artwork. Besides, after Andrew is safe we can inform the police and the Gardner Museum what happened to the works, and they can go after Adrian themselves." I pray that I am convincing. I don't look at Lush.

"I think that is a smart choice, Philip," Jonas says.

"I agree," Julianna says. "Mabry helped me photograph all the works. We can turn the digital photographs over to the police and the museum. They may be helpful in the future."

"Good," Jonas replies.

Geoff, with a longneck in his right hand, walks into the room. Lindsay appears right behind him.

"Dinner is ready," Lindsay says. "If y'all don't mind, we'll all just serve ourselves in the kitchen and then go sit in the dining room."

"That's perfect, Lindsay," Lush replies.

Brother Paul, a somber expression on his face, enters the den. He is carrying something in a black velvet sack with a drawstring. He walks in front of the fireplace, turns toward everyone, clears his throat and says, "I have a confession to make. I guess I have always known, deep in my heart and in my soul, what this is that I am holding. I feel so ashamed for concealing this all these years. This afternoon after my talk with Jonas, all these memories from my childhood came bubbling up, and once we found the treasure, well, there is no longer any need to hold onto this." He pulls open the drawstring and pulls out the gold, eagle finial from the Gardner heist, the finial Ted Johnson holds in the Polaroid he sent to Adrian. I hear a couple of people gasp, and I feel my mouth drop open, and I feel a pull in my cheek where the cut is. Tears run down Brother Paul's face as he sets the finial down on the coffee table. "You see, this was the last thing Dad ever gave Noel and me. We found him hanging in the barn the next day. Hanging there from the rafters, slowly twirling, his face purple, his legs cut off above the knees, his boots still on his feet, lying in a big pool of congealed blood. My Dad, the man I loved so much, was hanging there terribly violated and maimed and very much dead." He bends over crying. Lindsay and Geoff both run to him and embrace him. Brother Paul turns his face toward mine and says, "Philip, I am so sorry for the pain and agony I have caused you and your family for not revealing this until now. All I can do is ask for your forgiveness and for God's forgiveness."

I stand up, tears running down my own face, and I walk over and take the slim, young monk in my arms, and I push his head into my chest, and I hold his head with my right hand and I say, "Christopher, I forgive you and I know, from the bottom of my heart, that God forgives you, too."

CHAPTER 42

I sit in Billy's studio on the sofa with the beautiful, beige, chinoiserie fabric. Clark is stretched out beside me, sound asleep. The Gardner paintings rest on two of Billy's work tables in the cedar boxes in which we found them. The bronze Yu and the gilded finial sit beside them. Everything is just as Adrian requested: the police do not know about this rendezvous, Jonas has no special forces engaged ready to explode upon the scene, and I am quite alone, except for Clark. The events of the past twenty-four hours churn through my mind as I pick up a crystal glass full of single malt scotch. I just don't give a damn anymore. All I want is Adrian's blood, and I am not ashamed to admit that. Timmy is on duty downstairs. I suppose Adrian will just show up down there with Drew and request to be sent up. I told Jonas my Glock had been lost in the tornado, but I lied. It is in the right pants pocket of the baggy corduroys I have on. It is loaded and ready to fire. I intend to use it against Adrian and any guards he brings. So much has transpired during the past week and a half: Billy's and Elliot's deaths; my reconciliation with Dad, my bonding with Brenda and the kids; the revelations of Mother's murder, Lush's and my aborted child, Brooker T's real identity; Ted's and Dyanne's connections to the Gardner heist, and, my God, the list goes on. I feel as if I've been living in an emotional war zone. This morning Lindsay fixed a splendid breakfast of country ham, fried eggs and grits. It amazes me that we all survived a category four tornado last evening before discovering the location of the largest museum heist in the history of the world. This is all unbelievable, but it is my reality. I take another sip of scotch, and I am uncertain, to this very last minute, how all this will play out. We were all stunned when Geoff told us this morning when he and the dogs, including Clark, returned from surveying the tornado damage on Shepherd's knob that the dogs had led him to three dead men, all of Middle Eastern origin, in the rubble of broken trees, in close proximity to the grist mill. He said he guessed that they don't have to deal with killer tornados in the Middle East. He also discovered a white van on the road near Shepherd's knob, which Mabry traced as a rental car from the Louisville airport. I'm surprised Adrian warned me of his client's thugs. They must have been minutes away from killing us and taking the artworks. Nonetheless, here I sit now, waiting for someone whom I haven't seen since I was thirteen years old, someone who is directly responsible for most of the suffering in my life. So, God, how would you advise me now? Turn the other cheek? Uh huh! Yea, right. No, I'm not letting him get away this time. This time he will pay. Gosh, I never thought we would get out this morning. I walked down and saw at least two-dozen large trees fallen across the main road. That didn't deter Geoff and Lindsay. We crammed everything in Lush's Range Rover, followed them in their Jeep and made our way through a few miles of farmland and woodland to a paved road so we could head back to Bowman Field in Louisville where our jet was waiting to take us back to New York. Strangely enough, the two lane road on which we emerged from the woods, ran right past the Abbey of Gethsemane in the middle of what Lush described as the Holy Land of Kentucky. Poor Brother Paul, he never had a chance growing up surrounded by all this. I think, deep down inside, he is a tormented soul hiding behind a religious dogma that might give him some peace and comfort and even tone down the noise in his mind, and believe me, I know the noise is there, the noise is always there; I've lived his pain, but it will never allow him to fully realize himself completely, which I think must include recognizing and accepting that he is a gay man. What I've come to realize this past week is that the key to my own survival is to know and understand that this noise in my own mind is not the noise of my heart and soul, but the noise of someone else's pain and fear, primarily Adrian's, but to some extent Mother's, who could survive best by inflicting their pain upon me and others. I acknowledge this noise, but I refuse to own it. I may be wrong, but I do not believe leading the life of a Benedictine monk will ever stop Brother Paul's noise, but, in my heart, I'm rooting for him, and I hope that he will someday find a path that will.

Clark raises his head; his ears perk up as he looks at me with a questioning expression on his face.

"It's okay, boy," I say, stroking his head with my left hand.

And, then I hear what he hears: a low rumbling, whirling noise. My God, I think, it sounds as if a helicopter is landing on Billy's terrace. The sound gets louder and louder, and then I realize that a helicopter is landing on Billy's terrace. Is the terrace big enough, I wonder? No, it can't be. But I look out the French doors of the studio, and I see a helicopter descend close to the terrace and a nylon rope ladder falling down. Clark runs up to the doors, barking. I get up quickly, feel the Glock in my pocket, and then walk to the doors. A man with someone right in front of him is climbing down the ladder. He reaches the terrace, and I can see the other person is a child. Someone pulls the ladder up, the helicopter ascends straight up, veers off, and flies away. Adrian and Andrew walk up to the studio doors. I smile at Drew as I open the doors to let them in.

"Drew, buddy. Are you okay?" I ask as I bend down. He lunges toward me and I give him a big hug.

"Gosh, Philip. This has been so much fun. Uncle Adrian is the best. I've flown in the coolest jets and helicopters. I can't wait to tell you about the treasure hunt we've been on, and Uncle Adrian says you have the real treasure here. Please, please, please, show it to me now, Philip."

"Wow, slow down, Drew," I say. "We'll get to that in a minute."

I notice that Adrian is holding on to Drew and to my amazement and disgust, I realize he has a nylon belt around Drew's waist and it is also around fastened around Adrian's waist.

"Philip, what a pleasure to see you again, after all this time," Adrian says, peering at me with those pale, blue, soulless eyes. He has definitely aged, his face has drooped, the red beard from the photographs is gone, and I realize that physically I am a much larger man than he. This gives me immense satisfaction. And then I see it, in Adrian's right hand: a needle. He is holding onto the nylon belt, attached to Drew, with his left hand, and in his right hand he is holding a needle very close to the back of Drew's neck. Drew bends down to pet Clark, but Clark moves over to sniff Adrian's feet. Adrian is dressed in a preppy outfit: black lace up dress shoes with blue and green argyle socks, khaki pants, a black leather belt, and a white Oxford cloth, button down shirt. Strange, I expected him with a big red beard and a robe, but instead, I get the Adrian I remember. All that is missing is a pastel cardigan wrapped around his waist. I sigh. "So we finally meet again, Adrian," I say.

"Yes, we do, Philly. Poor Fatgram, try as she might, she simply couldn't prevent this from happening, now could she?"

Adrian smiles as I look at him, searching for answers, and then it occurs to me that Fatgram must have figured out what Adrian did to us and to Mother. And perhaps she tried to stop him but failed? Who knows? It doesn't matter now.

"Philip, I thought I told you that we all were to meet alone," Adrian says.

"We are alone, Adrian," I reply. "No one else is here."

"That dog is here," he replies.

"Clark? He's harmless," I say.

"Yes, well, I think it will be most helpful if we lock the dog in a room or a crate while we examine the treasure," Adrian says. "I wouldn't want him jumping up and damaging anything. Don't you agree, Drew?"

"Oh, yes, Uncle Adrian," Drew replies. "This treasure is far too valuable to let a dog get hold of it or slobber on it. Philip, it's worth almost a billion dollars!"

"Let's go inside," Adrian says, as he uses his left hand to push Drew forward. "You first, Philip." I walk in the studio with Clark beside me. Drew and Adrian follow.

I turn around and observe Adrian scanning the room. "There's a guest suite back there, isn't there?" He asks.

"Yes," I reply.

"Put the dog in there and shut the door," Adrian commands.

"Alright," I reply, my heart beating wildly. "Come on, Clark," I command, but Clark sits down in front of Drew and will not move. I walk over, put my right hand on his collar and pull him up. "Come on, boy. Let's go. It's okay." He whines, but begins to walk with me. We walk to the guest suite, I push down the lever handle, open the door, and walk in with Clark. I bend down and give him a big hug. "You stay here, boy. This will be over soon. It will finally all be over." I stand up, back through the door, my eyes on his, as I slowly shut the door. I walk back into the studio to find Adrian and Drew standing in front of the worktable. Drew holds the gold finial and is turning it over and over in his hands. Adrian stands close behind him, the needle hovering behind Drew's neck.

"Wow, this is so cool, Philip. I'm so glad you found this. Wasn't it cool how Uncle Adrian and I directed you guys to the treasure using the treasure maps on Uncle Adrian's computer?"

"Yes, it was, Drew. We couldn't have done it without your help," I reply.

"Uncle Adrian let me sleep in the coolest bedroom—it's like a tree-house," Drew says. My heart sinks and my anger rises as I speculate whether or not Adrian sexually abused Drew last night.

"Yes, it is cool. I stayed there when I was your age," I reply, trying to sound enthusiastic and normal to Drew.

"Let me see the Vermeer, Philip," Adrian commands.

I walk to the larger cedar box and lift the lid. Julianna has separated the paintings with large sheets of nonreactive paper. The Vermeer is on top, underneath some sheets of this paper. I have also hidden one of Billy's Japanese Butcher knifes with a six-inch stainless steel blade in the sheets of paper. I carefully remove the lid and slide it on top of the other cedar box. My heart thumps in my throat; each breath is a struggle.

"Julianna's separated each painting with layers of this nonreactive paper," I remark. "The Vermeer's right under this first layer. Here, let me remove it, so you can see the painting."

I fold back the sheets of paper, carefully concealing the butcher knife as I lift the paper up, revealing the Vermeer. Adrian pushes Drew right up to the table. I see Adrian's eyes are glued to the painting. He is right along side me now. I lay the stack of paper beside the box, reaching in between the sheets with my left hand, carefully sliding out the butcher knife, moving it behind my butt with my left hand, transferring it to my right hand.

"Yes, this is it. This is real," Adrian says, looking at the painting.

"Yes, and so is this," I say as I drive the butcher knife completely into Adrian's left side, underneath his ribs, in the soft part of his belly, and remove it as quickly as I plunged it in. He gasps, drops the needle, out of his right hand, falls to the floor, taking Drew down with him.

"You bastard," Adrian gasps.

"What's happening, Philip? Uncle Adrian?" Drew screams.

I take the knife and slice the cord attaching Drew to Adrian. I throw the knife across the room, grab Drew in my arms and run out into the hallway to the front foyer. I'm out of breath, Andrew is crying.

"What happened, Philip? Where's Adrian. What about the treasure?"

I push the button for the elevator and get down on my knees in front of Andrew.

"Listen to me carefully, Andrew. We are all in great danger. Go down to the front and stay with Timmy. Just stay with Timmy. Tell him Adrian and I have some business to take care of and we'll be down in a few minutes. Tell him not to come up here. I'll come get you guys."

Andrew's lips are quivering, and I see how frightened he is. I hug him.

"It's going to be alright, Drew, I promise." The elevator door opens. I guide Drew in, push the button and hop out. The door closes.

"Tell Timmy we'll be right down."

I turn around, and run back into the studio. Adrian is gone.

"Fuck!" I shout in a loud whisper. I look for a blood trail, but see none. Where did he go? Suddenly, I hear a loud noise outside and I turn to see another helicopter descending toward the terrace. I look out to see several men in black jumpsuits and black knitted facemasks jumping onto the terrace. Are they coming for Adrian? The stolen artwork? I must hide. I run toward the guest suite and pause in front of the bathroom. I hear the men crashing through the studio doors. They don't even pause to open them. Clark begins barking and whining. I peer around the corner and one of the tall men running into the room looks in my direction. His eyes meet mind, my breath stops—those eyes are familiar to me, Najeed. He turns his head quickly away and heads toward the work tables. The other men follow him. I quickly move into the bathroom, push the molding on the shelves to open the hidden passageway. I back into the space in front of the hidden door and wait. I want to be able to hear what is going on out there. I can shut this quickly if I hear someone approaching, they'll never find me in here. Clark continues to bark. I hope the intruders leave him alone. I hear them shuffling in the studio. I know they are taking the Gardner paintings. I hear them walking back out toward the terrace. I hear the sound of the helicopter. I wonder if it is Adrian's people. I guess they are loading him onto the copter, too. Damn it. Was that really Najeed I saw or is my mind playing tricks on me? Goddamit. I was so close. Why didn't I just kill Adrian with the knife? I just couldn't do it in front of Andrew. I don't even think Andrew knows that I stabbed Adrian. Something pricks the back of my neck and I realize it is a needle going in. Lights flick on, and I feel arms around me. I look up to see Adrian grabbing me. I struggle to turn around to get my hands on his neck. I manage to turn around and I grab his neck with my hands and look into his eyes.

"You fucking bastard," I say and begin to squeeze my hands as hard as I can. "This is for Mother and Billy and all the others." I continue to squeeze and he grabs my hands with his, trying to remove my hands. My visions starts to blur and my knees give way, and I collapse down releasing his throat. What the hell did he inject in me?

He laughs. "So you think you won, Philip?" he asks. "Hardly. Maybe I didn't get the paintings, but you'll never get in my way again. I've so looked forward to this. To do to you what I did to your pretty brother and your mother."

I have totally collapsed and everything is spinning around. Adrian drags me into the closet, turns me toward the mirror, and fastens a nose around my neck. I try to focus on his left side, and I see a large wet patch of blood. I did get him good, I think. He may kill me, but I think I mortally wounded him, too. I find the strength to grab hold of the wooden frame so I won't choke. Adrian laughs.

"Just the help I need from you," he says as he unfastens my belt buckle, unzips my pants, and pulls down my pants and underwear. He reaches inside my pocket and pulls out the gun.

"Too bad you didn't use this on me, pretty boy. Yes, indeed," he says, "Now they'll think you were playing with your todger a little too aggressively, my boy." He grabs my cock and begins to stroke it. "Hello, old friend," he says and leans over and kisses it. He presses his face into my groin and takes a deep breath. "Hmmm, I always savored the smell of you Hampton boys." He looks up at me. He doesn't appear to be weakening from the stab wound. I guess I didn't hurt him that bad, after all. "Time for a little autoerotic asphyxiation, Philly. Remember the fun we used to have? Only this time, there will be no gold doubloon. Only a long, cold, dark, nothingness." He laughs again, stands up and starts to grab both my hands, trying to pry them off the scaffold. I try to kick him but my legs will not move. All I can do is squeeze the scaffold. I keep telling myself to squeeze, but I fill my hands slipping. Out of the corner of my right eye, I see a sleek, orange fuselage soaring through the air, fangs bared, and I witness the bite as Clark's jaws clamp down on the left side of Adrian's neck. Adrian screams as he turns trying to scrape Clark off of him, but he cannot do it. Clark hangs on motionless, growling like the devil. I manage to slip out of the noose and I pass out.

EPILOGUE

The sun's rays and the gentle breeze on my bare shoulders feel soothing, restorative. I sit on a warm boulder gazing at my rippling reflection in Fatgram's swimming hole, listening to the gurgling stream, the calls of crows and kingfishers, breathing in the smell of wet clay and fresh water. I'm getting used to my beard I grew to cover the scar on my face. Clark sits beside me panting, but clearly enjoying soaking up the sun. I turn toward him, smile at him; we look into each other's eyes. I owe him my life. He knew I needed help. Adrian did not inject enough GHB into me to kill me. I suppose he measured the dosage for Andrew and not me. But he certainly was planning to hang me. Clark figured out how to push the lever handle on the door of the guest suite. He knew Adrian was killing me. He also knew very well how to kill Adrian. I take great pleasure in knowing that Adrian bled to death by having the jugular vein in the left side of his neck severed by a pit bull. If that is not karma, I don't know what is. Clark will be my companion from now on. It seemed only fitting that he accompany me to scatter Billy's ashes here on the farm. Tomorrow we fly to Key West and then on to St. Barts where Lush and Julianna will join us. I open the black plastic box carrying my brother's ashes. It's so odd to know that his entire beautiful, physical body has been reduced to a few ounces of these grey ashes. But his spirit lives on. I feel it every day. I know he is here with us now. Clark sniffs the ashes, cocks his head, looking up at me. I pick up the box and with a shaking motion pour about a third of the ashes into the water. I watch them swirl around and begin to sink. I put the lid back on the box, sit it down on the boulder, stand up, slide my shorts and boxers off, and dive into the cool water. Clark barks twice, emits a high-pitched whine then jumps in after me. I dive under water, open my eyes to look up at the surface. I observe Clark dog paddling through Billy's ashes, and I know that I'm swimming with my brother once again.

ABOUT THE AUTHOR

Jody Zimmerman is the author of Blood Brother's, a psychological thriller within the framework of a literary novel. His belief that a good story awakens emotions, excites the senses, and encourages self-exploration has inspired his work as an author.

In addition to his writing, Zimmerman has worked as a process design engineer, a nuclear engineer, an instructor of economics at a junior college, an entrepreneur (founder of an environmental consulting firm), a manager/owner of a commercial real estate firm, and a certified hot yoga instructor.

His passions are fiction writing, gourmet cooking, and hot yoga. He enjoys entertaining, tending to his organic garden, and walking with his dogs.

Jody resides in Louisville, Kentucky with his partner. He grew up in Spartanburg, South Carolina.